SCARS IN TIME

A Novel

Ryan Gutierrez

<u>Dedication</u>

To my family and everyone else who heard my crazy pipe dream to write this and said, "You should do it".

To my wife, for being my first reader, my first critic, and for laughing and crying along every word and chapter of this journey.

To Angie. My sister, my editor, my critic, my friend. The family's armor bearer.

Table of Contents

<u>PART I</u>

The Present

Chapter 1

Like all people, we could describe Brennan Ramirez in many ways. We could say he was overweight, enough that one would notice, but not enough to define him as "the fat guy." We could describe him as having black hair streaked with premature gray, cutting green eyes, a complete inability to grow a beard, and a face that had long ago established a stern, severe expression as its default setting. Any time he wasn't expressing some positive emotion, he looked furious with the world. He had a few decent reasons to be, but we'll get to that later. He was Hispanic, as his surname would suggest, a Texan, proud American, but still, none of that defined him. Instead, we could bisect Brennan into two defining features. First, he was intelligent. Not your average guy with a quick wit and good academic performance. This was the brand of intelligence that rubs people the wrong way. The sort of intelligence that can build arrogance in men who would otherwise have no choice besides humility. Towards the end of his adolescence, Brennan had embraced that arrogance. Brennan believed he had to be the smartest person in his school, which he was, the smartest person in his town, he was in the top three, and perhaps even the smartest person in all of South Texas though, realistically, he landed somewhere in the top five percent. He embraced the arrogance until his second defining feature forced humility on him.

A severe, often uncontrollable, anxiety.

He had always struggled with anxiety, but it began to snowball in college.

He was 19 when he went to his girlfriend's house to tell her mom she was expecting his child.

"How could you do this to me? After all I've done for you!" her mother had shrieked.

She was a diminutive woman, barely earning the 5 feet her expired driver's license credited her with, but she had a squawking voice, scratched up by years of smoking just about anything that could be smoked. To make matters worse, the knife scrape on china timbre reached decibels that defied the confines of the body that projected it. Brennan remembered that as nervous as he had been, as angry as the remark had made him, he almost laughed at Misty's response. That expired driver's license read Lupita, but she had named herself Misty when she worked the corners downtown. She preferred that name. Brennan found it hilarious that Misty, mother of 3 children and 2 abortions, all from different johns, had the sheer gall to claim she had done anything for Deidre, besides inadvertently set her up for struggle from before birth.

Misty had gone on to kick Deidre out. Brennan had always wanted to get Deidre out of the rust bucket hellhole Misty called her trailer, but he had never planned on doing it like this. He wanted it to be on his own terms, but passion had gotten the better of Brennan and Deidre, as passion is wont to do with young couples.

Brennan had worked night shifts, often going more than two weeks without a day off, while going to college in the daytime. Between studying, working, lack of sleep, and the pressure of learning to be the head of household, the physical symptoms of the anxiety began to grow, like a malignant tumor in his psyche. If he had been honest, he would've confessed he was not ready to move in with Deidre. Yet, he asked her to stay, even after they lost the baby.

The baby's prenatal passing eventually brought Brennan back to God. A very tumultuous two and a half years later, he and Deidre were married in a small ceremony that took place in a quaint, small-town, church. Brennan had not participated too much in the hasty preparation for the wedding, but he insisted on choosing the church. He didn't know why, but he loved the little church. Maybe it was something about its classical, small town, aesthetic. Happily married and free of religious shame, it was not long before he found a small Christian congregation to join. He became associate pastor in just three years after starting there. His tendency to pour himself completely into something and incredible ability for recall, including scripture, was definitely helpful with that venture.

Even with the peace he found on Sundays, he was having a panic attack about every three months at that point. Then, yet another mistake began to enact its toll on him. Brennan graduated with his Bachelor's in Criminology and decided to work for Child Protective Services. For six years, case after case chipped away at his sanity, every perpetrator was a reminder of the pain his wife relived in her nightmares, every child a reminder of his own, the one he would never meet, and Abby, who had been born a year into his investigative career, a year before his marriage. The panic attacks progressed, becoming monthly, then weekly, and eventually, daily. By the end of the six years, driving for more than a block resulted in a major attack and work became an impossibility. After years of Deidre's urging him to do so, he finally quit. First his paying job as an investigator, and soon after, his volunteer job in the ministry.

Now Deidre worked as a nurse's assistant, looking after senior citizens who had reverted to infants in their mind. He stayed home, watched Abby, and worked in his lab. The lab was really just a converted garage, filled with metal odds and ends, electronics, tools, and lined with shelves of books ranging from physics, electrical engineering, to theories on time travel. Time travel was, after all, his main goal.

He had worked tirelessly on what was almost certainly an impossibility. Today, he stood in the garage, his heart racing, staring at the small mouse sitting in the pod he had built. The pod was covered with a translucent little dome that would target the mouse for transfer, instead of him. This was the best way he had found for testing The Machine on an animal first.

As he prepared to send the tiny rodent into the past, he remembered the night that pushed him into pursuing time travel. The night that pushed him into pursuing a career with CPS. The night that had brought back a silent rage he thought he had lost.

Brennan was halfway through 16, Deidre had just started 15. They sat in Brennan's mother's automobile, a minivan that was ancient in car years. It had a design that would have been considered futuristic in the early 90s. Now it just seemed impractical. Nonetheless, the embarrassing old Toyota didn't just live, the thing was a survivor. It had more little tricks than Brennan could count, but the important stuff functioned how it should. The Turtle, as they affectionately called it, drove well, seat belts worked, the A/C kept the South Texas heat at bay, and the radio had a tape deck that Brennan paired with a cassette tape adapter to play the music from his cracked, old, iPod. As much as Brennan hated driving a van, it was the vehicle that made dates, and the panicked treks to get home just a shave before curfew, possible.

Brennan gripped the steering wheel hard, his pulse thumping in his chest, head, and wrists. He felt lucky to have been able to be with Deidre for a few months, but he knew an end had to come. She was vastly out of his league. She was clever, much smarter than she realized, funny, spunky and outgoing, in many ways the exact opposite of Brennan, and she was gorgeous. Big brown eyes, long black hair, perfect curves, even at her young age. This wasn't little league to MLB. This was mini golf to NFL. So far out his league it wasn't even the same sport. Yet, she liked the weird, broody, chunky kid with the attitude.

He was grateful, but all good things must come to an end. It was his first girlfriend after all. "*Just practice*", he had tried to comfort himself when she advised him they needed to "have a talk". He was lying to himself, even in his immature, adolescent heart, he knew he was too far gone. He loved her. Brennan braced for the emotional wreck of a first break up. It didn't come. Deidre was not very eloquent then and the metaphorical filter between her brain and her larynx appeared to have some huge holes in it. She bluntly blurted out when planned words eluded her.

"I was raped." she erupted.

There was no crescendo into it, only a massive staccato note of painful truth. Her words vibrated through Brennan's head, quickening his pulse and stifling his breath.

He wanted to say something helpful, something profound. A very selfish part of him was relieved this wasn't a breakup talk, but most of his mind, in both conscious and unconscious effort, was grasping at the air to pull down the words that would make this better. Instead, he coughed out a stupid monosyllabic question.

"When?"

"I was about to be four years old, the first time."

"Four? The first time?" Brennan asked, as he tried to convey in his tone that he was disgusted at what was done to her and not disgusted by her. He wondered if she understood that as his voice failed to convey anything beyond shock and anger.

"It went on for a while." She described in painful detail how he would touch her, how he had tried to be "in" her, but she had been too young, too small, so he had resorted to other perversions. She talked about telling her mom. About how Misty said it had to be a misunderstanding. Of course, she might've been influenced to say that since the man happened to be her boyfriend, really a long-term john would've been a more accurate term, and her drug dealer. Sometimes he'd even let Misty get the product free. Of course, Misty considered it free, but she knew deep down it was in exchange for her professional services. Deidre was sure he had hurt her sister too, possibly even her brother. Deidre told Brennan he had been the first person she told after her mom had ultimately accused her of lying for attention and because she didn't like him.

Brennan asked what made her decide to tell him.

"I'm really starting to like you," Deidre smiled coyly, but was unable to sustain the grin for more than a second, "and I wanted you to know you're chasing damaged goods."

She averted her eyes, her cheeks blushing, her eyes watering.

Brennan's heart cracked like a volcano. A deep emotional pain, accented with a fiery, roaring, rage that simmered, threatening to explode. That moment changed him. He had suffered similar abuse, but he didn't tell her then. It was less severe, and he had been able to eventually put a stop to it. Still, it was more than that. It was to hear this smart, gorgeous, young girl say she was "damaged goods". To

8

hear that a four-year-old had suffered the wound that resulted in those scars. To imagine that child had not only experienced one terrible trauma, but that it continued for years. To try to fathom a mother that would accuse that child of conjuring up the abuse for attention. *"Although,"* he thought *"maybe if Misty had given her attention, she could have protected her."*

That revelation had changed their relationship and exposed parts of Brennan that Deidre had not seen before. The previously shy and docile young man became her white knight, defending her from friends, her mother, his mother, and anyone who dared speak or act against her. They were closer than ever. When Brennan's mother decided Deidre wasn't good for her son because she came "from bad stock" and she revoked his driving privileges to prevent him from seeing her, Brennan mowed lawns. In one weekend, he gathered enough money to buy a bicycle and pegs the neighborhood kids called "homie haulers". Deidre used the pegs to ride with him on their dates to the local Dairy Queen. Even Deidre's witchly mother had to admit, when they rode like that, they looked pretty cute. Part of Deidre knew that this new role Brennan was playing probably wasn't emotionally healthy for either of them, but she ignored the thought. She had never had a white knight before.

Ever that white knight, there he stood, over a decade later, the impossible in his hands. All in the obsessive effort to heal the little girl that still lived in Deidre's head. The one that woke up in the dead of night, screaming at ghosts and scars.

9

"When? When?" Brennan asked himself aloud, looking at Modest the 8th.

The mouse's seven predecessors hadn't fared well. As he ran scenarios in his head, there was low groan and vibrations moved through the air. Modest the 8th was suddenly both inside and next to the small translucent dome. Brennan laughed and his heart slowed for a couple beats before it kicked into double time again. He attached the electrodes to his head, focused on the moment Modest the 8th had appeared and pushed on the round pad that he would wear on his chest when it came time for him to use it. The domed Modest disappeared. Brennan punched the air excitedly and did his best to quiet the thought loop in his head asking if he would've sent the mouse elsewhere if future him hadn't sent it first, then pondering the impossibility of the future being first, then not only the possibility but seemingly extreme likelihood of the same.

Then, his heart sank. Remote travel was great for testing one-way trips. A two-way trip would need to be tested with full gear and by a human. Not just a human, Brennan had to be the one to test it.

A buzzing sensation spread up Brennan's neck to his cheeks and down his shoulders to his hands. He was doing what one of his former therapists had called "passive hyperventilating". He slowed his breath as best he could, but to no avail. In truth, it may have worked, had he tried for more than 15 seconds, but in that panicked mindset, Brennan could have sworn he was doing the breathing exercises for at least a minute. He took a yellow pill bottle out of his pocket. He had only ever taken one of these pills, 2 years ago, his last day on the job with CPS, but carrying the bottle in his pocket still comforted him. The dirty, ripped, fading label could still be read: Alprazolam. Most people knew them as Xanax, or Bars, if they bought them off shady guys in alleys. Brennan hated taking them. Every time he was tempted to take one, he would hear his inner voice perfectly imitating his father say, "*You need to be stronger. Get control of yourself. You're fine. It's not like you're getting bombed in the Middle East. Now THOSE people have a reason to...*"

"I'm about to defy God and every law of physics," Brennan argued defiantly against the fading carbon copy of his father that still lived in his mind. "If there's a time for it, it's right freaking now."

He broke off one square from the bar and drank it with a nearby bottle of water. He paused, then drank a second square.

Brennan hurriedly buckled the chest piece on, adjusted the thin metal arm to press against the base of his skull, and re-attached the two electrodes to his temples. Brennan focused on a childhood memory and, knowing his boldness had a rapidly approaching time limit, he pressed the round pad on his chest. Brennan felt Nothing. Not just nothing different, but truly Nothing. He was just consciousness unrestrained by the confines of a body or any of the natural senses. Then, a warm breeze. His eyes were still closed, but he recognized from the sound of the traffic, the fresh, green scent of grass mixed with the stinging exhaust fumes, and a disembodied notion of belonging, of being home, that it had worked. He opened his eyes and before they adjusted, he heard his grandfather's voice.

"¡Ándele, mijo! ¡Vaya a jugar!"

He saw a chubby boy in blue shorts and a red shirt with a scruffy mop of black hair. The boy picked up a batman doll half his height and ran excitedly into a makeshift tent, made from metal and wood poles, rope, and blue tarp. That was him. That was Brennan. He stared in awe, tears brimming the banks of his lower eyelids, as his grandfather ran in after him. Brennan's grandfather had always seemed old to him when he was growing up, he was grandpa after all, but now, from the impossible retrospective view of a 30-year-old watching his early childhood happen before him, he looked impossibly young. Dark hair, balding, but not quite bald, tan skin, sunglasses, and quite limber for a man his age. Brennan wanted to watch forever. He wanted to see his dad. Where was his dad? He broke out of the surreal moment of peace that spread through his mind, the nostalgic love that filled the air in that quaint little town in northern Mexico.

"No. Not what I'm here for." he croaked huskily to himself. His mouth was suddenly dry, his tongue was sandpaper. He had been mostly sure traveling to the past would work. It had worked remotely with Modest the 8th, which was harder to do, and he was pretty proud of using consciousness and memory as a map. He had immediately ruled out using coordinates, considering that he'd have to not only account for location on earth, but for the earth's location in space. This was far more intuitive and would work well once he figured out how to travel using Deidre's memories. Yeah, this all worked fine. It was getting back that worried him. His heart began to race as he grasped the "e-cord", short for emergency cord. The e-cord was basically the return button but, being the fatalistic bundle of nerves that he was, he had named it and designed it for worst case scenarios. He closed his eyes and pulled. Again, Nothing. Then the stuffy, humid, air of the garage / lab surrounded him. He laughed a silent choked laugh. He looked at the clock on his table. Only a few minutes had passed. He laughed, audibly this time. He took The Machine off and stored it in a tool drawer. He couldn't help but laugh again.

"Whas funny, da-ee?"

Brennan turned and saw Abby, not Abigail. Both he and Deidre hated the name Abigail. She was a miniature copy of her mother, but with her brown hair in wild curls, rather than the sleek, straight, mane Deidre had. She was a bit too tall for a five-year-old and almost constantly smiling. She was rocking back and forth on the balls of her feet, as she often did.

"Nothing, baby girl. What are you doing down here?" Brennan asked softly.

"Mommy says you need to eat your food, da-ee. Is gonna get cold and poop on by the fies!" She couldn't hold in the giggle the word poop had triggered in her.

"Oh, no!" Brennan exclaimed in feigned concern, "Gotta get there before the flies turn my food into a toilet."

"Soup, da-ee. Mommy made soup. Is the afabet one." She looked at him and stopped rocking but began flapping her hands around. "Oh, no! Da-ee, you cut youself!"

Brennan looked at where Abby's cute, little, index finger pointed and was surprised to see a thin red streak rolling down the back of his hand.

"I'll get cleaned up and be right there, Abby."

"Ok. I'll shoo the fies."

"Yes, get those away! Thank you, Abby baby."

"You welcome, da-ee baby." She turned around and went back inside, hopping like a kangaroo, rather than walking.

Brennan cleaned and wrapped his hand. He walked into the family dining room and saw Deidre serving fresh lemonade into a cup and Abby standing between her plate and her father's plate, chubby little knife hands ready for any flies invading the no-fly zone over the food.

"Need any help, hon?" Brennan asked, a weight of shame behind his chest.

Shame was a familiar sensation recently. Deidre worked, cleaned, cooked, took care of the bills, while Brennan just tried to not have a meltdown. In his mind, he wasn't worthy of Deidre, the title of husband, or father. He wouldn't tell

Deidre that, but he often told himself while panicking behind the wheel or sitting pathetically under the shower.

"Nah, I got it, sweetie. I made Abby's favorite." Deidre gleamed a stadium light of a smile. Though an inaudible voice in his head assured him he didn't deserve the smile, he was always glad to get it.

Both Brennan and Deidre finished their dinner but kept their seats to give Abby some company.

"How was work, hon?" Brennan asked, cracking the suddenly awkward silence.

"Ugh," Deidre groaned, "Mr. Lopez crapped the bed and poor guy was so embarrassed, he kept denying it, and just staying in there. I did my best to coax him out and help him not to feel embarrassed, but eventually orderlies got involved. Good news was they cleaned him up. Bad news was that I still had to clean dry feces off of everything. So, my day was average actually." Deidre smiled.

"I wish you didn't have to work there." Brennan murmured in a low voice. "If I could work, if I could just get over this nonsense."

"Brennan, stop. It's not your fault. You had a tough job, saw some traumatizing stuff. Then Kaylee..."

Brennan cut her off, "What if we could change all that?" Deidre looked at him strangely, "Hypothetically, I mean." he continued. "Imagine there was a way to go back and stop all this."

"If wishes were fishes..." Deidre started.

"Imagine all that would change. No one hurts you as a kid, I go into research or open a private investigation firm instead. We'd be so much better off; wouldn't you want to change all that?" Brennan demanded passionately. He was doing his best to rein in his desire to yell out, "Because I can!"

"Brennan, please, just stop." Deidre closed her eyes and held her hand up. "I don't know what I'd change or if I'd change anything, okay? What's done is done, what's happened has happened. **Remember ye not the former things, neither consider the things of old. Behold, I will do a new thing; now it shall spring forth; shall ye not know it? I will even make a way in the wilderness, and rivers in the desert.**"

Brennan's eyes widened. The scripture stung like an insult. "Don't bring the Bible into this."

"One of us should."

"Look, Dee, how could you not change things? Make things better for all of us. Not just you, you know. Plus, how can you say what happened happened when it's still happening? You still wake up with nightmares or terrors most nights. You might not remember a lot of them, but I remember them all!"

"Mommy has nighmares? Why you're scared, mommy?" Abby asked, genuine concern glistening in the tears saran wrapping her eyes.

"No, mommy is fine, Abby. Are you done eating sweetie?" Deidre was trying to hide how upset she was from Abby. They didn't know if it was a side effect of the autism or just some talent she had, but little Abby was incredibly perceptive for a child of five years old.

"Yeah." Abby responded glumly.

"Ya ves lo que haces? ¿Porque te enfocas todo en lo negativo?" Deidre asked Brennan.

"It makes me itchy when you yell." Abby stated, not in complaint so much as an observation she was making.

"I'm sorry." Brennan apologized, the familiar shame setting in again.

Deidre hoisted Abby up into her arms. "Who's ready for a bath time?"

"Abby the mermay!" Abby yelled, pumping her little arms up.

Chapter 2

Brennan woke up, his hand had retrieved his phone and clicked on the screen before his eyes had opened. The brightness of the screen brought itchy tears to his eyes, but he was able to read the bold numerals that marked the time as 2:44 in the morning.

Deidre whimpered again. A tear had squeezed out of Deidre's eye and was now rolling down her cheek to her nose. The sudden urge to cry hit Brennan's throat and the corners of his eyes like an internal punch. He wondered for a second if tonight's nightmares were caused by him bringing up Deidre's childhood.

"Idiot." he said matter-of-factly to himself.

Brennan gently touched her arm and, as she usually did, Deidre shot up to a sitting position and yanked her arm away, gasping like people do in movies after coming back to life. Brennan never got used to it.

"It's okay, baby. You're safe, honey." Brennan comforted as he reached his hand out to wipe a tear away. Deidre shrank away from his touch.

"Yeah, stupid dream. I'll be fine." Deidre assured him, wiping her tears.

"If it was because of what I said earlier..."

"Stop, Brennan. It's because of what some pervert did when I was a kid. Not you." Deidre's words still sounded angry, but Brennan didn't push the issue. She turned around, lay back down, and was back to sleep.

Brennan always envied Deidre's ability to fall asleep almost instantly. He would be up for at least an hour, just trying to ignore his brain long enough to fall asleep. Then he had an idea.

Brennan got out of bed, pulled on a t-shirt, some tennis shoes, and went into the makeshift lab. He put on The Machine and did his best to think of Deidre's childhood home. He thought he might be able to trick The Machine to transporting him there. He had been to the rust bucket trailer Deidre grew up in, but not until she was already a teenager. He tried to focus on the rusted metal, the peeling paint, the constant underlying stink of mildew and compound that with what he knew from her childhood. He pressed the pad on his chest.

He experienced the odd Nothing, then cool air. He was inside a house. Instead of the wet, putrid scent of mildew, there was a warm smell of fabric softener and baby products. Brennan opened his eyes and saw mint green walls decorated with cars and checkered flags. He recognized the twin sized bed that sat in a Little Tikes plastic car bedframe and the G.I. Joe piñata, yellowing with age, that leaned against the wall. He was in his childhood home. His legs buckled. He fell to his knees and for a while forgot everything. This place was the last place he remembered being truly at peace. He crawled to the door and pulled himself up to open it. Out in the hallway was the old family tree, a literal tree made of beautifully styled and cut aluminum, still surrounded with portraits from both sides of the family. Brennan let out a shaky sob and suddenly realized his throat was bone dry. He tried to swallow, but his throat just clenched up. His heart had been beating fast already, but he hadn't noticed, and once he did, it kicked into an even higher gear.

He tried to go to the kitchen, there would be water there, but it seemed to be miles away. He turned back to head to the bathroom and his legs gave out again. He turned his head and saw the guest room, decked out in purple and gold. Grandma was their most frequent guest and she loved purple and gold. Colors fit for royalty and her royal ego. Dad of course was all too eager to please the monster-in-law. It wasn't that he liked her, it was that dad could manipulate people the way a virtuoso manipulates a violin. He knew just where to apply pressure, when to be gentle, and when to strike harder. The image of his dad sweet-talking his grandmother was almost humorous. He tried to hold on to the passing thought, hoping it would carry him out of the panic. It didn't. His peripheral vision was gone now, his heart was a jackhammer, and his mind was in a deep fog. He dragged himself to the restroom, shook out a few pills, and mustered enough fine motor skills to grab two small loose squares and throw them in his mouth. He pulled himself up to the sink, filled his Batman rinse cup a quarter of the way, and drank. Even with the water, the cubic chunks of chemical tranquility slid down his throat painfully. He took another swig of water and crawled into his old bedroom. He lay down on the fluffy carpet and cried. The tears flowed, decreasing, and finally stopping after about 20 minutes. He turned his head and stared at a little trophy cup on the spoiler shaped headboard of his race car bed. His mom still had that trophy at her house. He smiled weakly.

A door creaked open. He heard his mom and dad talking. He froze. He listened to his mother's voice, higher and gentler than he could ever remember it. His dad said something that made her giggle. The sound was brand new at first, then suddenly painfully nostalgic. He wanted to see them. Together. Happy. Young and full of hope. The doom of their relationship and the concept of divorce still years ahead of them. He grasped the e-cord.

"You gotta go, man. You can't stay. You can't stay." Tears started again.

He pulled the cord.

Nothing, then the thick garage air and the hard concrete floor. He sat up, his head swimming. He covered his eyes, then slipped his hands up and through his hair. He took a few minutes to settle his mind and then weighed his options. He could travel to the right time, then walk, drive, or hitch a ride to the trailer, any of which would probably trigger an anxiety attack. He could take the Xanax, but maybe too high to do much once he arrived. The other option was to figure out how to travel using Deidre's mind without her knowing. His best bet was probably waiting for a dream he could hijack. He'd have to prepare for both. He would need to practice driving and work on extending the electrodes.

He stood and wiped the sweat from his forehead with the back of his hand. A sharp sting struck his forehead. His hand was wet with a watery, crimson mix of blood and sweat. He assumed he must have hit his head on the sink or something along those lines. He took a deep breath and walked inside.

Chapter 3

Two weeks later, Brennan stood in his lab putting the
finishing touches on the new, longer electrodes. He had
managed to not only extend the cords, but make them
retractable as well. The reason they hadn't been too long to
begin with was to avoid snags and tangles. He was
oblivious to what the result would be if he attempted to
travel with frayed electrodes reading his brain activity. He
wanted to remain oblivious.

Brennan knew that hijacking Deidre's dreams could
probably get him to the right time, but possibly not the right
place. In order to be safe, he would have to be able to drive.

For two weeks he had convinced himself he would take the
next opportunity to drive and start practicing. For two
weeks he had found excuses with each opportunity.

However, excuses have a way of running out.

He was examining his handiwork with admiration when
Deidre walked in.

"Brennan, sweetie," Deidre started

Brennan turned and slyly covered the bulk of The Machine
under an oil stained rag.

"Yeah, hon?"

"I'm so sorry to ask. You know I wouldn't unless I really
had to, but I'm in the middle of cooking dinner and I need
fresh tomatoes."

A pang of fear gripped his lungs and heart in a sadistic twist. Deidre must have seen it.

"I'm so sorry, Bren, but I completely forgot them. You can go to the little convenience store like a quarter mile away. It's a lot closer and the tomatoes are only like fifty cents more." She tucked her mouth to the right, her incredibly expressive eyes and brow furrowing in along with it to show their shame, "I'm really sorry, Bren."

"No, don't apologize, hon." Brennan said, wearing an obviously counterfeit grin. It overenthusiastically spread from ear to ear, but didn't change his eyes. It was terrible, but the best he could muster at the moment. "How many do you need?"

"Just two. Thank you, baby, you're the best." Deidre skipped forward and gave him a quick squeezing hug and a peck on the lips.

Brennan smiled weakly, but genuinely this time.

He walked out and looked at his car. His heart grew heavy in his chest.

He got in and turned on the old, faded gray, sedan. A mallet beat against the inside of his sternum, through his neck, into his ears, and behind his eyes. He put the car in drive and accelerated slowly. Brennan kept reassuring himself, "almost there, almost there..." before he had even left the neighborhood. He got out on the main road. The fear tried to burst through his stomach and chest. He tried to swallow, but the flesh in his mouth and throat were sandpaper. His eyes watered, blurring the street. His head was overtaken with an almost overwhelming urge to just close his eyes and escape into a dark, heavy sleep.

Fighting against himself and a flurry of his abstract thoughts, he made it to the store. The quarter mile seemed to stretch for hours. He got out of the vehicle and walked in. Every bright light, every bold color, burned his eyes. The smell of deli foods, the bakery, and the collective stench of the shopping masses assaulted his nose. The PA system screamed in his ear. Something about a little boy looking for his mother, Rachel. Brennan tried to control his breathing and began to recite in a whisper, **"'For God hath not given us the spirit of fear; but of power, and of love, and of a *sound mind*.' 2 Timothy 1:7"** He emphasized sound mind and released a shaky breath. He tried his best to grab a plastic produce bag from the roll hanging over the lettuce, tomatoes, and peppers. He failed the first three times, but the fourth time was the charm. He grabbed two tomatoes. No checking, no weighing. They could've been soft apples for all Brennan knew. He could barely concentrate. He aimed all his focus at paying and leaving. One step at a time. Right. Left. Right. Left. *"What if I'm dying?"* his brain seemed to autonomously ask. *"I could be having a stroke. Dang it. Poor Abby... poor Deidre."*

"No." he told himself firmly, but still inaudible to others. **"Fear thou not; for I am with thee: be not dismayed; for I am thy God: I will strengthen thee;, I will help thee;, I will uphold thee with the right hand of my righteousness."**

"Is He thine God?" the fatalist voice in his head questioned.

Brennan paid at the self-checkout and left hurriedly. A short, brunette, store employee with a child's face stopped him at the door.

"Sir, you forgot your keys."

"Yeah... thanks. Thank you. Thanks. Need those." His voice was raspy and weak. He was starting to get dizzy.

"You just gotta get home, dude. Just need rest is all." he told himself, louder now.

In the confused blur of his mind, he had no idea how he got to his car. He turned the key with a shaking hand and far away, he could hear the engine turn over. He drove through a paradox. His car seemed to crawl along while traffic blazed past him at light speed. Every car's lights were like suns. Their motors were machine guns as they drove past him.

He narrowed his focus to laser precision. He just needed to get home. The muscles of his chest and stomach tightened, his knuckles turned white on the steering wheel, his breath was irregular, and his heart was a bass drum at jackhammer speed. Still, he focused.

He pulled into his driveway, hitting the curb on the way in. He was quivering in all his limbs and did his best to run in to the house. He staggered through the front door and caught his reflection on the TV screen. Even in that black mirror, Brennan could see the color had left his skin. Sweat had matted his hair. His legs were just as relieved to be home as he was and they gave out in front of the couch. He dropped onto the couch and did his best to breathe. Too shallow. Not enough air. He started taking gasping gulps of air. Pins and needles crawled up his neck to the top of his head. Tension clasped his facial muscles. He reached in his pocket for his pills. Something pulled his wrist, but he was unable to recognize the pressure of Deidre's hand holding his back.

His vision was little more than lights and smudges. He could hear a very distant voice. Someone calling him from a hundred yards away.

"Brennan! Baby, it's okay. It's okay. I'm so sorry I shouldn't -" the distant voice became muffled.

The dark rim in his sight grew inwards until all he saw was a tiny, illuminated, pinhole. An all-containing singularity of light. Warm hands embraced his face. His heart slowed. He was deeply and absolutely exhausted, but he was back.

"It's okay, Brennan. You're fine. You were hyperventilating. You passed out for a second, but you're okay." Deidre paused and broke the rhythmic, almost trance inducing cadence with which she had been speaking. "I'm sorry I asked you to go, sweetie. I didn't know it would get that bad."

"No," Brennan opposed, "I had to go. The more I avoid it, the worse it'll get." He tried to speak in a consistent, brave, tone. Deidre kissed his forehead and his already flimsy facade fell apart.

He wept. She held him and wept with him.

For about ten minutes, there were no words. No "I love you" nor any need for it. This was love. They were strong when the other was weak. They stood like a pillar when the other crumbled. For all their flaws, for all their mistakes, for all their regrets, they loved each other.

"Thank you." Brennan whispered.

"Anytime and every time, baby."

Brennan got up; his legs had upgraded from boiled noodles to firmly set jello. He sauntered over to his room, lay down, and slept. The distant voice came again.

"I'll wake you for dinner."

Deidre had tried to wake him. She got a few groans and, "Yeah, going", twice but he never did get up. Deidre put food away for him, told Abby that daddy was way too tired, and then went back to the room. She took off his shirt and slid off his pants. She was sensual about the whole thing, kissing her way up to remove his shirt and down to remove his pants. Not even that woke him. It made Deidre happy to see her husband asleep, but it hurt her that the only time she saw him sleep like this was after a full-blown panic attack. She cuddled up next to him, sparing the blanket in favor of his body heat and fell asleep.

Brennan woke up and turned his body around quickly enough to make the fitted sheets pop off the mattress corner. Deidre was motionless but moaning as tears creeped down her cheeks. Her mouth opened minutely, and she whispered a barely audible, "Please. Stop."

Brennan touched her arm and Deidre sat up in the familiar but ever shocking way.

"Baby, you okay?" Brennan asked moving his hand to her shoulder. He had barely touched her and she scooted away.

"No, don't!" she exclaimed.

Her response triggered a flashback in his mind's eye. He shuddered and was abruptly, though quietly, furious.

"I'll go get you some water." Brennan whispered breathily. He was worried that anything louder would betray the fury he was hiding.

Brennan grabbed shorts and t shirt from a pile of laundry in the living room and slipped them on. He walked into the garage; each step purposeful. He was not anxious, not conflicted. He knew exactly what he had to do.

He unzipped a large duffel bag that was in the corner of the garage. Years ago, his father, a paranoid doomsday prepper that ironically worked for the government, had gifted him this packed 'go bag'. It had a crank up radio / flashlight, thermal blankets, pouches of water, and a balaclava that Brennan would never have to use in the South Texas heat. Still, in this strangest and most improbable of situations, he took the balaclava and slipped it over his face. He wondered how ridiculous he looked. Basketball shorts, a Star Wars tee that read "Rebel Scum", and a balaclava. The whole outfit was pulled together by his bare feet. He went to put on the device and realized he'd have to put the electrodes on under the balaclava. He exhaled, exasperated. He ripped it off and walked inside the house to the small door next to the front entrance and took a hoodie out of the usually unnecessary coat closet. He carried it back to the garage, put on The Machine, put on the hoodie, admired the Iron-Man-esque way that the chest pad glowed blue under it for about a second, then closed his eyes, and pressed it.

Nothing. Not hot, not cool. Not even dark. Just Nothing. Then, a cool breeze. He pulled the hood tightly over his head and around his face. Past Brennan's car, the same, albeit newer looking, car that Brennan had driven on his tomato errand pulled into the driveway of the old apartment building where Brennan and Deidre had once lived. The street was lined with big, off white, box like buildings. Each building was split into quarters making up four apartments per building. Brennan had always wondered why the owners decided on white brick rather than regular, red brick. Maybe their aim was to make it look fancier, but instead the dirt and grime of the 'bad side' of town contrasted against the white, making the ugly boxes look old, faded, and unkempt. Although, to be fair, those were all adequate descriptions of the apartments' conditions.

Past Brennan got out of the car and paused outside of his apartment. Brennan remembered this night. Even before he had walked in, he had been preparing for a fight. Brennan had spent his entire day arguing with her on and off over the phone. Money, their mothers, their past, Brennan's career choices, Deidre's lack of career choices, chores, their future, absolutely everything they could argue about, they argued about. Except for one thing. Past Brennan took a deep breath, leaning against his car, and moved to the door.

The barefoot man in the hoodie approached Past Brennan quickly and silently. Past Brennan was pulled by the back of his shirt and shoved against the little gray Corolla.

"What the hell?" Past Brennan turned around, arm cocked, ready to punch, but he was pushed down onto the ground before his cocked arm could piston forward. He punched the air on the way down.

Both Brennans felt a reeling, unsteady sensation when they came into contact. For a second they were both staring at themselves through the other's eyes.

They both shook their heads clear in identical fashion.

"You feel like a man? Huh, punk?" the Hooded Brennan growled. "Bet you feel real tough hitting her."

Past Brennan scooted on his butt toward the door of his apartment.

"You've got what, a foot of height and a hundred pounds on her?" the man asked rhetorically.

"Dude, I've never... who the hell... what are you..." past Brennan couldn't make sense of his thoughts. He was simultaneously sleep deprived, angry, and scared.

"If you lay a single finger on her, I'll find out. I'll know. Now, get in your house and at the very least *act* like a freaking man." Hooded Brennan hoped that the hoodie and the poor lighting were hiding the tears streaming down his face and distracting from the breaks in his voice.

Past Brennan pulled himself up, looking less scared now, just confused. Brennan had never hit Deidre. The hooded man was probably a drunkard who had mistaken him for someone else.

"I hate this freaking neighborhood." Past Brennan thought.

Past Brennan opened the front door, hopped inside, and closed it, all in one fluid, fear-driven, motion.

The yelling started immediately. Hooded Brennan watched through a broken blind as Past Brennan and Deidre argued. They got louder and louder, but hooded Brennan couldn't quite make out what they were saying. They both stopped yelling, Brennan turned around to leave the room, and Deidre muttered something under her breath. Though her voice was much too soft for Hooded Brennan to hear her, the memory allowed them to clang loudly in his head.

"The way things are, maybe the baby was blessed not to live."

There it was. No Man's Land. The only field in the vast terrain of their past that neither had dared to fight on.

Hooded Brennan knew it had come from a place of pain, a place of suffering and regret. He knew that Deidre would've like to swallow the words before they escaped her gritted teeth, but Past Brennan didn't know that yet. He turned around and raised his hand then... he stopped. He was even more shocked than Deidre. Deidre was frozen, her eyes not looking at the hand, but straight into Brennan's. Past Brennan dropped to his knees and hugged her waist. He wept.

Hooded Brennan wondered how they had ever strayed so far from their love. Sure, things were tough. They had both faced trauma in their childhood and now, the little sun they had expected set before it even had its morning. Still, Brennan had always loved Deidre and Deidre had loved him.

Brennan slowly and agonizingly realized why.

It had happened recently. Past Brennan could feel it. He sensed and feared it but preferred to force himself to believe the lies. Past Brennan would soak in the imaginary peace for another month before his instincts were confirmed. Hooded Brennan unzipped his hoodie and saw his Star Wars shirt.

"Search your feelings, you know it to be true." he thought, in James Earl Jones' low tones.

Brennan let out a humorless snicker. He pulled the e-cord.

Pull. Nothing. Garage.

Brennan grabbed a water bottle from the fridge and walked back to the room. Deidre was clenched up and shivering. For a second, she reminded Brennan of a Chihuahua. The

33

way the tension in their little bodies shakes them, how afraid they seem, but yet so ready to strike out and bite.

He sat next to her and slowly moved a hand to wipe a tear. Again, she moved quickly, but this time towards him. She settled herself perfectly against the shape of his body, like an irregular Tetris piece that somehow fit. Her breathing slowed. The shivering subsided.

Brennan smiled and he held back tears of happiness. It had worked. He could change things. Make things better. This was proof.

His grin widened and a drop of what he thought was sweat or maybe some nasal discharge from his lingering desire to cry fell suddenly on his top lip and slid into his barely parted mouth. Brennan reacted in instinctive disgust, pushing it out with his tongue, expecting salt, but it was metallic and coppery, like pennies. More blood.

Chapter 4

Brennan had a love/hate relationship with weekends. On one hand, Deidre was home. She had finally become indispensable enough that she could demand things like at least two weekends off a month without being immediately shut down or fearing repercussions. Deidre was Brennan's anchor when his mind began to sail towards stormy seas and as much as it shamed him, he felt safe with her around. Brennan knew it probably wasn't healthy. His monster-in-law had called it codependency on multiple occasions, and though he wasn't completely sure she was wrong, Brennan hated hearing her say it, almost as much as she loved to say it.

Misty was constantly looking for opportunities to use words that she believed made her sound knowledgeable and, more importantly to her, superior to others. She learned codependent in the therapy sessions that Brennan had paid for when he was still working. She had attended a few appointments despite saying that she found Brennan's offer to pay "both patronizing and condescending". She had learned "patronizing" from a community college professor she knocked boots with who, despite his frequent visits with her, had apparently neglected to teach her "ironic".

The hate part of the relationship with weekends was an unfortunate consequence of the former. Deidre was with him, but she usually wanted to do stuff. Social stuff. Going out stuff. When their current situations had first started, she would ask if he would like to go get something to eat or go window shopping at the mall. He'd say no, she'd be understanding and suggest Netflix or Redbox. As the Brennan induced bouts of cabin fever persisted, she stopped asking and began to do what she called, "firmly suggesting". She would now simply say, "let's go to the mall", "let's go to the movies", "let's go to the park", and she'd get Abby ready to go. As much as Brennan loved Deidre, he could still tell her "no", but once Abby was all dolled up and excited for their family outing, Brennan forgot how to piece those two letters together.

This weekend, Brennan had almost been happy to go to the park. He felt like they should celebrate. Ever since he retconned what he considered one of his biggest failures, Brennan and Deidre had been closer. She hadn't had any night terrors and was more open with Brennan. Brennan had even begun forgetting details of the incident. A few days before, he could recall the stinging, hot sensation on his hand after he had struck her, but now, it was all foggy. Congruously, a new memory was taking root in his mind, like a weed that sets roots in a field and slowly strangles the preceding residents of its spot. Every time he thought back to that day, the image of a deranged, barefoot man in shorts and a hoodie became just a little clearer.

Though he had readily and happily agreed to go, his enthusiasm quickly waned upon arriving. Deidre was doing her best to ignore his incessant movements, but her peripheral itched every time he shifted his sitting position, tugged at his shirt, or rolled his shoulders, and her eye gave a small twitch every time he nervously popped a joint. She finally decided to react in a controlled manner, rather than ignoring him until she snapped.

"What's going on, Brennan, you're fidgeting around like you've got DTs." That was less polite than she intended. She decided she had waited too long.

"Maybe we should go." Brennan grumbled in a low, broody, voice.

"I thought you were excited to come. Look," she pointed out at the playground, "Abby's having a great time."

It's amazing how perspective can change a single event into completely antithetical situations. Deidre saw her daughter smiling, running and climbing. Being a kid in the simple way God had intended. Brennan saw his daughter as a satellite. She spun and moved around with the kids, but she was not a part of them. She was a separate entity merely caught in the gravitational pull of something bigger than herself.

"She's just playing by herself." Brennan exclaimed in an exasperated tone, doing his best not to manually signal at Abby with equal exasperation.

"No, she's...." Deidre started.

Another amazing thing about perspective is that once you see another person's perspective, it can be difficult to unsee it. Once you see the shadow ballerina spinning left, it's hard to trick your mind back to seeing her spin right.

Deidre's countenance fell as she saw that her daughter was in fact playing alone. She ran around the children. She walked through them. She struggled to climb behind them, but she did not interact. She was never tagged. No one looked for her when she hid obviously behind the seahorse on a giant spring. Even though Abby didn't seem to mind or even notice, Deidre's heart still ached for her. She felt the pressure of reluctant tears pushing up into her eyes.

A cautious relief descended on her as a little boy with a bowl cut and a dinosaur t-shirt approached Abby.

"Hi, I'm Jordy." the little boy squeaked.

Abby stood up suddenly, her back straight as if at attention, but her hands twisting and her little feet bouncing her up and down. The little boy saw her jittery movements and it sparked his curiosity. He smiled.

"Why are you so happy?" he inquired.

Perspective really is amazing.

"Are you essited to play?" He continued, his head bobbing around trying to find her dodging gaze to make eye contact. "What's your name?"

"Me Abby." Abby closed her eyes tight and scrunched her nose and mouth as if her faulty grammar tasted sour. "I'm Abby. My name is Abby." Her hands flapped faster, her light bouncing almost became hopping.

"Wanna play tag?" Jordy asked.

"Yeah!" Abby said, her eyes wide, her hands now flapping so fast you'd think she was trying to achieve lift off.

"Okay! You're it first, but I'll slow up a little, cuz I'm super fast. I'm the fassest kid in my class."

Jordy tagged Abby and, as agreed, moved away in a jog rather than an all-out sprint.

Abby stood in her spot looking after him, her delight showing in her toothy grin.

"Chase him, Abby!" Brennan called out. He was aiming for encouraging but his tone fell about a quarter way into frustrated.

Abby ran after Jordy on her tiptoes, curls bobbing behind her as she went.

Deidre was smiling again.

"I wish I could help her." Brennan remarked suddenly, drowning the happy mood. "Instead, I probably make it worse. It's my fault."

"It's not your fault." Deidre paused, measuring her words, "It can't be your fault." She concluded.

"Seriously? You think she doesn't notice when I panic? You think she doesn't notice I don't work, CAN'T work? That I can't even drive? At least before I could afford her therapies, now I just have to watch, knowing I'm too weak to do anything."

"Brennan, sweetie, you're spiraling." Deidre acknowledged in a low, calm voice.

"I can't fix myself, how am I supposed to fix her?!" Brennan almost yelled, and with those words, the last straw had been added.

"Fix her? Fix her, Brennan? You want to fix our daughter? She's not broken, Brennan." Deidre enunciated, a bitter note of anger in every syllable.

Brennan felt the aftertaste of regret following his careless words.

"I know, that's not what I meant. I just meant…"

"You just meant what? That you want to make her normal? Because our daughter is above normal. Did you mean that you want to make her life easier? Sure, therapy could help. Her dad stressing himself into an early grave, not so much."

Deidre took a breath and lowered her voice. "Do you remember what Abby asked you after the first time she saw you have a panic attack?"

Brennan responded with affirmative silence.

"She asked you why you were afraid. 'Daddy God protects you, daddy. Don't be afraid.' Do you remember when she learned to put her socks on and she'd wear mismatched socks but insisted they weren't the 'wrong' socks because she had chosen them that way? Do you remember her reaction when you explained that you quit and that we had to cancel the cable and buy her less toys? Do you remember how she completely missed everything you said about the cable and toys and just asked, 'Does that mean, you're going to be home with me, Daddy?' That big, goofy, smile on her face…"

"I don't want to change her just," Brennan paused, his angry voice had dropped to barely a whisper, "I just want to help her not be like me."

Deidre stopped. She had made her point and perhaps had taken it too far. A large tear slid down Brennan's cheek, shrinking steadily, leaving behind a trail of quickly drying moisture on his skin.

"She's different, but that's okay, Brennan. God gave us a gorgeous, unique, little girl. There just happen to be a few side effects to having a soul that beautiful." She bent down and held his hand. "Life isn't trail mix, baby. You can't pick and choose what you like and put the rest back in the bag."

Brennan smiled. "You've been reading my old sermon notes?"

Deidre reciprocated with her overwhelmingly brilliant grin. "No, that one just stuck."

Brennan heard a low buzzing sound. "Seriously?" he mumbled under his breath.

Deidre stood up and pulled her cell phone out of her pocket. "I knew I should've left it off today." She slid the green circle and put the device to her ear, "Hello? Yeah. Again? Isn't she out of sick leave already? There's no one else? Ugh, fine. You know hangovers aren't supposed to be covered under sick leave, right? Yeah, just give me 45 minutes." Deidre moved the phone away from her face.

"I have to go in. Sarah called in sick again, but according to Twitter, the night was still 'lit' at 4 in the morning." Her voice was tinged with disdain.

"I thought she blocked you." Brennan said dryly.

"I made a 'party guys' profile. I post pictures of the douchiest, lamest, fraternity, dudes that are probably all named Chad and then followed a bunch of 'party girls', including her."

Brennan couldn't help but chuckle. He raised an eyebrow at her. "Man, and they called me an investigator. Still, all that for Sarah?"

"I really like my days off," she replied with a smaller, softer, gentle smile. "Please get Abby so I can drop you off at your brother's."

Brennan's momentary spike in mood dropped. "What? Why?"

"Because you're feeling anxious, depressed, and overstimulated and I can't be working and worrying about how you are. Go get Abby, please."

Brennan couldn't argue with her. He did indeed feel anxious, depressed, and overstimulated by all the noise and running children.

The sting of her words must have been obvious on his face because Deidre apologized shortly after, "I'm sorry, hon. Look, I work more hours, I get more O.T., more money, and maybe we can afford a few therapy sessions for Abby."

Brennan nodded silently.

"Abby! Abby-baby! Let's go sweetheart, we're going to uncle's house." Brennan called out to Abby. Abby turned around ran to Jordy and gave him a hug. Brennan saw a pink shade rise in Jordy's cheeks and felt a strange twinge of jealousy. *"She's only five,"* he thought.

Abby ran up to Brennan. "I'm rea-ee, da-ee."

"Sweetie," Brennan began in the gentlest tone he could muster, "what have we said about strangers and giving people their bubble space?"

"Him is my frien'." Abby replied and began to rationalize, "I never had a kid frien' afore, just you and mommy, and I hug you and mommy."

Brennan decided she deserved to have that trusting innocence unsullied for at least one more day, but they'd discuss the concept of not everyone being a friend later. A pit formed in Brennan's stomach. He hated the idea of polluting his daughter with distrust and paranoia.

"It's just caution." He assured himself, just loud enough to hear his own voice. "Let's just go, sweetie."

It was a quiet ride to James' house. Deidre drove, humming along to old music barely audible over the car speakers, Brennan sat with his eyes closed in the passenger seat, thoughts racing a million miles an hour, a bouquet of fantasies, what-ifs, regrets, and plans. Abby had nodded off in her booster seat. Her curly hair, freed from the confines of its hair tie, enveloped the edges of her face and twisted down to her little shoulders.

Deidre parked outside a red brick apartment building. She had pulled up right next to James' red, F-150 Raptor. Brennan scoffed at the truck. He felt it was an accurate enough representation of who James was. Big, strong and handy, but often showy and bordering on obnoxious. Brennan got out of the car and picked Abby up and out of her booster seat. She stirred and hooked her arms around his neck.

"Be safe at work, sweetie." Brennan told Deidre through her lowered window. He hesitated a while. Deidre remained silent, sensing that he wasn't done talking. "I'm sorry about earlier. And about everything. About me being the way that…"

"Bren," Deidre interrupted, "stop. Just stop doing that to yourself. It's not your fault, okay? We're going to get through this. Yes, it sucks, but I don't know how many ways or how many times I can tell you that IT. IS. NOT. YOUR. FAULT."

Brennan felt frustrated. She always told him this. What she didn't understand was how upsetting it was. If it was his fault, he could change it. He could stop it. It could be under his control. He wanted to tell her, but he could see her glancing impatiently at the dashboard clock.

"Be safe at work, hon. No flirting with any old guys." Brennan remarked with a half smile.

"What if they're like, super rich and close to death?" Deidre asked jokingly. Brennan sometimes forgot the dark sense of humor that trauma had gifted his wife and how well it complemented his own. Deidre smiled playfully. "I love you, baby. Have fun with James."

Brennan chuckled. "I'll try. I love you too, hon." He rocked Abby upwards to improve his grip and moved to James' door.

There had been a time that Brennan really would have loved to spend a night with James. As kids, they had been inseparable. Brennan had basically raised James from the time their father left. James did everything that Brennan did. Brennan was James' Superman, but with time, James had outgrown Brennan. Despite trying to emulate his big brother, James had always been different from Brennan in one key way. James had the intrinsic ability to move on. When their father left, James moved on to Brennan. So it had been through every storm. To James, little orphan Annie sang *"Tomorrow"* as a hopeful anthem of what was to come. To Brennan, it was a reminder that the hope was indeed always a day away, never actually arriving.

The result was that James thrived. He was able to walk away from something he couldn't fix. He didn't worry for too long. He had succeeded in every place where Brennan had failed. His criminal justice career took off, he was happy, confident, in a healthy relationship, hell, he was even taller and fitter. Brennan was happy for him, it's every good parent's, or parent proxy's, dream to see their child more successful than them. What bothered Brennan was that James had switched the roles. Now James tried, and mostly failed, to turn his brother's life around with his perpetual optimism, much to Brennan's chagrin. James didn't understand Brennan's need to patch up people and situations, even if it required pieces of himself.

Brennan knocked.

"Brennie!" James exclaimed, startling Abby awake for a second. "Oh, crap, sorry. Didn't see the munchkin was asleep. Come in."

Brennan hadn't liked the nickname "Brennie" in years. It was a cutesie name when James was 3. It was endearing and nostalgic when James was 12. It began to feel condescending around the time James turned 20 and had grown taller than Brennan.

James stood at six foot three, 220 pounds of solid muscle, plus another 10 of what he called "dad bod".

Brennan walked in and James motioned him to his small guest room. Brennan carried Abby in and slowly set her down on the pink and purple, princess themed, twin bed. Despite the fact that James had no children, his guest room was full of toys, covered in cartoon posters, and had a small TV with stickers and some crayon writing on it. James could be annoying at times, but he loved his niece as much as he loved his brother.

"Michelle doesn't think it's weird that you have a little girl's room in your house?" Brennan asked, half joking, half not.

"Don't be morbid, man. You're making it weird. She knows about Abby and that y'all spend a good chunk of time here when Dee goes to work." As James responded, he moved the purple weighted blanket over Abby.

James had read that weighted blankets could be very comforting and helped children with autism sleep better. He had read the article online one day and ordered the $70 blanket not fifteen minutes later. He made sure to get purple since it was always at the top of Abby's ever-rotating top 5 favorite colors.
"Da-ee, is puhple!" Abby had exclaimed, never forgetting her manners, she had capped it with, "Thank you, Ucle Jimbo!"

Brennan held back the pressure he felt building in the corners of his eyes in seeing his baby brother's tenderness with Abby.

The brothers retreated to the living room where James had an episode of "*The Office*" playing at a volume low enough to basically be mute. Brennan sat down on the overstuffed, brown, leather couch. James kept walking towards the kitchen.

"What kind of psycho watches '*Scott's Tots*', like for fun?" Brennan teased, trying to hide some of the tension in his voice. His stomach was clenched and there was still a nagging buzz in his chest and neck.

James chuckled. "I don't know, man. I like cringey humor." He walked up to where Brennan could see him and held up a bottle of ZiegenBock. "Want a beer, bud?"

Brennan was back to exasperated. "You know I don't drink, James."

"Maybe you should start, homie. You look haggard." James waited a second to see if his brother laughed. He didn't. Brennan's serious face made James laugh involuntarily. "I'm joking Brennie. Sorry, bud." He laughed a little more.

"Nothing funny about alcohol dependency, man." Brennan criticized, subconsciously marking his hypocrisy by absent mindedly thumbing the bottle of benzodiazepines in his pocket.

"I don't know, man. Dad was an alchie and he was pretty funny." James' attempts to lighten the mood were falling flat before his one man audience. "He told great jokes."

Brennan gave a weak smile, if you could call the slight upward angles at the corners of his mouth a "smile".

"Yeah," Brennan began, "Remember that really funny practical joke he played on mom? The one where he was all like, 'Till death do us part' and then left her? HA!" Brennan mocked a single syllable of laughter, "Hilarious."

"Bren..."

"*Here it comes.*" Brennan thought. James would regift him some advice he himself had given James when they were younger. Or maybe James would give him an installment of his patented, *How to get over it, For Dummies.*

"I know I get annoying." James said in a quiet voice. He was picking at the sticker label on his beer bottle with his nails. "I just want you to be happy, bud. I want you to be well."

It was not what Brennan was expecting. Brennan felt a pang of guilt.

"I know you went through tough things…" James started, but was interrupted by Brennan.

"We all did, Jimbo."

"Yeah, but I had a childhood, Bren. In the middle of everything I got to be a kid."

"Jim…"

"You didn't have a childhood, because you instead chose to give yours to me." James declared, now louder, and with more conviction.

Bren held back the tears, but one fugitive rolled down his cheek.

"I don't regret that, Jim. It's not back then. It's now. I feel like a failure, Jimmy. I really do. I failed at my job, I'm failing as a provider, as a protector." Brennan paused, "I'm failing as a man."

"Stop it, Bren." James scolded, "Stop putting yourself down like that, bud. Do you remember what you would always tell me in hard times?"

"Stop doing that, Jim, Jesus is watching?" Brennan joked and chuckled through a soft sob.

James snickered, "No, dude. Psalm 28:7. **The Lord is my strength and my shield; my heart trusts in him, and he helps me. My heart leaps for joy, and with my song I praise him**." James paused, observing how Brennan's face changed. As a former preacher, Brennan knew the scripture, he just didn't live by it anymore. He didn't like the conviction it made him feel.

"Stop trying to do it on your own, man. You aren't strong enough alone and that's okay. You were a father to me before your age hit double digits. Then you became Abby's father while also being a father figure to the kids you dealt with in CPS. I mean, just the CPS job paired with our colorful past would mess anyone up. You didn't fail."

"I failed Kaylee." Brennan remarked.

James looked down. This was often where the spiral began.

Kaylee had been a turnip nosed preteen with dark red hair that hung like a curtain. She had olive skin, hazel eyes, and an abusive stepfather.

"CPS wasn't about me making up for our 'colorful past'. It was about balancing things out. Dee never had anyone save her. We never had anyone help us. No one was running to help mom. I needed to find a balance. To stop it, but it had usually already happened by the time we got there."

"Yeah, Bren, but you stopped the cycle. You ended it."

"No. That's what we tell ourselves, but it's not true. Kaylee's stepdad could've been stopped. I could've done it." Brennan trailed off. "I knew something was off. I couldn't find the proof. I couldn't convince her it was safe to talk. She was too scared." His eyes were red and shrink-wrapped in salty tears. "So, we closed the case, we 'moved on', and then the next time we got a call about her, she was dead. I failed Kaylee, like I'm failing Deidre, like I'm failing Abby, like I failed you..."

The spiral was in full swing. James got up from his end of the couch and sat next to his brother, holding his head to Brennan's.

"Brennie, it's okay. You did all you can." James had quiet tears running down his cheeks. "Buddy, you can't change the past."

Brennan stopped. Just stopped, crying, breathing, thinking, everything. It was abrupt and disquieting. He looked up at James, staring directly into his eyes. Just as suddenly, Brennan's shoulders and gaze relaxed, and he laughed. Not mockingly, not sarcastically. A genuine laugh as the weight of the world seemed to melt off his shoulders.

James smiled. "Alright weirdo, way to break the moment. *Office, Parks and Rec*, or we go dramatic with some *Peaky Blinders*, pick your poison."

"You choose." Brennan muttered absentmindedly. Whatever they watched, James might as well be watching alone. Brennan's mind was elsewhere, planning. Plans for tomorrow. Plans for yesterday.

Chapter 5

A man could not be in two places at once. No matter what happened, Brennan would have an alibi.

He waited until Deidre fell asleep and inched out of bed. He turned back to look at his beautiful wife. She looked calm, peaceful. No sign of night terrors. A sleep to be envied.

Deidre gave a short snort like snore and Brennan couldn't help but chuckle. He walked over to her side of the bed and, against his better judgement but completely helpless to the compulsion, he kissed her forehead, smelling her hair as he did. He could've sworn he saw a twitch of a smile.

Brennan walked into the garage / lab. He was better prepared for today. He slipped out of his pajamas and put on paint splattered jeans, tan work boots, a plain grey t shirt, and a Dickies tan canvas jacket with a grey hood. Under the hood and his grey tee shirt was The Machine. Tucked into an inside-the-waistband holster, slightly jabbing into the right side of his belly was a Luger LCR .357 revolver. Brennan owned several handguns but chose this one for two reasons. It was easily concealable, but more importantly, he had just purchased this gun from a pawn shop three months ago. It had been an impulse buy propelled by fear. He had stopped carrying since the anxiety had become as severe as it was. He felt that Deidre should carry something to protect herself. She had refused it and opted for mace. That didn't matter now. What mattered was that he was going to a time before the purchase.

He took a deep breath and focused on the date and place he wanted to go. He was about to push the pad on his chest, when he saw how badly his hands trembled and he became acutely aware of the tingling sensation rippling through his neck and into his face.

He took a quarter bar of Xanax into his hand, threw it into his mouth, and took a swig of water from a bottle he had left with the change of clothes.

He stood still, took another breath, and hit the pad with his open palm.

Pull. Tension. Nothing.

Blissful, peaceful, Nothing.

Pull. Pressure. Gravity. Fresh air.

He opened his eyes and looked around. He was getting better at this. He was behind the empty building that neighbored the old CPS offices.

He walked briskly around the building and saw a familiar, yet somehow alien, face walking into the building.

Brennan remembered how he felt that day, but from this 3rd person perspective, he could truly see how badly he hid it. Past Brennan's hands were trembling, his hair in disarray from the way he ran his fingers through it when he was upset, his eyes red from the effort to protect the emotional levy that constantly seemed on the verge of eruption, or at least overflow.

He waited until Past Brennan was in the building and then he walked hurriedly, his hood up, towards his car. The autumn wind was cool on his face. In deep south Texas, autumn is usually just a baby summer, but chilly days like this provided beautiful exceptions to the rule. He inhaled the fresh air to the full capacity of his lungs and felt a surge of confidence. He would make things right.

The car's key fob worked, regardless of what timeline it came from. Brennan got in and turned it on. It made a brief rattling noise and he had the foolish urge to write his past self a note. "The rattling gets worse. It's a timing chain. Deal with it now." He didn't, but he thought he could've used the warning.

He put the car in gear and drove before his nerves talked him out of it. He did his best to keep his mind focused on reviewing his plan, but the physical symptoms manifested rapidly. He squeezed his eyes shut and sat up in his seat.

He knew where the man would be. He'd be at the 8-Ball Bar. A nasty dive in the middle of nowhere. He'd be celebrating that he got off unscathed. Kaylee had refused to talk. He'd be celebrating that he beat the system. He beat The Man.

As he began to feel a pulse in his eyes, he decided he would be better safe than sorry. He took another quarter tablet of Xanax as the tremor in his hands intensified. He dry swallowed painfully.

The Stepfather would not be celebrating long.

Brennan arrived at the bar. There was no neon sign that indicated the place was a bar. Just an ugly white building, a giant concrete ball painted to look like the 8 Ball, and the sickly smell of smoke just a bit too sweet to be tobacco.

He parked his car towards the back of the caliche patch considered the parking lot and waited. The white noise sensation in his sinus cavity began to subside. The buzzing in his head began to quiet. His muscles and stomach relaxed.

He tried to remember details of the day. He knew that the sack of crap that dared call himself a man would arrive at his house, driving drunk, at around 6:30 PM. An early return to continue the party with a celebratory beating and then something worse. Even as he felt the anger go from simmer to full boil, Brennan held on to his benzo assisted composure.

A sudden hazy memory started taking shape. It was new, though it didn't feel like it was.

His car had been stolen that day.

The memory snapped at him and he jumped in his seat.

"I guess I'm not getting the car back to the office." Brennan told himself aloud. This was the first time he had experienced a memory forming as he lived the event that precipitated it.

Even with a half bar in his system, his heart accelerated from a nervous march to a frantic, deathly sprint. Brennan's vision immediately blurred, his eyes watered, and the color dropped from his face as it started to feel numb. He reached for a bottle of water in the back seat, pulled out the bottle of tablets, struggled for what seemed like ages to get the top off, and crookedly broke up two quarter tabs. He drank them hurriedly, spilling water down the front of his canvas jacket. He was exasperated by the spill for a split second.

"It'll help me fit in better if anything," an eerily clear thought broke through as he stared at his wet chest.

By the time that Kaylee's Stepdad came out, a full 30 minutes later, Brennan was comfortable and calm. Too calm if anything.

Brennan exited the car and looked at the pathetic being struggling to get the key into the door of his jalopy. The man was not what you'd expect him to look like.

Monsters rarely have warning labels.

He was handsome, light brown skin, dark brown eyes, thick black hair, and the kind of musculature that only comes through natural hard work, not a gym.

"Need some help there, bud?"

The man looked up. The transition of his expressions were comically abrupt. Like hard cuts, rather than smooth blends. Surprise, to confusion, to suspicion, to recognition, and finally to shock. The man managed to take one step back in the loose, swaying way that drunk men do, before Brennan's fist connected hard, fast, and with good follow through, directly below the man's left temple.

He dropped like a sack.

A man came out of the bar and met eyes with Brennan. This man was also inebriated, though not as much as Kaylee's Stepdad. He was a large, boorish looking man. He wore a dingy white t-shirt. His work coveralls were half undone, the sleeves tied to keep them up, holding on to each other as if for dear life around his considerable waist.

"Se tomo unas diez chelas de mas el guey." Brennan said with as charming a smile as he could muster.

The man laughed a tired-sounding, clumsy laugh.

"I'm his designated driver. I came to pick him up. Just in time it seems too." Brennan added unnecessarily. The man seemed focused on something Brennan couldn't see.

The other man walked back in.

As Brennan heaved Kaylee's Stepdad up, a strange smell wafted at Brennan. He realized that the other man had come out to drain the water main, so to speak. The man had done so, though he had forgotten to do it outside his pants.

Brennan shook his head in disgust and with some difficulty opened the passenger door of the jalopy and plopped Kaylee's Stepdad in. Brennan took the driver's seat and the keys he'd taken from his target and cranked the engine. It sputtered for a second then roared before settling into a rumbling purr.

Brennan had gloves between his hands and the steering wheel and made sure not to adjust the seats, the mirrors, or anything else in the car, and began to drive.

Nervousness began to creep in again, as the small town roads, lined with occasional shops and houses melted into what the locals called "the boonies" or "el monte".

A voice, probably his own, rang in his head.

"Vengeance is mine, sayeth the Lord." he shook his head. How many squares had he taken? Too many maybe. *"Thou shalt not murder."*

His heart skipped then hammered. Beat. Skip. BOOM. He coughed hard.

Brennan shook his head again and sat up straight, a new anxious jolt pushing past the cloudy, chemically induced, apathy.

He took a loose quarter bar of Xanax and then thought it better and bit it in half. The bitter powder from the broken tablet made him retch.

"No," he cried, "You left me. You turned Your back on me. You let fear consume me."

The lie itched in his throat.

His head was swimming. He tried to review the count of how many little Xanax squares he had taken, but numbers didn't seem to make sense.

He noticed that the curves in the road had ironed themselves out. A long, straight, county road lay ahead of them for at least a couple of miles. He pulled over and got out of the driver's side door.

The ground seemed to move under his feet. It felt like the earth was balancing on an old rope bridge and he was rocking it with each step. He held onto the roof of the car and felt his stomach lurch.

He instinctively pushed himself away from the car and vomited. He coughed and spat. The effort seemed to clear his mind a bit. He made sure that there was no vomit on him and returned to the car. He pulled the Stepdad across the bench seat to the driver's side and closed the door.

Brennan climbed back in the car through the passenger side. He felt like his body was lagging behind his brain. He felt his stomach cramp again, but was able to hold it down.

Brennan got as close as he could to the driver's side and pressed on the gas pedal while maneuvering the steering wheel with his left hand and brandishing his revolver in the right.

30 miles per hour. Then 40. 50. 60. 75. 85. 90.

Kaylee's Stepdad stirred he opened his eyes and a half choked yell managed to escape his mouth. He swung his arm wildly at Brennan, hitting him in the side of the head, and causing him to yank the wheel to the right. The old car jerked to the right before the man pulled it left, over correcting enough to send the car into a fishtail. The man looked at Brennan with his usually handsome face transformed into a terrifying visage. Bloodshot eyes, his brown face looking almost purple, teeth bared by an expression that was equal parts rage and terror, all capped by a dark purple-reddish welt where Brennan had struck him.

Brennan felt everything was distant. Blurred. He raised his hand felt the pull of his finger, the shockwave going back through his right arm, the pressure of the bang in his ears, and saw red chunks explode onto the driver side window, a red mist hanging in the air.

The man pulled the steering wheel left with the impact from the bullet and the fishtail climaxed into a flip over the front driver side wheel.

Brennan pulled the cord as the world began to toss around him.

Nothing. But this time he was falling through Nothing. He wasn't still. He realized he also wasn't alone.

Before he could fully understand the feeling that there was someone else there; air, concrete, pain.

He gasped trying to recapture the air knocked from his lungs.

Tears stung his eyes and as the adrenaline began to subside, the effects of the drugs returned. He removed his boots, pants, jacket, and shirt then hid them beneath a table in the garage. He hid The Machine back in a toolbox.

He moved very slowly, his head throbbing, his vision swimming, and grabbed an old mop bucket he used as a trash can.

Whatever was left in his stomach was transferred into that.

He walked inside and towards the couch, clinging to the walls for support.

He needed to sleep, but his room might as well have been Mordor and one could not simply walk there in his condition. He landed hard on the couch and slept.

He woke up 12 hours later to an empty house and closed curtains. Deidre was so thoughtful. He got up, realized he was hungry, started walking toward the kitchen, when a thought froze him.

"Kaylee"

His heart knocked hard against his chest before resuming a softer, but much faster beat. He needed to check on Kaylee. He needed to go.

Brennan jumped in his car, forgetting to brush his teeth, wash his face, or comb his hair. He had grabbed a pair of shorts and a t-shirt from a pile of laundry Diedre had been working on the night before. He slid his feet into the blue "TEXAS" flip-flops he kept by the garage door and got in his car.

His car. He had his car. They had brought it back.

"Wait, *who* brought it back?" He asked aloud. His brain refused to clarify and he drove off.

He took another quarter pill and the trip blended into a buzzing, milky track.

He made the 10 minute drive to Kaylee's school in about 8 minutes. He had hastily calculated it would take him 15 minutes to be there and wanted to find a good place to observe the after-school flow of children without throwing up any red flags for wary parents. Instead, now he was way too early and the anticipation was eating at him.

He saw his CPS identification badge and thought of getting down and asking to see Kaylee. No, it was irresponsible, unethical, not to mention he was dressed completely inappropriately.

Each minute stretched for hours. Brennan became more anxious with every glance at his dashboard's clock. He began to sweat, despite the A/C going full blast. His mouth dried out. His hands began to shake. A tingling numbness started prickling his jawline, then slowly spread down his neck and up his face.

He held off as much as he could. His valiant effort lasted 4 minutes.

Brennan tore the cap off the pill bottle and took out a bar missing a quarter. He tried to break off a piece, but his hands shook and the sweat on his palms and fingertips began to dissolve the coating of the tablet.

His heart was beating like cannon with the firing rate of a machine gun.

There was a dark subconscious certainty that it was about to explode. An artery would burst. It would choke on itself. He was going to die.

He took the remaining three quarters of the tablet and put his seat back and did his best to breath.

A slow, creeping, calm spread through his veins over the course of the next 15 minutes. In the distance he heard the familiar sound of a trilling school bell.

He sat up, pulling the lever beside him to let the seat assist him. He scanned the frantic crowd of children running out of the middle school. His vision was blurred around the edges, with a sharp focus at the epicenter of his drug induced goggles.

Suddenly, through the crowd, he saw it. The unmistakable, glowing, fiery, red, long locks. Kaylee seemed to move in slow motion in contrast to the rest of the school children. She was serious, walking diligently, but with a smile. She was not quite a child anymore. No one lived through what she had and completely remained a child. Still, she was alive. His heart skipped, albeit sluggishly. His vision sharpened and it took him a moment to realize that it had been cleared by tears. She walked down the steps of the school and took a gleeful hop off the second to bottom step down to the sidewalk. The hop triggered a smiling sob to escape Brennan's throat. She was alive. She had a chance. More than that, somewhere in her, she had hope.

Brennan wiped his eyes, took a breath, and put the car in reverse. He looked up one last time and saw Kaylee's mom. She looked tired. The kind of tired that comes from not one night, but a new lifestyle of short, interrupted, disturbed sleep. Her hair was a mess and she seemed paranoid. She saw Kaylee and motioned at her to hurry. Kaylee jogged to her and her mother hugged her and smiled. She kissed the top of her head and began to talk to her. She let Kaylee walk ahead of her and then she started looking around nervously.

Brennan had seen this before, though never to this extreme. A case would come in. A family member was abusing the child. The parent or parents would deny it. Uncle John could never, good ol' grandpa Joe is just playful, mom's boyfriend Bob is just trying to step up as the new dad. Then the proof comes out. The child speaks up. Some evidence is found. Sometimes, the person confesses. The parents' world crumbles. The unimaginable is reality. They do their best to keep a facade of normalcy for the child, but nothing is ever the same. The abuse doesn't just hurt the child. It splinters families.

A GIF of Kaylee's little hop looped in Brennan's brain the whole way back home.

He lay down on the couch, the little hop now melding with the mother's nervousness, then something else. A gun. A drive. A murder. His memories melded together into a blur that grew incrementally dimmer until it was just dark, black, sleep.

A few hours later a distant voice echoed, flowing closer and closer, louder and louder. A sweet, petite, voice.

"Da-ee! Da-ee!"

Brennan took a gasping inhalation and woke with a start.

Abby didn't seem to notice.

"Da-ee, I pass my spell-een test, da-ee!" She was flapping her hands happily, a now very wrinkled paper in one of them. She handed it to him.

He looked down at it. *"Her handwriting is improving."* he thought, then, "Wait, Abby who gave you a spelling test."

"The tu-dor, da-ee! From the-rah-pee," she enunciated each syllable, "I spelled 'should' and 'could', but I wrote the wrong 'wood'."

He suddenly remembered a blonde guy. Surfer dude long hair and goatee, wearing blue scrubs. Was his name Derek?

Abby ran into the bathroom and came back with wet wipes. She gave them to Brennan.

"You had a nose-beed when you were sleepin'."

Brennan took a wipe and dragged it across his left cheek. Sure enough, the white wipe was now streaked with pinkish red.

She wasn't as scared of the blood. Still nervous, her fingers were fidgeting, her jaw was shifting, but not afraid.

Deidre walked in and saw Brennan. Her mouth smiled, but her eyes showed concern.

"How are you feeling, baby?" she asked, the concern becoming the dominant emotion on display.

"I'm fine. I was just feeling out of it."

"You slept like half the day," her face lightened up a bit, "I guess you were tired."

She paused and her face became inquisitive. For a moment, Brennan admired how expressive his wife's face was, especially in contrast to his. How beautiful and adorable every expression was. "How did you get to the couch?"

"I don't know." Brennan replied honestly. He remembered he had done something. He had helped Kaylee. A flash of the little redhead hopping off a step. She was safe now, but the details were blurry. Then again, maybe he was remembering wrong. The Machine was messing with his memory. His brain was trying to consolidate different timelines.

"Have they called you from work?" Deidre questioned, ringing a bell in Brennan's mind.

He was working again. How? He tried to remember. He remembered quitting, but he also remembered being put on admin leave.

"I wish you didn't have to go back. It's a crappy job to begin with, but now with Kaylee's dad and Ron. I don't know how you could go back. Your anxiety has gotten worse. TWO panic attacks per week since the incident." Deidre held out to fingers to add emphasis.

Brennan had been having the dreaded terrors daily when he was at work. He remembered that. He remembered the gripping, irrational, chemical fear. Somehow, they were diminished now.

Brennan tried his best to appear like he was still tired and loopy. It wasn't much of a stretch.

"How long have I been on admin already?"

Deidre cocked an eyebrow. "You need a few more hours, Aurora?"

Brennan chuckled.

64

"9 months, Bren."

Another flash. A confused man in handcuffs.

"Right after Ron's arrest." Brennan said. It was strange. He was describing a memory and somehow discovering the fact for the first time.

The memories sharpened and took shape.

Kaylee's stepdad had died. The oxygen thieving pedophile had died almost a year ago in what was thought to be a drunk driving accident. The police had not revealed that their investigation had found evidence of the human trash heap being shot before the crash. That there had been another driver, someone wearing gloves. They didn't tell the public about the muddy size 12 boot prints they found. Then Brennan's stolen car had been returned.

Brennan had been the obvious suspect, but there were plenty of witnesses and camera footage showing he was in the office that entire day. The witnesses were credible, detailed, and corroborated each other. Brennan had been furious about the outcome at court that day. He had been vocal about it. Ron, another CPS worker who somewhat resembled Brennan, one of his two friends in the department, had left on a priority 1 case shortly after hearing Brennan vent. Brennan's car had disappeared right about then.

A couple of drunk guys remembered a big guy wearing work boots and a tan jacket. He had been there to pick up the drunken dung pile. They both picked Ron out of a photo lineup. The lineup didn't include Brennan though, witnesses and camera footage ruled him out.

After long careful examination, they found something, not on the car, but on Brennan's keys.

Fingerprints.

Ron's fingerprints.

The investigation dragged for months. Lots of false starts and circumstantial evidence. Finally, nine months ago, they had arrested Ron. Ron had sworn that he hadn't done anything, but the evidence was pointing at him, shaky as it was. Brennan had been put on administrative leave due to the investigation revolving around his case, his friend, and his car. He had no contact with work. Thankfully, though, terrified of a wrongful termination suit, they were still paying him and had not fired him.

"But Ron didn't do it." Brennan concluded finally.

"I know it's hard to believe, baby," Deidre said, wisping her hand down his cheek, neck, and to his shoulder, "but nothing else makes sense. I do wonder how he managed to get out of the car before the crash."

She was right. Gosh, he felt so guilty. If he hadn't told Ron about it, Ron wouldn't have lost it. Ron wouldn't have killed Kaylee's Stepdad. He felt a bit hurt too though. He had taken Brennan's car and worn boots that were at least a size too big for him. Had he been trying to frame him?

A punch landed inside Brennan's chest. "No." he blurted, sudden, staccato, and afraid. He had forgotten something. He knew it wasn't Ron. It had not been Ron. But then who?

A quick memory played out in a half a second.

Brennan is leaving a meeting in a hurry. Ron calls out.

"You're not going to get very far, Brennan."

Brennan turned.

"Not without these." Ron grinned. He grabbed the keys and mimed as if he was using them to start a car.

Now a rush. The unconscious drunk, the jalopy, the e-cord. The blood pulsed behind his eyes and in his ears, causing a momentary dark ring in his field of vision with every beat. Had he remembered that? Was it purposeful? Who framed who?

He was going to vomit and then his head and heart would explode. He was sure of it.

Deidre caught a glimpse of the swelling panic. She put a warm, soft, hand on either side of his neck, her thumbs reaching up to his jaw line. Goosebumps ran up his face and down his torso. She was his anchor, securing him to reality, and the current reality was that Ron had killed the monster that had lived in Kaylee's house. The monster that had snuck into her room drunk. The monster that had tried to hunt her and groom her into a self-cannibalizing little minion. The only thing that bothered Brennan now, was that Ron had gotten caught. All else slowly faded away.

Chapter 6

Three weeks passed and Brennan had finally gotten word from CPS. Due to the "complicated circumstance" and the "high profile media coverage" the department felt that it would be unwise and unsafe to continue his employment. They had explained themselves profusely but had been careful not to apologize or claim fault in any way. They had also generously agreed to award him extra vacation days, which would now be paid out to him. A sneaky thing they told him to consider a "severance". Brennan thought that kind of rhymed with "hush money."

Still, he took it. He didn't have the patience or finances to afford a lawyer and file a suit against the State. The money would pay the bills for a couple of months, but things would not be too easy after that. Still, even though the bills loomed over him like menacing trees in the dark forest of adulthood, a bigger stress was removed.

He would never have to work another case again. He would never have to ask another child to "tell me more about that" after an already reluctant admission of molestation. He would never have to attend or see pictures of another child autopsy. He would never refer to a Billy, Susan, Nick, or Joe as "Oldest Victim" or "Sibling". Kids could now just be kids. He could ignore the dark undertones, the signs that now seemed all too obvious, the untold stories unfolding in the faces and voices of the children.

As he pondered on that, Brennan knew that at the very least, his last thought was a lie. He had never been able to fully ignore the underlying darkness. After Deidre revealed her traumatic childhood, he had only become more outspoken about it, but now, after the training and years of experience, he wondered to himself if he'd be able to watch, to notice, and do nothing beyond making a report. Even on his leave of absence, he had tried to check in on the cases he had left open. He had been assured and reassured that they were being taken care of and the children would be okay, but if that were true, why had he heard workers referring to those types of cases as "abandoned cases" every time someone quit?

His pulse elevated and his breath became shallow. He struggled to suppress the thoughts. He started praying in a whisper, barely more than a murmur.

"God, help them. Protect them. Save them. Please... if you're there," the idea that God may not be there, that the children may be alone, kicked his anxiety up another gear. His thoughts sped forward. It was like looking out the window of a speeding car. The thoughts were unclear, undefined, gone in an instant, but still recognizable.

"We take captive every thought to the obedience of God. We take captive every thought to the obedience of God. We take captive..."

Deidre walked into the room. Everything stopped.

"Bren, you okay?" Deidre didn't want to be insensitive, so she waited to ask the question she had come in with.

"Yeah, I'm fine. Just..." Brennan hesitated, "thanking God."

"Oh, great! What did they tell you?" That seemed as good a moment as any to ask.

"How did Pepper Potts put it?" Brennan asked rhetorically, "We are 'consciously uncoupling'" he joked with a void smile that was clear in his mouth but absent in his eyes.

Deidre smiled, hers genuine, "That's great, baby! I mean, I know you're unemployed now, but it's honestly the best thing that could've happened for you."

Brennan nodded, trying to keep his grin from melting. "Yeah, they even gave me a 'severance'." he highlighted the word severance with finger quotes, "A paycheck's worth of vacation time that they'll cash out to me."

Deidre's smile widened and there it was, the stadium light smile. "That's awesome! We'll be okay for a few months and in the meantime, I can talk to Joanna and she can probably get me a spot working at the nursing home. You can relax, recover," she sat next to Brennan and hugged him. His skin came alive with goosebumps as her warmth radiated onto him, "We're going to be okay, hon." She held him with her eyes closed and her lips in a quiet, gentler, grin. A few seconds passed and she added, "You know, since you're thanking God and all, maybe we can go thank Him on Sunday. You know, at His place."

Brennan sighed. "I don't think I'm up to that yet."

Deidre held on to him tighter, her face tinged by disappointment, a look she currently shared with Brennan.

Brennan didn't like the idea of Deidre having to work at a nursing home. He didn't mind her working if she *wanted* to, but he didn't like that she *had* to. Plus, there was something unpleasantly familiar about it all.

There was a thought, a memory. Deidre leaving the park early for work a few weeks back. Of course, that didn't make sense. She wasn't working then.

Within a week, Deidre had gotten a job at the local nursing home. She was doing grunt work, dirty work, cleaning up messes the aging human body could no longer prevent. Still, it was a decent job. The pay wasn't great, but it was still extra. Brennan had expected his wife to save half, spend half on herself. A reward for her efforts. Change a geriatric diaper, punch your card, win a prize. But she didn't. Instead, Deidre would cash her check and store it in a pink toolbox she had received as a gift from Brennan's mother.

"Every woman needs to know how to use basic tools," Brennan's mother had explained, "you know, in case Brennan were to not be there one day." she had elaborated, comfortably, maybe even hopefully.

Deidre had bitten her tongue then, but Brennan was the one that had replied.

"Geez, mom, why would you even say that? Why are you thinking of me dying?" Brennan chastised, knowing full well that his mother was alluding to a separation and preventing her son's mixture with "bad stock".

"No! That's not what-" his mother had lost all color in her face for a second, then regained it, brighter and burning as she understood her son's joke at her expense. She'd been quiet after that.

Seven weeks went by. Brennan had been sleeping better. Dreamlessly. Deidre would get back from work, completely exhausted, and would turn in early. She appeared so peaceful that Brennan couldn't help but fall asleep with her, comfortable, warm, and most importantly, together.

Seven weeks was the limit though.

Deidre had come home with an odd smile one evening. Her smiles were genuine, open, warm, but this one seemed mischievous, her lips were a bit tighter, her eyes a bit narrower.

"I had an interesting phone call today." Deidre remarked matter-of-factly, "I guess Eve didn't know I have your old phone number now."

Brennan flinched and then tried to play it off.

One of the benefits of marrying your high school sweetheart is the lack of time you have to build up baggage in previous relationships. Deidre was Brennan's first and only girlfriend, but Eve was the closest thing he had to an ex.

After a particularly rough argument between Brennan and his mother over a very rude comment she had made to Deidre, Deidre decided it was best for everyone if she stopped being the burden on Brennan's life that his mother had accused her of being. The temporary break-up was tremendously difficult on Brennan. A longtime friend named Eve was there to comfort him, strengthen him, and build him up, all just in time to win Deidre back.

It wasn't that Eve wasn't a good person or that Brennan was simply not attracted to her. At the end of the day, she just wasn't Deidre.

"Don't get scared, playa," Deidre joked, "she just wanted to apologize for not reaching out to you about the thing with Kaylee."

"Why would she?" Brennan asked, confused.

"She was the medical examiner on the case. She said she wanted to reach out but knew it could compromise the case and get you and her in trouble. According to her, it was a messed up case. She said nothing added up."

Brennan nodded absent-mindedly.

"Anyway," Deidre's smile was back it its warm, brilliant self, "I just wanted to poke a little fun and see you squirm." She poked his ribs, "Oh, and relay the message of course."

That night he had a dream. He was standing in the middle of a road in the boonies. The air was still, so much so that it felt almost suffocating. There was a car in front of him, stopped mid turn, smoke from the friction between rubber and road was frozen in place. It was like a diorama made from real life. Brennan walked toward the car and saw sunlight glinting off of something next to the window. As he approached, he could see small fragments of glass hanging in the air. It was almost pretty, almost artistic, if not for the white bone, grey brain, black hair, and pink-red flesh coming from the window.

Brennan's heart went from trot to gallop.

This was the car. That was the Stepfather. Brennan could almost see the ejected soul mixed with the mist of blood and brain. He inched closer and closer to the car, his heart picking up about a beat per minute with every inch. He looked inside the window.

Before he could notice the disfigured head of the dying degenerate, he noticed another head, another face. He saw the killer. He saw…

Brennan almost leaped out of bed with a grunting shout.

A million thoughts ran through his head, then suddenly, just one. Clear, severe, and urgent.

"The Machine!"

For the first time since his arrival from the all but forgotten trip to the 8-Ball dive, Brennan remembered The Machine. Other straggling memories he had of that trip had drained away like water in a cupped hand, but this one stayed. It stuck in his head, refusing to go back.

He was already forgetting the dream. He still couldn't recall the details of his trip, but he knew whatever his objective, it had been completed. His reality was no longer clear, no longer unopposed.

"What was it? What did I do?" he asked himself aloud.

Before he could admit to himself that he already knew he pulled his focus to another part of reality that had faded back. Now he knew the Machine was there.

He hadn't noticed Deidre had woken up. She was asking if he was okay, but he hadn't heard her.

As life came back into focus, he lay back down.

"Yeah, yeah," he muttered, "I'm okay, Dee. I'm okay." he exhaled slowly through his mouth, "just a bad dream."

Chapter 7

The next day had gone smoothly. One little white square had held the questions stemming from the dream at bay. He had been tempted to take more, but he knew he'd be watching Abby.

Deidre had come back home, exhausted as always.

She greeted Brennan with a kiss and asked about Abby.

"Down for her afternoon nap." Brennan answered.

"Good. I'll get started on dinner." Deidre smiled tiredly.

"No, I already started boiling the chicken, I chopped lettuce and tomato, not as well as you, but it'll do, and crumbled cheese."

"Oh," Deidre sighed with relief, "you're the best." she put her head down on the counter, her hands running through her hair.

"But…" Brennan started, knowing she wouldn't lash out, knowing she'd be okay, but still feeling terrible about putting more pressure on her. "We're out of refried beans."

Abby's favorite food was tostadas. She only at them with beans, chicken, and cheese, and she always ended up with cheese in her hair and beans behind her ears. She made a right mess, but she loved them. Beans were not only one of the three toppings that Abby kept exclusive to her tostadas, they were the glue that kept things together and prevented a whole other level of mess.

"I tried calling you, but I guess you were driving." Brennan said apologetically.

"Yeah, I forgot to take my phone off silent." Deidre knew she had to go to buy the stupid refried beans. She had just gotten back home, she hadn't been off her feet all day except for the drive to work and back. She had dealt with enough brown substances for the day and just did not want to go.

Brennan saw how tired she was.

"I can try to go." Brennan suggested, simultaneously hoping she'd say no and hoping the one little square would help him complete the drive if she said yes. He thought of tomatoes for some reason. Was that the last errand he had run for her? He couldn't remember. Did that happen? Did he imagine it?

"No, it's okay hon. I got it. I'll get the grocery list off the fridge and pick up my weekly lotto ticket while I'm at it." Deidre pulled her mouth back into a grin to try and hide her feeling of resignation. She was much too expressive to hide it.

"Casting lots, huh?" Brennan joked trying to get a genuine smile.

"Didn't you say that casting lots was meant to be a form of divination? To determine God's Will or fate? I'm not doing that." Deidre retorted, her fake grin a sly smirk now.

"Well, if you win, won't you consider it God's Will?"

"Look," Deidre instructed, a full genuine smile on her face now, "you gotta play to win, right? I wanna win. You want me changing diapers for pervy, geriatric dudes for the rest of our lives?"

That bit stung Brennan, but he kept his smile. The only tell was a tiny twitch in his right eye.

"Or," Deidre started, she must have understood her words had a slight edge, "you know, until you get all better." She smiled and put her arms around his neck. "Then I can go back to school, work my butt off, and we can take Abby to Disneyworld. Work on Abby: The Sequel?"

Brennan did lose a bit of his smile at that. Deidre had wanted a sibling for Abby for a long time now.

"Yeah, once I'm better." Brennan agreed in as optimistic a tone as he could muster.

Deidre gave him a pop kiss on the lips, put her head on his chest and gave him a hard, squeezing, hug.

"I love you. Be back in a jiff."

As Deidre went over to the refrigerator to get the grocery list, Brennan had an idea.

The two words that had been steadily pulsing in his mind drove this idea. The Machine.

Brennan opened his phone and googled the lotto numbers for last week.

There had been no winners and the prize was a hefty one. $60 million Powerball.

He wrote the numbers down on a scratch piece of paper and tore it off.

Deidre came back through the living room and headed out.

"Love you, see you in a bit."

The door shut.

Brennan rushed into the garage.

He opened up his large toolbox and took out the shoebox that was crammed inside. He retrieved The Machine from this second box and focused.

Two weeks ago. He tried remembering what was for dinner, what was on TV, what movie Abby had on repeat that week. Anything to narrow down the timeframe.

He pressed the pad on his chest.

A pull. Nothing.

In the Nothing, he remembered everything.

The memories hit him like a freight train. He suddenly remembered every detail of how he had killed the Stepfather. His altercation with his past self. Modest VIII. Seeing his grandfather.

Stuffy air filled his lungs again.

He was back in the garage.

He opened the door just a crack and then turned back to look at the clock that hung on the wall of the garage. Deidre had bought it for him as a joke since he had a penchant for tardiness. It was oddly appropriate in this situation. All the numbers on the face of the clock were jumbled at the bottom, except for the 12. In the center of the clock it said, "Eh, who cares?". The missing numbers made it a bit more difficult to read the time. It was 2:15 PM. Deidre was still at work.

Brennan quietly stepped into the house. He walked slowly to the kitchen, looking around corners to make sure he wouldn't bump into Abby or himself. He could hear a song playing at the end of the hall. The crescendo to *"How Far I'll Go"* from *Moana.* He was safe. Abby loved that movie and all those songs and he loved watching her dance and sing along.

As he walked closer to the living room, he began to feel a strange sensation. His mind was clouded, his head seemed to grow heavier, and memories began to playback in his head like a movie.

He shook his head and took the pen that was latched onto the lavender colored notepad magneted onto the refrigerator. The long, narrow, ruled, paper read "Groceries" at the top and had a little cartoon shopping cart filled with flowers on the bottom right corner. Brennan had never understood that. Who buys flowers as groceries?

At the bottom of the list, right under skim milk, he wrote in all caps, "PLAY MY NUMBERS ;)". He took the scrap of paper out of his pocket and wrote the numbers down.

He took a deep breath. He smiled and stared at the notepad. He pulled the e-cord.

He felt a pull, like a string tied to the inside of his navel being jerked through his back.

Nothing. Quiet, peaceful, Nothing.

Something. Someone. Inside the Nothing.

The humid garage again.

There were boxes. Cardboard boxes with branding that said Bounty, Charmin, Pampers, Velveeta, all sorts of cardboard boxes with tape on them and then in thick, black, permanent marker, added labels that said things like KITCHEN, ABBY, CHRISTMAS, CUPS.

Brennan removed the device and stowed it away, back inside the shoebox, inside the toolbox. He headed for the door and just as he put his hand on the knob, it opened.

"JEEZ… on a cracker, you scared the crap out of me, hon." Deidre huffed out with her hand over her left breast.

She was wearing a navy-blue bandana in her hair, a black tank top, and loose-fitting jeans that were torn around the knees. They weren't the stylistically torn jeans she insisted on wearing, but jeans that had torn from actual work and wear. She was sweating pretty profusely.

"Hey, Dee." Brennan said trying not to sound too dumbfounded or out of place.

"So," Deidre usually started statements with so when they were going to be run-ons of the day's events or things to do, "I spoke to the realtor lady, Ms. Shannon, she'll be by tomorrow to help take pictures of the house. I just finished boxing up the kitchen, so we're going to be on outside food until we move in, but screw it, we can afford it now, right?" She let out a short chuckle and continued, "We have the beds broken down, got the air mattresses out, we've packed up clothes, toiletries, food, TVs, electronics, bedding, rugs, kitchen, lawn stuff, small decorations, all of Abby's fridge art, washer, dryer, fridge, and stove are unplugged and cleaned. What else do we need before the movers come get the big stuff?" She looked around the garage, "besides all your lab stuff? You have not made much progress, buddy." She kept surveying the garage with her hands balled up into fists and sitting on her hips.

Brennan knew she was only half joking. She had expected for him to be moving faster, but then again, Brennan didn't know they were moving, at least not yet, but the memories were already seeping in.

"Why don't we pay the movers to take all the stuff?" Brennan asked. It was the first thing he thought of that would sound like normal conversation. He wanted to ask where they were moving, when, what pay-out option they'd chosen, but he figured those details would come with time.

"Because, my handsome four leafed clover," she said as she pinched his cheeks, "we need to be smart with our money. We're not going to be those people that win the lottery, buy a mansion, and a lambo, then end up living out of their fancy sports car because they go bankrupt."

"Oh, but eating out until we move is so fiscally responsible." Brennan retorted with a smirk. Comfortable, natural, and a sneaky way to get the information he needed. Dad would've been proud.

"Three days of restaurant dinners isn't the same as paying thousands for a professional moving service." Deidre retorted with exaggerated, mock snarkiness.

That surprised Brennan.

"Three days? Dang, that's really quick. We just found out we won like two weeks ago. I can't believe it's going this fast."

"Yeah, well, that's why your lovely wife is handling this. Why she made an appointment to go up to Austin to get everything done like the day after, why she set up Abby to be a trust fund baby, why she is rocking it and moving everything along. Plus, it's not like we had to house hunt. That house has been my dream house for years."

Brennan knew the house immediately. It was a very nice home, but incredibly modest for a new millionaire couple. It was an American Craftsman style four bedroom, three and a half bathroom house. The exterior was a mixture of grey to white stony brick and wood panels painted a forest green. It had a wraparound porch made of a dark red cedar and a gigantic yard. It was out in the country, but not too far out. Brennan remembered driving out there when they were dating. They'd find secluded places out in the country to do what teenagers do when they take their cars out into the boonies. They'd pass by that house and it was always the same routine.

"It's beautiful, Bren." Deidre would say, momentarily disrupted.

"Yeah, it is." Brennan would say, usually distracted by either the anticipation of what was coming shortly, or the fear of being caught.

"I wonder why it never sells?" Deidre would almost always muse.

"It's old fashioned and expensive. People usually want modern and people around here usually can't do expensive."

Then one day, after Deidre opened up to him, after Brennan had decided that eventually he'd marry this girl, they passed by and the routine changed.

"It's so beautiful." Deidre marveled as he slowed the car while passing in front of it.

"Yeah, it is." Brennan replied. He wasn't distracted this time. He stared lovingly at Deidre. "I'm going to buy you this house someday."

Deidre had laughed. "That's so sweet of you to say." she had replied. From that day forward, every time they passed by the house, she would point at it.

"Look, there's my house."

The pregnancy moved them into an apartment, and after Abby, Brennan managed to get a nice, smaller, most importantly, cheaper house.

Five days later, two days were added due to small delays, they pulled up to the house slowly. Brennan had insisted on driving. He had snuck a little white square to make sure he'd be okay behind the wheel. As the car rolled to a stop, he saw tears cling onto Deidre's reddening eyes, she turned to look out the window and said in a breaking voice, "Look, there's my house."

Chapter 8

Being rich is not like it is in movies.

You would think it would be easy to get used to having millions of dollars, but there's a different kind of stress to it, at least at first.

Brennan and Deidre had gotten a financial advisor, a lawyer, and did away with all their social media. Despite remaining mostly anonymous, people had heard about their windfall and they had cousins, uncles, aunts, and friends they'd never heard of coming out of the woodwork.

Still, Deidre had handled it surprisingly well. Brennan wanted to help, but it seemed that financial security was not enough to chase away his anxiety. His demons seemed to have laid down roots. In the meantime, Deidre had set up investment accounts, a college fund, and had arranged for Abby to receive therapy at home. Brennan's involvement was mostly limited to the final decision making.

For most things.

Deidre had set up two secret accounts. One for her mother and another for her mother in law. Their basic bills were paid. Her mother's rent, his mother's mortgage, and all their utilities. They kept working so they could have money for food and spending. Her mother had lauded her for the idea and had sworn secrecy. Brennan's mother had been reluctant. She had told her that secrets, even when they're benevolent, breed distrust and problems into a marriage. It took collusion with James and a promise to tell Brennan soon for Deidre to be able to convince her to accept the help.

A lot had happened in that first month.

Brennan lay in bed. He felt like he was riding waves of air with every rotation of the fan. Everything felt like it was moving in slow motion.

The door to his room opened.

"Dad-dee," Abby had learned to pronounce the consonants in the middle of the word, but still struggled to conjoin the syllables.

As proud as Brennan was of her progress, he missed the way she used to say "da-ee".

"Someone knocking." She scrunched up her face.
"Someone IS knocking," she corrected.

Brennan sat up and saw Abby's wild curls being held down by a large set of headphones. The therapist said that they canceled noise but let voices filter through. The little device connected to them was clipped to Abby's shirt. It played a mixture of Mozart, Bach, Beethoven, and Chopin. The therapist had instructed her to wear them for thirty minutes, twice a day. He said it would help her concentrate and learn to filter out noise.

Brennan smiled at her and stood up. The room tilted a bit. He walked to the front door and opened it. A bearded young man in a flannel shirt and blue skinny jeans stood outside.

"Hey, Mr. R. Just delivering your pharmacy order." the young man handed Brennan an unmarked, white, pill bottle.

"How much do I owe you?"

"Buck fifty, sir."

Brennan had picked up his wallet on the way to the door and took out two bills, one bearing Ben Franklin and the other, General Grant. He handed them to the young man.

"Thanks, Mr. R." He hesitated a second, "I should tell you, sir. My doc is out on vacation. His PA isn't so loose with the Xan. You might want to slow down with this bottle. She might not buy my act or let me get samples if I go back too soon."

"Yeah, thanks, Joel." He looked up sleepily, "I'm weaning myself off," he lied.

Joel nodded and picked up his hand in a simple wave goodbye.

Brennan could afford to go to the doctor himself. His doctor probably would've given him the medication too. Between the nightmares and random bouts of anxiety, Brennan's need was obvious. Still, he didn't want to worry Deidre… and he was pretty sure he had worked himself up to more than the recommended dose.

Deidre hadn't had nightmares. She was calm. She was on top of it all. He just wanted to be the same way.

Brennan sat down on the living room couch. Derek the therapist had moved the living room coffee table and was now playing a game with Abby that involved her jumping forward to spots he had marked with masking tape Xs. He had removed Abby's headphones, presumably to keep them from falling.

Brennan watched his daughter hop along, her curls bouncing like little springs. He could feel himself coming out of the influence of the damned little squares. He set his mind that he'd challenge himself to see if he could go on without another one.

Brennan lasted until dinner time.

The utensils clattered in his hand as he helped Deidre set the table. His shaking hands annoyed him, the droning headache bothered him, but what really pushed him over the edge were the flashes.

A drunk man with his brains sprayed out of a moving car window. A third person view of his grandfather playing with him. His childhood home. His father's voice. An alien voice in his head whispering, *"Vengeance is mine."* The dying man again. Only he's in court, he's wearing a cheap suit, and he's smiling. Not a smile of relief, but an arrogant smile. The smile of a cocky magician who just pulled a fast one on his audience. *"I'll make Lady Justice disappear."*

He walked quickly to the bathroom, doing a terrible job of hiding his nervousness. He held the Xanax bar in his hands for what seemed like ten minutes. Finally, he snapped off two squares, hesitated again and broke the two down to one and took it with a handful of water from the bathroom sink.

Though he felt defeated, he wasn't devastated by it. Part of him wanted to give up. Part of him had written defeat into the challenge to begin with. Part of him depended on the little squares of chemical apathy, because that's what it was to him. Apathy. Not peace, not problems vanishing away or solutions becoming clear, just a little square of I-don't-give-a-crap.

His hands immediately stopped shaking. He pushed away the reasoning part of his mind that told him that was ridiculous. The medicine couldn't possibly hit him instantly. That this dependence had become as much psychological as it was chemical, perhaps even more so.

By the time dinner was served, thoughts were aimlessly floating in and out of Brennan's head. There was no rhythm or sense to them. Some were intense thoughts that might have disturbed him in a sober moment. Some were memories that he had all but lost, and others were random things that made no sense.

"If a Smurf eats too fast and chokes, what color does he turn?"

Brennan let out a monosyllabic chuckle.

"What's so funny, Dad-dee?" Abby asked.

"Smurfs."

Abby giggled now, her tiny little bottom teeth jutting out with her beautifully weird little laugh.

"Yeah, Smuffs is funny." she giggled. "They blue, Dad-dee, but not sad." She laughed a little harder this time.

Brennan laughed with her and another wandering wonder swam through his head.

"Did she get the joke, or does she think they'd be sad because their skin is blue?"

There was a third question that didn't quite materialize in his head. If Abby had understood the joke, it would've been a big deal. There was plenty that Abby found funny, but she struggled to understand jokes.

Deidre sat down and quickly scanned the table. Brennan could hear her mutter.

"Forks, drinks, bread, napkins…" she looked up smiling, content that nothing was missing from the table, "Alright, who wants to say grace."

"I do it, mommy!" Abby yelled out, throwing her hand in the air as if she were shouting out to claim a bingo victory.

"Okay, go ahead, Abby. Pray."

Abby's chubby, warm, little hand shot out to Brennan, palm out, ready to clutch his. He held it and the heat from her hand gave him chills around his neck. There was something oddly comforting about it, almost like he hadn't realized how cold he was until he felt her warm, tiny digits trying to wrap around his palm. He couldn't help but smile at her.

"Dear, Jesus, than you for been nice to us. For the food. For the wadder. For the people. For mommy and dad-dee. For Ther-ra-pee. For toys. For Drerick. For You. I lub joo. Amen."

They began to eat. There was silence, except for Abby periodically picking up a song halfway into the chorus or a verse.

Brennan has always been so amazed at how much better Abby could enunciate when she sang.

"The whole world in His hands. He's gots the whole, wide, world." then a few bites later, "Jesus lubs the little chi-dren. All the chi-dren of the world."

Then out of nowhere, "Momma! Oooh. Didn't mean to make you cwy!" she paused as her expression sublimated from passionate singing to confused analysis. "Dad-dee, why is he makin' his mommy cwy for?"

Brennan couldn't help but laugh again. "She's crying because he's going to jail for doing a bad thing."

"Like you frien' Won?" she asked.

This caught both Brennan and Deidre off guard. Almost as if she was reading their minds, Abby added, "I saw him. Him picture." Abby scrunched her nose, "His picture. He in the noose."

"In the what?" Brennan asked, humor now gone.

"The news." Deidre clarified.

Of course, Abby meant the news. She didn't know what a noose was.

Deidre continued, "He came out on a short promo for the six o'clock news when I was watching something on TV. I muttered something and she asked me if I knew him. I'm sorry."

"No, not your fault." Brennan replied, suddenly feeling hyper-aware and beyond sober. "What are they saying about him?"

"His trial has been pretty public," Deidre stated in a hushed tone. Abby was now soulfully jumping straight into the bridge of For King and Country's *Without You*, but Deidre didn't want her to overhear. "Rumor is he's going to go for a self-defense argument or plea to a lesser charge."

"Self-Defense?" Brennan's eyes squinted quizzically.

"Well, yeah," Deidre replied, "if he went there to confront the man, then was overpowered and taken, maybe he was fighting his way out of the situation. Maybe the gun was his only option. They never found it, you know. The gun, I mean. For all we know he took the gun from that bastard. Maybe if Ron hadn't done what he did, Kaylee or her mom would've been the ones at the wrong end of the barrel."

This made Brennan jerk his head up. His eyes glistened with tears, but his face was frozen in a stern, pensive expression. There was a high-pitched whirring sound in his head. The old and new memories wrestled in there with little regard for him. As they struggled, Brennan couldn't help but wonder which would win. The memory that was stronger, or the one that was true.

"I'm sorry, Bren. I shouldn't have brought it up, hon." Deidre's expression was that 'Oh, crap' expression people put on when they know they messed up and now they're just hoping the damage is minimal.

"Nah, it's not a big deal. That's a past life now." he assured her calmly as he simultaneously tried to reassure himself. He changed the subject for their mutual benefit. "I was thinking of getting a work-from-home job, or at least a hobby."

Deidre's eyes lit up. "Mmm!" she hummed with her mouth full of steamed broccoli. She chewed in a comically obvious way and held her hand up as if to signal that there was a response coming soon. She took a swig of lemonade. "That's awesome, Bren! I mean, you don't have to work, our investments are doing well, bills are getting paid and will be getting paid for a long time, but I think it'll be good for you to set your mind to something you'll enjoy." She paused and Brennan remained silent, waiting for the inevitable list of suggestions. "So," she started. Brennan smiled slightly and crookedly. He really loved this woman. "you could start writing again. Your poems were always so sweet, and Abby loved your bedtime stories. You could start on the guitar again, maybe eventually play with the church again," she snuck that last bit in before quickly leaping to the next thing, "you always wanted to play piano too, remember. The pool guys are starting on the build soon, so you can start swimming again, be the next Michael Phelps! Whatever you choose, I'll support you, as long as your hobby isn't other women or something that'll make us broke."

Brennan smirked. "So, I should cancel the Lambos and the Bunnies then."

"I WANT BUNNIES!" Abby yelled out excitedly.

Deidre and Brennan burst into laughter and were soon joined by what Brennan called Abby's "lost giggle". It was the giggle that Abby gave when she didn't understand a joke or situation but was just tickled to be part of all the fun.

They settled in for a movie night. It was, as it often was, Abby's choice. Her cartoon love was currently bifurcated between Disney princesses and Hawkgirl from the Justice League cartoons. Brennan would try to push her a little deeper into the superhero pool, or at least further into the Justice League so that she would maybe pick a Batman or Superman animated movie that would be at least a little entertaining. Alas, that wasn't the plan for today. After her request to watch *Moana* for the billionth time was kindly but firmly denied by her parents, she opted instead for *Tangled*.

Rapunzel wasn't even out of the tower before Abby conked out, curled up like a cat on the large ottoman.

The movie droned on in front of them, but Brennan and Deidre paid no attention. Deidre was slowly fading into dreamland in Brennan's arms and he was just basking in the moment.

It was quiet. Peaceful. Now was a good time. He felt calm.

"I know you've been giving our moms money." he whispered. Deidre tensed a bit. "Before you say anything," he continued, "just know, I'm okay with it. I understand why you didn't tell me. I don't think I would've reacted very well at first, but I think it's the right thing to do."

Deidre sighed, but it didn't seem to be in relief, rather in preparation, like a person might exhale to calm down before a nurse delivers a shot.

"Since we're doing peaceful confessional time," Deidre paused. Brennan waited for the characteristic, blunt, word vomit. "I know about the pills," she finally said in one breath, practically one syllable.

Brennan's heart dropped. He thought maybe she had bought an overpriced purse or make up. He wasn't expecting his wife to call out his budding drug addiction.

"Dee…" Brennan started, but was promptly interrupted.

"I know it helps you, Bren. I'm okay with you getting help from meds, but I think it needs to be under a doctor's supervision."

Brennan was the one tensing up now.

Deidre sat up and held his face in her hands. "I'm not an idiot, Bren. I'm not going to make you quit cold turkey, but we need to start weaning you off. Things are better. Life is better. I think you can do this. I think you can beat this. I

93

don't expect you to do it alone. I'll be here and, if the doctor recommends it, we'll get you some meds to help too. You will beat this."

Brennan was half comforted and half disappointed. He loved how understanding his wife was being. He loved that she was so supportive of him. He loved that they were on the same team. What disappointed him was how much her words seemed to be meant for someone with cancer or failing kidneys. Though he could no longer remember his exact voice, he remembered his father's words in that moment. *"It's all in your head. A real man learns to control his impulses and emotions."* A classic line from his dad that Brennan had heard during his first real panic attack at the age of seven.

"I'm weak." Brennan told himself out loud.

"You're not weak." Deidre interrupted his soliloquy. "We all have our demons. We all have our fights."

Brennan held her tighter. He could feel the comforting warmth radiate from her chest and arms. She crooked her neck up and planted a soft, wet kiss on his cheek.

"I love you, Bren."

Brennan softly set her upper body on the couch. and stood up.

"Where are you going?" Deidre asked, clutching on to his hand with both of hers.

"I didn't want to ruin the moment, but I gotta drain the main vein."

Deidre gave a goofy, immature chuckle. It was beautiful.

Brennan smiled at her and trotted across the room to the nearest restroom. After he had finished, he washed his hands and stared in the mirror, the warm water still running from the faucet.

"You can do this," he whispered to himself, "you can beat this. You don't need the pills."

He smiled. He felt like he was actually telling himself the truth. He cupped warm water in his hands and softly spread it across his face. The contrast between the warm water on his face and the cold air blowing from the A/C vents gave him goosebumps across his shoulders and down his back. There was something strangely pleasant about the trickling sensation.

He felt content, not necessarily overjoyed or even happy, just a calm contentment. It was the best he had felt in years.

He walked out of the restroom and back to the living room, continuing to feel around his body. He felt like he was free from the cage in his mind. He was aware of the things around him. How the carpet fibers slipped in between his toes as he walked to the couch, how the water now felt cool on his face, how the air felt crisp entering through his nose and traveling down into his lungs.

Deidre was asleep. Brennan considered waking her, but she seemed so peaceful.

"We'll have a camp out." He thought as he looked around at the furniture. He might even bring out an old sleeping bag so he could doze in the open carpet between Abby's ottoman and Deidre's couch. He grabbed a small, fleece, blanket that was folded up on the couch and spread it over Deidre.

Deidre pushed out a noise that sounded like a pained moan that slid into a whimper. Her eyebrows twitched down, giving her a worried expression for a second.

Brennan was back in his head. He stared at her face, trying impossibly to read her dreams and fears from her sleeping expression. She moaned again and then muttered weakly.

"No"

All the frustration roared back into Brennan and seemed fortified in its return.

A thought voiced itself in his head, *"Then goeth he, and taketh with himself seven other spirits more wicked than himself..."*

He bent closer to wake her up and stopped. A tear clung on to the corner of her eye, reflecting the cartoon that was still playing as it struggled to fight gravity, then it fell, giving way to another tear.

"This is it. Now. I'm doing this." Brennan whispered to himself. Even in the low, quiet tone, his voice broke with anger and pain.

He rushed to the garage. The new garage was roomier, but it was still a garage, warm and humid. Not the cold, sterile, lab environment Brennan would have liked. He walked in and walked over to a tool box. He opened the box, opened the shoe box inside, and pulled out The Machine. The cords were a bit tangled, the way headphones seem to autonomously tie themselves up in your pocket or in a drawer. Brennan untangled them impatiently. His hands were quivering now. He felt his pulse in his neck, every heartbeat causing a momentary choking sensation. He finally straightened out the cords and put the device on.

The harness style buckle that connected to the large pad like button on his chest felt tighter than usual. The metallic arm touched the base of his skull, spreading static like tingling from its contact point forward to his nose. He knew the tingling was a symptom of hyperventilating. He felt for the pill bottle in his pocket. He swallowed hard enough to cause an audible click in his throat. His mouth suddenly felt dry.

"I'm not weak." he whispered to himself. He let go of the bottle's outline in his jeans pocket. He walked back into the house, trying his best to remain calm and quiet. He took a bottle of water that Abby had left opened on the little table near the garage entrance and took a swig from it. He felt himself calm a bit. He brought the bottle up and saw what he called "fishies". Abby didn't drink correctly from bottles and the result was slivers of food or crumbs populating her cups and bottles. He paused for a moment, noticed how the shaking in his hand had grown in both frequency and intensity, and chugged the rest of the bottle.

Emotion can make fools of even the smartest of men. He had learned the importance, and difficulty, of controlling emotions first from Sun Tzu in the copy of *The Art of War* that his father had gifted him on his 13th birthday and then from the Bible in his studies for the sermons he would write. Still, knowing and doing are very different things. Brennan knew he should take a pill before going, but his pride interfered. Brennan knew that if he was going to face the man who haunted his wife's nightmares, he should be well armed, just in case. However, the feeling of panic and urgency that he felt led to him grabbing a folding pocket knife out of his toolbox and hurry to Deidre. Brennan assumed that using dreams to travel would be incredibly dangerous, but his frustration at the thought of having dominion over time, of being able to give his wife the world, and still see her suffer, burned in him like glowing coals piled from his stomach to his throat.

Brennan leaned down close to his wife. He kissed her forehead and then rested his forehead on hers.

"I'm coming, baby. It'll be over soon."

He pulled the electrodes as far as he could and held them pressed to Deidre's temples, first with both hands, then with just one hand stretched across her head like a diadem. He used his free hand to press the pad on his chest.

Chapter 9

The Nothing was different.

Or rather, he was different within the Nothing.

Before he was nothing in Nothing. Just a consciousness in a vacuum. Now, he felt corporeal. The Nothing stretched him out and crushed him down simultaneously. There was a feeling he might've called pain, had it been his body feeling it. It was indescribable. The only way Brennan could have come close would be to say it felt like his mind, his essence, his soul *was* his body. It had stretched itself into what it felt it should look like, feel like, be like. Now his body in this realm, woven from his very soul, was being crushed and stretched. A paradoxical anguish.

He felt pulls, crackling, breaks, and lacked any ability to express his despair. There was no voice with which to yell with. Brennan was suddenly keenly aware of time. As he stretched, it stretched. A strange thought entered his mind. He could feel things inside his soul knit body break, but nothing tore. He imagined it was like broken bones that stretch the skin but fail to burst through.

Brennan began to believe he failed. He was stuck here. He had gambled it all and lost. He was fairly certain that his soul had been on this cosmic torture rack for weeks. He was utterly stuck.

He felt reality vomit him into the air. His flesh and bone body struck a car and rolled off onto the concrete.

Not weeks. Seconds. He understood now it had been a few seconds at most.

Brennan pushed himself up to his hands and knees, feeling like Atlas in that moment, pushing up the weight of the world. He tried to open his eyes and realized they were already open. The dark, distant, blotches clarified and lightened. Then they gained color. A dark, thick, wine colored red dripped down to the ground. Blood. His blood.

He stood up slowly and sat down on the car that had served as his landing spot. He closed his eyes and breathed deeply. slowly, and steadily. He began holding his inhalations for a 4 count before slowly exhaling. He could feel his heart now. It was beating way too fast, but it hadn't sped up. Brennan just hadn't realized all the symptoms of his panic yet.

A thought came to his mind, breaking in, not like a thief coming to take and harm, but like a fireman coming to the rescue.

Deidre lived in the worst neighborhood in Brownsville. If he had been transported to the right place and time, then he needed to be on his toes. He bolted upright, his heart not showing any signs of slowing, and looked around. Brennan was shocked to find that he was not at the right place or the right time. He was back in front of his apartment. He had landed on his neighbor's navy-blue X-Terra. He felt a second of delayed relief, thanking God the vehicle didn't have an alarm, and then worry kicked in again. Had he traveled back to the night when he had originally struck Deidre, now only almost struck her. No, the weather wasn't right. It was cold out. What did she have to dread in their old apartment? Had he been sent to a random time, disconnected from her nightmare?

Then he heard it. The sound first and then the sight of it. An old, large, gold pickup truck parked a few spaces away from his white brick building.

It was this night. She was protesting herself. She was reliving their shared nightmare.

Brennan had known. He had always known, but she had denied it for months. When she had finally admitted it, had to admit it, he had ultimately chosen to forgive her. He had never cheated, but he had made other mistakes. It was also before they were married, so he had reasoned it should count less. Brennan hadn't wanted details. She had assured him, without him asking, that "it" was not better. "It" had never been love. Though Deidre's lack of eloquence couldn't give a reason, Brennan knew, in a dark part of his mind, that she had done it to punish him, to punish herself, and to force herself away from him. From the pain, from the loss, from the love. She thought she was better off alone. Brennan was better off without the suffering she would bring. She was damaged goods after all.

The Guy was about Brennan's height, a tad shorter, light skinned, with tight curls that barely came off his head. His dark eyes and pock marked face had the dopey look of a mentally myopic person, goofily living in the moment. Brennan walked towards him. The guy looked in his wallet and whispered, "Crap," then shook his head and continued walking. Brennan blocked his path.

The Guy looked up. His face morphed from startled, to confused, to nervous, then, peaking Brennan's anger, to defensiveness. The abrupt changes in expression seemed familiar.

"Man, you're not supposed to be here."

Brennan didn't hear him say that. Brennan didn't hear anything except for the crackling thump of his blood pulsating through his head. A repetitive, short, "*kroomph*" speeding away in his head.

Brennan hadn't wanted details. He hadn't wanted to know where. The moron's truck, he assumed, maybe The Guy's house. He never considered his own home. His bed. The place where his never-born child would have slept.

Brennan's mind was empty of thought. It was instead a hive of impulses and feelings he could not direct or hinder in any way. Then, there it was. A split second, a tiny fraction of a moment, where he had to decide if he would say something, do something, formulate a plan. In that wisp of a moment, the deciding moment where people claim they snapped, Brennan made a decision. He disconnected his rational, thinking, mind. He took Cerberus off the leash.

Brennan would not remember much of what happened for the next minute or so. He would not remember making that choice. He would feel that he snapped, but know deep down he hadn't

His fist struck hard against the The Guy's face. It hit flat, heavy, and straight, fracturing The Guy's nose and loosening his teeth. Brennan didn't feel the lacerations on his hand. The Guy backpedaled two steps, then fell squarely on his behind, the way an unsteady child tumbles when learning to walk. The Guy opened his mouth to speak but was not granted the time. Brennan heaved himself on to him. He straddled him in what actual fighters might call a "full mount".

A cruel moment of lucidity interrupted Brennan's panicked rage to fan the flames, asking if perhaps his wife had mounted The Guy this way.

Brennan growled a low, inhuman rattle and began to rain his fists against The Guy's face. They were not elegant punches, the way his father had shown him when he was too young to fully understand the concept and consequence of violence. They were wild, hammering and sloppy. The Guy wasn't blocking his face anymore. He just coughed and lay there, doing his absolute best to raise his arms and failing.

Brennan stood, stumbled backward, steadying himself with another neighbor's vehicle. He put his right hand over his chest. His mind creeped back in to urge him to stop. He was going to have a heart attack, or a stroke, or an aneurysm. Brennan turned and saw The Bloody Heap sit up. The adrenaline began to wash away, not pent up, but utterly spent in this event. As his mind cleared, Brennan felt calm. Panic was gone. There was a numb, electric feeling, but no anxiety, no panic, his heart was becoming steady. He closed his eyes and took a chilly, steady breath.

The knife had dropped out of Brennan's pocket. It lay next to The Heap. He had grabbed it and flipped it open with a soft *"flit"* sound. He was on one knee now. Brennan opened his eyes, saw The Guy, positioned to lunge forward and plunge Brennan's own knife into him. Brennan instinctively kicked out with his right leg. The Guy's knee buckled and he landed in a kneeling bow. The top of Brennan's foot connected heartily with The Guy's temple, causing his head to whiplash to the side. There was a crunch, then a pop.

The Guy fell forward, his neck turned at an unnatural angle and a long, gritty sigh escaped his mouth.

The panic was back. What had he done? Had he meant to do this? Had he meant to frame Ron? Had he wanted all this?

It was a strange phenomenon. While temporally displaced, Brennan remembered everything. It wasn't until he was back in his own time that his memories became confused and muddled.

Brennan popped a Xanax into his mouth and dry swallowed. His mouth suddenly feeling dryer than he had expected, he almost choked before forcing the stupid white rectangle down with a swig from the neighbor's water hose. He looked around and used the same hose to rinse away the blood as best as he could. He picked up The Guy with great difficulty and his mind, slowly calming itself under the influence of the Xanax, strayed to pondering on how dead people really did seem heavier. He knew it was due to them not adjusting their center of gravity, as a live person can, but his drugged brain delighted in how true the myth felt.

Brennan plopped The Guy on the bench seat of his ugly, gold pickup. He didn't bother with a seatbelt. He got in and drove away.

****

Deidre was in the shower. She peeked out and looked at her phone. It had been 45 minutes since she had texted him. Maybe he had wussed out. Part of her was happy about it. Every time it had happened, she felt disgusted and devalued. She considered the possibility and ethics to raping one's self as the burning hot shower water fell over her, turning her skin an angry pink. When it would happen, she would always immediately dismiss him after and go home to take her third or fourth shower of the day and cry in the quiet loneliness of her apartment. This time was different though. It would be in her house. The coup de grâce to her relationship with Brennan and all the pain she had caused him and caused herself. She turned off the water and the thought of that loss called her to her child's nursery. The nursery that he or she would never know. The nursery that stood frozen in time, at her request and against Brennan's wishes. The nursery that she entered several times a day, just to imagine her child there, to smell the smell of baby clothes she had preemptively washed with "baby scent" gentle detergent. The scent that had faded to the point that it was so faint she was fairly sure it was really gone and she only imagined it. She could re-wash the clothes in that detergent to cling to her clearly unhealthy past time, but she didn't dare move them out of the room. She could spend 5 minutes in there or an hour, but whenever she came out, she'd take another scalding shower to melt off the grime of loss, of death.

She dried herself off and braced herself for what was to come.

There was a noise. It sounded like dogs fighting, but she could've sworn one of the growls was almost human.

She heard a thud that seemed to be right outside the apartment.

Her hand flew to her phone and she dialed the number to the little hotel in the middle of town.

"Bren? Bren, can you come home?" she paused trying to see silhouettes through the window. "I know your relief isn't there till the morning, but I think someone's fighting outside. I'm kind of freaking out, Bren. Yes. Yes, of course, I'm staying inside. Okay. Thanks. Oh! Hey, Bren?"

He had hung up already.

"I love you." she whispered to herself. Her thumbs flew over the keys on her phone as she wrote a text message to the contact on her phone saved as "Katy". The text was short, grammatically incorrect, but to the point.

"Dont come. If I nvr c u again itll be 2 soon."

The Brennan from that time arrived shortly after. He fought the urge to sprint over to his front door.

"Hey!"

He looked up and saw a neighbor from the second floor on the stairs. She was a middle-aged single mother who had moved in recently. She hated the area, but her divorce was still in its ugly courtroom stages and housing assistance paid for some of these apartments. She looked like a personified stereotype, fuzzy bathrobe, slippers, cigarette, and hair in curlers. "Did you see what happened?"

"No." Brennan answered, "Did you?"

"I think some idiots got into…" she mimed punches "se agarraron a madrazos. I heard them and saw them through the window, but it was dark. They took off in a big ol' troca."

Brennan mulled it over for a second. "Did you see the color of the truck?"

"No it was dark. I think maybe brown or grey." she paused, "People like us, with kids or a wife, shouldn't be in a place like this." she lamented.

Brennan offered a sympathetic smile. "Buenas noches." He called out as he opened the door to his house.

"Si, buenas." the neighbor called out, sounding defeated.

Brennan walked in and was immediately embraced by Deidre.

****

Brennan was driving carefully, obeying the speed limit and traffic lights, but his tolerance for the Xanax had been raised in the last few weeks. It started wearing off and he felt that the speed limit was too slow, the lights lasted too long, the streetlights were too bright.

He looked at the Corpse. One of his eyes had been forced closed and the inflamed lid was now turning a disgusting greenish black. The other eye was bloodshot and dull, open, off center, seeming to stare dryly at Brennan.

He heard a nervous, broken chuckle. It took Brennan a second to realize the chuckle was escaping from his own tightened throat.

"You know, I'm not an idiot." Brennan told the Corpse in a voice that slid repetitively between audible and not. "I messed up, man. I know you're not the one that hurt me." Brennan's eyes stung as salty tears enveloped them. "I mean," he coughed up a hybrid between a laugh and a sob, "you're utter garbage. You knew she was with someone. You knew she was taken... but you didn't owe me anything. You didn't make any commitments to me. She

107

did. It's easier this way though. I can't hate her. I can't hurt her. I can't help but forgive her. You…" he exhaled shakily, "You I can hate. You I can hurt." he turned to look at the Corpse again, "You I can kill."

He was feeling the tightening and buzzing sensation in his face when he finally reached the long road he was looking for. There were a few houses in the area, but no traffic. He stopped the truck, took a deep breath, ensured that the e-cord was easily accessible and gunned the engine.

He stared at the speedometer as it grumbled higher at an impressive rate for the large vehicle. 60, 70, 80, 85.

Lights. Red and blue flashing lights lit up, faded, and then began to grow again. The loud, swinging woops of the sirens clicked on.

The panic flared up in Brennan for a second, but he could still think.

"No. This is good. This is good." he told The Corpse. "Me from this time has motive. Means. If the cops see you have an accident, there's no need to suspect foul play. They might not be able to explain some injuries, but they saw you crash! How else can they explain it?" Brennan finished with a nervous, panicked chuckle. He suddenly remembered when he was younger, when the panic attacks weren't so bad. He would often have laughing fits when he felt one coming on. This in itself caused him to laugh again.

95, 100, 105…

"STOP THE VEHICLE." A distorted voice commanded from the patrol car's loudspeakers.

Brennan could see it up ahead. The big yellow sign with a double pointed arrow, one point going right, the other left. The sign that bellowed, "Hey moron, this is a dead end! Make a choice!"

The cop saw it too and he hit his brakes.

"STOP THE DAMN CAR!" the officer's breaking voice screamed through the loudspeaker and, for a second, Brennan felt bad for him. He must have been really scared.

Brennan pulled the e-cord just as the truck plummeted into the sign and the embankment behind it at 115 miles per hour. The truck lurched, then launched bed over cabin. It landed in a resaca and began to sink slowly. The Corpse was no longer in the truck at that point. It had been thrown out through the windshield when the truck struck the embankment. It had hit a branch on a nearby tree before splashing down into the resaca.

The police officer called for help over his radio. He did his best to calm his voice.

Chapter 10

There was Nothing. Brennan's aching heart, his quiet sobs, were part of a greater void. A darkness that was comforting and all encompassing.

He was in the living room.

The Machine's electrodes weren't connected to anyone. Deidre was probably in bed.

There was a residue of a sharp, frantic, fear swimming through his veins. He had messed up. He had killed someone. He could not remember who or why their death made him so afraid.

"Consequence." he told himself.

There was a severe consequence, an unwanted consequence to what he had done. He didn't remember what the consequence was. He stretched the reach of his mind, trying to pull out who he had killed, what he had changed.

Some guy.

He removed the device and walked to his room to check on his wife. She was laying in bed, sound asleep. Her hair was cut into a bob. That was different. Nothing to fear, but different.

She stirred and he could've sworn he heard her whimper. It aggravated him. It felt like sandpaper scraping in his brain. He broke out in goosebumps and a chill ran down his neck and out into his arms.

The nightmares continued. He had fixed nothing.

He put the device in his nightstand drawer and walked to the restroom. He removed his jacket and hung it over the hook on the back of the bathroom door. Brennan ran the cold water from the sink. He was tired. Exhausted in fact. He looked in the mirror and saw dirt on his face and small flecks of red that he was almost sure had not come from him, not to say he was unhurt. The white of his left eye was completely red, though Brennan didn't remember being hit there. He cupped his shaking hands and filled them with the icy water and splashed it onto his face. The cold water was at first shocking, then calming. Brennan thought of the mammalian dive reflex. He opened his eyes slowly and felt his heart thump in his chest, steadily, and at an easing pace.

Suddenly, he knew. He didn't kill a guy, he killed The Guy! His stomach dropped, his throat tightened. He took his pills out of his pocket and opened them. He suddenly felt bloated tension coming from every part of him.

"Daddy?"

Brennan froze, terrified of what stood behind him. An apparition. The ghost of his rage and stupidity.

"Daddy, are you okay?" a pause, "Daddy?"

"*Da-ee*" a voice whispered in his soul.

He turned around, startled, as if that disembodied voice had been the first he had heard.

He knew this was going to happen. He had suppressed the fear of it, but he knew this was the consequence. Still, some part of him wanted some parts of this.

Before him stood a young girl, 4 or 5 years old. She was wearing a flannel Wonder woman pajama set. Her hair was straight and black. Her eyes were wide and green. Her expression was concerned. She was scared, excitable,

111

anxious, and yet, her hands were still. She didn't hum, she didn't flap, she didn't bounce. She just stood.

"No," Brennan squeezed out in a breaking, squeaking voice. "No, no, no, no, nononononono…"

The pills dropped from his hands and Brennan ran back to his room.

"Daddy?" the little girl called after him. Now her eyes were welling up with tears. She ran behind him to his room.

Brennan leapt over Deidre and landed hard on the bed next to her, startling her awake. Deidre sat up quickly as Brennan struggled to control his shaking long enough to open the nightstand drawer and pull out The Machine.

"Sweetie, Nikki," Deidre called, "please go to your room. You can watch TV. Daddy isn't feeling well."

Brennan's shaky hands were even worse at untangling The Machine's cords than they were at opening the drawer.

"Bren, are you having a panic attack? A night terror? Brennie, what is that?"

Brennan had straightened out the cords and buckled on The Machine.

"Bren…" Deidre spoke carefully, "Bren take that off, Bren. Bren!"

Nikki hadn't left. She approached the now crying, terrified Brennan.

Brennan was trying with all his might to remember his daughter's face, her name, her voice. The picture of her in his mind was fading. Not just fading but being replaced by this little girl before him.

Brennan saw Nikki approaching and backpedaled, tripping over his own feet and landing hard on the floor.

Nikki shrunk away and cried openly now.

"Daddy!" Nikki yelled.

"Da-ee!" a voice echoed in his head. He mind saw tight, little, brown curls. An exaggerated smile. Flapping hands.

"I'm sorry." Brennan lamented, meaning every bit of it. "I need to fix this. All of this."

He hit the button on his chest.

PART II

1994

Chapter 11

Brennan wanted to stay here. At least the weakest parts of his mind did. It was dark, calm and quiet. There was nothing. It was Nothing.

Gravity. Light. Air.

He landed on his feet but stumbled. The sunlight reflected off white sidewalk, glaring into his eyes. Brennan squeezed his eyes shut and removed The Machine. His eyes adjusted and he realized he was now leaning on a brick wall. He felt a pain stab at his chest and he coughed hard. A bloody glob of sputum landed on the grass.

Brennan was an intelligent man. He often acted stupid, but he wasn't stupid. He had known that the traveling was damaging him. He figured that the body wasn't meant to be temporally displaced. Time was not a medium that the human body was built to move through. Sputum was a sign of infection and it didn't take a genius to understand that the blood was not a harbinger of health. This had to be his last trip. He had to make it count.

Brennan took a breath and thought of his daughter. Abby's face came to mind, clear and perfect. A sob pushed up his throat, bringing the penny taste of blood with it. He loved Abby. She may not have carried his blood, but she was a part of him. Her love and life flowed in his veins, kept his heart pumping, and kept his mind sane.

He looked around at the cars. Most of the cars were made in the 80s. The newest, nicest car in the lot was an Acura Integra. A man in khakis and a white polo was walking away from it, holding the hand of a tiny girl wearing a Sesame Street shirt, blue jeans, and a braided belt.

115

A tear broke from his reddened left eye and rolled down his cheek. He let out a soft, broken sob. He hadn't come back to save Abby. He hadn't gone back to stop himself from making the stupid mistake of killing her biological father.

No, this was 1994. This trip was for all the marbles. He wasn't saving Abby. He was saving her mother.

Chapter 12

Brennan was visiting his first day of school. He walked to the back of the school and found a back entrance to the cafeteria. There was a trash can next to the entrance. He opened the trash can and retrieved a brown paper bag from the sack breakfast meals he remembered liking so much as a kid. The Machine wouldn't fit. He remembered the bags being bigger, but then, everything seems bigger when you're a child.

Brennan looked around and when he saw no one, he tipped the garbage can over. It was still morning on the first day so there wasn't much in the can. He took the liner bag out and put The Machine in there. He tied the top of the bag as close to The Machine as he could and ripped off the excess plastic.

The back of the school was fenced off, but he could walk out through the front. He would just have to swing out around the parking lot to avoid suspicious and paranoid parents. He was passing the second row of cars when he saw the anchor point that had drawn him to this place, to this year.

His mother was taking pictures with a small black camera. She was wearing a blue blouse over black slacks. Her hair was a jet black, defying gravity by faith and the power of hairspray. She had huge, dark eyes, and porcelain skin. His father was holding his hand and hunched over, whispering platitudes and last minute words of wisdom to little Brennan on his first day of school. His father was a thin man with handsome, boyish features. He had been strict, mean, severe, but seeing him again, he understood how young and inexperienced he was. He wasn't a tough guy with a drill sergeant look. He wasn't a monster, dark, overpowering and vicious. He was a pasty, skinny kid in his late twenties, scraping the bottom of six feet tall, with green eyes, and his sandy blond hair in unfortunately all-natural Jheri curls. His mother took one more picture of them in front of the flagpole and a teacher called Little Brennan to her. Little Brennan was halfway to her, when he stopped, turned around, ran at his father, stood at attention and saluted him. His father dropped to one knee and hugged him in response. The knot in Brennan's throat tightened and he made no effort to stall the tears. He remembered times his father yelled. Times his father had scolded him. When his father had snapped because a "boy your age" couldn't tie his shoelaces. When his father bought him a sick, dying dog to help him understand mortality in the days leading up to his grandmother's death and funeral. Still, his father had been wrong, perhaps mean, but never evil. He had loved Brennan. Even when he had left their family. Even when he remarried. Even when he drowned his PTSD in alcohol.

People had called Brennan's father a "functioning alcoholic", but his liver had disagreed with that sentiment and it ceased all bodily function when Brennan was sixteen.

Brennan felt like he couldn't breath. He felt like he was trying to suck air into his lungs through a straw. His heart quickened a tad, but not too much. His face muscles tightened and the buzzing sensation began to stretch through his skin.

"I'm going to be okay." Brennan thought to himself.

He reached in his pocket to pull out his pills.

They were gone.

"No... no... No!" his panic escaped from his mind to his mouth. Brennan tore into the plastic bag and rooted around looking for his pill bottle. He did so even though he could see the bottle lying on his bathroom floor in his mind's eye, clear as day, right where he dropped them. About 5 miles and a quarter century away. Now his heart was racing, his chest felt like it was encased in rapidly setting cement. He stood up at full height to run away, but tunnel vision came in. Everything seemed far away.

In the distance, maybe miles away, a woman with a sweet voice asked, "Are you okay? ¿Joven, está bien?"

It all went black and Brennan crashed down to the floor.

Brennan was nothing within the Nothing. Slowly, he felt his body coming together. He had fingers, but only fingers. Then hands, then a chest. Suddenly he had feet. Piece by piece he was reconstituted into his physical self. Once fully assembled, he felt dizzy. His stomach lurched at the idea that there was no up or down in the Nothing. He felt like he was about to vomit. He clutched his stomach, felt his flesh, and suddenly, his mind decided he was upright. He saw something in the distance. It seemed to grow steadily bigger. It was at least fifteen seconds before he realized that he was moving towards it.

It was a man, The Stepdad. He was floating there, perfectly preserved in the time of his death. His head was incomplete. Brennan knew this would have driven him half mad, but his emotions seemed subdued in the Nothing. He examined the once handsome man, frozen in time, a diorama of his death. He noticed, without much thought, how there were no shadows here. It was completely dark, yet the body was perfectly illuminated. He wondered how this man could have ever been so destructive.

Something appeared out of the corner of his eye. He looked at it and turned his body. He felt the same sensation as before as he floated to it. His body didn't feel like it was moving. There was no resistance, no wind, no steps being taken. Instead, the image grew and then was directly in front of him. It was The Guy. The Heap. The Corpse. His neck seemed too long. Brennan thoughtlessly realized his spine must have been severed near the base of the skull. Again, he looked at every contusion and laceration, a numb sort of admiration for his work. A life, a unique paradigm, a universe, snuffed out by his foot. Except it wasn't. Brennan looked closer and noticed a reflective, glass acne across The Guy's face. If the Nothing captured the moment of their death, he had still been alive. Probably on death's door, but alive still when he missiled through the windshield. A low buzz of something like pain vibrated in Brennan's soul. He thought that if he had not been in the Nothing, he'd feel sorry for The Guy, The Boy, really. Basically a kid. A stupid, immature, kid, who made a bad choice. This time Brennan wondered how he could have ever been so destructive.

He didn't see, but he felt the thing behind him. He turned slowly and saw a tiny ball of pink floating. He moved to it in the same, odd, motionless, oxymoronic way. As he approached, the object didn't just grow, it changed. The small ball was now clearly definable. It was a fetus. He thought about his unborn child and wondered what this meant. Had he somehow been responsible. Had he killed him or her? A pang of black emotion broke through, unable to be suppressed by the Nothing. A cacophonous, muddy, mixture of sadness, panic, anger, and grief. He felt himself moving faster. The fetus grew. It was a baby. Then it unfurled and continued its growth. First an infant, then a toddling little girl. Tears were now building behind his eyes and it struck Brennan that he may be incapable of crying here. The pressure behind his eyes was enormous and excruciating. He moved closer. Her hair grew out in big, tight curls. Her eyes opened wide. Then the killing blow struck as her mouth curled up into a beautiful, huge, toothy, silly, yet haunting grin.

There was a roar, low and rumbling at first, then growing and rising. Louder and higher into a scream.

It was him. That was his voice.

His entire body bucked upward in the seat of the woman's car. The seatbelt pulled Brennan back by the neck, choking him. He coughed and looked around bewildered.

"It's okay, son. It's okay. Calm down. Easy does it." The woman was trying to hold his chest down with her hand. "Don't want to pass out again, right?"

Brennan stopped moving. He looked around at the inside of a 1985 Ford Escort. His eyes stung and watered from the bright light. He could make out the shape of the plastic bag with The Machine inside.

"Bad dream." he said curtly.

"Really?" the lady asked confused. Brennan got a better look at her as his eyes adjusted and his mind slowed down. She was a pretty lady, probably in her late fifties or early sixties. She had long black hair streaked with white, tied in a low ponytail by a bright, red scrunchie. She was wearing a purple blouse and blue jeans. She was thin, perhaps too thin to be healthy. She turned to look at Brennan and he saw she had smooth brown eyes, a crooked smile, and a mixture of freckles and liver spots across her face. "I thought it was waking up in a car, being driven by a strange lady." She chuckled.

"Yeah, who are you? Why am I in your car? What happened?" he felt too exhausted to be properly worried. Plus, this woman wouldn't harm him. He wasn't sure how he knew that, but he knew.

"Okay, so let's go in order. My name is Alexandra, you're in my car because I'm driving you home, and you passed out from hyperventilating during a panic attack."

Brennan looked up. "Oh… thank you. I'm.. um… my name is Brennan."

Her eyes seemed to get even brighter. "Good to meet you, Brennan. Figured you wouldn't want a hospital. I have plenty of experience with panic attacks. I had them almost all my life. I knew you just needed to rest and relax."

Brennan sat up. "Why did you think I wouldn't want a hospital?" he asked suspiciously.

"Aw, well, I always feel silly after going to the hospital for a panic attack. I feel especially silly when the ER bill arrives." she laughed.

"Right, thanks." Brennan said. "You can let me off here."

"What? Why don't you tell me where you live? I'd happily oblige."

"I think it's best if I get off." Brennan insisted.

"No, I don't want you getting heat stroke and dying for real this time." Alexandra insisted with a sincere look of concern on her face. "Are you from around here? It's August in South Texas, honey. We praise the Lord when the thermometer stays in double digits."

"Yeah." he replied trailing off. This woman looked very familiar. Though the memories of all the changes he'd made, all the rips and stitches in time, were crystalline in his mind, all other memories were as they usually were. Blurrier, murkier, and more likely to be inventions of a mind trying to fill gaps the farther back you go.

"So, are you?" Alexandra asked again.

"Am I what?"

"From around here. Are you from around?"

Brennan took a moment to formulate his response. "Kind of. I find myself recently displaced." he responded carefully. "I had a home in town, but I'm not currently welcome there."

A look of sympathy and understanding washed over her face. "Oh, I've been there. I live in a lonely apartment because my family won't have anything to do with me. I made mistakes. Serious ones. Still, all in all, I wanted what was best for my family."

Brennan was suddenly curious as to why a woman that lives alone would be at an elementary school that she doesn't work in. The question almost escaped his lips, but he knew if he asked, he'd have to be ready to answer as well.

Alexandra seemed not to have an issue asking though.

"So, I'm assuming you don't have kids, at least not school aged." Alexandra stated. "Why were you at the school?"

Brennan shifted uncomfortably in his seat. "I got a bit lost." A terribly vague lie. He quickly redirected, "Why were you, I thought you mentioned living alone. No family." Brennan was suspicious and curious, but his manners got the better of him in the end. "If you don't mind my asking, I mean. I apologize. That sounded rude."

"No, no need to apologize. I asked you, you ask me, it's only fair." she sighed, "I lived with my daughter, her husband, and my grandson. A beautiful, little boy. I was not very good at minding my business and was asked to leave. Today was my grandson's first day of school. I just wanted to see him go in. I would've loved to talk to him, give him some advice on bullies and teachers. I used to work as a school nurse. I've seen it all." Her mouth smiled, but her eyes grew wet. "Still, I got to see him. That's enough for today."

"I'm sorry about what's going on with your grandson. I know I would've loved to have my grandmother around. My maternal grandmother died when I was a little kid, and my paternal grandmother lives far away and doesn't have much contact with us."

"I'm very sorry for your loss, Brennan." she smiled, not taking her dewy eyes off the road. "Hey, I need a grandson, you need a grandma, I need a housemate, you need a house. What do ya say?"

"It really was a different time." Brennan thought. He couldn't imagine someone inviting a person they barely met to stay with them in the age of surveillance camera equipped doorbells and state of the art home security

systems. "I wouldn't want to cause you any trouble or inconvenience." Brennan replied.

"Nonsense. I have a naturally nurturing nature, ya know. You're welcome in my home as long as you need. I have a sofa bed, but that thing has a mattress thinner than paper. The metal bar in the middle of it will rearrange your spine in a night. The couch itself is smaller, but much more comfortable."

"I really appreciate the offer, but I'm not sure how long I'll be here, I don't have money, you have no idea who I am. I just don't think it's right."

Alexandra looked at him, lips pursed, a look saying that a lecture was coming his way. "Now, you are a penniless, lonely wanderer, with an anxiety disorder, and off your meds as far as I can tell. My dear Lord says to help those in need. To clothe the naked, feed the hungry, care for the sick, and house the unsheltered. That's Matthew 25:35 and 36, don't ya know, and darn it, I'm going to be a sheep. No goats in my house."

Brennan smiled, first slightly, then a chuckle rose out of his throat and brought on a full smile.

"I do know it, Alexandra. I was a preacher in a former life."

"What happened?" she asked before preemptively stating, "and don't give me any of that 'God left me' nonsense, because God has never abandoned anyone. He'll leave the ninety-nine to get the one, but he comes back so he can care for the full hundred."

"Matthew 18:12." Brennan recalled, his smile holding to his face longer than it seemed to have held in lifetimes, "No, Alexandra, God didn't leave me. I left Him."

"Not a smart move." she remarked, giving him some side eye.

"No, no it was not."

"Why did you leave though?"

The response flowed from Brennan's mouth, surprising even him, "I saw so many terrible things. I saw so many broken people, left in pieces by other people worse than demons. I saw them and couldn't turn the other cheek. I figured you can't get the bad guys to step up. The only way the fight is fair is if you become a bad guy. Fight them on even ground."

Alexandra was silent for a moment. "I understand. The anger for justice so often becomes a hunger for vengeance, but, 'Vengeance is mine, sayeth the Lord'."

Brennan gave a smiling scoff.

Alexandra continued, "I have been there before in life, but I was lucky enough never to fall so deep that I couldn't climb back up and of course, there's no depth too deep for the Lord to reach. I'm guessing you're not quite ready to come back."

"No." Brennan's voice had a cold honesty that was simultaneously comforting and exhilarating. Brennan liked being open and honest, without having to worry about people recommending therapists.

Alexandra pulled the car into a small, four-unit apartment building, and parked in the spot marked with a large letter "B" spray painted on the ground with a stencil.

"Home, sweet, home." Alexandra said sarcastically. "You're probably hungry. I'll fix you up a sandwich.

Peanut butter and strawberry jam is my grandson's favorite."

Her hands shook as she unlocked the door to her apartment and for a moment, Brennan thought she seemed very old, much older than she actually was. She rushed in.

Brennan walked in and closed the door behind him. "Cool. Mine too."

He looked around the house, "I really appreciate all this, Alexandra. I can make the sandwich myself or fix you something as well."

"Nonsense!" she called back from the adjacent kitchen.

He saw the couch that he'd be calling his bed for a while and sat down. The cushions were overstuffed, firm, with a comfortable give.

"Might not be so bad after all." The fear of what was to come abated in Brennan for a while. He felt warm. He felt at home. "So, Alexandra is pretty long, do you have a middle name or something with less syllables? Alex, maybe?"

A chuckle came from the kitchen. "Well, my full name is Alexandra Beatrice Maldonado."

Brennan smiled and took a picture off the end table. The picture had a young Alexandra standing next to a mustachioed man in a nice suit, holding a toddler dressed in a white dress. Brennan thought the little girl's face seemed familiar. He tried to place the face and his blood froze in his veins.

"That's even longer," Alexandra continued, her voice growing louder as she walked back, sandwich in tow, "but my friends shorten it to initials."

She walked into the living room and Brennan looked at her. His eyes were wide and his face was pale, the blood drained by a mixture of shock and disbelief.

"So, it's A.B., but my grandson calls me Grammy Abby." Alexandra finished her thought and was immobile, waiting for a response. When one didn't come, she said the first thing that came to mind. "Hi, Brennie-boy."

Chapter 13

Brennan was very bright for a boy still closing in on three years old. He had a decent command of the English language and was equally fluent in Spanish. His father had taught him basic math and the alphabet. His grandmother had taught him to play.

Alexandra Beatrice, known to her loved ones as A.B. or Abby, was on the carpeted floor in the purple room. She was on all four and little Brennan was struggling to climb on her back.

"Gwammy Abby, you a hose!" Brennan laughed, his thick black hair in a messy disarray, sticking straight up in places and falling flat in others. His eyes were still swollen and a little crusty from last night's sleep, but he had run to the purple room and found his grandmother dressed and ready to play.

"Hold on, Brennie-boy! Time to conquer the Wild West!" she exclaimed, then neighed like a horse, to Brennan's delight.

He laughed a hearty, silly laugh, raised one hand and held on to his grandmother's shirt with the other, "Yeah! Conca the Wile Wess!"

She did her best to gallop on her knees and hands and managed pretty well for someone her age. She knew she'd be visited by aches and tightness later on in the day, but the adorable, chittering laugh was well worth it.

She went back and forth in the room before Brennan collapsed off of her.

"Ugh, the bandits got me, gwamma." He closed his eyes and stuck out his tongue, comically straight up with a "blagh" sound.

"Brennan!" His father's voice rang out, thundering and then echoing through the narrow hallway. He was coming back from a graveyard shift.

Brennan's eyes went wide and he quickly got to his feet and ran. Grandma Abby was slower to her feet, but she followed Brennan. She saw the three-year-old standing before his father, his back straight, his chin high, and his quivering little arms at rest next to his body. A crusty eyed, crazy haired, toddler, standing at a military attention. Grandma Abby could see how the little boy suppressed the flapping little dance his hands did when he got nervous.

Brennan's father was holding a red plastic truck in his hands, looking quite angry.

"Did you leave this in the living room, young man." he said in a low growl, his eyes bulging from their darkened, tired sockets.

"Yes, suh. Sorwy." Brennan's voice was barely audible.

Grandma Abby's eyes welled, the tears carrying the sting of her frustrated sadness and anger.

"You know what this means, right, boy?"

"Yes." Brennan squeaked, his voice cracking on the last sound. To Abby's surprise and growing fury, Brennan cleared his little throat and repeated, "Yes, suh." in a steady, lower voice.

"Go to your room, think about what you did, and wait for me."

Brennan did an about face and hurriedly marched to his room. His hands now breaking loose of his restraint, opening and closing repeatedly. They gave an extra shudder at the sound of his father's belt clearing its loops.

"Brent," Alexandra said in a growl of her own, "You're going to go in there and whoop on a kid who's not yet three for leaving a truck out?"

"I tripped over it. I work all night. I want to come home to a clean house." Brent explained calmly, coldly.

It had been Brent's idea to name their son Brennan. It was a combination of his and his wife, Nancy's, name. He had always been clever. Creative. He had picked out the name a full seven years before Brennan had even been born and six years before his last tour in the military. Six years before he left and came back different.

"Your son is terrified of you. Your voice sparks fear, not love. He stands at freaking attention for you. You had to teach him that. Is your ego so big, or did you forget? He is not one of your inmates, Brent." Alexandra's voice was menacing. She was a full foot shorter than Brent but had absolutely no fear of him. He could physically destroy her, he could use her daughter against her, he could try to manipulate and sweet talk her, but Alexandra knew just where to poke. How to break through his thick skin. She lowered her voice, "He's also not one of your God forsaken troops, Captain." she snarled, a subtle sarcasm adding an extra bite to her last word.

Brent winced. The color that had risen in his face dropped out of it. He gently moved his mother-in-law aside and started towards his son's bedroom door. He heard Nancy begin to scold her mother, telling her this was the last straw, that she needed to leave, she was no longer welcome.

Brent walked into Brennan's room. Brennan had been sitting on the bed. He bolted up straight, standing again at attention. He had put on jeans to soften the hits. Brent stared at his son, on his feet, doing his best to keep his face straight, brave. He was doing an admirable job, but he could not keep his bottom lip from quivering or his eyes from watering. A teeny, tiny soldier, ready to face his punishment.

Brent softly tossed the belt onto Brennan's bed. Brennan's eyes fluttered to the belt and back. Brent sat down on the floor, silent tears dripping from the corners of his bright green eyes.

"Come here, buddy."

"Um... suh?" Brennan was genuinely confused.

"Dad's fine, kiddo. Come sit with me."

Brennan sat next to Brent. Brent picked him up effortlessly and put him on his lap. The tears quickened. A tear fell on Brennan's forehead and he looked up.

"Dad? Daddy? Why aw you sad? I'm sorwy. I'll pick up my twucks." he used his little hands to wipe away his father's tears, "Don't cwy, daddy. I promise to clean my twucks."

Brent held him tighter and cried harder.

"I love you, Brennie. I love you like you have no idea. You are my pride. You are my joy. You are the only thing I've done right in my life so far." He was sobbing now. Brennan was scared. "Be better than me, buddy."

He held his son for a long time.

That was the first time Brennan saw his father cry. That was the last time Brennan saw his grandmother outside of a few holidays and eventually her funeral.

That day changed Brent's life. From that day forth, he tried to overcome his pain. Tried to overcome his hardness. He treated his son like a son, to the best of his ability. It was the day that eventually led to him realize that he couldn't. He couldn't be the father that his son deserved. The father his second son needed. It was the day that led to him leaving. It was the day that started him on the path that ended at the bottom of a bottle.

Chapter 14

"I haven't really had contact with you since." Grandma Abby lamented. "Well, little you." She beamed and wiped the tears off his cheeks. "You're such a handsome, young, man." Tears now filled her eyes. "So intelligent."

Brennan smiled, "How do you know I'm smart, grandma?"

"To begin with, you have a brilliant light behind your eyes. That and you were able to find a way to travel through time." She leaned back in her armchair. "Either that sort of travel is common and I never noticed, or my grandson is a genius." Her smile faded. "Why did you come? Not that I'm not ecstatic that you're here, just curious."

Brennan looked down at his feet. "I married this beautiful woman. You'd like her grandma." He smiled for a second. "She's smart, witty, funny, gorgeous, strong…"

"Broken." she interrupted.

Brennan nodded. He felt like he had been doing too much crying lately and fought to stop even more tears.

"Someone hurt her, when she was just a girl. I'm here to fix it." he declared plainly.

"Brennie-boy, you still have such a beautiful heart, but what's the cost?" she inquired, a sad understanding in her voice.

"No cost is too great to spare her that pain."

She scooted towards him and held his hand.

Brennan talked. He told her about everything. He told her about Modest the Mouse, about The Machine, the abuse, the nightmares, his anxiety, the Xanax, Abby. She was

134

delighted he had named her Abby. He only left out The Stepdad and The Guy.

"Brennan, it sounds like you have a beautiful life. Not a perfect life. Not a painless life. A beautiful life. Doing this can change anything and everything. Maybe you can go back. God can heal her, you know. Isaiah 53:5." She spoke to him, pained with the knowledge that her grandson didn't want to hear this. That he had thought of it all. That he knew he would probably lose his wife, his child, his life, but that at least Deidre would be whole.

"It's too late for that." Brennan said. "I have to do this, grandma. I can stop her pain. I can fix what's broken. How could I not?" Brennan lost his shaky command over his tear ducts. "She saw me, grandma. Past my crap. My trauma, my scars, my brokenness. She saw me. I've loved her for that and so much more since then. I can erase her pain."

Grandma Abby knew that arguing the point further would make no difference. His mind was made up. She wept silently, staring into her grandson's eyes, clear and green. If she couldn't stop him, she'd help him. Maybe if she did that, he'd come around. He'd figure it out himself. The best lessons were always learned that way. Understanding and wisdom always stick better when you come across them yourself.

"Brennie, the anxiety attack you had, you've been managing it with emergency meds, haven't you?"

Brennan couldn't help but smile, her mind worked like his, he could tell. There was a familiar glint in her eye, a pushing, knowing, curiosity riding in her voice and sneaking across her face.

"Yes, grandma. Why?" He asked but didn't require an answer. The grin melted from his face and he felt an overwhelming foreboding that he was going to have another attack. He might, and worse, it would not be his last. Not by a long shot. Not for a while.

"What was it, Brennie?"

"Xanax." He responded absentmindedly. He was running calculations in his head. He was taking the Xanax to the point where he felt calm, not yet euphoric. Maybe the detox would only last a few days.

Grandma Abby stood up and went back to the kitchen. She was gone for about thirty seconds before she returned with a small, purple, zippered, soft-sided cooler and a bottle of water.

"Alright, Brennan. We need to get you hydrated and keep you hydrated. You'll stay in my room with me. When was your last dose?"

Brennan thought about this and was confused as to how he could answer. He wondered if his travel through time was instantaneous. Time in the Nothing was non-existent. It felt like forever and it felt like a second. He had taken it while driving The Guy's truck, or had it been before that? How much time had passed since his drive, since his fight? He was suddenly hyper aware of the dull ache in his knuckles and his legs. Then he was hyper aware of everything. His breathing quickened. He felt pressure behind his face, in his sinus cavity, then the tingling sensation run down from the top of his head to his chest. Everything was too loud. Everything was too bright.

Grandma Abby hugged him tight. "It's okay, Bren. You're okay."

"I think, for me, it's been about 3 hours, but I don't know how the jumps affect that. I jumped twice pretty much back to back." His voice was slow, measured, but shaking. He was doing his best to reign in his mind.

Grandma Abby guided him to lie down on the couch. About five minutes later, the urgent panic had passed and Brennan only felt a general heaviness in his hands, face, and feet. At that point Grandma Abby walked him to her room. She took a blood pressure cuff and stethoscope from her purple pack. She measured his blood pressure and smiled kindly at him.

"137/85. Not quite perfect, but pretty good for someone who just had an anxiety attack."

She turned and took out a small, leather-bound, notebook from the cooler and a pencil from her bedside table. She wrote the date, time, and stats.

Brennan nodded. "Thanks, grandma." He held her bony hand. Her skin felt paper thin, her knuckles protruded, but it was warm.

She smiled at him, squeezed his hand, then grabbed the remote from the bedside table. She turned on the TV and a Mexican channel came on, playing a telenovela. A lady named Angelica was outraged about something a man named Sergio had done or said. Grandma Abby changed the channel and Brennan opened his eyes after hearing the familiar, low, tones of Kevin Conroy's voice.

"You used to love Batman." Grandma Abby reminisced, her eyes gazed at the TV, but Brennan suspected what she was actually seeing was a two-year-old in his briefs, sitting in a tiny chair, watching cartoons in her old gold and purple room on a Saturday morning.

"Well, somethings don't change, grandma." Brennan replied.

Grandma Abby chuckled and moved the hand that still held his to his shoulders and squeezed them. She was crying again. Brennan watched about half the episode, his eyelids constantly gaining weight until they did not re-open. He slept peacefully for the first time in a while, but it wasn't meant to last long.

Chapter 15

Brennan woke with a start and immediately jumped out of
the bed. He was still fully clothed, except for his shoes, and
his socks slid out from under him, causing him to stumble
over. He had barely hit the ground when he jolted back up
to his feet.

"No, no, no, nonononononono…" he put his hands up to
his face and raked them up, fingers wrenched like claws,
pulling through his hair, "I'm gonna die. I'm gonna die.
I'm gonna…"

Grandma Abby pulled him towards the bed and sat him
down. She spoke very calmly. "You're okay, Brennie.
You're fine. Focus on my voice. Focus on me. Focus on
what's real."

But that was the problem. Everything was real. Everything
was TOO real. Brennan's skin was tight over his body, the
small crevices and details on the walls jumped out at him,
her quiet, calm voice, was booming in his head. The
knowledge, the understanding, the realization of his
mortality hung on his head like a lead crown.

"Brennie-boy? Brennan?" Grandma Abby could feel his
body tensing, his shoulders, his arms that he was now using
to hug himself, his set jaw, his eyes that were closed to
block the mild visual hallucinations. Everything tightened
and Abby was just able to get a small cushion to his mouth
as he let out a roaring, gravely yell.

The yell seemed to have drained him and he slumped over,
his heart slowing, the world fading into normality again.

She took his blood pressure. 145/87 but he was relaxing
now.

He slept for a few hours. He was sweating quite a bit and would at times whine in his sleep, but he didn't have any more night terrors.

Brennan woke up just shy of six in the morning and used the bathroom. That was the first of five times he'd use it before noon. Each time, he'd return to his grandmother's room, his stomach feeling incrementally better, until it worsened, and he was in the bathroom again. He was refusing to eat anything and it took Grandma Abby plenty of patience and some of her patent stubbornness to get him to drink water and eat a few saltines. Brennan did his part and held it down for a few hours before his body decided it was time to start spewing things out up top now. He only threw up twice, but both times were with such force he was half expecting to see his esophagus plop into the toilet. During one on his sleeping spells, Grandma Abby had run out and bought him some Gatorade to replenish his electrolytes. She advised him to drink it slowly and she diluted it with water. Finally, after a quarter hour of tossing, turning, and groaning, he fell asleep.

Everything was black. No, not quite black, just empty. Void. The void. The Nothing. Brennan's aches and pains were softened to a dull throb. The splitting headache was a light tension. The angrily beating heart that was protesting against the lack of drugs was quieter, slower, almost distant and not actually in Brennan's chest. He felt his consciousness stretch and begin to take form. It was a strange sensation to slowly start feeling his limbs grow out of nothing. When he felt fully formed, his feet touched down on something. Normally he would've thought of it as the ground, but this was different. He felt it, but he didn't. It was warm, but also cold. His mind briefly spun as he walked on and in these forms of contradiction. There was something else too. Empty as this place was, it was alive. He felt watched.

"Investigator Ramirez," a raspy smoker's voice called out in a tone of sarcastic respect, "how are you today, sir?"

Brennan recognized the voice. He turned knowing he would see the Stepdad, and he did. Only, he was not expecting to see the Stepdad missing part of his face. This was the Stepdad as he was in death.

"What the hell?" A voice echoed from everywhere and nowhere. Brennan recognized it as his own.

"Yeah, not great to see your handiwork, huh? I was good looking, you know, but you had to come and blow my face away," the Stepdad hissed angrily.

"You deserved it for what you did. You deserved more." Brennan inhaled slowly, "I should've emptied the gun into your disgusting, weasel face!"

"I used to be a hit with the ladies. Natural good looks, husky smoker's voice, charming," the Stepdad smiled, "I could've had any girl. I coulda been your daddy, In-ves-ti-ga-tor."

"Yeah?" Brennan questioned, the environment of the Nothing allowing him to remain calm, "Could've had any woman, but you picked a child?" Brennan's face had shriveled into a sneer. "What was it, big boy? Pretty face and muscles making up for trouble downstairs?"

The Stepdad's expression was probably one of anger, but it was hard to tell from the remaining pieces. He was quiet and then yelled explosively, as if he suddenly remembered the cause of his new looks and new home.

"YOU KILLED ME!" the Stepdad roared through his purplish, blood speckled, face. "You planned, you plotted, you killed me."

"You were going to kill her, you rancid piece of inhuman waste." Brennan growled, low and menacingly.

"YEAH, YEAH, I WAS!" Stepdad chuckled, "I'm a monster. I'm an alien. I walk among you." He finished his sentence in a mocking sing-song tone, "Are you like me, In-ves-ti-ga-tor?"

"No."

"Are you sure? Who am I, In-ves…" he didn't finish.

"The Stepfather. The disgusting, gutless, perverted, evil rapist, that Kaylee called Stepdad." Brennan was furious, part of his mind wondered how intense his anger would be if the Nothing wasn't subduing it.

"My name is Rafael Robles. I was a life. A dark one. A twisted one. A broken one." Brennan looked up at that last description, "Perhaps an unforgivable one, but a life nonetheless. You killed Rafael Robles. You took that life."

"To prevent you from taking hers." Brennan reasoned, more to himself than the Stepfather, who was now nothing more than a Phantom.

"No," the Phantom's broken face twisted into a smile, "for practice." He paused for a moment, "You killed me to see what it would do, to see if it worked. If it did, you didn't think I deserved to live, and if you crapped the bed… Kaylee was dead anyway!"

Brennan lunged at him, his fist drawn back, ready to piston into the cracked and bloody remains of the Phantom's face, but he didn't connect. The Phantom was suddenly behind him.

"And, chingado, In-ves-ti-ga-tor," the Phantom continued in a mocking voice, "did you crap the bed."

"What?" Brennan asked and suddenly felt a sense of dread stemming from a presence behind him. Someone was there, but he didn't want to turn, he didn't want to look.

"I was broken, In-ves-ti-ga-tor, and what broken people do best..." he paused and signaled behind Brennan with a flat hand, "is break other people."

Brennan turned around, ready to fight, but the Figure wasn't going to fight him. The Figure was that of a girl, late teens or early twenties, hanging by her neck from a noose made from a thick, orange extension cord. The noose stretched upwards and faded, seemingly hanging from nothing. The Girl swayed back and forth softly in the non-existent wind. Her red hair hung down straight, obscuring her face, but Brennan didn't need to see it. He knew he she was. She was older, but it was definitely her. Kaylee's lifeless body suddenly and uncomfortably reminded Brennan of windchimes in a late fall breeze, eerie in their peaceful sways.

"No." Brennan barked. "It's fake. I'm hallucinating, living my worst nightmares, I'm in withdrawal, none of this is real."

The Phantom was suddenly directly behind him and Brennan realized there was a charred and metallic smell emanating from him.

"No, in-ves-ti-ga-tor. It's painfully real. You still don't understand this place. You seemed so smart." His voice was low and almost creepily seductive, but Brennan understood that he meant it to be mocking.

"It's outside of time. A connection. Like a temporal train station."

"Ah! Quick wit after all, In-ves-ti-ga-tor. Close. You see, if this is the train station, you're the train. This is a tear, a wound, a slice through time that will infect and ooze with the blood and puss of your meddling. You're stitching yourself into it, through it. Ripping the stitches out again and again! You're torturing time. But, for every action..."

"There's an equal, opposite reaction." Brennan recalled in a low whisper. He was starting to understand and the more he understood, the more fear seeped into his mind. He remembered all the cuts that he pretended not to notice. He remembered his last injury and his tongue recalled the metallic slime he had spat out upon his arrival to 1994. He was hurting his body with every trip. He was probably hurting his mind as well. Without him saying anything, the Phantom spoke, as if he could hear his thoughts, and maybe here, in the Nothing, he could.

"It's not just you that hurts. I broke her. You didn't stop me from doing that. To change so much meant Kaylee's mom wouldn't learn her lesson. I'd be replaced with another abusive boyfriend, one after another, until someone took my place in Kaylee's nightmares. You knew this. Your brain is faster than your heart, In-ves-ti-ga-tor. It suits you," he sneered and chuckled, "Kaylee grew up. She wanted to be normal, but her mother never fully forgave me and never fully forgave her. You see, she wasn't just disgusted, angry, and hurt. She was jealous. Jealous of Kaylee's youth, of her sleek, untouched body. Of her innocence. Of the things I fed from." His voice dropped in the last sentence and Brennan could've sworn there were two voices at the end of it. "I drove a wedge between them. Kaylee went to therapy, but she always blamed herself. She thought she had broken her mother and killed a man. She knew I died because of her. You gave her time, but just time to live in hell. Time to-"

Brennan's hand suddenly felt heavy. He swung it upward in a compulsive, but smooth, motion. Brennan didn't know how the gun was there, but he pulled the trigger anyway. Brennan just glimpsed the explosion of the rest of Rafael Barrera's face. Red mist drizzled with grey, pink, and black particles.

He woke up in a cold sweat, gasping, a knot in his throat, and pain coursing through his veins. Grandma Abby pushed him back down onto the bed as he tried to get up. Brennan settled and rolled on the bed towards the side. He tried to grasp the trash can next to his bed. He saw three identical trash cans floating over the floor and guessed the middle one was the real one. He picked up the trash can and vomited. Grandma Abby barely caught the bin out of his hands as he dropped it. She propped him up and gave him a bit of ice water.

"You're okay, Brennie. You're okay. It'll be over soon." She looked at him with compassion and sympathetic pain. "I can use Valium to wean you off. That may help a bit."

"N-No. No." Brennan croaked in a broken voice that she had to lean in to hear. "This is faster. I need to get this over with. I need to finish what I started."

145

Grandma Abby put Brennan down on the pillows and then removed one of them to help him lay flatter. Brennan took the pillow with a shaking, clammy, hand, and put it over his eyes. Every pulsing heartbeat thumped an invisible railroad spike into his sinus cavity and temples. He took a slow breath to calm his rushing heart and it skipped a beat, then came back with a hard thud that made him sit up straight with a coughing gasp. He put his hand over his chest and tried to calm down.

"Brennie, please! This isn't safe! We can wean you off with the Valium," she repeated.

"No," he begged desperately trying to swallow saliva and wet his sandpaper dry throat, "It'll take too long."

His head kept throbbing painfully and then a low whir began to sound in every beat. Every beat of the deep, vibrating tone lasted longer and went up about a half step in pitch. Soon, he could only hear his breathing inside his head, the outside world was drowned out by a high pitched ringing. His peripheral vision blurred, darkened, then was gone. The rest of his vision became distorted by the sudden tears in his eyes and the black ring began to grow inwards until the whole world was a pinhole of light.

Nothing again. The Nothing.

Brennan was on his knees with his back slouched and his head almost tucked between his legs. For a moment, a peace came over him as he enjoyed the dull, distant pain that had replaced the intense ripping and piercing that he felt in his waking state. His veins now pumped a warm, stinging fluid, rather than the intense battery acid they had been pumping a moment before. He enjoyed the moment as the expected dread of whatever nightmare the Nothing had for him settled in.

"AAARGH! Screw this place!"

"Yep. Freakin' sucths, man." Another Phantom agreed with a heavy lisp.

Brennan looked up and saw him. The Guy, The Heap, The Corpse. The personification of Deidre's betrayal. The anthropomorphic confirmation of his paranoia. The, honestly disappointing, answer to his insecurities.

The hits and wounds all looked relatively fresh, plenty of bruising, but not much swelling. As if he could read Brennan's mind, which Brennan was now assuming he could, the Phantom explained, "Blood poolth, but you don't thwell the thame way when you're dead."

"Good Lord, that lisp gets old fast." Brennan complained.

The Phantom's pulpy face contorted in hurt, annoyed, anger.

"Well, you gave it to me, you peeth of..." the Phantom was cut off by Brennan's exasperated voice.

"Alright! Let's get this over with." Brennan inhaled deeply. "I killed you! God! I am so freaking done with this place. Whatever. I beat the crap out of you and killed you! You're going to tell me about how you were just a guy in love! You're going to tell me how terrible I am for doing it! You're going to tell me how you had your whole life ahead of you and it wasn't my place!" Brennan paused to take a breath and chuckled humorlessly at the genuinely dumbfounded look on the Phantom's face. "I'm sorry! Is that what you want to hear? I'm sorry that I stopped you from SCREWING my WIFE! I'm sorry that I stopped you from adding another notch to your belt or bedpost or whatever the hell! I'm sorry that I ended your life before you unleashed the full potential of your burger flipping talents upon fast food chains across the state!" Brennan hadn't even noticed, but he was walking closer to the Phantom with every statement.

There was no fear in Brennan. There was only a stomach knotting frustration and hot, burning, seething, wrath.

"I'm sorry that your family will never get to be fully disappointed in you! I'm sorry..." Brennan was breathing hard, his voice softened, now shaky and airy from the stress of yelling, "... I'm sorry that you died and everyone will focus on the good that COULD have been, instead of the disappointment that WOULD have been."

He was face to mangled face with the Phantom, The Guy.

"You know what I am sorry about? I'm sorry that I took MY daughter, MY baby girl, away from this world, just because you were the freaking fluid donor that she came from." Brennan's eyes stung, "I hate you and I know you hate me, but you can't possibly hate me as much as I hate myself. So go ahead. Try to guilt trip me. Try to tell me how badly I messed up. You can't push me past the bottom."

Brennan's heart was in his throat and he felt ready to lash out again, but this time there was no weight of a magical gun appearing into his hand. Instead Brennan stood awkwardly in front of the Phantom, inches from his disfigured facade. Brennan noticed a glint, a reflection of a non-existing light, bouncing off a small speck in the corner of the Phantom's eye.

"Are… are you… are you crying?" Brennan asked incredulously, confusion temporarily supplanting his fury.

"I don't hate you, man." The Phantom confessed. "I'm truly thorry." The Phantom appeared to become frustrated and he reached into his mouth with dirty, crooked fingers, and tore out a chunk of cheek that had been intruding against his tongue.

Brennan looked on, unable to avert his gaze, his mouth twisting in disgust as the bit of bloody flesh ripped and then plopped onto the invisible floor.

"Much better." The Phantom grinned, as much as he could grin with a partial face, "Don't worry about that. I don't feel any pain. It's more like pressure. Like when the dentist numbs your mouth and then does an extraction." The Phantom looked back up at Brennan. "Look, man, I'm pissed that you killed me. I'm pissed I had to have a closed casket, but I don't hate you. You got the girl in the end and rightfully so. You're the better man, but you need to understand a couple of things." The Phantom gulped and Brennan couldn't help but think how much more human this vision was compared to the previous Phantom.

"First off, I didn't love her." The Phantom confessed. He twitched as if something had hurt after all. "Okay, no, before that, I'm not a Phantom. I'm not some ghost, please stop thinking of me that way. I'm not just a guy, I'm not a corpse. My name is Kyle."

"I know your name." Brennan growled. The sound of the Phantom's name was like a puff of air over a pile of glowing embers, feeding his anger to grow hotter, brighter and stronger.

149

"I know it's easier to think of me as a figure, as a symbol, but I'm a person. Or I was, I guess. For what it's worth, I think you're probably right. I wasn't exactly on my way to amounting to much, but I was still someone. Still, whatever, that's not my point." He paused to regain his train of thought, "I didn't love Deidre. I was infatuated with her. She was pretty, smart, funny, she was everything a guy like me did not deserve. She spoke about you a lot. Mostly with her girl friends. She said great things and terrible things. How you were the only guy she had ever been with, how you were crazy smart, like uber smart. How you had been the most romantic and sweet guy ever. How you had changed after y'all lost the kid. How you were very smart, but how it scared her sometimes. How you seemed empty. How you'd get angry. How you'd grown cold. I overheard these conversations and got closer to her. I had this thought that I could be the new you. I wanted the girl who had been chased like that. I wanted the girl that you had deserved at one point, because I would never deserve a girl like that."

Kyle looked into Brennan's eyes from his bloodshot, hazy, pair, and Brennan almost felt a twinge of sympathy. So much of this sounded like what he had felt when he had first met Deidre. The girl he'd never deserve.

Kyle continued, "Eventually, one of the hoeskis in our class convinced her to open up her horizons, or whatever. I was at the right place, at the right time, and just harmless enough."

Sympathy dissipated and Brennan wanted to kill him all over again. He felt the ire saturating every cell in his body. He used all his willpower to restrain himself and continued to listen.

"After the first time, she told me I couldn't quite measure up to you."

"No pun intended." Brennan joked flatly, without an ounce of humor in his voice and countenance.

"No," Kyle corrected, "she intended the pun. She intended the insult. But I went back again, to the same results. You caught me before the third time. First time in your home. I'm sorry for that too."

"Am I supposed to feel bad for you?" Brennan asked, trying intently to push out the small bit of sympathy that had somehow slithered in.

"No. I knew she was spoken for. I did wrong. But I wasn't the one that betrayed you. She hurt us both."

The sympathy disappeared. There it was. The raw nerve, hidden under layers of excuses and justifications. The callback to his conversation with Kyle when he had thought of him as The Corpse. Kyle owed him nothing. Deidre was the one that had made a commitment to him. Deidre was the one who had hurt him. Kyle had been an instrument of that betrayal. Little more than that.

Kyle had been used and hurt.

Once more unfortunately for Kyle, when one hits a nerve, the reaction is never calm. Brennan's fist connected with Kyle's already loosened jaw, sending him sprawling to the floor. Kyle cried out.

"Ugh! I guess I can still feel some pain."

Brennan marched over to him and put his foot on his chest.

"You think you're going to get to me with some pitiful, pathetic, sob story about how you couldn't *deserve* her? She's not a freaking prize. She's not a medal. I stopped trying to *deserve* her because she LOVED ME... and I loved her."

Brennan fought back the reasoning that his statement proved Kyle's point.

"I did what any person would have done. I did what any man would have done if he went home to find another man about to take... no, not take... about to *use* his wife." Brennan put more weight on the foot planted on Kyle's diaphragm. He momentarily wondered if the dead needed to breathe, but quickly lost the thought.

"I reacted the way anyone would've reacted."

"Stop... stop..." Kyle said, but they weren't pleas. He was trying to say something. "Stop... lying... to... yourself!" He finally coughed out and Brennan removed his foot, only long enough to make the tip of it connect with Kyle's already broken ribs. Kyle coughed and yelled. "You acted! Like you're acting now. You tell yourself you snapped... you chose to snap! You made the decision to let go." Kyle's bloodshot eyes met Brennan's burning green ones. "You knew as you were beating me that you would kill me. I could see it in your eyes. You also knew that she would be gone. The girl. The little one. You knew! You just pushed it away to kill me. Tell me why...you know why. I know too, but I want you to tell me! Why did you push back sense and CHOOSE TO KILL ME?!"

"BECAUSE IT FELT GOOD!" Brennan yelled in a roaring, deep tone as his body twisted back to Kyle, the bottom of his shoe connecting with Kyle's face.

"BECAUSE I'VE BEEN FANTASIZING ABOUT THE DAY I WOULD SQUEEZE OUT YOUR FINAL BREATH AND WATCH THE LIGHT LEAVE YOUR EYES!"

Brennan's unforeseen honesty felt like wings growing on his back. It was darkly liberating.

"I killed you because I hated you. Because I could blame you. Because I could hurt you. Because I loved her!" Brennan gave a quick, stifled, sob, "Because I knew I'd forgive her. I wanted to forgive her, but I still wanted someone to pay."

Brennan fell to his knees besides Kyle and gripped Kyle's shirt collar. "Because even though I knew she'd be gone, I wanted to believe she wouldn't. I wanted to believe that God would see it fair to leave her. To give me Abby without the pain."

Brennan's stifled sobs transformed into angry, bitter, weeping.

"Why couldn't I just have Abby? Why did I need to suffer to have her? Why can't I just fix things! Even now! Why do THINGS... KEEP... BREAKING?!" Brennan shook Kyle by his bloodied shirt collar as he emphasized his words. He stopped and dropped Kyle back down. Brennan lowered his head and his voice, "I can go back and change things. I can go back and fix them, but they just break again. It's the hydra. It's Sisyphus' freaking stone."

A singular sob escaped with Brennan's last word.

"Sometimes," Kyle stammered in a weak voice, lined with what seemed like true concern, "sometimes, the alternative to broken is just broken in another way." His breath rattled in his body, like an old vacuum cleaner sucking in particles of loose dirt. "We can't fix everything. We just need to make the best of the opportunity we have."

Brennan looked up at Kyle. The tears still streaked his cheeks, but they had stopped flowing. His piercing, green eyes bore into Kyle. There was a renewed darkness in them.

"No," Kyle warned, "What are you doing?" he asked nervously.

"I have an opportunity. I truly feel like it's the last one left."

Brennan's voice was deep, low, and steady.

"You're right. I need to make the best of it." An eerie serenity emanated from him, like a still lake in the moonlit night, its placidity hiding it's treacherous depths and ravenous predators. Brennan had found his lost resolve. "Don't worry. I'm not going to leave you here to suffer. I'm going to give you rest. True rest. Then, I'll take my one last shot." Brennan grabbed the side of Kyle's broken face and, in a now quiet voice as honest as his loud, broken, yells had been earlier, he said, "Thank you. Thank you, Kyle."

Brennan slid his hand from Kyle's cheek forward towards his nose. He clasped Kyle's cut nostrils between his thumb and forefinger and used his palm to seal Kyle's tattered mouth. It didn't take long, and all the while, Brennan looked into Kyle's eyes, not with hate or vengeance now, but with understanding, as the flicker of already dying light was snuffed out.

Brennan woke up, calmly and slowly this time.

154

"I'm sorry, Brennan." Grandma Abby said, holding a glass of water in one hand and an open pill bottle in another. "I had to, you were terrible. You were crying, and yelling, and saying nonsense."

"It's okay, grams." Brennan affirmed.

He understood now where the peace had come from. It was more than the uncharacteristically wise words of a twice dying, young man. It was the Valium's slow burn abating the mental flash burns and scorch marks left by the Xanax. His head still ached, he still felt disoriented and off balance, but the worst of it was subdued.

He stood up shakily and slowly straightened out.

"You did what you had to. Now, I'll do what I have to."

Chapter 16

Brennan explained that, if she allowed him to, he would stay with her until he found a way to protect Deidre. Grandma Abby was delighted at the idea of him staying. She immediately hugged him and gave out a strange yelp of joy that Brennan was pretty sure he had heard from his mother at one point.

Abby took his arm and walked him to the other room in her apartment, which she excitedly dubbed his room. It wasn't until he walked in to that spare room that he really understood how the room really was his, or at least it could've been.

The room itself was unremarkable. White walls, white tile, not very spacious. It was the decor that pulled at Brennan's heartstrings as he gazed around, drinking in the heartbreaking details.

There was a twin sized bed in the middle against the wall of the room. The duvet was a bright blue and grey, adorned with images of Bruce Timm's Batman in several action poses. the pillows were emblazoned with large, yellow and black, bat symbols. On the wall next to the bed were two posters. One had a very stoic looking Batman and the other was a much happier looking version of the hero with Robin, the Boy Wonder by his side. On the wall that Brennan would be facing when he slept on the bed, there were pictures of Grandma Abby with little Brennan. Next to a small dresser, there was a large, blue, plastic, storage container with "BRENNIE'S TOY BOX" printed in block letters made by a large permanent marker. On top of the box was a small tent card. Brennan walked over to it and picked it up.

"To my Boy Wonder. I love you, Brennie."

"I was hoping that I'd be able to have you visit." Grandma
Abby said, "I never expected it to be like this." She
chuckled softly. "Sorry about the twin bed. The room is not
very big and I was hoping to fit another twin bed once
Jimmy's old enough to come spend the night too."

Brennan stayed silent. He had never seen this room before.
Ever. He had never been given the chance to. He had never
seen Grandma's apartment at all, he realized. His heart
sank and he wondered how much time she had left.

"You don't remember this room, do you?" Grandma Abby
asked, breaking the silence yet again.

"To be fair, I don't remember much of my life at four years
old." Brennan replied and turned to look at her with a smile
that aimed for happy, if slightly teasing, but landed
squarely in sympathetic. His mind wandered and wondered
how much longer she had or if she was even aware of the
cancer consuming her body. "Grams, I need to tell you
something. It may shock you, but it's necessary for me to
tell you. There may still be time."

"There isn't, Brennie." Grandma Abby replied. "It's
terminal. The demon spread like wildfire. Doctors have
made me comfortable and assure me that I have a while
before I'm too messed up to take care of myself. Another
six months, they think."

"Grandma, you need to call mom." Brennan urged.

"I can't, Brennie. I call her just to tell her I'm dying? That's
manipulative. I don't want to worry her. Plus, I've tried
calling her to see if we can talk. She rarely answers and

when she does, she is always busy. Damn caller ID. I'd get more answers if that didn't exist."

"You're not at all like they describe you, you know." Brennan couldn't believe this was the egotistical woman he had heard about.

"I'm sure I was at some point."

"Grandma, did you forgive mom? For kicking you out?" Brennan asked apprehensively.

"The moment I walked out that door. I was a terrible mother when your mother was growing up. Any love I get from her is already more than I deserve." There was a resolve in her voice. She seemed set on convincing herself that she had earned this trouble. Brennan guessed it was how she maintained the illusion of control, by pretending she caused all her problems. Brennan often did the same thing.

Brennan didn't say anything else, but his mind raced for the right words, the right encouragement. Before he could devise a response he deemed appropriate, Grandma Abby cut in.

"Alright, enough of this. Let's go get you a decent wardrobe. Can't have you wearing those clothes. You've been sweating and puking in them for days." Grandma Abby said this with a slightly disgusted look on her face. Brennan suddenly realized she was right. The house had smelled sour to him and he began to realize it could just be him.

Abby and Brennan went to a Walmart a town over. Brennan was enchanted with the short trip. This was the longest he had spent in the past and it was incredible how much had changed since his childhood. The first thing he noticed was the lack of roads. What he considered the long way in his time was the only way in 1994. He was also incredulous of the stretches of land along the way that were just grass and trees. When they finally arrived at the Walmart, or Wal-Mart, as it was known in that time, Brennan couldn't help but laugh. Hundreds of small differences, some barely noticeable, became one massive, cumulative, nostalgic, culture shock. He saw a group of kids who were obviously skipping school dressed in a style meant to emulate Kurt Cobain. There was a man in dirty blue jeans, tucked in plain white shirt, and tan work boots pushing a cart filled with gardening supplies. The man reached for the beeper on his belt as he passed by Brennan. A woman with a haircut reminiscent of Zack Morris power-walked by Brennan in an effort to catch up to her friend, a young woman in overalls and two hair buns on the top of her head. Brennan laughed again.

"Good Lord, it's like I stepped into a stereotype." Brennan quipped to no response.

"Alright, we'll get the essentials. Underwear, socks, jeans, a few t-shirts. Maybe we can get you some slacks and button ups for church!" Grandma Abby cheered gleefully.

"Grams, I love you, but you know I can't stay too long." Brennan tried to say it as nicely as he could, both for her sake and his. A part of him wanted to stay. A part of him wanted to join this world of grunge, bright colors, boxy cars, and way too many mullets. He wanted to be part of this disconnected world where Facebook, Twitter, and smartphones did not exist. He wanted to be a part of a world where Grandma Abby was a part of his, but he knew he wouldn't stay. The part of him that wanted all those things had never grown past childhood. That part of him would remain ever repressed in him.

"Well, we don't know how long it will be. We'll make the most of it for now. Okay, let's go get you those things, then I'll pick up some groceries, then we can swing by Payless real quick to get you some shoes for church."

Brennan was astonished at how cheap everything was, at least when compared to prices from his time, but even with the 1994 prices, it was about $200 and 3 hours later before they headed back to Grandma Abby's home. About a mile shy of her place, they stopped at a store called Mikes. It was your average, small town grocery store, with the added bonus of having a butcher shop in the back.

"Meat is always cheaper here." Grandma Abby explained. "You can wait in the car if you want, Brennie."

"No, I'll get down. I remember this place. It doesn't exist in my time. It's just an empty building now."

"Where do y'all buy groceries?"

"Walmart across the street from our house."

"Dang. Guess our small town doesn't stay small after all." Abby remarked, raising her eyebrows. Brennan couldn't quite tell if she was impressed by the idea of a Walmart in her little, back road town or if she felt sorry that it wouldn't stay the Smalltown, USA it was in her time.

"It's still a small town." Brennan assured her. "Everything just grew around us. Brownsville has like 4 Walmarts in my time. Harlingen has 1 but like 3 H-E-Bs. Hell, even San Benito has a Walmart and H-E-B."

Grandma Abby scrunched her nose like if she had smelled something sour. It was an expression that reminded Brennan of his little Abby. If that wasn't enough, what Grandma Abby said next really drove it home. "Too many people. Sounds like there are just too many people."

Brennan smiled, wondering if little Abby had picked up that facial expression from him. He was painfully reminded that, genetics aside, Abby had irrevocably been his daughter.

They entered the store and got their pound of ground beef. As they were exiting Brennan saw two piles of paper pamphlets on a quarter operated candy machine with a cardboard and Sharpie sign that read "FREE-GRATIS". One pile of pamphlets was titled "El Atalaya", the other was "The Watchtower". Brennan suddenly had an idea. A smirk inched over his face. He took them all.

Chapter 17

"Okay," Grandma Abby started, "are you sure about this? You're going to need to have complete control over yourself. You can't lose it when you see this guy, Brennie."

They were sitting in Grandma Abby's car, down the street from the less rusted trailer that Deidre had grown up in. Brennan was wearing slacks and a button up. His hair was carefully combed and he had a satchel on his lap full of Jehovah's Witness' reading material.

"I'll be fine, grams." he took a deep breath and fidgeted his hands.

"How's the Valium treating you?"

Brennan felt a bit anxious. He was definitely riding a bit of an adrenaline rush, but the Valium was doing its job.

"I feel sleepy and wired at the same time. Like when you don't sleep well so you get a big coffee."

Grandma Abby smiled and touched his cheek. "Brennie, are you sure you want to do this?"

"Yes. I need to."

"Okay, so what's your big picture here? Get evidence and call the cops? Convince the mom?"

Brennan smiled with his mouth and cheeks, but his eyes were grave, emerald, stones.

"Something like that. Something that removes him from Dee's life."

Brennan got out of the car and walked to the trailer. His heart quickened with every step he took toward the trailer.

He cleared his throat and rolled his shoulders. He felt tension spread like wings across his back. He tilted his head to the left and then to the right, producing a loud pop with the first turn and a quick-fire series of cracks with the second. He exhaled as he walked up to the door.

His body instinctively angled to make itself a smaller target as he knocked on the door.

He braced himself and the door opened.

"The hell…" he whispered to himself.

A man with long hair that had been bleached opened the door. He was young, thin, and was wearing a woman's silk robe. His lips were painted with smeared lipstick.

"Can I help you, Mr. Fancy Pants?" the man asked in a practiced, high pitch tone.

Brennan went into an auto pilot mode he had inherited from his father. It was useful, but he always felt dirty after using it.

"Good morning, sir," he greeted with a large, genuine looking, grin. "Have you heard the good news of our Lord and Savior Jehovah?" he asked as he removed a copy of The Watchtower from his pack.

"Oh, no, honey," the man lamented, "I've heard it all, but it's not for me."

"Well, is it okay if I leave you some reading material at least?"

"Yeah, sure, why not." he huffed and extended a hand out. His fingernails were colored with chipped nail polish.

Brennan gave him the reading material and peeked inside the house. There was a mess, a few boxes, and something that caught his eye immediately. A platform boot with a clear bottom filled with water and fake fish. Brennan remembered Deidre telling him about those boots and all the strange, 80's party paraphernalia, and BDSM equipment they had found when they moved into the trailer.

"Moving out?" Brennan asked.

"Yeah," the man flourished his hand and signaled toward the trailer, "I'm leaving this tin box, Fancy Pants. I'm out in a couple of weeks. So," he said with a smile that showed yellowed teeth and burns on his lips, "if you want to come check in with me again, you're gonna have to do that before then."

Brennan smiled again and gave a light chuckle. He extended his hand to the man.

"Good to meet you, Mr..." he trailed off giving the man a blank to fill.

"Call me Carlos. Or Carla. Both work."

Brennan thought about the burns on his lips and now the pock marks on his arms. "*Poor dude's an addict,*" he thought. "We have almost the same name, I'm Elder Charlie," Brennan lied.

The man looked at him quizzically, "Aren't elders the white kids on bikes? Ya sabes, los Mormones, or whatever."

"*Crap,*" Brennan thought, but what came out of his mouth was, "Yeah, them too. We have similar titles."

"Mmhmm," Carlos hummed with a fair amount of sass. "Y'all are like men. All the same. When are y'all gonna realize it's the same Papa Chuy y'all are fighting about?"

Brennan was surprised by his very real laugh. That had been legitimately funny.

"One of these days, Carlos. You have a great day." Brennan turned around and headed to the car. He let out his frustration as he got in.

"Damn it."

"I'm guessing Buffalo Bill was not our man," Grandma Abby joked.

Brennan cringed at her calling him Buffalo Bill.

"1994. Different times," he thought.

"He's getting evicted. He's going to get severely depressed, he's going to overdose, he's going to die." He sighed. "The trailer will be empty for 2 months before the landlord decides to rent it at a stupidly low price to a single mother, in exchange for her cleaning it, and possibly sexual favors."

"They don't live here yet." Grandma Abby summarized, a look of slight disgust on her face.

"They don't freaking live here yet." Brennan repeated angrily.

They walked back into Grandma Abby's apartment a half hour later. Brennan paced the living room like a caged wolf. He was wringing his hands and then running his fingers through his hair. He was beginning to sweat and his heart was revving up.

"Brennan, let's sit down." Grandma Abby tugged his arm toward the couch. Brennan sat down reluctantly. His eyes were boring a hole through the floor. His breathing was becoming increasingly shallow.

"I need to find her. I need to stop him." His voice was a low growl.

"We need to talk about that too, Brennie."

Brennan suddenly remembered how he hated that nickname. He was not Brennie. He was Brennan. Earth's first-time traveler. A genius investigator. A dangerous man. A murderer. He was not a powerless, useless, senseless child. Still, he said nothing.

"I will continue to help you find Deidre and this man. I'll help you to get him to justice. I will help you to protect her," Brennan felt the proverbial 'but' coming, "but you need to tell me you are not going to kill this man, Brennan. We will find evidence. We can call the police, child protective services, get her safe. I don't know if that's a good idea, I don't know that this will fix the problems you're facing, but you'll do it with or without me, so I'll help. What I do know, is that if you take another man's life, you cannot come back from that. Your father can tell you that."

"No, he can't. Not in my time." Brennan replied with the intent of shocking her into silence. It only worked for a moment.

"Nonetheless, his drinking, his anger, he was a broken man. When you take a man's life, you sacrifice a part of your own as well." Abby spoke with such conviction that

Brennan suddenly wondered if she had first-hand experience in the matter.

"I know, grandma. I know."

He stood up and walked towards the restroom. He needed to wash his face. In times of anger and anxiety, Brennan had found that triggering the mammalian dive reflex could help smooth the jagged edges a bit. Grandma Abby remained seated, wrapping her mind and heart around the man the little, mop headed boy she loved had become.

Chapter 18

Brennan woke up early the next day and walked out to meet Grandmother Abby in the kitchen making eggs and toasting bread. Brennan suddenly remembered a breakfast she made that he loved. He couldn't remember was it was called, but he could remember sitting at the table as a kid and his grandmother giving him an over medium egg cooked into a piece of toast with the yolk bubble poking out through a hole in the bread. The circular piece of cut out bread had been his favorite part. He would use it to mop up the yolk after he finished eating the egg.

Brennan was touched, though not surprised, to see that was exactly what she was making.

"Morning, sweetie. You used to love these as a kid," Grandma Abby said in a cheery tone. Her voice contrasted against her countenance. She was pale and looked frail. Brennan noticed she only had enough ingredients to make breakfast for one.

"You joining me for breakfast, grandma?" he asked casually, easily hiding the concern he was feeling. Once he entered that autopilot mode that was so skilled in deception and manipulation, he was often stuck in it for a while.

"No, Brennie. Sorry." she hesitated then added, "I'm feeling under the weather. I can't hold down much of anything nowadays."

"Grandma, I can go get a second opinion with you. Maybe a third. Even in 1994, technology has come a long way."

It was her turn to be tough now.

"No. I am going to live the rest of my life moving. Able. Not bald and wilted. I'm going to make the most of it. Spend time with my grandson," she stroked his cheek and her papery skin caused Brennan's heart to dip into his stomach.

First thing in the morning, the sun painting her face through the kitchen window, no makeup, her straight hair loose, appearing more white than black this way, she looked fragile. She looked older than her age.

Brennan hugged her and she hugged back.

They ate breakfast, or rather Brennan ate, Abby watched.

"Do you remember the time I made you this breakfast and you took it to your table in the room to watch Sesame Street?" Grandma Abby asked.

"No, sorry grams."

"Oh, it was hilarious!" she chuckled preemptively, as if to offer it as evidence of the hilarity. "Okay, so your dad was away training, when he was away, your mom would call me to stay with her. They were long trainings, some over a month. I was there during one of those longer stays and I made you your favorite. You were just barely three at the time. You asked me, 'Gama Abby, can I take my food to the TV?' and I tell you, sure, since your dad wasn't there. So you go to your mom's room, where the TV was. I don't hear you for a while and you know what they say about kids, when you stop hearing them, start worrying. So I go check in, thinking you've made some sort of mess. Instead, you're sitting butt-naked in front of your little foldable table, using your training potty as a chair, and watching Sesame Street. You start calling out, 'One, two, three,

169

THREE bats' or whatever the Count was counting that day. I ask you, 'Brennie boy, why are you sitting like that?' You look at me, your mouth is all full of yolk, and I ask again, 'Why are you on your potty?' You look at me confused as heck and reply, 'I have everything here, grandma!'"

Brennan and his grandmother laughed. As old and fragile as she looked, her green eyes seemed to glow when she laughed.

"You know, grandma, I'm really glad I got stuck in this time. I'm really glad I get to spend this time with you and really get to know you," their eyes met, "I'm glad I get to be reminded of why I loved you so much."

Her eyes teared up and she smiled. She held his hand. Her hand was cold and bony. Brennan could've sworn she had shed weight overnight.

"This miracle is the best sign I've ever had that the Lord must still be on my side. I couldn't ask for a better last chapter than this." Her voice was creaking and hushed.

Brennan held her hand for a long while.

A few hours later, Brennan and Abby were parked outside a brick office building.

"Okay, so before we moved into the old mall, this building held the CPS offices. I'm quite sure that they're currently officed there. I'll be in and out in a few minutes. Then we can go back home and work on switching the picture."

Grandma Abby nodded and then handed him a small pill. "You forgot to take it this morning. I figure you need to be calm for this."

Brennan took it, dry swallowed, and got out of the car. The inside of the building was familiar. Posters with sad children's faces and phrases like "break the cycle" or "save a life" in bold print.

He sat down with the parents who were waiting for their visitations and the foster parents who were waiting for them to end. He chose a chair that was at the corner that led to the front door. A man walked out of the door that led to the bullpen. He was wearing a polo shirt, slacks, and dress shoes. He had a lanyard with an ID badge. Brennan noticed that it had the man's picture and identified him as a CPS worker but did not have his name. He smiled to himself. It was too perfect. He stood up and leaned on the corner, waiting for someone else to come out. A few minutes later, a woman came out. She had her ID tag on a lanyard as well.

"Third time's the charm." he whispered to himself.

Sure enough, ten minutes later, another man came out. He wore a button up shirt and a tie. His ID was clipped to his tie. Brennan turned around, giving his back to man. As the man headed out to the front door, Brennan watched his shadow. When he got close enough, Brennan spun suddenly, straight into the CPS worker.

"Oh, crap, so sorry, sir." Brennan apologized.

The man looked annoyed. "Watch it, man. Why don't you have a seat, like a normal person."

"Sorry, sir. Restless legs." Brennan smiled bashfully.

The man walked out and got in his car, a black 1994 Ford Mustang.

Brennan walked out after him and sped to Grandma Abby's car.

"Alright, let's go, let's go, let's go," he urged with a snide grin on his face.

They pulled away as the man walked back into the office, looking for his missing ID badge that he surely dropped when the clumsy, fat guy bumped into him.

"Okay, grams," Brennan began once they were a few blocks away, "if the dude puts two and two together and realizes I took his ID, he's going to report it. He seemed like an arrogant prick, so he may not report it for a while, but I doubt I have much time."

Grandma Abby pulled into a parking lot and removed an Exacto pen knife from her armrest.

"I thought we'd do this at home, grams." Brennan said as his grandmother made herself a makeshift desk on the car's dashboard.

"No need, Brennie. Carpe Diem! You know," Abby continued as she carefully sliced out the other man's picture from the ID, "I used to make fake IDs back in the day. I would make fake IDs for abused women running away from their husbands in Mexico. Divorce was frowned upon by both sides of the family. Machismo was expected and perpetuated by the culture. Still is."

She wrapped a polaroid of Brennan's face around the cut-out piece and inserted it back carefully. She used the Exacto knife to cut off the excess and invisible tape to hold the piece in. She inserted the badge into an ID badge holder they had purchased and clipped it on to a lanyard.

172

"Yeah," Brennan marveled, surprised by her quickness and obvious skill, "you have definitely done this before, grams." Brennan chuckled, "Who knew grandma was such a gangster. You're a straight up, badass granny."

Grandma Abby laughed gleefully, but her laugh transitioned into a continuous cough that brought Brennan and her back to reality. Brennan gave her a bottle of water and rubbed her back. She managed to drink down some water and stop coughing. She pressed her hand against her side.

"You okay?" Brennan felt stupid asking his cancer-ridden grandmother, who had almost passed out coughing and was in obvious pain if she was okay. She was dying.

Brennan had been trying to remember her date of death from the funeral or from the two times they visited her grave when he was a child. It was late August now. He couldn't remember the exact date, but he was almost sure she had passed in September of 1994. There was a question in his mind, a burning little ember that he had been ignoring, but an opportunity like this was extraordinary, and quickly running out.

"Grams," he hesitated, scrounging around in his mind for a polite way to ask, "growing up, I never really heard good things about you. It was always about how you were just not a good person, and now that I've met you and you're telling me about all this cool stuff you'd do, and..."

"You're wondering where that came from," she interrupted.

"Yes."

"Well," now it was her hesitating, "it came from truth, Brennan." Her eyes immediately reddened and swelled with tears. "The old me would've told you that your mom was a fool and your father was a liar and a manipulator. That you were turned against me by them the way your mother was turned against me by your grandfather, but it's simply not true." She inhaled deeply and held it for a few seconds. It was a calming technique Brennan had often used to try to evade a panic attack. "My life wasn't the easiest. Don't think that's an excuse, it's not. It's just background. My parents loved me, but they were so strict. I felt that I had many opportunities to become a great person. Not a great woman. A person. I am intelligent. I was beautiful. I was charismatic. I had potential, but my parents were strict and set in the ways of our culture. Women, even strong women, were meant for the home. I wanted to be a doctor, an actress, maybe a writer!" she said enthusiastically, the glimmer of lost hope shining vague and distant in her eyes. "I was allowed, just barely, mind you, to be a nurse. My parents had amassed themselves a decent financial legacy, enough at least for their sole surviving daughter to not have to work. I would climb the social ladder by marrying rich instead. I was pretty, well-mannered, they had sent me to a finishing school to learn how to cook, set a table, be a 'lady of the house' as my father put it." Grandmother Abby turned to look at Brennan and gave a weak smile. The kind of smile one gives attached to an apology. "Your grandfather was very rich when he started courting me. He was handsome, powerful, intelligent, manly. All the things one would find in a good husband. My parents were thrilled. They were hoping to see me married before they passed. They didn't. What I hadn't told them is that your grandfather had all the makings of a great husband, and his wife agreed."

Brennan knew about his mother's half-siblings. He knew about how his mother was a product of her father's second family, but hearing it from the perspective of his grandmother somehow made it more real. His mother had just been born and was accepted as his daughter, illegitimate or not. His grandmother, on the other hand, had been actively rejected.

"I spent my late twenties and early thirties chasing around a man who wasn't faithful to his wife, somehow trying to make him faithful to me, trying to convince myself that he'd be different, but I knew better. He was abusive, verbally, emotionally, and on rare occasions, physically. I spent that time raising his children too. I resented him for it. I resented his children, *our* children, too."

Tears were not flowing down her face, but there were no sobs. The pitch of her voice bent upwards a bit, but it remained strong and steady. It was the weeping of a woman who had learned through experience to cry in silence.

"Did you know I once told your mother that I would rather have borne a toad than her? What kind of mother says that? Worse, what kind of mother *means it*? Because I did at the time. I wanted a career, I wanted life, my life. I didn't want to live life for other people, not even my kids. You know what your mom did after I told her that? She was furious. Locked herself in her room. That day, your grandfather came back and he was angrier than usual because I had told one of his mistresses about his two families. The fight culminated with a shotgun barrel aimed at my face." Brennan's eyes widened with shock and he watched intently as his grandmother continued matter-of-factly to describe that day. "I have never seen your mom move that fast. She slid in front of me and locked eyes with your

175

grandfather. She had his eyes and, in that moment,, looking down at that mirror of himself, he lost his nerve and stormed out. We left that day," she sighed, "Still, I refused to adapt, and in the end, it destroyed me. My ego was inflated by the thoughts of what I could've been. What I was kept from. I kept acting like that proud and tough young woman. I pushed away my family. I pushed away my friends. I lost everything. I filled your mother with similar insecurities, you know. The difference was that your mother had your grandfather's Irish blood in her too." She chuckled lightly at this. "She was more rebellious than I was. She was tougher, stronger, more adaptable. She wasn't scared to put me aside. She wasn't scared to tell people 'no'. I'm glad for that. She wasn't better because of me, she was better in spite of me, and spite was what I reaped."

Brennan sat in silence. This family history was revealing but begged a question.

"What changed?" he asked, his voice just barely a decibel above a whisper.

Grandmother Abby looked at him, smiling despite the streaks that were now drying on her face. It was a loving smile that Brennan had once seen in his mother, when he was very young, and that had been reflected again in little Abby. It was the smile she gave when Brennan read her a bedtime story. A smile of gentle, but unadulterated, love.

"You." Grandmother Abby answered. "You, Brennie. When your mother announced she was pregnant, I could feel the warmth and love radiating off of her. It was something I hadn't seen in a very long time. Something that I had forgotten that I had known. I loved my children,

Brennan. I truly did, but it was a love that grew within me over time. The love that your mother had for you was immediate. The second she knew you were being formed within her, you became her hope, her joy, her pride, her love. I wanted to be a part of that. Reluctantly, and over time, your mom allowed me in. I was there when you were born. I wasn't allowed to be there by the time James came around though. I haven't even met him yet," there was a distinct tone of regret in her voice. "Anyway, I was there when you were born, I was allowed to be around you, your dad even made up a room for me at your house. Your mom and I would argue from time to time, but I learned to be quiet, to be humble, because it let me be close to you. The quiet didn't last long though."

"I'm sorry, grandma. I really am."

"Sorry for what, Brennie?" She put a hand on his face. Brennan hated how fragile it felt. "You did nothing wrong. I sowed a lot of resentment and hate, then I reaped it. Galatians 6:7." She referenced the scripture and raised her eyebrows in an expression that was almost comically stereotypical of a grandmother. "Now, I'm just trying to be better, as I get to the end of it all. Why must I be such a procrastinator? Always waiting to the last minute," she teased with forced humor.

Brennan gave a weak attempt of a chuckle, that was little more than a puff of air through his nose. "I'm the same way."

"Don't," Grandmother Abby commanded with an abrupt seriousness. "Do not wait until the end to make things right. You'll spend what little time you could have enjoying peace dwelling on regret and lost time. You can buy medicine, you can pay for doctors, hell, nowadays you can even pay for friends, but you can't buy love and you can't buy time."

Brennan suddenly noticed how firmly she was holding his face with both hands now. A deep sense of foreboding stirred in him.

"Okay, grandma, I get you," he replied quietly.

She lowered her hands and looked down. Brennan pushed the dark sensation out of his mind. He reassured himself it meant nothing, after all, if someone could say they could buy time it was him, wasn't it? As if she had heard his thoughts, Grandmother Abby spoke.

"Moving through time, even in the way you do, does not buy or guarantee time. Be wise with the time you get, Brennie."

Brennan swallowed with great difficulty. His throat had gone bone dry.

"Um, there are a few," Brennan's voice cracked on 'few' and he cleared his throat, "a few schools I want to look at today. I may be able to find out where Deidre lives."

The pair were silent for the 20-minute drive to the first school on Brennan's list. Putegnat Elementary was smaller in 1994 than it was in Brennan's time, but not by much. A couple annexes and paint jobs aside, it looked almost the same. The only other thing that was missing was the tall, chain link fence with the magnetized lock that seemed to encircle most schools in 21st century South Texas. Brennan's heart was beating hard, steadily. He counted his breathing for a few seconds and then walked right into the school and headed for the office. No one asked who he was or why he was there. He was stunned at the complete lack of security, but then again, this was an elementary school pre-Columbine. He approached the front desk and that conniving, lizard brained, auto pilot took over again. A large, expertly counterfeited, smile spread across his face.

"Good morning," Brennan greeted cheerily. He looked at the small name plate the clerk had next to her on her desk, "Carol. What a beautiful name. It sounds like a song."

He was almost disgusted by the oozing charm in his voice. He showed his badge to the front desk clerk in a hidden way and leaned in close as if he was confiding some great secret to her.

"I'm from Child Protective Services. I need to speak to a child who I believe is a student here."

He made his request in a hushed tone, with a worried look on his face, and then smoothly transitioned back to the beaming smile as he stepped back and away from the desk. He felt a gross satisfaction at how the clerk had mirrored his movements and expressions. He had her.

"Yes, of course, sir." She reciprocated with a smile of her own. Now it was her that leaned forward and he consciously mirrored her move.

"What's the child's name?" she asked in a secretive, whispery, tone.

"Bethsaida Morales."

No sooner was the name out of his mouth that the woman rolled her eyes exaggeratedly.

"Ugh, I am not surprised, sir," she exclaimed with exasperation painting her voice.

He leaned in further, made eye contact, and asked in the same secretive tone, *their* secretive tone, "Tell me about it."

Carol hesitated.

"You're the eyes and ears of this place. Office managers are so undervalued," he said looking around in feigned disappointment.

She had straightened up at being referred to as, 'office manager'. A deep, currently hidden part of Brennan felt revolted with himself. A part that was deeper still wanted to laugh.

"What have you heard?" he asked again, lowering his voice.

"Well, no hard evidence on this," she started and Brennan did his best to suppress a smile, "but I've heard the mom," she looked around as if to make sure no one was listening in to their secrets, "that the mom is a lady of the night." She finished by bouncing her eyebrows twice as if to ask, "*Do you get it?*"

"Ah..." Brennan nodded slowly. "Some people," he said, shaking his head. "That... career choice... never ends well for the children. If you could get little Beth in for me, I'd love to speak to her. Help her out."

"Well, she's no longer here." Carol revealed, a disappointed look in her eye. "She moved to another school. I actually think the family is staying with a friend of the mother's. They're basically homeless."

"Darn," Brennan replied. "I'd really like to get to her as soon as I can. Do you happen to know what school she went to?"

Carol shuffled around her desk a few seconds and then opened a drawer and flipped through folders. Finally she pulled one out that read, "TRANSFERS" in bold, block lettering.

"Ah! Still hasn't gotten filed. I thought so. She moved to," she paused skimming through the papers, almost as if to build suspense, "Laureles Elementary!" she exclaimed finally.

Brennan grinned again, "Thank you so much, Carol, you're my hero," he paused and then said in a candy coated voice, a thankful look on his face, "and Bethsaida's hero."

He began to walk out of the office.

"Oh, sir," Carol called after him, "I never got your name to sign you in, I need to make a note of it."

"Oh, of course. It's Juan Garza," he lied, picking the most common name he could think of.

"Funny," she replied, "you don't much look like a Juan."

"Well, my friends call me Johnny and so should you." He waved at her and turned back. "Have a good day!" He exclaimed as he walked out the door.

The smile, the charm, the calm, all of it fell off of him, like a snake shedding its scaly skin, as he crossed the threshold of the school back outside. His heart was pounding with a caffeinated combination of anticipation, disappointment and urgency. He entered Grandma Abby's car and slid into the passenger seat wearing determination like a mask over his anxiety.

"Laureles Elementary, grams," he directed curtly, cold, as if he had forgotten he wasn't speaking to a chauffeur, but to his grandmother.

Abby didn't call him out on it, her mind had been too focused on something else while he was inside the school gathering information from Carol.

"Brennan." Her thin face seemed to be straining to maintain a stern expression. "I won't help you if you're going to kill him."

"Grams, I never said I was going to…"

"I didn't say you said it, but I can see the rage in your eyes. I can see the calm acceptance under your anxiety. I can hear the determination under the fear in your voice." She locked eyes with Brennan and in that moment, Brennan saw that behind her physical weakness, there was a great mental strength. Her body was failing her, essentially killing itself, but her mind was youthful, strong, perhaps a bit weary, but not blunted by the pain nor age.

"I need to do what has to be done. I can stop him from hurting her, or anyone else, for that matter." Brennan had looked away. He suddenly felt that he could not dare to look at her, he felt if they locked eyes again, that glowing mind behind her frail eyes would certainly decipher his.

"I know that you're a good soul, Brennan. I know that killing someone, ending a life that was perhaps supposed to go on, would be incredibly difficult for you. Something that could break you, yet you're calm. That's how I know you've killed before."

Brennan felt a warm, shameful, flush crawl up his face, but with that shame came a small sense of relief. He hadn't had anyone to talk to about his journey until Grandma Abby, and even then, he couldn't share the worst of it. What he had done and what it had done to him. Now he could. Still, he turned his head further away from her, completely hiding his face.

"There was a little girl in one of my cases. She was raped by her stepfather. He threatened her, told her he'd kill her mom if she ever said anything. One day, kids at school are talking about having seen a movie that had sex in it. They're all hyped up and feeling adult. She keeps telling them to shut up, sex is not a good thing. It's not a funny thing. The kids tell her she's stupid, she doesn't know anything about sex, she has a breakdown. During the breakdown, she yells out that she does too know about sex, because she's had it. They take her to the counselor's office immediately and she makes a shaky outcry to her school counselor. She calls it in to us, but by the time we get there, she's all tight lipped. She's denying ever having said anything. I pushed it. Took it to court on the counselor's account of a little girl ranting during what would seem like a tearful temper-tantrum to someone who refused to recognize it as a nervous breakdown. There wasn't enough evidence. We couldn't get an outcry on record. We failed. Case closed." He stopped. His teeth clenched so tightly that his jaw began to ache. He took a shallow inhale through his nose and let it out in a short, measured, puff through his mouth. "Less than a week later, we get another call on the family. She was dead. He blamed her for being exposed, ending up in court. So, he killed her. I figured it would be good to see the effect I could have. The effect death could have. Plus, he ended up in jail and that was way too good for him. I could give him what he deserved. I could start him on hell early." Now, he couldn't help it, Brennan turned and looked at his grandmother. Her conscious mind was doing its best to hold the stern look, but her eyes were full of pain and sorrow for her grandson and this little girl. "I went back. I killed him. I shot him in the head. She got to live."

"What was her life like? Do you know?" Grandma Abby asked.

Brennan saw a flash of the redhead little girl, grown to her 20s, hanging by a makeshift noose in the middle of the Nothing.

"Lies and manipulation. Your imagination paired with withdrawal symptoms," he assured himself.

"No, I don't know," Brennan lied, as much to himself as to Grandma Abby, "but I know she got to live one."

"I'm very sorry about all that, Brennie, but murder is not the answer. I'll help you, but we do this right. I am not going to be party to my grandson tearing away at his soul like this."

"That's the only real option, grams."

"We can go to the police after you get more information."

"They'll fail. The system failed her before. She had a dozen CPS cases."

"We'll get the evidence, I'll help you, Brennan."

"I NEED TO KILL HIM!" Brennan yelled abruptly. He appeared to be more surprised by his outburst than his grandmother was. "I can deal with this. He'll never hurt anyone else. It's the best, most permanent way, grandma."

His voice had returned to its normal volume, but it quivered with an airy quality to it.

"I love you, Brennie Boy. I absolutely do. This doesn't make me love you any less, but I will not help you. Not if it means you kill someone."

The drive to Laureles Elementary was once again silent. Brennan didn't know if his grandmother would go there at all. He half expected her to drive home and refuse to help him with even a ride. She eased into a parking space and kept looking forward out of her windshield.

"Brennie, this is the last leg of the trip for me if I can't convince you to find another way. I cannot…"

Brennan interrupted her in a solemn voice. "Pictures. Dee remembered pictures. He would take them on a Polaroid instant camera. They seemed halfway innocent at first. Bath time pictures. Her on his lap. Then they got worse. He's not there yet with her, but if he's abusing Bethsaida, as I'm sure he is, he's probably taken pictures of her too. If I find where he keeps them, we can call in an anonymous tip."

Grandmother Abby hugged Brennan with startling quickness and strength.

"We will find a way, Brennie. We are going to put that bastard away for a LONG time. We are going to protect your wife."

Her teary-eyed smile had him almost convinced.

Chapter 19

A little song and dance very similar to the one he had performed at Putegnat Elementary ended with Brennan sitting in the office usually occupied by the counselor with Bethsaida sitting across from him.

Bethsaida did not look like her sister. She had jet black hair, teacup saucer eyes that were just a shade light of being black, dark olive skin, and an angry resting face that resembled Brennan's more than Dedire's. She sat quietly, her hair in a ponytail so tight, Brennan almost wondered if it had pulled her eyes to be as large as they were, her lips tightly pursed, already resolute to say nothing. Brennan looked at her intently and then smoothly transitioned to an easy, relaxed smile. He could see beads of sweat collecting on Bethsaida's neck and forehead, he could see a slight quiver in her thin neck, and one handheld the other so tightly that it would soon be tingling with the pins and needles static that accompanies restricted blood flow. She was nervous and scared. He had to use that to throw her off balance, just long enough to ease her into a sense of security.

"Hi, Bethsaida. My name is Juan Garza. You can call me Juan," Brennan started.

"I'll call you Mr. Garza," Bethsaida quickly replied

"Dang, this little girl is not going to be easy," he thought.

"Okay, Bethsaida. Mr. Garza is fine too." Brennan smiled gently, "I work with the Texas Department of Family and Protective Services. Do you know what that is?"

"You've seen my family's old cases by now. You know I know." She was strong, but there was still a fearful tremble in her voice, "Why do you use the super long name? Is it supposed to confuse me? Just say CPS or Child Protective Services."

"Okay," Brennan chuckled, "Bethsaida, you seem like a very smart girl. So, I'm not going to mess around. I'm going to move a bit quicker than normal so I can let you get back to class as soon as I can, okay?"

Bethsaida's shoulders dropped a bit and she looked down and nodded. She had let her guard down, ever so slightly. Brennan hoped it would be enough to get the information he needed.

"When we talk to kids, we usually record our conversations with them, in case we forget what was said, or in case there's any confusion. For example, if I ask you your favorite color and you say it's red, but I make a mistake and say it's blue, we can go back to the recording and verify…"

"I thought you said you were going to move more quickly than normal. I know why you record, Mr. Garza." Bethsaida switched her hands so that her left clutched her right hand. "I do not allow you to record."

"Okay, totally fine." Brennan assured. He was relieved, it would have seemed strange if he had to falsely confess he was recording with the tape recorder in his pocket if she had agreed to it. He could've omitted the question, but it may have tipped her off. "*Or I could've bought a freaking tape recorder.*" Brennan thought, annoyed at himself. "I'm sorry." Brennan shook his head and held up his hands, as if in a modest surrender, "You're right. Let's move it along. Do you know the difference between a truth and a lie?"

"Yes, a truth is fact, a lie is made up."

"Great!" Brennan really tried to create a contagious enthusiasm. It was surprising how very often, guilty adults were easier to manipulate than traumatized children. "Will you tell me the truth today, Bethsaida?"

"I have no reason to lie, Mr. Garza."

"Good to hear. Tell me, Bethsaida, what is your full name?"

"My full name is Bethsaida Minerva Morales."

"That's a really cool name, Bethsaida. What's your birthday?"

"November 10th, 1986."

"And what grade are you in?"

"I'm in 3rd grade."

This answer hit Brennan harder than the number. In Brennan's mind, a person from the 80s was in their 30s. He knew Bethsaida wasn't at this time, but he hadn't done the math out in his head. It wasn't until she gave her grade that the grotesque, anachronistic, pain of interviewing his abused sister-in-law as a child really hit him. Brennan twitched as a chill passed through his spine and shoulders like a trickle of cold water.

"Sorry, it's a little cold in here." Brennan continued. "On a scale from 1 to 10, with 1 being absolute hate and 10 being completely love, how much do you like school?"

"7 and a half or 8."

"Really?" Brennan asked rhetorically, with genuine surprise, "That's awesome!"

"I'm a good student and I get free food."

Brennan weighed out if that was a joke, maybe she was relaxing, or if she really was expressing her joy to be able to rely on a meal.

"Now, I'm going to ask some questions about home, okay?"

"Sure."

"Do you know your address?"

"No."

"Are you sure?" Brennan asked as casually as he could. He was finding it very difficult to remain calm. His throat clenched repeatedly. His field of vision kept time with his heart, surging and vibrating with every beat.

"I kind of know it, but I don't feel comfortable giving you that information," she replied honestly.

Brennan tried not to seem exasperated. He had already tried to get an address from the office, but Bethsaida was listed as being homeless and staying with a friend zoned to that school.

"Where you live, is it a house, an apartment, a trailer, or something else?"

"Trailer."

"How would you describe your home?"

"It's a piece of crap, but we're getting another trailer soon. We were going to get a house with housing, but you guys reported my mom for selling the food stamps and they disqualified our application."

Brennan was a bit horrified at the fact that the rust bucket he had visited so many times in his youth was a step up from where they lived now. He was also worried about how much Bethsaida would protect her mom if she was so ready to blame CPS for her mom's suspension, rather than blaming her mom for selling their food.

"I'm sorry that happened, Bethsaida." He paused and she remained silent. "I know you said it's not good, but can you describe it a bit more specifically. What specifically don't you like about it?"

"It looks like an old man color. It's like beige or something. It always smells, even though I clean every day, the water is always cold, and I saw a rat once. I brought in a stray cat. We gave him food and we never saw the rat again. I'm pretty sure that cat killed it."

"When you say that you clean, what do you mean?"

"I have chores. I wash dishes, sweep, mop. That stuff. Normal cleaning," she answered in an aggravated tone. Brennan decided not to pursue an elaboration.

"Bethsaida, who lives with you at home?"

"My mom, my sister, my brother, and my mom's boyfriend."

"What are their names?" Brennan asked in a soft voice.

"Seriously, can't you check your records? You guys have to have their names."

"I'm sorry, Bethsaida, it's just for…"

"Ugh, fine. Lupita, Deidre, Gerard Roel, and Marcos."

"Marcos?" Brennan repeated. The bastard's name felt slimy and sour on his lips.

"Is there an echo in here? Yes, Marcos!" Bethsaida exclaimed.

Brennan couldn't help but laugh, caught in a cocktail of shock and humor at what this skinny seven-year-old had said and how she had said it.

Bethsaida was full on shaking now and her eyes were watery. Apparently, Beth's penchant for lashing out when she was scared or nervous stemmed from young childhood. In adulthood, it had cost her relationships, jobs and other opportunities. She took a deep breath and spoke again.

"I'm sorry, Mr. Garza. Mr. Juan. It's just, I want to go back to class, I don't like talking to people I don't know. It makes me very uncomfortable. Can we please just skip to the part where you ask me about what people said? Please, sir?" Bethsaida's efforts to retain a countenance of strength were now failing horribly. She was obviously scared and on the verge of tears. Her breath shook and her voice cracked.

"I'm sorry, Bethsaida. Let's go ahead and do that." Brennan inhaled deeply. Even when he worked a normal case, he hated asking this question. Even though the question was a way to find predation and the predator, it felt predatory itself. "Do you know what your private parts are?"

A look of dumbfounded surprise smacked Bethsaida's face with all the grace of a wingless goose. She was ready to be questioned about the beatings, the lack of food, the "medical treatments" that included things like "disinfecting" her athlete's foot by pouring salt and lemon into the little cuts in the webbing of her toes, she had at times purposely and other inadvertently told a friend or two about that. She was even prepared to be asked about the drugs her mom and Marcos were using on an almost daily basis, a nosy neighbor could have reasonably guessed that, but no one knew about the pictures. No one knew about the late-night visits from Marcos. No one knew about their secret game. No one knew about their deal.

"Yes," Bethsaida said, trying her best to steady her voice.

"Can you tell me what they are, you can use the names you call them."

"Chest," she stammered as Marcos' voice whispered in her head, *"They're your boobies, girl! They'll grow soon, don't worry."*

"My butt," Bethsaida continued. *"Your ass is already looking good. You're not gonna be a plank like your mom,"* Marcos had told her.

"Va-" she cleared her throat, "Vagina." *"Cookie,"* the disembodied monster continued, *"oh, and that,"* Marcos and Bethsaida finished the sentence in unison, "Mouth."

"Mouth?" Brennan repeated, his eyes suddenly narrow, his relaxed facade gone.

"Ye-yeah. You know. Like, um," Bethsaida swallowed hard. How could she have been so stupid. Why did she say mouth? Why would she do that? "Like when your mom says not to share drinks. You know, not to put stuff in your mouth. Oh, and you can get sick from kissing." Bethsaida's pitiful save was as good as it could've been for a child, but she knew he knew. Her face burned with shame, anger, and fear. Her cheeks were flushed, causing her dark olive skin to appear a deep, wine maroon. Silent tears flowed from her eyes.

This case wasn't going to court. This wasn't going to be a proper forensic interview. *"Screw leading questions."* Brennan told himself. He spoke aloud, "What did he do to you, Beth?" He resorted to the shortened version of her name that he had used in his adult life.

"I don't know what you're talking about," she refused curtly.

"He hurt you, Beth. I know he did. You know he did. Tell me what he did, and I can help you."

"He dated my mom." Sarcasm was practically dripping off her voice. An abnormally mature effort to cover the pain and fear.

"C'mon, Beth. I can help you guys. I can…" Brennan started saying with a slight, kind, reassuring smile, before Bethsaida cut him off.

"No. No, you can't, and you don't. All you want to do is take us away from my mom and each other. You're going to put us with some rich people that just want pet kids to play with until they're bored! I'm not going to tell you anything!"

She crossed her arms and her face looked stern, but there was pain behind her eyes and there had been a sick desperation in her voice. The voice sounded familiar too. She had been trained in what to tell CPS and what not to tell. She wasn't great at it at only 7, but she remembered enough to say things like "pet kids" and refer to foster parents as "rich people" who were easily bored by children. These thoughts weren't just learned, they were placed in by a soft, whispering voice of a loved one or by threats of a perpetrator.

She looked back at him, her eyes glimmering with a sorrow and shame that no child should feel.

"You want to separate us. Do they pay you a bonus if you get rich couples to take us in? Is that why you want to split us up?"

This was not the first time Brennan had heard this ridiculous rumor, but his heart broke every time he did. It reminded him that for many children, the prospect of losing family, of being away from their siblings, was worse than the abuse they suffered at home.

"I'm not going to split you up," Brennan reassured her. "If I could be sure that I could keep you and Deidre together, I would try to get you guys out of your home, but I'd rather get him out. Just tell me about what he did."

Bethsaida stared at him intently. Brennan could see her pulse beating in her neck and could feel his own pulse throbbing painfully in his head now.

"Nothing happened. I want to go back to class, I'm done talking."

Bethsaida knew that was something she could do. If she wanted to discontinue the interview, she was well within her rights. Of course, by this point, her rights had been violated by her brother in law from the future because he pretended to be a CPS worker. She stood up, her chin held high, back straight, and said, in a voice as defiant as her posture, "I'll be on my way back, Mr. Garza. Thank you."

She put her hand on the doorknob and was drawn back in by Brennan's words. Words that he immediately felt guilty and dirty for using.

"He's going to move on to her, you know." Brennan explained in a soft voice. His heart ached to be playing this game with a 7-year-old. "He'll start with pictures, then go on to touching, and before you know it, your baby sister will be in the same situation you are. Maybe by then she'll be able to answer questions and speak out in her own defense. Hopefully it will only be too late and not too, too late."

Bethsaida sat back down in her little green chair in the center of the closet the school dared call an office. Silent tears were freely flowing now.

"You're wrong. He said…"

"He lied, Beth." Brennan was speaking quietly. Calmly. Firmly. The proverbial voice of reason. Of course he had lied.

"He told me if I let him do that, he wouldn't have to do it to Dee," she trembled in a low, quivering, voice. "He told me if I told anyone, Dee and my mom would get it. He said that my mom would be mad too." A sob broke, she held a second back, then it was a full-on cry, "He told me that she would hate me be… because… cause I was his... girlfriend."

She wept and Brennan knelt beside her.

"Beth. Beth, it's okay, Beth. Beth look at me. Look at me."

Beth continued to cry. Brennan put his hand very lightly over hers and spoke in the same soft, calm, but firm voice again, "Look. At. Me."

Beth's tears slowed and she turned to face him.

"I'm going to deal with him. I need you to be calm. I need you to be quiet. Don't tell them I talked to you. I will handle this with him. Soon, you'll be safe."

Beth nodded and wiped away her tears.

"You're incredibly brave, Beth. Thank you. Thank you so much." Brennan knew Beth had been abused as well. He hadn't known about her sacrifice though. He hadn't known how much Beth had tried to protect little Deidre. Brennan liked adult Beth, but now he loved her so much more for what she had done for Deidre.

"Did he take pictures of you, Beth? Pictures of him hurting you?"

Beth nodded weakly. She had the thousand-yard stare of a person who has seen too much, too fast.

"Do you know where he kept them?"

This time, Beth shook her head no. "I know he would take them into his and my mom's room, but I think he would hide them. One time, I saw him jump while he was looking at them and he heard my mom getting home from the store. He ran to the corner. I don't know where he put them, but he didn't have them after."

Brennan considered asking if there was a closet, or box, or anything near that corner, but felt he was pushing her already. Beth seemed to read his mind instead.

"I'm not allowed in their room. When he… does what he does, he likes to be in our room."

Brennan nodded and stood to his full height. "Don't worry about it. I'm going to help you. I just need one more thing. Do you think you can remember your address?"

Chapter 20

"That bastard." Grandmother Abby fumed in an angry, trembling voice.

Brennan had just reported his findings to her. She had known Brennan wasn't lying about Deidre being abused. She knew that it happened to many children, she knew that it was terrible, but listening to Brennan's account of his interview with Bethsaidsa made it real somehow. This wasn't a thing that happened a long time ago, or even that would happen in the future to Brennan's future wife, this had happened to an elementary school girl who was freely allowing it to protect her baby sister.

"That no-good, disgusting, little-peckered, human-shaped, sack of shit!" She ranted with a more feverish intensity now.

Brennan was a bit taken aback by her strong response and saw a window of opportunity.

"I can still kill him, grams. Make sure he never hurts anyone. Ever."

Grandmother Abby sighed, "No, Brennie-boy. When you take a life, it takes a part of yours too. We discussed this already."

"Grandma, look, I'm sorry, but I've…" Brennan was cut off.

"Yes. I know. You've killed before. An evil man who maybe deserved it, who am I to say. I know this man maybe deserves it too, but there are other ways. It's easier this time, isn't it, Brennie?"

Brennan didn't answer. Killing Rafael felt terrifying, fast, and uncontrolled, like a roller coaster. Killing Kyle had been a matter of quieting his rationality, choosing to ignore it and letting emotion take over. Now, he didn't have to fight himself to kill Marcos. He was fighting himself to find another way. He was eager to kill him. Unlike his choice to kill Kyle, his bloodlust was now undisguised. He wanted Marcos dead and he wanted to be the one that did it. Make sure it was done right. Brennan looked down at his feet.

"I'm sure it'll get easier each time. It'll take less and less. I know it can take a monster to fight a monster." Grandma Abby paused and Brennan looked up to see her looking straight ahead, a strong look on her face. Paired with her frail demeanor, she reminded Brennan of the Spartans his dad would tell him about. She was old, tired and dying, but she was going back on her shield. "When you become that monster, you're stronger, fiercer, you might even feel smarter, but you're vicious and toxic to be around. You start to poison everyone around you and before you know it, you're either like the monster you fought, or you're your own monster, alone in a cave, sheltered from the outside world for both your sakes."

Her words weighed on Brennan like concrete blocks placed on his chest.

"So, I have a plan to get him arrested." Brennan half-joked lightly and cheerfully in a weak attempt to hide the conviction behind humor. He was deeply disturbed by his grandmother's words and sudden change in countenance. He knew she was not wrong. He knew she had experienced something similar. He had also seen the effects of his grandmother becoming that monster. He knew her change back was too little, too late. He knew his mother had been damaged by that monster she had once been. He had seen the spite and bitterness sprout from deep roots in his mother's heart, like a weed that blocks out the sun and sucks up the nutrients, killing the grass under it.

"We know he has the pictures now," Brennan continued, "I do the J.W. bit, go to some neighbors, find out what time the house is empty, if no one is there, I can sneak in, find the pictures, and then re-hide them elsewhere. Somewhere he can't find them or dispose of them in a hurry. I call in an anonymous tip and it should be a slam dunk case for the police and the prosecutor. Maybe Misty learns her freaking lesson and stops hooking and dating abusive crap sacks. Then, I can chill with you for a bit, make sure all is well, and then jump back to my time."

"What's your timeline?" Grandmother Abby asked before coughing hoarsely into the elbow furthest from Brennan. She gave six or seven hard coughs, her white, paper, skin coloring in with a pinkish tint of red. Brennan could hear a wheeze in her throat with every cough.

"Grandma, you okay?" Brennan asked

"Yeah, fine. What's the timeline, Brennie?"

"Okay, so tomorrow is Saturday, a good day to catch a lot of neighbors at home, try to piece together a schedule for the family. Then Sunday I can go back and hide the pictures. If not..."

"No, not Sunday," Grandmother Abby interjected. "You're going to church with me on Sunday. It's the Lord's day of rest." She gave a single, rattling, wheezing cough.

"Well," he began to argue, but decided against it. One day probably wouldn't hurt and he was unsure how long his grandmother was going to last. "Monday, then. That'll work better. Bethsaida will be in school and Deidre might be with a babysitter or in a daycare, though the babysitter is more likely. I hide the pictures and then call it in."

Brennan sighed nervously. He felt excited and anxious. This was the home stretch though. After this, he could return to his time. He recalled how difficult it was to remember the changes he made when he returned to the present, how quickly the old memories were supplanted. This made his heart start trotting forward at an increasing pace and he began to count his breathing in his mind. He tried to slow his racing heart to match his slow and graceful lungs. It was to little avail, he remained on the edge of a panic attack, but did not fall from that precipice.

"Sounds good to me, Brennie boy." Grandmother Abby agreed, holding his hand.

"You know, I can stay, grandma. I actually kind of want to. My time will be there, regardless of when I jump back. It's really not a big deal and you don't have to do this alone."

"I know, Brennie, but I think I'm supposed to. This is my cave. I don't want you to join me in it. You should go back to your time. Enjoy life. Live it in a way worthy of what you're sacrificing."

Brennan was disappointed and hurt. Not just that she didn't want him to stay, but that it was because she felt she deserved to die alone and that she believed he might fall into a similar situation. That she was warning him about doing what he had prepared for years to do. That she considered saving Deidre a sacrifice, when he felt it was the only thing to do.

He said nothing more for the rest of the way home.

Saturday morning, he woke up and fixed breakfast for his grandmother. She was sleeping in apparently. He hadn't seen her wake up later than 7:30 since he had met her, but Brennan thought it would be good for her to sleep in. Brennan made egg, bacon and misshapen pancakes. The pancakes reminded him of Deidre's pancakes. They were always so buttery and crispy on the edges. Deidre was a truly talented cook and baker. Brennan was suddenly and desperately homesick for a home he knew he would never have again. He was also glad that his grandmother had rejected his offer to stay. He didn't want her to be alone, but he wanted to start forgetting the pain of resetting his wife and daughter as soon as he could. He was not surprised to find a knot in his throat and the pressure of reluctant tears pressing against his eyes.

Grandmother Abby walked in just as Brennan was putting out a glass of milk for his grandmother to drink with her breakfast. She sat at the table and politely stated, "You didn't have to do this Brennan, though I appreciate it."

"I know," he replied, "I wanted to. The pancakes could've been better, but I can demolish eggs and bacon. The secret ingredients are cheese and love," Brennan said with a smirky smile.

"You know, Brennie, I always used to put cheese in egg. Who taught you to cook?"

"Mom, I guess. She worked a ton and was rarely home, so I needed to feed myself and James somehow. I started cooking out of necessity, but after a small grease fire scared the bejesus out of us, she started teaching me to cook and would always sprinkle shredded cheese into the egg before it fully cooks."

Grandmother Abby smiled and began to eat. "Well, now I can say I left her one good thing. Cheesy eggs."

Her appetite seemed to have increased. She looked less pale and Brennan could swear she had fewer white hairs. He smiled and sat to eat with her.

"So, tell me, Brennie, is your mom still an adrenaline junkie in the future?"

Brennan couldn't help but laugh. "You know, grams, I had never thought of her as being an adrenaline junkie. I always thought of it as just making stupid decisions."

"Well, those two often look alike and the line between them is usually blurred."

"Okay, so for example, this one time, we had fake family over..." Brennan began.

"Fake family?" his grandmother asked.

"Yeah, you know, school friends or classmates that my mom had that we now call Tio or Tia, maybe Primos, just because they stuck around so long."

"Oh, okay. Familia postiza," she clarified.

Brennan considered that for a while and felt that made more sense. Postizo was something fake that you used to replace something that was missing. Dentures were 'dientes postizos' and a hair piece was a 'cabello postizo' or simply 'postizo'. The term felt accurate in Brennan's mind.

"Yeah," Brennan replied, "familia postiza. So, some Tios come over from Monterrey and they're acting like such prissy, little girls. They're complaining about how there's nothing to do in the Valley, no night life, no adventure. This is while we are on the island, mind you. Probably the most adventurous part of this county. So, they're complaining to my mom while we're stuck in traffic. My mom is obviously getting annoyed, so she says, 'If you want an adventure, we can have an adventure.' She puts the car in neutral and starts revving the engine. The Tios are taunting her, asking if she's going to race in our old Buick. I start freaking out because I'm the only person that realizes that what she's really doing is burning out the gas tank."

"Oh, no…" Grandma Abby chuckled.

"Oh, yeah. So, she keeps revving and then the Tios start getting worried and one of them notices the plunging gasoline gauge, which was quite low to start with. Before long, the car sputters and dies. The Tios ended up having to push the car for about a mile while my mom steered, laughing like a freaking maniac the entire time. She thought it was the funniest thing ever and the thrill of it, of doing something stupid, of being stuck on the island, it made her happy."

"Well, that's not too bad," Grandmother Abby reasoned. "She could have done something crazier."

"Last year, well, last year in my time, she drove through a freaking hurricane because her sister was going to be alone on her birthday. I urged her not to go. I told her Tia Mary stopped celebrating her birthdays after 40, but mom insisted. Thing is, she's never cared about Tia Mary's birthdays. Being in that danger made her happy. Made her feel alive, I guess."

Grandmother Abby seemed a tick less cheerful now. Her smile was still there, but it looked weary and sad, like the smile people give at a humorous memory recounted at a funeral.

"I'm not surprised, you know. I was glad. At first, I figured that at least her and Mary had grown close, but I guess that may have been a bit of wishful thinking. You're right though. She loved the danger. It makes sense to her. Her childhood was filled with danger and drama. That's probably where she feels the most alive. I did that to her."

"Grandma, it's not all bad." Brennan consoled, placing his hand over hers.

"No. She often did those dangerous, stupid things to help people. You know, one time, she went to visit Mary at your grandfather's house. This was before Mary started caring about the fact that she lived with the rich parent, which made her sister a poor, less popular kid. Anyway, so your grandfather had this big van he used for travel. Back then, and even now really, if we're talking about Mexico, seat belt laws were very lax. He had a bed in the back for the kids to sleep on for long trips to the US, and for his extra marital excursions, I'm sure. So, your mom is spending time with your dad and Mary. Your dad was not very well off, so their dates were street food and sodas most of the time. So, they're walking back to your grandfather's house, and she sees the van and gets this crazy idea. With your dad's help and against his light protesting, they removed the sliding doors to the van, then she, Mary, and your dad drive into the poor part of town and find the pesera, you know the micro-bus that people use in Mexico, and they cut in front of it and pick people up."

She started laughing and the laugh transitioned once more into the hard, phlegmy coughs, and then into a light chuckle before she continued.

"So, they spent the day giving free rides to poor people, who were probably making a sacrifice in their budget to ride the pesera. She would take the older people all the way to their house, instead of just to the bus stop, she refused all payment, said that that day's ride was courtesy of 'El Ingeniero'. That's what your grandfather was known as in most of the city."

She laughed a little bit more and Brennan laughed with her, then there was silence.

"You know," Grandmother Abby started, "She's got a heart of gold. A sharp, silver tongue, skin as thick as a rhino's, she's hard-headed as a mule, but that's my fault."

She looked up at Brennan.

"What's hers, really, truly hers, not inherited from me or your grandfather, is that heart of pure gold. Whatever you do, Brennan, do not give up on her. No matter what changes in the future, do not give up on your mother. She may be harsh, rough around the edges, or just plain broken," a full sob escaped her throat, "but she stood between a barrel of a shotgun and her cruel mother, she's taken the blame for and defended a snobby sister, she played mother for a baby brother when she was way too young, and she's been hurt more times than we can count, trusting people that she finds good in when no one else does. Do not give up on your mother. Don't give up on my Nan."

Brennan felt heat rise to his cheeks in a shameful blush. He thought of every ignored call, every eye roll, he thought of how his mother could be so rough, but it was always in the interest of helping. Always to further someone else, not herself. He thought about how she had been wanting to see him and he had refused. He thought of all the lame, pathetic, excuses he had made, the ones she would know he was making up on the spot. She may have been rude and tactless, but she was not stupid.

Neither was Grandmother Abby. She saw the hidden sorrow seeping through his face and placed a hand over his. She refrained from further crying and wiped away her tears with her free hand.

"You didn't know all this before, Brennie. We do the best we can with what we have."

Brennan gave no response. He hadn't done his best. As in so many aspects of his life, he had measured out judgment, based on intellect and ease.

"You're dressed so nice, what are we doing today?" Grandmother Abby asked. She was unsure of how to calm the storm-like guilt thundering in Brennan's mind and settled for changing the subject.

"Um… a little bit of recon, remember. Going to try to get information out of the neighbors with the Jehovah's Witness gimmick."

"Oh, yeah. I had totally forgotten. You think that'll work?" she asked, wary of not causing further despair in her grandson.

"I hope it'll give me an in. People seldom enjoy talking religion, but they love gossip. I'm going to do my best to appeal to that. I've gotten talented at schmoozing people to death." Brennan chuckled humorlessly.

"Now, that, that you get from your father's side."

A few minutes later, they were headed out the door, a Watchtower loaded satchel at Brennan's side. They were barely out the front entrance when Grandmother Abby's entire body leaned right, almost as if she had momentarily decided to try walking horizontally. Brennan caught her and noticed for a split second that she seemed to be sleepwalking, her eyes baldly open, staring forward, before they blinked and flickered back to life.

"Oh, dear Lord, did I fall?" she asked, genuinely confused.

"Grams, you okay? Does anything hurt? I should get you to a hospital."

"No, Brennie Boy, I'm fine. I'm not as strong as I used to be. The temperature change from the inside to the hot outside probably caused me to have a little fainting spell."

"I think we should get you to a hospital. I can deal with this stuff another day. C'mon grandma." Brennan urged as he carried her to the car.

"No, it's a waste of time and money. What? Do you think it might be cancer?" She laughed at this. It sounded like the shadow of a hardy, belly laugh, as if that's what her body was going for, but it just couldn't muster it.

Brennan did not laugh.

"At least let me drive, grams." Brennan urged.

"Fine, just don't get pulled over. Can't explain away why your driver's license isn't issued for another 12 or 13 years. I could use a rest, I guess," she conceded with feigned hesitation.

She suddenly wanted little else besides some sleep.

The drive to Rosemallow Street was uneventful. Brennan took half a Valium before getting behind the wheel, and besides an unpleasant buzzing sensation in his neck, he had done fine. Grandmother Abby had indeed fallen asleep after all. She looked peaceful, pale, *"almost dead"*, Brennan thought. At least five times during his drive, Brennan had considered turning around and heading to the hospital, but she was right. She had terminal cancer. He had noticed her alternating high energy and very sleepy periods. The way she slept so deeply and awoke early and often slowly. He had even noticed how little she used the restroom. She was on strong painkillers. She was being made comfortable. There was little else to do. This was the first and most important factor. The second was that every time he wanted to turn around, the idea of driving on the expressway through living nostalgia fired off a warning shot of panic. What if he had a bad panic attack? The kind he'd had before, when his lizard brain beat his conscious mind and convinced him that it really was a heart attack this time. There was no cell phone to call 911. There was no GPS tracking in this old car. No help. Each time, he'd snap out of it, take a breath, and keep driving.

He looked at the rows of trailers, each looking older and more in need of repairs than the previous one. He had been hoping against hope that Bethsaida's description of the trailer would be unique, but he had known better.

There were at least five trailers that fell within described parameters. Just as he was feeling a pang of frustration and anxiety began to hook into his mind, he noticed something. Cats. Large house cats to kittens seemed to gravitate toward one trailer in particular. Deidre had always loved cats. She had told him how even when she was little, she'd find some food for them. That didn't seem like a big deal, but when your older sister sometimes took old tortillas out of the trash to microwave them and douse them with lemon and salt, finding food to give was a big deal.

Bethsaida hadn't been able to remember her house number, she had only described the trailer and given Brennan the street name. Deidre, on the other hand, would fondly remember the veritable mélange of cats that would gather outside every home she ever lived in.

Brennan parked the car in between the two trailers to the left of kitty cat manor and lightly shook Grandmother Abby's shoulder to wake her. Her eyes opened slowly, and she smiled.

"Hey, Brennie boy," she croaked in a raspy, tired voice.

"Grams, you just stay here and nap. I'm going to go do my thing. I'll be right back. I'm leaving the car and A/C on, is that okay?"

"Yeah, honey, you go do your thing." She closed her eyes and drifted off again, declaring one last thing as she entered sleep. "Just be home by dinner."

Brennan sat and stared at his grandmother for a few minutes. She hadn't been in great shape when he first found her, but she seemed to have aged at least five years in the span of a few days. Her seat was leaned all the way back and she fit on it as if it were a bed.

Brennan had a disturbing thought. He was reminded of the time he saw a large, gray cat get struck by an 18-wheeler. The way the stupid cat ran out onto the busy street. How inevitable it immediately became that he would be struck. How Brennan's heart wanted to save it, but his mind, which intelligently deduced it was too late, just wanted to close his eyes and not see what would happen. Instead, he stood there, frozen, unblinking, and unable to look away as he powerlessly saw the cat jump, only for his body to be struck, rather than squished. The cat sailed across the air to the other side of the street. That's what he felt. His grandmother was in the middle of life's heavy traffic and he couldn't help her. He could only watch.

Brennan took a deep breath and got out of the car. He walked towards what he was almost sure was Deidre's childhood home, or at least one of them, and then went past it. Their neighbor was putting some sheets up on a clothesline. She was a short woman, about 5' 2", with light brown skin and eyes that were barely not black. There were wrinkles on her face, but Brennan noticed her hands still looked strong. No crooks or bends where there shouldn't be any and they possessed a steadiness a surgeon might envy. This was a woman who had worked 50 years in a 40-year life.

"Good afternoon, ma'am." Brennan greeted cheerily. He was back in that manipulative, investigative, mode that he hated so much but used so often. The scales were back on, the fangs were out, the poison was primed.

"Ah," the lady exclaimed, exasperated, "Mira, mijo, lo que andes vendiendo, no lo quiero y no lo necesito." she paused for a second, thinking he may not have understood, "What you sell, I no want. I no need. I okay."

Brennan smiled with his eyes and gave a short, light-hearted chuckle. "Disculpe, señorita, no vendo nada. Le traigo las buenas noticias." He clarified he wasn't selling anything, only bringing the gospel.

Brennan took out a copy of "El Atalaya" and handed it to the woman, knowing she'd take it, but not read it. Brennan continued the conversation in an informal Spanish, knowing it would help put her at ease.

<< "Thank you,">> she said, taking the booklet and sticking it into her large apron pocket, <<"but my family and I are Catholics.>> De hueso colorado."

<<"I understand.">> He held his hand out to her. <<"My name is Carlos.">> Brennan loosened his posture, smiling an easy half smile. She shook his hand. Brennan noticed her strong grip and reciprocated firmly and respectfully.

"Maria Lourdes Cavazos" she said with a little tilt of her head.

"Mucho gusto, Señorita Lourdes." Brennan had taken a chance there. He had noticed throughout life that when a Maria introduced herself by her first and middle name, she preferred to use both or just her middle name. He had also taken a gamble on being familiar and not using her last name. She nodded and grinned politely. Brennan stood with that half smile for 2 seconds and then put on an inquisitive look and pointed at her. He opened his mouth as if he was about to say something, ask something. Then he dropped his hand and head, <<"No, nevermind, I shouldn't ask. It's not right to ask about someone else's personal matters. I should just speak to your neighbors directly.">> He signaled the kitten swarmed trailer with his thumb in front of his torso in an overt effort to hide it from anyone who may have been standing behind him.

Maria Lourdes' expression retained the polite interest look she had been giving him, but she couldn't hold her eyebrows from taking a quick upward bounce. He had her. Brennan pretended to cave.

<<"It's just, I came by here once and I was really worried about them. Especially that little girl. The younger one.">>

Lourdes had been nodding to all this and now wore a wry smile. Brennan continued.

<<"I'm sure, as a fellow child of God, you understand this. They just look like...">> he trailed off and wringed his hands in feigned stress, <<"like they need Jesus.">>

A deep part of him cringed at that. A part of him that didn't wear the scales. A part of him that was not currently in control. A part of him that bled every time this Brennan came out. Brennan noticed his rapidly pounding heart for a second, then the autopilot came back on and it was back to business. He smiled again, this one a sympathetic, 'I'm sorry' smile.

<<"I completely agree with you.">> Lourdes said looking at the trailer in disappointment. <<"There are times that little girl comes over here chasing the cats and she'll smell that I'm cooking. One time she climbed on some cement blocks and looked in at my kids and me eating dinner. Nothing fancy. Just noodle soup, with the little stars. I saw

her and she jumped off and ran. I called her back and she came back all shame faced and dirty. I offered her a bowl. You should have seen her face. She looked like she just won the lottery. You would have thought I had offered her a bowl of the finest caviar sprinkled with gold.">> Lourdes paused and shook her head. <<"I don't make a lot of money. My husband was a bastard and I was an idiot for loving him. I clean houses, but the money that I make is my money. Mine. So I decided I was going to buy just a little extra. Make a little extra dinner every night. Just in case.">>

It didn't matter if he had shown up as the 'In-ves-ti-ga-tor' or as plain old Brennan. Deep down, it was Brennan, and Brennan had a few glaring weaknesses. Deidre was one of them.

Brennan's proverbial mask had fallen off. He cleared his throat, wiped at his eyes, and tried to get back in to character.

<<"You really care about them.">> Lourdes wasn't asking. She was simply pointing out her observation. <<"I don't care what religion you are. If you can help, please do. CPS does nothing because the girls won't talk. The police do nothing because the mom lies and teaches her kids to do it too. If you can do something.">>

<<"I will.">> He replied. <<"Do you know what time they'll be around, what time they leave? I want to make sure I come by while they're here.">>

<<"I'm usually working. I don't know their schedules that well until after about 4 in the afternoon. I'm always here in time to receive my kids from school. Usually, the mom is here at 4 and then she leaves again at around 9 and leaves

the kids with the man.">> She cringed disdainfully as she said that. <<"She had stopped going out at night and doing her… second job, I guess you could call it, after she started playing house with that man, but I think he was actually the one who put her up to it again. That's the rumor any way. If I was you, I'd go ask the neighbor over there.">> She pointed across the caliche trail that was supposed to be a street at a trailer flying a small, tattered, American flag. <<"He's a disabled veteran. All he does is sit and stare angrily at people. He probably knows their hours better, but I don't know that he'll tell you.">>

Brennan thanked her profusely and Lourdes just nodded and seemed to flip her own switch, going back to working mode. It was as if their talk, their productive gossip session, had been nothing but tiresome small talk.

Brennan walked to the neighbor with the small flag on his trailer. The autopilot had been shaken by Lourdes' story. He had to force the snakeskin back on right. He stopped walking, closed his eyes, and took a breath. He considered taking another pill, but knew if he overdid it, he'd be a somnambulist and he'd fail. He restarted his determined march to the man's house. As he approached, he saw the man sitting on a foldable beach chair. The chair was bright blue and had a fading Bud Light logo on the back. The man was wearing khaki cargo shorts, a T-shirt that said, 'Life is a beach', a ragged gray baseball cap that Brennan was sure was once black that had the words 'VIETNAM VETERAN' stitched in fading and fraying yellow. His skin was wrinkled and tan, it reminded Brennan of tough leather. He had a gray and white beard that connected to the top of his shirt. Above that, his nose sloped down in a straight elegant line until it hit a sudden crook near the tip.

His dull blue eyes stared out and Brennan noticed he had yellows instead of whites. Brennan assumed the yellowish tinge to his eyes was due to the man's liquid diet. Despite his chair's endorsement, he had an open Tecate in his left hand and a black bin almost full of smashed cans of what appeared to be his usual drink. The man saw Brennan approaching and stood up slowly in a manner that made him look like he was unfurling rather than just standing. Brennan quickly realized the illusion was a result of the man's deceiving height. Sitting he looked like a hunched over 5'10". As he stood at his full height, he pulled his shoulders back. Brennan could almost hear the man's spine crackling as he turned his hunched stance into impeccable posture. He was at least 6'3" and the paunch that hung over his waist was barely noticeable when he stood. Instead, Brennan now noticed the old man's musculature was very impressive for a man that was at least 60. This man had not just been a soldier once. Somewhere in his mind, in his core, he still was.

Brennan approached slowly and waved with one hand when he was still about 10 feet away and then extended it once he was close enough. He saw a surprisingly shiny, gold, pin in the man's cap. It looked like 3 incomplete triangles stacked on top of each other.

"Hello, Sergeant, my name is Carlos Hernandez. I was wondering if you had a few moments to discuss our Lord." Brennan recited as he pulled a Watchtower from his bag.

"Sergeant Mauricio Mata, but Sergeant was a long time ago now. You can just call me Maurice, Mauricio, or Mr. Mata, up to you, kid."

Brennan first didn't notice and then was pleasantly surprised by the realization that Sgt. Mata's voice sounded exactly as he expected. It was gruff, low, and clear.

Sgt. Mata grabbed a red foldable chair, this one on team Corona, and opened it in one thrusting motion.

"Take a seat, Carlos. Just park it right there, I think I've got a moment to spare," Sgt. Mata said.

"First of all, I'd like to say thank you for your service, Mr. Mata." Brennan spoke almost without thinking, this man was obviously proud of his service and Brennan was trying to get him comfortable, flattered.

Sgt. Mata sat back down and stared forward. Without shifting his gaze, he said, "I thought JWs didn't agree with soldiers and war. You're an odd one for sure."

"Well, sir," Brennan began as he sat in the red chair, "I get to spread my faith openly because of men like you. Doctrine may not agree with it, but I appreciate your efforts nonetheless."

"Our Redeemer, the Lord of Hosts is His name, He is the Holy One of Israel. Isaiah 47:4. Now this man used to go up year by year from his city to worship and to sacrifice to the Lord of hosts at Shiloh, where the two sons of Eli, Hophni and Phinehas, were priests of the Lord. First Samuel 1:3. Hosts is sabaoth in Hebrew. You know what that means, Carlos?"

Brennan was suddenly worried he was going to get caught up in an actual theological conversation. He needed information and to get Grandmother Abby home. He figured playing dumb would take too long.

217

"It means armies." Brennan replied.

"Smart man right there." Sgt. Mata complimented somewhat sarcastically. "It means armies. Now, you might argue that it means angelic armies, but when God or Jehovah, as y'all insist on referring to Him, moved on Earth, toppled kingdoms, ended tyranny, he mostly used human armies. Sure, there was Sodom and Gomorrah, a couple other examples of angels doing the wet work, but I think that just shows He meant both. As far as I see it, your theology may disagree with me, but God's on my side."

"Perhaps you're right," Brennan conceded, with a smile, doing his best to quickly be able to transition the conversation to Deidre.

Now, Sgt. Mata turned to look at him. "Nope. You aren't fighting me. That should have blown the top off the rabbit hole. Y'all are trained in a way that you need to correct, unless it gets pointless, but considering you're still in your seat, I'd say both choices are unlikely. Who are you really? Why are you here?" Sgt. Mata turned his face to look forward again and took a sip from the Tecate. He rolled the can, wiping off condensation into his palm. He sat there, waiting for Brennan to fill the silence. Brennan knew the technique well and boy, was it freaking annoying.

"I'm not sure what you mean, Mr. Mata," Brennan began.

"I mean you recognized my rank, you thanked me for my service, you knew the correct translation to sabaoth and provided it without justification, and you caved to my theology based on my few examples and my personal bias. I like conversation, but I prefer it honest. Tell me who you are, or I'll politely ask you to remove yourself from my property."

Brennan sat silently for a moment, the lizard brain and the conscious brain trying to cooperate to cobble together a good answer. Brennan didn't know what it was about this man that made him trip up so much. It should've been obvious to him, but it wasn't.

"I'll ask politely once," Sgt. Mata finished, his gaze still not moving, his eyes locked on something that Brennan knew probably wasn't actually there.

"I'm..." Brennan paused.

"Can't be doubtful of yourself. Just plunge in," he thought to himself.

"I'm a private investigator. I was looking into some concerns regarding the family that lives across the way from you. The ones with the young son and two little girls, one of them quite young. I was asked to look into the possibility of abuse by a concerned family member."

"Honesty," Sgt. Mata insisted, "with all due respect, Mr. ..."

"Ramirez, Brennan Ramirez." Brennan revealed suddenly, his voice tinged with anxious urgency. Just saying his real name out loud made him feel lighter.

"With all due respect, Mr. Ramirez, no one asked you to look into jack spit. I'm willing to bet you couldn't provide your credentials as a private investigator if I asked for them. I said honesty, Mr. Ramirez. If you want to go to Brennan and Maurice, you're gonna have to give me full honesty."

"She's family." Brennan blurted abruptly, "Distant family, I technically haven't met her yet, the little girl, I mean. I worked for CPS for a long time. Until it broke me. When I heard about Deidre being abused and CPS was doing nothing, the police were doing nothing, her mom was, at best, doing nothing, I knew I couldn't just fit in and do nothing."

"Honesty, Brennan. I like honesty." Sgt. Mata sighed, "I've seen the little girls playing outside. Little one, Deidre, she loves the cats. That black and white one, you see it there, the one that looks like it's got a moustache, that's her favorite. She chases it and tries to cuddle it. It's a little heel though. Given her a good many scratches. She's named it Chloe, and by God, I just don't have the heart to tell her Chloe's packing a sack under his tail." Sgt. Mata smiled, drawing deep creases in his leather skin.

The smile held for a second, but dissipated as he continued.

"The older little girl rarely comes out. She used to be outside all the time. Not playing, mind you, but watching her little sister. If that girl ends up a teen mom, it won't be because she's a floozy, it'll be because mothering is all she's known her whole life. The mom is a piece of work. She works at a tortilleria nearby. She walks to work every day, takes Deidre with her and leaves her at a friend's house down the road there. The friend's a butch. Treats the little girl okay, not as bad as she's got it at home, and has got it bad for the mom. Lord knows why. When the mom's not working the tortilleria, she's hollering with her man. When she's not doing that, she's selling what the Lord intended for her husband over at the bar on the other side of this here neighborhood. I'm pretty sure her man is fully aware and fully supportive."

Sgt. Mata took a swig and let out another sigh, "The man, geez, that little heel, if you can call him a man, is 10 pounds of dung in a 5-pound bag. God forgive me, I've been damned close, and I do mean damned, to beatin' him within an inch of his life and then two inches further. I done my killing a long time ago, I didn't like it, I begged the Big Man to never put me in a situation where I might do it again, but Good Lord, that Marcos sure does tempt me."

Brennan sighed and leaned back. His rage had company. It felt nice.

"I know what you mean," Brennan told Sgt. Mata. "Human garbage."

"What do you know about the situation?" Sgt. Mata was once again staring ahead.

Brennan pondered for a moment, wondering what he should say, what he should hide. Sgt. Mata was obviously intelligent and appeared to be a good man, but Brennan couldn't be sure. *"Too many wolves in sheep's clothing,"* a voice whispered in his head.

"I know that he hurt them. The girls. I know he's careful, but this particular species of beast keeps evidence. Mementos. Trophies of his prey." Brennan wasn't talking to Sgt. Mata anymore. He was merely thinking out loud. "I'm sure I can find it, expose him, get him locked up. I just need time and for the house to be alone."

"That's simple enough," Sgt. Mata replied.

Brennan jumped in his seat. He had sank so deep into his own mind that he had not expected a response. "I'll call you. I assume you have a telephone number. I call you, you get your tail over here, you do what you need to do."

"Really?" Brennan asked, half astonished and half completely disbelieving.

"Yeah, I've got a soft spot for little kids. They're our future, you know." Sgt. Mata took another swig of beer. "I've seen too much senseless death, lives thrown away, ending before they really begin. If I can help, I will. I just need one thing."

"*Here we go...*" Brennan thought.

"Don't kill him," Sgt. Mata implored, surprising the hell out of Brennan. "He's not worth it. You don't want that little girl, either of them, to get it in their heads that they're the reason a man died. A thing like that will haunt a person for life."

Brennan's mind flashed back to the ghostly image of Kaylee, swaying back and forth, like a perverse wind chime. Brennan suddenly felt he wasn't breathing deep enough. He cleared his throat hard, took a quick, sharp breath that was too shallow to even really reach his lungs, and sat up straight. He began counting his breaths.

"One, two, three, four, hold, two, three, four, out, two, three, four..."

"You okay, kid?" Sgt. Mata asked. "You've got that shell shock crap, don't ya? I don't remember that fancy name the head shrinks give it."

The letters C P T S D flashed in bright red in Brennan's mind.

222

"No," he muttered to himself in what would have sounded like a whimper, had it been any louder.

"One, two, three, four, hold, two, three, four, out, two, three, four."

His heart was going a million miles an hour. Despite the South Texas heat, his sweat ran cold and clammy. Incidents of goosebumps after goosebumps seemed to layer his skin from his ankles to his neck. Counting wasn't working.

"100, Mesquite, 8th Street, Legion Aire, Legion Hall..."

"Kid," Sgt. Mata interrupted and touched Brennan's arm. He had once more unfurled from his seat and was crouched over Brennan. As soon as Sgt. Mata's hand touched Brennan's shoulder, it was like an electric current ran through him.

Brennan shot to his feet toppling the foldable chair and startling Sgt. Mata. Brennan off-handedly noticed Sgt. Mata's hand had balled into a fist in his surprise. Brennan didn't care though. Suddenly, the adrenaline rush didn't feel like a heart attack. It had real purpose. It made sense. Fight or Flight was on.

"No," Brennan declared in a voice that was full, loud, but still shaky. "I won't kill him, but I'm going to nail that bastard to the freakin' wall. I am going to make sure he's locked up and the key is thrown away. I'm going to make sure the cops have no other choice. I'm going to make sure he wished he took Matthew 5:29 to heart." Brennan only whispered the last sentence, but Sgt. Mata heard anyway.

"Alright, well, let's slow our roll a little bit. Look, I'll call you, you get him arrested. We're going to get the dirtbag. We're gonna save those niñas. Deal?"

Brennan looked up at Sgt. Mata and for a second, he didn't see an old man, wearing his wrinkles as the scars his demons dealt him. He was a soldier, not yet touched by war, idealistic, brave and determined.

Brennan shook his hand.

"Deal."

Chapter 21

"Sorry I fell asleep, Brennie." Grandmother Abby apologized for the umpteenth time as Brennan weaved the shopping cart around the clothing displays in the Walmart men's section.

"It's okay, grams. You need your rest. You gotta stay strong and witty. Gotta give the calculator upstairs some cooldown time."

Brennan stopped to think about how smooth he talked to people, lied to them, told them what they wanted to hear, when he was wearing the snakeskin. The mask. The In-ves-ti-ga-tor. Now, he was making idiotic idioms to try not to sound worried to his grandmother. She hadn't just fallen asleep. She had passed out. A part of Brennan had been worried from the beginning that she would not wake up, but it was a part he had chosen to suppress.

"Oh, look, Brennie!" she exclaimed, "I found some!" she chimed enthusiastically as she held up a pair of tan cargo pants in what looked like just the right size.

Brennan needed the cargo pants for their stated purpose, cargo. Brennan had a few tools he decided he would take. A flashlight, tape, a makeshift lock pick set, his pills, and not a knife, but a knaw-eef. As in Crocodile Dundee's, "That's not a knife, THAT is a knaw-eef."

Brennan took the pair of pants and they began walking again, Brennan doing his best to arch right towards the hunting and outdoor sports section of the store, where they had the beautiful Bowie knives or maybe a KA-BAR.

Grandmother Abby stopped suddenly with an excited, "Oh!" that made her sound like she'd reached some sort of epiphany., "We should get you some sneakers!" she said finally, "You know, for sneaking." She laughed at her simple, silly pun, and then continued, "I mean, they're called sneakers, aren't they?

"Yes, actually. The nickname came from the manufacture of rubber soles, which were, as it turned out, much quieter than the leather soles of the time," Brennan replied flatly.

"You're so full of fun facts, Brennie," Grandmother Abby said as cheerfully as she could muster in her thin, frail voice.

Brennan smiled, "Shoe facts are hardly fun, grams." He peered over the counter with the knives and sheaths. Brennan's father had taught him to shoot almost as soon as Brennan was old enough to grasp a gun in his hand, but there was something just irrevocably elegant about a knife.

"What ideas are you getting, Brennan?" Grandmother Abby asked, her voice emboldened just enough to sound reproachful.

"Knives can be very valuable tools, grams. You'll never know when you have to cut something."

"Or someone?" Grandmother Abby asked rhetorically with a hint of sass and attitude that seemed to momentarily de-age her.

"No," Brennan denied, holding her small shoulders. They seemed to have narrowed in the last two days. "I told you, grams. No one is going to die. We get him clean. We get him for real."

She hugged him in a deceivingly strong embrace. If he could see her face as she buried it in his chest, he would've noticed her look of doubt.

"Come," she called, back to the thinning tone of joy she'd been speaking in, "let's look at a nice tie for tomorrow. Something that's just," she paused, "you."

They made their way to the formal clothing, Grandmother Abby supporting her meager weight on the shopping cart. Grandmother Abby had shown him at least a dozen ties of all colors and patterns before she gasped and hustled her small feet and wobbly, bony legs towards the youth section. She came back holding a tie in her outstretched hands, almost reverently, like she had just discovered the Spear of Destiny. She presented this magical strip of cloth to Brennan and whispered, "It's perfect."

In her ever-shrinking hands was a black silk tie with silver bars running down and to the right in diagonal strips. At the very bottom, where the tie was at its broadest, there was the iconic, black and yellow Bat symbol that had repeated itself so much throughout Brennan's childhood.

"You're right, grams. It is perfect."

Even though Grandmother Abby seemed to be restored, no longer teetering the line between this world and the next, Brennan knew better. After an arduous effort, he convinced her to sit down, watch some TV. Bob Barker was on The Price is Right and Grandmother Abby said that he was a man that was handsome at any age. Brennan prepared dinner. A simple chicken recipe that Deidre had taught him for the nights that he had to watch Abby alone and the mood wasn't right for pizza delivery. Deidre, who was the whole purpose behind the trip. Deidre, who seemed to have been part of some distant past, or maybe a beautifully vivid dream, the kind that teases you into believing it's your life, but then shatters and quickly starts to vanish. Then you're left with the longing and need, but not even memories to comfort you.

Brennan and Grandmother Abby sat together, ate, and talked.

"I can't wait for you to meet Pastor Albert." Grandmother Abby beamed. Her eyes were wide and behind the dulling iris, flecked with grey, there was a bit of the old fire in them. "Such a wise man, and a good, godly, pastor, who can still be honest and down to Earth." She waved her fork at Brennan, "None of that holier than thou, pharisee, crappolla there."

"I can't wait," Brennan replied, doing his best to sound genuine.

Part of him was being honest. It had been a while since he'd been to church, and he missed it. He missed the people, the atmosphere of familial love. He missed feeling like he was on a good path. He missed feeling like there was purpose behind everything. On the other hand, he felt abandoned. A deep part of him knew he had left God, God hadn't left him, but what was he supposed to do? He had prayed. He had taken all the right steps. He had followed the rules. Still, the anxiety stuck, like the thorn in Paul's side.

God's grace was supposed to be sufficient, at least that's what Paul had said. Brennan, on the other hand, had eventually decided that God's grace wasn't accepted as payment for bills. God's grace may grant forgiveness, but that and a couple bucks buys you a cup of coffee in this maddening world.

"Control." A deep voice thundered from somewhere a million miles inward.

"What was that, Brennie?" Grandmother Abby looked up at him with a tired smile.

Brennan hadn't recognized the voice as his own. It seemed so distant and alien. He cleared his throat and straightened his back in his chair.

"Nothing, grams. I think I was babbling. I may have nodded off for a bit."

Grandmother Abby's smile widened a bit and she held his hand across the table, her cold, bony fingers clasping his warm, meaty digits. Brennan ran his thumb across the back of her hand and stopped almost immediately. He had the sudden irrational fear that he would rub off and remove that paper-thin skin.

"You have had a long day. Emotionally and physically exhausting. I say we hit the hay earlier than usual so we can go to The Lord's House nice and refreshed. What do ya say?" She squeezed his hand and gave an encouraging smile.

"Sounds good," Brennan replied, finally smiling again, "I'm gonna shower first though, I feel... grimy, I guess is the word."

Grandmother Abby's smile was sympathetic now. Brennan felt oddly humiliated. Her "poor you" smile, her comforting understanding, and the fact that this was all coming from a woman on Death's door, or at least his driveway, just rubbed him the wrong way. He did his best to smile and broke off eye contact as soon as he could. He took his dinner plate and tossed the partially eaten remains in the bin before rinsing it off.

"Don't worry about the dishes, Brennie. We can do them tomorrow." Her voice strained as she stood up from the table.

"Okay," Brennan replied simply. "Good night, grandma." He turned and walked away without meeting her glance.

Brennan set the shower to a temperature he didn't usually favor. It was Deidre's temperature. A memory ran into his head, not bothering to knock.

He was nineteen. Deidre had snuck away from home to visit him at his dorm room. His roommate was gone for the weekend. They stood outside the shower, completely comfortable in their bareness before each other. She was beautiful. She set the water.

"Perfect," she chimed, her voice high and bright, as steam began to fill the small restroom.

Brennan reached in to test the water and immediately retracted his hand.

"Holy hell, Dee. It's like you put it up to scalding and then backed off just enough to not die!"

Deidre had laughed. She had a beautiful, genuine, goofy, wonderful laugh. They kissed.

In 1994, in his grandmother's bathroom, with the water falling over him like a thousand, burning, steel pellets, he remembered that kiss, and more than what came after, he would miss that kiss. He knew he would. He turned his face towards the shower. The burning water struck his face and hid his tears.

Chapter 22

Brennan lay in bed, his eyes closed, but unable to sleep. His skin still tingled from the hot shower and the overhead fan, which he had set to the highest speed, blew a cool breeze that would send a shockwave of goosebumps rippling through his body every few minutes. It was an oddly pleasant sensation, but it kept him in that murky, dreamy, limbo between sleep and wakefulness. At some point in that liquid, floating night, he heard the wall clock in Grandmother Abby's kitchen chime, lightyears away.

"BOM... BOM... BOM..."

It was three in the morning. The goosebumps came again, but this time they felt heavy. Brennan was pushed down and then he fell. He didn't jerk awake, he wasn't startled, he just flowed downwards and then...

Nothing.

He was in The Nothing.

"BOM... BOM... BOM..." this time, the chime wasn't from a clock. It was voice. A high, chipper, squeaky voice.

"BOM, BOM, BOM... The bwain got hurted..." A little girl sang, dipping low on 'hurted'.

"BOM, BOM, BOM... Now Imma fiss it..." she continued.

Brennan turned around and saw a small girl in a white lab coat standing on a high step stool working on something over a metallic table. The lab coat had a sheen to it and a little bit of pinkish purple trim. He recognized it. He had bought Abby the whole Doc McStuffins kit for her birthday.

232

"Abby?" he asked. Even with his emotions suppressed in and by The Nothing, his voice wavered and cracked. "Sweetie?"

"Hey, da-ee." she replied without turning.

"What are you doing, Abby baby?" He felt a building pressure behind his eyes as reluctant tears pressed through.

"I'm fissing you. Fissing. Fick-sing. Fixing. I'm fixing you, da-ee baby." She still didn't turn.

"What do you mean, Abby?" Brennan inched closer to her. He was afraid. He didn't want her to vanish. He didn't want to startle her or himself out of this shared space.

"Well, you har... har-t. Heart. You heart was hurted, da-ee. But, then your brain," she giggled. "Butt." She chuckled sheepishly at the word some more. "I gots band ais and tape."

Brennan's heart was pounding harder than it had since he had arrived in his grandmother's home. When had that been? A week ago? A year ago? A lifetime ago? A lifetime from now? He took another step and pointlessly wondered what his level of anxiety would be if his emotions weren't subverted here.

"I'm gonna fix you, da-ee."

"Abby, baby..." Tears were flowing now. His heart and stomach suddenly felt like lead. He felt pressure in his chest and throat. He could feel the hysterical sobs The Nothing was forcing down. "I'm going to fix things. I need to fix things. Mommy will be happier. You'll somehow find your way to her. I know you will." A sob managed to escape. "It's okay, Abby baby. Daddy's got this under..."

Suddenly, with no warning her face turned just enough for him to see that her eyes were a gleaming, shining green. They were his eyes. They shouldn't be, but they were. With words completely unaffected by any sort of impediment she declared, "Control. You think you have this under control." She paused. "Control. It's time to wake up, daddy."

Brennan's eyes burst open and he sat bolt upright in bed. The sun was out. He could hear a man singing through a radio, *"Si el Espíritu de Dios esta en mi corazón, yo danzo como David"*.

Brennan smelled eggs cooking. His heart was beating faster than normal and his face and neck felt damp with cold sweat. He was sure he had just woken up from some sort of nightmare. He couldn't remember what it was. The harder he tried, the more one word would replay in his mind.

Control.

Chapter 23

Brennan stood frozen outside the church, he was sure he looked like an idiot, an overgrown child, six feet tall, with his slacks, white shirt, and a tie that looked like something a kid might refuse to wear unless he could have the Batman one. He felt extremely self-conscious. He tried to move, but he could not. He was rooted to the spot on the fake grass entry path to the quaint, small-town church. It was not just a church. It was THE church. The church that either five years ago or seventeen years from now would appear as a backdrop in pictures of a happy, newlywed couple. A tall, young man with hard features, green eyes, and a little too much weight, and a beautiful, curvy girl with gorgeous brown hair and eyes like polished mahogany.

"Are you okay, Brennie?" Grandmother Abby asked him. She was holding him by the arm and holding her large purple purse in the other. She was wearing a dark purple dress with deep, forest green trim. She had done her makeup and she looked wonderfully alive.

"I got married… I get married… here. This church, your church." His eyes were shrink-wrapped in tears as he remembered his vows, his family, both sides together for the first time in at least a decade.

He had loved that day. There had only been one thing that bothered him. From the planning stages, to the day of, Brennan's mother had been apprehensive about the building. She had suggested other more modern churches, she had suggested event halls, she had even offered her house, but Brennan had been set on that church and Deidre had fallen in love with it from the first time he took her to see it. It had never made sense to Brennan, but it did now.

Grandmother Abby hugged him and looked up at the church as Brennan was doing, "You know, I think a part of us really does stay behind. It blossoms in the lives we plant our seeds in. That's our real legacy. Maybe that's why you picked this place, you could feel that."

She took his arm and they walked in.

There was a slow worship song playing over a fuzzy sound system and a crowd of people walking around, reciting, "God bless you" and "Nice to see you" to everyone. There were maybe thirty or forty people, but in the small space, it created a good amount of congestion.

They had arrived early, and Grandmother Abby took full advantage of the extra fifteen minutes. It took that whole allotted amount of time to greet, introduce, and shuffle their way to the pews where they'd sit. Grandmother Abby introduced him honestly, or at least mostly honestly. She introduced him as Brennan Ramirez, but would not explain the relation unless asked. When prompted, she would say that Brennan was her nephew. Brennan could see a twinge of discomfort in the corners of her mouth every time she did this. He supposed she had a harder time lying in the house of the Lord than prosperity preachers did.

Brennan heard another lie come from her much more easily though. Every once in a while, someone would remark on how she looked better, stronger. She had told him she didn't go to church as regularly as she wished she did, and if this was true, then they must have been lying as well. Still, she replied positively. She claimed she was feeling stronger. She was feeling better. She was marching on through the strength of God.

236

Church started and the church worship team, consisting of an acoustic guitarist, a piano player and a singer, played some tunes that were outdated even in 1994. Brennan was glad they had at least done a couple of ageless songs, How Great Thou Art, and Amazing Grace. The others were before his time and he only stood there awkwardly as those around sang, lifting up their hands along with their voices.

After worship was completed, a balding man with round spectacles and a brown suit walked up behind the pulpit. Brennan recognized him immediately as the man he had made some wedding arrangements with. Brennan had approached the pastor, who was no longer balding but bald, and asked about availability and pricing for the church. The pastor had asked him questions about his belief and his relationship with Deidre. Apparently sufficiently satisfied, the pastor told Brennan he'd lend them the church free of charge. Brennan had been all smiles and gratitude, and the pastor had been just as good humored until right Brennan was about to leave. The pastor had taken a hold of his arm, his expression suddenly stern, and told him, "You will one day be a great man of God."

The statement had been generic enough that Brennan decided to brush it off, but his ominous tone and the conviction in his eyes had been harder to shake.

Brennan looked up at the man, who he suddenly realized may have been wearing the same suit seventeen years from now, and thought, "*Boy, were you wrong, old man*" as a humorless half smile tugged at the left side of his mouth.

The pastor had preached in the accented, exaggerated way that Brennan disliked so much, but Brennan hardly noticed. He was too busy thinking about tomorrow. Tomorrow and life thereafter. He would stop The Pervert. He would stop Marcos. The Human Dung Pile would never lay another hand on Bethsaida and he would never get to Deidre.

He wondered if this change would cause the family to function better. CPS would have no choice but to intervene, considering that Brennan would be sure to provide clear evidence of abuse. The children may spend time apart, but he knew that deep down, the part of Misty that was still Lupita could be a good mom. Since kicking her daughter out of her house, Misty had really changed. She was still a bit selfish, she was still insufferable at times, but she was repentant and most importantly, she was trying. She'd call Deidre every day to check on her. She had added Brennan and his anxiety to the list her prayer group kept. Deidre had a cautious sort of love for her. Brennan tolerated her for Deidre's sake. Maybe this would kickstart the change earlier. Maybe Roel, Deidre and Bethsaida's older brother, would come back. He had left as soon as he had been thirteen. He had ended up in juvie a few times, but had gone on to be a kind, good-hearted, foul mouthed Marine. He thought his return could might lead to a more unified family and protection for Dee and Beth.

There were so many possibilities.

The pastor continued his preaching, growing louder and breaking words into syllables throughout to the repetitive replies of "amen" and "glory to Jesus". It all seemed to be happening far away from him but then, the pastor lowered his voice. The forced emotion was gone from it, the loud outbursts evened out, his signaling, emphasizing hands rested on the pulpit. Brennan woke from his busy thoughts and listened.

"We need to get out of our own way. We complicate our lives and seek solutions for problems we built, in places that offer no real solace. Why do we distrust God's plan for our lives? Because things don't go perfectly for us? The Lord Christ said, 'In this world you will have trouble, but take heart, for I have overcome the world.' He never promised it would be easy. You thought you'd follow Jesus and you'd wake up to happy, pink, Jesus flowers growing on your porch?"

A pause as he surveyed the room, his eyes lingering on Brennan a tad too long.

"Perhaps it's because it's not our way? God says, 'My thoughts are not your thoughts, my ways are not your ways. Just as the heavens are higher than the Earth, so are my thoughts higher than your thoughts. So are my ways higher than your ways.' Yet we distrust, because we think we are so smart. We become arrogant because we're a bit above the rest. I bet the snake feels far superior than the mouse, until the boot heel crushes its head."

Brennan felt the hair along his spine tense upwards.

"Trust in the Lord with all your heart, mind, and soul. Lean not on your own understanding. In all your ways acknowledge Him and He will make your path straight."

No amens. Only silence.

"You know what it comes down to?" he continued. "Control."

In that moment, his eyes locked with Brennan's. Brennan couldn't release his eyes from the pastor's and, could it possibly be, he saw a glimmer of recognition in his eyes.

"Control." A small, child's voice resonated in Brennan's head.

"We like control, brothers and sisters," the pastor straightened up and disengaged his eyes from Brennan, "and we will fight God for it. We will chase after it. It's like chasing the wind. We will seek to fix life our way, forgetting that God's way is better. Forgetting that God sees the end. Forgetting that God does not suffer the insecurity of time as we do. In this world you will have trouble. In this world you have had trouble. But my God is a God of healing and restoration. There's nothing life or man or Satan himself can take from you, that God cannot heal. In loss, there is gain. In death, life. In brokenness, restoration!"

Now the amens came.

There was more singing, tithing, one last song, then some news about a fundraising bake sale for the youth camping trip. It was all a drone to Brennan.

As a former pastor and longtime church goer, he was not new to the feeling that a preacher was talking straight at you, but he had never felt it the way he did this day.

His legs felt shaky and his heart fluttered in his chest. He considered taking a Valium but decided it would cause him too much drowsiness. He had already taken the daily dose his grandmother had assigned in the early morning.

"That was such a good word, wasn't it, Brennie?" Grandmother Abby asked excitedly.

"Yeah, good message. Strong message." Brennan struggled to string words into a sentence.

"I'm so happy you came with me today, Brennie. Never did I imagine my grandson visiting church with me. You and me, side by side, listening to the Word, praising the Lord, it was great!"

Brennan couldn't help but smile his weird, thin-lipped, half smile. She was so genuinely happy.

"Let's go get some lunch, what do you say?"

"Sounds good, grams."

Lunch was taken place at a well-known town establishment called Julia's. It was a pretty successful startup in 1994 and a community staple in Brennan's present. Both Grandmother Abby and Brennan ordered an enchilada plate, a specialty of the restaurant. They awkwardly discussed current events. Current to Grandmother Abby, history to Brennan.

Grandmother Abby wondered if the Republicans would come back in power in 1994, saying she still didn't know how to feel about "this Clinton fellow." Brennan tried to discuss his views but found that it was very difficult to do so without spoiling it.

"You know, I probably won't even be alive by then, you can tell me," she argued while wearing a smile that seemed absurd to Brennan, considering the subject of her joke.

"Grams, don't say that. You know, you do look stronger. I believe in you," he squeezed her bony arm where a bicep muscle should be, "I think you can make it to at least 96."

They grinned at each other in a strange, mirror image, and ate their food. They moved on to discussing Brennan's life instead. Did he have pets, what music he liked, what was

241

his favorite movie, 1994 or before, it was all in all a very pleasant conversation.

The unpleasant conversation didn't start until they were home sitting in the living room, Brennan on the couch, and Grandmother Abby on the La-Z Boy recliner with her feet up.

"So, Brennie, what's the plan for tomorrow?"

"I'm taking the cordless phone to my room, if you don't mind. Sgt. Mata, one of their neighbors, is going to call me once Misty, the girls, and the douchebag are out of the house. I'll head over…"

"We will head over," she corrected. "No good trying to find incriminating evidence if you get pulled over without a license."

"Or have to get an ambulance because you had a panic attack on the road," he thought.

"Right," he said aloud, "we'll drive over at that point. I'll sneak in. I made a lock pick out of a pen and some clips. It should work fine. That tin can doesn't exactly give me a Fort Knox vibe. Once I'm in, I'll put my investigative skills to work. You'll be my lookout. You'll park by Sgt. Mata's house and honk at him, pretend that you're getting his attention to ask something if anyone comes back before I'm out."

Brennan tilted his head left and then right, causing audible cracks both ways.

"If I take too long, maybe you can run interference until I get out. I'll find the pictures and move them to another hiding spot. I know a lot of the usual spots for pervos to hide that crap, so it shouldn't take me long. Once I move the evidence, I get out, and Sgt. Mata calls in an anonymous tip. Police come in, the idiot protects his usual hiding spot, only for the cops to find the pictures where I put them. Numbnuts goes to jail, Deidre's life gets better, and," he sighed, "and I can chill with you here for a while."

"Brennan," Grandmother Abby started.

"No, grams. Don't say anything. I know what I'm doing is," another sigh, "messy. I probably won't have my wife and daughter to go back to. They'll be gone, but Deidre will be happy. Abby will pop up somewhere, I'm sure."

His reassurances still rang false.

Tears spilled over his eyelids and down his cheeks, "God knows Earth needs souls like hers. No way he just keeps her up there." He wiped his eyes and cleared his throat. "I'll stay here to remember them. If I'm understanding this time travel thing correctly, once I do go back, I'll eventually forget them. They'll fade quickly. Then I'll start my life over. Deidre will have peace."

"Are you sure this is what you want? You know I'll support you. I'll only ask you once more. Are you sure?" Grandmother Abby had her own glistening tears in the corners of her eyes.

"Yes," Brennan replied resolutely. His voice was steady, deep, and barely a whisper. He was staring, not at the floor, but beyond it. He didn't see the carpet, he saw Deidre in the shower. Deidre in her wedding dress. He saw Abby's first steps. He saw Deidre waking up with a look of sheer panic on her face. He saw Deidre in his mom's van.

"I wanted you to know you're chasing damaged goods."

"I need to do this."

Chapter 24

The phone rang.

The black and red digital clock next to Brennan's bed disclosed that it was 9:47 in the morning.

Brennan answered groggily, "Hello?"

"Is this Brennan?" A deep, calm voice asked.

"Yes, Sgt. Mata, how are you?"

"Doing just fine, kid. Chicken's flown the coop and fecal brains just left to score some dope."

"Thanks," he cleared his throat, "thank you, Sergeant. I'll head right over."

Brennan jumped out of bed, pulled his cargo pants on, a plain black t-shirt, and put on the black sneakers his grandmother had bought.

He went into the restroom, splashed water on his face, took a swig of mouthwash in lieu of brushing, and spat it out once he felt his tongue and palate were sufficiently burned by the alcohol.

He slowed down, he didn't want to startle his grandmother. He walked to her door, knocked lightly and then walked in.

"Grams? We gotta go. The trailer is empty. Now's the time. I'll take my pill on the way, we can pick up some breakfast tacos or something if you're hungry."

She was on her side, covered. Her face stirred a little. Except, no, it wasn't her face. It was her hair, it was being blown around by the fan. Brennan went to her side.

"Grandma? You feeling alright? We'll probably get another chance tomorrow," he stammered hesitantly. For the first time since he started this messed up journey he was scared by tomorrow he'd lose his nerve to do what he set out to do, "if you don't feel well, I can get you water, make soup, call the doc-"

Brennan's words became solidified and dried in his throat like cotton. He had touched her shoulder. It was cold. He removed the blankets and rolled her over. She stiffly complied with the force of his hands. It stiffly complied. This wasn't "she" anymore.

"Grams?" his voice broke and his vision blurred, "Grams?!"

She didn't look like she was sleeping. Her skin was wax-like. She looked like the Madam Tussaud version of herself. There was a ring of urine around her on the bed. She was colder than a person should be, the innermost warmth was all that remained.

Brennan collapsed, sitting down hard next to her bed. He didn't know how long he cried. His loud, broken sobs sounded like they were coming from next door, muffled and distant. He didn't hear himself, he lost concept of time and reality. At some point he thought he may have started speaking to her. To it. He didn't feel much, except a buzzing sensation in his face, behind his eyes, in his nose, and in his lips. A pins and needles sensation he was very familiar with.

In time, it may have been minutes, it may have been hours, the tears dried. The sobs became dry coughs, then shallow sighs, then faded completely.

He still had unfinished business. He had to handle Marcos and then he had to go back to whatever his new home was going to be. He had to go back to take care of mom.

"Don't give up on your mother. Don't give up on my Nan."

Brennan grabbed the phone from where he had dropped it on the floor and dialed *69.

It rang twice then, "This is Mata."

"Sergeant," Brennan's own voice sounded alien to him. It was emotionally flat and sandpaper rough, probably from the sobbing, "I had a delay. Do I still have time?"

"Yeah, it's only been, what, half an hour? A little more? If you can get here soon, you should have enough time."

"Thank you, Sergeant. I appreciate your help."

Brennan hung up and went to his room. He took the lock pick set, his pills, and duct tape. He added all these things to the deep cargo pockets and then removed the pills and held them in his hand. He looked at the Valium bottle and felt his heart quicken as he thought about the drive. He put his palm on the cap to twist it off, then decided against it. He needed to be all there for this. He shoved them into his hip pocket this time.

He removed his t-shirt and opened the toy chest that Grandmother Abby had for his younger counterpart. The toy chest that would never be used again. On top of the toys, laid out flat, was The Machine. It hadn't been that long, but it looked unfamiliar to him. He strapped it to his chest and connected the electrodes. He replaced his t-shirt. He was going to have to find a way to hide the electrodes.

His mind was a static filled mess. He figured he'd just bow his head and walk fast. He didn't have time for all this.

He began to rush out of the apartment and stopped at Grandmother Abby's door. He walked in and went to her side.

"I love you, grandma. Rest easy now." He hunched over and kissed the waxy skin of her forehead.

His hands began to shake in an angry grief. He took the phone handset, dialed 911, and left it on.

Chapter 25

Brennan was able to trick his brain with the old jump in the deep end trick. He got in the car, turned it on, and pulled out of the driveway with as little thought was possible. He began to drive, and it wasn't until he was on the highway that his mind betrayed him.

His heart sped up. He felt his shoulders and jaw muscles tighten. His knuckles were white from the tight grip he had on the steering wheel. He repetitively cleared his throat, took in sharp bursts of air through his nose, and rolled his shoulders to relax them. He knew the sharp intakes were a bad idea, breathing shallow and quick was a great way to accelerate hyperventilation, but he couldn't help it. His heart would normalize and then kick into high gear again with one, pounding beat, giving him the urge to take that sharp sniff of air. The pins and needles began in his neck. They simultaneously bled down and rose up prickling his cheeks, behind his eyes, in his sinus cavity, and down his shoulders to his arms. His vision blurred. He began to take deep breaths.

"I'm going to pass out. I'm going to pass out..."

The deep breaths were too quick, he was making it worse.

He let out a frustrated, roaring yell that shook the rear-view mirror. As he held the yell, a black ring appeared around his field of vision and began to tighten inwards.

"The exit. It's this exit. Take it."

He veered the car and almost struck the barrier. He turned the car to the right at the first street. A left, another right, he was looking out of blurry pin pricks now. He took a left onto the caliche road and the small red car fishtailed. He

249

pulled over and put the gear in park. He clumsily turned it off and dropped the keys. He opened the door, the world was almost total blackness now, the oxygen he so desperately wanted seemed to be made of Jell-O. He tried to get out but stumbled and fell. Using the car for support, he stumbled over to the safe, grass, side of the path, one loose step at a time, hand over hand on the burning hot hood of the car, like a drunk man. He saw a green blur in his minute, oil painting like, field of vision and collapsed onto the grass.

He felt himself sink into unconsciousness.

Darkness. No, less than even Darkness. Nothing. The Nothing.

Then a sweet, melodic, though off-key, voice of a little girl, "Lights will guy-i-ai you home, and igniy-i-ai you boze, an' I will twyyy… to fiss you."

He woke up with a start, jumping to a sitting position and saw the resaca to his right. The sun reflected off of it and into his eyes, causing him to squint and feel a pressure in his head. He rolled onto his knees to get up a little easier.

"Mister, are you okay?" The voice of a little girl chimed out again. Only this time, it wasn't The Nothing. It was real. He could've sworn it was little Abby, only without her impediment. He turned.

"Abby?"

The girl who stood in front of him looked about three. Her hair was a tangled nest, there was dirt on her forehead and hands, and her shirt, which was supposed to be lilac, was a dingy, purplish gray, with food stains on it. She had a slightly parted mouth, missing a tooth or two, a large

250

forehead, a button nose, and on either side, two, brilliant, brown eyes, like polished mahogany.

"No, mister. My name is Deidre. People call me Dee."

Brennan stared wide-eyed and held his hand tightly over his mouth to stifle any sound. What sound would've come out, he had no idea. A sob, a laugh, a scream? He had no clue. He managed to stand up and lean on the car for support. His head ached savagely.

"Deidre," he finally managed, "why are you here?"

"Well, I saw you fell. Are you sick? You have little stickers with wire on your head. Also, when my mom falls like you fell, it's because she's sick. She needs Gatorade, sleep, and for everyone to shut the fuck up."

She spoke so sweetly that Brennan almost didn't catch the curse word. It made his heart sink, feeling like it was anchored down near his gut.

"No," he groaned, slowly transferring his full weight onto his feet, "I'm not sick. I meant, why are you wandering outside?"

"Ms. Martha, my babysitter, she's with her friend, Kimmy, in her room. She tells me to go outside when she plays in her room. If I don't listen, she locks me in the bathroom, so I just go outside. There's rats in the bathroom."

She paused, pursed her lips, and looked up and to the left, as if contemplating something. After a brief moment, she looked back at Brennan and wondered, "I don't know why she does that. I saw them playing once and they were wrestling. I don't like to wrestle, I'm too short. Anyway, I was going to go play with my friends. Are you a robot?"

Brennan smiled at the way her ideas seemed to blend into one sentence with more twists and turns than a rollercoaster. It was so very much like the Deidre he knew.

"No, I just think the wires look cool. Who are your friends?" Brennan asked. He didn't remember Deidre talking about any childhood friends from the trailer park. Then again, three years old may have been too early to remember, especially for someone with as much early childhood trauma as her.

"Yeah! I can show you!" She cheered, a giant smile apparating across her face. "There's Rusty, Muffin, Mittens, Menso, Speedy, Preciosa, Pulga…"

Brennan realized she was referring to the cats outside her home.

"No!" he yelled, surprising even himself. His heart was further crushed as he saw Deidre's face transform from hopeful happiness to vigilant fear. "I'm sorry, I didn't mean to yell. You shouldn't go to your house right now. It's dangerous to go places alone. Also, Ms. Martha might get mad if she comes out and you're gone."

Deidre frowned, "Yeah, you're right." She looked around and saw a large, gray, cat with amber yellow eyes, "Church! His name is Church. He's Mr. King's cat, but he's also my friend. I'm gonna go play with him."

She turned away from him and took a step forward before stopping suddenly. She looked back at him, with that pensive expression she had made earlier. "You're really weird," she stated observationally, "I like you." She smiled and ran after Church.

"Look both ways!" Brennan called out after her, but she was already on the other side of the caliche road. Brennan got back in the car, picked up the keys, and turned over the engine. He slowly scooted down the road, his heart beating hard, though at a slow, steady pace, in a combination of post panic attack lethargy and excitement from what was technically his first time seeing his future wife. She had been so small and frail. Exhausted as he was after a panic attack, his rage was renewed. Even if Deidre had never been his wife, even if she never would be now, how dare anyone hurt a smart, innocent, little girl, like her.

"Find the pictures. Hide them. Call the cops. Stick to the plan."

But that's not what he saw in his mind. In his mind, this monster that called itself Marcos, lay on the ground, pissed and soiled, with a drooling, red grin spreading across his throat, from one ear to the other.

Chapter 26

Brennan parked his dearly departed grandmother's red car behind Sgt. Mata's trailer. He got out, his legs still shook, but they at least felt like they were made of solid matter now. He took a deep inhale, held it for a few seconds, then let it out slowly. He ran his fingers through his hair. He hadn't noticed until this moment how long it had been getting. It covered the top of his ears now. He felt like he had built The Machine only yesterday, yet it seemed like he had arrived in 1994 months ago.

He took another paused breath and attempted not to focus on the complexities of time. Anxious curiosity was the last thing he needed right now.

He saw Sgt. Mata's shadow approaching and discreetly removed the electrodes from his head and hid them in his shirt.

Sgt. Mata walked up to him and Brennan noticed the odd grace that the tall man had. His arms and legs flowed in synchrony, giving the illusion that he was almost floating, rather than walking.

"Hey, kid." Sgt. Mata grumbled in his gruff, rumbling voice, "Took you long enough."

"I got delayed. Family emergency," Brennan replied and immediately felt tense.

He remembered how Sgt. Mata had been able to read him during their first meeting. Though he was telling a half truth of sorts, he still felt incredibly self-conscious and somehow guilty. He did his best to keep his face relaxed, his arms lazily on his waist, and his feet pointed toward Sgt. Mata.

"You know what you look like, kid? You look like a man who's trying to look calm."

"You gotta be kidding me," Brennan thought.

"No. I mean, yes," Brennan replied, this time purposely allowing the shaky timbre of his voice come out. "I'm trying to be cool about all this, but I'm pretty freaked out."

Sgt. Mata seemed to accept this second half truth. "Well, freaked out is okay to an extent. Anxiety and adrenaline keeps you on your toes. Just don't lose your head. As for your family emergency, I hope everything is okay, but you can't think about that right now. No distractions. Focus on your objective. Find the incriminating evidence, do what you gotta do."

Brennan nodded nervously, his eyes fixed on his feet.

Sgt. Mata continued, "If I see the man coming, I'll honk the horn of your car twice. If it's the girls or the mom, I'll do it once."

"What if it's the whole family?" Brennan asked.

"I'll honk twice anyway," Sgt. Mata replied.

Brennan paused. "No," he disagreed calmly, "my exit may have to be different if it's the whole family, just do once for the girls or the family, twice for scumbag. That way, if it's the whole family, I can replace the evidence where it goes. I wouldn't want him to take his anger out on them if he can't find it. If it's just him, I don't care if he's mad. The cops will have him before he can get his hands on anyone else."

Sgt. Mata looked at Brennan with plain, open suspicion. "I told you no killing, kid."

Brennan heard his grandmother's voice in his head and tears came to his eyes, "*It's easier this time, isn't it, Brennie?*"

"I'm not going to kill him. I just want as much chance to get this done now and not to have to come back and finish later."

Sgt. Mata's stare felt like it could drill a hole into his soul. "I'm gonna be honest, kid. I don't quite believe you."

"I won't kill him. I want justice, the right way. I want to give the family closure." Brennan felt that was an honest response. He'd honor his grandmother, heck, he'd honor Sgt. Mata, but most of all, he'd still save Deidre.

Sgt. Mata turned away and walked to his chair. "Once for the family, twice for the pervert. One if the band, two if the flea."

He had a cooler with a Tecate can in the built in cupholder, popped open and sweating in the Texan heat. He sat and placed a dark pair of sunglasses over his oddly opaque blue eyes. He adjusted his Vietnam Veteran cap on his head. Though he was doing the same thing he had been doing when Brennan first met him, he was different. There was a tension in his body, like a coiled spring, a drawn bow, a loaded gun. Here was the soldier again.

Brennan walked casually, as if he was a trailer park resident, no agenda, no reason to hide. He hopped up the steps and didn't bother to knock. He opened the glass screen door and reached in his pocket as if to pull out a key, but instead took out the makeshift lock pick. He tested the doorknob and noticed it was incredibly loose. This didn't surprise him one bit. Looking at the state of the trailer, it was a wonder it was still locked, and even more mysterious was what someone could possibly believe would be of value to steal from this rust bucket.

The answer to that question bypassed his brain and came to him straight from his mouth.

"Drugs."

Instead of engaging in the tedious task of finding and pushing the pins in the lock, he took a credit card that was a part of his lock pick set, pushed the door, and wedged the little, plastic card into the gap. The door and knob were so loose, he could see part of the latch bolt. He used the card to push the latch bolt in and away from the strike plate. The flimsy door slowly swung open.

Brennan walked in and felt a wave of emotion slide over him. It was a disgusting, muddy, mixture of anxiety, heartbreak, and nostalgia.

The first thing was the smell. In the decade between his present past and the time when he had met his wife, her mother had not changed cleaning products. The aroma of late nights, sneaking in through windows, awkward dinners, and movie dates when the movie was barely watched filled his nose. It was the smell that had been impregnated in her clothes for their precursory friendship and the first few years of their relationship. His eyes watered, his heart beat faster. It felt good to cry. One of the frustrating parts of the anxiety was the inability to cry. The pressure, confusion, rage, and need to purge, to yell, to bawl, was always aggravated by the fact that in those moments, he couldn't. The rolling anxiety that built up to a full-blown attack was full of tightly packed, pressurized emotion that could not be released. Crying helped.

He wiped his tears and there was the second thing. Everything, their stove, their couches, everything was a newer version of the old things they had when Brennan had met the family. That was less nostalgic, and bordering on the heartbreak territory, but then came the coup de grace. The feeling of the home. The tense fakeness in the air. The subcutaneous sensation brought on by generations of evolution, fine tuning of the human instinct, to detect what the conscious mind cannot. Something isn't right here.

His heartbeat increased at least 10 bpm in one sudden jump. His vision became sharper, his hearing clearer, and he began to breathe slowly and steadily to try to stop the adrenaline rush from becoming panic. He looked around the entrance to the mobile home, an amalgamation of living room and kitchen. He doubted the pictures were somewhere so trafficked. He'd come back and check if he didn't find them, but he doubted they'd be here. The bathroom and his bedroom were better bets. He walked down the narrow hall, lined on each side with splintered, stained, and peeling fake wood paneling. The small bathroom as on the left, across from what looked like a storage room. Cardboard boxes and plastic garbage bags marked "Boy Clothes", "Kitchen", "Bathroom", and other common things filled the room, with a small space in the corner for a twin sized bed. Brennan thought that if the timeline he remembered was correct, this was the year that Misty had started selling clothes and trinkets at the flea market on Saturdays for extra money. The sales gave a great return on investment, considering most of the things were stolen.

Despite Beth's clues that the pictures were in his room, Brennan suddenly thought that Marcos may have hidden the pictures in the boxes and dreaded the idea of looking through all that mess. It was still more likely that the restroom or bedroom were the hiding place, but the thought of going through all those made him feel even more rushed. The tingling began on his upper neck and his shoulders. He made a split-second decision to focus on finding the pictures, rather than calming down. He skipped over some dirty clothes on the floor and into the restroom. He decided that even though the bedroom was a greater possibility, the bathroom would be quicker to survey.

He lifted the lid of the toilet tank and found a bag taped to the inside of the tank. The bag had crumbling, pastel yellow, rocks. It was not a small baggie. Brennan thought that in 1994, that bag may have paid for a month or two of rent in the rust bucket. His mind went to Marcos. Sgt. Mata said that Marcos would go out looking to score. This meant he probably didn't keep the stuff on hand, afraid of being caught. This stereotypically hidden bag must have been Misty's. This stoked the nauseating mixture of emotions that Brennan was feeling once more. He opened the bag a bit, loosened the tape, and the bag plopped into the toilet tank water. His mind tried to push in some reasoning against this action. What if she got angry? What if she thought it was one of her kids? Brennan thought that Misty would blame the tape and herself. Plus, what was done was done and there were more pressing dangers to keep from Deidre and Bethsaida.

Brennan looked in every nook and cranny of the bathroom cabinets, under towels, under and behind the sink, everywhere he could think of. Despite being relieved to be finished, his fear resumed its crawl up his face and down his extremities. He made his way to the bedroom.

There were three miniscule bedrooms in all. The one used mostly for storage, one crammed with a full-sized bed with stuffed toys on it and a magazine page featuring Boyz II Men haphazardly taped on a wall, then the other right across. Brennan figured the stuffed animals and boy band room was shared by Bethsaida and Deidre.

He turned and looked at the final bedroom's door. It wasn't fully closed, just left open a tiny crack. Barely enough for light to squeeze through. The invisible, miniscule, fear mites that crawled up his neck and down his arms quickened. His breath grew deeper and faster. His heart, which was already holding a quick, albeit steady, pace, lurched forward at a higher gear. He swallowed hard enough to hear an audible click in his throat and pushed open the door with a burst.

He half expected Marcos, or some monstrous, demonic, representation of Marcos' sin to reach out and grab him. To tell him they were fully aware of his intentions and that he would die. Instead, nothing happened. Brennan entered the small room. There was another full-size bed, a dresser, and a small closet. There were blankets, sheets, and other bedroom odds and ends stacked up next to the wall. Brennan looked at the headboard of the bed, which was very awkwardly positioned, up against the wall, directly to the right of the door. On the headboard, barely hidden under a copy of TV y Novelas magazine, was a rubber representation of the male organ. Brennan grimaced.

"Gross." He whispered to himself and continued to look around, pushing out the idea that the children in this house had almost undoubtedly seen that sort of thing before.

He closed his eyes tight for a second to forcefully suppress the part of him that Rafael Barrera had referred to as the "In-ves-ti-ga-tor". This home had more red flags than a Chinese military parade. He had to be an investigator, not The In-ves-ti-ga-tor. He had to find the pictures, not take note of all the risks present. This had become instinct, and a part of Brennan knew that this instinct to take stock of all dangers to children would follow him for the rest of his life, but right now it was not useful to his main objective.

It was difficult to know what was odd or out of place when there didn't seem to be a place for anything. Brennan made his way toward the closet and there it was. A rusting metal tool box, with a very much not rusted, metal padlock. If the man worked with tools, it would make sense to have the box somewhere easily accessible to him for days when work was something besides finding a cheap source of rock. The shiny lock, however, did not make sense. Sure, he could tell Misty it was to protect the kids from the sharp instruments in there, but dangers abounded for them in this house. No, this man was hiding something in there.

Brennan knelt by the toolbox and looked at the padlock threaded through the latch. Though it had proven unnecessary before, he was relieved to have brought his lock pick set. He took it from his pocket and tried to steady his shaking hands. He inserted the pin rake and applied small pressure to the tension wrench. Padlocks, especially ones small enough to fit on a toolbox latch, weren't very difficult to pick. The issue here was his almost vibrating hands and hyperactive thoughts.

"Focus, man. Focus." His voice was shivering too.

He felt around trying to think of the pick as an extension of himself.

His father's face and voice were suddenly front and center in his mind.

"A weapon is nothing more than a tool. A tool, whether it's a gun, a knife, a screwdriver, anything, is most effective when it is an extension of yourself, son. You cannot fear the gun. You do not fear your hands, your fingers, or your feet. It is an extension of you!"

Brennan's thoughts came into focus when he felt a click. He quickened his pace and a half minute later, the tension wrench slid, and the lock popped open.

"Yes!" Brennan exclaimed, trying to keep his voice quiet and somewhat failing.

He opened it and saw a pair of large work gloves. He hadn't worried about fingerprints, considering his four-year-old self wasn't in the system, nor was a kindergartener a feasible suspect for a crime of this nature. Still, he felt that this was an opportunity to be taken and put them on. Once they were on, he rummaged the tools around and saw that they actually lay on a plastic tray. There was a small notch at the center of the tray. He grabbed it and pulled up. It took him a few tries, the thick work gloves had hampered his fine motor skills, but he finally took out the tool tray without dropping it back. Underneath the tray were three items. A flattened bag of pot with rolling papers included in it, a somewhat significant wad of cash, mostly fives and tens it seemed, and a parcel envelope.

His heart was intent on matching the beat of a hummingbird's, the tingling covered every inch of his body, the air coming in and out of his lungs was heavy and viscous, his tongue was sandpaper, the roof of his mouth was chalk.

This was it. He took the envelope and opened it. He looked straight ahead at the wall, allowing the polaroids that tumbled out onto his hand to be caught only by his now shrinking peripheral vision. On the edge of life's screen, he could see flesh colors on the polaroids. Some redder, some pink, others darker. This was it.

He continued his efforts to not look at the pictures and slid them back into the envelope. Once they were put away, he felt calmer. His heart began to slow, if only by a few beats per minute. The air got a little thinner. He'd found the evidence and he knew exactly where to hide it. He turned quickly towards the door and his foot slid away from him on a discarded, dingy, white t-shirt. His clumsy gloved hands fumbled the envelope and its contents slid out and seemed to float down to the floor in slow motion.

Brennan regained his footing, and everything stopped. There was no motion, no feeling, no sensation of any kind, this was the closest he'd ever feel to being in The Nothing while in the real world.

Some pictures had mercifully landed face down, but others had not. Brennan saw Bethsaida's suffering, what she had endured for her sister. In one polaroid, she was smiling, but there were tears in her eyes. Then he saw a different skin tone. It would have been a cute, toddler, bath picture, but cute, toddler, bath pictures didn't have the toddler's privates as the central focus. He was already starting to groom Deidre.

No rage came. No pain. Just the scales. The psychological snakeskin resurfaced. He could almost physically feel it covering him, consuming him. He was completely numb.

Chapter 27

Brennan walked towards Sgt. Mata at a leisurely pace, looking like he belonged.

Sgt. Mata stood, trying not to appear as excited as he was.

"Did you do it, kid?"

"Yeah, I did it." Brennan reported flatly. There was no triumph, no nervousness in his voice. There was Nothing.

"What did you find? You think they'll get him?" Sgt. Mata asked, and Brennan noticed how peculiar nerves sounded in the low, grumbly, voice of this man.

"Pictures. several have his face in them. They'll get him."

"I didn't see you come out the door." Sgt. Mata's eyes narrowed slightly. Brennan wondered who had hurt Sgt. Mata so much that he almost completely lacked trust. He momentarily pondered whether it was more likely that it had been the government he had served or a loved one.

"I used a window. I forced the door since it was so loose. I figured I could close and lock it better from the inside, since I don't have a key. That way it's less obvious someone was in there."

Sgt. Mata paused for a moment, decided Brennan wasn't lying and continued, "Should I call 911? Or will you do it?"

"I'm going to leave. I have to get my car away from here. Don't call 911 until he's back. I want him to be caught. I don't want there to be any possibility that he realizes the pictures are missing and he lashes out at the girls."

"Where do I tell them to look?" Sgt. Mata asked. His voice was steadier, his eyes were recovering their astute appearance. He saw something was off.

"It's somewhere they'll know to look. Won't be hard for them to find. I gotta go, Sergeant. This has been too much for me. I need to find a bar and drink the memories away." Brennan looked down and walked away, still keeping a wandering pace. He did his best to seem devastated, the snakeskin was in deep this time.

Sgt. Mata looked at the young man walk away. He was sure of two things. This was the last time he'd see Brennan, and this kid was not a drinker. He wanted to react to the surely accurate assumptions his mind had come to but didn't know that it would help.

"Kid," Sgt. Mata called to him, "This is the right way. You did the right thing. If you were careful, you'll be fine."

Brennan said nothing, got in the car, and drove away.

Chapter 28

Brennan ditched the car only seven minutes later. This time, it wouldn't be enough to leisurely walk up, to pretend to belong. His large frame and overall lack of athleticism made sneaking harder, especially in broad daylight, but nonetheless, he managed to make it back to Deidre's trailer unseen. He wasn't too worried about someone seeing him, unless that someone was Sgt. Mata.

Brennan looked through the open kitchen window and saw that the strip of duct tape he had put across the trailer's door and doorframe was still intact. No one had arrived yet. He climbed in with difficulty and cursed junk food as the windowsill scraped the paunch he carried over his abdomen. He tumbled in the trailer and felt embarrassed in spite of the fact that no one was around to see.

He stood up, brushed off his body, and walked up to the front door. He carefully removed the duct tape, bunched it up and stuck it in a cargo pocket. He walked back to the bedroom, closing all the other doors on the way. Once inside the room, he left the door open just a sliver. The pictures were neatly fanned out on the bed, all face up, as he had left them. A slide show of horrors and trauma, of broken innocence that could not be repaired.

"Except I AM going to fix this," he thought.

He reconnected the electrodes to his head, not caring if Marcos saw them. Maybe it would scare Marcos. Maybe it would make him think Brennan was crazy. Either way, Brennan no longer cared. Brennan armed himself with the boxcutter he'd taken from the toolbox and walked into the closet. He left the closet door ajar, similarly to the bedroom door.

He closed his eyes and waited.

He didn't know how long it was before he heard the front door shifting and then opening with a whining creak. Brennan heard the footsteps. A single pair, heavy, slow, and slightly uneven. Brennan wondered if Marcos was carrying something or if he had a limp. Marcos opened the door to the room, speaking in a shrill, sing-song voice.

"Pipa, pipa, on ta mi pipa?"

Marcos was hungrily examining a small bag of rock and then turned to the bed.

"Que chingao?" he squawked, his voice cracking, still too shrill for a man his age. "Who did this? Who did this?" Marcos asked himself in English now.

"I wanted you to know, Marcos," Brennan explained in a rumbling growl, not of a scared animal, but a calculating predator. "I wanted you to know why this is going to happen."

Marcos swung around, his eyes wide, his face void of color. In a moment, Brennan realized that his prey was not as weak as he had thought. The man's nose was crooked and pressed in. He had pivoted on the balls of his feet and his fists had come up to a defensive position immediately.

Brennan had enough time to think one word, "*Boxer.*"

A fist pistoned towards his face and Brennan caught the arm with a swipe of the thin box cutter blade. Blood fanned out with the swipe, leaving streaking drops across the low ceiling and peeling wall. Brennan had barely had enough time to reverse the arc for the other arm when the fist struck his face. Brennan had managed to glance the blow off his

268

arm before it struck him, but he hadn't been fast enough to avoid it completely. The room seemed to turn as Brennan lost his footing. He instinctively turned on his side to avoid landing with his back across The Machine's components. He couldn't afford to break The Machine or his back. Instead, he landed hard on his side and felt a hot jolt of pain in his leg. He had completely forgotten about his pills. He had been working in that reptilian autopilot. The plastic bottle was not only broken, but a shard of thin, sharp plastic was now buried in his thigh. He let out a growl in pain and frustration. This man wasn't in his prime, nor close to it, but his muscle memory was good enough to kick in for this life or death situation.

Marcos had been slowed down by Brennan's successful swipe. He was examining the obscene flap of flesh opened on his forearm. He was breathing fast, in high pitched, grating gasps. Brennan used the opportunity to try to go to his feet. His head swam a moment and the room seemed to shift again as a sharp pain struck behind his eyes. He stumbled back, his back pressing painfully against The Machine. Marcos now took his opportunity and lunged towards Brennan, his uninjured left arm cocked back, his small, bony, morningstar of a fist, ready to strike.

Brennan raised his legs and brought his knees up towards his chest, allowing Marcos to get closer to him. Just close enough for Brennan to reach his ankle.

Brennan dug the thin blade of the box cutter into Marcos' left ankle, feeling it glance off the ankle bone. At the same time, Brennan kicked his legs, both feet striking Marcos' groin. His right foot struck Marcos' scrotum and the left heel dug sharply into the soft area protecting Marcos' bladder.

Marcos fell, squarely on his rear at first and then sprawling onto his back.

Brennan slowly got to his feet, his head still pulsing heavily. Every beat coincided with a black corona in his field of vision. He smelled something that reminded him of spoiled orange juice.

He saw that Marcos was on the ground, grabbing his groin with both hands. His right arm was bleeding profusely, he had wet himself, and the box cutter blade stuck out of his ankle, bent to an obtuse angle.

His lizard brain took back full control. Brennan walked slowly toward the beaten man. Marcos looked small, weak, broken. A victim.

Marcos saw Brennan coming to him and tried to roll over to crawl away, using his right leg and left arm. He seemed to forget the pictures for a moment and tried to cry out in his shrill, girly tone.

"HEL-PFF!" Brennan's heel connected with Marcos' jaw before he could get the entire word out.

The kick was enough to spin Marcos onto his stomach. He tried to prop himself up on his left arm, his jaw now drooping awkwardly on one side, and just as soon as his head was up and his neck exposed, Brennan's arm wrapped around it. The crook of Brennan's right elbow was pressing Marcos' Adam's apple, with the fleshy parts of his arm pinching the airways shut. His right hand grasped his left bicep and his left hand put pressure on the back of Marcos' head. Marcos protested briefly, weakly, and most importantly, quietly.

When a person is choking, really choking, they point to their throat, pound on the table, or stand up suddenly. That's when you know it's Heimlich time. If they're coughing or speaking, that means they can probably dislodge the obstruction themselves and they're still getting some air.

Marcos made no such sound. His left hand flapped around, his right leg weakly kicked the ground, his face turned red, then purple, then a deeper blue set in. Then, the movement stopped.

Brennan straightened up, bringing this new corpse, this new dark choice, up with him. He put the tattered remains of the man on the bed. The pictures haloed Marcos' head and shoulders, making him appear like some sort of evil version of a saint in an early renaissance painting. Rather than being haloed with light, it was the demonic images on those polaroids.

Pain began to surface, quickly followed by panic. Brennan's heart skipped a beat, then a few later, skipped again. He reached shakily into his pocket and pulled out a bloodied Valium tablet. He looked at it in disgust, still considering the dissolving chemical peace in his unsteady hand.

Red and blue. Red and blue lights danced in his peripheral vision, contrasting the sunlight peering through the draped windows.

"No time," Brennan reminded himself aloud. He looked back at the shell that had once, not very long ago, been Marcos. "You deserved it. You know you did."

He pulled the e-cord.

There was a rush.

He was moving, he was being stretched, the pressure was immense and excruciating. When this had previously happened entering The Nothing, he'd felt as if he had no body. This time he felt bones break, organs reorganize themselves, he felt fleshy, fatty tissues being squeezed and twisted. He tried to scream, but no sound came.

He heard voices far away, yet somehow booming in his eardrums.

Grandmother Abby - "It was easier, wasn't it, Brennie."

The Stepfather - "You've got balls, In-ves-ti-ga-tor..."

The Guy finished the Stepfather's sentence, though his tone was pained, rather than mocking, "... you even called him by his name."

There was the immense pressure, then darkness. A darkness so deep, not even The Nothing was felt.

Complete Darkness.

<u>Part III</u>

The New Present

Chapter 29

Brennan began to hear, though he still felt nothing. The voices were muffled, as if he was trying to listen to them under water. He tried to focus on what they said, but his brain wanted to go back to sleep.

"Massive internal hemorrhage…" a voice informed.

Another voice grumbled something unintelligible to Brennan.

The first voice spoke again. Brennan decided this was a female voice. "…defensive wounds… bruising…" then her voice deepened and moved further away.

There was nothing. Absolutely nothing. The void and emptiness so great it felt like an entity in and of itself.

Brennan was suddenly aware of his body in The Nothing. He looked around for what seemed like years, just floating in The Nothing. His eyes understood nothing more than vast emptiness and himself. He was somehow illuminated. He could see his body, but there was no light source. It was as if even darkness could not exist within The Nothing.

After years of floating aimlessly, Brennan found his voice.

"What is this place?" he asked no one, "Why am I here?"

"This is not a pace, da-ee," a chirpy little voice answered.

Brennan was suddenly aware that his feet were on something. He was grounded, yet beneath him there was only limitless void. Feeling some sort of terra firma allowed him to remember that he could move. He turned and saw a small girl, no more than five years old, with her back to him. She had gorgeous, brown curls that hung to her waist. She was wearing denim capris, pale pink converse, and a tiny lab coat.

"How is this not a place? What's happened to me? Who are you?" he asked calmly. He realized he should be terrified, in a panic, but he struggled to feel much of anything.

"Loss of questions, da-ee. We are nowhere and nowhen. You bwoke your bwain, da-ee. I need to fiss," she scrunched her face in a grimace, he couldn't see it, but he knew, "I need to FICK-S it. Fix it."

Brennan understood she had some sort of speech impediment and made what should have been a bombshell of a connection, but here, it felt like a mild curiosity.

"Why do you keep calling me daddy? I don't have kids. I don't even have a wife or girlfriend."

The little girl giggled sweetly and turned around. She was wearing a plastic purple and pink stethoscope and a t-shirt under her lab coat that read, "My dad is my superhero" and had small, rainbow colored, domino masks drawn around it. Her face was very pretty, cute button nose, but something was off. She had brilliant jade green eyes and Brennan thought, "*Those aren't hers*".

"I keep calling you da-ee, because you is my da-ee. You just don't member, but don't feel bad, da-ee. You bwain bwoke. Bwoke. Br-oke. Broke. You bwain broke."

Brennan saw that the little girl had been covering a man, lying on a table. It wasn't a bed, like you might see at a hospital, it was a table, like you'd see in a morgue.

"I don't understand this. I don't understand this at all." Brennan suddenly felt a tug, as if his sternum was being pulled towards his spine. Not pushed externally, but really pulled from the inside. There was pressure, a sense of motion that almost made him sick, and he heard the little girl's voice again.

"Is okay, da-ee. I'm comin' to getchu!"

Brennan opened his eyes with a start.

Pain. Pain was everywhere. Every inch of his body hurt. His eyes burned, the lights in this room felt brighter than the sun. Breathing felt like he was inhaling powdered glass. Most of all, his head throbbed hotly. It felt heavy, like a lead cannonball had been propped on his neck. He felt someone touch his arm and heard a familiar voice yell out, "NURSE! I need a nurse in here! DOC!"

Brennan went limp and passed out.

This new sleep was delightfully and mercifully empty. Brennan woke up hours later, with no concept of how long he'd been out. His consciousness returned, but he did not open his eyes. They already stung from the red glare filtered through his eyelids.

He tried to ask whoever was nearby, he could feel someone nearby, to turn out the lights. Instead what came out was a raspy groan that sounded something like, "Too ah I."

His tongue stuck to the bottom of his mouth. He tried for another word.

"War..." he croaked.

"War?" the familiar voice asked. "Oh, water! Yeah, water."

There was rummaging and then, "Nurse? Nurse! He's waking up, can you please call the doctor? Thank you."

276

The red light disappeared with a click.

"Here, drink."

Brennan felt a piece of plastic, a straw, he figured after a few seconds, being offered to him. He drank greedily. At first, the cool water went down as if minute razor blades were mixed in, but as the dryness was quenched, the feeling of cold water tobogganing down his esophagus was incredible.

Brennan opened his eyes in the darkened hospital room. He looked towards the place he had heard the voice coming from.

"Jim?" Brennan asked. His voice was clearer, but still rough. He took another sip of water. "What are you doing here? What am I doing here? What happened?"

"Well, shoot dang, man," James whispered. "I was hoping you could tell me. Doctor said memory loss was a possibility after your head trauma. I think what he wanted to tell me was that memory loss was probable, but better than you dying, which we thought was going to happen."

"How long have I been out?" Brennan asked, his voice smidge stronger.

"Three weeks, man," James replied in a solemn voice. He moved closer to his brother and despite severely blurred vision, Brennan noticed a large scar that ran upwards from the left-hand corner of his mouth, towards his ear.

"Dude, James, what the pus-spewing hell happened to your face?" Brennan exclaimed as loud as he could, which was still barely audible and came with a pubescent sounding crack midsentence.

"Okay, first of all, watch your language, dude. You know I don't like that. We've been making progress," James seemed proud of that, "Second," he paused here, and his eyes narrowed as they burrowed into Brennan's, "you really don't remember, do you?"

Brennan laid his head back on the pillow, his headache was intensifying. He slowly shook his head 'no'.

"It was the Medellin case," James stated before seeing he would have to elaborate. "The Case. The one that brought me back to God, had me quit our business, and earned me a Glasgow smile."

"Our business?" Brennan replied, thoroughly confused.

"Geez. What's the last thing you remember?"

"A case, but not from whatever our business was. CPS had called PD for our assistance. A set of eight brothers, left abandoned." Faces, facts, dates, all flickered through his head sporadically.

He knew he remembered, but he didn't know how.

"What the hell, man?! That was like three years ago!"

A tall man with teal scrubs and a lab coat came in. He had a strange, almost Slavic accent.

"Ah, meester Ramirez. I see sleeping beauty az finally woken up." He turned to James and covered his mouth, as if he was going to tell a secret, "Maybe sleeping beast in thees case, huh?" he chuckled. "I am Doctor Banich. How are you feeling?"

The doctor sat next to Brennan and began shining his pen light in his eyes, causing Brennan to flinch. "Good response, but a strong sensitivity to light."

"He says he can't remember anything from the last few years," James implored, the concern in his voice seeping through, despite his serious, almost angry expression.

"Yes, memory loss iz common. Ah, the brain," he bugged his eyes out and placed his fingertips on the top of his head when he said the word brain, "has suffered trauma. Thees can heal or may not heal. We are not sure. Only time can tell. For now, we are going to run scans, some tests, and then you will rest. Yes?"

"I've been asleep for three weeks, I think I'm all topped off on rest, doc," Brennan spoke this while simultaneously concluding that he actually did feel tired. Exhausted as a matter of fact.

"No, your brain was in coma. Not sleep. Very different. If you are not tired, you soon will be. The nurse will help with studies. Nurse Yefferson."

Nurse Jefferson walked in. She was wearing black scrubs with hot pink Superman logos printed all over. The logos were designed to look like they were dripping, as if they had been spray painted on. She appeared to be in her forties, some smile lines and the tiniest hint of crow's feet. She had otherwise smooth, dark brown skin, and her tight black curls were loose, framing her face almost perfectly. Her eyes were a hazel so light it was almost yellow, and they fiercely contrasted against her dark skin.

"Mr. Ramirez," she began as she took down his vitals, using a stylus and tablet, rather than a paper chart, "I will be taking care of you this afternoon and evening. We're going to wheel you out of here soon to get a CAT scan."

She walked up next to Brennan and clicked around on an EEG machine. It wasn't until now that Brennan realized he had electrodes on his head.

Brennan jumped up in his bed.

"What? You okay, bud? What is it?" James asked doing a pitiful job of hiding his nervousness.

"The electrodes. I had electrodes on my head. There were electrodes," Brennan muttered, his eyes bulging with hysteria.

"Okay, calm down, Mr. Ramirez. It's okay, it's a standard test. No pain involved." Nurse Jefferson placed her hands-on Brennan's shoulders, gentle but firm.

Brennan had goosebumps spread out across his body at the feeling of her warm hands. Everything else was so cold.

Brennan leaned back and took a deep breath. The doctor, who had already been on his way out the door, came back around.

"What do you remember about electrodes on head?" the doctor asked.

Brennan didn't like the way his voice sounded when he asked that question. For a second, he wondered if it made him racist that the doctor reminded him of a Bond villain.

"I had a thing, on my head. There were electrodes. It helped me..." he trailed off and his headache intensified, "ugh... it helped me move, or, or maybe... um... maybe go somewhere."

"You're not making sense, Brennie," James remarked in a stern, albeit shaky, voice.

"Is okay. Like Magic 8 Ball, I can ask another time, yes?" the doctor asked with a smile.

Brennan nodded at the doctor. His head was swimming and the nod made him feel nauseous. He tightened his already closed eyes with a grimace.

"You're okay, Brennan," Nurse Jefferson soothed, "is it okay if I call you Brennan? I call you Brennan and you can call me Nurse Shayla, or just Shayla. How's that sound?"

"Brennan is fine," he replied in a smoother tone. The rhythmic pulse in his skull was subsiding. "I'm fine." He opened his eyes. "I like your scrubs."

"Oh," Shayla looked down at her scrubs, as people usually do when their clothes are complimented, as if they'd forgotten what they were wearing, "yeah, I was in pediatrics earlier, they were short staffed and they offered me a few hours of OT to help out. I like to wear something fun any time I work with kids."

"Brennan loves Superman. Comics in general," James stated matter-of-factly. Brennan turned slowly to look at him and saw a crooked smile on his lips.

"Really? Me too! Honestly, one of the reasons I volunteer to take hours in pediatrics is so I can wear my Batmans, Supermans, Wonder Womans, and Spider-Mans. I mean, I like to help the kids too, of course." She smiled playfully, " What's your favorite Superman book?"

Brennan didn't know if she was genuinely interested or if she was trying to get his mind off the pain and anxiety. He

281

was sure James had told them about the anxiety. Regardless, he figured he'd play along.

"Red Son. I'm a sucker for alternate universes. You?"

"All-Star Superman," she replied with a real smile and an air of reflection, "That story, where Clark goes back in time as the bandaged Superman to spend some extra time with his Pa Kent before he dies. Ugh, gets me every time. I'm talking tears just…" she mimed a flow from her eyes down with her hands.

Brennan chuckled and closed his eyes. He felt a falling sensation.

"What do you think, Mr. Brennan? I say I give you a few minutes to rest, relax, and then we can start the tests. Okay?"

"Yeah, a bit of rest sounds good actually. Can I cut the lights?"

"Sure. I'll turn them off for you. We'll be back in a few."

Brennan closed his eyes. Dreading the coming questions, but happy that they'd be normal, brotherly, stupid questions. Nothing about memory or electrodes.

"So," James started, right on cue, "Nurse Shayla, huh?"

"No," Brennan replied curtly.

"Why not, dude? I mean sure it's unethical right now, but not once you're up and all better."

"Dude, she's got to be late thirties, maybe early forties. The age difference is too wide." Brennan protested weakly.

"You've always liked older girls. Nat? Older. Jane? Older. Priscilla? Older. The only exception I can think of is that girl who used to go to our church. You know the one?" James asked, "She was always with her mom. Her mom was either drunk or crazy, maybe both. You ended up not pursuing her because you found out she was younger than you, by like a freaking year or two, I might add."

"It wasn't really that," Brennan recalled. He remembered that girl and felt a deep, grievous, nostalgia at the thought of her. "She was always so busy with her mom. I felt wrong asking for her attention. When I finally decided to just up and do it, she was gone. She stopped going to church. Probably good I didn't. I'm pretty sure she stopped going because her mom was getting to be an issue at church. Eventually, she wouldn't have had time for a relationship either. Save time. Avoid heartbreak. Avoid drama."

"I can't for the life of me remember her name though." James pondered, searching his mind's records for the answer.

Brennan, on the other hand, Brennan who had lost years of time in his head could remember the name perfectly.

"Deidre. It was Deidre."

Chapter 30

A few days later, test results all showed that there appeared to be no permanent damage, Brennan was healing well, and he was stable. All they had found was a patch of scar tissue in the temporal lobe. They were unsure how it happened, or where all the blood they drained had come from, but as far as they could see, his prognosis was good. These circumstances convinced James to tell Brennan what little he knew about what happened.

He had been found in front of a house. The residents of the house called 911 and reported a dead man on their lawn. They had assumed he was dead because he was just about upholstered in bruises. He looked almost completely purple, red, and greenish. The police and an ambulance arrived shortly and found that somehow, Brennan had a pulse. There was blood coming from his mouth, ears, and nose. James didn't tell Brennan, but Brennan figured other orifices had been bleeding as well. He had a strange mechanical device attached to him. The police didn't know what it was, but considering the harsh electric shock it gave a cop who incorrectly tried to unlatch it, they figured it may have been a torture device of some kind.

Brennan had been brought to the hospital, where doctors took a look at him and expected to find crush injuries probably by autopsy. Instead, Brennan was mostly stable, but had suffered intracranial hemorrhaging. Surgery relieved the pressure, but to their surprise, the doctors had found no real damage. There was a pretty serious concussion, bruising, but not much else. It seemed the worst of the trauma was implied, but not actually seen. The doctor with the Slavic accent, Dr. Banich, had been brought in due to the peculiarity of the case. There were a lot of concerns that Brennan had been assaulted, maybe even kidnapped. James said that he had been missing for at least two weeks, maybe more, considering how little contact he recently had with family.

"Don't give up on my Nan," a shaky voice whispered in his head. It sounded familiar but had no identity in Brennan's mind.

"Wait, why aren't we talking?" Brennan asked confused and a bit hurt.

"Well, you got pissed that I left the business. You told me you understood and that it was fine, but I could tell you were upset. You call me about once every two weeks, just to check in. I call you, but you're usually too *busy* to answer." James marked the word "busy" with air quotes.

"I'm sorry, man," he paused, "What about mom?"

James' eyes widened, presumably in surprise. "Dude, you haven't talked to mom in months. Not since a big fight y'all had. You were helping her with some job application and admonishing her for not having retirement savings, and she started giving you life advice instead. Said you had to find a nice, docile wife. Do something with your life. You got upset, that you did do something. You graduated college,"

Brennan saw a flash of a massive congregation of people in black robes and graduation caps.

"you worked with PD for a while,"

Another flash, this one of him kicking a door. He was wearing a button up with a Kevlar vest over it. There was a tiny, little girl, maybe two or three, sitting naked, sobbing, in a corner, surrounded by her own waste.

"you tried to help,"

Brennan remembered being on top of a man. His fists were raining down over the man. He could hear yells and feel tugs at his vest. *"Stop! Detective! Ramirez! RAM! Dude, STOP!"* He had been suddenly lifted in the air.

"but you couldn't cut it. At least that's what you said. I think your heart was just too big for that crap."

Brennan stared off. These initially unfamiliar memories now felt tied, no, not tied, woven into him.

"Anyway, she told you it was time to stop moping around and get on the horse. She said the PI business was too little for you. You told her you were leaving, that all she had to do on the app now was hit submit. She told you that you were like dad. Leaving was what you did best. Y'all haven't talked since."

Brennan's stare remained transfixed on an empty space on the wall.

"That's terrible," Brennan mused softly. "Call her. I want to see her. Tell her to come visit me."

James' eyes went wide again, and a goofy smile parted his lips. He chuckled, "Dude, c'mon. Do you not know mom?"

Brennan looked at him, his expression still mostly blank.

"She's downstairs," James revealed with a smile.

Brennan looked at James and gave a weary half smile.

"You still want me to get her?" James asked.

Brennan nodded and James stood up and headed for the door. James was in the doorway when Brennan called after him.

"Jim!"

"Yeah, man."

"The thing they found on me. The device. What happened to it?"

"Police took it as evidence. I tried to get a hold of it so I could run the manufacturer of the parts, maybe follow the trail to whoever bought the stuff. I wasn't able to."

Brennan felt a disturbing sensation. The police shouldn't have it. He needed it, but for what?

"Yeah," Brennan conceded finally, "that makes sense. Thanks, bud."

Fifteen minutes later, Nancy Ramirez stood at the door. She seemed embarrassed, her hands were clasped in front of her and her head was lowered. An emotional pain struck Brennan as he realized the weight bearing down on his mother was an anvil of guilt.

"Can I come in?" Nancy asked.

"Yeah, of course, ma. C'mon in."

She walked into the room and towards Brennan. She approached the bed but kept a respectful distance. Brennan lifted his arms to her. The motion gave her a flashback of Brennan when he was a small child and would stretch his arms up when he wanted her to carry him or embrace him. She missed her little boy. She noticed his arms were still up and broke into torrential tears. She slid alongside him and held him close and tight. Brennan cried with her.

The apologies came after the tears, but by that point, all had been forgiven.

"I need to speak to this doctor," Nancy declared, suddenly in tiger mom mode.

Brennan took a moment to really look at her. He felt he had not seen his mother in ages. She had the same porcelain skin, only now it was lined with cracks in some places. Her jet-black hair now had streaks of white and was shorter than he'd ever seen it, the tips sitting right below the top of her shoulders. She looked older, she definitely looked tired, but her enormous brown eyes were still beautiful, viciously commanding, and full of energy. She was wearing scrub bottoms and a Batman t-shirt. She had worn that shirt for him. She hadn't told him, but he knew she had. His heart broke wondering how long she had worn it. How many days had she kept it on in hopes that her son would wake up, in hopes that he would allow her to see him?

"You're black and blue all over," she cried pointing at the healing bruises around his body, "you were bleeding into your brain, you were in a coma for three weeks, and still all this expert doctor has is that there was a concussion. I don't trust him!" Nancy remarked defiantly.

"Why not, ma? I hear he's good," Brennan replied.

"Well, if he's so good, he should have figured out what happened," she leaned in close to him and whispered, "and he looks like a bad guy in a James Bond movie"

Brennan laughed aloud at this. The laugh was great, despite the rib pain and throb in his head that accompanied it. He felt like he hadn't laughed in ages.

"I thought the same thing."

As if on cue, Dr. Banich walked into the hospital room.

"Ah!" he remarked, stretching his hand to Nancy, "You must be momma Ramirez, yes?"

"Nancy, good to meet you doctor." she stretched out her hand and Brennan could almost see the cogs turning in her mind as she planned her scolding.

"Good to meet you, Mrs. Ramirez. I am Doctor Artyem Banich. If that's too hard to say, all the interns call me Doctor A.B.," Dr. Banich replied, except in his accent it sounded like Doctor Ebby or Abby.

A light went off in Brennan's head and he tried to catch it but it faded as abruptly as it appeared. Why was that name familiar to him?

"Da-ee, I'm comin to getchu!"

Brennan sat up suddenly, causing a firecracker of pain to go off in his head and sides.

"Brennan, are you okay?" Nancy asked, startled.

"Fine, fine. I just…" he looked at Dr. Banich, Dr. Abby, and then back down at the blankets covering him on the hospital bed, "… I keep hearing things. Voices. A little girl right now."

"Paracusia, meaning Auditory Hallucinations, is not uncommon after head trauma."

Nancy took her chance. "What exactly was his head trauma, doctor?"

Dr. Banich looked at Brennan as if asking consent to tell her and Brennan just nodded.

"We see that your boy has concussion. He is hit on head. He had a small hairline fracture in jaw and chipped tooth, consistent with a, uh…" Dr. Banich punched his hand before remembering the word, "punch! Consistent with punch. He also had shard of pill bottle embedded in leg. A healing injury. Older, I think. There was also traces of benzodiazepines in blood."

"Brennan!" Nancy exclaimed, "I thought you were off pills?"

"Mom, I don't even remember taking pills." he protested.

The doctor looked around suspiciously and then bent forward towards Nancy and Brennan, ready to divulge some great secret.

"I overheard police. They believe your son perhaps was taken. Benzo maybe used as sedative. Maybe administered covertly," Dr. Banich offered. He turned his gaze to Brennan now. "Meester Ramirez, are you feeling well now?"

"Yeah, I guess I'm okay. Just a bit of a headache."

"Okay. Great. I told you were in pain, lost memory, not ready, but they insisted."

"I'm sorry," Brennan said, looking at Dr. Banich through heavy eyelids, "who insisted."

"Police. They are here to take statement."

"Oh, okay," Brennan muttered, somewhat apprehensively.

"No, not okay," Nancy retorted. "My son doesn't remember what happened, you're saying he may have been kidnapped and," she signaled at the bruising across his body, "beaten, but they want to talk to him now? Even if they do get him to remember, they're just going to make him relive whatever happened. The cops can do their job without him."

"No, mom. I don't remember anything, but I at least need to try to help the case. At least for the sake of justice, if nothing else."

She looked at him angrily. Momma bear was protecting her son. She considered her options and despite really wanting to put her foot down and save her son, they had just made up. Going against his wishes would be of no great benefit. A moment or two later she spoke, her voice dripping with reluctance and reproach, "Okay, fine, but I'm staying!"

"Mom...." Brennan started

"Okay, fine, but I'll be right outside."

Brennan smiled and felt grateful to have his mom, overprotective and at times overbearing, there to watch out for him right now.

Two men walked in. One was about 5'9", lean athletic build, with dark, almost black, eyes, short cropped, black hair, and smooth brown skin. He wore black slacks, a light blue button down with the sleeves rolled up, and his gun and badge on his belt.

The other was easily 6'2" and about 250 pounds. Though his stomach appeared to contribute to his weight a bit, most of it came from his heavy musculature. The entirety of head was clean shaven, except his eyebrows. He had keen light brown eyes, a sharp, slightly crooked nose, thin lips, and naturally tan skin. He wore a standard blue police uniform with his badge and name plate that read, "Barrera".

The one in slacks, a detective obviously, had a concerned look on his face. The officer in uniform wore a contrasting stoic expression.

"Hey, Bren," the detective greeted, giving a pitiful wave of his hand.

Brennan looked at him, sat up in his bed, and grimaced in pain at the effort.

"I'm sorry, do I know you?"

"I guess not," the detective replied, his concern seeming to deepen, "I'm Detective Aguilar, this is Officer Barrera, we'd like to ask you some questions about the last few weeks."

Brennan met eyes with Officer Barrera, who defiantly refused to avert his gaze.

"So your name is Barrera?" Brennan asked, "Makes sense. You know, Barrera, like a barrier, or a wall. You kind of look like a freaking wall."

Surprisingly, Officer Barrera cracked up at this. Even more surprising was the fact that Brennan was not surprised at all. He did know this man. He couldn't put his finger on it, but he had a feeling about him.

"Goddang," Barrera boomed in a deep voice that almost tangibly vibrated through the air, "same ol' Ram."

Brennan smiled. The nickname Ram clarified some of the murky sludge that was currently passing for his memory.

He was freshly graduated. He's dressing out for his first shift on the force.

"I'm just saying, nicknames will help in a bad situation," Barrera had insisted. He was shirtless, about to put on a white tank top to wear under his uniform shirt. In that time, Barrera had a Venice Beach level six pack and thinning, black curls.

"When the hell are we going to need a nickname? We're not going covert. This isn't Call of Duty, IronMaster13," A younger Aguilar had mocked, calling Barrera by his XBox gamertag. Brennan didn't so much remember as he just suddenly knew that they had often teased Barrera for his love of video games.

"Say I'm calling you for help. By the time I finish 'Officer Aguilar' or 'Ramirez' I might be shot." Barrera argued.

"Maybe be a better cop," Aguilar hit back, "or just flex and scare the bullets away."

"Ramirez, back me up here."

"Look, man, if you want monosyllabic nicknames, I'm gonna call you 'Wall'," Brennan had replied.

"What's monosyllabic?" Aguilar asked.

"Use context clues, moron," Brennan had responded.

"Wait, why Wall?" Barrera asked.

Brennan looked at him incredulous, every part of his face spelling out, 'Isn't it obvious?'

"Because you look like a freakin' wall, dude. You're like six foot twenty, two and a half tons of solid, Cemex brand, hecho en Mexico, muscle. Also, your name. Works on two levels," Brennan explained with a smile.

"Fine," Aguilar declared, "I'm in. I say we call Ramirez 'Ram'. Works on two levels too. His name, it's monosyballic…"

"Monosyllabic." Brennan corrected.

"… and he's always good at butting heads with people."

Brennan laughed and shook his head.

"If you're counting the monosyllabic thing, it's three levels. If you can't speak or spell, at least learn to count," Brennan shot back playfully

"Oh, sorry, Mr. College, I didn't graduate with a 7.0 and Magma Come Loud," Aguilar apologized mockingly.

Brennan and Barrera exploded in raucous laughter.

"The scale goes up to four and it's Magna Cum Laude," Barrera corrected this time.

"That's what I said, Magma Come Loud." Aguilar paused, "Hey if we're doing name stuff, I want to be Aguila!"

Brennan closed his locker and fastened his gun belt. "That's literally just one letter shorter than your regular name."

"I think we should call you Ace," Barrera suggested as he closed his locker and looked down exasperated at the uniform shirt. The buttons at the chest were holding on by little more than hope and force of will.

"Yeah, man. I like that. Ace. Cause I'm the freaking Ace in this deck, right?"

"No, because Sarge will get mad if we keep saying Ass over the radio." Barrera replied.

This memory surfaced in one sharp burst.

"Wall and Ace." Brennan looked back up at them.

Aguilar's face changed completely. A huge grin slid across his face and he hugged Brennan too hard. Barrera laughed and just shook Brennan's hand. Aguilar let go of Brennan and Brennan saw that his eyes were red and swelling.

"You crying, Ace?" Brennan asked.

"Hey, cabron," Ace protested in a shaky voice that was something between a sob and chuckle, "it's Detective Ace now."

The Wall spoke up now, "Ace made detective six months ago, man. Doctors said his head should shrink back to normal size any day now."

Brennan chuckled and electric currents of pain ran through this ribs, making him wince at the same time.

"What about you, Wall? Not testing yet?"

"Nah, man," Wall grumbled in his low, rumbling voice, "I'm not into the brainy stuff. I'm a blunt object. I'm a wrecking ball. Point me in the right direction and I will tear it down."

Brennan smiled, "We both know that's not true. Plus, if Ace passed, you could definitely do it."

The three of them chuckled again and Brennan took a moment to quickly evaluate his feelings. This felt natural. He remembered these men. They had been his friends. Yet, there was something off. Something underneath, trying to get out. A monster swimming under the surface of the murky memory lake.

"Hey, man, I worked for it, carnal. I hit the books hard," Ace defended. There was a hint of pride in his eye that made Brennan feel happy for him.

"How many books did you mess up or tear before your mom told you that's not what that means?"

Again, chummy laughter that was both perfect and completely wrong.

"I'm glad y'all are here, but let's talk shop, man," Brennan said.

"Well, Ram, you were last seen three weeks before you were found dying on someone's yard. On September 24th, Conrad Hierro says that you went to his drinking establishment and drank three whiskey glasses of..." he checked his notes, "Passion Fruit La Croix."

Ace pronounced it 'La Croycks', prompting another painful chuckle from Brennan.

"Conrad stated that one of his bar tenders had Jim on speed dial and was planning to call him if you ordered anything that even sat on the same shelf as the alcohol. He stated you were looking pretty down. After that, he stated you gave a pretty generous tip, five bucks on three bucks of drink, got up and left without saying a word. You walked to your car, apparently drove to your apartment, because that's where we found it, and next people to see you are some folks really freaked about about their new garden gnome."

Brennan gave out a humorless sound that would have been, 'Ha', if he had opened his mouth.

"No forced entry at your home, no emails, no phone calls, nothing displaced. You were just gone." Ace took in a deep breath, as if he were trying to inhale hope out of the air, "Do you remember anything?"

Brennan tried to remember and felt a pressure behind his eyes, like bad sinus pressure. He retraced everything backward from that moment. The pressure intensified.

"Agh!" he let out an exasperated grunt, "It's like it's right freaking there. Like behind my eyes somehow, but I just can't reach it."

"Hey, man, it's okay," Ace comforted, "you're still recovering, Doc Boris over there said your memories may come back with time. I mean, we jogged your memory and you remembered us, right? Maybe you just need the right trigger."

"Yeah," Brennan sighed.

Wall put a heavy hand on his shoulder and Brennan forced out a lame half smile.

"Hey, you remember my number?" Ace asked, "Hell, I'll leave my card anyway. That way every time you open your wallet you gotta see, DETECTIVE Francisco Aguilar." He smiled at Brennan and left a card on the rolling tray next to the hospital bed.

"I'm gonna leave you my card too, if you need to talk or if you wanna hang, just let me know." Wall offered, placing his card next to Ace's.

"Rest easy, Ram," Ace said. He stood up and they started to walk out.

"Hey, wait," Brennan called, "Jim said that y'all found a device on me. What was it? Where is it?"

"Uh, yeah, well we weren't first on scene, but we all saw it and heard about it. Looks like some sci-fi thing," Ace said.

"Yeah, some Braniac looking thing," Wall agreed, "They have no idea what it was. At first they thought it was some complicated torture device, it shocked the hell out of Davis, but then the more they looked at it, they started thinking it was some sort of medical telemetry device."

"So they're clueless," Brennan summarised.

"Yeah, pretty much," Ace replied.

"So," Brennan began, trying to think about how he could frame the question, "if it's not evidence, it may have been my property, maybe from a doctor or something, could I see it? Or get it? Where is it?"

"It may be a medical telemotor device," Ace began.

"Telemetry." Wall interjected

"Whatever, it could be a medical thing, or it could have been what fried your brain in a way that doctors can't figure out yet so, the U has it. They're studying it to try to figure it out."

"The U?" Brennan inquired, growing increasingly frustrated at how many things he no longer knew.

"Yeah, the University. UTRGV. They did us the favor of looking into it. There were no fingerprints on it or anything. All the DNA on it seemed to be from you."

"Y'all got DNA and sent it to a University to study?" Brennan inquired incredulously.

Wall answered this time, "Ram, you don't get it, man. This is some UFO, Roswell, Unsolved Mysteries, Twilight Zone kinda thing happening. In real life. In our podunk town. It's a matter of time before Feds get involved. We are going all out, man."

"I see that," Brennan agreed seriously, then tried to lighten the mood, "That's why they put the best men on the case, right?"

Wall and Ace smiled uncomfortably. Ace broke the awkward silence first.

"We still miss you, man. I studied till my fingers bled to pass the exam, but you just got it. You were a great detective, man. Great."

"The best," Wall interjected.

"I'm sorry about how things went down," Ace lamented.

This memory did not explode in. Perhaps because it had put down roots before, this memory gently bloomed.

"It is what it is, man," Brennan replied, looking away in a mildly angry shame. "I lost my cool. It's thanks to you guys that I just lost my job and didn't end up going to prison."

"Wall did all the work. You were on that dude like clap on a hooker," Ace exclaimed and was immediately backhanded on the arm by Wall.

"Gross, dude."

"Can I tell you guys something you probably already know?" Brennan asked.

The men remained quiet, but Wall nodded. Ace just looked down.

"I was going to kill him," Brennan continued, "What he did to that little girl. The look on her face. The panic in her eyes. That freaking scream. I can still hear it. I would've killed him."

"We've all been there, Ram," Wall assured, "We've all given a kick we shouldn't have, tackled a little harder than we should have, been tempted to ventilate a bastard because of what he did, and not what he is doing. We're not bad people though. We manage to hold ourselves back."

"I didn't pull punches. The only reason that guy's alive is because you pulled me back. If you didn't lift heavy, he'd be dead."

Ace and Wall looked at each other uneasily.

"Hector Zertuche is dead," Ace declared quietly. "Apparently he had another child abuse case a while back. Another little girl, about 10 years old or so. CPS took it to court tried to pin him for it, PD got involved and tried on the criminal law side and still, he got away with it. No hard evidence, girl clammed up. Well, the dirtbag ended up killing her. He ran, changed his name, changed his look. Ended up coming back to town, the dumb bastard. He does

what he did, you break his face, we put him in the pen.
Turns out, the other little girl's dad was penned up too.
Domestic abuse. Mom had a type, I guess. Anyway, dad
finds out Zertuche's real name is Rafael Robles..."

A warning bell went off in Brennan's head.

"In-ves-ti-ga-tor..."

"... he killed him. He died hard. Harder than if you'd done
him in. Got what he deserved."

"I had no idea," Brennan said grimly. "His real name, did
we have any cases with him under that name?"

"Nope. That's why we didn't catch it. He didn't have
fingerprints on file. No prior arrests, no military service,
nada," Ace said, regarding Brennan with a renewed worry
on his face.

"I guess it is what it is," Brennan repeated doing his best to
fake a smile.

Wall and Ace reciprocated the faux grin.

"Call me if you start to remember, Ram. I'll check in with
you in a couple weeks anyway, just in case," Ace instructed
and finally managed to finish his exodus from the hospital
room.

Nancy walked back in.

"I heard laughing. What was that all about?" she asked.

"I knew them from my days in PD. I didn't remember them
at first, but it started coming back to me. I think there's a
lot I'll remember once I get the right catalyst for the
memory."

"I think so too," Nancy paused and held her son's left hand in both of hers. "Can I be completely honest with you?"

"Yeah, sure," Brennan replied, trying not to reveal the apprehension that her question spawned.

"I hope you recover all your memory, but I'm glad you don't remember our argument."

She immediately looked away, emotional and in shame.

"I do remember, mom."

Nancy looked up at her son, surprised but relieved.

"I remember, but it's not worth fighting about. We're going to have our differences. You and I are very different people. That doesn't mean we can't be a good mother and son to each other. You were trying to encourage me. You believed that I could rise above and move on. I did not hold that belief and was scared to let you down, so I left. Then thing about dad hurt me because I'd hate for you to be right."

It was Brennan's turn to look away in shame.

"I loved dad. I still do. I wish I could've spent more time with him. I wish I had been older, maybe been able to help him, but I was mad he left. Mad he left the house because he didn't want to disappoint us as a father and husband. Mad that he left the real world and dove into the alcohol-soaked universe he often lived in. Mad that he didn't face the terrible trauma he had for my, perhaps selfish, sake. Mad that he died so soon. I love dad, mom, but I hate that he always left." Brennan looked up at his mother, the green of his eyes, made more vivid by the refreshing, yet stinging tears encapsulating them, connecting with her large, brown eyes, "I hate that he left until he couldn't come back. Then I almost did."

Nancy began to cry and hugged him. Before she fully lunged forward towards her son, Brennan caught a glimpse of her sobbing face and was struck by how ugly it was. Not aesthetically ugly necessarily, but the pure sight of his mother, weak, crying, vulnerable, seemed wrong. Ugly. She was suddenly a little girl, with a face too old to match her face, crying because she had to leave her father. She was a young woman, catching up to the wrinkles on her skin, crying because her husband left. She was an older woman, greying hair and lines that matched the emotional scars of her life, crying because her firstborn son almost left.

"Don't give up on my Nan," The soft, dulcet, alien voice repeated.

Brennan hugged his mother tightly for a long while. He ignored the ache in his ribs, the dull throb of his unexplainable, fading bruises, and he held her.

There would be other fights. There would have to be. There would be other arguments. There would be other yelling matches. There would be conflict again, but Brennan would never leave again, and Nancy would always love him for it.

Chapter 31

Brennan and his mother watched TV for hours. They watched CSI and Brennan pointed out all the erroneous, science fiction methods they employed, and bet on who would be the murderer. Brennan won every time. His mother assumed it was his police experience, but Brennan was relying on classic storytelling tropes that these procedurals thrived on.

They watched Jeopardy and Brennan accurately guessed many of the science and historical questions, while his mother aced most things pop culture related, leaving Brennan to feel as if the stereotypical roles had been reversed.

Finally, his mother changed the channel on the small hospital flat screen to a Spanish speaking network.

"Eeeh!" she exclaimed, "I almost forgot my novela!"

Brennan quietly chuckled as an overly dramatic male singer belted out deep, quivering, lyrics to a ranchera song with the title of the Spanish soap opera forcibly inserted into them. He smiled as his mother stared intently at the equally dramatic slideshow of scenes that played along with the music, matching slaps, kisses, sobbing faces, and forcible embraces to the beat and pitch of the booming Charro's voice.

Brennan had spent a pleasant time with his mother, and he allowed her to watch her soap opera without mocking her taste or complaining about boredom. Instead he allowed his thoughts to drift for the hour-long duration of the show. When the song started up again, this time with rolling credits, Brennan spoke about the first thing that came to his mind as he stared at the small white board that showed his nurses' and doctor's names.

"Does the name Abby mean anything to you?" Brennan asked his mother.

She turned to look at his, eyes wide in an inquisitive expression, as if to say, "can you repeat that, I wasn't listening."

"Does the name Abby mean anything to you?" he repeated.

"Well, yes. Why do you ask?"

"When the doctor said people called him Dr. A.B. or Abby, it rang the wrong bell in my head. I freaked and I have no idea why."

"Well, to be honest with you, I don't know why either. Abby has never been a bad name to you." She paused, "I never knew why, but you loved it. You said you would name your daughter Abby if you ever had one. You and James considered J.B. Investigations for your business name, but worried that people would mistakenly reverse the letters, you used James' middle name, Alexander, and did A.B. Investigations. Of course, you insist on pronouncing it Abby Investigations."

She hesitated again and the long-gone tears surfaced in her eyes once more. "It was also what you called my mom as a kid. Grandma Abby. Funny enough, your business, your doctor, and your grandma all got to Abby by way of the A.B. acronym, rather than being named Abigail or something. Weird how life goes in circles, isn't it?"

Brennan had a moment, like an old-fashioned flashbulb going off in his head, slow yet somehow immediate. His heart felt heavy and beat too fast. There were tears pushing against the back of his eyes. He was bending over to kiss the old woman on the forehead. The skin there was cold and waxy, no longer skin on a person, but skin on a corpse, and he was angry. He was so incredibly, rabidly, deliriously, angry.

Brennan snapped out of it. He had his second bout of word vomit.

"You didn't like her much, did you?" he interrogated accusingly.

Nancy seemed taken aback by this. She felt the sting of regret and offense hit her chest, but in the interest of maintaining this new, budding, and honest relationship with her son, she answered.

"We had our differences. Your grandmother was a survivor. A smart, beautiful woman with incredible instinct. Unfortunately, that meant that she often did things to survive that would fall into questionable territory, let's call it. Her survival depended on the understanding that the end justifies the means. She lived most of her life that way. Occasionally, her kids would get caught in that wave. I resented her for that. I resented her for making me paranoid, for making me feel unsafe. I resented her for not doing all she could to protect her children or even doing all she could to protect herself. I resented her for not leaving my father. I resented her for chasing after him, literally gun in hand sometimes, to scare away his mistresses instead of having some self-respect and leaving. I resented her for forcing me to make that choice for her. She was a proud, arrogant, materialistic woman."

Brennan felt unconvinced. Surely his mother was leaving out some redeeming quality, surely his grandmother could not be…

"Then you were born," she continued, "she was so different. I don't know if the generational space allowed her to see you better, I don't know if she loved you because she could see you, spend time with you, but not be stressed about you. I don't know if your little face just helped her understand the purity and fragility of feeling."

She inhaled and exhaled a deep sigh and her face melted from sweet reminiscing into a painful remorseful expression.

"She started calling out your dad for being too harsh. She moved in with us so she could help me with you. Honestly, for me it was an excuse to spend time with that happier, sweeter version of her."

A tear rolled down her cheek and Brennan realized something that pained him. His mother had an incredible amount of ways to cry. Crying wasn't just a response for her, it was something she had a lot of experience in doing painfully, silently, angrily, mournfully, and just about every other way one can cry. She was silent, stoic. She sat with perfect posture and stared off into nothing. Her tears rolled silently, the only indication that, in that moment, she was carrying an elephantine burden of guilt and regret on her shoulders. A burden she could never put down because her opportunity to do so had died along with her mother.

A boundless fifteen seconds later, she spoke again.

"I had a chance, you know? After I kicked her out of my home, I had a chance to make things right. I wasn't sure she was sick, but I had seen how thin she'd become. Your dad and I were dropping you off for your first day of school. I looked around and saw how for a lot of kids starting out, it was a family affair. Mom, dad, grandma, grandpa, everyone was there. I looked around and saw her. Your grandma. She was standing across the parking lot, but I could tell it was her and I knew she was there for you. A man had some sort of fit or episode and your grandmother rushed to help him. I decided I'd talk to her the next time she went to see you off to school."

"What happened?" Brennan asked, but he already knew. He almost felt like he had been there. Sure, a four-year-old version of him was there, but he remembered things oddly, like they were from a third person perspective.

"She never went back. A few weeks later, 911 got a call from her house. When they arrived, she had been dead a while. It was inexplicable. They said the 911 call was made in late morning, but they believed she had died in her sleep. Doesn't matter." She looked down and away from her son, "The point is that I said 'tomorrow' and tomorrow didn't have her in it."

A sob tried to escape her throat and she gritted her teeth together and managed to regain her composure. Brennan leaned over, causing a warm, creaking pain in his ribs, and hugged his mother. She hugged him back and his muscles protested, but he ignored them.

"At least," her voice cracked, and she cleared her throat, "at least I got the chance with your dad. At least I had this chance with you."

Brennan quickly but gently backed out of the hug.

"You had the chance with dad?" Brennan asked in a whisper. He felt a twinge of jealousy and a bit of anger. He had always wanted to have a farewell moment with his father and was hurt to know that he may have died feeling unforgiven and alone. Now his mother was telling him that may not have been the case.

"I knew it wasn't right. I knew I shouldn't have done it, but your dad and I started seeing each other towards the end."

Nancy's cheeks blushed and Brennan couldn't help but forgo his anger. Despite the fights, despite quitting, despite their uncountable, regrettable, stupid mistakes, they had been in love.

"He told me he was sick, but he asked me not to tell you or James. We'd see each other every once in a while, when you kids were at school. Sometimes we'd get lunch. Sometimes we'd catch up movie. Sometimes we'd just talk. Most times we ended up fighting. I never told you boys about him being sick because he asked me, and I never told you about him and me because I knew you'd get your hopes up. I couldn't bear to disappoint you to that extreme."

She looked at him with a pleading look. A 'forgive me' look.

"I got to see him a few hours before he passed. I told him that he was an idiot, but that I loved him. That I had always loved him, and I would always love him." Her voice bent upwards and cracked.

Her eyes squinted and welled up before spilling over. This was her heartbroken cry.

"I told him you and Jimmy loved him. That you didn't hold anything against him. That you were excited for every visit you had with him."

She gave a high pitched, choked up sob.

"He said he was sorry he had missed a few visits, to tell you boys that he was sick, that's why he didn't go."

A blue gray parade of sobs made it out this time.

"I promised to take you boys after school. He got worse. They sent a chaplain to pray with him just as the school bell was ringing. I would've taken you boys out early if I had known."

A coughing, choked sob now.

"The chaplain guided him through final prayers and then asked him how he felt. Your father's last words were, 'I'm gonna miss my wife and boys.' He fell asleep a little after. When we got to the hospital…"

Brennan remembered this part.

"… he had just passed."

Nancy collapsed once more into his arms. Even as his memories swirled in a murky, smokey mess in his head, he remembered his mother completely different as she was here. He remembered the woman who had gone to night school while working a day job. He remembered the woman who had defended him and fought for him all through school, even when it was his fault. He remembered the woman that stood up to his father when he missed his visitations. He remembered the woman who had been a lioness. He remembered the woman who had opposed him and butted heads with him. He remembered the woman he at times considered his enemy. Not because she was evil, but because her idea of what was best for him was different than his. Not because she was a control freak, but because her grown, independent, man of a son was still her little baby boy. The woman who had been a tower, his and James' tower, now crumbled before him like a house of cards.

"I almost lost you," she wept. Her voice was muffled as her face was pressed against Brennan's chest. Brennan silently wondered how many times the roles had been reversed, the innumerable times his mother had held him to her chest this way.

"I almost lost you," she repeated, "and you were going to go thinking I didn't love you. Over something so stupid."

"Mom," Brennan began, pushing her back gently, "I know you love me. I've never doubted that. We don't always agree, but I know you love me. You know what, I think maybe grandma may have known too, and if she didn't, something tells me she blamed herself and not you."

Brennan sensed that she was conjuring up a rebuttal, a way to blame herself, but he didn't give her the chance. He brought her close to him again, wincing through the throbbing aches, and just held her.

"Don't give up on my Nan."

This time he replied to the mental intruder in his thoughts.

"I've got her... I've got her."

Chapter 32

Brennan was surprised by how long he was kept in the hospital. What he was less surprised by were the insane number of tests that they ran on him for those two weeks. MRIs, CAT Scans, EEGs, blood tests, even a full skeletal survey at some point.

James was wheeling him out of the hospital and towards his mother's Toyota minivan. Brennan saw the beat-up old Previa, with the dusty looking green paint, making noises louder than a muscle car would, and smiled. His mom could have bought a much newer vehicle with all the money she had sunk into her beloved Flying Turtle, a nickname she'd given it before she had even officially bought it, but his mother was not the type of person who gave up on something.

Brennan got out of the chair and stepped up and into the minivan's back seat with little trouble. Even after spending five weeks in the hospital, three of those in a coma, he felt oddly strong. He had a sense that he was not used to his body running this well. He sat back in the generously cushioned tan seat and closed his eyes. At once he felt overtaken by a wave of nostalgia and along with it, he heard something in a stranger's voice that sounded like a memory.

"I'm really starting to like you, and I wanted you to know you're chasing damaged goods."

He startled himself awake, unaware that he had even been asleep. They pulled up to an apartment building. Though he did not immediately recognize it, it began to slowly take form in his mind.

"Do you live here?" Brennan asked James.

James had taken the shotgun seat. He looked back over his shoulder at Brennan. "Yeah, man. It'll come back to you once you see it."

There had been a lengthy discussion about where Brennan would stay. His apartment had been paid for, but James and Nancy both refused to allow him to go back and stay alone. The doctor had recommended that someone stay with him. Brennan had insisted that he was okay and could be on his own. This was of course a lie. It was all an act and Brennan had to play the part of big brave brother. In all actuality, he was terrified. He wanted to be taken care of. He remembered a lot, but a part of him still felt new to the world. Dark existential thoughts would ooze into his mind.

"What if this is a coma dream? Maybe that's why it feels fake. Maybe that's why it feels alien. Maybe I never woke up..."

He had struggled to take control of the panic that accompanied these thoughts. It became a little easier every time, but he still feared getting caught up in one.

James had eventually convinced Nancy that Brennan would do well with him. Nancy had enough things to worry about and she was close enough that she could visit any time she wanted. Brennan understood what James was really saying. Their newfound peace would not last long if they lived together and James could provide a neutral middle ground. A Ramirez family DMZ.

Nancy handed Brennan a thick, maroon folder with a string and button tie. He got out of the Previa and moved towards the apartments.

"If you need to pick up some stuff from your place, we can take the truck." James offered, signaling at a dark blue Tacoma with his thumb.

"Huh, you have a blue truck." Brennan looked intrigued.

"Yeah," James replied. He gave his brother look of mild amusement laced with a bit of concern. "Why? You don't like the blue?"

"No, it's great. I just... I think I remembered it red for some reason," Brennan paused, "and bigger too, I think."

James laughed, "Red's too gaudy."

Nancy now hopped out of the driver's seat of the Previa and hugged Brennan.

"If you need anything at all, call me."

"I will, mom."

"You're sure you don't want to stay with me?"

"I'll be okay at Jimmy's. Get some rest. Relax, ma."

"Remember! The doctor said no booze! At least for now, okay?"

"Mom, you know I don't drink."

Nancy and James suddenly and simultaneously looked at each other awkwardly.

"What?" Brennan asked, "I drink?"

James nodded bleakly, "You know, I'd lie to you if I thought it would work, but it wouldn't. I'm sure you'll remember soon enough. You started drinking after dad's passing. We knew you had been taking pills, but you were actually pretty disciplined with your self-medicating. Thing about Xanax is that it tends to be a lonely drug. You wanted company you could ignore. You wanted people to be there without really being there. So, you went to the bar. You took soda and lime at first, but it wasn't long before you switched up to something stronger. The rest, as they say, is history."

"Yeah, but whose history?" Brennan asked himself aloud.

"Don't worry," James took him by the shoulder, "that part of your life is over. I called Mario. Dude owes us a favor from the case we helped him out with."

Brennan looked up at James, his younger, but by no means little, brother with a blank look.

"Guess you don't remember. Dude was getting catfished. We investigated, reported it, AND did it without telling anyone about it. Saved the guy from making a series of expensive and ultimately humiliating decisions. As an added bonus, we put him in contact with Kimmy. They're engaged now.

"Kimmy? From church?"

"Yeah. It worked out really well. Anyway, I called him and told him that he owes us, big time. Told him that if he sees you at the bar, he needs to call me and refuse to serve you anything harder than cranberry juice."

Brennan had no conscious desire to drink alcohol. As far as he could remember, he hated it. Yet, there was a possibly autonomic response to the mention of alcohol, especially its restriction, that made Brennan feel just a bubbling cauldron of aggravation in his stomach.

"You know," Brennan began, "I don't even remember this Mario guy or what bar he works in for that matter."

"Mario is a good dude. Got his TABC license for a fundraiser during Charro Days and then couldn't find a job. Got his TABC back and went to work, not at a bar, at THE bar. The only place in town to sit and drink anything alchie besides beer. Conrad's place, man. The nasty, old, 8 Ball."

Brennan heard tires screeching in his head followed by a thundering gun shot. He smelled the hot, bitter, stench of spent gunpowder mixed with the sour smell of internal flesh being made external. He saw a man's face, once handsome, now bloated with the force of the bullet traveling through his skull.

Brennan didn't realize he had collapsed. James was holding him up, his legs hung like wet noodles. He hadn't noticed anything until the flash ended.

Nancy was already running from the Previa's driver's seat, sprinting as fast as her short legs could carry her.

"Hey, bud, you alright? What's going on? You okay?" James asked, panicking too much to restrict himself to one question.

"The 8 Ball," Brennan said, "Someone died there. They were shot."

"No, bud. Did you see that? No one has been shot at the 8 Ball."

Brennan could hear his mom freaking out behind him and felt a pang of guilt.

"Ya ves?! You should go stay with me. I can take care of you. This is not okay. ¡No está bien!"

Brennan stood up and pulled himself up as tall as he could. He legs were shaking, and he hoped his mother didn't notice and knew James would.

"I'm okay, just a flash. I probably need to rest. Maybe it's police stuff coming back, you know." Brennan reassured his mother as much as he reassured himself, "I'll be okay with Jim. If I need anything, I'll call. I swear."

Nancy did not seem to be reassured in the least. "James Alexander," she belted pointing an over stretched index finger at him, "call me immediately, IMMEDIATELY, if something happens. Please, James."

"Yes, mom, I'll call." James was obviously exasperated now, "You're stressing him out. Go home."

James and Brennan turned around and James put his arm around Brennan's shoulders, but this time he subtly pressed his hand under Brennan's right arm to stabilize him.

"How can you say you're not the favorite?" James asked Brennan with a half-smile on his face.

Brennan chuckled. He still felt warm pangs emanate from his ribs when he laughed, but it was much less painful than when he had first woken up.

"She didn't act even close to this when my face happened," James whined playfully.

"Well, in her defense, we had always expected you to come out ugly," Brennan replied.

James gave his brother a gentle hit on the ribs, knowing it would not feel as gentle to him. Brennan laughed between gritted teeth.

"I'm kidding," Brennan winced, "Oh, that freaking hurt."
He laughed again and then looked at his brother with a
sympathetic, slanted, smile.

"What did happen to your face, if you don't my asking.
You told me some stuff, but not, like, details."

"Well, I guess you were there, so it won't make much
difference. You'll remember one way or another." James
didn't seem happy about it and didn't speak again until they
were in his apartment and the door was closed behind them.

Brennan sat on the black faux leather couch next to the
entrance. He began to not just see but remember the
apartment. He wondered to himself why some memories
came gently, either slowly, or just knowing, while others
were violent, painful, and apparently erroneous.

He remembered the large screen television, the X Box
hooked up to it, he remembered the comic books hanging
in matte picture frames. He couldn't see it, but he knew that
there was a collection of Marvel movie cups from the
theater in the cupboard next to James' refrigerator.

There was a hot pressure behind Brennan's eyes. He closed
them tightly, instinctively fearing they'd pop out of their
sockets. In the red light that seemed to come from behind
his eyes he saw a twin sized bed with princess decorations
and a purple blanket. He could feel the purple blanket. It
was important somehow. It was heavy. He remembered this
being in James' guest room, but all the same knew it would
not be there. He felt the back of his eyes begin to cool. The
pressure lessened.

James was putting things away and hadn't noticed Brennan's episode. He sat down on the loveseat across from the sofa where Brennan sat.

"What do you remember about the Medellin case?" James asked in a somber tone.

Brennan tried to remember. He focused on the name, repeating it over and over in his head.

"Medellin, Medellin, Medellin, Medellin..."

There were two men in expensive black suits. One reminded Brennan of Wall and the other looked like a Hispanic Wilson Fisk. Bizarro Wall was holding something, no not something, someone. Hispanic Fisk was barking something out.

"Drug dealers?" Brennan asked.

"Yeah," James affirmed, leaning back in his cushioned seat, "low level cartel. Andres Ocasio was a nobody on a big scale, but he was the big fish in a small pond around here. So when Ignacio Medellin told him to shove it, that his restaurant wouldn't be paying protection money, that he had the police for protection, Ocasio got mad. He and his enforcer, Adolio "Gorila" Diaz, took Ignacio from his restaurant after hours one night. They threw him in the back of a panel van, because Ocasio watches too many movies. Anyway, Medellin's wife, Anita, called the police and filed a report. To her surprise, when she goes to pick up her copy of the report, she realized it had been," he paused, and looked up as if an appropriate euphemism would be floating around in the air, "elaborated upon," he finished.

"Ocasio had cops in his pocket," Brennan remembered rather than realized.

319

"Yeah, so you reached out to some of your department contacts, they couldn't help much. Maybe if Ace had been a detective at that time, he could've helped…" James trailed off.

"They didn't help," Brennan continued for him, "but they did tell us that they thought they knew where Ocasio was hiding. Every time they planned a move, he'd disappear, but they thought he was at the old cannery."

Brennan could almost see the memories unfolding like a great bed sheet, being unfurled and tossed up dramatically, then slowly settling down in place.

"Yep," James smiled slightly, "we were doing recon, trying to figure out if Ocasio was where PD said he was and if he had Medellin. We figured that would be the easy part. Hard part would be getting him out. Your contacts had also told you that Troopers and maybe Homeland or FBI would be involved very soon, but they were being delayed. You said that if news of the feds got to Ocasio, he'd get spooked, kill Medellin, and run. So we went and had ourselves a stakeout. We listened to Kansas, Styx, and Queen. We ate crappy Stripes burritos and awesome Stripes tacos. We stayed there for almost 36 hours and saw no movement. I had suggested we call it quits once or twice, but you were insistent. Finally, we got proof someone was there. Unfortunately, the proof came in the form of the most disgusting, blood curdling, scream I've ever heard."

James paused. His mouth pursed and his nose wrinkled as if he had just detected some sour, rotting odor.

"We ran in. Neither one of us said we would. We didn't plan anything. We just heard the scream and we ran toward the cannery. We were one mind in that moment. Like when we were kids. Or maybe we just watched too many superhero TV shows. Unfortunately, it wasn't until I saw you draw that I realized I didn't have my gun."

James chuckled humorlessly.

"It was poking into my side with the conceal holster, so I had tucked it under the seat of your car. You told me to stay there and call 911. You run in, saw Gorila digging a freaking Bowie into Medellin's quad and I hear you yelling for them to get on the ground. Ocasio runs out a side door, Gorila goes for his gun, and you go into that creepy autopilot you have and Mozambique him. You immediately back track, figuring you could cut Ocasio off rounding the corner, and he had me." James' face seemed to drop all expression. It was a blank slate of a face, eerily reminiscent of a mannequin, at least to Brennan. "He had that stupid little springblade between my lips and was holding me neck. I hadn't seen him. I had been on the line with 911. The guy really did watch too many movies and was going for a Joker vibe, I think. He said you let him go or he'd kill me."

The rest came rushing back to Brennan.

"Let me go, eh." Ocasio pleaded in a surprisingly squeaky voice. The poor man's Wilson Fisk was wearing a large pair of grey slacks and a sweaty, mustard yellow shirt with the sleeves rolled up. There was blood on his knuckles. Brennan could see James wincing in pain. Ocasio was shaking badly and the newly sharpened springblade was essentially shaving off the corner of James' mouth.

"Let me go and hermanito is set free."

Brennan was sure that he was going to die, but he couldn't let James die first. Brennan thought it would only be a matter of time before his heart exploded from the sheer pressure. His body was focusing the panic and adrenaline into his fight or flight as best as it could, but it wasn't enough.

Ocasio looked around and saw that the car that had taken him there wasn't in this parking lot and would have to be either on the other side, way too far, or hidden. Instead, he saw the car the brothers had arrived in.

"Pass me your keys..." Ocasio ordered, his voice breaking into squeaks twice. His pubescent voice seemed to have been badly miscast to his enormous body.

Without a moment's hesitation, Brennan tossed the keys at Ocasio. Ocasio, who had been expecting him to slide them over, reacted instinctively and reached out for them as Brennan brought his Sig Sauer P250 up in a short arc.

James elbowed Ocasio's solar plexus as he ripped himself out of Ocasio's arms. Ocasio, whose reaction to fear had been to tense up, held the springblade in place as it sliced through James' cheek like a hot knife through butter.

Brennan had his opening. Three shots rang out and James knew the count in Brennan's head.

"One, two, decisecond pause to readjust, One."

James turned around and kneeled, ready to render aid, only to see that all those Failure Drills or Mozambique drills Brennan had done over and over had paid off with exceptional lethality.

James sucked in breath and it sounded wet and disgusting. The way a person may slurp up saliva dribbling out after the dentist gives them a tad too much anesthetic on the bottom lip. Only, he wasn't slurping up saliva. His face featured an awkwardly smooth crimson waterfall, starting at a gorish flap that was his now bisected left cheek.

James ran inside to check on Medellin.

"What the hell are you doing? Jim?! JAMES?!" Brennan yelled. He ripped his button up shirt, revealing a blue-ish tee-shirt with the different designs of the Superman crest through the ages. He found a clean spot on his button up and ran to James. He pressed the shirt to James' cheek and for the first time, James expressed pain.

"Ah! Crap, dude. That burned!" James exclaimed, except it sounded like, "Ah! Craf doof. Tha burn!

"Hold it in place!"

Brennan untied Medellin, but left the knife in. He doubted it had hit the femoral artery, but he would rather not risk it.

When police and ambulance arrived, they had been interviewed and re-interviewed. It was a long process and James stuck with Brennan every step of the way. It was months, especially with Ocasio's family being rich enough to hire a shark of a lawyer, although they were no longer well connected. Turns out the cartel didn't mind a dead underling. Especially one that didn't understand that he was still just that, an underling. The shootings were ruled self-defense of the third person, despite the squaline lawyer's argument that the Mozambique pattern was an "assassination technique". James tendered his resignation to his brother the day after the ordeal was over.

"You know the kick of it all," James murmured during that difficult conversation, with a dour smile that now seemed to extend too far up on his face, "Medellin's Restaurant is still open. We can still eat for free there whenever we want, but he gave in. After seeing how some cops were dirty, after getting kidnapped by a drug dealer with delusions of grandeur and rescued by an ex-cop and his little brother, not the police, he gave in. Ocasio and his people lost what little market they had in town, but the Amaya family picked it up. Medellin happily pays the Amayas a generous percentage tip from all restaurant profits."

He stopped and looked away from Brennan as angry tears began to burn his eyes.

"We almost died to save one person. We almost died to fix a single injustice." He looked up again, his anger overpowering his shame, "We can't do this alone. We're not enough. We've never been enough. I can't keep working like this, Brennie. I can't keep up with your nihilistic view on life."

"Wait a second," Brennan interrupted, "I don't have a-"

"Talk is cheap, big brother. You killed two men without blinking."

"To save a life and then to save your life."

"It should've shaken you more."

"I'd do it again, for you, Jimmy. I'd kill 100 men for you, little brother."

"I KNOW!" James had yelled unexpectedly, not just to Brennan, but to himself. His shame, anger, pain, sadness, it

324

all flowed together, mixing into a murky, muddy, mess of emotion. He began to cry openly.

His voice quivered and growled at the same time, "I know you would, and if the roles were reversed, I'd kill 100 more, but it would hurt me. It would wound me. Killing should not be so easy. I want to save my soul. I want to save your soul. I won't have you kill for me again. I won't put myself in that position again."

"Jimmy, this was a freak occurrence, man. These things rarely-"

"I'm not taking chances, Brennan. I'm leaving. I'm going back."

"Where? To wha-"

"Mom says she talked to the pastor. He's a licensed therapist. I start going to church and he can see me for free."

James' tears had ceased now, but his voice was still unsteady.

"Okay, there's nothing wrong with therapy or church, but don't…"

"I need to leave, Bren. I'll come back for you. We can make our way back. Do you remember going to Sunday school together? We loved it. We loved that joy. We loved having that hope. We loved being close to God."

Brennan looked up, no longer hurt or pleading, but defiant, "I didn't. I just liked being the good guy. I loved being an image of goodness. I loved that I didn't have to be the person I was in my mind. I could be good. Then dad left, then he died, then the panic attacks started getting worse, I

325

lost my job with the department, then I started drinking, and no one stopped me. God didn't swat His big hand out of the sky and squish me like a fly against the wall. He didn't stop that evil in me, so I found a way I could be good and do good here."

"Is that what you wanted, Brennie? For God to swat you away? To die?"

Brennan didn't answer. He didn't need to. James continued.

"You don't get it, Bren. It's not about being the good guy. It's not good versus evil. It's not about evil men becoming good. It's about dead men being brought to life," he paused, "I want to be alive again."

Brennan was silent. His anger had died down. He understood his brother. He wanted to live again too. There was a terrible feeling of longing in his soul. The closest he could come to describing it was being homesick, except, he didn't know his way back, and he didn't think he'd ever find it. He was lost and he did not want the same fate for his brother.

"Okay," Brennan finally broke an awkward silence, "I understand you, bud. I want you to know you're always welcome back. I'll miss you, but maybe this is the best plan for your right now. I hope you find what you're looking for."

James hugged Brennan and Brennan was shocked by a strong jolt of nostalgia. He realized that hugging his larger, stronger, brother was incredibly like hugging his father had been. They both had strong backs and large arms that could squeeze the life out of you, but their hugs were instead very tender and emotional.

The brothers lightly bumped their foreheads and James strolled away towards the door.

"Hey, Jimmy," Brennan called after him and he turned, "if you find your way back, draw me a map or something."

Both brothers smiled at each other.

"Yeah. You once did the same for me," James replied.

James left and Brennan sat down and remained silent for the rest of that day.

Chapter 33

"Did you ever find your way back?" Brennan asked.

"Why do you think I'm here, buddy? I've been chasing after you, trying to bring you back. You resisted me. A lot. Dove headfirst into the bottle and chased everyone away. You'd give me a chance when I was helping you out though. Some of our best, most honest, conversations took place while I held your puke bucket. I think it may be true what they say, 'Los niños y los borrachos no mienten.'"

Brennan chuckled. "I've been around both kids and drunks enough to know that both of them lie. Albeit for very different reasons."

Brennan considered what his brother had said and still couldn't come to terms with it.

"You know, when Ace and Wall went to see me, it triggered a memory. Seeing your apartment did too, but when I try to remember drinking, it's like I see it, but I can't feel it. It feels fake. Like remembering a scene from a movie or something."

"Well," James responded with a quick upward jolt of his eyebrows, "thank God for His grace and miracles. Maybe all you needed was a concussion to get you off the bottle. If I had known that, I would've bopped your noggin way back."

The brothers laughed. Brennan felt good to laugh. He felt good to have his brother again. He felt like he had been gone for a very long time. Memories were starting to come back to him, some gently, those usually true, and some violently and painfully, those seemed to be false, but rather than make him feel complete, the memories highlighted just how much time was lost.

There were too many blanks to fill. Last he remembered, he still worked for the PD. His relationship with his brother and family in general was strained, though mostly free of animosity. He had been taking a medication to help with anxiety, but for the most part, he was toughing it out, riding out the panic attacks in his squad car, when necessary.

There wasn't just a small blank space, but huge gaps between that life three years ago and whichever memory came back. Like a puzzle that seems complete, until you find a few pieces that indicate a second half. He needed to fill in those gaps. He began to feel out of breath. His heart quickened. Pins and needles danced on his lips and he tried to bite them away.

"You're spiraling, Bren," James acknowledged, in a smooth, gentle, but incredibly quick movement, James was sitting next to his smaller, older brother. He wrapped his right arm around Brennan and held Brennan's left fist tight in his own. "Breathe. Count them. 1, 2, 3, 4, hold, 2, 3, 4, out, 2, 3, 4. In, 2, 3, 4…"

"I need my pills," Brennan pleaded, melding the sentence into almost a single syllable. He was trying, and failing, to keep his cool.

"Bud, you haven't taken pills in a long time. Doc said you couldn't drink and take them. You chose the wrong medicine," James caught himself and pulled against the negativity that would certainly not help his brother, "Just keep breathing with me."

James squeezed his brother close. "I'm right here, bud. We're breathing. Our heart is beating. It's okay. We are going to ride this out."

The pressure from his bigger younger brother's embrace was soothing. It sent shockwaves of goosebumps through his entire body. They felt calming against the spreading numbness and tightness. His breath began to deepen and slow, and soon his heart followed suit. James took his previous seat on the couch across from Brennan.

"Hey, bud. Are you going to go into withdrawal on me?"

"What?" Brennan asked, confused and still dazed from the small panic attack.

"The docs said they found a piece of a pill bottle in your leg. I told you, you haven't taken pills in a long time, I need to know, if you remember, am I wrong?"

Brennan tried to remember again. This time he felt like he was pulling the memory out of the ground in his mind. Like a tangled, stubborn weed that refuses to be pulled free. A dull ache began in his head and he stopped.

"Work smarter, not harder," he told James.

"Um... what?"

"Did you tell the doctor that I suffered from anxiety?"

"Yeah, he asked for a complete history."

"So, if a benzo came up on my tox screen, which I'm sure they did, he may not have mentioned it unless it was extraordinarily high levels."

Understanding spread over James' face.

"Always the detective," James smiled.

Brennan grabbed the maroon folder their mother had given him and untwirled the string from the button. He pulled the papers and started looking for a tox screen. James saw it first, it had been peeking from behind some discharge papers.

Brennan let him take the tox screen as he reviewed another lab result.

"Low levels of benzo." James read, "If you were using, at least it wasn't a very high dose, or it wasn't very often, at least it doesn't seem to be."

Brennan barely heard him.

"Look at this," Brennan directed, handing his brother a document with a list of lab results.

"Okay, yeah, I can read a basic tox screen, but this could be in Mandarin and be as meaningful to me," James said handing it back.

"I had slightly to moderately elevated levels of myoglobin, potassium, lactic acid, histamine, nitric oxide and thromboplastin."

"All that means to me is that it sounds like they really did test you for everything."

"It could mean a lot of things," Brennan paused, "but these specific chemicals are indicative of a crush injury. I've seen it in a couple of autopsies that Eve let me sit in on."

"Okay, first of all, still creepy that you don't just wait for the reports like a normal person. Second, no, you didn't have any broken bones, no torn ligaments or muscles…"

"First of all," Brennan replied, "I go in case Eve happens to miss something. Two sets of eyes are better than one. Second, I had all that crazy bruising."

"First of all," James repeated again, jokingly adding a brush of sarcasm to the phrase, "if she is missing something that you're catching, maybe she shouldn't be the M.E. She's like a doctor. She had to study for that. Git gud. Second, you'd have to be freaking Wolverine to heal from crush injuries that quickly or that well, especially if all that was left was bruising."

Brennan knew that James wasn't wrong. The thought of being crushed was terrifying, but it felt right. It seemed the jagged piece fit the open space in the puzzle perfectly.

"Yeah, my brain's just making crazy connections," Brennan admitted, "Hey, at least now we know I was pill popping, though doing so mildly, it seems."

James nodded and put his arm on his brother's shoulder as Brennan replaced the documents into the maroon folder and tossed it onto the coffee table.

Chapter 34

The withdrawal was nowhere near as bad as Brennan would have remembered, had his memory remained intact, but with nothing to pull as reference, Brennan felt like hell. Though he didn't spend all day and night in a constant stupor, as he previously had, his skin would occasionally alternate from being on fire to prickling with a needle sharp cold. He had a migraine for about a week and though he did not vomit, he dry heaved a few times an hour.

Though he hated how it felt, Brennan knew it was pretty mild compared to what could be happening and assumed that his body had really gone through its withdrawals while he slept the cold, half-dead sleep of a coma.

The symptoms grew fainter and farther every day for a week. At the end, he felt better than he had in a very long time.

James was now working with a non-profit that advocated for children and women who were victims of domestic violence. James did a bit of casework, mild investigative work when it was called for, but for the most part he was used as what evangelicals might refer to as a "hedge of protection".

He sat in front of the victims during court. He ensured that they were not intimidated. If the person showed up at the house, the police were called, and James was usually not far behind. James did this while helping and coordinating alternating groups of bikers that dedicated their free time to doing what James might otherwise have to do alone.

The pay wasn't great, which was expected for a non-profit, but it was fulfilling work. James got to live and relive the fantasy where he stood up for the childhood version of his mother over and over again.

Just two months after Brennan moved in with James, AB Investigations re-opened. Brennan kept the name, even though the A was just helping out of brotherly love and courtesy. Still, Brennan saw the spark in James' eyes and mind go off when a case got really interesting. For the most part, James would drive Brennan to certain locations that were part of his cases. Brennan had seemed to develop a fear of driving that was usually controllable, but at times led to panic attacks. He didn't know where it came from since he loved driving when he was growing up. He had no memory of ever fearing it. On the days when he felt the edge of the anxiety beginning to stretch over him, he'd ask James for a ride.

Two months after AB Investigations opened and four months after he was out of the hospital, Brennan and James had a very serious talk and made an equally serious decision. Brennan would let his apartment go and move into James' spare room. He'd help with bills and grow his depleted savings back up. They focused on the logistics and what they called "understandings", and refused to refer to as "ground rules", but internally both knew this was going to happen and had in fact been looking forward to it. Brennan was also secretly hoping James would join him on cases again, at least on an official part time basis, rather than being his chauffeur

Brennan and James took James' truck to go pick up his belongings. Brennan did not recognize the apartment building. The buildings were dreary, tan bricked, blocks. Each building looked exactly like the last and were more differentiated by the graffiti on them than by any decoration or difference in structure.

"Well, I knew the life of a P.I. wasn't exactly luxurious. Although, now I can see why you always offered to pick my stuff up, instead of bringing me here. You probably didn't want me to get depressed and spiral or something."

"Mmm… no. That wasn't exactly it," James responded with a cringing, tight lipped smile.

Brennan looked at him curiously, but neither spoke until they entered the apartment.

The door was an awful, dusty green and bore the number 1 and then a shadow where there was supposed to be a 3. James opened the door, giving it a shove to unstick the ill-fitting door from the frame. It squeaked open loudly.

"Oh," Brennan whispered, his voice just audible, "that's why."

The apartment was mostly bare. In truth it looked more like an abandoned hotel room.

The floor was smooth concrete, not tiled. The walls were a bland off white and didn't feature a single frame or decor of any kind. There was a full-sized bed with white and blue striped sheets and looked like it may have a thread count in the double digits. Folded on the corner of the bed was one of the itchy, wooly blankets that charities give out in the winter. Two pillows, pillowcases matching the sheets, were spread on the top of the bed.

To the left of the entrance there was a Sterilite plastic drawer tower that stood five drawers high. Brennan hadn't seen it, but he suddenly knew that was, from top to bottom, boxers, socks, t-shirts, dress pants, and jeans. Next to the drawer tower was a completely inornate armoire. It was nothing more than a tall wooden box with doors. On the side of the bed nearest to the entrance was a nightstand with a lamp and the coiled cord of a cell phone charger on top of it. Again, without seeing, Brennan knew there was also a spring loaded, under-desk concealment plate and holster. On the other side, closest to the wall and bathroom, was an ironing board. In front of the bed, next to the wall, where there should have been a proper dresser, maybe a console with a television, there was a thick yoga mat, a weight bench, and some dumbbells. Just ahead of these, still against the wall opposite the bed, was a mini fridge with a small microwave and a single burner electric range on top of it. Brennan walked towards the restroom and turned on the light. The sink was outside of the restroom, visible directly ahead from the room's entrance. The countertop was cheap laminate and held a cup with a toothbrush, toothpaste, and floss, and a small soap holder. The sink was immaculate white, but the faucet had begun to armor itself with limescale. In the restroom, to the left of the sink, there was one standard toilet and a bathtub with only a slightly opaque, vinyl curtain.

Brennan looked at James after he finished exploring the room with disgusted incredulity. "Why did I live this way, James?"

James looked down and appeared to be ashamed.

"After you were asked to quit the force, you isolated yourself a lot. You and I were close because of the business, but even then, I rarely came to visit you in the apartment. I'd suggest it and you'd say you would rather meet somewhere public or at my place. I knew you felt bad, but I had no idea about this until you asked me to pick up some of your stuff. You chose to live in these," he paused to think of a delicate word, "austere living conditions. It was not poverty or lack of support from us. I could swear, big brother, no one punishes you like you punish yourself."

"I can see that. I had a life of zero indulgence." He chuckled. I'm guessing that's why this version of me is in shape."

"What?" James looked perplexed and felt there was a hidden weight in that comment.

"What?" Brennan replied in kind.

"You said this "version of me", what does that mean?"

Brennan thought about it and questioned whether he had really said that.

A flash.

"I'm comin' to getchu, da-ee!"

The flashes had become less frequent and less painful, but they still happened. The flashes were now usually centered around that beautiful little girl with the tight curls and jade green eyes that weren't quite hers.

"You okay?" James asked.

"Yeah, why?"

"You zoned out for a second there. Everything okay?"

"Yeah, it's just, this is very disturbing but, it oddly feels like home."

"Which is why I wouldn't let you come before. I was afraid you'd see this, flash back to the pain and disappointment you were going through and you'd revert. Stop talking to mom, stop talking to me. You scared me, bud."

It was now Brennan's turn to feel ashamed.

"The Medellin case was the proverbial last straw. I still loved you then. I still love you now, but the way you unblinkingly took out those men… it didn't feel like you anymore. It didn't feel like my big brother that would stay up later than me working on my school projects. The big brother that taught me to respect the custodian as much as a CEO. The big brother that taught me that all life is precious and that there is always hope. When we were unsure you'd come back from the coma, I was devastated, but once you woke up and lost so much time. Lost so much of who you were," James hesitated for a second, choked back tears, pushed against shame, "I was glad for the coma. I know that's terrible. I know that's selfish. I just felt like I finally had my big brother back."

Brennan put his hand on James' shoulder and James shook. He cleared his throat and pointed at the armoire.

"Enough mushy stuff, Brennie. Let's see what we need to move out. Let's pick up some heavy stuff, get some testosterone pumping right now." James chuckled and wiped a tear from his eye.

Brennan walked over to the world's most generic armoire and opened the double doors. A few dress shirts, a coat, one blue blazer, one black blazer, and a black zip up hoodie were all hung up across the bar that made this armoire more of a makeshift closet. Below them were two small drawers. Brennan opened these and found a shoulder holster, an appendix-carry concealed holster, a side hip carry concealed holster, an open carry hip holster, and a drop leg holster.

"Geez, I really liked holsters," Brennan muttered half joking.

"I don't think it was the holsters. It's like ladies with nice purses. The purse looks nice, but what really matters is the contents.

The second drawer had a foam liner with cutouts holding empty magazines.

Brennan stood to full height again and split the coats and shirts apart, unable to prevent a cheesy, dramatic flair to the motion. On a small shelf, there was a green ammo bag with the name "Brent Ramirez" on it and right next to it was a black safe with a numerical keypad and a small, calculator like display.

"Hmm, I hope you remember the code to that. I tried to get it open to take them out and take them home, you know, put them somewhere safe, but I couldn't get the code."

Brennan looked at James with mild surprise.

"Really?"

"Yep," James replied with more than just a pinch of disappointment, "I tried your birthday in all its combinations, four digits and six digits, I tried first four and last four of your social, I tried first six and last six, I tried your academy graduation dates, I tried your high school and college graduation, I even tried your old school ID number. Couldn't crack it."

"Oh, little brother," Brennan huffed with mock disappointment, a sly smirk spreading across his face, "your big brother hasn't come back. I never left you."

Brennan punched in 10-18-93 and a small green light turned on. Brennan turned to smile at James. James reciprocated.

"Well, shoot dang. That should've been an easy one for me, huh?"

Inside the safe were a compact .40 Sig Sauer P250, a 9mm Sig Sauer P320, and a .45 Springfield XDM. Each had a magazine next to it. There were also flashlight and laser attachments to them. Behind them, Brennan could see the back half of the safe was full of ammunition.

"Well, at least I know where my money was going." Brennan's mouth eased into an easy, lopsided grin.

James tried to return his brother's smile a second time, but the best he could do was a pathetic little curve on each end of his mouth.

"You're not going to go back, are you?" The concern was evident in James' voice. It wasn't the voice of a man, it was the voice of a kid brother.

"No." Brennan said, "I don't know why I went down the path I went, but I don't want to do that again. I'm spending time with family, you even got me going to church again, I want to be better."

James' smile greatly improved.

It only took two trips to move all of Brennan's things. His Spartan, minimalistic, personality void lifestyle may have been indicative of deep-rooted depression, but at least it made moving easy.

Brennan enjoyed life and even realized he could have pride in his basic investigative work. It was mostly infidelity cases. He'd follow around a spouse, take a picture of them kissing someone they shouldn't be kissing or followed them to a hotel room and took time stamped pictures of them arriving, of their vehicle, and of them and their extramarital partner leaving. Simple, easy, and usually pretty clean on his end. The sloppy part was for the divorce lawyers.

Six months after moving in with his brother, something more complex than cheating partners came across his desk.

An old man, 81 years old to be exact, had died. Doctors found the cause of death to be a heart attack. This was no big deal, except that his wife insisted that he had been poisoned.

The old man, Ricardo Marzo, had once been a young man with a dream. He wanted to open a business of his own, be his own boss, and provide for his family.

One failed restaurant and a minorly successful boutique later, he decided to close the boutique, take the profits and invest in real estate. He soon realized that while he was terrible at selling food and not great at selling products, he was incredible at selling dreams.

He could take a shack and paint a picture of a home in the buyer's mind. One successful flip turned into two, two turned into four, and four turned into many more. Eventually he invested his profits in a couple of duplex condos on South Padre Island. Then more money came in and he flipped the duplexes into a fourplex in town, a low income, subsidized housing project that turned an empty street into two rows of apartments that he was being paid rent for. Even though the tenants sometimes missed their payment, the government did not.

In the years leading up to the end of his life, Marzo was more than just a little well off. Retired from his lifelong career, children grown up, and his wife a long-time member of the dearly departed, Marzo fell into a depression. He found a renewed joie de vivre in a woman named Camila. A woman who admired his tenacity, his intelligence, and his strength. A woman who listened to the stories of his youth for hours on end. A woman who fell head over heels in genuine love for him. A woman who also happened to be forty years his junior.

Of his three children, two were successful. His eldest, Ricardo Jr. was a nephrologist in honor of his mother, who had died of kidney disease, and his daughter Sofia was a family law attorney. His youngest was undoubtedly what someone might call the black sheep of the family.

Growing up wealthy, Arturo Marzo had squandered every opportunity he was handed for education and advancement. Arturo aspired to be the prodigal son. He wanted to get his riches and go be free, just avoid the part where the prodigal son runs out of money and goes back humbly to his father. He would figure his way out of that one. Somehow.

Arturo was upset that his father had cut him off unless he chose a career path that wasn't attempting to be a four-chord rock star on the wrong side of forty five years old. The ultimate man child, Arturo felt his actually long-gone youth was passing him by whilst his father refused to die.

He had never cared for his father, but after a massive heart attack failed to fulfill Arturo's wishes, Arturo returned home and was suddenly reformed and willing to assist in the care of his father. Camila was wary of him and had been further warned by Ricardo Jr. and Sofia to be vigilant of Arturo.

Mr. Marzo had round-the-clock professional care, but Camila administered his medication personally since Mr. Marzo had developed a strong aversion to swallowing pills. After a few weeks, there was an error at the pharmacy. Their system showed that Mr. Marzo was out of refills for his beta blocker, but Ms. Marzo's bottle clearly showed she had one refill. The system also showed that both bottles were given on the same day, within minutes. While that should not have been done, it was not uncommon for the pharmacy to make certain exceptions for Mr. Marzo. After some back and forth, the pharmacy decided it must have been an error. Someone had simply double logged the medication given out. They "fixed" the issue and gave her a new bottle.

Mr. Marzo became symptomatic slowly. First blurred vision, then lightheadedness. Camila found Arturo in his father's room supposedly comforting him and giving him water. Shortly after that visit, Mr. Marzo fell asleep and, despite frantic intervention from the night care nurses, never woke up.

When the doctors decided an 81-year-old man who had recently suffered a heart attack died from a completely natural second heart attack, Arturo became upset. He kept insinuating and then flat out telling doctors that there was probably an issue with his medicine. He began spreading a rumor that his hateful, gold digging, baby stepmother was anxious to get her share of his money.

Though the malicious rumor was not widely believed, certain aspects had gotten the attention of some police. Specifically, some people in administration that Arturo had made deals with, in exchange for making tickets and DWI charges disappear.

Mr. Marzo was thankfully not yet in the ground and Camila went to visit an old friend of hers, a young woman she had babysitted once or twice, who happened to be the county medical examiner.

Eve recommended AB Investigations and now Brennan was doing his best to get James on board.

"What do you say, Jimmy? Want to bring in the A game to AB Investigations? It's gonna be good, man. Plus, the family is well off. A good pay day, an interesting case, greasing up the cogs in your brain. Let's go!"

James smiled. He loved seeing his brother so passionate about something. Every time his brother smiled, every time his brother geekily yelled out, "Excelsior!" after hitting a breakthrough in a case, every time he saw his brother being happy, James thanked God for that coma.

"It sounds awesome, Bren,"

"...but..."

"but I've got to do some work. I'm helping to plan an awareness event slash fundraiser, and I want to see how many biker groups I can get involved. Some people around here go crazy for tricked out hogs."

"Mmmkay, first of all, never refer to a motorcycle as a hog again. It's weird when you're a guy designing flyers behind a desk. Second, dude, this is a crazy good case and Eve is starting the autopsy in," he looked at his watch, "45 minutes."

"First of all,"James replied, "this is America, and not just America, this is freaking Texas. I'm free as can be, homie, I say what I want."

Brennan laughed and put up his palms as if to say, 'alright, you got me'.

"Second, I don't like autopsies. You know that. I don't get why you like being there for them."

"Okay," Brennan sighed, "I'm not having that discussion again. You find dead people icky, I get it. Anyway, I figured you'd be busy. I got an Uber. It's like a minute away." Brennan headed for the door. "Love you little brother, I'll see you in a few hours. I'm gonna go crack open a cold one with the boys." Brennan grinned mischievously.

"DUDE!" James yelled after him, "You gotta stop referring to autopsies that way!"

Brennan laughed raucously as he closed the door.

Chapter 35

Eve was among the top three most intimidating women that Brennan knew. At first glance, she was physically diminutive, standing at 5'2", but she was also 110 lbs of well packed muscle. She had dark, olive toned skin, eyes so dark they bordered on black, curled up, jet black hair that reached halfway down her back even in a high ponytail. She was wearing a surgical apron, protective glasses, and a face mask yet, even through the glasses and mask, you could see her fiercely intelligent, often distrusting eyes. Even through the baggy apron that only tightened on her small but solid waist, you could see a body that wasn't trying to be pretty or hot, it wasn't trying to impress anyone, or catch someone's attention. Eve's body was prepared, fueled, and sculpted for the sole purpose of never being powerless. This was a woman who could school you, beat the crap out of you, and then patch you up and send you on your way. Brennan looked at his friend, had an instant feeling of gratitude that she was his friend, and then wondered if perhaps some trauma led her to this obsessive, Sisyphean goal of excellence.

"You know, Ramirez, I think Camila actually loved this oversized leather bag," she quipped. Her voice was muffled by the mask, but you could still discern a sultry tone that gave her low pitched voice a decidedly feminine quality.

Brennan sported the same protective gear, but he was not allowed to touch the body, much less pull out organs to weight them. Instead he just stood, absolutely raptured by this grim job that Camila performed quite artfully.

"Yeah, it seems like it. Pretty weird, but I guess everyone's got a kink," Brennan replied, equally muffled.

"Well, in the end, it's the person that matters. Outward beauty is only skin deep. Believe me, I would know."

Brennan gave a humorless "Hm" closed mouth chuckle. He walked towards the corpse that was once Ricardo Marzo and began to closely analyze it, inch by inch, without touching, of course.

"Just from the read you got on Camila, what do you think, think the kid did it?" Eve inquired as she removed the liver and looked at it carefully.

"Well, to clarify, this 'kid' is only a kid in his grown man brain. As to his guilt, I'm not sure, but I'm quite sure Camila had nothing to do with it. No part of her body language showed nervousness or fear, just grief," Brennan replied as he looked closely at the feet.

"Some people are great actors, they can lie to your face and look honest as hell. I've met some Oscar worthy liars. I've dated some Oscar worthy liars."

"Well, the face is actually pretty easy to hide. Some people practice fake tells and then show those tells with small so-called white lies only so their major lies can be hidden, but there are things that ninety nine out of a hundred people will not consider in their non-verbals. The lower you go on the body, the less a person can hide their intentions and thoughts."

Brennan had his face about two inches away from the corpse's left foot.

"I figured the honesty would peak right around the groin. Man or woman, that thing will make you lie and then betray you. By the way, forensic toxicology will be a few weeks, but I'm willing to bet this dude overdosed on the betas. Hearts crap of course, but his liver has what looks like recent damage. Kidneys are relatively fine. Only normal wear and tear. His meds were lipid based, broken down by the liver, not kidneys."

She looked up from the kidneys that she was currently handling and to Brennan, who was hunched over the left foot. "You know, I get it, the lower you go, the harder it is to lie, but I think the only lying homeboy is doing is lying dead."

"Homeboy had athlete's foot." Brennan stated matter-of-factly.

"Ew, gross, gumshoe." Eve cringed behind her protective goggles.

"Really?" Brennan's face was unmistakably incredulous, even behind the protective gear, "You just held a pair of kidneys in your hands, but athlete's foot grosses you out."

"I'm good with dead stuff. That fungus is probably still alive. It's a type of ringworm, you know." Disgust still tinged Eve's otherwise pretty face.

"I need you to spread his toes for me," Brennan requested.

All trace of disgust and hesitation instantly left Eve and she rushed to Brennan's side and pulled apart the second and third toes as Brennan was suggesting.

"Excelsi-freaking-or." Brennan's face lit up.

"Is that a needle mark?"

"Yep. Maybe the perp thought it would be harder to see with the fungus. Maybe he just wanted to push Marzo along," Brennan postulated. "Heavy dose of beta blockers mixed with a little bit of heroine, hell, even some insulin would've put a fragile old guy six feet deep."

"Good job, gumshoe! I guess getting your noggin rearranged didn't knock out the good stuff."

Brennan smiled at her, "I cannot wait for the toxicology reports," he stood to full height, "alrighty, Eve. Wrap this burrito up tight, we'll take it to go. Let's do this."

"This isn't Chipotle or religion, Ramirez. You don't get to just pick the things you like and then up and leave." Eve was fairly certain most people would have missed the humor in her tone, but not Brennan.

"Just a burrito joke, but somehow it got political," Brennan muttered jokingly and rather quickly.

"I need to do the rest of the exam." She looked up at him and placed her bloody gloved hands on her apron.

They locked eyes for a fleeting moment that highlighted all the romantic tension they had felt on and off in the years of their friendship.

"I'm happy for you, Bren. You're not someone I would've liked to have seen on my table."

"Does that mean you have a list of people you would like to see on your table?" Brennan teased.

Eve kept a straight, stoic expression. It wasn't until Brennan's eyes widened and his eyebrows perked that she began laughing at her silent joke. They shared the laughter and their eyes locked for just a second. Eve broke the strange silence. "You don't have to stick around for the rest of it. Maybe you and James can start working on a plan. Anything else interesting comes up, I'll let you know."

"Okay, sounds good." He paused a moment, "Hey, kidding aside, I appreciate you helping me get back on my game. This case is amazing."

Eve grinned at this. Even with the mask on, the height of her cheeks and eyes told the story.

"Well, Camila is an old friend, and more than that, she knows my mom, so I wanted to refer her to the best. I hate getting yelled at."

"Yeah, I would not want to be on that lady's bad side. Your mom can do some damage. She's like a black belt in guilt tripping people."

Eve laughed and removed her bloodied gloves so she could give him a hug or at least a handshake.

Brennan immediately noticed the single tan line on her left ring finger. Eve noticed his gaze.

"I'm sorry," he apologized, "I heard about you and Izzy."

"Yeah, wasn't meant to be, I guess. She didn't respect me," Eva explained. "She wanted to take a break. Like Ross and Rachel or something. See other people." She scoffed, "You know I'm no one's back up plan, Ramirez. I wasn't about to be hers."

Brennan nodded silently.

"I'm surprised you never took your shot, Bren," Eve remarked.

Brennan felt a strange twinge. Like internal goosebumps in his mid-back. Not just his first name, but a nickname version of his first name, sounded almost wrong coming from her.

"Well, you were pretty open about being bi, even when we were younger. I felt you were out of my league to start with. Smart, pretty, tough as nails, AND I had twice the regular competition."

Eve chuckled.

"I guess it's a hindsight thing, Ramirez." She smiled a sweet, crooked smile, "Now, I think back and wonder what it would've been to settle down with the smart kid who was sweet, kind, and tough, but not too tough to enjoy musicals."

They shared another laugh.

"I think in the end there was more to it though," she continued, "you never really did get over being hung up on that one girl. I'm sure you remember. Church girl, pretty, with an attitude like a Rockaleta. You know, sweet as candy, but layered with spice all the way through. You know the one... and like I said, I'm not anybody's back up plan."

She finished with a smile. Brennan returned it.

The great investigator, well-versed in nonverbal communication, confident in his ability to read people, completely missed the megaton hints Eve had dropped throughout their friendship, but it may have been for the better. There was a spark, but something told him it would've been explosive. Awesome, brilliant, fiery, and gone before you could appreciate what it was.

He said his goodbyes and left, their relationship intact and in the perfect place it was meant to be. A deep and loving friendship.

Brennan decided to walk part of the way home. It was an unseasonably nice day in deep South Texas. The weather was sitting Reliant K style, sunny with a high of 75, instead of the common cook-an-egg-on-the-sidewalk hot. He would probably get bored and get an Uber somewhere down the line. He figured this all went under the expenses line item on Camila's bill anyway.

It was a nice day, nice breeze, break in the case, reconnection with a good friend, and his anxiety was idling at a lazy purr. As some say, everything was coming up Milhouse, which made it the perfect opportunity for fate to check in.

Brennan had walked three blocks and was making his trek towards a crosswalk when a woman caught his eye. Brennan was a man, and like most healthy, red-blooded, American men, he appreciated a good-looking woman. What Brennan was not in the habit of doing was being a creeper and staring at them, especially anywhere below their face. Still, the woman waiting for the light at the crosswalk drew his attention and quickened his heart with a nervous excitement rather than fear or panic. She was wearing jeans that were probably a tad too tight around her curvy bottom, a pair of black Chuck Taylors, and a green shirt with tour dates on the back.

The woman heard his steps and turned around, causing him to shamefully and instinctively turn away rather quickly. He pointed his face up and away as if he was looking at the sky, sure that he was blushing noticeably.

"Brennan?" A sweet voice asked.

Brennan looked down at the woman and his heart stopped, then suddenly, everything stopped. Not just in him, but around him, the entire world, the very fabric of space and time, everything ceased motion. In a split second, the moment passed.

"Deidre?" He awkwardly uttered, replying to her question with a question.

"Oh my gosh, Brennan!" Deidre ran at him and threw her arms around his neck.

Her touch was electric. Buzzing spread from her skin to his neck, through his bones, to his fingers, toes, and that place Eve commended for honesty.

"It's been such a long time!" she added, and Brennan read a sincere glee in her eyes.

"Yeah, it's been a while," Brennan agreed. He tried to swallow. His mouth had gone sandpaper dry. His heart raced and the buzzing sensation pulsed through him intoxicatingly.

"Well, I'm not sure if I'm in love or dying, but I think it's definitely one or the other," he thought to himself.

"How are you? I heard about your…" she hesitated for a split second, but long enough for Brennan and his currently panicky and hyperactive awareness to catch it, "accident. You look all better now." She said this giving him a once over, head to toe, as if she was inspecting the evidence of her statement.

Brennan's heart slowed a bit and the anxious buzz reduced in intensity as he noticed she was the one blushing now.

"Yeah, I'm doing much better." He smiled nervously. "How have you been, how's your mom?"

Brennan was suddenly annoyed by the fact that as soon as she had released his neck, she had tucked her left-hand part way into her side pocket in that peculiar way she had, like she was leaning her whole self into the pocket. He felt an urgency to check for a ring.

"She's the same." Deidre's million-watt smile faltered a bit, "I'm actually on my way to the gas station," she pointed with her left hand towards the Stripes across the street and Brennan's heart sank, "I just picked her up this morning all the way at El Hoyo. She's started going further than the 8-Ball to throw me off." Her smile was completely gone now, "She had just hit five months sober. A personal record for her."

"I'm sorry," Brennan looked down at his feet, "I didn't mean to bring that up, I just…" he felt word vomit coming, "I mean, at least she's making progress, maybe this time she'll hit the six months,"

"Nope, that's not right," he scolded himself,

"Or 9 months, or a year, you know one day at a time," he stammered and once more felt heat rise in his face.

"Idiot…"

To his surprise, her sunshine rivaling beam returned. "You know, when we were," another split-second hesitation, "talking, I always had to give you the bright side. It makes me happy that you can find it on your own now."

Deidre raised her left hand for the dorkiest, most adorable, high five proposal Brennan could remember seeing.

Brennan gave her a high five and his face automatically feigned surprise as the second bout of word vomit hit him.

"Oh, wow! Are you married?" He pretended to just now be noticing the ring.

"Oh, this," she said looking down at and removing it from her hand, "it's my grandmother's."

She handed him the ring and signaled the inside. A fading inscription read, "4-20-50".

"Ah, your grandma got married on 4/20," he remarked stupidly.

"Yeah," Deidre chuckled, "coincidentally, to a man who ended up being a drug dealer. Anyway, I wear it when I gotta rescue my mom from bars. It doesn't stop all pervert strangers from hitting on me while they're hyped on their liquid courage, but it deters some. I just forgot to take it off."

Brennan did his best to suppress what would have been an extraordinarily wide smile for him.

"Anyway," Deidre continued suddenly, "I should go, I gotta get back to Misty before she gets pissy." She scrunched her face in a way that was awfully familiar to Brennan, though he failed to recall from where, "Hmm… that didn't quite rhyme like it did in my head." She giggled and smiled her starlight smile, "Anyway, we should hang out, catch up some time."

"Yeah, definitely!" Brennan could not suppress the smile this time, "I'll give you my card." He took a business card from his wallet and then cringed, "Ah, that's kind of pretentious, isn't it? 'I'll give you my card'."

Deidre somehow brightened her smile. "Not at all, Mister Fancy Businessman. My people will call your people."

They both laughed bashfully, "I'll text you, and then you'll have my number," Deidre told him as she flicked the card up between two fingers.

"Sounds good. It was great seeing you!"

"Is great too much? Should I have just gone with good? Or nice?"

"I know! Great seeing you too!"

She hugged him again and gave him a kiss on the cheek.

"I'll text you!" she called out as she crossed the street, looking back at him.

"Look both ways!" he called after her.

That made his head swim and the buzzing, the malicious buzzing, kicked up a notch. He waited until Deidre was far enough away from him that she couldn't see him well and then he bent down as if he was tying the laces of his black work boots. Instead, he reached into a small pouch he had sewn in and pulled out a quadrisected, white tablet. He broke off a fourth of the Xanax and tossed it in his mouth, clearly underestimating the severity of his dry mouth. He squeezed his eyes shut as the jagged little square crawled down his esophagus.

Chapter 36

"Deidre? The church girl? The younger one?" James asked, already knowing the answer.

"Yeah, man. She's still really sweet. Still really pretty."

"Does she still fill out a pair of jeans miles better than she had any right to?"

"Really, dude?" Brennan reproached with an exasperated expression, "I thought church was doing you good."

James smiled, his eyebrows raised high on his forehead, waiting for a response.

"She's gorgeous, okay, yeah, she's…" Brennan exhaled heavily, "probably out of my league."

"Don't say that, dude. You're a decent looking guy, super smart, a business owner, you can't grow a beard, so you'll look young for a while, and you're genuinely a good guy."

"I'm an amnesiac, recovering addict, with a slight weight problem," Brennan retorted.

"Ah, Brennie, I can always count on you to find the dark cloud in the silver lining. She's got daddy issues AND mommy issues, now that I think of it. She spends her free time babysitting her mom, so you'll probably be super interesting to her." James paused and seemed to think something over in silence, "You know, she probably runs her house, so she probably cooks super well too."

"I don't need her to cook for me. If I wanted a mom, I'd go for an older woman."

"Didn't we discuss how you would always go for older women?" James inquired with a sly smile.

Brennan seemed to be realizing this just now, "Oh, Lord, that certainly explains a lot."

James chuckled. "So, when's the big date?"

"Um… no date yet. I gave her my card so she could call me." Brennan blushed and immediately turned away from James, pretending to focus on making his way to the kitchen.

"You gave her your card?" James marveled with a hint of distaste in his voice.

"I know, kind of douchey, it just happened." Brennan's face felt even hotter and he knew that he probably looked like a beet at that point. "It is what it is, let's focus on business."

James laughed. "Alright, bud. How was the autopsy?"

"Actually, it was very interesting. Eve won't have the toxicology report for a few weeks, but she's convinced damage to the organs and a small pockmark I found between the vic's toes strongly suggests a combo of beta blocker OD with some assistance from morphine or heroin. I think the prodigal son killed his dad."

"Just like that?"

"Well, still need to get the tox report and find actual evidence to get the cops into this loop. It'll be a bit difficult since the prodigal and stepmom live in the same house. My plan is to ask her to move out temporarily. I'll keep an eye on the kid, he'll get sloppy, and I'll find the evidence the police need."

"This guy you keep calling a kid," James began, confused, "isn't he like 40?"

"Physically, yeah."

"Oh, so we have like a Tom Hanks in *Big* scenario?" James teased.

"No, more like immature, ungrateful, man-child scenario." Brennan clarified, obviously annoyed with his little brother going out of his way to make a bad joke, "Payday is pretty good. 5K up front, another 10 if he's arrested. An extra 15 down the road if he's convicted. Of course, plus expenses"

"Dang, she really wants him put away," James mused, his eyes wide with the surprise of the dollar amounts and the widow's determination.

"Well, to her, this isn't just about clearing her name. It's about taking the guy that killed her husband and nailing him to the freakin wall."

"Dude was getting ready to bite the dust either way." James paused when he saw his brother's stern face turn to him, "Hey, I'm just playing devil's advocate. The defense may argue that there was no point in killing daddy. Just needed to wait him out. Not win, just outlast."

"He wanted Camila out too. Bigger share for him. I think he really hated her. Maybe resented his father for managing to find happiness, even at his age. For filling the void that he had been trying to fill his entire life."

"Phrasing," James replied.

Brennan shook his head with a slight smile, "I think the execution is actually pretty smart. Arturo probably had potential before he smoked and drank it away."

"So, we break this case, hand it over to the police, nice and tidy so they don't mess it up, and get paid?"

"We?" Brennan questioned

"I'm in."

"Then, yes. That's the gist of it."

"Sounds like a plan." James clapped his hands and rubbed them together, "So, about Deidre."

As if on cue, one of Chewbacca's signature growls roared from Brennan's pocket.

"You're going to want to change that nerd ringtone if you actually get the date," James told his brother, pointing at the phone's outline in his pocket.

Brennan smirked but the concern apparent in his eyes showed he was considering it may actually be a good idea. He removed the phone from his pocket and saw a notification from a number not saved in his contact list. He pressed the notification and lay his finger over the fingerprint reader on the back of the phone. The phone screen brightened and an orange bubble with white text came up on a black field.

"Hey, Bren. This is my #. Hope to hear from u soon. - D"

Brennan made an effort to subdue his reaction, but all the same, he could feel his face warming and the left corner of his mouth pulled up with suppressed joy. He clicked the number to add it as a contact and quickly typed, "Deidre" but drew a blank for her last name. Immediately frustrated, as he usually was when he found a new dark spot in his memory, he took a deep breath and exhaled slowly. He closed his eyes and fought to remember. He could almost feel the name, it was there, he just couldn't reach it. He pressed on despite an achy throb rising in his temples.

"There," he thought and immediately after, perhaps even before that thought was fully processed, the world disappeared.

Everything was hazy, bright, and there was a delicious aroma in the air, like an old library, full of books that waft their unique fragrance to lure in curious readers.

"... and do you Deidre Nadine Morales, take Brennan Donovan Ramirez to be your lawfully wedded..."

Brennan felt a hard shove against his chest and then a very distant pain on the left side of his hip. He felt himself come awake and instinctively kicked out and flailed. He sat up and realized he was on his brother's couch.

"What the hell, man?" Brennan's panicked voice cracked.

"I'm sorry, man, I couldn't reach you in time to catch you, so I pushed you hard enough for you to hit the couch and not the coffee table." James was now kneeling in front of his brother and holding his shoulders. "Are you okay, man? I haven't seen you collapse that way in a while."

"Yeah, I hadn't had flashes like that in a long time." Brennan swallowed the trickle of saliva left on his desert tongue and exhaled. His heart's gallop slowed to a trot.

"What did you see?"

Brennan looked up at James, rolled his shoulders, and said, "Nothing. Well something, but I can't remember anymore. Geez, these things feel like crap. I'd almost forgotten." Brennan rolled his shoulders again and chuckled in what seemed like relief to James.

He picked up his phone, saw it wasn't cracked, and then noticed the blinking cursor on the screen still sitting next to

'Deidre'. He placed both thumbs on the edge of the screen and deftly added, "N. Morales". He stared at the name for a long time as wave after wave of goosebumps rippled and erupted across his skin.

Chapter 37

Brennan had convinced Camila to go stay at a hotel for a few days, giving Arturo free reign of the home. For three days, Arturo had now been home alone.

The home that the ghost of Arturo's potential haunted was a two-story American Craftsman style house. It had a wraparound porch made of dark red cedar, an exterior of stony brick ranging in different shades of gray and forest green wood panels. It was a beautiful, rustic, image to behold, but there was more to it than that.

The closest neighbor to the house was roughly a hundred yards away. Brennan and James had rented it as an Airbnb for their stakeout. As Brennan sat in the neighbor's sunroom with a pair of binoculars and his Nikon, he felt an inexplicable wave of nostalgia as he stared at the house. His mind drifted as he stared and he may have stayed in that semi-catatonic state for quite a bit longer, had it not been for the unexpected tear that rolled down his cheek. Brennan jumped in his seat and wiped it away with his index finger. He stared at the moisture on the rounded, swirling pattern of his fingerprint and pondered on the alien sorrow dwelling in him.

"Anything?" James asked as he walked back into the sunroom with two cans of chilled Sprite Zero.

"No. He hasn't left the house. No visitors besides the blue Impala making the delivery a couple of hours ago," Brennan replied, successfully hiding his emotion.

"Has Ace gotten back to you on the partial plate we managed to get?"

"No, not yet."

"Dang it." James sat on a wicker chair with overstuffed, floral pattern, cushions strapped to it, "Want to play Mind Sparks?"

Mind Sparks was a game that James and Brennan had made up and played on long road trips into Mexico when they were children in a pre-smartphone era. They continued playing it when they were bored and couldn't sleep in the room they shared in their teens, and eventually, on the stakeouts they had while working together.

The object of the game is to let your mind wander and wait for a random thought, usually a question, to materialize and they'd discuss it, sparking conversations that sometimes ended after three minutes and sometimes went on for hours.

"Yeah, sure," Brennan groaned as he sat up straight in his wicker chair, a twin sibling of the wicker chair James was using.

They both went quiet as they stared out of the enormous bay window that framed the sunroom.

"What do you think we would've done if this place wasn't an AirBnB?" James asked first.

"Camp out on the bed of your truck in the corn field across the road. Pay the owner for the space and discretion," Brennan replied almost immediately, making it apparent that he had considered the question already.

"Yeah. Stakeouts aren't as easy as in the movies when you live out in Nowhere, Texas."

Brennan responded to James' observation with the short, nasal, puff of air that people sometimes consider a chuckle and a subtle nod.

Another couple minutes of silence, then James took another turn.

"Why do you think we have some white people names?"

Brennan chuckled, a true chuckle this time.

"Yeah," James began to elaborate, "You're Brennan Donovan... Ramirez." He laughed and then resumed, "I'm James Alexander Ramirez. I mean, at least when I was in Ms. Garcia's Spanish class, I could be Jaime Alejandro." He laughed again.

Brennan smiled at his brother and leaned forward, "Well, my first name, is a combo of mom and dad's name, you knew that."

"Yeah, but what did they combine for Donovan?"

"I think Donovan is an homage to our Irish ancestry on mom's side. Then you were also a combo of mom and dad in a way."

"Really? How come I never knew that?"

"Because people often create a deep, meaningful name for their beloved and long-awaited child, then upon meeting the little hellion, they immediately forget all that," Brennan said with a wry smile.

James backhanded Brennan's right shoulder and asked, "So, how am I a combination of them?"

"Well, both wanted to name your something different. Mom wanted James, after the apostle James. She liked James because he was close enough to Jesus to witness the transfiguration and because he was impetuous and outspoken, like her, a child of thunder."

Both boys smiled, separately and not looking at each other, at the thought of their tough, crazy, momma bear and the way she always said what was on her mind, regardless of the often-negative consequences.

"I guess she missed the part that James was also the first to be martyred," Brennan muttered.

"Such a Negative Nancy, Bren."

"Dad, on the other hand, wanted to name you Alexander, as in, the Great."

James nodded with a smug and satisfied smile, "Nice."

"Dad had been super into Sun Tzu and Alexander of Macedonia at that time. Big on power, battle, and manipulation. He saw life that way." Brennan's smile waned as he again began to focus on Arturo's house again.

"Seriously, Bummer Brennan?" James asked, proudly revealing his new and improved alliterative pun, "Can we stay on a happy topic for like a second?"

Brennan sighed deeply and sat back, sinking lower into the chair again. He closed his eyes for a moment and let his mind wander.

Before he really processed the odd thought, he spoke it.

"Smurfs are blue, but they're not sad." Brennan stated under his breath.

James laughed again, "What? That's the weirdest one we've had in a few years, for sure." He released one final chuckle, "Oh, hey, if you put a Smurf in a chokehold, what color does it turn?"

Brennan's smile had just begun to re-form when a small vibration recalled his attention and humor. Binary Sunset began playing in his pocket.

"It's Ace," Brennan told James and swiped the green circle on his phone's screen to the right side and put the phone to his ear.

"Hey, Ace. Did you manage to get a hit on the car model and LP?" Brennan paused. "Holy crap! Seriously? Well, I'll wrap it up for you if you want it." Another lapse of a few seconds, "Yeah, I know, man. No, I'm betting it's the smack, but it may have been both. He's probably out right now. Yeah… Yeah… Yep, as soon as I'm done. Thanks, man. Tell Wall I say 'hi'. Later."

James stood in front of Brennan, eyes wide and hands on his hips. They stared at each other for a second, but James could tell Brennan didn't see him. He saw through him. He was seeing the house. He was planning. Finally, James had enough and threw his hands out to the side in an inquisitive gesture.

"So?"

"Car belongs to Clara Bonilla. She's an elderly woman who had her license expire five years ago and didn't bother to renew it. Not a big deal, she feels she's not well enough to drive. Her grandson though, is Chuy Malenko."

"Ah," James grimaced, "Malenko Products, your one-stop-shop for drugs and guns. Why just get high, when you can be high and violent."

"Malenko doesn't work streets anymore, but I figure a rich guy like Arturo is, or is about to be, gets preferential treatment. I figure he gets a nice delivery of smack, then uses it to go on a chemically induced vacation for a couple of days. Probably why we hadn't seen him leave the house at all. He was probably working through his last delivery."

"Okay," James hopped to his feet and gave an enthusiastic clap, "what's the plan?"

"I don't have one," Brennan replied plainly and honestly.

"You always have a plan," James argued, "What's that thing dad taught you that you taught me? Have contingency plans for…"

"…for the contingencies of your contingencies," Brennan finished.

"So, what's up? What's the plan?" James repeated, as if there'd be a better answer this time. Completely unsurprising to him, there was.

"We wait for the next contingency," Brennan said. "Odds are he'll leave the house at some point. We can't just bust in while he's in there. If he's been having deliveries from Malenko, he may have gotten paranoid and gotten some firepower from him too."

James nodded solemnly.

"So," Brennan continued, "Once he leaves, I can go in, find and," he paused looking for a euphemism that would make the illegal thing he wanted to do seem less illegal, "shall we say, rearrange some evidence."

"Yes, you're going to tamper evidence, go on," James interjected.

"I like to think of it as making it more accessible to the police," Brennan retorted.

"What if he doesn't come out though?" James asked.

"He will. If he got the new delivery, it's probably because he was coming down already. He might feel a bit of the cabin fever and anxiety that comes with coming down hard. He may need to go for a walk, or…"

"Or take his ugly purple Jeep to buy some snacks or get a Redbox?" James finished for his brother.

"What?"

James gestured to the sunroom window. A Joker purple Jeep Wrangler with no doors and no top besides roll bars was pulling out of the picturesque home. Whether the Jeep accented the junkie driver, or the junkie driver accented the obnoxiously painted Jeep, it all melded to create a truly distasteful sight.

Arturo turned the vehicle towards them, and they saw that there were green, metallic, flames painted on the front end. The Jeep colored to look like what a first grader's crayon illustration of what a 'cool car' might be sped past Brennan and James' rented home.

Brennan and James made themselves small as Arturo passed the house and then jumped up just a split second off from perfect unison. Brennan grabbed a Bluetooth earpiece and dialed his brother on his phone as he ran towards the back door.

"Can you hear me clearly?" Brennan asked.

"Loud and clear, Brennie."

There was an arrhythmic clicking sound coming from Brennan's end of the call.

"I'm texting Camila," Brennan explained without being prompted, "she still has remote control of the alarm system on her cell." There was a pause filled only with Brennan's breathing as he ran across the field between the two homes. "Ah, got it, she disarmed the alarm and even opened the deadbolt on the back door. How sweet of her."

James finally caught sight of Brennan in the field and chimed in, "Hey, Bren, stick to that water drainage ditch, if you can. I think right now there's not a lot of cover between you and the street."

James watched as Brennan at first slowly moved down and then slid to the bottom of the ditch.

"Ah, dang it. We got recent rain, Jimmy. Good thing I was wearing work clothes. Grass stains are hard to see on dark green cargo pants." Brennan huffed as he made his way to Arturo's house, really Arturo's father's house.

James saw his brother get to the end of the ditch through his binoculars. He removed them for a second to ensure there was no incoming traffic, then replaced them over his face and saw Brennan hoist himself up to the concrete drainage pipe and jump out of the ditch.

"How creepy is that drainage pipe?" James asked with a chuckle.

"I ran straight at it, ready to dropkick Pennywise just in case the bastard popped out to flirt with me."

James laughed, more at the way his brother replied instantly, obviously thinking the same thoughts James had, than at Brennan's actual joke.

"Ah, trying to get all this mud off my freakin' shoes," Brennan complained. "Okay, I guess I got off as much as I could, a druggy shouldn't be able to tell, but a paranoid dude coming off of it will probably notice everything."

"It'll be fine, Bren. We don't have any timeline for Arturo. Do what you gotta do and get the heck out, man."

The back door led straight into the kitchen. Brennan looked around and saw a bunch of dirty dishes in the sink. The trash can, a stainless-steel canister with a motion activated lid, was now overflowing and trash had been at first placed and then just tossed around it. Brennan superficially reviewed the area for needles, bags of powder, or burnt spoons. He found none, but his primary concern was Arturo's room. He walked towards the front entrance and stopped at the edge of the wall opposite the front door. He peered around the corner and looked up at the security camera. It was unplugged. Brennan again considered Arturo's mental capacity and what his potential, sans drugs, could have been. He relaxed and walked up the stairs. At that point, it became incredibly obvious where Arturo's room was. The door was ajar, his light was on, and Brennan could hear the ceiling fan going. He could also smell a faint hint of smoke and vinegar.

Brennan walked down the hall and into the room. As soon as he opened the door, the sharp scent that had been barely a hint assaulted him with full force. There was a mess of foil, spoons, and syringes strewn around the room. Arturo had cracked the window open to let the stench escape.

"Dude," Brennan whispered, "It's a pig pen. Needles freakin' everywhere."

"Careful, man. Don't poke yourself."

"Tons of paraphernalia, but that won't be enough. I need evidence to tie him to his dad's murder."

Brennan knelt down beside a garbage can. He carefully took out trash with his gloved hands, piece by piece.

"Nothing in the trash of any interest. I'm going to go check the restroom." Brennan reported to James. He walked into the on-suite bathroom and was once again assaulted by scent. "Dude, this bathroom stinks like puke and piss."

Brennan's face scrunched up in disgust and he lightly kicked at the trash can next to the toilet. The garbage shifted but he was unable to see anything. He kicked it a little bit harder and cringed as it teetered, seemed to balance on its edge, then tipped over. Soiled papers spilled out over the floor and some immediately became wet.

"Dang it, man."

"Brennan!" James yelled out suddenly, "Bren, you're going to have company, really freaking soon, buddy. Time to get the heck out."

"No, I still haven't found anything I can use, man."

"Bren, get out, dude. Now!" James' urgency cracked his voice.

"Turn off the lights, open the garage, get the car ready to go. I'll be right there."

"Bren, he's pulling into the driveway, man. Please, buddy, get out."

"Do what I said," Brennan commanded.

James began to protest again, but Brennan could also hear the garage door opening. Just as he heard rattling downstairs, he noticed among the disgusting white paper with brown, that there were smaller bits of white paper with brown that were not product of a disgusting, man-child, getting sick. It was burnt paper. Brennan tipped out the rest of the garbage and brushed through it, his growing panic beginning to take control from his squeamishness. He finally found a larger piece of paper, also burned at the edges with a few visible words and pieces of words. One word segment caught his eye, "-oprolol".

"I found the receipt for the medication!" he unfolded the paper and saw blue scribbles, except, they weren't just scribbles, it was a name, a signature.

"IT HAS HIS FREAKING SIGNATURE!"

"Brennan, please, buddy." James pleaded.

"James it's okay, I don't hear anything. I d-" Brennan froze. He had heard the rattling of the doorknob downstairs, then nothing. He held still and held his breath.

There was a creak. A foot putting weight down on an old wooden step.

Brennan's heart jumped, then seemed to swan dive into his stomach. He felt a buzzing pressure against his sinus cavity. His limbs went from nothing to pins and needles in that same moment. He stood up, the partially burnt receipt in his rubber gloved hand. He looked around the disgusting bathroom and did the first thing that came to mind. He opened the medicine cabinet and stuck the piece of paper behind a pack of razors. As he was about to close cabinet, he found his other hand was reaching up and taking a pill bottle. He pushed the bottle into his pocket and made his way for the window. Brennan just about jumped out of his skin as he heard Arturo kick open a wooden door. Brennan turned and saw the door was still ajar, but the crash had been close. He crawled out of the window and hanged from the ledge. Brennan felt severe, painful strain in his forearms. The anxiety attack made him feel weak and worse now, he felt he couldn't breathe. Brennan pushed off the wall and turned as he plummeted down to the ground. He landed off center and knocked what little breath was left in his lungs out of his body. His right ankle ached. He moved toward the ditch in what looked like a hobble in fast forward.

"WHAT THE HELL!" Arturo screamed, his voice echoing out into the field.

Brennan collapsed into the ditch. His right ankle was now screaming in pain. He could already feel his boot constricting his swelling ankle. He used his left leg to push himself back into the large, concrete, drainage pipe he had joked about with his brother. He heard footsteps crunching on the grass.

"WHERE ARE YOU? YOU COWARDLY BASTARD! I'M GONNA FIND YOU AND VENTILATE YOU!"

Brennan wondered how Arturo had known there was someone in the house. What had he missed?

"The alarm." Brennan whispered to himself. Camila had turned off the alarm. Arturo opened the door and didn't have to disarm it. No annoying voice telling him to 'disarm system now'.

Brennan heard Arturo walking overhead. Arturo was whining and moaning in fear and frustration. Brennan heard Arturo's retreating footsteps and then the squeaky hinges of the back door open. Brennan didn't dare stand up and, in his current condition, he would probably be faster prone than trying to walk. He army crawled through the mud, moving as quickly as he could towards the other end of the ditch.

"Bren, can you talk? Bren? You okay, buddy?" James sounded incredibly worried and Brennan felt terrible that he couldn't respond.

Brennan made it to the end and crawled out of the ditch. In the distance, he heard the cymbal like crash of shattering glass. He saw a faint shape flying out of Arturo's window. Brennan walked around the back of the house and to the garage, where James' truck was already running. It also seemed to be all loaded up. James jumped out of the driver seat and clicked the button of his earpiece, hanging up the call.

"Brennan, crap, man. What happened?"

"I hid the receipt. We need to leave and call it in."

"Yeah, okay, but why are you limping?" James inquired as he tried to help his brother towards the truck.

"No, wait," Brennan objected and removed his completely mud coated gloves.

"Dude, really, you're full of mud, you're worried about touching me with muddy gloves?" James put his brother's right arm around his neck and hoisted him up, taking a good amount of weight off Brennan's right ankle.

"Well, I found the receipt in the bathroom with toilet paper over it. Pretty sure homeboy had the 'horse' trots and pretty sure not all of that was mud."

James looked at the gloves discarded in the lawn outside the garage and grimaced. He put his brother in the passenger seat and climbed back in behind the wheel.

"When we get paid for this, "James said as he started the truck, "your first expense is going to be detailing the inside of my truck."

Brennan chuckled and leaned his seat back a few degrees. He closed his eyes and clicked his earpiece.

"Okay, Google. Call Ace, Mobile."

"Calling Ace, Mobile," a deadpan but somehow pleasant voice replied.

"Detective Aguilar."

Brennan almost laughed at how Ace lowered his voice when he answered the phone.

"Detective, I would like to call in a tip regarding a case you're investigating."

"Ram?"

"No, Detective Aguilar, you see, I would like to call in an anonymous tip regarding a case."

"Okay," Ace replied, understanding Brennan's intention.

"At the Marzo residence there's a large number of drugs, syringes, and a special receipt. It's hidden in the medicine cabinet in Mr. Arturo Marzo's bathroom. I believe that Arturo is armed."

"Why is the receipt special, Mr. Anonymous?"

"Because Mr. Marzo overdosed on his beta blockers and a little something-something extra that you'll find all over the place. The receipt to the extra beta blockers is signed by Arturo."

"Okay, well, we will look into this information…"

"You need to go now. Arturo is throwing things out of the window, disturbing the peace. He may decide to discard this important evidence, Detective Aguilar."

"Got it."

Brennan hung up without any farewell. He leaned the seat back a bit more and fell asleep.

Once they were home, Brennan headed straight for the shower while James called Camila with the developments.

In the bathroom, Brennan undressed and heard a rattle in his pants pocket. Grogginess left him and an anxious anticipation set in. He reached into the pocket and pulled out a pill bottle.

Arturo Marzo. Take one quarter tablet, up to three times per day, as needed. Do not take more than prescribed. Alprazolam 2 mg.

His hands were shaking now. There was no reason to be scared, no reason to be anxious. Ace would deal with Arturo now. The full payment for the case was all but guaranteed. Still, his hands shook. Still, Brennan broke off one small square, tossed it in his mouth, then scooped water with both hands from the cold tap and sipped.

Chapter 38

When the police arrived at Arturo's home, the paranoid drug addict was absolutely livid. He was strung out, afraid that if he used the heroine his body was crying out for, the heroine that had just been delivered a few hours prior, his home invader would return to kill him. Ace took a giant leap of faith, arriving at the home without a warrant, hoping to follow up quickly on his "anonymous" tip. Ace knocked and called out, "Police! Mr. Marzo open up!".

Ace had his weapon drawn and was standing at the edge of the door in a bladed stance. It was what he was trained to do, and for good reason. A bullet ripped through the door, sending splintering wood flying out towards the officers. Wall called for backup on his radio before the second shot rang out. That time, the bullet struck the concrete near their feet and ricocheted towards Ace, cutting a ragged trench in his right calf.

"Agh! Bastard! He's shooting from the stairs!" Ace yelled.

By that point Wall had been fully aware of the fact that the bullets were hitting the door at a downward angle, implying that they were coming from higher ground. Wall took his radio again, "Officer hit! Need medical!"

"I have rights! Get off my property! This is Texas! I have rights!" the crazed man yelled in a breaking, raspy voice.

Ace thought that while Anonymous Ram had mentioned syringes, it was pretty likely an impatient Arturo had chosen to smoke some heroin too. Or perhaps he had used an upper to give himself an edge on the heroine. Ace considered this as a third bullet struck the pavement, this time further ahead on the walkway.

"He's coming down the stairs." Wall said calmly, "Stay down, Ace. I'm going to stop this guy."

Ace tried to protest but Wall was already around the corner. Wall peered in through a window and saw the staircase. The first floor ceiling and banister covered most of Arturo's body, but Wall could see his two feet. Arturo was also in a bladed stance. His right foot was one step lower than his left and was more clearly visible.

"Are you gone? Did you leave?" Arturo yelled out. He sounded like a scared child trying to figure out if he's been left behind by his parents. A strung-out Kevin McAllister.

Wall heard Ace call back to Arturo in a strong, stern voice, "Mr. Marzo, this is the police, drop your weapon and come out with your hands behind your head!"

"Aaah!" Arturo ripped a banshee like shriek and unloaded a fourth and fifth round towards the door.

Wall could hear sirens in the distance, but he was not going to allow this to continue. He placed the butt of his department issue AR-15 on his shoulder, looked through the scope and fired two shots about a half second apart. The first cracked through the window and splintered one of the banister's columns. The second also caused a crunching sound as it struck, but this sound was muffled, rather than resounding. Arturo's muscle and tendons effectively dampened the crack of his shattering right ankle. As the bullet inadvertently avenged Brennan's similarly located injury, Arturo toppled over while his foot remained flat on the ground. His leg bent at a disgustingly unnatural angle and Arturo hit the stairs, face first, and dropped the gun.

Wall ran back to the entrance of the house and saw Ace trying to shoulder tackle through the door, unable to use his injured leg to kick it or support his weight while the other leg did the hard work. Wall's size 14 tactical boot made quick work of the door frame and the two men entered the home to find Arturo doing his best to stand to his feet, one of which appeared to be attached to his leg with bloody chewing gum. Arturo fell again, face flat, furthering the damage the steps had done to his nose and orbital bones. Wall kicked the gun away and cuffed Arturo as Ace slid down to the ground next to the wall, his gun trained on Arturo.

With a look of disgust and tears cresting in his eyes, Wall took a pair of blue rubber gloves and an emergency tourniquet out of a cargo pocket in his pants. He put on the gloves and knelt on Arturo's left leg as he applied the tourniquet to the mangled right leg. Still wearing the bloodied gloves and frustrated that he couldn't run to the patrol car to get another pair, he reached into Arturo's pockets. He removed a transparent pouch filled with something resembling the salt crystals he had made for his fourth-grade science class, only with a glassy, blue tinge. He reached in again and pulled out a burnt-out glass pipe and a small torch lighter. Arturo protested weakly.

"Freaking meth, man," Wall growled.

"That explains a lot," Ace grunted. As the adrenaline wore off, the bloody groove that was now where some of his calf muscle used to be began to ache with a pulsing, searing heat.

The rumbling of multiple footsteps echoed in the entryway of the house like distant, rolling thunder as the cavalry arrived.

"All dressed up and no one left to dance with," Wall called out at them.

All the same, they began to comb through the house.

"Check the medicine cabinet in Meth-Head Marzo's room. We're not just looking for drugs, we're looking for evidence to tie him to his father's death," Ace instructed in a commanding voice that adequately suppressed his pain. "Just try not to touch anything until we can get it properly bagged and tagged!"

Arturo flailed wildly and grunted protests after hearing this. Wall simply pressed down on Arturo's back with one of his leg sized arms and held him in place.

"Meth-Head Marzo," Wall laughed, "good one."

Ace chuckled, "I tell you, Wally. Mr. Anonymous is going to owe me a big one after this."

Chapter 39

"How did it go?" James asked.

"Went well. He's fine. He's home for a couple of days. It was just a flesh wound. Pretty jagged because it was a ricochet, but he'll be fine. I still feel pretty bad about it though," Brennan replied.

"Well, it's part of the job, right? You can't really be a cop and expect to not get hurt." James looked at his brother and saw that no guilt had left his face, "Although, if you feel that bad about it, we can send him some pretty flowers," he joked, "Camila's check just hit the AB account. I'll transfer my cut later today."

"Yeah, I don't know about flowers, but maybe we can DoorDash him a Texas Roadhouse dinner. Ace loves that roadkill plate they have." Brennan smiled and looked up at his brother, "You know the first time he tried it, it was because of the name? Who sees steak, burgers, and all sorts of stuff and then goes, 'gee, roadkill! That sounds appetizing.'?"

"Speaking of steak, what are you going to do now that we're rich?" James asked with a coy smile.

"Ha, yeah, rich. First, I'm going to pay bills, including some payments for medical ones. What they charge me per night at the hospital, you'd think I had been staying in a suite at the Broadmoor."

"What's the Broadmoor?"

Brennan ignored the question and continued, "I talked to mom last week and she's been having a hard go of it. Work sucks almost as much as her coworkers. I'm gonna surprise her with a little island getaway. It'll just be here in SPI, but I'll get her a nice room, room service, spa day, and dinner somewhere."

"That's really sweet," James said. "You must really like being the favorite."

Brennan laughed and did not respond.

"You know, Bren. She doesn't need stuff. She needs people. She gets lonely."

"I have breakfast with her twice a week and we do family dinners on Sunday. I unfortunately can't be constantly there," Brennan retorted, but then looked up at his brother, smiling. "You remember Vic?"

"That guy mom dated? Yeah, nice guy."

"Did she ever tell you why they broke up?" Brennan asked as he looked up at his brother's distracted eyes.

"No, didn't care. I was like thirteen."

"Well, she told me. I asked why she didn't go out anymore and she said Vic and she weren't really hanging out. She dumped him because he took too much time away from us."

"Really?" James asked, his brows furrowed together in doubtful confusion, "I don't remember her being around that much. You practically raised me."

"Well, yeah. Mom worked days, did night school, and slept somewhere in between. She was never around because of that, so when her little time with us took a hit, she dumped him. She didn't want to bring him around to kill two birds with one stone because we had lost dad and she was scared we'd get attached and then if the relationship went the way of the dinosaurs, it might devastate us."

"Dude..." James mused, "That's... horrible."

"Yep. So I stalked him."

James looked up at his brother, the doubtful confusion on his face returned.

"Facebook stalked him... at first." Brennan grinned in a way that made him look both playful and devious, "He's a good guy. Going to church. Playing guitar in their band. Pays his taxes. Nothing criminal beyond a couple speeding tickets. Credit score in the 700s."

"Mmmkay, you may have gone too far, buddy."

Brennan ignored him again, "He was doing nursing school at the time, remember? Well, now he's a nurse practitioner. Best part of all, he's still a bachelor."

"Are you going to Parent Trap mom?" James asked, cringing at his brother.

"No! I change my mind, this is the best part of all, he still likes mom."

"What?"

"Yeah! I finally looked him up and 'bumped into him at the store'," Brennan used finger quotes to highlight his deception, "He says that he still Facebook stalks mom. He said that he's been wanting to reach out to her, but he doesn't know how. He thinks it's too late. So..."

"So," James interrupted, "You came up with a hairbrained scheme to get them in the same romantic hotel on an island getaway. Instead of, you know, telling mom. Or giving him her new number. You over complicate your life, Brennie."

"It's brilliant. Mom will be relaxed, she'll have alone time. Dude is still fit, you know. Kept all his hair..."

"Yeah, then when our new baby brother gets old enough, we can all sit and tell the story about how hard you worked to get mom laid."

"Dude, don't say it like that," Brennan protested with a grimace.

"Meanwhile, you're Chastity Charlie. Don't get me wrong, I'm not saying you go out and break Commandments, but I feel you could be on your way to a real relationship. You know? Something to keep you grounded. Something to anchor you to life."

"You're my anchor, Jimmy." Brennan's face was suddenly crestfallen.

"I know, bud. I know and I love you for it. You stepped up and filled a grown man's shoes when you were just a child. It's because of you and mom that I am where I am. I appreciate that, but you need to build a life for yourself too."

The sadness in Brennan's face faded, leaving only the disappointment.

"I'll be fine, little brother. Life is complicated. Kids, a family, it all sounds great," The secret pocket he had sewn into his boot suddenly felt huge. Like it was bulging into his leg, uncomfortable and conspicuous. "but I'm just not good enough."

"Bullshss…. ugh… bullspit," James finally spat out, stifled anger peeking through his expression. His jaw shifted behind his lips, his brow furrowed, he tensed up and then verbally released the tension, "That's bullcrap, buddy, and you know it. Why do you do this, Bren? Why do you shoot yourself down before giving yourself a chance?"

Brennan ignored him.

"Why, Bren?"

Brennan began to walk away.

"Why?! What are you so freaking scared of?!"

"I'M GOING TO FAIL!" Brennan exploded, "I'M AFRAID I'M GOING TO FAIL! Okay? God…" The yells were heartbreaking and terrifying. He had gone from upset to furious in an unquantifiably brief moment. Brennan ran his fingers through his hair and James was suddenly regretting this line of conversation. He could see a hint of madness in Brennan's face. A hint that had been there long ago. A quiver at the corner of his mouth, a twitch in his eyebrow, and an angry contradictory smile trying to push its way out of his skin. That smile and laugh that Brennan sometimes couldn't help when he hurt.

"Bren, I'm sorry, okay?"

"I'm scared, James. I failed you on the Medellin case. I didn't protect you like I should have. I failed mom as a son. I abandoned her. I couldn't do that. I'd fail. I couldn't do that to my kids, my wife. The way I failed you, mom, grandma, Kaylee…"

Concern and confusion quickly spread across James' face, "Who's Kaylee, and how did you fail grams?"

Brennan was speechless and looked almost funny as he stared out perplexed, mouth agape, as if he couldn't figure out how to make words go. His slackened jaw and confused squint had cast out the rage.

"Brennie?"

Brennan looked up and closed his now chalky mouth. He tried to produce enough saliva to swallow. "I... I don't know," he shook his head slowly, "I'm just tired. Sorry, bud. It's been a long few weeks."

"It's fine, man. Look, pay your bills, send mom away on relaxation duty, but please, take a chance. Call Deidre. Ask her out. Worst that could happen is she says no and judging by the fact that you have her phone number, I doubt she will."

Brennan nodded reluctantly. James patted his brother's shoulder lightly and gave him a sympathetic smile that almost insulted Brennan. Brennan dutifully smiled back, and James walked away.

Brennan went into the restroom and washed his face. He took cold, stinging, water in his cupped hands and lightly splashed it over his face. He could feel the heat and buzzing begin to recede. He did this a few times then looked up at himself in the mirror. The face that stared back seemed alien to him. He closed his eyes and began washing his face again. After another three splashes, he brought the heels of his hands to his mouth. He drank and felt the pill disappear into his system. He didn't know how he'd gotten it. He didn't remember taking it from his boot.

Brennan walked into his room and shut the door behind him. The combination of cool air being blown by the ceiling fan and the blue toned darkness felt great. He hadn't realized until that moment that his head had been pounding. Every heartbeat was a small hammer tapping on the inside of his skull, a hazy black circle kept perfect tempo in his field of vision. He closed his eyes and took a deep breath. Goosebumps broke out on his neck and arms, spreading across his body. He could feel his muscles giving way and becoming lax. He was suddenly very tired. The full sized bed at the far end of the room seemed to call his name. He removed his shoes and curled his toes in, their joints cracking as they did. He pulled off his socks, then removed his khaki cargo pants. He pulled off the black and grey Superman shirt he had worn to Ace's house. He lay down and felt as his pillow push out air as his resting head flattened it. He felt the folds of the blanket softly line his back. He couldn't see himself, but he felt like he had slithered up and then down under his blanket with a million tiny motions that seemed to cumulate into a single, smooth, transition. The cool silky sheets sent another wave of goosebumps up his back, then crawling, incrementally slower, up his ribs towards his chest and extremities, stopping just short of connecting at his sternum. He noticed he was holding in a slow, deep inhalation. He exhaled out slowly, triggering yet another gaggle of goosebumps. Time seemed to slow. He could hear something.

"Hwoo, hwoo, hwoo, hwoo…" at first keeping tempo, then allargando.

He felt heat on his face and smelled the fresh, almost visibly green, scent of freshly mowed grass. There was something heavy in his hands.

He opened his eyes and saw small, chubby, hands holding out a .22 caliber Marlin Glenfield Model 60 rifle.

"Alright, Bren, you need to breathe in and pull on the exhale." His father's voice was deep, stern, and resonant, but it filled Brennan's heart to hear it.

Brennan, age 6 or 7, held out the rifle, looked down the sights, inhaled, and then pulled the trigger as he exhaled.

"CRAK!"

Brent grunted in exasperation. Brennan turned his face, warm with not only sunshine now, but a rosy blush, up to his father. Brent squeezed his eyes and pinched his cheeks up towards his eyes in an expression of clear dissatisfaction. He opened his eyes, exhaled through pursed lips, and spoke again.

"Alright, Bren. That was actually better, son, but you're still breaking your movements down on the trigger pull. It needs to be one, smooth, clean pull. Don't anticipate the shot. Don't fear the shot. Remember to center your trigger finger."

"The gun moves too much, dad." Brennan protested.

"No, Bren! The gun doesn't move! You move. If I put the gun down on the pavement will it walk away? Will it start tossing and turning like a baby? No, it'll stay still. The gun doesn't move. You move it."

Brennan's naturally sad and droopy eyes sloped farther down and he bit his bottom lip anxiously. Brent tried constantly. He hated that he still let his words get away from him. This was his son. Not a soldier.

He knelt down next to his son, took his son's wrists, the little hands still held the rifle, and he pulled the hands and the rifle up slowly, so it looked like Brennan was presenting him the rifle, like a ceremonial sword.

"This rifle, this weapon, ANY weapon, is an extension of yourself, son. You control it. You use it. You attack or defend. It's like the punches I was teaching you last weekend, remember? Follow through, then pull back, one motion, one weapon. You don't just hurl fists. It's the same thing here. The gun does what you want it to. Don't make the gun fire. You fire. Try again."

Adult Brennan would have joked about how his dad's speech would have been a good preface to a Rocky style training montage, but adult Brennan didn't have the privilege of joking with his father. Child Brennan, on the other hand, was enamored with superheroes, whether they be the classic tights and cape kind, or the preternaturally talented quickdraws of the cowboy, Western movie variety, and of all the heroes, none held a candle to his father. The speech spoke to him. It imbued him with power. After all, that sort of speech always prefaced a cool training montage.

Little Brennan moved the rifle up to his shoulder, centered his fingerprint over the trigger, took a breath, then pulled back with no hesitation as he exhaled.

"*CRAK!*"

The paper target stapled to a large palm tree moved. It was still a bit off center, but he hit paper.

"Good job, son!"

No words would be sweeter for at least 10 years. Brennan looked up again, his eyes squinted by the smiling, rosy cheeks. His huge grin revealed two missing teeth.

Brent looked at his son and once more felt emotional dissonance. Pride for his beautiful, intelligent boy. Full of life and potential. A real, 'look what I made' moment. Then the conviction that he did not deserve his son and his son deserved better. Maybe he deserved someone like the dads he had been unable to bring home, or the young men who had stained the sand and his psyche with blood before having the privilege to be fathers.

He smiled slightly at his son, he hoped little Brennan wouldn't see the tears.

Of course, he didn't. All Brennan saw was Superman.

"Control, son. It's all about control."

Brennan woke up. He usually hated napping. His body had a great habit of waking up at the perfectly wrong time. He'd wake up, heart speeding, eyes heavy and crusty, feeling like he got hit by a truck. Not this time though. He assumed it was some of his chemical tranquility, but he woke up feeling rested, relaxed, and pleasantly drowsy.

"Control, right, dad?"

He picked up his phone from the floor. It must have fallen when he collapsed in bed. He dialed Deidre.

"Hey! Hi, it's Brennan."

"Hey, Brennan! I'm glad you called. I thought we were going to end up the quintessential Facebook friends that always say they need to hang out or catch up, but never do," she chuckled.

"Things got crazy busy. We were working a case that got a bit dramatic."

"Oh, I get it. Living that cool, noire life. Brennan Ramirez, P.I." she chuckled again, this time a bit more heartily and though it was a phone call, Brennan could clearly see her face when she laughed.

"Nothing quite so cool, unfortunately. No trench coats and fedoras in the South Texas heat." he paused. *"Control"*, he thought to himself. "Although, I was still hoping for the dazzling femme fatale. I was thinking maybe I could take her out for dinner?" His last worked peaked and hung like a question rather than a statement.

"Smooth, Mr. Brennan." She smiled. Brennan didn't know how he knew, but he knew she smiled her million watt smile. "I would love to."

"It's a date then. Are you free on Friday?" Brennan asked.

"Kind sir," she replied in a mild mock outrage, "I am an American and a Texan at that, I am always free."

Brennan laughed and quickly stopped, not because it wasn't funny, but because she was laughing too and he wanted to hear her cute, immature, not quite goofy laugh.

"Jeez," he remarked to himself, *"Chill out, man. You're smarter than this."*

He didn't really mind though. He felt a connection to her and though it was too early to know if he would love her, he loved that there was potential for it.

"Does 6 PM sound good? How about Saltgrass?"

"6 PM sounds fine and Saltgrass sounds amazing. I like a man who isn't afraid to see my carnivorous side."

"Great! I'll pick you up at 6, have a nice chat on the way to McAllen, good, calm dinner, and be home well before midnight."

"Oh, Mr. Brennan," Deidre was now speaking as a stereotypical Southern belle, "Home before midnight! Such a gentleman you are." She laughed again and this time it really was goofy, and Brennan found he like it even more. "It sounds wonderful." Deidre finished in her normal voice.

"Awesome! I'll see you then."

Though time continued its steady march, Brennan felt the days stretched into weeks. He was embarrassed enough to barely be able to admit it to himself, but he found he was counting the hours until 6 PM Friday. Finally, it was T minus 90 minutes and Brennan sat on his bed. He was freshly showered and wore new blue jeans, a black button up with a black Batman t-shirt for an undershirt, and he was now staring at his black clad, opaque, square toed, Ariat cowboy boots. For Brennan, the ideal shoe was a comfortable size 12, preferably laceless, that looked just good enough to pass for business casual, but easy enough for him to run in. Dapper with the sole of an athlete, the pun-inclined might say. Cowboy boots did not fit that description, but Brennan wanted to make a good impression and a good pair of boots can be the Texan version of patent oxfords.

Brennan slipped on the boots and couldn't help but think of his dad. His dad who had once worn a tuxedo with a cowboy hat, bolo tie, and snakeskin boots to a wedding. Though the thought of his father was not always, heck, not even usually, tied to good memories, he smiled. He was dressing like dad and it felt right.

He had a flash, but not of a first hand memory. After his father left, Brennan would often stay up late, pretending to be asleep until his mother was deep in her own slumber. He would then get up and grab the VHS home videos they kept in what used to be his dad's gear closet. He would watch them for hours. A few times, the sun came up to greet Brennan while his eyes were still set on the screen. He did this on and off for a few years. One night, James woke up. He asked Brennan what he was doing, and Brennan fought the instinct to scold him and send him back to bed. Instead, he invited him to sit with him. As they sat together and watched, Brennan would narrate stories for James, really Jimmy at the time, of times Jimmy could not or could just barely remember. The first video they ever watched together was what flashed in Brennan's mind. A secondhand memory of little Brennan, not quite two years old. He was in a diaper, no pants, no onesie, and doing his best to shuffle around in his father's boots. The ostrich skin boots, a deep almost orange shade of brown, almost reached to the place where Brennie's diaper met his thigh. On his head, a cream-colored cowboy hat hung down obscuring his eyes. His dad, obviously much taller than him at that point, recorded from a bird's eye view.

"Ah, que guapo, mijo!" his father had exclaimed, and with that Brennie turned his head. His eyes were barely peering under the comparably giant hat, his head was tilted up high so he could see his dad, and he smiled what had to be the biggest smile to ever cross a toddler's face.

"Dang! What's up, Urban Cowboy?" James' voice snapped Brennan out of his nostalgic stupor.

Brennan snickered, "Shut up, dude."

"You look good, big brother. Kind of a young, lady-killer, Travolta, meets Midworld Gunslinger."

Brennan smiled and scoffed. "First date, man. Just want to look presentable, make a good impression before I introduce her to my vast and innumerable collection of superhero and Star Wars T-Shirts."

"You look good, buddy." James grinned slightly. His heart filled with the sight of his brother, almost estranged in the time B.C., before coma, living in his home, dressed up in a way oddly reminiscent of their father, ready for his first date, and above all, happy. Hell, almost giddy.

"Thanks, Jimmy. Hey, speaking of gunslinger, do you have a black sport coat I can borrow? I want to keep my shirt tucked, but I need to hide my concealed carry."

James pushed off the door frame he was leaning on and stood at full height, "Did you consider not carrying on a first date."

Brennan made an odd sound that was a hybrid between a chuckle and a scoff, with the hybrid facial expression to match, "I'm not gonna not carry, Jimbo."

James pulled his lips to the corner of his mouth in an expression of pensive concern and replied, "Yeah, bud. I've got something you can wear. Might fit you a bit long at the sleeves though."

"Thanks, Jimmy, I appreciate it."

A few minutes, some hair pomade, and a black sport coat later, Brennan was headed out the door.

"You sure you got this, right?" James asked for the umpteenth time.

"Yes, man. I've got this. Her house is a five-minute drive and once she's in the car with me, I'll be fine. I don't get panicky if someone is in the car with me."

"Okay, well, call me if you need anything, bud."

"I will." Brennan looked at his younger, bigger, brother, "Thanks for everything, man. I don't know how I'll repay you."

"You won't," James' usually jovial face was suddenly stoic, "bud, if we start keeping score, I'd be eternally indebted to you. Growing up, you were my hero, my big brother, my dad, my tutor, my teacher, my pastor, my freaking everything. There's no me today without you." He paused and smiled at the image of his brother, happy. "You laid your childhood down so that I could have mine."

Brennan hugged his brother and his memory overflowed once more. A ten-year-old Brennan hugged a skinny little James in khaki shorts, a dark blue polo, and round Harry Potter like glasses, topped off with a standard issue my-mom-cuts-my-hair, mushroom cut.

"A 96! I told you, Jimmy! I told you! No dyslexia's gonna beat us!" Brennan held his hand up for a high five.

"Yeah!" James yelled as he jumped and slapped his brother's hand.

"No ADHD can beat us!"

"Yeah!" James yelled as he repeated his motion and gave his brother five.

"I told you, buddy. Don't be nervous. Study and do your best. You killed that test!"

"Yeah!" James repeated, "We crushed it!"

"Dude, if you cry you're gonna mess up your makeup," Adult James joked, effectively breaking the emotional tension.

Brennan slapped his brother's arm lightly. "Whatever, man. I'm gonna head out." Brennan took his keys off the wall hooks and walked towards his car. The air was pleasantly chilly and gave James' coat added purpose.

"Drive Safe!" James waved at his brother, "Remember to leave enough space in between y'all for Jesus!" This made Brennan chuckle as he entered his car, "Oh! You should check your eyeliner didn't smear before you pick her up!" James called out.

"It was one time in high school!" Brennan replied loudly.

"People don't forget!"

Brennan closed the door of his car and looked up to see James waving once more as he closed the door to the apartment.

Three minutes into his five-minute drive, Brennan pulled over. He could feel his hands tensing and his breathing became shallow. The pins and needles sensation traveled through his arms and neck like an army of ants. He had not worn his usual, surprisingly comfortable, work boots. There was no secret pouch sewn into these boots. His hands shivering, he fumbled with the arm rest and sighed in relief when he saw a couple of loose, white, rectangles in the armrest compartment. He took one in his trembling hand and bisected it. He looked at the conjoined squares and suppressed the anxiety in his mind that screamed, "*Take it! Drink it! We NEED it!*"

With tremendous effort, Brennan took the halved rectangle and bisected it further, ending up with one solitary square. He threw it as far back into his mouth as he could and took a swig from a water bottle he had brought along. Hands still shaking, pins and needles poking at his eyes and extremities, he drove the rest of the way to the address Deidre texted him.

Deidre must have been at least half as excited as Brennan because he was still psyching himself up in the car when she walked out of the door of her small duplex apartment. Walked may have been putting it mildly. Deidre skipped out in a lime green and yellow polka dotted sundress that reached just above her knee, a white belt across her waist, and a lime green headband that separated her side swept bangs from the rest of her chestnut hair.

Brennan's heart skipped a beat and the vibrating, pins and needles, sensation returned for a second. He came back to himself and tried to rush out of the car to open the door and be gentlemanly. He almost tripped over himself but managed to make it to the passenger side of his car just before her. He held the door handle but didn't open it at first. He just stared.

"You like beautiful," he said, but that wasn't enough. His mouth continued before his brain could catch up, "You look ethereal... dream like."

Color rose in Deidre's cheeks. Growing up with her mom, Deidre was constantly surrounded by metaphorical bull manure and she could tell this wasn't it. She though Brennan was awkward, broody, and a bit dark, but he was genuine.

"Thank you," she replied. "You don't think I look like an old Sprite commercial?" she asked with a chuckle.

"No… no… not now."

A flash. It was Deidre. The apartment was replaced by a trailer. Deidre was younger, 15, maybe as young as 14. A child on the cusp of blossoming into adulthood. She wore the same dress, but it reached down to her knee in the memory.

"Wow, you look ethereal," Brennan heard himself say.

Young Deidre gave him a tilted, inquisitive look.

"It means dream-like." Brennan explained.

Young Deidre laughed. "Oh! Thanks. It's the only nice dress I have. I thought I looked like a Sprite commercial."

"Brennan? Are you okay?" The present Deidre pulled Brennan out of his own head.

Brennan's feet faltered for a second and he laughed nervously, "I'm fine. More beauty than I'm used to, I guess."

The million-watt smile. "You're so kind. Just don't let my radiant beauty blind you while you drive, okay?"

They both laughed awkwardly then stood motionless.

"Oh! Right! The door. Sorry," Brennan blurted out and opened the door. Deidre climbed into the car and he closed the door and re-entered the driver's side.

Brennan backed out of the parking spot and began to drive.

"I'm really glad you were able to make it," he told her, making an effort to smile. He had plenty to smile about at the moment, but he knew his face set to an intense, focused default when he drove.

"Yeah, I managed to get my neighbor to babysit. She's a godsend. Only charges me $20." Deidre exhaled and closed her eyes, as if she was slowly relaxing.

Brennan tried not to react. "I didn't know you had a kid." He uttered, unsure it was the right way to say, or ask really, what he needed to ask.

Deidre looked at him puzzled and then burst with her goofy, beautiful, laugh, "Oh, no, Brennie. For my mom!"

"Oh," Brennan whispered as he felt heat climb up his cheeks and almost to his hairline.

"I'm sorry," she said with the last of her giggling, "I shouldn't call it that." She let out one last syllable of laughter. "If I'm gone too long, my mom starts to think she can get away with a bender. I tell the neighbor to go and distract her while I'm gone. It usually works too. Even though she's dependent, I think the root of the booze is still to fill the loneliness."

"I understand, I'm…" Brennan trailed off. There was no good way to end that sentence.

"Man, that conversation got dark quickly. It's a thing with me. You gotta laugh or you cry, right Brennan?"

As she asked this, Brennan turned to her and realized she was still genuinely smiling. He wondered if at one point she had stopped needing to fake it, because she had finally made it.

"Right," Brennan replied. "What kind of music do you like?"

"No, no music, Brennan. Let's get the small talk out of the way, that way, we can get to the meaty stuff at dinner. Literally and metaphorically."

He turned to her again and was met with a smile again.

"Okay, as the lady wishes. Where should we start?"

"How about I ask a question, you answer, then I answer, then you ask? Deal?"

Brennan smiled, "Sounds good to me."

"Favorite Color?" Deidre started.

"Green," Brennan replied.

"Hot Pink," Deidre said, and although he was focused on the road again, he could hear her smile in her voice.

"Favorite animal," Brennan stated

"White tiger," she almost sighed.

"Lion."

"Favorite number," Deidre continued.

"Twenty-Four."

"Thirteen"

Brennan's turn again, "Favorite male name."

"Jordan," Deidre replied.

"James."

"Ooh, both Js." Deidre mused, "Favorite female name?"

"Abby," Brennan said without thinking.

"No way! Me too!" Deidre replied excitedly, "But Abby, not Abigail."

"Abigail sounds like an old lady," Both said simultaneously and laughed in unison as well.

All stress, anxiety, and panic had fled from Brennan's mind. Even the first date jitters that a person not suffering from anxiety or stress disorders would feel had faded. The butterflies in his stomach had gone from a kaleidoscope to just a singular pair of flapping, fluttering wings. It's not that he wasn't excited. It's not that he wasn't happy. He just felt like he was finally, for the first time in a long time, right at home.

Chapter 40

"Medium, please," Brennan told the waiter.

The waiter turned to look at Deidre now.

"Mmm... Medium well," she said.

"Should I leave the bottle?" The waiter asked displaying the bottle of wine he had poured Deidre's glass from in a way that reminded Brennan of the way women on game shows would hold and display prizes.

"No, I'll be fine with my glass," Deidre replied. "Brennan?"

"I don't drink," Brennan responded just as he realized a simple 'no, thank you" would have sufficed. He smiled bashfully, hoping it would make his reply seem less sanctimonious. The waiter had only turned about 90 degrees when Brennan had a change of heart sudden enough it could cause whiplash, "Actually, I'd like to keep it." He turned his gaze to Deidre, "It would be a good memory."

The waiter said something clever that made Deidre chuckle politely. Brennan didn't hear it, he was swept away in a flash that seemed to last only a fraction of a second.

He was heavier. He could feel that his shirt was a bit tighter and his protruding belly was closer to the table.

"Actually, I'd like to keep it," Brennan told the waitress. He turned his gaze to Deidre. Her hair was colored in what he had heard people call an "ombre" and there were two rings on her finger. One diamond solitaire and one band bisected by a row of small diamonds. "It would be a good memory," Brennan told his wife.

The flash ended and Brennan cleared his throat and rolled his shoulders uncomfortably.

"You okay, Brennan?" Deidre asked and Brennan was very much aware it had not been the first time today.

"Yes, sorry. I drank my coke too fast."

Deidre looked at his untouched glass of Coke Zero, then squinted and pouted slightly, a coquettish expression that seemed to say, "nope, try again."

Brennan smirked and bowed his head a bit to his right and threw up his hands, "Fine, you got me. I was trying to play it cool. I've got a moderate case of the first date jitters."

This made Deidre smile that brilliant, million-watt smile. "Oh, Brennie. You're so sweet. This isn't our first date though."

For an instant almost too quick to register, a nonsensical thought crossed Brennan's mind, *"Does she remember what I remember?"* Of course, she didn't.

"What was it, when we were kids?" Deidre asked with a mischievous, squinting smirk.

The waiter finally understood that his presence was not required for this repartee and walked away, leaving the bottle in a small ice bucket.

"McDonalds," Brennan answered with a shy grin and color in his cheeks. "We got dollar burgers and McFlurries."

Deidre giggled her sweet, goofy laugh. "Oh, Bren. You're so adorable." She held his hand and kept her smile.

Brennan was sure that he wasn't imagining this. She felt it too. She felt that odd comfort he felt. The familiarity. She had to.

She retracted her hands from his softly and straightened her posture. "Okay, time for the hardball questions," she said with a teasing leer.

He mirrored her corrected posture and made intentful eye contact. "Shoot."

"Why didn't we work the first time? I know we were kids and it was mutual, but what was your part of it?"

Brennan raised his eyebrows in genuine surprise. The question was much more hard-hitting than her lighthearted introduction had let him prepare for.

"Wow." He cleared his throat and straightened up in his chair again. "A couple of things, I guess. One, I felt you were really out of my league. You're gorgeous and I was the chubby kid with encyclopedic knowledge of Batman and Star Wars."

She gave a serene, crooked smile.

"Second, I felt you were this great daughter to your mom. Things seemed to have been picking up for you guys. I felt you kind of pulling away and decided maybe I would be a distraction."

She gave an almost imperceivable nod.

"So," Brennan exhaled, "is turnabout fair play? What was the reasoning on your end?"

She smiled, but the wattage was sticking to the triple digits. "If I'm being honest, a bit of it was my mom. She had just started going to church and she seemed very motivated to change. I thought that if she was ever going to get better, that was the chance. I didn't want to distract myself from that," she sighed, "that being said, there was another reason."

She stopped talking and her pause sped up Brennan's heart. He was half expecting her to tell him he was right, and she was way out of his league. As it turned out, she did, but not in the way he expected.

"As far as me being out of your league, I felt that too, but not like you. I thought I was too far beneath you. Like I was too messed up. Damaged goods." Deidre's smile was completely gone now.

Her last words sent a chill up Brennan's spine.

"I was," she continued and a voice, her voice, only higher, younger, spoke in Brennan's mind.

"...raped."

"abused as a child. Nothing too heavy. I wasn't raped or anything." She shifted in her seat, "One of my mom's boyfriends was grooming me. That's when..."

Brennan nodded, silently telling her he knew what it meant.

"Oh, ok," she muttered, then continued in a clearer voice, "he took pictures of me in the shower. He would 'accidentally' leave porn on the TV when he left the room. He planned on doing more once I was a little older, a little more developed." Deidre's eyes glistened and a tear rolled down one cheek. She didn't move, she didn't wipe it away, she didn't change her expression. Her stoic, cold stare at nothing broke Brennan's heart. This was a deep hurt she was used to. A hurt she no longer fought. "My sister, Bethy, you remember her, right?"

"Yeah, vaguely, Bethsaida, right?" Deidre nodded and Brennan resumed, "She visited the church a couple times."

"Yeah, she had moved out by the time you and I met. She had actually moved out like three years before. She was living with a sphincter of a boyfriend, then a pothead friend of hers, then managed to rent a little place for herself. Anyway, around the time we met, I found out that she had gotten a lot worse than I had. She was going to expose him. Open up to a counselor, a teacher, or something like that. She had talked to our mom, but Mom said she was just an attention seeker." Deidre scoffed, "He could tell. I'm assuming he had experience, or maybe he had a nose for it, he was a predator after all. Sorry, I ramble when I'm nervous." She took a quick, but deep breath. "He threatened me. Said he'd move on to me if she didn't cooperate, if she didn't play along," the rage simmering below the surface of her face momentarily bubbled to the top, "if she didn't love him back."

Brennan did his best not to cringe, but he felt a small twitch in his eyelid. The story sounded familiar and filled him with rage, but Brennan was accustomed to holding things in, a master of bottling things up.

"You were such a sweet guy. Genuinely nice. I was over developed for my age," a hint of her flirty smile resurfaced, "but you always looked me in the eye when we talked." Deidre full on giggled now, "You always looked so nervous when I walked away too. You made a clear and honest effort to look in any direction that wasn't my jeans."

Brennan laughed and for what felt like the millionth time today, he blushed with embarrassment. "Did you have eyes on the back of your head or something?"

"Oh, Brennie. Such a kind boy," the rage seemed gone, but Brennan knew better, "I knew my charms. I checked reflections, took sly glances, I grew up hating the feeling of eyes on me. You fought those teenage hormones tooth and nail though. A true, chivalrous, gentleman."

Deidre laughed and Brennan couldn't help but laugh with her. He saw a bravery in her. An ability to laugh, not in spite of trauma or at the trauma, but through it. Not a coping mechanism, as much as an acknowledgment that it was there, that it would be carried, and that she would stand. She would not falter.

It was quick, much too quick for Brennan's calculated thinking, but if he hadn't loved her before, he loved her now.

"A boy like you didn't deserve my baggage. You still don't." She smiled sweetly at him. "Talk about getting heavy on a first date."

"No, it's okay," Brennan reassured her.

"I just feel like I don't have a ton of time, so I don't want to waste it. I've invested months, one time a couple of years, into relationships that end when I finally open up. It's a lot of baggage. I'm not gonna try to sneak it onboard."

It was Brennan's turn now to take a deep breath, a deep inhalation before jumping into the icy waters.

"I was five years old, when my aunt started molesting me."

The waiter came to their table again, bringing along two steaks, Brennan's with a side of green beans and a side of steamed vegetables for Deidre.

"Anything else I can get for y'all this evening?"

Both shook their head no and the waiter mercifully walked away promptly this time.

"She wasn't really my aunt. My grams on my mom's side adopted her. Anyway, my mom and grams had a big falling out before my grandma passed away. Mom's way of making up for it was to help her adopted sister out. My aunt had been estranged from my grandma when she passed, but my grandma always sent her money and did her best to check up on her. To honor that, my mom would pay her to babysit, clean, that sort of thing. Whatever job she could get her. Mom even offered her our spare room, but thank God she declined. She was seventeen when it all started, I was five. It continued for a while. She would touch me, force me to touch her, kiss her. As I grew and developed, she began to take it farther. I was finally going to speak up when I was about seven. I had it planned out. I would tell my mom, if need be, my dad. They'd fix it. I was sure. I decided to tell them after a church event we had. It was a repentance night at a local church, which basically meant it was Scared Straight: Apostolic Edition." Brennan chuckled humorlessly. Deidre kept her beautifully clear, smooth brown eyes locked to his. "They played some cheesy end times movie. These Christians living in secret sin get left behind after the rapture. They decide to shape up since their faith is finally confirmed through the disappeared millions. Long story short, they die bloody. Executed by decapitation, firing squad, and other stuff for not denouncing Christ. The ending was played so that the worst

409

outcome was for the ones that saved themselves and did deny. They get sent to the low-budget, D-movie version of hell."

"Oh, no," Deidre whispered. Her drooping eyes and the tears that floated under them told Brennan she knew where this story was going.

"I didn't tell my parents. I felt responsible. I felt it was my fault. I was the sinner." Brennan felt Deidre's hands wrap around his right hand. "I figured if it had happened, I must have wanted it in some way. I must have invited it. I kept quiet. It kept happening. Then one day, I walked in on her doing the same thing to James. It all stopped that day." Brennan said that with a sense of finality.

Deidre continued to hold his hand while trying, ultimately in vain, to hold her tongue as well. The curiosity overwhelmed her tact.

"You finally told after that, I'm assuming," Deidre stated in an inflection that made the statement a question.

"No," Brennan looked up at her. "My parents still don't know to this very day. I didn't want them to blame themselves. It ended. A few months later, after persistent insistence, my mom finally decided I was old enough to look after myself and my brother. She would still go to the house for family gatherings, hell, sometimes she still does, and every now and again, if she was really strapped for cash, she'd help my mom around the house."

"So, what happened? What made her stop? Did you do what my sister did?" Deidre's tact was completely eroded now, destroyed by the pressure of unanswered questions.

No one beyond Brennan, James, and that pseudo-aunt knew this part. Brennan had never told anyone, but somehow, he felt safe saying it now. Telling it here. Telling her.

"I realized something she had realized a long time before. It was the very thing that had made her move on to James in the first place. I had grown bigger than her. Stronger."

"What did you do?" Deidre asked, but part of her knew. Part of her wanted to hear it. To know that someone had lived the fantasy she had concocted in her mind for her abuser. The fantasy she couldn't ever enact, him being gruesomely murdered and all.

"I remembered the love bites, the hickeys she'd leave on my body in places my parents wouldn't see, and I aimed for those places. I beat her black and blue and no one would ever see. She couldn't tell without having her secret come out."

"You did what you had to. You stopped it, Brennan."

"I didn't exactly make it a custom of mine to beat on people, especially not women, but…"

"She wasn't a woman," Deidre responded, "she was a monster. You did what needed to be done."

Brennan looked at her and decided he would not, could not, share the true revelatory moment. The worst part of his story wasn't his defense of James. That part was like something out of an action movie. The heroic figure serving out some measured karma. No, the worst part was after. When he felt no shame, no regret. In the moments for years after when he felt a peace at the sight of her not meeting his eyes, flinching when he moved towards her, showing up less and less often to family event. The control

411

he felt in stopping when every fiber of his being screamed to continue. To end her.

Brennan, master of bottling it all up, pushed that part of him back down and inserted the proverbial cork onto the bottle's neck.

He smiled and made eye contact again, "My point is we're all broken. You just look for someone who's edges match up your edges. You take the pieces and make a beautiful mosaic."

The million-watt smile was back in full force. "Brennan, you are so corny Monsanto is trying to patent you and I love it. You're also honest and bare and real. I love all those things too."

They turned their attention to their rapidly cooling food and broke the grim tension.

"So, tell me about the case. All the cool details." Deidre squinted and pointed finger guns at Brennan, "Brennan Ramirez, P.I. Taking a bite out of crime."

Brennan covered his mouth, trying not to laugh with a mouthful of food. "I'm pretty sure that's McGruff the Crime Dog."

"Brennan, my job is to take care of old people and then go home and babysit my mom. I need excitement in my life." She looked at him pleadingly, "I heard a dude got his foot blown off!"

"Mmm, not exactly. My old cop buddy, Wall, shot his ankle out. He should be able to keep the foot, but I'm sure he's going to have some trouble going through metal detectors for the rest of his life. If he ever gets out of prison, that is."

"Riveting!" Deidre explained, putting her chin on her two propped up hands. "Tell me more."

The rest of the night was light, fun, and free of the traumatic topics they had opened with. Brennan would have thought it unwise to start out the dinner with a discussion on their childhood abuse, but it worked. He felt lighter and he knew Deidre was relieved to get it all out in the open. He had realized a few bites into the dinner that Deidre's icebreakers in the car, real talk at dinner, her first question, everything was orchestrated for her to be able to put her baggage on what Brennan called front street and see if Brennan was still interested. He of course had been and now Deidre felt untethered from her doubt and fear.

They sat silently in the car, listening to old songs on the radio, occasionally commenting something along the lines of "I love this song," or "I remember my mom always listened to this".

"Is this the real life…" the iconic Mr. Mercury asked over the radio. Deidre perked up in her seat and her hand shot to Brennan's bicep. He'd never admit it, but he tried to impress her by flexing at her touch.

"…or is this just fantasy?" Deidre joined Freddy now and Brennan was caught up in the silky texture of her voice. Deidre had been a choir girl in church for all of about a minute, but Brennan had never heard her sing.

"Caught in a landslide, no escape from reality…"

Deidre caressed Brennan's cheek and gooseflesh sprung down his neck and onto his chest.

413

"Open your eyes, look up to the skies and see…" Deidre's voice matched the high pitch of 'see' perfectly. Brennan found himself enraptured by it. It was angelic. Once more the word came into his mind.

"Ethereal."

"Sing with me, Bren!" she urged, and Freddy continued his song.

"Are you kidding me?" Brennan asked with a sly smile, "As if it's not bad enough already to have to go up against Freddy freakin' Mercury, you want me to put my voice next to yours?"

Deidre made no attempt at humility and instead combated his reasoning. "Bohemian Rhapsody is not a song where you compete. It's a song where you just join in. You sing your heart out to the painful but freeing words. Come on, Brennie Mercury!"

"Momma! Just killed a man!" the Deidre and Freddy duet continued, "put a gun against his head, pulled my trigger now he's dead!"

Deidre gave Brennan a gentle shove.

"Momma, life had just begun… and now I've gone and thrown it all away!"

"MOMMA! OOH OOH OOH OHH!" the duo had become a trio and Deidre punched the air in victory, "DIDN'T MEAN TO MAKE YOU CRY, IF I'M NOT BACK AGAIN THIS TIME TOMORROW, CARRY ON, CARRY ON, as if nothing really matters."

The trio continued until Brennan dropped out again before the crescendo in the song, but Deidre was unfazed.

"... has a devil put aside for me, for me, for MEEE!" Deidre hit the climactic, screechingly high note with astounding proficiency that left Brennan in literal awe.

"WHOA!" Brennan cried out as Deidre air drummed and head banged her way into the instrumental.

Brennan and Deidre sang their way down the expressway with rock anthem after rock anthem until the DJ decided to take things slow, just as they entered their quaint, little town.

Brennan stopped singing but Deidre did not. She seemed tired, a dreamy, pleasant smile still on her lips as she eased into another selection from Queen's discography.

"Love of my life, you've hurt me…"

Her voice was louder than the radio now. It was smooth as silk, sweet as honey, and carried a weight of earnest, honest, emotion.

"... you've broken my heart and now you leave me…"

The words rang true in some part of Brennan's soul. The hair on his arms stood at attention for a second and his vision blurred as his eyes produced tears. Her words resonated in him.

"Love of my life, can't you see… bring it back, bring it back, don't take it away from me because you do not know, what it means to me…"

"I've been so homesick. She's home."

Brennan knew immediately that this was only part true. Even with her, there was something else. Something missing.

"Da-ee!"

"Well, this is me, good sir." Deidre said as they pulled up to her and her mom's duplex.

Brennan parked and undid his seatbelt.

"I'll walk you to the door," he told her.

They walked, hand in awkward hand, and paused at the door.

"I had a really great time," Brennan said.

"I did too, Brennie. We should plan to do it again some time."

Before Brennan could answer, Deidre's pouty, curvy, lips hushed his as they pressed into a kiss. Brennan kissed back and did so deeply. A tension and buzzing rose in his neck. He could feel the flash coming.

He suppressed it. He reburied whatever dead memory wanted to spring forth.

Tonight, he wanted to make new memories.

<u>Chapter 41</u>

The high that Brennan was experiencing had nothing to do with Xanax. This was the first time since the coma that he felt he belonged. The first time since he had woken up, battered, bruised, and relieved of years' worth of memories, that he felt like this was his place, this was his home, this was his life.

Brennan rode that high all the way home, too wrapped up in the lingering feeling of the kiss to remember to be anxious about driving at night.

He parked the car and just about floated to the front door. He tried to straighten out his face, but as much as he tried, he couldn't remove the silly, love struck grin plastered on it. He walked in and saw James sitting on the couch watching something on Netflix.

"Brennan, do you have any idea what time it is?" James asked with a fake scowl.

"Dude, it's like 10:30," Brennan replied, the smile still stuck to his face.

"Exactly, young man! What the heck are you doing back so early."

Brennan's smile widened. "We were both kind of tired. It was a good night though."

"A good night? That's all I get? Give me some details!" James urged.

Brennan sat down heavily onto the recliner. "She's great, man. Hilarious, sweet, and smart, but in a way where I think she's brilliant and doesn't know it."

"Hmm," James replied simply to show his intrigue.

"She did this thing where we had all the small talk on the way there and once we were there, we started with the real stuff, you know. Heavy questions about who we were. I think she was measuring to see if I could deal, you know? Like be there long term."

"On a first date?" James asked, cocking an eyebrow.

"She doesn't mess around, man. You know what, though? I like that. I'm too far into the little that's left of my youth to be playing games. I want something real. Since the coma, and with your help, I've come to realize this life doesn't feel right, it doesn't feel like mine, because I need to own it. I need to make it my life. I gotta stop being a plastic bag, you know?"

"I do not." James furrowed his brows in confusion.

"Just going where the wind takes me. Job to job, case to case, day by day. I need a big picture to feel like I'm living, not surviving."

James smiled wide enough that his cheeks obscured his eyes. He rushed his brother suddenly and hugged him, almost knocking back the recliner.

"That's what I wanted to hear, bud!" James squeezed him enough for it to hurt and Brennan wondered how this behemoth was ever the skinny kid he had defended from bullies.

James let him go. "Things are going to keep getting better. You're back with our family, you're going to church, re-discovering your relationship with God, you're off the booze." James made an excited half shriek half grunt and posed in a ridiculous flex, "I. Am. So. Freaking. Hyped. Bro!" He let out a Ric Flair type "WOOO!" and collapsed back onto the couch. "Gotta keep pushing forward."

Brennan chuckled, amused at his brother's childish display of affections and excitement and in love with the fact that his brother loved him as he did.

"It feels good, Jimmy." Brennan clapped his hands to his knees and stood up, "I gotta shower, man. Get into something comfortable, then I'll probably chill out a bit before bed."

"Yeah, man. Go for it. You earned it!" James replied, once more focused on the TV, "Oh! Wait, dude."

"Yeah, bud."

"You got a call from a professor. A Dr. Abernathy, I think his name was. Anyway, he wanted to talk to you. He said it was urgent."

Brennan grimaced. "I wonder what could be urgent. I've never heard of him."

"He was from the Physics Department, I think."

"Ugh, it's probably about that thing they found on me."

"I don't know, I gave him your number, but warned him you were on a date."

Brennan took his phone from his pocket and inspected it. His screen showed an alert for three missed calls from the University.

"He called me three times. I had it on Do Not Disturb mode though. I have you set up as the only exception for that." Brennan paused to think and then, with a decisive stab of his thumb, cleared the notifications. "You know, I'm not gonna call him back."

James turned around to look at his brother standing in the hall with his phone in hand.

"I'm not," Brennan repeated. "I want to make this life mine. I start by cutting out stuff that pulls me back. Including that dang coma. It's a new day, man."

"Smart man," James said with a smile. "I'll see if I can figure out what it is and tell him to stop bothering you."

"Thanks, bud. I appreciate that."

James nodded and turned back to the television.

Within an hour, Brennan was showered and lying on his bed listening to the sound of his fan.

"*Hwoo...Hwoo...Hwoo...*"

Brennan slept.

"*Almose, da-ee! You gonna be so pwoud!*"

Chapter 42

Brennan woke up to the brass tones of Binary Sunset.

"What the heck, man…"

He grabbed his phone and saw the caller ID read, "Univ. Tex. RGV".

"Ugh, Nope. Not today, Satan."

He clicked the volume button on his phone to silence the ringer. The incoming call notification changed to red and became a missed call notification. Brennan's phone now displayed the time as 6:23 AM. He also noticed the battery symbol on his phone had an exclamation mark and a small red number 6 next to it. He considered plugging it in, but the cord was on a chair about four feet from his bed and it may as well have been four miles. He tossed his phone onto the carpeted floor and turned around, silently thanking God and James for the idea of blackout curtains in his room.

The second time he did not wake up until almost noon. He felt good. Rested, happy, no kinks or aches. Well, almost no kinks or aches. He picked his phone off the floor. The battery now had a small 2 next to it and the clock read 11:48 AM.

"Holy crap," Brennan remarked, "I slept for twelve hours."

Shocked and slightly embarrassed as he was, he understood why. Since the coma, he had struggled for more than four hours of sleep at a time. With his mind now at greater ease, his body wanted to catch up on rest.

He jauntily made his way to the kitchen and called out for James. There was no answer. He looked out the window and saw his car had been moved and James' truck was gone.

Brennan brushed his teeth and read the news on his phone before going to eat breakfast. He helped himself to a couple of scrambled eggs with turkey bacon and toast. He checked his email as he ate. He was fresh off the Marzo case but was ready for more work. It was his day off and he had planned to relax, but he found relaxing much more difficult than he expected. Every part of him wanted to call Deidre. He knew she was working and to make it worse, he felt oblivious to all the unspoken rules in modern dating regarding how long to wait to call and all that nonsense.

He let his phone drop back onto the table with a thud and continued to eat. Not twenty seconds after he had gotten off of it, the phone began to buzz, and John Williams' signature crescendo reverberated from it. He picked it up and spun it, so the screen faced him again.

"Univ. Tex. RGV"

Brennan grunted and turned the ringer off again.

Brennan felt odd doing nothing. He sat in the living room and turned the TV on. About fifteen minutes of Netflix surfing later, he decided he'd just rewatch episodes of the Office, like he often did when he just needed to watch something entertaining enough to help him not be bored, but familiar enough that he didn't have to watch it very closely. Brennan was getting restless and his leg bounced up and down. He watched Dwight cut the face off a CPR dummy and wear it as a mask and found absolutely no humor in it for the first time in the at least six times he'd seen it. He turned the TV off and flung the remote onto the couch in a mild display of frustration.

He texted James asking where he was. It was past two in the afternoon and his brother had not communicated with him at all.

He was putting his phone down when it buzzed again in his hand.

"I swear, if it's UTRG freakin' V…" he started, but it wasn't. His display showed a pretty face with a green headband and "Deidre N. Morales" directly under it.

Brennan answered hurriedly, almost fumbling his phone.

"Hey, Deidre. How are…" Brennan wasn't allowed to finish his question, though he no longer needed to. She was not well. She was crying. "Dee, what's wrong?"

"My mom, Bren. I left to work this morning. The neighbor was going to stay with her," she sobbed. "Sorry. The neighbor was going to stay. I left but she called me to tell me that my mom is missing." Her crying intensified and Brennan felt an ugly helplessness and uselessness climb into his gut. "She said that my mom should've been awake. She never sleeps all the way to one, so she went to check on her. She wasn't in bed. I don't know when she left. I'm sorry, I'm sorry to…"

"Dee, you have nothing to be sorry for. Did you call the cops already?"

"Yes!" she sounded exasperated, "She has a bad history. She's just an alchie, ex-whore to them."

"Dee…"

"Bren, I called all the bars. No one has seen her. I'm so sorry to have to ask you, but please help me…"

"No, it's no problem. What's her usual place, again?"

"8 Ball." Deidre replied. The tears were gone, but her voice was still shaking.

"Ok, meet me in the parking lot there in about 15 minutes. Can you do that?"

"Yeah, okay. Thanks, Brennan."

Brennan didn't hear her gratitude. He had already cut the call and was getting dressed. It took him all of five minutes. Jeans, sneakers, first t-shirt he found, and a belt to hold up his pants with the weight of his concealed carry weapon.

Brennan's heart pounded as he ran to his car. It wasn't just the impromptu cardio session. He was pushing the drive and anxiety out of his head as best he could, but he felt like he was going to die. His heart would explode, he'd keel over, dead. His face buzzed, his arms tingled and seemed to have tripled in weight. He jumped in his car, threw open the armrest compartment and found a singular rectangle of sweet, chemical, calm. He tried to break it in half and managed to divide it into a square and three. He threw the larger of the segments into the back of his mouth and hurriedly drank from a bottle that had stayed in his car overnight. The water was warm and washed down unpleasantly leaving a warm trail in his throat on an already hot day.

Brennan drove the way he felt. He was weaving in and out of traffic at a speed that should have gotten him pulled over. By the time he reached the 8 Ball he had been contemplating if the grace of God had spared him the ticket and the time it would have added to his trip. He was just getting back into the whole Jesus thing thanks to James but decided he wasn't far enough to give the Big Guy credit for this happenstance.

He parked in a space that felt right and familiar. The pill had begun to take effect.

A flash hit him more like a whirring buzz, a similar sensation, but slower and farther.

There was a rust bucket car, a drunk man, a gun, and an anger so severe it was practically palpable.

"Brennan?"

Brennan came back to himself and turned to see Deidre. Her eyes were red, but she no longer cried. Instead her face bore the marks of anger layered over her fear and concern.

"Deidre are you-"

"Stupid barkeep won't talk to me," she interrupted.

"What?" It registered at a mitigated pace, but Brennan managed to understand before she replied, "Oh, wait, which one? Who's on duty?"

"Mario's got the shift right now."

"Okay," Brennan said and felt like his brain zoomed in as the rush of adrenaline and the unprescribed Xanax battled it out in his head, with the adrenaline taking momentary power, "I'll take care of it."

"What are you going to do?" Deidre asked and Brennan noticed a hint of concern in her voice.

"I just need to ask some questions," Brennan said putting his palms up at shoulder level in a 'calm down' gesture.

"I already asked questions, Bren," Deidre's voice betrayed her, showing more of her anger and frustrations than she intended. Brennan seemed not to notice, however.

"He'll answer me," Brennan simply stated and walked away.

"What makes you so sure?" Deidre called out with that same curiosity that had removed her tact just the night before.

"I'm invested."

"In the bar?" Deidre looked at Brennan quizzically as she lightly jogged to catch up to him.

"No. I call it, Human Capital."

Brennan and Deidre entered the bar and Brennan signaled at Deidre to sit at a table in the corner while he walked up to the bar.

"It's-a me-a, Mario!" Brennan called out to the barkeeper.

"Oh, no, Brennan," Mario replied shaking his head and trying to look busy.

"What, man?" Brennan feigned bewilderment, "Speak. What's going on?"

"We reserve the right to refuse services to anyone, my friend, and I am exercising that right with ya."

"Why the cold shoulder, bud?" Brennan conveyed concern in his voice but wore a wry smile on his face.

"Look, amigo, your brother Jaime told me not to serve you. Even if I wasn't scared of that Chewbacca lookin' bastard tearing my arms outta their sockets, your mother warned me too and I fear she'd tear off more sacred parts."

Brennan chuckled. "No need to risk the family jewels. Club Soda and Lime, if you please."

Mario obliged and took a deep breath, "I'm sorry, Brennan. Ya know I appreciate ya and your familia."

Brennan kept his smile. "Actually, bud, can I trouble you for one more thing?"

"Sure thing, amigo. As long as it's not alcoholic."

"Well, actually, she is," Brennan quipped and showed Mario the picture Deidre had texted to his phone.

"Oh, man," Mario sighed out the words. He looked up and almost immediately spotted Deidre, making direct eye contact. "Look, hermano, I told the chickadee I hadn't seen her. She comes by when she sneaks off the wagon but haven't seen her since the last time."

"When was the last time?"

Color started to rise in Mario's cheeks, turning his light brown skin into a deep maroon.

"At what time today was the last time?" Brennan rephrased.

"About three hours ago," Mario said quietly.

"You serve her. You know she's got a monkey on her back and you still do it." Brennan had done away with the smile and was now speaking in a deep, low rumble.

"Hermano, ya gotta understand! My boss finds out I'm turning out paying customers and I end up in a bad way. I got bills, homie. I'm doing online school. I want out, but I need this job right now."

"Was she alone?" Brennan inquired.

"She showed up alone," Mario replied in a voice just above a whisper.

"Did she leave that way?" Brennan pressed.

"Uh… look, hermano. It's not my place to say. Some people like their privacy. They get mad. I can't have people mad at me. I've got Kimmy, ya know." Mario looked torn and Brennan did feel for him, but now was not the time to allow emotion to stop his investigation.

"You're right, hermano," Brennan told a relieved looking Mario, who did not catch the hint of sarcasm in 'hermano'. "You've got Kimmy. Family changes things."

"Yeah, bro. Thank you."

"How is Kimmy, by the way?"

"Great!" Mario replied, but then he caught up to where Brennan was in the conversation and his cautious joy faded, bringing back a mix of shame and concern, "Why?"

"Well, I was the one that introduced you guys. I'd hate to have her be heartbroken because of me, she's a sweet girl."

"Look, Brennan…"

"I mean, you were the white knight, Mario. Or rather, she was your Peach, right?" Brennan was wearing a fake grin he had put minimal effort into constructing. "You made her believe in chivalrous, good men out in the world. Or at least here in the Valley."

"I know where you're going with this…"

"Imagine how she'd feel to know the chivalrous knight who loves her mother so, did nothing, if anything actively stood against people trying to ensure the safety of a woman right around her ma's age."

"Fine," Mario growled. "I swear, Brennan, sometimes you are such a good man and others…" he trailed off and looked down as if searching for the right euphemism to censor his response, "other times you're like them clown faces all these ghetto dudes get tattooed on they ass. More two faced than Harvey Dent."

"I do what I need to," Brennan stated. This was not an excuse; it was not an apology. It was not even a justification, since that would mean Brennan felt he had to justify himself to someone who he currently saw as a withholding, interfering witness. This was just a statement of fact that closed this tangent they'd gone off on.

"Alright. I get it, hermano," Mario said this with at least quadruple the amount of razor-edged sarcasm Brennan had added to his use of the word. "Just keep my name out your mouth, eh. Kimmy and I don't need trouble. We're about to hit good times."

"There will be no mention of your name, I'm just here to have a chit chat with an old friend I haven't seen since I hitched a ride on the wagon." Brennan laughed suddenly, pointing to Mario as if Mario had just said something hilarious. What scared Mario wasn't the suddenness or reasonlessness of the laugh, it was the fact that it sounded exactly like every other time he had heard Brennan laugh. "Oh, boy, that's a good one, Mario," then in a softer voice, "get to the point."

"One of the Amaya guys. I don't know his real name, but they call him Gigolo, as in…"

"I know what it means."

"Yeah, so, he's known for liking his wine and cheese well aged."

"I get it," Brennan strained through gritted teeth. "He's a cougar hunter. He likes old ladies. I get it."

"He was hitting on her. She didn't give two craps. Looked real down in the dumps, ya see. He made her a, um, financial offer. She said no. She said she don't do that stuff anymore. He got a little aggro, but then says, 'hey, your loss' and buys her a drink as an apology."

"Let me guess, she was drunk after that drink," Brennan said in a cold, emotionless, voice. It wasn't a roundabout inquiry. Brennan knew he was right.

"She definitely seemed to be feeling it. I figure since she's been on the wagon a bit, ya know, her tolerance ain't what it was."

"Do you know where he went."

"Not for sure, hermano." Mario had added no sarcasm, no edge, that time. This was the good guy Brennan knew. The one that worked knee deep in crap and still managed to keep clean. "My guess is La Villa house. It's a nice place on the outskirts, the bars are asked to refer ladies, you know ilegales, who might be looking for work. I've heard about it, been approached, but I never-"

"I know, Mario. You're a good man, bud. I'm sorry I put you through the wringer."

Brennan stood up and took his wallet from his back pocket.

"Nah, man. Don't even think about it. On the house," Mario said.

"It's a tip then." Brennan insisted and lay a twenty on the bar, moving away before Mario could reject it again.

"Hey, buddy," Mario called after him. "You know where-"

Brennan cut him off again, this time for Mario's benefit. Most patrons of the bar could hear him calling out. "I know where the freaking Lowe's is, Mario. Y si no, I'll GPS it." He beamed at Mario and threw a hand up as a farewell.

Deidre stood up and headed out as soon as Brennan was out of the doors. She caught up with Brennan with a light jog again.

"Y'all were yucking it up pretty good back there." Deidre did her best to hide any sign of contempt or frustration, but once more her voice betrayed her.

"And the Oscar goes to…" Brennan teased in a humorless tone.

"What did he say?"

"She's with a guy. We're going to get her now."

"Good. Don't want to know what kind of jerk would take advantage of my mom's situation."

"No. You don't."

It was a fifteen-minute drive to La Villa, but Brennan made it in just over ten.

"Brennan? Brennan she's here? You didn't say she was here!" Deidre's worry seemed to be renewed and had brought some of its friend, terror, along.

"You know this place?" Brennan asked with no emotion being audibly conveyed as he parked on the shoulder of the street, not wanting to box himself into the driveway.

"Yeah, sometimes Mom worked this place when we were kids."

"Good, then you know to stay in the car," Brennan told her.

A chill ran up Deidre's spine. He was suddenly so different.

As the chill ran up her spine, a twin trail of gooseflesh traced Brennan's spine. He would've been touched to learn of this connection between him and his once and hopefully future wife, but instead he was focused on the cause of said chill. He didn't know if it was the pill, the thrill of being on the hunt again, or just a plain ol' adrenaline rush, but he felt focused. No anxiety, no nervousness, no fear or distress. There was no excitement or joy either. Just clear, rational, thought.

"Brennan, I can't stay."

"Please, Deidre. I don't want you hurt, and if I really want to help your mom, I need to do this without being worried about you."

Deidre did not protest, and Brennan marched up to the door. He knocked to the beat of "Shave and a Haircut". A woman opened the door. She was gaunt and painted with exaggerated makeup. She reminded Brennan of someone. He couldn't remember quite who. Carlos? No, that didn't make sense, it was surely Carla.

"How can I help you, sir?" the lady asked.

Brennan smiled the sleaziest, most charming, and smarmy grin he could conjure. "Hey, gorgeous. I hope you're on the stable."

"Stable? Sir, we don't have any horses."

"Oh, I know." Brennan cocked an eyebrow.

The woman smiled but didn't open the door further or move out of the way.

"Well, all the same. If you want riding lessons, you need to make an appointment with management, mister."

"Oh, I don't need any riding lessons, lil missy. Believe you me." Brennan edged closer to her and the woman reciprocated the intensity of his smile and flirty gaze. She got close to him and whispered so close that Brennan could feel and almost taste her cigarette and vodka breath, "Professional rides are by appointment too."

Brennan was growing frustrated with his failure when something hit the override button wired into his instincts. Distant, but inside the house, upstairs, there was a scream.

Brennan looked back and as he expected, Deidre had left the car and was edging ever closer to the thinly veiled brothel.

"Call 911!" Brennan yelled at her, startling the woman at the door.

He shoved past her and ran up the stairs, taking them two at a time, thanking God and providence that he had chosen sneakers and hating himself for not taking James up on his offers to join him on his daily runs.

He reached the top of the stairs and did all he could to ignore the way air felt like molten lead in his lungs. Another muffled scream, much shorter this time, interrupted by a resounding slap that was almost surely leather belt on flesh. Brennan ran to the end, shoving a girl, surely no older than sixteen, who had come out of her designated room wearing a sheer robe, trying to investigate the commotion. She fell back inside her room and Brennan barked back at her,

"Shut the freakin' door!"

He heard footsteps behind him as he neared the end of the hallway. They were coming from the second-floor landing.

"Deidre, please tell me you didn't follow me in." Brennan thought.

He arrived at the last door. Heard a muffled cry and another slapping sound. He tried the door and it was unlocked. He figured it was probably a security measure for the Amaya family to protect their merchandise. He swung it violently open.

The interior of the room was a bizarre scene to behold. Deidre's mom Misty was kneeling, almost as if in prayer, by a heart shaped sofa that took up most of the room's floor space. She was shirtless, but still wearing a plain, white bra, that would have made a matching set to some equally white 'granny panties'. There were welts on her back. A man, lanky thin, with leathery tan skin, shoulder length black hair, with a few grey streaks peppered in, sunken dark eyes, a straight nose, and nicotine yellowed teeth was holding Misty's hair in one hand and a belt in another. He was stripped down to his boxers, but at least he was wearing

434

those, thank goodness for small favors. They were a light blue, though going a bit yellow green in the crotch.

The man, nicknamed Gigolo, was stunned by Brennan's brave and sudden entrance.

"Que onda, Gigolo?! How's it going brother?" Brennan had learned that if you approach a person, in almost any situation, and talk to them like you're elementary school buddies, they tend to react slowly, trying to remember you. He was hoping this distraction would be enough for Misty to squirm away so Brennan could knock out or choke out this gangster with mommy issues until the police arrived.

Gigolo did seem confused and he did slow down. He wondered who Brennan was and would've asked if the boss sent him, but Deidre caught up with Brennan, looking very shocked, emotional, and stressed. She was behind Brennan, but Gigolo could see her, Brennan only faintly felt her behind him. Gigolo simultaneously pulled Misty up towards him by the hair and reached to his dresser towards the metal thing sitting on top. This was not a great angle to see it from, but Brennan immediately recognized the rectangle visible to him as the top slide of a handgun.

Brennan's right arm became a blur, going to his inside waistband holster. Brennan trained with heavy calibers, in large part because he remembered his father would swear by a .40. Yet, today he had taken the 9mm P320. After training with heavier calibers, the recoil of the 9mm felt minuscule and easily manageable, allowing increased accuracy.

Three shots rang it in quick succession. The first one thundered in the enclosed space, leaving the occupants of the room and hallway feeling a deafening pressure in their ears. Almost deafening enough to keep out Deidre and Misty's horrified screams. With the deafened ears, the two following bangs resounded in the room, but sounded distant and muffled to the strange group of four.

Almost instantly and keeping in the same cadence as the sound of the shots fired, two large splatters of blood and bone hit the wall behind Gigolo. The third splatter had brain added to the recipe.

In what was definitely an inappropriate, though memorable, conversation to have with a nine-year-old, Brennan's father had taught him that if you carry, you should carry hollow points. They're better for self-defense because there's less liability and danger of your bullet tearing through your enemy and then a nearby bystander. The side effect was that the bullet went in clean, then mushroomed and came out with an exit wound like a saucer plate. This explained why Gigolo had two red circles on his chest and one in his face, while a large chunk of his back and the occipital bone of his skull were obliterated.

Brennan stood motionless and emotionless as Deidre's mom ran to her. Her white bra was now peppered with red. Misty sobbed and screamed. Deidre stood with her mother clinging to her waist, leaving maroon smears on Deidre's jeans. Deidre's usually beautifully brown eyes, like well-polished redwood, were now dull and empty. They stared at nothing and somehow at everything. Deidre coldly pushed her mother off and tried to open the window to the left of the room. She wasn't quick enough to do so, and she vomited at the end of the hallway. Brennan turned to Deidre and walked to comfort and help her.

As Brennan reached out and touched her shoulder, she recoiled from him and Brennan's heart broke at both the action and it's strange sense of familiarity.

He had been here before. He had loved her before. She had recoiled at his touch before. In another life and another time and for other reasons, he had been here before.

Chapter 43

Brennan didn't know and didn't much care for how long it had been. He hadn't cared for much since that familiar and devastating moment with Deidre.

The police, on the other hand, did care. Taking his statement, questioning him, talking to witnesses, running gunfire residue tests on the webbing between his right hand's index finger and thumb, it had all amounted to about six hours of work. Through every minute of it, Brennan had obediently and robotically cooperated.

"Dude, he told you he shot the guy. He literally said he fired the gun. Why the hell did you have to swab him? Why go through all this? He's been here for six FREAKING hours. He saved a life. Now you've got plenty to shut that brothel down, make a big dent in the Amaya trafficking ring. He did your job and better than y'all. You should be thanking him."

"James sounds upset," Brennan thought absently.

"What? Afraid your wife's gonna lose work?!" James yelled as the officer left. "Hey," James called another officer's attention, "Can you get me Detective Aguilar? Ace?" A pause. "Medical leave? Still? It was a flesh wound."

The left side of Brennan's mouth actually twitched up in what was almost a smile.

James finally finished his detoured walk towards Brennan and hugged his older brother, who did not hug back.

"Bren, are you alright?" James asked as he scanned his brother stem to stern.

"I'm fine." Brennan's voice was monotonous and just a hair above a whisper.

"I'm sorry, bud." James sat next to his brother and put a comforting hand on his shoulder. "This has you pretty messed up, huh? I can imagine. I mean…"

"No," Brennan interrupted. "Do you remember after the Medellin case?"

"Yeah." James nodded lightly.

"I was freaking out about you, but I wasn't exactly haunted by the fact I had to take out a small-time mob boss to save you."

"This time you are?"

"No," Brennan repeated. "This time I'm not even freaked out about anything. I just…" Brennan searched for the right way to say what was on his mind, but there wasn't one. There was no honest way to sugarcoat it. "When I saved you, you were shocked, but you understood. Deidre, she," Brennan exhaled loudly, "she looked afraid. Disgusted. Like I was a monster."

"She probably hadn't seen someone die violently in front of her. That'll mess someone up on the quicks, bud. I heard you Mozambiqued the dude." James grimaced and sucked his teeth, "Mozambique with hollow points is gory enough to turn most people's stomachs. I'm sure it wasn't about you, bud."

"I felt nothing, James. I should have, but I didn't. Not even anxiety." Brennan finally looked up over at his brother. "She could tell."

"Bud, you're in shock. While it doesn't let you feel anything sometimes, it's a pretty normal reaction to a pretty abnormal situation. It's not easy to take a life. You'll feel plenty once you process everything."

"No, James. I felt nothing. I still feel nothing, except for the concern and pain I feel about losing whatever I had with Deidre."

"Buddy, it'll come."

"James," Brennan locked eyes with his brother now. Brennan's eyes, a brilliant emerald green, had gone dull. It was like their light had gone out, "I don't care. I killed a guy who needed killing. Waste of space and resources. An abuser, a pimp, a real monster. I shot a rabid dog to prevent the further spread of his infection. Nothing more, nothing less. It was procedure. It was necessary." Brennan's voice lowered in both pitch and volume. "It was easy. I felt nothing."

James heard a sincere, subtle intensity in Brennan's voice and could read the honesty all over his face. His brother was not in shock at all. Just upset.

"Okay, Brennan. I believe you." James scooted closer and wrapped an arm around Brennan, this time not to comfort him, but to disguise a private tête-à-tête. "Did they drug test you?"

Brennan felt his stomach and chest stiffen with unease.

"No."

"Then we need to get out of here before they decide to. I'm going to ask them to let you go, make a scene of it. If they are not arresting you, they'll release you."

James stood up and talked to an officer sitting behind a desk.

"Hey, my brother has been here for six hours or more, can he go?"

"I think they still had some questions for-"

"Is he being arrested? Is he being detained?"

The officer looked both annoyed and intimidated but answered strongly and respectfully.

"No, sir, he is not being detained."

"Okay, then. If they have further questions, Detective Aguilar and Officer Barrera have his number and our address. I'm sure it's also written down on one of the million reports you had him fill. He can answer questions after a long shower and longer sleep." James beckoned his brother with a wave of his hand.

Brennan stood up and accompanied him out.

James and Brennan were only a minute into their drive when James broke the silence.

"When did you start?"

"Start what?" Brennan asked, still flat and emotionless.

"Don't do the dumb act, big brother. It's unbecoming."

Brennan did not answer.

"I'm not a freaking court, Brennan. You can't plead the Fifth. I found some pills in your car. I told myself that maybe they were in your car for emergencies only."

"That's exactly what they're for."

"STOP LYING, BRENNAN!" James' voice boomed in the enclosed cabin of the truck and hurt Brennan's ears which had still been aching from the gunshots. Even then, Brennan didn't flinch. "That's why you felt nothing. You've been acting so weird and I figured it was just the recovery process post-coma, but I should have known."

James paused to let Brennan respond, but Brennan kept his silence and James still had much he wanted to say.

"You know, I think I did know. I think I didn't want to see it. I didn't want to accept that my brother had hit a giant reset button in his brain to ditch alcohol and pick up pills. So, how long Brennan?"

Brennan still offered silence as his only reply.

"I'm not the best detective. I'm not the freaking Batman, Sherlock Holmes, or the eminent Brennan Ramirez, but I'm going to guess it's been at least since the Marzo stakeout. You took them from him, didn't you?"

Brennan thought it wise to remain silent.

"Fine, Bren. Whatever. We can talk tomorrow. You've been through a lot today, but we will talk."

Brennan and James arrived at the apartment. They both quietly ambled towards the door which James opened and allowed Brennan to enter first. Brennan went straight to his room without a single word. He would shower, he needed to shower, but for now he just wanted a bit of rest. He wanted to drown the silent rage that had been sloshing around in his chest like lava. He'd rest and let it die.

Brennan's brain snuck into slumber much too quickly and sneakily for Brennan to notice or fight it. It was a half hour before his phone began to go off. It was still on vibrate, but also still in his pocket.

It was the University again. Suddenly, he could not suppress the frustration any longer. He answered with full intention of going off on the unsuspecting professor.

"What do you want?" Brennan seethed.

"Mr. Ramirez, so glad to finally get to speak to you, I was calling because-"

"Burn it. Melt it. Sell it for parts. I don't care what you do with the device, just leave me the bloody, puss spewing, hell ALONE!"

Brennan moved the phone away from his ear, ready to disconnect when the professor's voice called out, "No, Brennan! Please! No!"

"What?" Brennan asked, nearly as exasperated with himself as with the professor.

"Your device-"

"It's not mine. Didn't you need to learn to read to get to your ivory tower, professor? I'm quite sure the report says-"

"That's the thing, Mr. Ramirez," Abernathy said, reverting to his professional voice, "I strongly believe it is. I think you built this. I think your brain is the best insight into how to use it."

"Sorry, I'm not the chemistry kit, science type." Brennan replied and then said to himself, "*I doth protest too much, methinks.*"

"I looked into your background. Everything up to college pointed to you pursuing a scientific career. Why you decided on public service, law enforcement, is beyond me and surely none of my business, but Mr. Ramirez, please. They're going to take it back soon. If they do, we might never learn its purpose. If I'm even close to being right, this is science beyond what's currently practical. Hell, most of it is barely theoretical. Together we can unlock this. This could change everything."

"Change everything? Whatever it is, it put me in a coma and caused crush injuries and lacerations. It'll change everything, alright. One messed up, beat up, person at a time."

"I don't believe even you believe that, Mr. Ramirez. I believe if you stop, think, and consider, you'll realize that there's much more to your situation and definitely much more to this device than just your injuries."

Brennan was a lot of things. Out of those many things, he felt anxiety and intelligence defined him best, but not completely. He considered one characteristic of his as having the potential to be equally constructive and destructive, not just for him, but for all who suffered or reveled in its excess. This, of course, was curiosity. In that moment, Brennan was enraptured by the curiosity to find the purpose of The Machine, *his* Machine. He knew it was his. He felt he had known all along. He had wanted it gone from him. He had wanted it away.

As if he had read Brennan's mind, the professor spoke up, "Can you meet me at my office in an hour? I'll text you the room number. It's in the science building. I left it unlocked, just in case."

Brennan closed his eyes and tried to mentally stretch out his auditory perception. He heard a static like noise coming from down the hall. It was the bathroom and the static sound was the shower spraying the shower curtain, wall, and in all probability, James.

"Fine. I'll see you there. I'll give you fifteen minutes."

The professor let out a shrill, nervous laugh that made Brennan feel uncomfortable in a low part of his gut. The closest familiar feeling Brennan could compare it to was a faint but foul smell that turns your stomach.

"Oh, thank you, Mr. Ramirez. I'll see you here. I look forward to seeing you here and exploring-"

"Yup," Brennan interrupted, "see you in an hour." Brennan clicked the red circle on his screen and tossed the phone onto a pillow.

Brennan had learned that it wasn't always the wisest choice to live by his gut and take the leap, but that didn't mean he should ignore it completely. He had read studies about how the subconscious brain, the "lizard brain" as Brennan referred to it, detected smells, sounds, behavior, and all sorts of sensory stimuli that our conscious mind ignores. This in turn causes the "gut feeling" that perhaps would've saved our lives when people still had to hunt for their food and humans didn't have as steady a hold on the top of the food chain. That instinct told him he shouldn't wait. He should leave immediately, try to catch Abernathy off guard. Brennan put on his sneakers, tucked his inside-the-waistband holster and 9mm into his pants, then changed his mind and took it out. He cursed the weapon he had used only hours earlier and shoved it into his sock drawer. He figured the odds of him having to shoot a person twice in a day would be pretty slim.

Brennan headed to his closet, reached into the hidden pocket of his boot and took out two long Xanax rectangles. Knowing he'd need to be clear headed and that he would not only be driving, but driving at night, he broke one of the bars in half and dry swallowed painfully. It was a gruesome, albeit relatively mild, choking pain, but it was oddly satisfying. It felt right. It felt like penance.

As Brennan walked out of his brother's apartment, he paused in the doorway. He felt a pang of deep sorrow.

He whispered, "I'm not coming back, am I?"

Brennan held back tears and scoffed, deciding that it was useless to ask questions to no one. If a man asks a nonsensical question in the middle of the forest and nobody is there to hear it, does he still sound stupid?

Brennan got into his car and drove. He was antsy, inhaling deeply, holding the cool night air in his lungs, then exhaling completely, for the first fifteen minutes. After that, the pill began to take effect, subtly at first, then more completely. He felt like he couldn't be stressed. He also couldn't seem to keep his mind empty. It wandered from thought to thought. He formulated different conversations he'd have with Deidre, apologizing, trying to justify himself, and doing what he could to win her good graces. A song came on the radio, which had been playing at a low volume the entire drive, and suddenly he was caught up in a fantasy where he was singing the song to Deidre, serenading her in perfect pitch and expertly playing guitar.

"Don't want to close my eyes, I don't want to fall asleep, cause I'd miss you babe, and I don't want to miss a thing..."

He felt, in a word, relaxed.

He arrived at the university and purposely parked one lot away from the science building.

There was more to his budding addiction than just chemical tranquility. He had been able to restrict himself to doses of Xanax lower than the average addict's choice, most of the time at least, because the true addiction was that balance of anxiety and peace. There was a happy middle where Brennan could swear his senses were as sharp as any sword, his mind as clear as newly polished glass, and his heartbeat strong and steady, like the ominous bass drum opening of an epic symphony. It was all the benefits of hyper-awareness with none of the fear, tachycardia, or existential dread.

As he walked to the science building, purposely sticking to the shadow painted parts of the sidewalk, that was how he felt. In a balance perfectly held over a razor's edge, ready to strike at any moment. It was the feeling that he had when he, not his gun, had dispatched Gigolo so efficiently that the police had initially insisted premeditation.

"I aim with my eye, shoot with my mind, and kill with my heart." Brennan remembered the line from a favorite series of his. As a young teen, his face always in a book and his head always in the clouds, he had always identified himself with The Dark Tower's Jake and imagined that in that universe, his father would have been Roland.

447

Brennan stopped moving suddenly and listened, once more stretching his hearing towards the sound that had caused him to pause. Footsteps, coming from a hall that led to the student health building. A young brunette woman came out, holding books to her chest. She looked at Brennan and then walked away, quickening her pace. Brennan noticed she had her keys sticking out from between her fingers, and he felt sympathy for her. He did his best to walk away quickly and a bit more loudly now, so that she would know he was not following.

Brennan finally arrived at the science building. He took a detour before reaching the front entrance. He walked around the back of the building and saw no one. He looped around once and then entered through a side door. The building was dimly lit, but Brennan could see bright fluorescent light coming out of a few rooms currently being used to study, or to grade papers by professors. The room number Professor Abernathy had given him was 2.121.

"Second floor," Brennan thought, and he soundlessly climbed the stairs. His feet rolled step by step, keeping him almost completely silent.

Brennan reached the second floor and looked at the first classroom to his right. 2.115. Beyond that there was 2.117. He continued down that hallway. At the corner of the hall was 2.119. He peeked past the corner and noticed the light to 2.121 was off. He made his way down the hallway that 2.121 was on and checked the even numbered offices and classrooms opposite. 2.124 opened as soon as he twisted the handle. He walked in and kept the lights off, leaving the door just open enough for him to see 2.121.

"When is a door, not a door?" Brennan thought randomly.

He had been there for less than ten minutes when a thin man with a full head of white hair, all combed back, a padlock beard of varying shades of grey, and a billowing white lab coat, obviously a size or two oversized, approached 2.121.

Brennan silently slid down the hall back to 2.121.

"Hello, professor," Brennan said in a deep, gravelly voice.

Professor Abernathy just about hit the ceiling. His hands flew to his chest and he spun around in a panic. "Jesus, Mary, and Joseph!" A repressed Irish accent resurfaced in the professor's moment of surprise. "You damn near scared the American out of me, Mr. Ramirez."

"Brennan is fine."

"Brennan, then, you can call me-"

"I think Professor should suffice," Brennan interrupted.

"Very well, Brennan." Professor Abernathy forced a smile and then pointed at the door across the hall. "My lab room is 2.120. I often get to class late and tell my students that they must pardon me, it's a long walk." Abernathy forced a chuckle this time and Brennan let out something between a laugh and a scoff, mostly out of politeness. "If you'll follow me, your device is locked away in my lab locker."

Abernathy set his phone and car keys on his messy desk and led Brennan across the hall and into a lab room that could accommodate 12 students, if they sat two per lab table. Abernathy flicked the lights on and bright, blue tinged, white glow illuminated the room. The floors were cheap white tile, the walls were white, the ceiling was white. The only contrast in the room was the black tables.

Brennan noticed the shelves were painted white as well and was struck by another random thought,

"The school could use an interior designer."

Abernathy walked to a double door locker about eight feet tall and three feet wide. He took a key that hung on a UTRGV orange and green lanyard and opened the locker.

The machine seemed to stare at Brennan through it's one, central, blue eye. A single word came to Brennan's mind.

"Time."

"Okay, Brennan," the professor said excitedly, "if you truly don't remember, you may want to take a seat for this."

"I assure you I cannot remember, but I'll stand if it's all the same to you."

Abernathy raised his hands and shrugged in a, "if you say so" motion. The professor made eerie eye contact with Brennan and sighed deeply, "I believe that in my hands," the Professor said as he held up the strange object. The four straps, all connected to the blue circle in the middle reminded Brennan of the crisscrossed gun belts worn by Mexican revolutionaries in the movies. "I believe that I hold in my hands," the Professor repeated, changing his wording just a tad, "the first ever time travel device."

Brennan laughed out loud.

"You're joking." Brennan rolled his eyes and began to walk out.

"It works through thought, I think," Abernathy called out. This made Brennan turn back. Something about that statement rang true. "See, there are so many factors that would have to be precisely calculated to plan even the most basic of time travel. By focusing on a specific when and where, emotionally tied more than likely, the subconscious, the… the, um…"

"The lizard brain," Brennan provided.

"Yes! Good term. Lizard brain, I like it." Abernathy was smiling a shameless, greedy, grin now, "It's a very personal method of travel, at least I would imagine, but think of the possibilities and applications. You could go back and fix old mistakes, remove traumatic events, win the lottery, or hell, an old enough man could go back to the prime of his life and stop Lee Harvey Oswald!" Abernathy exclaimed loudly. His grin, wide to start with, seemed to spread up his cheeks.

"He wouldn't go back to his prime," Brennan said, referring to the old man example. "He'd go back, see himself in his prime maybe, but he'll still be the same old man."

The professor's wide smile became toothy, "So you admit it! This is yours! I knew it!"

"It's an educated guess, Professor," Brennan insisted, lying to the professor, but no longer lying to himself. "I assume it would cause some difficulty to operate within close range of your other self though, considering it works off of memories."

Brennan swiftly took The Machine into his own hands.

"What else can you tell me about this?" Brennan asked as he turned the device in his hands.

One hand slipped away from the device and snuck into his pocket. Like most of the people in his generation, Brennan could operate the basic functions of his smart phone without looking.

"Well," the Professor began, "I'm not sure how it's powered. I have a sense it's somehow powered by the user. Bioelectricity or movement, I'm not exactly sure. I found no connector that would use allow this. Not to mention how dangerous it would be for the user."

"Really?" Brennan said with an exaggerated sense of wonder.

Brennan swiped his finger on the fingerprint reader and hit the "Call" icon twice.

Abernathy's phone began to ring in his office across the hall. Brennan looked out of the door and saw struggle in Abernathy's face. "Ugh," he grunted, "I should probably get that."

Abernathy ran out and Brennan began to strap the device on himself. He found the electrodes had been replaced. They had new small gel pads that helped them stick.

"Ah! Blast it all, I can't find it! Did you see where I set my phone?" Abernathy asked, concern and frustration teeming in his voice. He wasn't concerned with the phone. He was concerned with leaving Brennan for too long.

"Nope, sorry. I think you may have placed it on your desk. Did you check around your piles of paper? Maybe it's under one." Brennan suggested this and smiled, remembering how quickly and smoothly he had slid the phone into the trash can.

The Machine was fully strapped. Brennan hit redial on his phone again and heard the phone in the office start ringin.

"If that's my wife, she's gonna kill me!"

Brennan left the call screen and entered texts. He fired a text out to Deidre.

"I wish I could make up for all my wrongs. I know it's early, but I have a feeling this is a one-way trip, so now's the time... I love you, Deidre. You're it. It was always you. I can't explain our connection with anything rational. Please, forgive me. I hope to see you soon."

He clicked send.

"How did this get in the trash?" Professor Abernathy asked out loud.

Brennan realized he had no time for a loving lengthy message anymore.

He took his phone and typed out a message for James.

"I love you. You are the best brother a person could have asked for. People often choose their best friends. God sent me mine."

Send.

"Brennan, did you call me?" A moment's pause as realization sank to Professor Abernathy's, Professor Abby's, mind, "BRENNAN! NO! NOT UNTIL-"

Brennan dropped his phone and hit the blue button on his chest.

There was twisting, stretching, bending, and all of it was excruciating. He was Nothing and the Nothing was him.

Suddenly he felt himself growing, being yanked apart like soft dough that's to be shaped. First he had a chest, then arms, then legs and what's in between. He had a mouth and breathing was possible and immediately, terrifyingly, necessary.

Once his body was shaped, he dropped further down and hit an invisible floor.

He managed to turn himself around onto his back and breath. His eyelids fought to droop down and he wanted, more than ever, to sleep.

He couldn't move. There was pain, excruciating pain. Then, a voice.

"Is okay, da-ee. Imma fiss you!"

He lay there, trembling, the taste of his own blood in his mouth, and suddenly everything was black. There were odd, droning, distant voices… "Congratulations, It's a boy."

His body was being touched by the warmest hands he'd ever felt. He was scared and there were giant voices advising about cutting a cord, cleaning, and suction.

"Holy crap." he realized all at once, "I'm being born!"

<u>Part IV</u>

Nowhen

Chapter 44

Except, no, he wasn't. He felt the sensation of being lifted. He saw his mother through blurred eyes. His father was there too. He could hear him, smell him. Still, somewhere far away, he was lying on the ground. A ground that had no temperature, no form, it just was. There was also a hand. A small, warm, chubby little thing gripping his hand while its twin gripped his arm. It took him a moment to understand in the midst of all the confusion.

He was in the Nothing, someone was with him, and he was reliving his birth. For a second Brennan tried to further his understanding, but all he could gather was that this was like the most intense virtual reality experience. He saw the world from newly opened eyes, felt his mother's caress, but it wasn't real.

Brennan tried to sit up and shake it off. He couldn't move. He tried again and could not muster even the slightest twitch. He tried to speak, but only a low groan came out.

"Is okay, Da-ee."

It was the person holding him. There was someone else too. Further away, but there.

"Is he okay?"

The voice sounded low pitched and muffled. It reminded Brennan of how you hear the world when a dentist administers some anesthetic gas.

"Is just hurts, gwampa."

Grandpa? Had that been what she said? Brennan fell deeper with a very literal sinking feeling.

Being a baby was extremely boring, but Brennan relaxed and watched the moments go by. Even the truly uncomfortable parts, like a first-person point of view of a diaper change and breastfeeding, were somehow soothing.

A few months before a year passed, Brent Ramirez delighted in hearing his son say, "Pa-pa!". His mother acted playfully annoyed that Brennan's first word wasn't for her. Ma-ma came two weeks later. A few months after that, Brennan felt as his shaky knees supported him, and he took his first steps.

When he made it all the way to his father, his father had wrapped him up in an embrace tight enough to scare Baby Brennan for a second and his mother cheered, jumping up and down like a fangirling teen.

Far away, Brennan felt a warm tear slide down the side of his face towards his ear, but before it arrived a small set of lips kissed it away.

Another couple of weeks passed and his father was leaving. He was wearing clothes like Baby Brennan's G.I. Joe and had a large, dark green duffle bag with him. Stranger still, he was crying.

The real Brennan understood, but he could nonetheless feel Baby Brennan's confusion.

There was no real articulation in Baby Brennan's thoughts, but Brennan's adult brain could pull meaning from them.

"Why is he crying? Why is he so sad? He always leaves in the morning and comes back when it's going to be dark."

Baby Brennan's confusion, and inability to articulate or verbalize said confusion, reached a tipping point. His bottom lip pooched out and quivered, his tiny brows slanted down at the outside ends, his eyes squinted, and he began to bawl.

His father held him close and kissed his chubby, rosy cheek.

"Everything is going to be okay. I'll be back before you know it. 'Ta bueno, campeon?'"

His father was smiling now, but his tears had not stopped flowing.

Brent left and mom took Brennan to play in his room. Brennan grabbed his G.I. Joe, now G.I. Dad, and went to sleep on his toddler bed instead.

A few days later someone new arrived. Well, perhaps new is not the right term. Brennan had seen her before, but not often. She looked like mom, but her hair was short, and she had wrinkly skin. At first, she called herself Grandma, but Brennan can't pronounce that yet. She tried Abby and that seemed to work.

Abby was really nice. She sang funny songs, played funny games, and gave him horsey back rides. When mom got sad and went to her room, Abby took Brennan to the guest room and they watched cowboy movies on TV. Brennan liked cowboys. They wore boots and hats like his dad. He really missed his dad.

Months passed by and mom was starting to look happier. She played with Brennan more and went to her room less. Sometimes her and Abby got in fights, but it was okay because they got happy later.

Brennan still couldn't say Grandma but managed "Gwama" so Abby became "Gwama Abby". He wasn't too sure what a Gwama is, but he thought maybe Gwama was like an older mommy.

Brennan saw every single one of Baby Brennan's days as he became Toddler Brennan.

It was his birthday and he was excited. He didn't understand birthdays yet, he just knew there was a party, he saw a cake, and a lot of presents that he would get to open. Everything smelled good, his mom and gwama weren't fighting and a lot of people were holding him, smiling, and playing with him. He liked all of them. Well, most. There's one girl he didn't like. His gwama said her name is "tia" and Toddler Brennan found it odd that so many women are named the exact same thing. Tia held him and smiled at him. Brennan doesn't like how she smells. Toddler Brennan couldn't place the smell, but the adult brain connected the dots again. She smelled like the fake fruit smell from an air freshener. Overly sweet and pungent. As she set him down, Toddler Brennan gasped. He felt an ant bite on his leg, but there was no ant. He looked at this bad smelling tia and cried. His mom came and took him. She carried him and said he was getting too big. She gave him a candy out of someone's goody bag and he soon forgot about the ant bite.

Toddler Brennan decided to stay away from the smelly tia and the day continued in its previously joyous form. Then there was another problem. Mom took him outside and there was a giant G.I. Daddy made of something like paper hanging from a tree. All the kids lined up and mom took him to the front. It's amazing. The G.I. Daddy was almost as big as real daddy.

Then things got weird. She gave him a big stick and helped him hold it. She guided his hands to tap the figure. He figured that mommy didn't know how to play with the G.I. Daddy and Brennan drops the stick to clue her in. Mom laughed and crouched carefully, Brennan still in her arms, to pick it up.

"No, mijito. Asi," she told him calmly and then, for no obvious reason Toddler Brennan can make out, she wacked the G.I. Daddy in the head. Toddler Brennan was shocked! That was definitely not the way to play.

"Go, andale, bebe."

Toddler Brennan refused the stick.

"Mira, mijo. Like this." Mom wound up with the stick and Toddler Brennan saw what she was about to do.

"NO! DADDY!" Toddler Brennan yelled with a fervor unexpected in a two-year-old. He pushed off of his mother's arm, diving for the hand holding the stick. This caused his mother to stumble momentarily, almost dropping him and falling herself. He managed to grab the arm holding the stick with both hands and his painfully thin baby teeth chomped down near her wrist.

"OW!" Mom cried out and dropped the stick as half her brain moved her right hand to clutch Brennan and the other half moved it to clutch the injured arm.

As a result, Toddler Brennan fell and for the first time in his life, knocked his wind out. His back and chest hurt, and his mother is immediately upon him trying to hold him and check him for injury, but Toddler Brennan was too fast and wiggly. He squirmed out of her hands and stood in front of G.I. Daddy, crying loudly and unashamed. His legs and arms were spread open, trying to cover as much of the piñata as he could, though he barely reached its knee.

He stood there, a boy only a couple of days removed from his actual second birthday, staring defiantly at a row of children and a crowd of adults, protecting what was intended to be a G.I. Joe piñata the way a Secret Service agent may protect the president.

Adult Brennan stared out of his younger self's eyes feeling emotions that his adult mind had to process into words to fully understand. As rage and fear pounded in the toddler's mind, boiling hot tears swam out of his disproportionately large, green eyes, and his lungs ached as they tried to regain control of his breath, the immature, instinctive emotions in Toddler Brennan's heart were translated into a single word in Adult Brennan's mind.

"Heathens."

Chapter 45

The giant G.I. Daddy was not only spared but became a decoration in Brennan's room.

A few months after that, mom got a call. She started crying. She was talking to gwama and then gwama saw him watching. She took him to her room and put on cartoons. She wouldn't tell Brennan why his mother was crying though.

Mom left for a few days. It was just Brennan and gwama. She took him to the park to play on swings, she rented movies from a lady down the street. The lady had a huge collection and rented them at fifty cents a tape. She made him his favorite meals, first chicken strips, then gorditas, and on the third and final day, a mini cheeseburger.

Mom came back and she was not alone.

"Daddy?" Toddler Brennan asked the man she came back with.

He looked like his father, but his face was tanned, his hair was very short, and he was wearing his arm in a sling.

"Hey, Campeon," the man said with a weary smile.

"Daddy?" Toddler Brennan repeated and he ran to him as fast as his little chubby legs could carry him, his face contorting into a tomato red mess of tears. "Daddy!"

Brent went to one knee and caught his son in his uninjured arm. He winced in pain as his son collided into him.

Toddler Brennan buckled his hands together behind his father's neck. Brent stood up, bringing Toddler Brennan up with him. They were both happy, but things were not the same. Brent was not the same. Toddler Brennan, in his inarticulate, toddler mind sensed the difference in a way that the Adult Brennan, once more crying as he lay paralyzed on the floor, interpreted as a smell. He smelled different.

Soon, everything else in life changed. Everyone was happy his father was back, but everyone sensed the difference now.

Toddler Brennan sometimes stayed up at night, worried it would be a bad night for his dad, and often it was. His father would wake up in the middle of the night and Toddler Brennan could hear him through the thin walls, crying. He called himself a murderer. A killer. A failure. Mom tried to help him, but he only got angry.

Brent had always loved his son but had also always been strict. His son called him "Daddy", but when something is asked of him, Brennan replies with "sir". Lately though, Brent expected his son, quickly going on three to stand at attention. He didn't say as much, he didn't consciously teach him this, but he did teach him, nonetheless.

Brennan was playing with his toys. G.I. Daddy was beating up a plastic T-Rex and the T-Rex went flying through the air and struck a giant mountain, which in reality is a vase. The vase tottered, the mountain fell.

Brent rushed into the room. For a second, there was a look in his eye that Adult Brennan recognized as concern. He thought his son might be hurt.

"Brennan did you do this?" The concern was gone from his face, it was stern anger now.

"Yes," Brennan replied in a voice barely above a whisper.

"Speak so I can hear you!" Brent's voice climbed in volume.

"Yes," Brennan repeated, louder, his voice breaking.

"Yes, what?"

"Yes, sir."

Brent took a menacing step towards his son, at least that's how it looked to his boy, "Stand up straight! Look at me when I'm talking to you!"

Nancy looked nervous and conflicted. Gwama Abby was a silent observer, but her eyes were shrink wrapped in tears and Adult Brennan could recognize that it was taking all her control to stand still.

"What the hell were you doing?"

"Playing, sir."

"Playing? With what? The vase? Does that look like a freaking toy to you?"

"It was an assident, sir." Brennan said. The mispronunciation of accident hit Abby's heart particularly hard.

Unknown to her, this also hit Brent's heart and reminded him that his son is only two. Unknown to her, Brent felt he couldn't stop, but he wanted to.

Brent closed his eyes and inhaled, "There are no accidents, only carelessness. We are responsible for our actions, we need to be in control!"

Brent advanced toward his son, his muddled intention was to go to his knee, give him one or two more stern words, something he'd remember, then maybe hug him. Brennan just saw the angry doppelganger of his father move to him and he flinched.

Brent froze and his heart dropped to his stomach, but before he could say anything, Abby had swooped in and led Brennan away.

"See, Brennie boy, this is why we need to be careful. This is why you need to play in your room. You aren't wearing chanclas! You can cut yourself. Let's go put on chanclas and then we'll get the broom and I'll show you how to clean this."

Adult Brennan heard a voice, miles away. It took him a second to realize it's his voice. His adult voice, breaking, and skipping through sobs.

"He needed… help. He needs help. Broken. He's broken. I should've seen…"

The faraway little hands tightened on his right arm, but now there was the other person, the one the little girl called Gwampa. His much larger, much stronger, handheld Brennan's shoulder and the low, distorted, voice spoke again.

"Nothing you could do. Not your fault, son."

Days went by, turning into weeks, turning into months. Life was getting better. Brent was working the night shift. Toddler Brennan didn't know where his dad worked, only that he slept during the day, worked at night, and dressed like a policeman.

Toddler Brennan noticed that Mommy is getting fat. He liked touching her belly and he noticed it was getting harder, not jiggly, like his belly.

Mom and dad had a meeting in the living room with Brennan and Gwama Abby. Mommy explained that she had a baby in her belly. Brennan, shocked by this revelation, asked his mother the only rational question he could ask in that moment.

"Why you ate him!"

They laughed. His father laughed and this made Brennan happy.

She explained that she didn't eat the baby. Babies grow in their mom's belly.

More time went by. Brennan left out a toy truck. His grandmother finally lost her temper with his father and said something his mom called a "low blow".

Brent and Brennan had the heart to heart that Brennan would not be able to understand until it was much too late to do anything.

Abby was forced to leave, despite Brent's insistence that there was no reason for her to go. Nancy said Abby was never there for her and now she wanted to be Supergrandma by yelling and demeaning her husband. Brennan heard this and was intrigued by the prospect of a Supergrandma.

Days, weeks, months.

The house was quiet. There was a lady in the house who helped clean and make food. Mom called her Hermana Martina. Brent had been teaching his son a lot of things recently, including Spanish. Brennan knew Hermana meant sister, but the lady was old, far too old to be his mother's sister. Plus, he was starting to think mom's and dad's sisters were all named Tia.

Brennan was worried because Mommy was in the hospital. Brent was taking days off work to be with his son. Brent was still not who Brennan remembered from before he left, but he was not as angry anymore. He taught his son to do push-ups and sit ups while Mommy was in the hospital. He taught him a lot of things now, but everything seemed to come back to one lesson.

Control.

Brennan's dad told him that Hermana Martina is going to stay with Brennan because he needed to pick up mommy from the hospital. When they came back, they were not alone. It seemed to Brennan that every time Mommy was gone for a few days, she came back with someone new. This time it was a baby.

He was tiny, his skin seemed to vary from pink to red, and he had a thick tuft of black hair on his head.

Mommy lay down in bed holding the baby. Daddy boosted Brennan up to the bed to meet the boy named James.

Brennan saw him and set his mind about a few things.

First, James was perfect. Second, James was his. And finally, James was too small to protect himself, so he would make sure no one was allowed to hurt James.

Days, weeks, months once more passed.

Through many dirty diapers, baths, feedings, Brennan seldom took his eyes off James. He was James, tiny protector. A sentinel, guarding the perfect boy, named James. This self-imposed responsibility doubled once James learned to walk, but Brennan didn't mind. He just walked beside him.

Brennan was getting ready for his first day of school. He was excited. He had an awesome Batman backpack. He discovered Batman through the Animated Series and was instantly hooked. He wanted to be Batman. Though he was too young to see the irony, he wanted to be Batman for his mom, dad, and James.

He was inspecting his first day of school outfit for what must have been the tenth time that day. He could not be too sure, only three days left to prepare, after all.

There's a crash and James cried out. Brennan ran out, a part of him imagined a cape flowing behind him, a cowl covering his glowering face. He arrived in the hallway that led to the front door and saw James' eyes wide and terrified. There was a tall glass shattered into a million pieces on the floor. Brennan remembered a certain broken vase.

"No," he mumbled nervously as he began to shiver, "Oh, no, no, no…"

Adult Brennan watched helplessly out of his past self's eyes as he had his first panic attack ever. Little Brennan picked James up, a considerable feat for a boy of four, and slowly shuffled away from the glass. He carried James down the hall that felt a mile long in this instance. His heart was pounding out of his chest, he felt like he was going to vomit, and he kept getting wave after wave of goosebumps all over.

He puts James down in his room and spoke breathlessly, "Stay here, okay, Jimmy?"

James stared blankly.

"Jimmy, you have to stay here, okay? There's glass. You can get cut. Okay?" Brennan asked again, hoping to see some understanding from James.

"Kay, Bwennie." James finally replied, terror still tinging his sweet, high pitched voice.

Brennan raced back and grabbed the broom and dustpan. He began to sweep up the glass and vaguely remembered how his grandmother had once taught him to do it. He was forgetting something though, he couldn't remember what, and as his heart seemed to beat in his head and his vision trembled with every pulse, he gave up on trying to recall.

He was done! He stepped back to inspect his work and...

"TSSSS!" Brennan sucked in breath through his teeth. Chanclas, he forgot his chanclas.

Brennan saw a jagged piece of clear glass protruding from his foot and now his eyesight began growing dim and he felt woozy. He heard his mother beginning to say her farewell to the neighbor she was talking to outside and he shuffled, stepping only with the side of his left foot, towards the back door. He opened the door and dumped the glass on the dustpan into the aluminum trash can back there. He dropped the broom and dustpan, too panicked, too hurt, and too hurried to put it back where they belonged. Brennan hobbled to the restroom and as he was about to enter, he saw James looking at him, horror radiating from his saucer like eyes as he noticed the piece of glass in

Brennan's foot. Brennan held up his index finger to his lips and did his best to smile.

His mom walked in the house. "James? Jimmy? Where are you, baby?"

Brennan walked into the bathroom, closed the door, then collapsed. He pulled a towel off the shower curtain rod and put it under his foot. Terrified and on the verge of fainting, from his panic attack, not the bleeding, Brennan took hold and pulled the jagged piece of glass out.

A flow of blood bubbled out of his foot and he grimaced and wept silently as he held pressure to his foot with the towel.

"If you ever get a bad cut, you apply pressure and call for help."

Brennan decided half of his father's advice would have to do. Fifteen minutes later, there was a knock at the door.

"Brennie, are you in there?" his mother asked.

"Yes, mom. I'm in here."

"Are you okay, it's been a long time?"

Brennan said the first thing that came to mind, "I'm estriñido."

"You mean estreñido? You're constipated?"

"I can't poop, mom!" Brennan cried out with tears of frustration and pain in his eyes. His foot really stung.

"Okay, okay. Do you want me to come in there? Rub your belly?"

"No!" Brennan yelled and began to cry again.

"Okay, it's fine, Brennie. No need to get mad. I'm going to call your dad and ask him to buy some prunes okay?"

"Okay," Brennan sighed, "thank you."

He hated prunes, but now, not only was his father going to buy them, he was going to have to eat them in order to back up his story. He sent a short prayer to God, asking that the prunes not give him diarrhea on his first day of school.

After a while longer, the bleeding stopped and the cut on his foot just looked like a disgusting flap of dead skin, like the world's worst athletes' foot or a large piece of peeling sunburn.

Brennan took a length of toilet paper and peeked out of the door. His mother was in her room changing James' diaper. Brennan hobbled out to the hallway and then to his room. Brennan stashed the blood-soaked towel under his bed, hoping he could keep it hidden there until he had a chance to throw it out in the back-yard trash can. As far as he knew, no one checked in there.

He applied pressure to the dried-up gash with the toilet paper and rolled a sock over it to hold it in place. He decided this would work. He would just try his best not to walk.

Brennan was able to keep his goal fairly well. He walked to the kitchen for dinner and back to his room. He told his mom he was too sleepy to shower and that he promised he'd shower in the morning. His mother agreed.

To his own surprise, Brennan found out he was not lying after all and he sank into sleep soon after.

What Brennan, or rather both Brennans, did not see was Brent get back home. He was now on evening shift. Still not great, but he got to sleep at home with his wife and boys. When he returned, Nancy was looking for the broom to clean up James' mess that came with every meal. She told Brent she had no idea where it was. She hadn't used it since lunch.

"How is Brennan?" Brent asked as he joined the search party for the broom.

"Better. He said it came out eventually."

"Mijo drinks too much milk, Nance. You gotta keep a closer eye on that."

"I know, I know."

Brent looked outside through the back door and saw the broom and dustpan.

"Ah! Found it! What do I win?" Brent asked with a smile.

Nancy loved to see her husband smile. It reminded her of the old him. The him that didn't feel guilty for the death of a group of young men under his command. The him that didn't seem hellbent on preparing their son, just barely school aged, for a hard life he would hopefully never have.

"Your prize is my undying gratitude," Nancy said and kissed her husband on the lips, his small, wiry, whiskers poking at her.

Brent smiled again and bent back out to get the dustpan. This was when he leaned to far and knocked the lid, already set askew, off the aluminum trash can.

"Dang it," he picked it up and was about to replace it, "What the hell?"

"What is it?"

"Glass. A lot of it. What broke?"

"Nothing that I know of," Nancy replied.

"I took this trash out yesterday. Something broke today. Was Hermana Martina here?"

"No, just me and the boys."

Brent handed his wife the dustpan and made his way around the house. He looked for little gleaming bits of glass, missing vases, anything that could indicate what had happened. One of the traits Brennan would inherit from his father, besides their disturbing false charm, was his addictive curiosity. Once Brent, or eventually Brennan, caught scent of an investigation, they could not let up.

Brent walked up the hallway towards Brennan's room and noticed a small red dot under the bathroom's door. He crouched to inspect it and confirmed his suspicion. The browning dot was dried blood. He walked into the restroom and inspected the trash can. There was a lot of toilet paper in there, which was wrong for two reasons. One, their plumbing was good enough that they could flush toilet paper. This is what they had always done. The trash can was for old shampoo bottles, empty toothpaste tubes, or barren, brown, cardboard rolls. Two, the toilet paper was scrunched up, but clean. Brent was so confident of this that he reached in and grabbed the tip of it with two fingers. He picked up the piece he had grasped and saw the jagged and bloody piece of glass underneath.

Brent made his way into his son's room. The boy was asleep with the covers tossed off to the side. Brent smiled at this every time he saw it. Like his father, Brennan ran hot in his sleep and always cast the blanket and covers away. He also slept without socks. At least, he usually did. Today, was an exception. Brent saw the sock on his son's left foot had a red rose blooming on the sole. He knelt down next to his son, wondering if he should wake him or deal with this tomorrow. Once on his knees, he saw the towel. There was a lot more blood than he had expected.

Brent immediately understood what had happened. Brennan was not the only one who remembered the vase. Despite the evidence of his son's injury, the understanding of the story behind it had come by way of jumping to conclusions, but it didn't make him any less right.

Exhausted and feeling burning hot tears swell behind his eyes, Brent kissed his son's forehead and stood up. The voices in his head, the ones that constantly told him he was not good enough, that he did not deserve his son, that he was doing both his boys more harm than good, became louder. Soon, they'd be too loud to ignore.

Brent walked to the kitchen, planning on how he'd tell his wife. How he'd open up and bare his soul. He'd talk about how terrible he felt. He'd tell her he needed help. He never stopped feeling like a failure. He had led boys to death and was now worried he would lead his sons to similarly disastrous ends.

He stood before his wife, a naked soul speech brimming on his lips.

"Everything okay, honey?" Nancy asked.

"Yeah, Brennan broke something. It's no big deal." He reached for his bottle of whiskey and Nancy scoffed. Brent wouldn't argue today. He'd just drink. She'd say he had a problem, but he knew better, or so he'd lie to himself. He could stop if he wanted to. He chose not to, after all, he was in control.

Brent, the Brent who had awakened in what Brennan called the Nothing, the Brent who had been recruited by his beautiful, little granddaughter to help his son, let go of Brennan's shoulder.

The physical contact had allowed him to see everything that happened that day, at least from his perspective. He backed away and held back tears, both in the timeline Brennan was reliving and in the Nothing.

Suddenly, Brennan began to convulse. His eyes rolled to the back of his head and his body jerked about like a fish on dry land. Brent forgot about the side effect of touching his son in this place and knelt next to him. He propped Brennan's head onto his legs. He knew the floor wasn't really a floor and doubted that Brennan could injure his head on it but was not about to risk it.

"Gwampa?" Abby asked frightened.

Brent looked at her. She had been so brave. He knew she was different, but autism didn't begin to explain just how different. His heart ached as she began to rock back and forth while flapping her little hands.

"It's okay, Abby. He'll be okay."

He touched his son and as their memories melded, he saw the problem. Brennan had experienced four years of his

own life for the second time and had arrived at his first day
of school in 1994.

Chapter 46

Brennan began to panic. There were two. Two of everything. He was seeing, feeling, living, everything double. It hurt. It physically hurt. His head felt like it would split, and he knew why.

He had created two timelines by jumping back to 1994. The Nothing was going to consolidate them, one way or another.

Time sped up now.

First day of school.

Second day of school.

The third. In one reality, nothing happened, in the other, Mom invited Grandmother Abby to go see Brennan off.

School, school, school, death.

Grandmother Abby is gone in one reality. She never got to see her little grandson off to school, but she was blessed to spend a few weeks with the adult version of him. She died hoping he'd make the right choice.

Nancy became bitter. Angry. Her heart was broken, but she hid it well. This helped Brent feel able to leave sooner.

School, school.

Death again. Grandmother Abby died in the second reality, or perhaps it was the first, Brennan couldn't tell anymore.

In this reality, Nancy and Abby made up. Nancy was deeply mournful that she had lost her mother, just as she felt she was getting her back. Brent loved his wife his entire life. Even after he left. He couldn't leave her and add to her pain. This difference caused him to stay almost a year longer in this reality.

Brennan's dad left. Mom told them he's on a business trip. She lied, and insisted it was extended another week, then another, then another.

Brennan stole some of the dot matrix printer paper and made a banner 10 pages long that said, "Welcome Back, Dad!" for a father that was not returning. This is the breaking point. Nancy finally told her sons the truth.

Brennan experienced his father leaving his family again. Same cycle again, only this time Brennan and James were older. James was thoroughly confused. He was wondering if Brennan was dad now.

Mom began school, in addition to work. Their tia, the one Brennan had disliked since almost infancy, began to take care of them.

Brennan in the Nothing yelled.

"NOOO!"

He was about six in one reality, five in the other. She lowered her pants and underwear and as Brennan stood behind her, his eyes level to her bottom. She told him to kiss it.

Brennan was grossed out, but she insists and says that it's "what daddies do".

He wanted to be a daddy now, didn't he? With dad gone, he needed to be daddy for James. He closed his eyes and kissed her behind. He didn't like the smell or the sensation. He looked down and saw blood.

"Are you okay?!" Young Brennan exclaimed.

"Yes, it's something that happens when you become a grown up."

Brennan was now terrified of the day he would begin to bleed from his privates.

Days, months, years.

She repeated the abuse and slowly goes farther. At one point, she put her mouth on his prepubescent member. It hurt him, he hated what was happening, but at the same time, he couldn't deny a disgustingly pleasurable sensation. His stomach turned and threatened to vomit.

Days, months, years.

He was at church. The two realities coincided for this moment.

The church screen an apocalyptic movie that left him terrified of being left behind for his sexual sin. He knew he didn't initiate it, but it did feel physically good at times, as much as he detested it. As much as she repulsed him. Surely, he must have wanted it on some level. Surely, he's guilty.

Days, months, years again.

"Here it is," Brennan thought.

His rebirth. Once more the realities coincide with each other.

She had walked out of the restroom after Brennan had refused her repeatedly in there. She had tried to convince him to insert himself into her, but Brennan was worried he'd get her pregnant. She said that doing it that way she suggested didn't get you pregnant and then stared at it and left. He hadn't seen her since and it had been almost half an hour. The door of his mom's bedroom was closed. His heart sank and he began to wish his mother could get out of work early. Maybe he'd call her and tell her he felt sick. He had read somewhere that drinking a glass of water full of salt could make you vomit. He'd try that.

He opened the door.

James looked terrified. His skinny, naked body was being caressed by this woman they called Tia. She was topless, and all at once, that was fine.

It would help Brennan aim better.

He told James to leave. Adult Brennan remembered this as something that happened but lacked real detail. Now, he saw it live and in high definition.

"Why did you come in here? Why are you looking at me like that? I'm going to tell your mom if you don't-"

She finished the sentence by letting out a wheezing cough as Brennan's fist connected with her solar plexus. Dad had taught him if you hit there, it stuns your enemy. He was taller than her. Stronger as well. He felt like an idiot for not noticing before. His guilt deepened. He wondered if the physical sensation was so pleasurable that he had ignored the fact that he was stronger, rather than being truly ignorant of it. He held her hair with one hand and yanked it back. She was too shocked and panicking over her inability to breathe to hit back. He looked into her eyes and relished the fear in them.

He was twelve now, and so much stronger. An early bloomer, he believed in part because he had been technically sexually active since early elementary school.

"This ends today. You never touch me again. You never touch him. You don't even LOOK at him."

He waited for her response. He waited for her "yes" or an "I understand".

Instead she replied, "I'm- eeh," her raspy inhale sounded was sharp and raspy, "going- eeh - to- eeh - tell."

Rage began to flow under the fear in her eyes and Brennan decided he'd extinguish it. He didn't react. He didn't snap. He decided. After all…

He was in control.

He released her and she wound her hand back to slap him. He continued as his father had taught him.

Jab, cross, hook, uppercut. Repeat. Jab, cross, hook, uppercut. By the end of the second combination she was on the floor and red welts were turning to bruises on her torso.

He repeated the words she had spoken to him on numerous occasions.

"Don't worry. I'll kiss you where no one can see."

He continued his assault. That's what it was. This wasn't karma. It wasn't heroism.

It was vengeance.

Brennan's adult mind, or something in it, mercifully cut in here.

"Vengeance is mine, sayeth the Lord. I will repay."

Unfortunately, the distraction was momentary and Adult Brennan watched the moment he had eventually polished to seem heroic and just for what it really was, a monstrosity... and who commits monstrosities, if not monsters.

Chapter 47

Brennan's body began to settle as his brain became accustomed to the dual realities. The seizing stopped and Brent cradled his son as if he was still the boy he had been when he left.

"He's calm," Abby stated as she hunkered next to Brent.

"I can't hold him for too long," Brent's voice quaked with emotion.

"Is okay, gwampa."

Brent looked at Abby. He found it difficult to wrap his mind around the fact that she was not Brennan's biological daughter. He saw so much of Brennan in her. There was nothing physical. It wasn't that she had his nose or eyes. She had his mannerisms. The way she looked at her dad, the way she held him, that way she hunkered down and in no way felt out of place in this very adult situation. That was all his little boy, or at least it had been his little boy.

"What do you think he's seeing now?" Brent asked.

Abby shrugged, an intense, focused, look in her eyes. That was definitely Brennan.

Brennan woke up in his maniacal version of *This Is Your Life* feeling sick to his stomach. It had been over a year since he exacted retribution on the woman who had sexually assaulted him since childhood.

"Brennan, are you okay, honey?" Nancy asked.

Brennan found this odd. "Mijo", "Brennan", "Brennie", were all normal, but "honey" was when something was wrong.

"Yeah, mom. Why wouldn't I be?"

"Well, because of last night. Oh," she sighed, "was it one of those forgetful ones?"

Brennan struggled with generalized anxiety, but a few years ago had begun having night terrors. He'd wake up disoriented, his mind in a tailspin. The most common issue was a sudden and ugly realization that he was going to die. Not that he was dying in that moment or even soon. Just that mortality had been thrust upon him, by no choice of his own, and now he had to live it and eventually die. This realization would make him feel like he was losing his mind. He could be careful, he could watch out for James and his mom, but no matter what, there was absolutely nothing in his power that he could do to avoid that.

Simply put, there was no control.

These intense half-waking states of existential dread often brought friends along, including minor visual and auditory hallucinations. Things seemed too bright, things seemed to grow, and on occasion, he heard voices and music.

These episodes happened between one to four times per year, but recently Brennan had found out he didn't always remember them. Sometimes he would go through an entire panic attack and feel nothing in the morning.

Last night had been one of those nights.

"I'm sorry, mom," Brennan lamented.

"No, it's okay. These things just happen sometimes."

Nancy did her best to smile at her son, but she was very worried about him. He seemed to have forgotten how to be a kid to the point that some days not even sleep brought him true rest.

"How did you get me to stop?" Brennan asked.

"Same way we usually do," Nancy replied.

Brennan winced at her response as if he had been struck.

His father had been missing visits. He had been calling less. Yet, in the clutches of those terrible panic attacks, in the throes of fear and horrific delusions, one thing calmed him down without fail.

Nancy knew he didn't like her doing it. She would explore every option. Trying to hold him down, singing, praying, talking to him, splashing him with water, even the tried and true Mexican fix-all, Vicks Vapor Rub.

None of those things worked, at least not with any consistency, but one thing always did.

She would dial his number, press the phone handset against Brennan's ear so he could hear, and Brennan would hear a voice.

"Mijo," his dad would start, no anger, frustration, or danger in his voice, "it's okay, mijo. How are you feeling?"

By that point, Brennan's heart and brain had usually slowed enough that he could speak intelligibly and at a normal volume.

"Not too good," a pause to gather his courage and make his dad proud, "but I'll be okay."

"That's right, mijito. You're absolutely right. You're going to be okay. This will pass, you'll be tired, and you'll sleep."

"I love you, dad," Brennan would say, the tears now drying, the hysterics passing. He wanted to say more, but he'd bite his tongue. He didn't want to make his father feel bad and more than that, he didn't want to give his father more evidence that he couldn't handle all this. He couldn't say what he wanted.

"I miss you, dad. Come back home, daddy. Please. I can't do this anymore."

Young Brennan was annoyed, but understood. He didn't remember the events and the exchange from the night before.

Adult Brennan did. Even while Young Brennan's mind had been more unconscious than awake, Adult Brennan had seen everything. Even in Young Brennan's mostly sleeping mind, he could hear the thought. Even in Young Brennan's mostly sleeping mind, he did not dare say it.

The day would come when Brennan would be ready to say it. The day would come when he had the courage, true courage, to stand before his father and tell him that all this wasn't his job. It was his father's. He missed him. He needed him. He wanted him home.

One day he'd be able to say all that, but by then, it would be too late.

In the place that Brennan called the Nothing and Brent and Abby had decided should be called Nowhen, Brent held his son in his arms and wept silently. Abby stood behind him, leaning her curly locks on his shoulder as she hugged him. She began to sing Brent a song. Her voice was childish, her pronunciation was off on a large part of the lyrics, but her pitch was perfect, and her touch and tone were soothing.

"I'm tie-ud, I'm won, my heart is heavy! From the wok it takes, to keep on breathin'..."

Brennan observed in his strange dual reality as his younger self began to dress.

"What are you doing?" Nancy asked.

"Getting ready for school."

Nancy smiled and laughed. It was brief, but the scarcity of her laughter after Brent left made it beautiful. "It's Sunday, Bren."

Bren scoffed and smiled slightly and crookedly.

"I just wanted to check up on you because I heard movement. I'll be back to wake you for church in a couple of hours."

Brennan rolled his eyes, too late for his mother to see, and collapsed back onto his bed.

"You know," came a soft, muffled voice from the other twin sized bed to his right, "if you could lower the dramatics, I could sleep better."

Brennan chuckled and threw a small decorative pillow that was on his headboard shelf at James. The pillow hit James on the back of the head and James sat up and took the pillow, inspecting it in his hand.

"Oh, thanks, Brennie. I love having a little pillow for my head," and proceeded to lie back down, turn on his side, and place the small pillow between his legs.

Brennan couldn't help but laugh, "Gross, dude. You can keep it."

Young Brennan turned in his bed and slid back into sleep, smiling at his brother's dumb joke.

"James…" Adult Brennan whispered, too entranced in what he saw to hear his own voice or even notice he had spoken. What he did hear, about a mile away, was a familiar tune that caused him to have an earwig. As he unconsciously hummed, his brain sang.

"Let me see redemption win, let me know the struggle ends, that you can mend a heart that's frail and torn… I want to know a song can rise, from the ashes of a broken life, and all that's dead inside, can be reborn…"

Young Brennan begrudgingly woke up two hours later and dressed for church. His "Sunday Best" wasn't too different than his school day casual. Jeans, t-shirt, and usually an open flannel shirt that just screamed, "I grew up in the 90s and haven't let go."

Brennan's raven black hair was shoulder length at this point. It was wavy and loose for school, tied back in a ponytail for church. It was more presentable that way, according to his mom.

One of the biggest issues that Young Brennan had with church wasn't doctrinal in nature. It was that his mother was in the church choir. He was glad she got to sing, and she had a lovely voice, but it meant being in church an hour early, with nothing to do except sit and listen to the sound checks, warm ups, and last minute tweaks to the music. So, Brennan sat in a comfortable pew toward the back of the sanctuary as the guitarist tuned his instrument and the choir warmed up with some arpeggios. Brennan closed his eyes, leaned his head back, and tried to rest.

The two realities that Brennan's mind had grown accustomed to over the course of the last few years of replay were beginning to feel different again. There had been small differences throughout, but a sense of discord began to settle in Adult Brennan's mind.

"Hey," a male voice called out to Young Brennan's right. "Hey!" it repeated a bit louder and Brennan noticed that there was an inflection in the voice that was too subtle to be an accent, but unique, nonetheless. He also noticed that the voice was referring to him.

Brennan opened his eyes wearily and saw a familiar face he didn't remember a name for.

"Do I know you from somewhere?" the young man asked. He was probably around 18, maybe 19. He had a buzz cut haircut, what his instructors undoubtedly called a "high and tight". His dark green polo shirt was tucked into his khaki pants and the belt he wore formed a straight gig line into the seam of his fly. It took Brennan a second to notice, there was also a young girl, probably a year or two younger than him, standing behind him, as if waiting for her turn.

"I don't think we've met," Brennan lied. He knew he had seen this person somewhere.

"Oh, I know," the young man said, "imagine me with long hair and black rimmed glasses."

Brennan did and knew where, but not when he knew him from.

"Did we go to school together?" Brennan asked.

"No, I graduated the year before you were a freshman. I did your band tryout. You weren't half bad, if I remember correctly."

"Thanks," Brennan said and felt awkwardly out of words, the way one does when conversation leaves, but the conversant doesn't.

There were a few seconds of awkward silence then the young man continued, "Right... anyway, my name is Roel. You seemed bored and I was bored, decided I'd come talk to you. Chit chat, you know."

Behind Roel, in both realities, Brennan saw a beautiful woman. She had brown sleek hair, wore tight jeans on her well sculpted bottom, and had to be quite short, since she was ear height to a not-very-tall Roel, even with the black wedges she wore on her feet.

"That's quite rude," the girl reprimanded, her forming a duet with her alternative reality twin, "I don't even get a hello? Are you scared to talk to girls?" She asked with a sly grin.

"Oh, sorry," Young Brennan said, reaching for her hand. She was pretty.

"Beautiful is closer to the truth," Brennan thought, *"she's like something in a dream. Ethereal. Roel must be a lucky man."*

"Deidre, can you just let me find a friend before you swoop in?"

Deidre laughed at this and responded, "I want friends too. You just take all the good ones and never introduce me."

"I'm Brennan," Brennan said, raising his outstretched hand a bit to emphasize that it was still there, hanging in the air and waiting to be shaken.

"Brennan," Roel said, clearly exasperated, "this is Deidre, my little sister."

Deidre shook Brennan's hand and Brennan felt how warm and fragile it felt in his. He held it gently for probably about half a second too long. He withdrew his hand.

"Glad to meet you, Deidre," Brennan replied.

He felt his face grow hot and noticed that Deidre was blushing as well.

The feeling of dissonance grew in Brennan's mind and he finally saw why. Deidre's mom tumbled over a bump in the carpet and went sprawling.

In one reality, Deidre rolled her eyes in disdain and frustration as Roel rushed to his mother's side.

In the other, the changed timeline, Roel did not rush after his mother because before he took a step, Deidre had already been halfway to her.

"Is she okay?" Brennan asked in both realities.

"Ugh. She's just a klutzy old lady, but hard labor has hardened her bones. I'm sure she's fine." Deidre answered nonchalantly.

In the other timeline, Roel replied and told him, "She'll be fine. It's Dee I'm worried about. Ever since Bethsaida and I left, she's been mom's sole caregiver. She needs to have a life."

Young Brennan saw a sorrow in his eyes that he thought was just Roel's love for his sister. Adult Brennan saw this for what it was. He hurt knowing it should've been him that stayed. His sister took his place. He hated himself for it, but could not come back. Adult Brennan, now barely more than a third party subconscious sharing Young Brennan's eyes, knew this would eat him away. He could see the demon of regret salivating. Brennan knew that particular demon well.

"I was a dumb kid when I left," Roel spoke in a low, deadpan voice, "I did every stupid thing I could do. Figured the best way to get my life together was to join the military. I became a Marine."

He stopped talking and Brennan felt that he should say something at this point, if nothing more, just to fill the dead air.

"That's awesome, man. You did it, turned it around. You-"

"I'm not the stereotypical hunk of muscle, but I did pretty well," Roel interrupted, "especially in combat training." He looked down at Brennan, who was sitting still, "I saw the way you looked at her. Worse still, I saw the way she looked at you. If you hurt her, I think I am more than capable of ensuring you regret it."

Young Brennan held back a defiant, half smile.

"Sounds fair," he replied, but what was in his mind was filled with that hostile rebellion that often lay dormant.

"Maybe if you had stayed, you'd be more believable."

Adult Brennan's muscles tensed, and he felt a heavy discomfort that would have been a searing migraine, had he been more conscience of his own body. As the two realities split further apart, becoming increasingly incongruent, his body reacted more intensely to the divided confusion.

Abby held him tighter and Brent stroked his son's hair and face. The tears had stopped flowing from Brent. His eyes stared baldly into Brennan's bloodshot eyes. The green in the iris seemed to jump out against the pinked white and red spider web vessels of Brennan's eyes as they fixed their focus on some invisible target a thousand miles away. He held his son, trying to somehow convey and transfer as much peace as he could to his boy's mind.

Brent knew what was coming next.

Chapter 48

Brennan's body shuddered as every differing event in his revisited life sent electric pulses down his spine.

A young and extremely nerve-wracked Brennan was taking Deidre on a date. His date on a budget had taken them to a nearby McDonald's.

Ashamed, Brennan was overly apologetic about the choice of venue, but Deidre was surprisingly charmed by it.

"I used to eat dried tortillas out of the trash can," she told with a smile, like she just revealed something innocuous, like her favorite childhood TV show or what her shoe size was. "My sister would stick them in the microwave, which softened them up. We'd steal lime off our neighbor's tree, then salt them with little packets we'd take from restaurants. Believe me, a McDouble is a delicacy."

Brennan had no idea how to react and told her so.

"Don't react, Brennie," she comforted, suing his pet name for the first time, "just listen. Just let me say it to someone who isn't going to look at me with pity."

Despite her mirthless statement, a genuine and gorgeous smile held on her face.

"If we share a drink," Brennan suggested, with a light smile and not breaking eye contact, "we can splurge on McFlurries after."

Brennan, who would have been incredulous that her smile could be any more magnificent, was touched as her smile broadened and she let out a staccato note of giggle.

That was the first time Brennan saw the signature million-watt smile.

One reality ended the night with a slow, soft, immature, somewhat awkward, but picturesque kiss.

The other ended with a hug and Brennan pained acceptance that this would not repeat itself as he noted the tears she held back.

One reality continued with cold, blue, nights. Brennan's heart, already prone to cold, slowly hardening and as it froze over. This was perfectly capped with a call regarding his father.

The other reality was warm. The cold was cast out and Brennan rediscovered the romantic view of the world he once had. The rose-tinted perspective of poets and young people in love. People who believe love can overcome every tragedy they've faced through the proverbial and cliched power of love. As the months passed and Brennan discovered Deidre's broken past, his loyalty and love for her solidified.

Then, the roles of knight and damsel were flipped with a call regarding his father.

Brennan stood heartbroken next to his father's body in the changed reality, the one without Deidre at his side. He held his father's cold, stiffening hand. He whispered to the father that would not hear him.

"You shouldn't have left. Look what it's done to you," a quiet tear rolled down his cheek, "You made a coward's choice, but I forgive you. More than that, I won't let your name die. I will be who you wanted me to be. I will obtain control. Despite everything, I'll always honor you."

In the original reality, although Brennan was less and less
sure which was the true reality anymore, Brennan sat
heartbroken next to his father. He held his cold, stiffening,
chest in a clumsy child's hug. He cried and talked to the
father that would not hear him.

"Dad, why did you leave? I could have helped you," he
sobbed, "we still loved you. We could have helped!"
Brennan's composure broke even further and Deidre's soft,
warm, hands slid down his arms that held his father. He felt
her warm breath on his neck. His tears began to slow, and
his mind began to calm as he remained there, sandwiched
between warm life and cold death. "You messed up, dad,
but I forgive you. I'm never going to forget what you
taught me. I'll try to keep myself in control. I'll help others.
I'll be the person you would have wanted me to be. I'm
going to do it for them, for her, and for you, dad. Despite
everything, I'll always love you."

With that keystone memory relived, Adult Brennan began
to seize again.

One reality continued. He loved Deidre. He protected her.
He forgave her. He loved Abby. He went back.

A grunt escaped Adult Brennan's mouth as some
semblance of consciousness and awareness returned to him.
His head exploded in agony as Past Brennan hit the blue
button on his chest to go back. That reality became two,
then three, then four.

This time the groan was replaced by a banshee like scream,
ripping out of Brennan's contorting body and pressured
lungs.

Brennan tried to focus on the blue reality. The calm reality. The cold reality.

In the warmer reality, he had jumped out of bed in the middle of a panic attack. With shaking hands, he flicked his way to the file saved on his phone for these occasions, that final voicemail.

"Hey, mijo. How are you? I guess I missed you…"

In the colder reality, Brennan jumped out of bed, awakening mid panic attack. He clenched his fists and gritted his teeth and lay his shivering body on the cold, tiled floor. He focused on one word, repeating over and over, as his heart raced and his limbs numbed.

"Control"

The blue reality was bleak, but it didn't hurt. It was numb instead. Cold. Brennan tried to zoom in on it, to make it the only reality, he needed to release the pressure or he would die.

Gunshots. The Stepfather's brains are forcefully evacuated from his skull.

A kick. The Guy's neck snaps, leaving him paralyzed, but not yet dead. Not dead until his truck slams into a sign and through to a resaca at over 100 mph. This crash killed the Guy, but the kick, the initial interference, had killed Abby.

Subconjunctival hemorrhages erupted in Brennan's eyes as his body bucked. Brent held his son and barked at Abby to look away, but she wouldn't. Her eyes were fountains, her hands were twisting and flapping about, and she rolled from the tip of her toes to the heel so quickly it was a wonder she didn't fall. One word departed her lips, repetitively and with increasing speed, in an inaudible whisper.

"Da-ee, Da-ee, Da-ee, Da-eeDaeeDaee…"

Grandmother Abby is dead, the Monster is dead (long live the Monster), the button is pushed and…

"DHAAAA!" Brennan gasped and sat up with a jolt. He looked around at the nothingness of the Nowhen and began to sway.

Brennan's brow furrowed as his eyes met his father's.

"Dad? You shouldn't be here," he muttered, "you're dead too. Dead is dead," he looked over at Abby who was now still and wide-eyed, "Hey Abby, baby," he greeted with a confused, somewhat insane, smile.

"Hey, Da-ee baby," Abby greeted in a squeak that sounded scared and shy.

"Son, we were worried," Brent informed him, "we still are," he added as he noticed Brennan's head wobbled as if it were set on a loose spring, "It's hard to tell here, but you had to be out for at least an hour."

Brennan scoffed and grinned an anesthetized version of his, 'C'mon, don't be dumb' smile. "Dad… Dead… Dead Dad," Brennan's eyes widened and for a moment he looked like a happy drunk who's about to puke, "Dead Dad the Living…" with that he dropped back into his father's arms. The light, drunk like humor abandoned his voice and any trace of a smile disappeared.

"Daddy," Brennan whispered, "it was at almost thirty years."

Brennan slept.

Chapter 49

"Almost thirty years," Brent mused aloud, "He relived it. Every emotion, every hurt, every pain. I saw glimpses when I held him. It's like our memories synced up when we touched. Life would speed by, but some events would slow. Not for him though. He lived it in real time."

"Yeah," Abby replied as if she knew exactly how it all worked, and for all Brent knew, she did, "Da-ee bwoke his bwain. So I needs to fissed it. Fixed. Fixed it. I fixed it. It was like a puzzle, gwampa. I like puzzles. Da-ee says I'm really good." Abby beamed with pride.

Brent, on the other hand, continued to stare at his son with dismay. At least Brennan seemed to sleep peacefully now.

"What did we do?" Brent questioned himself.

"His bwain was in pieces, gwampa. We putted it back together. Puzzle!" she yelled out the last word like some infantile battle cry.

Brennan opened his eyes slowly and sat up like a drunk with a hangover.

"Ugh! My freaking head…"

"You alright, son?" Brent asked.

Brennan looked up at his dad, "I thought it was a dream. You're really here." Brennan smiled and then winced in pain, "I feel like I need to cry, but it hurts. Why does it hurt?"

Brent knelt next to his son and embraced him tightly. Brennan felt the strong back under his hands and smelled

500

the earthy, subtle, scents of his father's favorite soaps and colognes.

"I never thought I'd feel this again," Brennan murmured into his father's ear with dry, painful, sobs.

His father released him and, almost immediately, Abby tackled him with an excited and aggressive hug. She began planting kisses all over his face. Brennan hugged her and the dry sobs continued.

"Abby, I'm so sorry. I 'm so sorry about what I did."

"Is okay, Da-ee. You want to help mommy, thas all."

"How did you get here?" Brennan asked as he pushed her back and then held her at arm's length. Despite his question, he felt he had a decent idea of how.

"Is the Nowhen, Da-ee," Abby replied, her tone indicating that this short response answered all questions. "When Gwampa and I have no more when to be in, we go to the Nowhen."

Brennan pulled Abby back in for another tight hug and kissed her forehead and nose. She giggled delightedly and the sound wreaked havoc on Brennan's heart. He hugged her tighter still.

"Da-ee," Abby whispered in his ear, "I need to breef."

Brennan held her at arm's length again. She was beautiful. Perfect. How could he have ever doubted it. Her brown curls, her fair skin, her red-brown freckles, her mother's brown…

"Abby," Brennan's voice was heavy with concern, "your eyes are green."

"Yeah," Abby replied simply.

"They've always been brown. Mommy's eyes. How did that happen?"

"I can do magic twicks in here, da-ee. He show me how. I call Gwampa, I can change clothes."

Brennan looked up at his dad.

"I'm not "He"," Brent said, putting his hands up in an 'it wasn't me' gesture, "I don't know what it is. She knows this place. She's been my guide, if anything," Brent told his son in reply to his silent question.

"I wanna look like you, Da-ee," Abby said, beaming the junior version of the million-watt smile.

"Abby, you don't need to-" Brennan began to comfort her.

"So, you member I was you baby, da-ee."

Brennan's throat clamped shut, his eyes burned furiously with their desire to produce tears, and his breath shuddered. He wanted to tell her he had never forgotten her. How could he ever forget her? But he had.

Instead, he changed the subject, "I get Abby, but how are you here, dad? How did Abby get you here? You passed before I ever traveled back. The changes I made didn't alter your life."

"No, son, but they altered my time with you." Brent sighed. "When I was holding you, I could see…" Brent gave up trying to verbalize an explanation, "I left later when your mom was grieving her mom. When she reacted to it by closing off and acting coldly, I became frustrated, blamed myself, and left."

"Dad, it wasn't your fault. You had to know that."

"I did know. I rejected it. If it wasn't my fault, then it wasn't under my control. I always felt the need to be in control."

"I can relate," Brennan mumbled.

Brent laughed mirthlessly.

"I know, mijo. It's what I taught you. I wanted you to be in better control of yourself to avoid the mistakes I made. I put faith in the wrong man. I thought I was the best choice. Captain of my soul. I didn't realize I was wrong until the end. I tried to tell you, but I ran out of time."

"That doesn't make sense, dad," Brennan replied, adding dad at the end for no reason besides the feeling of calling his father by that title, "I mean, you left earlier, but died at the same time."

"No, not completely," Brent paused a moment, "Did you ever check the inside pockets of my old ammo bag? The one you took from your mother's house?"

"I didn't even know there was an inside pocket. Why? What's in there."

"It depends," Brent replied. He looked down at the ground, "It depends on what you choose, mijo. This time, unfortunately, I can't give you the answer. I can't really even give you advice. This time the decision is purely yours.

"What decision?" Brennan asked. He looked from his long-gone father to his daughter who was and yet never had been. "What choice do I have to make?"

"We fissed, fiss, FIX, fix-duh, fixed," Abby strained, the factions of her face pulling in towards its center, "fixed you. We fixed you, da-ee. Now, you choose!" Abby beamed excitedly, "You choose where you go!"

Chapter 50

Inexplicably, Abby seemed to be more knowledgeable of the choices and their consequences than Brent, but between the two of them, they got their point across.

Brennan had traveled, adjusting and re-adjusting his position in space-time. His injuries were caused by the stress and forceful nature of the travel. The human body was only meant to move one way through time.

During his last trip, Brennan had made a major change, and as a result of the tearing apart and restitching of time, he had almost died upon returning. The repeated and progressively increasing pressure on his body was too much.

"So that means," Brennan calculated, "that if I travel anywhen again, I'll be stuck. A return trip would kill me."

"The other option would be to return to your last departure," Brent explained.

"Right," Brennan scoffed, "the world where I had just killed a pimp with a penchant for older women. Where Deidre looked at me in horror. Afraid of how easy it had been."

Brennan ran his hands through his hair in exasperation.

"There's no good choice," Brennan yelled, "I can't just go back to when Deidre hates me. I know you, Abby. I can't let this happen to you."

An idea began to take form in his mind.

"What if I go back, I can destroy The Machine!" He grimaced, "Ah, but old me will just rebuild. I was obsessed with this. With having control and fixing Deidre. I'll just restart this."

Even with the way that the Nowhen seemed to mitigate emotion and feelings, panic rose in his heart. His entire face buzzed, his field of vision began to constrict, his breathing became shallow and quick, "I'm doomed. Misery or a never-ending cycle. I'm doomed. I can't get out, I'm doomed. It's too late. Oh, God. Oh, sweet Father God, I can't change it, I can't..."

His heart was beating wildly, he was out of breath, His head swam and began to lull. He fell to one knee and his stomach cramped, attempting to send up its contents.

A large, strong, rough hand touched the back of his neck.

"Mijo," Brent began.

This time, despite dehydration and exhaustion, tears came. They flowed down Brennan's cheeks as his mind echoed his father's voice. The deep, soothing voice that had always told him he'd be okay.

"I know, dad. Be in control."

Brennan began to count his breathing and tried to stand to his feet, but stumbled back down, this time on both knees. Brent took his boy's face in his hands and pulled it up so they were eye level.

"No. You will be okay. Let God take control. Let Him be your strength. Surrender to Him, Brennie. Don't try to be in control. Instead, try to be at peace."

The anxiety had begun to melt from Brennan's mind, but this new paradigm his father offered didn't exactly please Brennan.

"I tried God, dad. God never-"

"Abandoned you, mijo," Brent finished for him, though not how Brennan had intended to finish,
"Even when I did. Even when you did. He never left you. Men do evil things. They hurt and break, but He's a God of restoration. He's a God of New Life. A God of second chances," Brent whispered to his son.

"Dad, the things I've done…"

"Those things are forgivable. You have a second chance, mijito."

"I've killed, I became a monster. I let rage own me. Vengeance drive me. Hate guide me. I've been like this. I just hid it. This is who I've been since…"

"Don't justify it, Brennan," his father scolded him. Even with the harsher tone, Brennan loved that Brent was there to give him that scolding, "Don't blame your nature. All our nature is sinful. Our free will comes into play when we make the choice to turn from it. You call yourself a monster, but here's your chance to change all that."

"I can't dad. I can't condemn Abby to being here. I can't take Deidre's disgust either."

"I is not condem, Da-ee," Abby reproached, "You can go back. Mommy will love you. Just tell her you sorry. She will say yes. She will give you another chance. She will love you, Da-ee."

"No, Abby. What about you? The Guy is dead, and he was…"

"I know, Da-ee. I get to leave with Gwampa. We go to stay with Him, with Da-ee Yah. Da-ee Yah told me."

"Daddy Yah?" Brennan asked.

Abby merely pointed upwards.

"Da-ee, go back. You forget again. Little bit at first, then a lot. You be good, mommy loves you, marries you," she giggled in a high-pitched tone while jittering her fingers in front of her face, "then you have BABIES!" She laughed, "cute, doorbell, BABIES!!"

"Doorbell?" Brent asked

"Adorable," Brennan replied as he processed what Abby was telling him. "Abby, Mommy and I may get married, have babies, but they won't be you, because, -"

"I know, da-ee," in that moment, Brennan saw Deidre's face in Abby's. The smile she was giving, her eyes brimming with tears, was the same smile her mom had given when telling dad about eating tortillas out of trash cans.

"You gotta laugh, or you cry. Right, Brennan?" Deidre's voice spoke in his mind.

"You babies will still be awesome, da-ee," Abby told her father confidently.

"Abby, baby, you can't know that," Brennan refuted with a soft, well-meaning smile on his face.

"Yes, I can, da-ee baby. Cuz they will be you babies," Abby paused, "like me."

Brennan kept his smile, but hot, stinging, tears squeezed out of his eyes, sending waves of pain all through his head.

"Go back, da-ee. You will forget all you did. Mommy will love you. Gwama will love you, Uncle Jimbo will love you,

you will be happy. You will be…" she grimaced, trying to pull the word out of the air. She repeatedly closed her two tiny fists together and then apart. Suddenly, her eyes lit up, "You be COMPLETE!" Abby cried out delighted, her gorgeous, oddly green, eyes still glimmering with tears.

Brennan was weeping now. Every sob sent earthquakes of pain through his skull and jaw.

"Abby, I can't leave you. I can't forget you. I can't do this. I can't, I can't. baby girl. I won't."

Abby came to him and hugged him. Tears streamed down her chubby, freckled, rosy cheeks, but she didn't make any sound.

Brennan felt an odd sensation. Something uncomfortable between Abby and his chest. Abby stepped back, her fight-the-darkness smile firmly printed on her face.

"Thank you, Abby. Thank you for bringing me love. Thank you for bringing me peace. Thank you for giving me a second chance to be a better person."

"I didn do that, da-ee. Da-ee Yah sent me. I just love you," she told him and gave a kiddish shrug that almost audibly said, 'Shucks, I'm just doing my job'.

Brennan went to his father and hugged him tight. He took a moment to appreciate that this was the first time he hugged his father while being the taller of the two.

"Dad," Brennan whispered into Brent's ear, "how did you know what happened? Even after you were gone?"

Brent smiled. His boy had always been so smart. Keeping the embrace locked in, he whispered back to his son,

Ryan Gutierrez

"We're connected, deeply connected. When I touched you, I saw my part of what you saw."

Brennan laughed in the monosyllabic way that keeps the laugh in your chest and behind closed lips. He remembered the odd, almost hallucinating disorientation he had felt when he made contact with his past self on the night, he corrected his stupid mistake. The shimmering manner in which discordant memories seemed to overlap when he had been close to his past self the day, he left the winning lottery numbers on the fridge.

He whispered back into his father's ear, "I knew it."

Brent held his son tighter and gave him a kiss on his cheek. This time it was Brent who held his child at arm's length. "I love you, son. Listen to Him. He knows what He's doing. Make the most of this second chance."

Brennan nodded and Brent released the hold. He then did something that almost meant more to Brennan than the hug and kiss. He held his hand out to his son. Brennan shook it firmly.

"A man's handshake, mijo. You are my life, my legacy, and I am humbled."

Brent let go and Brennan walked back, very aware of the weight and discomfort of The Machine that had seemed to suddenly appear on him. He knew it had always been there. Just hidden. Forgotten for a moment.

Abby held Brent's hand and waved good-bye to the only earthly father she felt she needed.

"Good luck, da-ee! Have fun! Make loss of babies! I wanna meet them up there and we can play!"

Brennan smiled at Abby and blew her a kiss. He looked at his father, who gave him a subtle, nearly imperceptible nod.

"Check the ammo bag!" Brent called out.

Brennan took the e-cord that would transport him to his last departure in a lab. The e-cord that would transport him to a universe where he would forget Abby ever lived. Where he would have a second chance to make things right. A universe where Deidre was hurt, but not as hurt as she had been. A universe where his mother and he were on good terms. A universe where he lived happily with his brother. A universe where so much pain and trauma never befell him.

He turned his back on Abby and his father. He closed his eyes and focused. While he still held the e-cord, he firmly pressed the blue pad on his chest instead.

He disappeared.

Abby looked around with a nervous smile, rocking back and forth on the balls of her feet. "Gwampa, where's the bwight light?"

Chapter 51

An incredible pressure squeezed Brennan into nothing more than thought. A flattened soul flying towards a when that seemed to be a century ago.

Humidity, sweat, air, the concrete floor. He opened his eyes in his garage. He stood across from himself. Past Brennan stood with his mouth agape, eyes wide as saucers, staring at a very different version of himself that had appeared from nowhere.

There was a low, warping sound and Modest the VIII appeared on the table. Brennan turned to look at it and Past Brennan took the opportunity to reach for the gun that was still in a toolbox in the makeshift lab. Before he reached it, Brennan tackled his past self to the floor.

Past Brennan never pressed the button and Modest the VIII, first successful pioneer of time travel, flickered out of existence. Or at least the version of him who had nervously appeared outside of the little dome disappeared.

Past Brennan swung a heavy fist at Brennan, but he blocked it with his forearm and hopped forward into a full mount.

"Stop it. You idiot, I'm here for a reason. Stop!" Brennan commanded his past counterpart, "LOOK!" Brennan squeezed his hands on Past Brennan's temples and focused.

He's born, he meets mom, he meets dad. Dad leaves. He meets Grandma Abby. Dad comes back. He's not the same. Grandma leaves. James is born. The world splits in two. Grandma dies. Dad leaves.Tia hurts him. He's afraid. Tia tries to hurt James. Brennan is split in two as he hurts Tia. He meets Deidre. Dad dies. Changing. Too different. Two worlds split to four. He murders Rafael Robles. He murders Kyle. Grandma dies again. He meets Sgt. Mata. He murders Marcos. Everything changes. Dad. Abby. A choice.

Past Brennan opened his eyes suddenly. He coughed and turned to his side as Brennan stood up from him. He spat out blood that had drained from a profuse nosebleed down to his throat. He began weeping in between bloody coughs.

"It's a lot, I know." Brennan said.

"I was gone for years! Decades!" Past Brennan grunted in a hoarse, growl of a voice.

"It was seconds. I forced it to be faster with you. Be glad for that at least," Brennan told him, his voice tinged with disdain. Honestly, he dang near hated the man on the floor. The version of him that had been so selfish and dressed up that selfishness to look like love. Except, Past Brennan was no longer that man either. He had seen it all. Lived it all. He was changed.

The two Brennans stood face to face.

"You know what you have to do, right?" Brennan asked.

"Yeah," Past Brennan, or rather New Brennan answered, "you're really going to do it, aren't you?"

Brennan laughed and after a few seconds, New Brennan joined him.

"What else is there to do?" Brennan asked. His grin faded and he locked eyes with the Past and New version of himself, "Take care of mom. Talk to James. He loves you more than you deserve. Stop being an idiot. Stop playing God."

New Brennan nodded.

"You haven't traveled yet," Brennan stated, "that means you'll remember everything. You're not going to forget like me. You're going to live knowing what you did. Can I trust you to handle that?"

"I'm going to live knowing what I chose not to do." New Brennan corrected.

New Brennan moved to the machine and opened the spine of the machine. He grasped a bunch of the wires.

"No, wait!" Brennan cried, "Do me a favor? Don't destroy it until I'm gone."

New Brennan nodded.

"He can fix you, you know," Brennan spoke solemnly, **"While there is breath in the lungs, there is hope. Better to be a living dog than a dead lion,"** he recited, **"those who hope in the LORD will renew their strength. They will soar on wings like eagles; they will run and not grow weary, they will walk and not be faint."**

New Brennan's mouth twitched up on the left into a crooked smile, tears were held back by the dams of his lower eyelids.

"God shows his love for us in that while we were still sinners, Christ died for us. Since, therefore, we have now been justified by his blood, much more shall we be saved by him"

Brennan pulled the e-cord.

He opened his eyes in the Nowhen. Abby and his dad were still there. He sprinted to Abby as her eyes widened with

514

understanding and shock. He collapsed to his knees and slid towards Abby. She embraced him.

"Don't let him forget, okay, Abby?"

"Da-ee, no, you was suppose to live, da-ee! You second chance!"

Brennan smiled and laughed, "It's not living without you, baby girl. I love you, Abby Baby."

"I love you, da-ee baby," Abby began to cry.

Brennan's smiled widened, "Be brave. I'll see you in a little bit. Well, kind of."

Abby grew dim. She smiled once more and was gone.

"I'm proud of you, son."

Brennan looked up at his father.

"I always have been," Brent told his baby boy. "You're a better man than I could be. You have been for a while. I'll see you soon, son. Though hopefully not too soon."

Brent didn't fade away. Instead an intense, blinding light, forced Brennan to close his eyes and recoil. When he opened his eyes, Brent was gone.

Brennan coughed violently. Already on his knees, he fell on all four and coughed up blood. He could feel his heart beating irregularly, his lungs filled with blood, it was every worst-case scenario he ever had, only now there was no panic. No fear. Only the peace of knowing he did what was right. He looked up and saw three men. Rafael, Kyle, and Marcos.

Brennan grinned at them with red stained teeth, "You lost!" Brennan's body shuddered as he loudly coughed and retched, "I hope you found repentance," he spat, looking at Marcos.

He then turned his attention to Rafael, "I hope you find redemption." Rafael grimaced as if in pain.

He looked at Kyle and, at first, said nothing.

"Kyle... I hope you find peace... and real love." Kyle merely nodded with a solemn smile.

The three Phantoms faded out too.

Brennan collapsed. As his breath was smothered out by blood, as his heart burst and beat no more, Brennan found his own million-wattF smile in the memory of his wife and daughter.

<u>Epilogue</u>

Three Years Later

Brennan shifted nervously behind the pulpit. He cleared his throat and straightened out his notes.

Three years had led to this moment. Three years, a lot of therapy for both Brennan and Deidre. Three years of a bit of rehab, Bible studies, and a job as a columnist with a website and some freelance writing on the side. Three years of prayer, apologies, long talks with his mom, long talks with his mother-in-law, and exposure therapy. Three years of small steps, giant leaps, and a few backslides.

Three years of accepting the past and learning to heal with the present.

Three years of understanding that Deidre had been ahead of him on this journey. That James had been right.

"It's an honor, a humbling, pride shattering honor, to be here again." He looked up from the pulpit and smiled as he surveyed his family, both in Christ and in blood. Beth and her young son sat next to Lupita, who had given up the name Misty.

His mom, crying and wearing a Batman shirt in support. James next to her, one arm around her, another arm around his pregnant wife.

Abby giddily rocking back and forth in her seat, beaming up at him, showing off the little windows of missing baby teeth. Her curls swayed back and forth. Her mother's eyes gleamed in her face once more.

Next to Abby, in the front row and closest to the center, was Deidre. Her smile easily outdid Brennan's. She held a tissue in one hand and dabbed away at her quickly ruining makeup. In her other arm, she held a baby girl. The infant had a full head of scruffy, black hair, green eyes, and a pretty name.

Nikki.

Not Nicole, Brennan and Deidre didn't like Nicole. Just Nikki.

"I left. Stunned and misguided by my own pride and pain. I left. Still, God, in his incredible mercy and grace has brought me back. Not because I'm good. Not because I'm well. Because I'm not good. Because my spirit was sick, and I needed the Doctor of doctors."

James gave out a booming, "Amen!" that resulted in scattered chuckles and applause.

"Today, I want to talk to you about second chances. It's only fitting right? Again, this is not because I want to show off my recovery. I did very little to help myself. That credit goes to my family and our God. I want to show off God's power for restoration, because He is a God of restoration, of New Life. I want to let you know I did not deserve his grace, but isn't that the beauty of grace? It makes life not fair in the best way. I want to let you know that if He brought me back, He can do the same for you. He wants to, but pride needs to be set aside. Arrogance needs to be set aside."

He paused a moment.

"Control needs to be set aside. Let him hold the reigns."

"Jesus take the whee-eel!" James sang loudly.

Many, including Brennan, laughed, "Exactly!" Brennan said, emphatically pointing at his brother, "just not literally, drive safe, y'all."

The laughter swelled up again for a moment then diminished.

"Let's open our Bibles to John chapter 5, and we're going to read verses 24 and 25."

Brennan pulled an old Bible with cracked, peeling, leather covers and loose binding from the small shelf under the pulpit. He set it on top and smiled at the cover. Taped on it was a piece of paper he had found rolled up in a hidden pouch in his father's old ammo bag. A hidden pouch, much like the one a Brennan of a long gone when had once sewn in a boot.

In a messy and shaky version of his father's usually exquisitely neat, small caps handwriting, the note read,

"Brennan, my firstborn son,

I have little time left and even less energy to write the volumes that my heart wishes it could convey.

I love you. I'm proud of you. You are the best parts of me. I've seen how James has grown, and I know I owe much of that to you, the boy who took this man's place.

I regret leaving you. but more than that, more than the bottles that led me to lie on this hospital bed, more than the decisions that led to my nightmares, more than the pride that held me back from seeking help, I regret teaching you to seek absolute control.

That level of control is fickle and not fit for human wisdom. Give control to God. Let him guide you. There's no mountain of sin, no wall of pride, no desert of depression, or valley of death too great, too dark, or too bleak for His light and love.

Stop seeking that control. You're already a better man than me, but you can be a better man than you. Seek Him. Find Him and He will show you who you are meant to be. I wish I could live to see it. No matter what it is, I know it will be great.

I love you, mijo. I thank God for allowing me to be the other man you called father.

Live Well."

And he did.

Ryan Gutierrez

CPSIA information can be obtained
at www.ICGtesting.com
Printed in the USA
LVHW110746270521
688660LV00007B/239/J

DIGGING
UP THE
DEAD

A HISTORY *of*
NOTABLE AMERICAN
REBURIALS

✠

MICHAEL KAMMEN

University of Chicago Press | Chicago and London

Michael Kammen is the Newton C. Farr Professor of
American History and Culture (emeritus) at Cornell
University, where he taught from 1965 to 2008. A member
of the American Academy of Arts and Sciences, he received
the Pulitzer Prize for History in 1973 and the American
Historical Association Award for Scholarly Distinction
in 2009.

The University of Chicago Press, Chicago 60637
The University of Chicago Press, Ltd., London
© 2010 by Michael Kammen
All rights reserved. Published 2010
Printed in the United States of America

19 18 17 16 15 14 13 12 11 10   1 2 3 4 5

ISBN-13: 978-0-226-42329-6 (cloth)
ISBN-10: 0-226-42329-8 (cloth)

Library of Congress Cataloging-in-Publication Data

Kammen, Michael G.
  Digging up the dead : a history of notable American
reburials / Michael Kammen.
      p. cm.
  Includes bibliographical references and index.
  ISBN-13: 978-0-226-42329-6 (cloth : alk. paper)
  ISBN-10: 0-226-42329-8 (cloth : alk. paper)
  1. Exhumation—United States—History.
2. Exhumation—Political aspects—United States.
3. Burial—United States—History. 4. Funeral rites and
ceremonies—United States—History. I. Title.
  GT3203.K365 2009
  393'.10973—dc22

                  2009023515

For Carol
with enduring love
because her dedications
are the ones that have really mattered

Good friend for Jesus sake forebeare
To dig the dust enclosed heare;
Blest be the man that spares these stones
And curst be he that moves my bones

Shakespeare's gravestone

At one point we got on the theme of immortality,
in which she believed without being sure
of its precise form. "There is no death," she said.
"No, my dear lady, but there are funerals."

Peter de Vries, *Comfort Me with Apples* (1956)

CONTENTS

For quite some time now, anthropologists and archaeologists have examined mortuary practices as an intriguing aspect of their professional inquiries. Historians have begun to do so more recently, most notably American Civil War specialists and a smaller but intensely engaged cluster of scholars who write about Eastern Europe after the collapse of Communism in 1989. What follows here is largely an inquiry into conflicted moments of historical aberration or rehabilitation in mortuary practice—the exhumation and reinterment of significant individuals, for a broad array of reasons. I have tried to trace patterns and make sense of what happens when someone, more often a family or an entire constellation of devoted followers, feels dissatisfied with where and how a person deemed worthy of note has been buried. In 1983 a U.S. congressman remarked at a hearing before the Subcommittee on Cemeteries and Burial Benefits that "the quality of a civilization is revealed in the way it reveres its dead." If that is valid, though perhaps not standing alone as the sole criterion of civilized life, how did it happen that many distinguished Americans have been buried but soon forgotten, or else it was belatedly noticed that their graves are sadly neglected? That is one key *problématique* of this inquiry.

Another complication contributing to the problem—rather a major issue as it turns out—is that during the colonial period and well into the nineteenth century, there were customarily few special markers or monuments to commemorate the careers and exact locations of figures as eminent as Roger Williams and the Revolutionary firebrand Sam Adams. As late as 1849 a poet and story writer as prominent as Edgar Allan Poe was initially buried in an unmarked grave. Is it any wonder that admirers of such individuals would eventually feel obliged to remedy these shameful situations?

Therefore I shall attempt to discern what those responsible for reburials believed they were achieving. Were they always and unambiguously seeking to do justice to the dearly departed? Were their dutiful deeds more beneficial to themselves than to the deceased? Did they recognize or acknowledge a difference between the two motives—or perhaps see any symbiotic relationship between them? To what extent was exhumation and reinterment an act of devotional fantasy, sometimes even a delusion? One criterion of postmodernism involves accepting what is called the "constructedness" of the past. Are reburials quite literally about the physical *re*constructedness of the past—a form of historical revisionism, setting the record straight in some sense? How often do aspects of American history and biography come to be understood differently by contemporaries because of a reburial? The answer to that is, quite often.

And then we have whole communities competing for the honor of burying or reburying a personage whose presence would lend luster to their new or improved cemetery. When exhumation did occur followed by reburial at a different venue, there was often anxiety over the nagging question "Did we get the *right* remains?" That was true of Daniel Boone in 1845, of Charles Thomson (secretary to the Continental Congress) in 1838, and of numerous Europeans as well, such as the German poet and philosopher Johann Friedrich von Schiller, who was disinterred several times during the nineteenth and twentieth centuries. Sometimes a coffin was opened just to satisfy curious or anxious survivors that it was actually occupied, as happened more than once with Abraham Lincoln. In 1886 Henry Adams wrote to John Hay, Lincoln's onetime secretary, expressing his personal "historical indifference to everything but facts, and my delight at studying what is hopefully debased and degraded," even shocking in terms of moral content and sense. He had the strange saga of President Lincoln's several reburials very much in mind.

The reader will encounter much that is bizarre, indeed shocking, in the pages that follow. To cite only one example: when Dr. Joseph Warren was killed at the Battle of Bunker Hill in June 1775 and became the first martyr of the Patriot cause in the American Revolution, British officers contemplated cutting off his head and mutilating the body of such a "traitor to the Crown." As Jean-Pierre Vernant has observed, the mutilation of an enemy's corpse is the inverse of the "beautiful death" so prized and lauded by the ancient Greeks. He was invoking the disfigurement of Hector's body at the hands of Achilles, an act that could rob the dead hero of his individuality and make proper memorialization all but impossible. Discussions of the "beautiful death" became commonplace during the American Civil War, when so many young men left their families behind with considerable uncertainty whether they would return intact, or even alive.

When Northerners and Southerners both wanted possession of the same famous figure, it is noteworthy that the South normally prevailed. Although the intensity of feeling about such matters cannot be measured in anything like precise terms, I have a sense that "ownership" of renowned men—like President James Monroe—mattered somewhat more in the South. Not always, to be sure, but often. The Lost Cause syndrome is only partially responsible. This pattern appears in conflicts over the most appropriate venue for Revolutionary War generals of northern provenance who either died in the South or else fought their most famous battle there, like General Nathanael Greene. Nostalgia appears to be a somewhat more distinctive quality in southern culture. Perhaps that comes as no surprise.

✠

I am deeply indebted to an array of friends and colleagues who provided counsel and suggestions and read all or part of the work-in-progress. I thank especially Paul S. Boyer, Holly A. Case, James A. Hijiya, Isabel Hull, Walter LaFeber, David W. Maxey, Robert R. Morgan, and Richard Polenberg. Although I have never met Robert E. Cray Jr., I owe him particular appreciation for his exhaustively researched essays on several important episodes from the period of the early American republic.

Several staff members of the Cornell University Library system have once again provided indispensable assistance, especially Gabriela Castro Gessner and the ever-patient and resourceful Susette Newberry. At the University of Chicago Press I owe a very special debt to history editor Robert P. Devens, editorial associate Anne Summers Goldberg, and my meticulous manuscript editor, Ruth Goring. Their help with this project has extended above and beyond the call of duty. Most of all, Carol Kammen has not only read every word, as always, but listened patiently to an excessive number of lugubrious tales. I am deeply grateful to everyone cited above but hold none responsible for information insufficiently dug up or inadequate insights.

MK, April 2009

Introduction

In pride, in reas'ning pride, our error lies,
All quit their sphere, and rush into the skies!
Pride still is aiming at the blessed abodes,
Men would be Angels, Angels would be Gods.

✛ Alexander Pope, *An Essay on Man*, epistle 1

*J*efferson Davis, president of the Confederate States of America from February 1861 until its collapse in April 1865, died in New Orleans on December 6, 1889, at the age of eighty-one. Five days later, following a frenzy of local and regional arrangements, Confederate veterans and many others packed an immense procession that accompanied the body to Metairie Cemetery for what turned out to be temporary burial in a vault guarded round the clock, awaiting a decision about the erstwhile CSA president's permanent interment (fig. 1). Bells tolled from every church tower in New Orleans to accompany the long and solemn parade to Metairie. The issue of his final resting place, however, had actually begun on the very day that Davis died and swiftly became what we now call a "hot button issue." Although his reputation revived during the 1880s, he had been reviled by white Southerners after the Confederacy fell and he fled from Richmond only to be apprehended by Federal troops in Georgia. During his lingering last illness he wisely said to his wife, Varina, "You must take the responsibility of deciding this question, I cannot—I foresee [that] a great deal of feeling about it will arise when I am dead."[1]

Davis understood the delicate situation all too well. Southern press coverage of his death signaled swelling admiration and pride in the former leader—utterly inconceivable less than a generation earlier, at the time of unbearable defeat. Six Southern cities each hoped to "host" the body into eternity, above all Montgomery, Alabama, where Davis had reluctantly assumed the presidency, and they all intensively lobbied the quickly created Jefferson Davis Memorial Association (JDMA). The decision belonged entirely to Varina and her children, however, and they waited more than eighteen months before choosing a prime site at Hollywood Cemetery in Richmond, capital of the Confederacy, where the Davises had lived for four years and where a great many honored Southern dead already lay buried. The civic leaders of New Orleans, feeling bitter disappointment at surrendering a prized symbol of states' rights and resistance to Northern aggression, decided to build a monu-

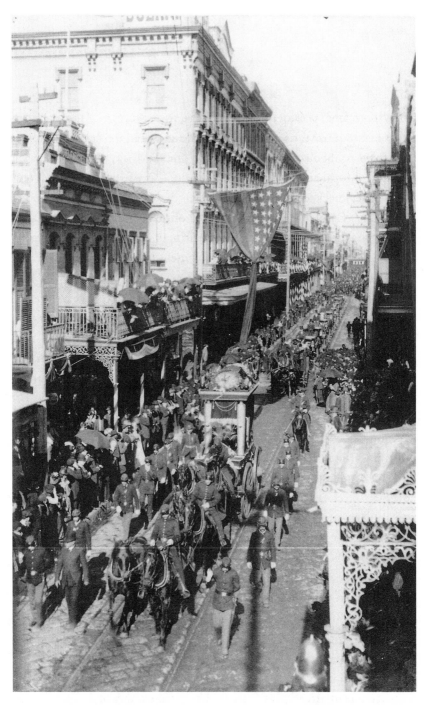

Figure 1. Jefferson Davis's funeral procession by horse-drawn wagon in New Orleans, December 6, 1889. Division of Prints and Photographs, Library of Congress.

mental memorial to Davis that would equal in scale the ones already erected to Abraham Lincoln in Springfield (see fig. 18, p. 96) and just recently conceived for Ulysses S. Grant in New York City. Their ambition, however, wildly exceeded their collective or potential purse.[2]

Necessary fund-raising and the complexity of related preparations meant that the Richmond reburial would finally be scheduled for May 31, 1893. On May 27 Davis's coffin was removed from the Metairie vault and opened to make certain that the JDMA really had the right body, which then was placed in a brand-new hand-carved coffin and loaded onto a specially designed railroad car with oversized glass windows. A mournfully decorated locomotive hauled the ensemble of passenger cars. Each step in this meticulously planned event was taken, as the press reported, with "every possible mark of *respect.*" That word will recur in many episodes in the chapters that follow. Relocation and reburial (or "translation" of a body, to use the traditional, Latin-derived word) are invariably all about the resurgence of the reputation of and hence respect for someone whose lamp and visage had dimmed in some way.[3]

As the leading authority on Davis's demise has observed, "Southerners grew increasingly anxious as the departure date neared for what was expected to be one of the most elaborate and ceremonious funeral processions in American history." Intensifying the precedent and coverage of Davis's death in December 1889, newspapers across the South and quite a few in the North reported every step in lavish detail. Many sent their top reporters to accompany the special train on its mournful but politicized mission to the Old Dominion's distinctively honorific grave.[4]

The train coursed along at a top speed of sixty-two miles per hour, slipping smoothly across and then sloping eastward down the Piedmont like a child's coiled Slinky, pausing at major state capitals so that the coffin could be viewed for a few hours by dignitaries and large throngs of worshipful citizens. In Atlanta, the delegations from Texas, Louisiana, and Mississippi failed to adjust from Central Time, which had only recently been regularized, so thirty members of the honor entourage accompanying the cortège were unhappily left behind when the train departed at 8:00 p.m. Eastern Time. The embarrassed laggards caught up in Greensboro, North Carolina, on a regular train. Even

though Southern pride was displayed with Confederate flags throughout the journey, talk of the bygone secession was already giving way
to sentiments favoring national reconciliation. Although that seems to
have been most true in progressive Atlanta, capital of the New South,
it was manifest elsewhere as well. As early as 1886 one former Southern
general had referred to the "circle of a new nationality." Others soon
echoed that refrain.[5]

Massive crowds in Richmond attended services followed by the
huge procession to Hollywood Cemetery for final interment; there a
specially brick-lined, extra-deep grave waited on a spacious hillside,
a site of unusual beauty overlooking the James River (fig. 2). Jefferson
Davis rolled to his ultimate resting place on a bed of roses: en route to
the cemetery the caisson carrying the coffin rumbled over a continuous carpet of flowers, strewn by young women and girls in white who
preceded the line of march. Mourners insisted upon their loyalty to the
Union—their support for reconciliation and American nationalism—
even as they displayed the Stars and Bars alongside Old Glory. Yet in
this instance state pride seems to have been an even stronger emotion
than sectional pride, because certain rebel states still rankled with resentment that they had not been chosen for the final entombment—
despite elaborate offers and schemes to build a very special monument
in Davis's honor at local expense.[6]

The JDMA recognized that a major monument, inevitably to be
erected in Richmond, should be a gift from all of the former Confederate states rather than a local memorial from Virginia and for Richmond.
The committee hoped to raise a million dollars so that the monument
"should be a grand thing indeed," with a "shaft so high that the birds
could not fly over it." It might even dwarf the Washington Monument.
Despite earnest desires to undertake "the patriotic and pious work" of
building an "everlasting memorial," reality and inertia set in soon after
the funeral.[7] The ambitious goal of erecting a temple in Davis's honor
soon faded. Finally, on June 3, 1907, the Jefferson Davis Monument
would be dedicated: an eight-foot bronze statue standing on a five-foot
pedestal with a sixty-foot column adjacent. Its installation did not gen-
erate a great deal of apparent interest.[8]

Davis's moment of glory, verging upon sanctification, had peaked
between the time of his Southern farewell tour in 1886 and his Rich-

Figure 2. The tomb of Jefferson Davis, Hollywood Cemetery, Richmond, Virginia (c. 1905). Division of Prints and Photographs, Library of Congress.

mond reinterment seven years later. With that the South seems to have spent its capacity for intense retrospection about the failed leader. The Lost Cause may very well have lived on, but its former president very gradually receded from view. A lingering apotheosis of sorts occurred in 1916, when Gutzon Borglum began carving Davis's visage on Stone Mountain, not far from Atlanta, alongside those of Robert E. Lee and Thomas "Stonewall" Jackson. After that, however, while Lee and Jackson remained as iconic immortals, Davis's profile began to dim, becoming spectral in public memory.[9]

✠

Historically considered, reburial has come to mean a figurative form of resurrection—primarily the resurrection of reputation, at least for a while. It has also meant, with the passage of time, renewed honor and frequently some form of reconciliation, or at least movement in the direction of reconciliation—familial, sectional, and above all national. That will be true of many of the episodes to be considered in the six segments of this book. While there have been some significant differences in the particular dynamics of individual situations, there have also been numerous similarities between "translations" and reinterments in America and elsewhere. The complexity of repatriation, a revived reverence for reputation, and the resolution of differences are constant themes that supply this book with much of its focus, which I call the cultural politics of exhumation.

This project is primarily about *pride*, as the opening epigraph from Alexander Pope is meant to suggest—different levels and layers of pride. National pride, for example, in the case of John Paul Jones's reburial at the Naval Academy in 1905–6. Sectional pride when we witness the instances of President James Monroe and the fiery abolitionist John Brown. State pride in battles over the decomposed bones of Revolutionary War General Nathanael Greene (Georgia versus Rhode Island) and the renowned scout Daniel Boone (Kentucky versus Missouri).

Regional pride is at stake in the burials of Revolutionary rifleman Daniel Morgan and bank robber Jesse James; local pride with the likes of Edgar Allan Poe (Baltimore, where he lived and died, versus Philadelphia, where he wrote his most famous works) and Frank Lloyd Wright (Taliesin East versus Taliesin West as burial sites); and family pride coupled with patriotic pride in the Revolutionary War cases of Dr. Joseph Warren and General Richard Montgomery (both killed in battle in 1775) and the much later contretemps involving F. Scott Fitzgerald and the Catholic Church. Finally, we also encounter ethnic and racial pride in the exhumation stories of Sioux Chief Sitting Bull and later Matthew Henson, an African American who assisted Admiral Richard Peary in first setting foot on the North Pole in 1909.

When groups of people, cities, privately owned cemeteries, or states contested where the remains of a celebrity should most properly repose, *pride of place* was often at stake. And when small bands of men came in the middle of the night to covertly dig up a body and steal it away, *pride of possession* became the prize. Matters of pride often caused but also resulted from intense rivalries—between regions, states, and families. Then add the commercial competition of newly established cemeteries seeking to become tourist attractions as well as profitable investments. People must buy burial plots, and often they like to be interred where celebrities have already been situated. I have in mind such sites as Mount Auburn Cemetery in Cambridge, Massachusetts, Green-Wood Cemetery in Brooklyn, and Laurel Hill in Philadelphia, a new cemetery in 1840 that crassly vied for the skeletons of not one but two Revolutionary leaders who had earlier been buried privately in family plots.

Readers should not be surprised to encounter a particularly lugubrious manifestation of pride that recurs with notable frequency in these pages: people handling or even taking personal possession of skulls belonging to figures they greatly admired, even revered in some instances. The historical origins of this practice can be traced back to medieval and early modern times, when the skull served as a reminder of life's earthly transience. Skulls also had religious significance, of course, because the contemplation of death as a spiritual exercise was recommended by the Jesuits and would be enhanced by the use of a skull, especially apparent to us in iconographic symbolism that survives. Paintings often depicted saints at prayer with a skull nearby. One thinks of Francis of Assisi, hermit saints (most notably Jerome), and Mary Magdalene as a penitent. Skulls were also used in a more secular context to symbolize Melancholy, one of the four temperaments.

In our nineteenth-century American episodes, however, religious or even spiritual reasons for contemplating skulls seem less significant or meaningful than physically holding the skull of a famous individual as the ultimate act of possessive connectedness to the deceased—most certainly an expression of secular admiration and pride, as we shall see with figures as different as Daniel Boone and Edgar Allan Poe. The latter-day disciple could boast, "I once held in my hands the very skull of . . ." (though the honor was not always voiced in quite those words). In the case of evangelist George Whitefield, however, actually displaying a skull at the vault of his tomb (see fig. 36 on p. 171) does hark back to premodern sentiments about holy relics, whereas holding up a skull for a kind of photo op in 1904, as with James Smithson (see fig. 23 on p. 111), had more to do with declaring that "we've really found our man and here's proof positive." The skull resists decay longer than any other part of the body. Quite often it was the sole surviving puzzle piece still intact and deemed recognizable—sometimes because of teeth or, as with the skull of Jesse James, a bullet hole.

One might very well say that this project is written in a major key—call it Pride, public and collective—yet the work intermittently modulates to a minor key, the somewhat secularized version of veneration for sacred relics among the Christian societies of medieval Europe and early modern times. For illustrative episodes of the latter, we will consider the burial and subsequently the ritualized uses of evangelist Whitefield in the Congregational Church of Newburyport, Massachusetts (formerly Presbyterian); of John Paul Jones in a new and elaborately decorated chapel at the Naval Academy in Annapolis; and of Augustus Lord Howe in several rebuilt incarnations of St. Peter's Church in Albany. If the body of a venerated person can serve in some sense to consecrate a secular site, an already consecrated site can effectively elevate the status of a civil figure's mortal remains.

The narratives here differ in time, by place, and by circumstance. The preponderant majority, however, are American, and they manifest certain clear patterns, never identical, because (as it is said) history does not repeat itself even though historians often do. Although I will touch upon different cultures, different eras, even different countries, most of the episodes that I explore clearly involve the desire to enhance respect for someone deceased, the variability of reputations, and the complexity of restitution or repatriation. Intensely felt sentiments of pride emerge on multiple levels. And they reveal that the symbolic significance of possessing "sacred relics," even in secular settings, has incalculable potency—yet often provides pleasure as well.

The compelling need to do the right thing with dead bodies has proved to be more than merely symbolic, though that significance has been notably present on many occasions as well. Moving the remains of deceased figures has mattered in social, cultural, and political ways—often in varied combinations. Moreover, we are contemplating a phenomenon at least as old as recorded history in the Western world. Two examples from antiquity should suffice. They provide precedents, of a sort, but also suggest contrasts with our modern narratives.

Herodotus tells us that after countless defeats by the Tegeans during the reign of Croesus, the Lacedaemonians consulted the oracle at Delphi, who advised that in order to prevail they must relocate the bones of Orestes, the son of Agamemnon. With a mix of luck and savvy they found a ten-foot coffin, "opened the grave, and collecting the bones, returned with them to Sparta. From henceforth, whenever the Spartans and the Tegeans made trial of each other's skill in arms, the Spartans always had greatly the advantage; and by the time to which we are come now they were masters of most of the Peloponnese."[10]

A second illustration, also situated in classical Greece, comes to us from Plutarch and bears a striking resemblance to the narrative of Orestes' efficacious exhumation. Early in the fifth century, when Cimon led Athenian forces against Persia, he successfully conquered the strategic island of Scyros. He then learned that

> the Athenians had once been given an oracle commanding them to bring back the bones of Theseus to Athens and pay them the honours due to a hero; but they did not know where he was buried, since the people of Scyros would neither admit that the story was true nor allow any search to be made. Cimon, however, attacked the task with great enthusiasm and after some difficulty discovered the sacred spot. He had the bones placed on board his trireme and brought them back with great pomp and ceremony to the hero's native land, almost four hundred years after he had left it. This affair did more than any other achievement of Cimon's to endear him to the people.[11]

Although the consultation of oracles had long since ceased to be normative in nineteenth-century America, despite a certain predilection for séances in some Victorian circles, necromancy or supernatural guidance would have come in very handy when the grave sites of venerated heroes were unknown or uncertain, as I shall note. Evident among these stories is a vocation that is more valuable than an oracle or a spiritualist in calling attention to neglected burial sites. As it happened, journalists took the initiative in launching the quests to move John Paul Jones and D. H. Lawrence from France to rebury them in America, more than a generation apart. Church sextons have also played particularly useful roles.

Although quite a few of our incidents are more instructive or amusing than tragic, and reveal far more about human nature than they do about *nature morte*, one rather likely musical accompaniment might be Chopin's Piano Sonata No. 2 in B-flat Minor with its *marche funèbre*. Processions and audiences have heard it played time and time again during reinterments. At the end, however, when we come to comparisons between the United States and other cultures, we might very well bear in mind that the expression "whistling past the graveyard" is an idiomatic American usage meaning the effort to remain cheerful in a dire situation. I cannot claim that Americans whistled more than Europeans when they reburied people, but I do submit that a great many of the occasions we will visit were more celebratory than sad.

— ONE —

A Short History of Reburial

PATTERNS OF
CHANGE
OVER TIME

Let's talk of graves, of worms and epitaphs.

✚ King Richard II in Shakespeare,
The Tragedy of King Richard the Second, 3.2.145

$\mathcal{D}$uring the 1780s, the very decade when the new American nation had its genesis, a highly unusual tomb was being planned to rebury the French philosopher and social critic Jean-Jacques Rousseau (1712–78) on an island in a small lake at Ermenonville, near Senlis. Designed and completed between 1780 and 1788, it aroused considerable interest because it indicated a radically new view of mortality—or more precisely, the circumstances surrounding what happens after death and the appropriate response for survivors. The cypress, a tree traditionally associated with mourning, disappeared, supplanted by a grove of poplars. Rousseau's tomb would be a *garden* rather than being situated in a formally bounded urban or ecclesiastical burial ground. As historian George Mosse has written, "Here men and women could contemplate nature and virtue in an atmosphere of sentimentality but not pathos. The tranquility and happiness of the living were to be retained even in death."[1]

The emerging Enlightenment view of death as tranquil sleep, a condition of repose, gradually began to replace the long-standing grim notion of dying as not merely inevitable but very likely harsh or cruel, resulting from war or disease, for example. Thomas Hobbes's seventeenth-century notion of life as nasty, brutish, and short eventually gave way to perceptions that anticipate or more nearly approximate our own. During the Jacobin phase of the French Revolution, death even underwent democratization: it was decided that all citizens, irrespective of social rank or wealth, should be buried modestly, reflected in the basic similarity of new tombs. In such practices we can perceive the origins of military cemeteries ever since the nineteenth century: row upon parallel row of identical graves. Thereafter, the state took upon itself the responsibility to regulate burials, as it has ever since in European nation-states.[2]

It is not sufficiently understood, however, that during the seventeenth and eighteenth centuries only an estimated 5–7 percent of the dead escaped the fate of a common trench. Dreading exactly that, Madame Pompadour, the influential mistress of King Louis XV, stipulated in her will that she be buried in a lead coffin near the central cross of her favorite churchyard. But even she was exhumed, reburied, and dug up once again later, and her remains were ultimately lost. As we shall see, such mishaps were not at all unusual. Yet another basic aspect of early modern interment that is significant but too little appreciated: the normative absence of individualized markers. Nonconformists in Great Britain were given a burial ground in London during the 1660s, very close to the house that became John Wesley's. The apocalyptic artist William Blake was buried there in 1827, but his precise location went unmarked and hence forgotten.

In the United States a movement developed in the 1840s to honor Boston's Revolutionary leader Sam Adams with a heroic monument, but no one knew quite where his bones reposed in the Old Granary Burying Ground.[3] That brings us to what might seem at first glance an observable discrepancy. Anyone who has walked the Freedom Trail in Boston will have noticed interesting gravestones in the King's Chapel Burying Ground or in Copp's Hill Burying Ground, where members of the Mather family were buried. Several splendidly illustrated books have been compiled about unusual and attractive individualized gravestones dating from the colonial period, especially in New England.[4] But these actually represent a rather small minority of the burials in seventeenth- and eighteenth-century America. Most early settlers were placed in unmarked graves, often hastily and under difficult circumstances. Wooden grave rails consisting of one or two horizontal markers between vertical posts were more common than tombstones, and they disintegrated fairly quickly with the passage of time.[5]

We should also bear in mind the complex legacy of Calvinism, especially in New England. John Calvin himself had unsuccessfully insisted that his own grave *not* be marked so that followers would not treat his remains as relics, a practice that seemed all too redolent of superstitious Catholicism. Some Calvinists even wanted the customary funeral liturgy abolished. Religious dissenters from the Church of England in the colonies decided to secularize burials by refusing to consecrate burial grounds as sacred space. The imperative not to do so by Calvinists in Old England and New meant that commemoration of individual lives and mundane worldly accomplishments had scant place in New England graveyards. Hence the astonishing (to us) paucity of particularized place markers at discrete burial sites.

For an illustration of this practice carried to an unusual extreme in early America, consider the case of Baron Von Steuben, the successful drillmaster and tactician of George Washington's army who retired to upstate New York, where he speculated in undeveloped real estate like several other Revolutionary War generals to be encountered in the next chapter. When he died suddenly in 1794, it was found that his will specified that he be wrapped in his military cloak and buried in a plain coffin in a "retired spot" on his estate. He had instructed two devoted aides that "they never acquaint any person with the place wherein I shall be buried." He had often insisted that he wanted no stone to mark his heavily wooded grave, perhaps near a beloved hemlock tree.[6]

Several decades later, however, commissioners of a nearby town, close to Oneida, decided to create a wagon road whose line ran directly across the grave and actually disturbed the coffin. One former Von Steuben aide, still living, removed the body farther into the woods and gave fifty acres to a Baptist society under a covenant with the provision that five acres should be fenced in and forever remain uncleared. Disregarding Von Steuben's wishes about the absence of a marker, however, in 1824 he placed a modest monument above the grave. When it began to crumble, local and New York German-Americans erected a new and grander one in 1872. The site has since become part of a New York state park dedicated to the general's memory.[7]

A widespread desire to ensure the perpetuity of graves dates only from the 1790s and early 1800s, and then the pattern spread rather slowly. The related practice of visiting graves to pay respects on the anniversary of death or some other occasion (to tidy up the site and leave flowers) also emerged gradually and became customary only as late as the 1840s. That explains a problematic issue that we shall encounter with some frequency when exhumation and reburial were desired: grave sites of prominent individuals that had become shamefully overgrown, neglected, unkempt, and difficult to locate with certainty.[8]

The changing nature of American Protestantism provides us with *some* help in understanding what might appear to be a kind of disconnect in many of the nineteenth-century episodes that will be found in the chapters that follow. Most of the reinterments seem to have been, fundamentally, *secular* commemorative events. Except for an obligatory invocation, a hymn or an anthem, and closing prayers or a benediction by clergy, I find little trace of the traditional religious views so firmly held by most Americans during the first two-thirds of the nineteenth century—visionary and optimistic notions about God's judgment and humankind's ultimate fate. There was little effort to literally sacralize these reburials, even though the phrase "sacred relics" was commonly voiced. The remains of deceased heroes were more like trophies to be secured—honored, to be sure, but not with the rituals and spiritual discourse seemingly appropriate for the Christian expectation of bodily resurrection on Judgment Day.

From recent scholarship we know a good deal about the eschatology of Americans before the Civil War; and those beliefs persisted even as they clearly evolved during the later nineteenth century, especially because biblical criticism and later Darwinism gradually made literalism and naive optimism less pervasively accepted. Nevertheless, notions of heaven and hell did not simply disappear, and many assumptions characteristic of evangelical Protestantism lingered on, albeit somewhat diluted, despite doubts during the so-called late Victorian crisis of faith.

Antebellum Americans shared a very comforting vision of eternal life, especially once orthodox Calvinism became democratized during and after the 1820s. Democratization diminished the notion of selective predestination and meant that anyone could become one of God's elect by accepting Jesus Christ as personal savior. Heaven was not envisioned as some ethereal entity or state of the soul. Rather, as recent studies have shown, heaven was a very material place, hovering just above the cloud cover, in which individual bodies and souls would be joined and perfected. In 1857 Sarah Gould compiled numerous writings about heaven in a book titled *The Guardian Angels, or Friends in Heaven*, published in Boston. "We believe Paradise to be our fatherland; our parents and patriarchs; why should we not [make] haste and fly to see our home and greet our parents?" she asked. Heaven was regarded as a real place of immense beauty, and the very point of living was to achieve heaven. As one minister proclaimed: "No night in heaven! Then no sad partings are experienced there;—no funeral processions move, no death-knell is heard, *no graves are opened.*"9

Countless sermons and tracts reveal the expectation that resurrected persons would exist not merely in spirit but in full possession of whole, perfected bodies. And because identifiable bodies would be preserved, the notion of "heavenly recognition" seemed virtually self-evident to those who subscribed to this notion of life beyond death. Families would be reunited, perhaps even entire communities. More often than not, the authors of these tracts held strongly materialistic ideas about bodily resurrection.[10]

True enough, in thinking about it they could not ignore the biblical pronouncement that "flesh and blood cannot inherit the kingdom of heaven, nor does the perishable inherit the imperishable" (1 Corinthians 15:50). Yet they were willing to risk intellectual or theological inconsistency and leave unresolved puzzles to God's providence. They had clear if ambiguous reassurance from 1 Corinthians (15:51–52): "for the trumpet will sound, and the dead will be raised imperishable, and we shall be changed." Those unresolved puzzles never ceased to be sources of concern, however, especially among the most devout. As Lyman Beecher, the prominent Calvinist preacher, candidly wondered in 1820: "What happens when we die?" A man with greater faith and assurance than many, he was hardly alone in asking.[11]

Because Calvinism was in transition precisely when the new garden-type cemeteries emerged during the 1830s and 40s, inconsistencies abounded. Some people resisted any thought of reburial because they wanted the body to remain intact in its original place of rest "so that it could be identified." But New England medical societies, concerned about the health effects of the interment of countless bodies in tightly crowded urban centers, began urging in the 1820s the benefits of rural burial, accepting the logic of bodily decay, and answering those who insisted that the dead would rise up on Judgment Day. During the 1820s and 30s, Boston-area Unitarians and Universalists offered strong support for the natural process of earthen burial rather than putrefaction in sealed vaults. Representative figures like the Reverend William Ware (1797–1852) could reject traditional Calvinism but still have it both ways with facile words. Death, he declared, "we regard as not so much as even a temporary, momentary extinction of being, but simply as the appointed manner in which we shall pass from one stage of existence to another—from earth to heaven."[12]

As midcentury approached, eschatological thinking made only modest rhetorical adjustments to the reality of new, naturalistic cemeteries. At Spring Grove Cemetery in Cincinnati, John McLean insisted in 1849 that "we should view the grave as the opening portal of heaven." At the dedication of the Ever Green Cemetery in Gettysburg, Pennsylvania, in 1855, Methodist minister J. H. C. Dosh declared that "we do not idolize the departed, nor would we cling too devotedly to their mortal remains; 'knowing that these *vile* bodies shall be changed,' and shall come forth from their graves glorious and immortal bodies."[13]

If these are, indeed, representative sentiments, then we must wonder what families, friends, and admirers were thinking when they exhumed incomplete skeletons in the cases that follow. Quite often the bones being sought were intermingled with others because burials had been commonly crowded together, wooden coffins disintegrated, and in smaller churchyards when space ran out, burials occurred on top of one another. Perhaps there really is no problem then. If at the time of resurrection God is going to make bodies whole again and reunite them with souls, why make such a fuss over the temporal location and condition of human remains?

The answer certainly appears to be that exhuming and relocating remains, when it occurred, had rather little connection with the prevailing Protestant eschatology and everything to do with the needs of the living. Reburial was all about possession and memorialization: matters of reputation, memory, sentiments concerning the most suitable venue, pride of ownership, plus the commercial development of privately owned cemeteries, and eventually even tourism.

When we reach chapters 3 and 4, we will confront the question of change: what happens when fewer people regard heaven as a physical place serenely hovering above the clouds where husband and wife will recognize one another and parents embrace sons and daughters lost to life in infancy or childhood? Once upon a time people could sincerely sing or recite, "O death, where is thy victory? O death, where is thy sting?" because they genuinely believed in life everlasting (First Corinthians 15:55). Perhaps the sting of death became more painful and less readily scorned once traditional belief systems were undermined by science, secularism, and skepticism. In any case, whether we look to the Age of Faith or later to an Age of Anxiety, the imperative of exhumation seems to have been unclearly linked—one might even say oddly *unrelated*—to religious values, whether strongly held or intensely desired.

This puzzling situation requires from us a kind of twofold suspension of belief: first, suspending our presumption of some rational and necessary consistency between putative eschatology and public behavior, and second, recognizing that there must have been a partial abeyance or willful avoidance of the culture's belief in the ultimate reconstitution of bodily remains on Judgment Day. Reburials occurred *despite* the discovery of incomplete or even fragmentary remains. Whatever was found when exhumation took place was clearly regarded as fundamentally symbolic, even though the living scarcely acknowledged that in so many words. The reality, however, is that in many instances (Nathanael Greene, Daniel Morgan, John Paul Jones, James Wilson, Daniel Boone, Edgar Allan Poe, and others) reburial was quite literally a civic occasion, and therefore a secular rather than an ecclesiastical event. Principal speakers devoted their eulogies or remarks to the individual's historic importance, not his divine destiny.

✝

Changing attitudes about death, urban health, and especially the democratization of interment, did not all reach or affect the United States immediately. For that matter, such concerns were not even addressed or observed consistently throughout Europe during the later eighteenth and nineteenth centuries. Wealth and rank in bourgeois societies would result in all sorts of elaborate, honorific initial burials and fancy vaults, and mourning in antebellum America became an almost formulaic phenomenon in a "culture of melancholy" with a distinctive iconography that is all too familiar today from art museums and the historic house museums of famous Americans.[14] The notion that a person was entitled not only to a proper resting place but to the right *kind* of resting place emerged not long after the new nation did.[15]

It needs to be noted that the word and concept of *cemetery* as we understand it only surfaced in the early nineteenth century and came from Europe, almost certainly from France. Before that there were private graveyards, church burying grounds, and areas simply called burying yards. Individualized markers were unusual, as I have noted, even for people of some distinction. What is known today as the very extensive

Congressional Cemetery in southeast Washington, DC, did not receive that designation until the 1830s. From the time of its creation by private citizens in 1807 it was called the Washington Parish Burial Ground. Private, enterprise-driven cemeteries emerged gradually as a commercial phenomenon during the second quarter of the nineteenth century.[16]

✢

The history of death in America has been examined from multiple perspectives, most notably, perhaps, through scrutiny of the highly commercialized funeral industry and the social pressures it can exert and through accounts of the terrible carnage caused by the savage Civil War of 1861–65.[17] Anthropologists and historians have looked at mortuary rituals and at the history of cemeteries, especially the rural cemetery movement that visibly began in 1831 with the creation of Mount Auburn Cemetery in a suburb of Boston.[18] We also have insightful studies of monuments and memorials, along with analyses of American gravestones and what they can tell us about the changing symbolism associated with death and its aftermath.[19]

What has been largely overlooked in this intriguing body of literature is the disparate and sometimes arcane yet significant story of exhumations and reburials—episodes tucked away in various antiquarian and memorial volumes and tracts, and occasionally in the coda to a biographical chronicle, often written by a descendant, disciple, or devoted hagiographer. My curiosity and interest in bringing these sagas together within some sort of meaningful framework have been heightened by the recent and ongoing surge of serious scholarship devoted to all of the politically motivated repatriations and reburials that took place in Central and Eastern Europe—most notably in Hungary, Poland, and Romania—following the fall of Communism in 1989, a subject that I will save for comparative purposes in the final chapter.

The reasons for digging up dead bodies for reburial in the United States have been less often ideological yet no less partisan than in Europe.[20] Some of the most dramatic and controversial American cases have essentially been driven by patriotism (especially arising from Revolutionary War history; see chapter 2) or by strong sectional sentiments, particularly involving deaths during and after the Civil War era, followed by intense nationalism at the turn of the nineteenth and start of the twentieth century (chapter 3). Adding to the rich diversity of American motives have been phases of hero worship and ancestor worship, as well as the determined desire of survivors to bring a loved one home and honor that person properly because the initial burial had been inappropriate or the grave had been disgraced by obscurity and neglect (chapter 4 especially). The commercial desire to attract tourists and reasons rooted in local pride have also provided ongoing stimuli in the competition to possess or repossess the bodies of famous figures.

Still other remains were moved when descendants belatedly recalled the explicit wishes of the deceased—in the case of painter John Trumbull, for example, to be buried close to his own art at Yale College in New Haven, Connecticut. Religious motives and racial discrimination provide yet another constellation of causes, with the repatriation and reburial of prominent Native Americans revealing motives that involve both ethnicity and religion (chapter 5). Above all, perhaps, and pertinent to most of these chapters, are the vicissitudes of individual reputations, which in many instances fluctuated in volatile ways and ultimately required the restitution of a proper grave and monument, at the very least, and more often complete exhumation and reburial in a place somewhat distant from the original site.

Because our primary concern is with figures whose careers have been historically significant—most often quite famous (though occasionally infamous, like the outlaw Jesse James)—I shall *not* highlight the mass reburials of large numbers of lesser known people fallen in battle or (with one important exception) those where entire cemeteries had to be relocated in the name of "progress," such as the construction of a new highway or a major building on what had become prime real estate.[21]

Moving multiple bodies, especially anonymous ones, has often prompted striking cases of political conflict, and I will touch upon a few representative instances, most notably Confederate soldiers who died in the North during the Civil War; but that is not my principal focus, which is the process of digging up prominent individuals in order to "do them justice" and, in some instances, also to open a coffin to be certain that the "right" remains are still actually within. Sometimes, once the identification was successfully made, reburial took place at or near the original site; but more often the body was moved to a far more appropriate venue for interment. I will also leave to others treatment of the exhumation of bodies to check DNA in order to determine issues of lineage, whether racial, criminal, quasi-political, or otherwise important for proving innocence or probing some mysterious or enigmatic connection.[22]

While my story (actually consisting of *many* stories) is primarily American, with some parallels and comparisons to other cultures, it is important to acknowledge at the outset what is universal and so fundamental that it transcends even cross-cultural differences and similarities. As Robert Pogue Harrison has wisely observed, "Humans bury not simply to achieve closure and effect a separation from the dead but also and above all to humanize the ground on which they build their worlds and found their histories. . . . [Humanity] is a way of being mortal and relating to the dead. To be human means above all to bury. Vico suggests as much when he reminds us that '*humanitas* in Latin comes first and properly from *humando*, burying.' "[23]

Why do I find these frequently bizarre and macabre episodes so intriguing? In part because of a fairly distinctive change in practices that piques the historian's interest in patterns of sociocultural ebb and flow. Reburials became increasingly common during but especially *after* the second quarter of the nineteenth century, a little-noticed trend. Although I will consider them in a more topical manner than a strictly chronological one, when they are plotted along a time line we find comparatively few between 1800 and 1835, many more between 1845 and 1909, something of a surge during the 1930s, and then fewer after that. During the period from 1845 until 1909, the initiative came primarily from politicians or local boosters, more often than from family—a pattern that was reversed in the twentieth century, when survivors and descendants were more likely to supply the initiative.

Most important, however, I am intrigued because the ways in which Americans have honored (and sometimes dishonored) their dead are marked by substantive and symbolic details that tell us much about the values and culture of the living. And, as I have indicated, comparisons with the relocation of bodies for political reasons in Europe are revealing because we have not had as many ideologically motivated murders that later required honorific redress, even though nationalism, sectionalism, and political partisanship have at times quite clearly served as essential stimuli for reburials in the United States.[24]

After the national capital became permanently established at Washington, DC, in 1800, a problem arose when members of Congress from northern states died during the winter season. Moving bodies to New England in severe weather on poor roads was difficult enough, but also the ground in their home states was usually frozen too firmly to permit interment. So in 1807 what later came to be known as the Congressional Cemetery was established in southeast Washington near the Anacostia River; here temporary burials could take place until climatic conditions in summer permitted the removal of coffins for proper burial on "native ground." Some families chose to leave their statesmen permanently in Washington, however: currently nineteen senators and seventy-one representatives remain there. Eventually six thousand individuals who had not been members of Congress also received burial rights in this very first national cemetery. They range from mayors of Washington, craftsmen and architects of the U.S. Capitol, and veterans of the Revolutionary and other early wars to Indian chiefs and foreign diplomats. What began as a 4.5-acre square grew by annexation to its present size, 32.5 acres, in 1875. But even to this day, the section initially devoted to temporary burial is still set aside as a memorial to those who were initially laid to rest in the city planned by Pierre L'Enfant.[25]

If we inquire about other national cemeteries involving reburials, real and envisioned, we might note the following. In 1862, when unexpected numbers of Union troops died in battles in northern Virginia (near Washington), Abraham Lincoln and Secretary of War Edwin Stanton took steps to seize the estate of Robert E. Lee, overlooking the Potomac, in order to provide a burial ground for soldiers. On August 6, 1866, corpses of 2,111 unknown soldiers recovered from the battlefields at Bull Run and along the Rappahannock River were brought to Arlington and buried beneath a single monument in what would become Section 26 (fig. 3). These were the first combat Unknowns brought to the sprawling federal site soon to be known as Arlington National Cemetery.[26]

It is worth noting that the United States has nothing like Westminster Abbey in London. In 1889 the Reverend R. Heber Newton, an Epis-

Figure 3. Vignettes of Mount Vernon; the tomb of George Washington; graves of the 2,111 unknown soldiers—the first Americans buried at what became Arlington National Cemetery. Division of Prints and Photographs, Library of Congress.

copalian active in the Social Gospel movement, urged the creation of a national mausoleum in New York for illustrious Americans. The closest we came to that was a statuary hall of fame administered by New York University.

In 1945 the anthropologist and folklorist Zora Neale Hurston wrote to W. E. B. Du Bois, asking him, "Why do you not propose a cemetery for the illustrious Negro dead? Something like Pere Lachaise in Paris." She envisioned such figures as Nat Turner and Frederick Douglass and wanted it to be located in Florida because the vegetation there is green all year round. As she urged Du Bois and possibly others: "As far as possible, remove the bones of our dead celebrities to this spot. Let no Negro celebrities, no matter what financial condition they might be in at death, lie in inconspicuous forgetfulness. We must assume the responsibility of their graves being known and honored. You must see what a rallying spot that would be for all that we want to accomplish and do."[27]

Needless to say, neither Newton's nor Hurston's idea ever got off the ground (or, rather, into it). Yet the imperative of "repossessing our dead" lingers on in proactive and politicized ways in the United States. Witness the black MIA flags commonly seen flying right below Old Glory at many post offices and airports in the decades since the Vietnam War, and of course many bumper stickers on cars and trucks convey the same message. The desire to locate and repatriate the remains of military personnel still stirs strong emotions in many quarters.[28]

✠

The practice of exhumation and reinterment has had a long, complex, and intriguing history elsewhere in the world. Although a fear of disinterment was prevalent throughout the ancient Near East, in Egypt and especially in Palestine, reburials often became unavoidable. One authority on this subject has argued for an ongoing pattern of secondary burials even though these appear to have contradicted orthodox theology. Jews in antiquity collected remains of the dead and deposited them in individual receptacles. Ossuaries for bones were deemed all the more desirable because they could be used to transfer human remains readily, either to a family tomb or else to the Holy Land. It became incumbent upon Jews to bury their dead in Palestine, if at all possible.[29]

In ancient Greece, as we have noticed, there does seem to have been an overwhelming imperative to bring back the bones or remains of Homeric heroes who had perished far from their homelands or city-states, though the literary and archaeological evidence is not consistent on this point. With the American Civil War in mind for contrast, especially, it is worth remembering that at times the Greeks and the Trojans paused or interrupted battles in order to exchange dead and dying heroes and provide them with appropriate on-site interment.[30]

The culture of ancient Rome had very strong taboos against moving or dividing bodies—taboos that gradually receded, however, over a period of centuries. An official market in famous bones began in the year 787 CE. By the twelfth century, dividing and even distributing body parts for burial became a widespread Christian practice. Quite often, one person's remains might be buried in two different places in order to satisfy competition for pride of place, even though the major liturgical manuals denied the validity of doing so.[31] It is well known that the bodies of saints were divided up in order to maximize the distribution of relics. During the High Middle Ages, the stowing of redeemed relics in an altar meant that the saint was virtually present during celebration of the Mass. But as historian Caroline Bynum has remarked, "Enthusiasm for bodily partition affected not just the saints." By 1200, especially north of the Alps, the bodies of prominent ecclesiastics or nobles were often eviscerated, boned, or boiled after death, and the resulting parts were buried in several places, often near different saints. Gradually, as older graves were opened for practical purposes, such as making space for new arrivals, charnel houses became commonplace. Initially charnel houses were all about the relocation of skeletons; only subsequently did they become dumping sites for bodies during periods of plague and pandemics.[32]

As Johan Huizinga observed in a classic work on the later Middle Ages, the desirability of being buried in the soil of one's own country gave rise to practices that the Catholic Church interdicted as being contrary to canon law. In the twelfth and thirteenth centuries, when a prince or another person of high rank died in battle or on a crusade far from home, "the body was often cut up and boiled so as to extract the bones, which were sent home in a chest, whereas the rest was interred, not without ceremony, however, on the spot. Emperors, kings, and bishops have undergone this strange operation." Although Pope Boniface VIII forbade it, his successors sometimes gave dispensations. Numerous Englishmen who died in France during the Hundred Years' War were granted this "privilege" of being buried in more than one place. The Swiss historian Jacob Burckhardt observed that Pope Pius II decided to make Rome "the common refuge for all the remains of the saints which had been driven from their own churches." But he could not get all of them. The obsession with relics became especially strong during the sixteenth and seventeenth centuries, enhanced by the Council of Trent, which officially directed that the remains of saints be venerated.[33]

The body of Saint Geneviève (419/422–512), for example, was exhumed and enshrined on several occasions at various locations in Paris during the millennium following her death, mainly due to the number of sanctuaries and churches devoted to her memory as the city's patron saint, and to their occasional relocation. In 1793, however, revolutionary Jacobins removed her remains from the site of the newly secularized Panthèon and burned them.[34] It is not surprising that when the beloved St. Francis died in 1226, his followers buried him secretly in Assisi and very deep underground beneath a kind of premodern cement in order to prevent his exhumation and bodily desecration.

✛

The multiple reburials of René Descartes, the brilliant philosopher, mathematician, and natural scientist, are instructive and prescient for our purposes because they had so much to do with national pride, the sometimes lurid early modern obsession with sacred relics (*la précieuse relique*), hero worship, and pride of possession—securely controlling the remains of a genius and great man. Religion, or one might better say religious differences, also played a part. All of these considerations will be critically important to the interpretive spine of this book.

Descartes led a peripatetic life. A Frenchman who lived and did much of his most important writing in the Netherlands, he moved to Stockholm in middle age (1643), lured by the invitation and brilliance of young Queen Christina. Special patronage as a court intellectual at a time when such figures were valued had special appeal for a man grown weary of war-ravaged Europe south of the Baltic Sea, separating Scandinavia from so many sites of ceaseless conflict. It also put some distance between him and harsh critics of his empirical *Discourse on the Method*, which some construed as a scandalous challenge to orthodox Catholicism, even though that had not been his direct intent at all.[35]

When Descartes died in 1650, with his anger raging against a climate that had caused him to contract pneumonia, he was buried in the obscurity of a small, rustic cemetery outside Stockholm. Sixteen years later, when a new and ultra-nationalistic French ambassador arrived in Sweden, he found it deeply offensive that his famous Catholic countryman was buried in Protestant oblivion. So he negotiated the highly complex arrangements necessary to have Descartes translated to Paris for proper reburial. Once again, reputation and respect were prime motivations. When Descartes' remains were dug up in 1666, however, a few people with immediate personal access kept souvenirs. The ambassador himself modestly plucked the bones of one finger for himself, but a Swede actually took the philosopher's entire skull—somehow seemingly unnoticed at the time—and it remained in Sweden until 1821, when repatriation finally occurred because of serendipitous coincidences.[36]

A Cartesian cult had already surfaced in France by the 1660s, mainly among academics, so what remained of Descartes—a heap of bones confined to a copper box only thirty inches long—was reburied inside a venerable church right next to relics of Saint Geneviève. Although Louis XIV disapproved of Descartes' views, national pride prevailed. In 1792, however, amidst the chaos of the French Revolution, a dedicated soul named Alexandre Lenoir removed what he believed to be the philosopher's remains from the Church of Saint Geneviève for safekeeping, but made some small jewelry from a bone plate—actually considered a gesture of respect rather than a callous act.[37]

Late in 1793, with Robespierre's Terror running at full steam, the National Convention ordered that the great Descartes be honored by reburial in the deconsecrated Panthèon. Despite that order, however, the philosopher's bones remained safe and secret in a convent near the Seine. Subsequently, as the French polity calmed, Lenoir relocated Descartes to the garden of his *soi-disant* Museum of Monuments. In 1819, though, when it became clear that the Bourbon monarchy would continue, Descartes was relocated and reburied yet again, just a short distance along the Left Bank from the Church of Saint-Germain-des-Prés.[38]

All told, Descartes' body was buried once in Stockholm and reinterred at least three times in Paris, twice at venerated sites and once in a secular venue. Scholars have lost count because there was at least one reburial of the wrong bones. The detailed detective story of where and when, including false starts and misidentifications, has been told exceedingly well by Russell Shorto in his gripping narrative of great moments in the history of early modern science titled *Descartes' Bones.* The skull was bought at auction in 1819 by the owner of a Stockholm casino. In 1821 it was again sold at auction in Stockholm, but this time it was solemnly retrieved by a dedicated French biologist, Georges Cuvier, and deposited in the Museum of Natural History. The skull was actually misplaced in the horrendous Paris floods of 1911–12, yet somehow it miraculously reappeared in a pile of bones. It could be readily identified because in 1666 and subsequently various owners had inscribed their names on the skull and someone else had composed an entire poem in Latin on the top.[39] What could not be inscribed on that skull was "R.I.P.," because that would never be Descartes' destiny. To this day he rests in pieces rather than in peace. It is not even clear whether the remnants other than his skull are all actually his. But the saga of his migratory bones may very well be the most bizarre of all such tales.[40]

✝

During and after the French Revolution, funeral processions and a cult of heroes played a crucial role in shaping what became a new, secularized cult of tombs, cemeteries, and the dead in nineteenth-century France. The National Constituent Assembly established the desanctified Panthèon as a burial place for distinguished Frenchmen. One notable occasion involved the 1791 reburial of Voltaire's body with official honors in the Panthèon. (He had died in 1778, his views anathema to the church, so he was originally buried surreptitiously at a Cistercian monastery near Troyes.) But after the monarchy was restored in 1814, royalist fanatics stormed the Panthèon, opened the lead coffins, and disposed of Voltaire's remains in a pit of quicklime.[41]

Perhaps the single most famous reburial of all occurred in 1840, when Napoleon's remains were recovered from St. Helena and reinterred in the Dôme des Invalides in Paris—a momentous reversal in the politics of French memory. (We might recall two lines from Sophocles' *Oedipus Rex*: "The tyrant as a child of Pride / Who drinks from his great sickening cup.") His son, Napoleon II (1811–32), remembered as "L'Aiglon" (the Eagle), received the title King of Rome at birth but apparently died in Vienna of lead or arsenic poisoning at the hands of Prince von Metternich's governmental agents. In 1940 Adolf Hitler sought to win favor with the politically paralyzed French by having the remains of L'Aiglon sent to Paris for burial with his father at Les Invalides. He was subsequently moved to a separate crypt below Napoleon's. (His heart and intestines, however, remain in separate urns in Vienna.)[42]

Less well known than Napoleon's repatriation is the grim obsession of Jules Michelet, the prolific and popular nineteenth-century French historian. "I had," he explained, "a beautiful disease: I loved Death." His favorite walk in Paris was through Père Lachaise, the extraordinary cemetery for celebrities; and he enjoyed exhumations. He delighted in the ghastly story of Danton opening the grave of his wife in order to embrace her corpse. Danton recorded her disinterment in grisly detail. Necromancy at work again? We cannot be sure.[43]

During the 1790s the graves of two seventeenth-century English antimonarchical martyrs, John Hampden and Algernon Sydney (the former killed in battle against Charles I in 1643 and the latter beheaded by Charles II in 1683), were opened, the bodies examined and then reinterred. Emblematic of the rights of Englishmen, those two were much admired by Whig reformers. In 1828 Lord Nugent opened Hampden's tomb once again, studied the remains, cut off some locks of hair, and then described the incident for the *Gentleman's Magazine*. More than a century following the death in London of philosopher-theologian Emanuel Swedenborg in 1772, his remains were repatriated to Sweden. Only then was it discovered that a Swedish sea captain had removed Swedenborg's skull as a souvenir for his cranium museum. (Yes, the Descartes drama déjà vu.) The skull was eventually recovered and returned to the Royal Academy of Science in Stockholm. "It's a great relief to have it home," remarked a grateful academy official. "It's been a very macabre story."[44]

Such sagas may seem like mere curiosities, fabulations from *Ripley's Believe It or Not*. But the death and repatriation of Lajos (Louis) Kossuth, the Hungarian revolutionary, bear (and bare) a political punch portending the dramatic events that unfolded in Eastern Europe with the fall of Communism. After Kossuth's 1848 revolution against the Austro-Hungarian Empire failed, he fled into exile in Italy, eventually dying in Turin in 1894 at the age of ninety-two. When his body was brought back to Budapest for burial in early April of that year, half a million people attended the funeral, and Kossuth was lauded as the father of the nation. His funeral—held at the National Museum because Kossuth was Lutheran and the Catholic Church refused to display any symbols of grieving—launched a three-week period of mourning and became a pivotal moment in the construction of Hungarian national identity and historical consciousness. For his burial in Kerepesi Cemetery, clumps of soil were actually sent to Budapest from all the sites where the blood of patriots had been shed during the wars of independence in 1848. Kossuth would be revered as the soul and spirit of the nation, and when the anti-Soviet revolt occurred in 1956, Kossuth became the symbol of democratic socialism—his shield sewn on the flags of nationalists, foreshadowing what would follow in 1989.[45]

A parallel yet different portent took place in Paris and Poland during the 1880s. Adam Mickiewicz (1798–1855), the beloved romantic poet, became a freedom fighter in the unsuccessful uprising of 1848, when his native Poland was partitioned and dominated by neighboring Russia as well as the Habsburg Empire with its seat in Vienna. Much of his mature life was then spent in France, so when he died in Constantinople his remains were shipped to Paris for burial at the cemetery in Montmorency, where many other Polish émigrés had already been laid to rest. During the later 1860s, when changes occurred in the governance of the Austro-Hungarian Empire, Polish patriots began to consider—indeed, yearn for—the possibility of exhuming Mickiewicz and bringing his remains back to Krakow for an unprecedented reburial in the Wawel crypts beneath the cathedral there, the historic burial site of Polish kings, considered the "holiest shrine of the Polish nation."[46]

Sentiment for the translation of Mickiewicz's ashes built only slowly during the 1870s and early 80s, because Poles were themselves divided on the issue, at least initially. Liberal nationalists, intellectuals, and students supported the idea with enthusiasm and referred to the poet's remains as "relics" and the prospect of their return as "elevation" or "exaltation." Conservatives and Galician officials, however, were reluctant because of the permission required from Vienna (the emperor's opposition never actually became public), and the Polish Catholic Church was reluctant because of doubts about the integrity of the poet's faith. As momentum for repatriation increased during the mid-1880s, Galician officials at least wanted to control when and how the translation would take place. After all, the remains were most likely destined for a castle and cathedral belonging to the king of Galicia and grand duke of Krakow. The prospect for a nonobservant poet was unprecedented.[47]

In 1884 the cathedral chapter finally bowed to popular sentiment and offered its approval for use of the Wawel crypt, but then balked at making any further arrangements. After the emperor eventually relented, permission formally came from the Austrian minister of the interior, with the stipulation that the celebration "not take on the character of a political demonstration." It is crucial to keep in mind that unlike nearly all reburials in the United States, Kossuth's and this one involved delicate international negotiations, requiring Russian as well as Habsburg approval above all because Poland had been partitioned. Moreover, the Polish community of exiles in France had to consent to relinquish their control over Mickiewicz's remains.

Once their approval had been secured, he was exhumed on June 27, 1890, before a small group of family and dignitaries and placed in a new metal coffin. (The old one was promptly cut into small pieces—like holy relics—so that many people could have souvenirs.) The next morning, delegations of French, Poles, Hungarians, and Czechs along with members of the French press crowded into the cemetery to pay homage to the great poet.[48]

Significantly, the official French spokesman on that day turned out to be the noted historian Ernest Renan, formerly a professor at the prestigious Collège de France, where Mickiewicz had also lectured. Renan was less than acceptable to the conservative Polish Catholics, because he was regarded as an atheist. He is best remembered for his famous lecture at the Sorbonne in 1882, "What Is a Nation?" in which he declared that a nation is "a soul, a spiritual principle," and that its existence is a "daily plebiscite." Those were comforting sentiments to the partitioned and politically subordinated Poles. In his remarks on June 28, Renan explained that in moving Mickiewicz's remains to Krakow, Poles were voting for their nation. He elaborated: "To have shared glories in the past, a shared will in the present; to have performed great deeds together, to wish to perform still more—these are the essential conditions for the making of a people."[49]

The train bearing Mickiewicz in his new coffin passed through France and then Zurich, Switzerland, where it was met with fanfare, flowers, and speeches in six languages. When it reached Vienna, however, rallies at the train station were disallowed. Polish requests to speak and place wreaths were prohibited, and railroad officials transferred the coffin from the French train to an Austrian one without the poet's family even being present. But Krakow more than compensated with an extravagant reception, called by one scholar "the public event of the decade, if not the century." Poles arrived in record numbers to witness the procession and entombment in the largest manifestation of national unity since the January insurrection of 1863.[50]

On July 4, 1890, elaborate ceremonies began with the coffin being placed on an elevated catafalque in Wawel Cathedral, topped by a prominent cross and an image of the Mother of God, Queen of Poland. Poles had come from all over the country and showered the bier with flower petals as the procession, accompanied by Chopin's solemn *marche funèbre*, made its way to the cathedral. The event had immense populist appeal, with considerable involvement from Polish peasants manifest in the form of forty-four large wreaths sent from all across the land. The inscription on one of them read: "To Mickiewicz: from the Warsaw youth, born in bondage." The entire affair prompted an enormous burst of Polish nationalism.[51]

When the great poet William Butler Yeats died in the south of France early in 1939, the drama of his eventual return to Ireland measures up well in significance with Kossuth's narrative but even more with that of Mickiewicz, for religious reasons (or more precisely, doubts about the orthodoxy of both poets). One of Yeats's very last poems, published posthumously, made clear that he wished to be repatriated after death, and his wife and family wanted to honor his last request. But because he, too, was regarded by many as an atheist, even "satanic," and by some as "un-Irish," objections appeared in the Irish press and from the Catholic Church. Meanwhile, obituaries published in Britain claimed him as an "English poet," which enemies in Ireland used as a taunt. Plans for exhumation and interment in County Sligo actually went forward for many months, but the outbreak of World War II put all arrangements in abeyance for nearly a decade.[52]

Initially the delay occurred because Yeats and his wife had wanted his remains to lie in Roquebrune, France, for up to a year before being shipped back to Sligo; but the war and fierce objections from the Catholic Church in Ireland combined to complicate reburial amid secular as well as ecclesiastical red tape. There was also considerable confusion following the war at the cemetery in France: the curé there informed Yeats's widow that the temporary permit for burial had expired after five years and Yeats's remains had been removed to an ossuary. Some, especially French authorities, insisted that owing to wartime "disturbances" the body should remain at Roquebrune. Although it had indeed been exhumed without anyone informing the family, French officials eventually identified Yeats's remains and placed them in a new coffin with the original plate affixed. Rumors persisted for years that the wrong body had been shipped to Ireland, and legends endure of a mysterious reburial and even of an empty coffin.[53]

In any event, no one can doubt the powerful symbolism of Yeats's ceremonial return to Ireland in September 1948. The coffin was carefully removed from Roquebrune on September 6 and relocated with a military guard of honor to Nice, covered by the Irish national flag. At Villefranche it was placed on an Irish naval corvette for shipment to Galway, where it was met early in the morning by Yeats's widow and children. They were greeted at Sligo by yet another military guard of honor, though the family resisted the idea of a state funeral. A Church of Ireland service was conducted by the local rector despite doubts about Yeats's right to Christian burial. An enormous crowd assembled for the funeral, and the ceremony on September 17 proclaimed that Yeats's reputation "belonged neither to government nor family, but to the country whose consciousness he had done so much to shape," and which would declare itself a republic at the end of that same year.[54]

✚

As one anthropologist has written of ancestor-related rituals in Madagascar: "Ancestors are made from remembering them. Remembering creates a difference between the deadliness of corpses and the fruitfulness of ancestors. The ancestors respond by blessing their descendants with fertility and prosperity." A handy reminder of the constructedness of history! A visit to the Melanesia and Oceania galleries of any large art museum underlines the fact that ancestor worship plays a prominent role in the religious lives of many so-called primitive cultures. We see ancestor poles from the Asmat people of New Guinea and striking ancestor tablets from the Kerewa people of the Papuan Gulf. In Madagascar, when an ancestor becomes restless, he is removed from his tomb, dressed in silk, and paraded through the town; toasts are drunk to his health, and he is brought up to date on local gossip. Then the body is returned to its grave until it calls upon the living once again.[55]

In one form or another, the importance of acknowledging ancestors appears to be nearly universally felt. The notion of *repossessing* the dead for political purposes is also widespread but occurs under more particular circumstances, most often as a consequence of regime change. In the United States, however, for much of the nineteenth century ancestor worship was deemed inappropriate for a present-minded and future-oriented society. As Ralph Waldo Emerson declared in a widely heard lecture on the lyceum circuit, "The reverence for the deeds of our ancestors is a treacherous sentiment. Their merit was not to reverence the old, but to honor the present moment; and we falsely make them excuses of the very habit which they hated and defied."[56] Sentiments about ancestor veneration began to change more rapidly in Britain than in America, so that in 1878 Gilbert and Sullivan included some satirical dialogue and recitative in "The Pirates of Penzance" directed at social pretense in "acquiring other people's ancestors."

During the later nineteenth century, however, American sentiments about forebears began to shift rapidly, at least among the elite and upper middle classes, which created in the 1880s and 90s a series of hereditary and honorific patriotic societies like the Mayflower Descendants and Daughters of the American Revolution, followed swiftly by a burst of similar exclusive groups. Just after the turn of the century a rash of essays appeared in popular journals bearing such titles as "The Quest of Ancestors" (nonfiction) and "The Power of Ancestors" (fiction).[57] Nevertheless, Americans still did not regard statues as surrogate corpses, as many Europeans did, nor did they have a tradition of toppling or desecrating statues, despite the famous episode of pulling down the equestrian statue of George III in New York City in 1776. Unlike Europeans, Americans reluctantly relocate statues after they have become offensive for racial or political reasons.[58]

And yet the history of exhumation and reburial in the United States tells us much about the phasing and variability of ancestral idealization, about certain sites of collective memory and how Americans have felt about them. The phenomenon can even be related at times to revisionist historical writing, though not to the same degree that it has been in Europe, especially since 1989 in the countries once under Soviet control. Reburials have not been a major stimulus for the rewriting of history here in the United States. Yet in some instances dead bodies *have* served as the Protestant equivalent of Roman Catholic relics in medieval times, and quite often, as we shall see, dead bodies have indeed been deployed as potent American political symbols. Lincoln and Davis are among the most obvious examples. Statues and the bodies that lie near or beneath them (virtually more often than actually) do make the past more immediately present and vivid. And that is exactly what the makers of monuments and memorials had in mind.[59]

✛

Germane to our understanding of pan-Atlantic sentiments are the news items that Americans in times past could read in the press concerning the reburials for cultural or political reasons of notable Europeans who died in the "wrong place." The rise of intensely felt nationalism made it increasingly imperative for iconic figures to lie on native ground. In 1887, for example, the *New York Times* reported that the remains of composer Gioachino Rossini, who died in Paris in 1863, were disinterred at Père Lachaise Cemetery in the presence of dignitaries from the Italian embassy and musical admirers who included Jules Massenet, Leo Delibes, and Camille Saint-Saëns. Rossini's remains were taken to Florence, Italy, for reburial. By then, the notion of repatriation had begun to take hold in the United States as well. In 1852 the playwright and actor John Howard Payne, for example, died in Tunis, North Africa, where he had served as U.S. consul for a decade. In 1883 his body was exhumed and brought home to America for burial at the Oak Hill Cemetery in Washington, DC. How appropriate considering that he is best remembered for writing the enduring song "Home, Sweet Home" in 1822.[60]

Sergei Rachmaninoff, the great pianist and composer, fled Russia for the United States in 1918 because the Bolshevik Revolution disturbed the peace of mind he found essential for his work. When he died in 1943, burial took place at the Kensico Cemetery in the suitably named town of Valhalla, New York, where he was eventually joined by his wife and one of his daughters. By 1992, as the fiftieth anniversary of his death approached, speculation began to increase about the possibility of exhuming the trio for reburial in Novgorod, close to Oneg, the composer's birthplace. The inspiration for this move owed much to the removal of Bela Bartók, who also died in the United States during World War II and was first buried in 1945 at Ferncliff Cemetery in Hartsdale, a suburb of White Plains. In 1988 Bartók's two sons arranged for his remains to be reburied in Hungary, his native land—a politically motivated decision that actually pleased the Communist regime that had one year remaining before the velvet revolutions toppled governments throughout

Eastern Europe. As of this writing, however, Rachmaninoff remains in Valhalla, but for how much longer no one can be sure.[61]

In the wake of World War II, the American press provided numerous reminders that politically motivated reburials could bear immense symbolic significance. In 1949, for example, the body of Theodor Herzl, considered the founder of political Zionism during the 1890s, was exhumed from his burial place in Vienna (where he died in 1904) and flown to the new state of Israel for reinterment in Jerusalem. According to the media, this ceremony was perceived as the biggest event of its kind "since the burial near Nablus of the mummified remains of Joseph, which the Prophet Moses took along on the exodus of the Israelites from Egypt."[62]

Whereas the reburial of Herzl as a virtual founding father received unanimous acclaim, the 1964 reburial (on what became known as Mount Herzl) of Vladimir Jabotinsky would be quite controversial, because he had led what was called a Revisionist movement in Judaism. Upon his death in 1940 he was buried in the United States. Because Jabotinsky had been a particularly divisive figure, Prime Minister David Ben Gurion refused repeated requests from Menachim Begin that the Israeli government provide an official state funeral for his reburial, just as it had done for Herzl. Ben Gurion's successor relented, however, and Jabotinsky's remains received a full-dress state funeral in 1964, on the twenty-fourth anniversary of his death. That ceremony symbolized the normalization of relations between the Labor Party and political descendants of the conservative Revisionist movement, and marked the beginning of a process of political rehabilitation and legitimization for the latter.[63]

Somewhat less controversial, and a prime example of exhumation for purposes of national pride and regime building, was the state funeral orchestrated by the Begin-led government in May 1982 for remains reputedly belonging to the fighters and followers of Shimon Bar Koziba (popularly known as Bar Kochba), who led the second Jewish revolt against Rome in 132–35 CE. The remains had been discovered in 1960 by the noted archaeologist Yigal Yadin. The exhumation and ceremony twenty-two years later was understood as an attempt by Prime Minister Begin to establish political dominance for the Likud Party by means of ideological hegemony for what is called the New Zionism, closely identified with Begin and the period of his political leadership in Israel.[64]

✠

When we read about various funeral and burial practices in nineteenth-century Europe, especially the more macabre ones fetishized by people like Jules Michelet, we might wonder how Americans reacted when they had occasion to observe or learn about them. We don't have much information concerning firsthand American responses, but early in 1878 a group of upper-class women from Boston happened to be in Rome and found themselves spectators at a lurid display that became something of a tourist attraction. After King Victor Emmanuel II died in January, visitors could climb a long staircase to the grand salon of the palace, which was hung with crimson (not black) brocade. The sides of the room were lined with huge candles, and the king's body, "crowned and dressed in royal robes, was seated on the throne." The Boston ladies were utterly dumbfounded.[65]

Although nothing quite like that in U.S. history has come to my attention (so far), we do have from the mid- and later nineteenth century numerous accounts of men and women's attempts to visualize deceased family members, especially parents and children. The next best thing to ethereal or mystical contact was the presence of art intended to memorialize if not immortalize a loved one. But on occasion a family would reopen a recently buried coffin in order to gaze one last time at the visage of someone beloved, most often a child, but sometimes to attempt communication with or guidance from a parent. Ralph Waldo Emerson recorded the following in his journal on July 8, 1857: "This morning I had the remains of my mother and of my son Waldo removed [transferred] from the tomb of Mrs. Ripley to my lot in 'Sleepy Hollow' [cemetery in Concord]. The sun shone brightly on the coffins, of which Waldo's was well preserved—now fifteen years. I ventured to look into the coffin. I gave a few white-oak leaves to each coffin, after they were put into the new vault, and the vault was then covered with two slabs of granite."[66]

In 1704 in colonial Virginia, William Byrd II, who rapidly became a prominent planter, politician, and writer, lost his father. The father's will had expressed the clear hope that when his son returned from being educated in England, he would successfully follow his parent in running a major plantation on the James River. Byrd did so, "but his father's distant voice, urging him to improve and sending him specific tasks as agent of Virginia, was now silent." So Byrd made one final effort in the winter of 1709–10 to consult his father by exhuming the corpse for continuing counsel. The effort failed. The corpse remained obdurately silent, and consequently the heir was obliged to become totally self-reliant. He eventually surpassed his father as a planter, built one of the grandest homes in early America, became a notorious womanizer, and achieved immortality as a compulsive keeper of self-revealing secret diaries.[67]

An episode that took place in 1801 would have been much less likely to occur later in the century. Louisa Park of Salisbury, Massachusetts, wished to postpone the interment of her infant because her husband was away at sea and she wanted to wait for his return to make a final decision about how and where the little boy should be buried. Consequently she "borrowed" the vault of a wealthy friend for temporary interment. She recorded the following in her diary: "Captain Hoyt's politeness I shall never forget. . . . His consenting so readily to lay the corps [sic] in his tomb was a satisfaction to me. For some reason, to see him deposited there was not half so distressing to my feelings as it would have been to see him buried under the [ground]; and when his father returns he can see him, and remove him as he may think best."[68]

The nature and course of such shifts in sentiment and practice, as well as significant continuities, will become increasingly apparent in the chapters that follow.

— TWO —

Heroes of the Revolution

THE SITING AND RECITING OF PATRIOTISM

Land where my fathers died
Land of the pilgrims' pride . . .

✦ Samuel Francis Smith, "America" (1831)

$\mathcal{A}$lthough reburials of certain key figures from the age of the American Revolution tended to become politicized in several respects, these nineteenth-century episodes tell us more about patriotism than they do about nationalism or sectionalism, which will provide the focus of chapter 3. Distinguishing between patriotism and nationalism is difficult and subtle, but in the large literature devoted to those topics, a slender line sometimes suggests a valid and meaningful difference. The former, derived from the Latin *patria*, concerns love of country—its heritage, traditions, symbols, and institutions. The latter, nationalism, has more to do with what one wants a country to achieve in terms of policy initiatives and worldly standing in relation to others. Nationalism tends to be more chauvinistic and competitive. It has prompted aggressive action to acquire colonies and territory overseas, to be number one in an arms race, or to be the "top gun" in space.[1]

Patriotism takes pride in what has been—in past achievements that have shaped the present, legendary and mythic as well as historically recorded. Nationalism seeks validation in what should or might be— here and now, but also soon. Although nascent nationalism certainly helped to provide a potent impetus for the movement leading to American independence, its transformational manifestations would arise in the later nineteenth century in a different form, whereas patriotism achieved its full flowering earlier, well before the doctrine of Manifest Destiny set the United States on a course leading to the successful Spanish-American War of 1898–99 and its implications overseas.

Whereas patriotism is closely concerned with civic affiliation and cultural identity, nationalism has more to do with the State and its objectives in relation to other nation-states. Patriotism involves sentiments predicated upon a perceived past. Nationalism takes pride in ongoing achievements and future prospects. Patriotism fosters allegiance. Nationalism prompts competitiveness.[2]

This chapter will concentrate primarily on battle-tested heroes who died and received burial far from home, frequently giving rise to conflicts over just exactly *where* should most properly be considered "home." In some instances there could be no doubt where home was situated, yet disputes hinged upon the issue of which venue was more apropos: home or the site of a hero's greatest military triumph and contribution to American independence. At the close of this chapter we will also consider a few foreign-born figures, similar to Baron Von Steuben, who helped facilitate freedom in highly significant ways and died in the young United States—a circumstance that grateful Americans often felt needed to be rectified, though sometimes with disastrous results, as in the case of Tom Paine.

✢

We must begin with the sad, intensely politicized story of the "prison ship dead" and their unfortunate neglect. During the War for Independence, Americans taken prisoner by the British in the New York area, especially sailors, were detained under wretched conditions in prison ships anchored near Brooklyn. When they died of disease, malnutrition, and other causes—it is estimated as many as 11,500 in all—the corpses were placed in shallow graves on the shores of Wallabout Bay. Although their bones soon lay scattered and exposed, plans to honor the "prison ship martyrs" after the war elicited little interest. In 1807–8, however, a surge of attention occurred because of a potentially serious conflict with England, and thirty thousand spectators witnessed a solemn procession by barge and by wagon from Brooklyn to Manhattan and back, organized by the Tammany Society, which originated as a Jeffersonian Republican political club. Thirteen coffins filled with bones were ultimately taken to a Brooklyn burial vault, where prayerful eulogies by clerics accompanied the reinterment of "the relicks of our brethren."[3] Here we have just the first example among many that we will encounter of mourning rituals as political performance.

Hopes for the construction of a suitable monument rose and fell because Federalists condemned the attempt at memorialization as shameless posturing by the Tammany Society. From the Federalist perspective, what was going on amounted to partisan manipulation of the past, because passage of the Embargo Act in 1808 aroused sentiment that played to the anti-British feelings of Jeffersonian Republicans. Repeal of the Embargo Act one year later meant that this heated issue subsided and the prison ship victims would receive no monument. Those lost ghosts lapsed into total obscurity following the War of 1812 and peace with Great Britain. Nevertheless, the Tammany Society's cornerstone ceremony on April 13, 1808, followed by a special holiday declared on May 26, although less than a full-scale reinterment, included genuine funereal elements. There were floats, banners, and a considerable sequence of marchers. The Republican Greens performed the "Grand Wallabout Dead March," composed by Captain James Hewitt. As historian Robert Cray has observed, New Yorkers saw an "impressive display of sepulture immersed in pageantry."[4]

As Brooklyn grew rapidly during the nineteenth century and population spread quite close to the burial vaults, local residents typically blamed the inadequate entombments for what they considered impure air and gases believed to be capable of spreading disease. Anxiety concerning possible cholera outbreaks recurred periodically. Given the neglect of those bones in their poor housing, the aging Walt Whitman later lamented the situation, "mark'd by no special recognition," in his *Leaves of Grass*:

> Greater than memory of Achilles and Ulysses,
> More, more by far to thee than tomb of Alexander,
> Those cart loads of old charnel ashes, scales and splints of mouldy bones,
> Once living men—once resolute courage, aspiration, strength,
> The stepping-stones to thee to-day and here, America.[5]

So in 1873 the remains were removed to Fort Greene, and thirty-five years later in 1908 the Martyrs' Monument was dedicated, with President-elect Taft as the prime guest of honor. Federal, state, and municipal funds supplemented by private subscription made possible the construction of a 198-foot column above the new crypt where the peripatetic bones now reposed. Some twenty thousand spectators braved the elements to witness the dedication. But that was then. Within little more than a generation, the monument fell into neglect prior to World War II; by the end of the twentieth century it was "forlorn and forgotten."[6]

✣

One of the most representative episodes for our purposes involves the earliest martyr in the struggle for independence, Joseph Warren, president of the Massachusetts Bay Colony's Provincial Congress and Masonic Grand Master, shot in the head on June 17, 1775, at the Battle of Bunker Hill. According to legend, some British officers suggested decapitating him for being a despicable traitor to the Crown, but a more civilized fellow Mason intervened. So they buried Warren with several others in a shallow unmarked grave. On April 8, 1776, after the British had decamped from Boston, Warren's brothers and some friends exhumed his body, which was identified by Paul Revere, who had made two false teeth for Warren. After a public ceremony at King's Chapel, his remains were interred at the Granary Burying Ground. Almost half a century later, in 1825 a nephew undertook a quest to find the "lost" bones at the Old Granary. They were exhumed a second time and removed to a special crypt in the Warren family vault at St. Paul's Episcopal Church, where they lingered for thirty years until they were disinterred yet again for reburial in the new Forest Hills Cemetery at Roxbury, Warren's birthplace.[7]

The eulogy delivered by a minister at the first reburial in 1776 (and reprinted on the occasion of the third in 1856) is instructive for several reasons. Although it begins with the sentence "*Illustrious Relics!—* What tidings from the grave? Why has thou left the peaceful mansions of the tomb, to visit again this troubled earth?" it never mentions God, heaven, or anything remotely eschatological. Instead the emphasis, above all, is upon Warren's patriotism. "*Amor patriae* was the spring of his actions," the cleric intoned, and there are repeated references to "our patriot." The day before he died at Bunker Hill, Warren is said to have declared: "Dulce et decorum est pro patria mori" (It is sweet and becoming to die for one's country). A secondary motif in the eulogy concerns Warren's distinguished role as Grand Master of all Masons in Massachusetts (in 1794 a Masonic lodge in Charlestown erected a monument to his memory on the very spot where he fell in June 1775). The homily, given in Calvinist Boston, was totally secular.[8]

✝

Charles Thomson, a prominent Philadelphia patriot from 1765 onward and secretary of the Continental Congress throughout its existence from 1774 until 1789, was married in 1775 to Hannah Harrison, daughter of a wealthy Quaker landowner, Richard Harrison. Thomson requested that when he died he be buried with Hannah (who passed away in 1807) in the graveyard at Harriton, his father-in-law's estate, which was legally divided among Harrison's heirs, and where the Thomsons lived after 1781. Having been married in their forties, they had no children. Charles's wishes were honored in 1828. Eight years later, however, several prominent figures in Philadelphia, following the Mount Auburn model in Massachusetts, established Laurel Hill Cemetery on the banks of the Schuylkill River and expressed eagerness to acquire prestige (and new customers) by having historically important people reburied there.[9] One of the promoters called upon the owners of the Harriton estate, requesting permission to remove Thomson's remains from the family burial ground to the new cemetery. An elaborate cenotaph configured as a sixteen-foot obelisk in the shape of Cleopatra's Needle was prepared in advance to mark the site of Thomson's new, more publicly visible interment site.[10]

After various family members had considered the request, they decided that because Thomson had so explicitly asked to lie with his wife's ancestors, it would be inappropriate to agree to reinterment. Deborah Logan, a socially prominent near relative, raised particularly vocal opposition. There was, however, a nephew of Charles Thomson, unrelated to the Harrisons and apparently unfriendly to the new owners of Harriton. He had not been consulted, and he approved the removal on grounds that he had been his uncle's executor and nearest relative. Because taking Charles's body also meant removing Hannah's, and because the exhumers were not at all sure of the legality of their undertaking, it seems that the deed had to be done by stealth.[11]

On August 12, 1838, gravediggers assembled at a home in Bryn Mawr, about a quarter of a mile from Harriton in neighboring Merion Township. They expected to complete the task that night, but digging up the two (and possibly three) graves proved more difficult than expected. They were still finishing when dawn broke and were spotted by a farm laborer on his way to work. Hearing their voices and seeing their lanterns, he approached them, whereupon the diggers "were seized with a panic and hastily loaded the bodies in wagons which they had in readiness, and drove off rapidly, leaving the graves open, a high pile of earth, and other signs of their depredations. The facts were at once reported to the owners [of Harriton], but there seemed nothing to do but fill up the open graves and repair the damage done to the cemetery."

Because individual graves were not clearly marked in those days, especially at Harriton, and there had not been sufficient time for careful examination of the exhumed bodies, it is unclear whether the real Thomson remains were actually removed.[12] That will turn out to be an ongoing pattern in our narrative. "Did we get the right body?" became a great issue in the case of Daniel Boone's remains in 1845, as we shall see, and with many subsequent exhumations as well.[13]

As Mount Auburn enjoyed almost immediate popularity following its dedication in 1831, and because eminent figures who were logical prospects for burial there died conveniently in the early 1830s, the proprietary trustees felt less urgency about obtaining other men comparable to Thomson and General Hugh Mercer, also reburied in 1840 at Laurel Hill. Still, during the 1840s a number of eminent Bostonians, especially such prominent clergymen as the Reverend John Murray and Unitarian leader Joseph Buckminster, were exhumed from sites like the Old Granary and reinterred at Mount Auburn. Adding celebrities enhanced the sale of lots. Like attracts like, even the likely deceased.[14]

✢

Richard Montgomery was born in Dublin in 1738, served in the British army during the French and Indian War (most notably at the siege of Louisburg in 1758), and then returned home. In 1772, however, he sold his army commission and chose to relocate in New York, where he bought a sixty-seven-acre farm in King's Bridge, now part of the borough of the Bronx. Three years later he was elected to the New York Provincial Congress and married Janet Livingston, and in June 1775 he was commissioned a brigadier general in the Continental Army. He achieved swift promotion to major general on December 9 and along with Benedict Arnold led an American army into Canada, where he seized two British forts and the city of Montreal. On December 31, while attempting to capture the city of Quebec amidst a fierce snowstorm, Montgomery was killed. The British recognized his body and, quite unlike the episode involving Joseph Warren six months earlier, provided him with an honorable burial in Canada—an act that brings to mind the military courtesies we recall from Homer's *Iliad*. Montgomery swiftly received romanticized recognition as another great martyr to the American cause, and numerous towns and counties would be named for him throughout the United States.

In 1794 Jedediah Morse wrote the first biography of Montgomery, coupling him with the war's greatest hero, George Washington—a pattern of pairing that would be repeated in histories and eulogies for other leading generals, such as Nathanael Greene. When Washington died in 1799, one widely published poem declared that "*Montgomery's* godlike form directs the way" to heaven. Effusive praise for Montgomery, linked with Warren as the first great and lamentable losses, appeared in every early history of the War for Independence. When Anglo-American tensions began to intensify again in 1810, members of Congress both for and against the prospect of war invoked Montgomery's memory in debating the issue. Once the war actually began in 1812, citations of his patriotism and bravery served quite effectively in the enlistment of soldiers. As one recruiter in northern New York explained to his father, invading Canada might result in the loss of American lives, but it was better to "bleed on the tomb of Montgomery" than submit to British intimidation.[15]

In 1814 the poet Alexander Coffin published a long ode titled *The Death of Montgomery*, comparing him to such epic heroes as Hector and Achilles. In the years following the war, veneration of Montgomery increased even further, and his widow, Janet Livingston Montgomery, who had never remarried, launched repeated efforts to have his body returned. In 1816, at the age of seventy-four, she called upon her social connections for support, and Sir John Sherbrooke, governor general of Canada, consented to release the remains. In 1818 Janet used family ties once again to prevail upon a former lieutenant governor and current assembly member to persuade New York to formally undertake the necessary procedures. The legislature then passed a resolution authorizing the state to get final Canadian approval for exhumation, with reburial to take place at St. Paul's Chapel in New York City.[16]

Governor DeWitt Clinton gave Janet's nephew the rank of honorary colonel and sent him to Quebec to manage the project with assistance from the man who had supervised the initial burial in January 1776. Despite his eighty-nine years, he readily located the general's grave in

1818. Although the coffin had largely decayed, the skeleton was intact except for part of the lower jaw, which had been struck by grapeshot. As workers moved the remains, a musket ball fell from the skull. The coffin and skeleton were wrapped in a tarpaulin and placed in a heavy box for movement to New York. Following arrival at Whitehall south of Lake Champlain, cavalry units escorted the crate to Albany. Communities through which they passed held memorial services, with Revolutionary War veterans participating in the ceremonies. At Troy the remains were transferred to a large mahogany coffin bearing an engraved silver plate. On July 4 that coffin lay in state at the capitol building, guarded by an artillery company, and large numbers of citizens filed past to pay their respects to a fallen hero. On the morning of July 6 an even larger procession followed the coffin to the steamship *Richmond*, which carried it down the Hudson to Manhattan. Several aging men who had participated in the 1775 assault on Quebec marched in this ceremony. When the vessel passed Montgomery Place, the estate where Janet still lived, she felt overcome with emotion and fainted.[17]

Upon arrival in New York City the remains were taken to City Hall, and the funeral on July 8 was grander than anything that had preceded it there. "It began at dawn with cannon shots announcing a day of mourning." Businesses closed early, horse and wagon traffic was banned from the parade route, and flags flew at half-mast. In midmorning a huge procession made its way to St. Paul's. "The marchers walked in silence, accompanied by tolling church bells and booming salutes fired by the ships and forts in the harbor." Thousands of spectators lined the parade route or watched from windows overlooking it. This was the most elaborate and solemn ceremony since George Washington's death in 1799. Press coverage would be national because Montgomery's tragic loss had transcended the bounds of state and regional fame. As Andrew Jackson, himself a military hero of the War of 1812, would write: "The memory of the *patriotic* and gallant Montgomery is coeval with our liberty as a nation, and will exist in the heart of every *patriot* so long as our Republic exists."[18]

Phrases expressing gratitude and welcoming redemption from ingratitude appeared in many speeches and newspapers, but above all, the inspiration of patriotic pride was most frequently cited. As New York's adjutant general, Solomon Van Rensselaer, observed: "In rendering due honor to illustrious heroes and statesmen, we not only reward distinguished merit, but excite to new achievements of patriotism and glory." Seven years later Henry J. Finn produced a play, *Montgomery; or the Falls of the Montmorency*, in which the general makes only a brief appearance; but the use of his name in the title shows that it still held strong audience appeal.[19]

The Mexican War of 1847–48 intensified interest in the War for Independence and prompted an array of new publications. In George Lippard's highly popular *Washington and His Generals, or Legends of the Revolution* (1847), the author conveyed a widespread sentiment that Canadians might revolt against Britain and therefore should receive American aid: "Then perhaps some true American heart will wash out the blood of Montgomery from the rock of Quebec."[20]

Anthony Wayne, linked historically with Montgomery, was born in 1745 in Chester County, Pennsylvania. His vocation began as a surveyor and with work at his father's tannery. Like Montgomery, he became involved in late colonial politics as a patriot, serving as a member of the Pennsylvania legislature from 1774 until 1780. In 1775, however, he raised a militia and his regiment joined Montgomery's unsuccessful assault on Quebec. During the next eight years he commanded the Pennsylvania Line in a series of major battles at Brandywine, Paoli, and Germantown (near Philadelphia). He led the American attack at the battle of Monmouth, but the highlight of his military career came with his victory at Stony Point in 1779, a cliffside redoubt commanding the Hudson River—the triumph coming as a great boost to American morale at a time when there had been numerous losses.

Wayne then moved south, scored significant victories, and severed the British alliance with Native American tribes in Georgia. He successfully negotiated peace treaties with the Creek and Cherokee nations, for which the state of Georgia rewarded him with the gift of a large plantation. Following his final promotion to major general in 1783, he moved to Georgia in order to manage his plantation; but in 1793 President Washington recalled him from civilian life to head an expedition in the Northwest Indian War, where British support had made Indians living beyond the Appalachians a major problem for American settlers pushing west. In 1794 Wayne led a successful assault on the Indian Confederation at the Battle of Fallen Timbers, near Maumee, Ohio (just south of modern Toledo). Following that decisive victory ending the war, in August 1795 he negotiated the Treaty of Greenville, which ceded most of what is now Ohio to the United States.[21]

Fifteen months later Wayne died of complications from gout during a return trip to Pennsylvania from Detroit, and he was buried in a plain oak coffin in an isolated grave at the foot of the flagstaff next to the blockhouse at Fort Presque Isle (now Erie, Pennsylvania). In compliance with his request, similar to Von Steuben's, Wayne was clad in his best uniform—suitable attire for a man who had devoted most of his mature life to military affairs. Soon after the burial an austere stone monument was erected bearing the initials A. W., with a simple wooden railing surrounding the burial site.

Late in 1808, however, Thomas McKean addressed the Pennsylvania Assembly and lamented that his home state had largely ignored the graves and achievements of notable revolutionaries, especially Anthony Wayne.[22] That prompted Wayne's son and daughter to seek reinterment in the family's burial plot at St. David's Church in Radnor Township. When they sought advice from the venerable Dr. Benjamin Rush, he assured them that the remains had long since turned to dust; therefore the bones could easily be "taken up . . . put in a box in their natural order," and surrounded by wood shavings for safe and expeditious shipment home. "I rejoice," Rush added, "that public honor is at last to be done to one of the heroes of the American Revolution—I love his name—he was a sincere patriot, a brave soldier, and what is more, an honest man."

So Isaac Wayne went to Erie in August 1809, but feeling emotionally incapable of presiding over the exhumation himself, he commissioned a doctor who had also been a friend of General Wayne to do the work. When J. C. Wallace opened the grave, he found the body remarkably well preserved—contrary to Dr. Rush's assumption. Because it could not be transported in that condition (given that embalming was not possible), the doctor, with Isaac's approval, "dissected the body and boiled the parts in a large iron kettle to render the flesh from the bones. Thereupon the skeleton was cleaned, arranged in order in a new casket, and shipped home in that fashion." What remained in the kettle, along with the surgeon's knives used in the operation, was returned to the old coffin and placed in the original grave.[23]

At the end of a difficult 350-mile journey, Isaac Wayne's entourage was met by an honor guard of Pennsylvania militiamen drawn up to escort the boiled general to Waynesborough. The next day, accompanied by the same military guard, Wayne's new coffin was taken in "solemn processional" through roads lined with friends and relatives to St. David's Church in Radnor, where a minister delivered a suitably patriotic discourse. Subsequently the Society of the Cincinnati and three local militia companies erected a tall stone monument at the grave (fig. 4).[24] A handsome statue of Wayne now stands in the Valley Forge National Military Park, where the general endured the bitter winter of 1777–78. Fourteen counties in as many states are named in his honor, along with countless cities, including Fort Wayne, Indiana. According to legend, however, many bones were somehow lost during the arduous ride from Erie to Waynesborough. Every year on January 1, Wayne's ghost is said to wander the highway (now primarily Pennsylvania Road 322) searching for his missing bones.

✝

As the centennial of George Washington's birth approached in 1832, members of Congress began thinking of ways to memorialize him

Figure 4. Grave site of General Anthony Wayne, Radnor, Pennsylvania. From the *Freemason's Magazine*, September 1811. Courtesy of the American Antiquarian Society.

properly in the nation's capital. (The design of the Washington Monument on the Mall lay more than a decade in the future.) Serious proposals circulated to exhume the Father of His Country from his rustic tomb at Mount Vernon and rebury him in the crypt below the Rotunda of the U.S. Capitol. Washington's descendants, however, led by nephew Bushrod Washington, defeated that plan in court, arguing successfully that reburial would violate the president's wishes, stated explicitly in his will. At just that time, moreover, many assumed that the nation's capital might eventually be moved beyond the Appalachians and then to the Midwest as America's population spread westward. Would Washington have to be reburied in conjunction with each demographic shift? Consequently, what might have been the ultimate American reburial never took place.[25]

As late as 1889, the centennial year of Washington's first inauguration, a letter from Bushrod Washington to the governor of Virginia, written in 1816, suddenly surfaced. The Virginia legislature had passed a resolution requesting that Washington's remains be moved to Richmond, where a publicly funded monument would be built above the new tomb. Anticipating the 1832 controversy, Bushrod said that he was moved by the request and that if the decision were his alone, he would allow the transfer to occur. But citing the written terms of the will, he declared that it would be illegal to violate the late president's preference. It is unclear whether the avid congressmen had been aware of that exchange when they proposed reinterment in the nation's capital in 1831–32.[26]

✛

John Trumbull was born in Connecticut in 1756, the son of colonial governor Jonathan Trumbull. He served during the Revolutionary War as an aide to Washington, valued especially for his cartographic abilities. Resigning his commission with the rank of colonel, he spent 1778–79 painting and the following year went to London to study with the American expatriate Benjamin West. Trumbull was arrested there in reprisal for the execution of British spy John André in 1780 and spent seven months in prison. Following his release he continued his studies with West from 1782 until 1785. A year later, encouraged by Thomas

Jefferson, he began a series of historical canvases designed to illustrate major episodes in the American Revolution.

Noted for their liveliness and presumed authenticity in terms of detail, his early works included *The Battle of Bunker Hill* (1786), which he insisted he had witnessed from a distance (a dubious claim), and *The Death of General Montgomery in the Attack on Quebec* (1788), both located today in the Yale Art Gallery, the very first college art museum in the United States and one that Trumbull was instrumental in founding. Sensing what his mature mission and vocation would be, he spent the years from 1789 until 1794 traveling extensively around the United States making portrait studies of leading statesmen and collecting visual data for future paintings. He maintained a studio in New York City from 1815 until 1837; in 1817 he received the plum commission to paint four huge canvases for the rotunda of the U.S. Capitol. They were complete by 1824 and have been admired by many millions of visitors ever since. They include *The Declaration of Independence*, his most famous; *The Surrender of General Burgoyne at Saratoga*; *The Surrender of Lord Cornwallis at Yorktown*; and *The Resignation of General Washington at Annapolis*. From 1817 until 1836 he served as president of the American Academy of Fine Arts in New York. In 1831, despite being a Harvard graduate, he consigned his own collection of paintings to Yale (for an annuity of $1,000) and designed a gallery to house them. He lived in New Haven from 1837 to 1841 while working on his *Autobiography, Letters, and Reminiscences* (1841).

Soon after his pictures were installed at Yale, Trumbull declared to the noted scientist Benjamin Silliman, his devoted nephew-in-law, "It is my wish to be interred beneath this Gallery," adding that "these are my children—those whom they represent have all gone before me, let me be buried with my family. . . . Please, therefore, apply to your authorities of the College for leave to construct a tomb beneath this building—at my expense. I wish to have it large enough for two. I will remove the remains of my wife from New York and place them in it and when I die, I wish to be placed by her side. Let the tomb then be finally closed, not to be opened again until earth and sea shall give up their dead." The tomb was built accordingly, and Sarah Trumbull's remains were reburied at Yale in 1834.[27]

Nine years later the artist died in New York at the age of eighty-seven, and his body was transported by steamer to New Haven, where it was taken to Silliman's home and given a laudatory funeral. The artist was lowered into his allotted place well beneath his portrait of Washington, with portraits of Trumbull and his wife just below the general's. Under them were placed a trophy sword from the battle of Rhode Island and Trumbull's palette and brushes—art and war displayed in symmetry. Silliman soon added a black marble tablet with this inscription: "Colonel John Trumbull, Patriot and Artist, Friend and Aide of Washington." When Yale built a larger art museum in 1866, the college corporation voted to remove Trumbull's paintings to the new structure and that "the remains of Colonel Trumbull and his wife be also removed." Sixty-one years later Yale erected a third art museum, and the director found himself obliged once again to relocate both the pictures and the coffins. The "translation of the relics" was set to take place during the next spring recess in order to avoid any student demonstrations.[28]

At first it appeared to the assembled spectators, led by Trumbull and Silliman descendants, that the reburial would take place outside of and adjacent to the new museum. Then someone happened to suggest moving inside to a spot where the floor had been removed, revealing that a well-constructed brick crypt was prepared. Still resting outside, the coffin containing the thrice-buried Sarah was not in good condition, and when it was gently lifted, the bottom gave way. Her bones were moved to a new casket by waiting undertakers, who had been advised to prepare for any eventuality. The colonel's mahogany casket was well preserved, and "the two flag-draped coffins were carried across High Street, followed by a small procession, to the new impressive tomb in the still incomplete Gallery." A full account of what happened that day, along with the signatures of witnesses and extracts from Silliman's notes on the original burial eighty-five years earlier, were bricked up in the new and spacious vault.[29]

The press carried extensive reports in the following days, but within a decade distorted versions of what had happened in 1928 began to appear. In one wild account, Trumbull's own bones had tumbled out of a broken coffin, only to be swept back into the box by a crabby janitor using a broom and dustpan. In truth, however, on June 26, 1928, the 172nd anniversary of the "patriot-artist's" birth, a decorous memorial service was held directly above the new vault. President Angell presided over a distinguished gathering composed of Trumbull and Silliman descendants, friends, faculty, and students. The university chaplain reenacted the original service of 1843, and eloquent tributes were heard. Trumbull's request remained honored. He lies beneath his art, though not quite so close to it as he had envisioned.[30]

✛

The political and military career of Nathanael Greene paralleled those of Montgomery and Wayne. Born in 1742 in what is now Warwick, Rhode Island, he initially worked at his father's iron foundry and then in 1770 moved to Coventry, where he managed the family forge. He served in the Rhode Island General Assembly during 1770–72 and again in 1774–75. In May 1775 he helped raise a militia in his colony and was promptly named a brigadier general. Months later he achieved the same rank in the Continental Army and participated in the American siege of Boston. When the British evacuated that city in March 1776, he was placed in charge of Boston. In August he was promoted to major general and given command of the troops in New Jersey. Although he suffered defeats in Manhattan and at Fort Lee across the Hudson, he played a major role in the victory at Trenton late that year and subsequently at Brandywine and Germantown in 1777. Following the harsh winter at Valley Forge, Congress appointed Greene quartermaster general, and he established a system of supply depots for Washington's army.[31]

When Benedict Arnold's plan to surrender West Point to the British was discovered, Greene succeeded Arnold in charge of West Point and presided over the tribunal that condemned John André, the British spy, to die. After Horatio Gates was defeated in 1780 by the British at Camden, South Carolina, Washington gave Greene the command of Gates's army. After reorganizing the Southern Department, and following Daniel Morgan's victory at the Cowpens in January 1781, Greene nearly exhausted Cornwallis's forces by leading them on a hectic winter chase through harassment across North Carolina to Virginia.[32]

At the battle of Guilford Court House, Greene caused Cornwallis to suffer very heavy losses, and subsequently his troops completed the reconquest of the South. After the war the citizens of Georgia voted to give Greene, as they had to Anthony Wayne, a plantation there, and he spent the rest of his life moving back and forth between Georgia and Rhode Island trying to restore his finances. Greene died near Savannah in June 1786 and was buried there in what became known as the "old cemetery" and later the "Colonial cemetery," first established in 1758 as the burying ground for Christ's Church (Anglican).[33]

At the close of the nineteenth century, a time of increasing veneration of ancestors, especially heroes of the Revolution, sentiment grew quite strong in Rhode Island to have Greene exhumed and to repatriate his remains for reburial in his native state. Colonel Asa Bird Gardiner, president of the Rhode Island Society of the Cincinnati, led a delegation to Savannah not only to negotiate for Greene's return but to search for his burial place, by then totally obscure. As Savannah grew, burials had ceased in the "old cemetery," and it fell into disuse and sad neglect, the graves heavily overgrown. Boys had entered and desecrated some of the tombs, and when Sherman's army camped in Savannah during the close of the Civil War, soldiers had emptied out some of the major family vaults in order to use them for shelter. Further desecration resulted from their disregard for the final resting places of Southern families.[34]

Colonel Gardiner's committee came to Savannah in March 1901. It needed to secure permission from the vestry of Christ's Church and the mayor of the city to open and intensively examine a line of four major vaults known to contain the remains of distinguished persons buried during the later eighteenth century. Because there was no visible exterior marker for Greene's likely grave, intuition and careful study were employed to eliminate three of the four. Along with local cemetery staff, Gardiner's committee worked through massive brickwork at the Graham family site to get below an upper level of coffins to several that had fallen apart. Good fortune favored them. Amidst gravel and rubble they found part of a coffin-plate on which the numbers "1786" appeared. Very close by they found not one but two sets of bones intermixed, the skeletal remains of a grown man and those of someone either an adolescent or a teenager. The Rhode Islanders knew that Nathanael's son, George Washington Greene, had drowned in the Savannah River at the age of eighteen in 1793. Clearly, he had been buried in this vault close by his father. Mingled with the bones of the adult the searchers found three metal buttons from a military uniform, and on the bony hands, heavy French silk gloves had survived intact. Experts recalled that when Lafayette revisited the newly independent United States in 1824–25, he invariably presented French silk gloves to the generals he had known and worked with during the war. Perhaps he had done so a generation earlier for Greene and others. The committee felt confident that it had found the remains of Nathanael Greene and his son. The bones were separated and placed in two zinc-lined boxes.[35]

Those boxes of relics (with new coffin-plates suitably inscribed) were then placed in a vault of the Southern Bank of the State of Georgia, subject to the joint order of Colonel Gardiner and Alfred Dearing Harden, representing the Society of the Cincinnati, awaiting a decision about what to do next. Greene's widow had remarried a few years after his death and moved to a plantation on one of the Sea Islands. By 1901 there were numerous direct descendants scattered all over the United States, but mainly in Georgia and Rhode Island. When officials and family in the latter requested the remains for reinterment in Greene's home state, all the living descendants were consulted. An overwhelming majority preferred that his bones be buried in Savannah, close to their original location. Interestingly, the three exceptions expressed a preference for the battlefield of Guilford Court House in North Carolina, the site of Greene's most brilliant tactical decisions.[36]

Representatives from all the patriotic organizations in Savannah formed an ad hoc group simply called the Association of Patriotic Societies. They chose Johnson Square, where the cornerstone for a monument to Greene had been placed in 1825. The association exercised full control over the ceremonial reinterment on November 14, 1902, and decided to place the remains of father and son beneath flagstones on the south side of the monument.[37] The expense for that event would be borne by voluntary subscriptions from the citizens of Savannah, with no funds requested from either the state or the municipality. The mayor issued a proclamation requesting all merchants to close their places of business on November 14 between 2:00 and 6:00 p.m. "in order to give their employees an opportunity to be present and participate in the ceremonies incident to the occasion, and all persons having flags are requested to display the same at half-mast between the hours of three and six." Great numbers of people did, in fact, turn out to march in the procession and line the streets as spectators. The crowd was swelled by local and visiting members of the recently formed DAR.[38]

Greene's new casket, made of Georgia curly pine, was placed upon a caisson by a detail from the Chatham Artillery and accompanied by troops to the "old cemetery" (fig. 5). A bronze tablet was placed upon the original Graham family vault, declaring, "Here rested for 114 years the remains of MAJ.-GEN. NATHANAEL GREENE." Following the procession to Johnson Square, a prayer, and the playing of a dirge, the new permanent tablet to be placed upon a memorial shaft of granite was presented on behalf of Greene's descendants to the municipality. Walter G. Charlton, president of the Georgia Society Sons of Revolution, declaimed: "To-day come again the people of Savannah, and with them the distinguished sons and beautiful daughters of other parts, that, with *pride and reverence*, new honors may be paid to the memory of Nathanael Greene. We who will look upon the procession solemn, yet, triumphant . . . need no incentive to keep in our hearts and memories the services of this great soldier, whose strong arm and stout heart bore the burden of Georgia's fate in one of the darkest hours of her existence."[39]

Figure 5. Caisson bearing the remains of General Nathanael Greene, rolling to his reburial in Johnson Square, Savannah, Georgia, November 14, 1902. From *Remains of Major-General Nathanael Greene* (Providence: Committee of the Rhode Island General Assembly, 1903).

Figure 6. Monument to General Nathanael Greene, Johnson Square, Savannah, Georgia. Photograph courtesy of Mike Dover.

After the two coffins had been situated in their new crypt, the governor of Rhode Island stepped forward while the tribute from his state was placed upon the monument: "a large wreath of bronze galex, crossed with cycus palms, tied with rich purple ribbon on which were embossed in gold" the state arms of Rhode Island (fig. 6). The wreath stood on a tripod at the base of the shaft. Greene's great-great-grandson unveiled the memorial tablet, which declared General Greene second only to George Washington in greatness. After the playing of "America," the principal oration was given by the man who had initiated the search and exhumation, Asa Bird Gardiner, president of the Rhode Island Society of the Cincinnati.[40]

The Association of Patriotic Societies had been determined "to make the occasion a patriotic one, and to avoid giving it, as far as it was possible to do so, a funereal aspect." They succeeded admirably. Patriotism had been paraded with military exercises at two separate sites in Savannah, and solemnity had been achieved without grimness or maudlin words. On July 4, 1902, Colonel Gardiner had given a satisfying report of the exhumation and reburial plans to the Society of the Cincinnati in

Newport. Both sides seemed satisfied—and it is no accident that all of this occurred at a time when there was great emphasis upon sectional reconciliation and strengthening the Union.[41]

Although Daniel Morgan's origins were more humble, his military career would be closely linked with Greene's. Born in 1735 in Lebanon Township, New Jersey, Morgan was also the son of a forge worker, but he quarreled with his father and left home at age sixteen. After working at odd jobs in Pennsylvania, he moved down through the Shenandoah Valley and settled near Charles Town in what would become West Virginia a century later. Morgan, seemingly inexhaustible, worked mainly as a teamster; but when the Continental Army called for the formation of ten rifle companies, Virginia's House of Burgesses asked Morgan to organize one. He quickly recruited ninety-six men and marched to support the siege of Boston in 1775. Because of their effectiveness, his group came to be known as Morgan's Sharpshooters.

Late in 1775 Benedict Arnold chose Morgan to lead his own company and two others on the ill-fated expedition to Quebec in which Richard Montgomery lost his life. Morgan was captured by the British and remained a captive until early in 1777, when he received his freedom in an exchange of prisoners. Promoted to the rank of colonel, he played an important role in the defeat of General Burgoyne at Saratoga. Because he mistrusted the Continental Congress and did not curry favor with anyone, he was repeatedly passed over for promotion until late in 1780, when he became a brigadier general under Nathanael Greene, who instructed him to harass Cornwallis's army in the south.

Cornwallis chose to send Banastre Tarleton's British Legion to track Morgan down. He did so successfully, but Morgan devised a brilliant plan to maximize the effectiveness of his outnumbered men as guerrilla fighters and excellent shots with muskets and rifles. He chose to make his stand at a place known as the Cowpens, South Carolina, on January 17, 1781. Knowing that his foe tended to be precipitous, Morgan lured Tarleton into making a premature charge against a carefully arranged triple defense of riflemen, cavalry, and infantry. The outcome was an immense victory. Of Tarleton's 1,076 men, 110 died and 830 were captured. Although Tarleton himself escaped, Morgan's forces gained control of all his equipment.[42]

Following the war, Morgan returned to Charles Town, invested in land, and eventually acquired 250,000 acres. He joined the Presbyterian Church in 1782 and built a new house in Winchester, Virginia, which he named Saratoga. In 1790 Congress awarded him a gold medal to commemorate his great victory at the Cowpens. Four years later he returned to service by leading militia units to suppress the Whiskey Rebellion in Massachusetts. Elected to Congress in 1797–99 as a Federalist, he died in Winchester at his daughter's home in 1802 and was buried in the local Presbyterian graveyard. In 1881, the centennial anniversary of that astonishing triumph at the Cowpens, a statue of Morgan was erected with congressional funds in the central town square of Spartanburg, South Carolina. The square and the statue remain in place to this day.

At Morgan's funeral he was eulogized as the others had been, with resounding sentiments that Winchester would always remember its "Beloved Patriot and Hero." As early as 1843, however, a patriotic weekly titled *Brother Jonathan* ran this item: "In the graveyard at Winchester, Virginia, says a Southern paper, the traveler will find a grave overgrown with grass, without a stone or an inscription to preserve the ashes of its inhabitant from insult. Within the grave reposes the remains of the brave General Morgan, whose name ranks in the annals of the Revolution second only to that of Washington."[43]

One year later, however, as part of the "rural cemetery" movement begun at Mount Auburn in 1831, the new Mount Hebron Cemetery was dedicated in Winchester. On that occasion in June 1844, the principal speaker promised that "the tomb of Morgan shall be here. . . . Near, too, will be the graves of Soldiers and Patriarchs who fought and struggled in the early conflicts of our country. So that the youthful volunteer will have no need to make a pilgrimage to the plains of Marathon or the pass of Thermopylae, to inhale *patriotic* fervor."[44] Morgan's renown would be restored and respected once again, and the new cemetery would have a celebrity, just as Laurel Hill in Philadelphia had achieved two with the 1838–40 reburials of Charles Thomson and Hugh Mercer.

The full text of this highly representative eulogy illustrates two other points of importance. First, William L. Clark's totally secular address also called attention to the paramount significance and distinguishing feature of the new phenomenon of the public cemetery, because it portended the democratization of interment. "No man of proper feelings can be insensible to the final disposition of that tabernacle in which he hath abided during his earthly pilgrimage," he declared. "But to receive proper interment ourselves, we must extend it to others."[45]

The second point emerges from an introductory address given on the same occasion by Reverend A. H. Boyd, which is totally different in its tone and texture, indicative of the distinction mentioned in chapter 1. The body, Boyd explained, "is destined to rise from the tomb, and to be reunited to the deathless soul, to enhance either its happiness or misery. And thus it shall be, my hearers, with all the bodies that shall be placed within this enclosure. In their appointed time, they shall leave this hallowed spot . . . where they may have been reposing for centuries in undisturbed silence, and shall enter another abode, which their Creator has prepared for them."[46] The two sets of remarks on this occasion, Boyd's being much briefer, marked a careful separation between the secular and spiritual spheres. At most reinterments, however, only the first was heard.

Unfortunately, Morgan would not lie undisturbed forever. During the Civil War his remains were removed because of the fear that Yankee soldiers in that hotly contested valley might carry them away—assuming that they could find them! In 1868 he was reinterred in Mount Hebron Cemetery, and the six Virginians responsible each took away a handle from the original coffin as a personal memento—a latter-day reminder of what had once been done with the body parts of disassembled saints. Morgan's gravestone had become chipped, however, the words weathered and difficult to read. As the cemetery expanded, the older portion where Morgan's casket was located came to be neglected, and once again grasses grew up around the marker. In 1900 the firemen of Winchester initiated a movement to memorialize Morgan properly, but nothing came of it.[47]

In July 1951 Winchester received a rude awakening. Having learned of Morgan's lapsed renown and the neglect of his grave, the DAR chapter in Spartanburg enlisted support from local civic groups to launch a campaign to have Morgan disinterred and reburied in or near Spartanburg, where they believed he would be accorded greater respect. But when a delegation of determined gravediggers from South Carolina, armed with picks and shovels, arrived at Mount Hebron, an alert caretaker called the Winchester and county police. Very quickly a crowd of

Figure 7. Monument to General Daniel Morgan, Mount Hebron Cemetery, Winchester, Virginia. Photograph courtesy of Steven Dunn.

"patriots" gathered at the cemetery, hotly determined to retain their nearly forgotten hero's relics. Outnumbered, the South Carolinians retreated and headed for home. *Life* magazine recounted the episode in a lively article titled "Who Gets the General's Body?"[48]

Morgan's memory would ultimately be vindicated in 1953, when the Winchester-Frederick County Historical Society proceeded to erect an impressive granite monument bearing the general's likeness over the grave (fig. 7). Children descended from members of Morgan's first rifle company saluted the monument, and the congressman representing the district unveiled it. Thus, having been exhumed during the deadliest of all American wars, the remains of "the Old Wagoner," as Morgan was once known, were belatedly rescued by his adopted community rather than being removed to the site of his greatest triumph and ultimate source of fame.[49]

✦

The battle for Button Gwinnett's bones also took place at midcentury, but in this instance the conflict involved two competing communities in Georgia: Savannah, once again, and Augusta as a determined rival—the latter much less gracious than Rhode Island had been about its native son Nathanael Greene. The conflict began to heat up in 1957, but the phase of greatest intensity occurred between 1960 and 1964. Like Daniel Morgan, Gwinnett had been born in 1735 but in Gloucestershire, England. His odd first name came from his godmother, Barbara Button, his mother's cousin. Because of family need and a feisty disposition he would not repay a loan, decided to cross the Atlantic, and settled in Savannah in the mid-1760s. Gwinnett purchased a sea island south of Savannah and became a planter and a lumberman. After taking an interest in politics, he became a member of Georgia's colonial assembly and decided to support the Patriot side when push came to shove with Britain. As an ardent Whig, in 1776 he was sent to Philadelphia as a delegate to the Continental Congress, where he strongly supported the Declaration of Independence and signed it. Once back in Savannah, he became speaker of the new state assembly.[50]

Gwinnett also had military aspirations, but in the spring of 1777 his fiery temper led him to challenge a suspected traitor to a duel. They met in a meadow on Sea Island Road near Savannah and faced off with pistols at a distance of only four paces. Each man was shot only in the leg, as honor required, but Gwinnett's wound in the left thigh became gangrenous, and he died just three days later at the age of forty-two. Because of his early death, his signature is the scarcest among all signers of the Declaration. There is no known portrait of him that can be certified, though spurious ones have surfaced. For many decades, amateur historians played detective in trying to locate his unknown burial place, but without success. In 1957, however, a retired school principal from Savannah, Arthur J. Funk, who had been intrigued by Gwinnett ever since 1913, began the process of serious sleuthing.[51]

At the Chatham County courthouse in Savannah, Funk found the original accounting by the executor of Gwinnett's will. A bill indicated payment for erecting some sort of monument to the deceased, and the only plausible site turned out to be the same neglected "old cemetery" of Christ's Church where Greene had been buried. Exploring the re-named Colonial Cemetery, Funk found a brown stub of stone situated seven paces from the grave of Georgia's first governor. After receiving park department permission, Funk very carefully removed soil from beneath the stub and made out a few letters on the face, including a *G*, a *T*, and a *7*, which certainly suggested the likelihood of Gwinnett's grave. An archaeologist from New York who happened to be in Savan-nah at the time urged Funk to dig further and open the casket to see whether the leg was broken at the knee. Funk decided to seek help from the Georgia Historical Commission, which sent its own archaeologist to excavate the site and examine the remains.[52]

They found the skeleton of a man about five feet six inches tall whose left femur exhibited a section of damaged bone in the area immediately above the knee. Although Funk felt jubilant, a Savannah physician who was also an expert on Indian remains argued that the evidence was in-adequate. He may very well have been piqued that after so many years of fruitless searching by others, Funk had found his man so easily. With Funk's consent, the damaged femur was sent to the Smithsonian In-stitution in Washington; specialists sent back a skeptical report, specu-lating that it was actually a female skeleton. Funk and his supporters responded angrily, calling attention to the gravestone evidence that had been ignored and a plait of hair on the skull that seemed to belong to a male. When Funk showed the bones to a ballistics expert in Georgia, the latter declared that the wound had clearly been inflicted prior to burial and most likely by a "circular device" such as a pistol ball.[53]

By then much of Savannah was intrigued and intensely divided, so Funk appealed to the mayor for an impartial investigation. The mayor turned the matter over to the Savannah-Chatham County Historic Site and Monument Commission, an agency of state government chartered by the Georgia legislature in 1949. In September 1959 the commission issued a thirty-four-page report and added some information of its own. Essentially, it supported Funk's view that the grave as well as the skeleton was indeed Gwinnett's. Funk stored all of the exhumed re-mains in the guest room of his home and awaited the next phase of the controversy: the claims of rival Augusta to Gwinnett's bones, on the grounds that it already had the bodies of Georgia's other two signers of the Declaration of Independence entombed beneath a granite obelisk, erected in 1848, known as the Signers' Monument. Shouldn't all three rest in peace together?[54]

In April 1960, Mayor Millard Beckum of Augusta began his campaign to have Button's bones removed there. Augusta's case hinged heavily upon the authenticity of a portrait believed (by some) to be the only known likeness of Gwinnett, signed by the painter Jeremiah Theus. It had been purchased by Atlanta's Fulton Federal Savings and Loan Association from a New York gallery for five thousand dollars and then acquired by Augusta as a kind of surrogate for Gwinnett's actual remains. After citizens of Savannah made a compelling case that for various reasons the portrait could not be genuine, the city appropriated funds for the erection of a proper Gwinnett monument, thereby dashing Augusta's hopes for relocating the bones (fig. 8). The people there took their loss gracefully under the circumstances, because reburial of Gwinnett locally would have required digging up the wife of one of the other two signers, and everyone seemed to agree that that was no way to treat a very old lady.[55]

Figure 8. Monument to Button Gwinnett, Savannah, Georgia. Photograph courtesy of Kurt Lau.

In October 1964 a crowd gathered in the Colonial Cemetery to witness Gwinnett's reinterment, quite satisfied that they possessed the correct set of bones and had commemorated him in a dignified manner. Present for this patriotic occasion were representatives of the Georgia chapters of the Sons of Revolution, the DAR, the Society of Colonial Wars, and the Colonial Dames of America—each member waving an American flag. There were many chuckles when a leading collector of rare American manuscripts from Joliet, Illinois, declared: "We no longer need to ask, 'Button, Button, who has the Button?' Button has been found." Arthur Funk then proudly unveiled an appropriate bronze tablet; taps was sounded, and a detail of ROTC cadets fired three volleys into the air.[56]

✦

We turn next to episodes concerning four individuals, each European born, who figured dramatically in the history of Revolutionary America—all of them involving issues and controversy over exhumation and reburial, and most culminating in confusion or fiasco, but in two cases sad neglect followed by fortuitous redemption: one might even say a satisfactory second ending.

Complex and historically convoluted is the story of George Augustus, Lord Viscount Howe, a principal leader of the British attack early in July 1758 on the French fortification at Ticonderoga, located just south of Lake Champlain. He turned out to be the most prominent martyr fighting on behalf of the colonies in the French and Indian War, so the location of his burial prompted considerable research and controversy, especially between 1889 and 1911. In October 1889 some laborers digging a sewer in the town of Ticonderoga found a tombstone that appeared from cryptic lettering to be a battle-site memorial to Howe, along with a skull and some disintegrated bones. The discovery caused a local sensation, and the laborers had to prevent people from ripping away pieces of the coffin (such as it was) in order to carry off relics.[57]

This discovery sparked a battle among local historians and archaeologists that would eventually be clarified, though not definitively, with a lengthy publication in 1911. Howe was serving under General Abercromby on July 6, 1758, when the decision was made to launch a frontal assault on the French lines defending their fort. Howe was shot through the chest and died at the scene of battle. His partially embalmed body was carried south of Lake George to Fort William Henry on a "rude bier," where preservation of the body was completed prior to its being sent by wagon to Fort Edward. After that it went by bateau to Albany and from there, presumably, to be shipped down the Hudson River and then to England for final burial. That much is known largely from the papers of Major Philip Schuyler, who was in charge of moving the corpse, and from oral history within the Ingalsbe family. The ancestor of one member is known to have accompanied Schuyler with Howe's body to Albany.[58]

When the corpse reached Albany, however, its condition was so poor that General Stanwix felt obliged to have it buried there in St. Peter's Church. What is known as its "church book" survived several major fires and contains entries regarding use of the church pall (or coffin drapery). Those who believe that Howe was buried elsewhere contest the validity of that evidence. But accounts of Howe's death and burial appeared swiftly in New York and Boston newspapers. (Albany still lacked its own paper in 1758.) When the old church was taken down in 1802, there are eyewitness accounts of Howe's remains being placed in a special coffin with a rich silk damask cerement, seen and handled by the historian Elkanah Watson and his assistant, formerly a British officer residing in Greenbush, New York, who knew the exact location of the grave. Howe was then reburied beneath the second St. Peter's Church along with twenty-four other bodies that had been interred at the original structure.[59]

When the second church was in turn demolished in 1859, Lord Howe's coffin was disinterred once again, distinguishable by a black silk ribbon referred to in Watson's account, and reburied under the vestibule of the third church. That is where matters stood when the accidental discovery in Ticonderoga of an apparent headstone and some bones occurred in 1889. Subsequent expert investigation determined that the memorial headstone had no characteristics of such stones from the mid-eighteenth century and that the remains bore no indications of a person of high rank and social status. Moreover, these remains had been found in a venue to which the British had absolutely no access at the time of the battle and defeat.[60]

Adding to all this uncertainty concerning Howe's whereabouts, some people have cause to assume that he must be buried in Westminster Abbey. How could that be? Only with the arrival of a fresh and stronger British force under Lord Jeffrey Amherst in 1759 would the British and their colonial allies begin to repulse the French occupation of northern New York and turn the tide. Meanwhile, the General Court of Massachusetts had appropriated 250 pounds for a monument to be erected in Howe's honor at Westminster; this compounded the confusion, leading many to believe that the military hero surely must be buried there rather than remaining in Albany, despite two recorded exhumations and three burials.

✠

An English officer who conspired *against* the Patriot cause two decades later did come to rest at Westminster Abbey, but that didn't come about easily. When Major John André was captured by American irregulars in 1780 while disguised in civilian clothes, papers concealed in his boot revealed that he was negotiating with Benedict Arnold for the betrayal of West Point to the British. George Washington ordered that André be hanged as a spy rather than shot as an officer and a gentleman—an injustice bitterly resented by the British, and by quite a few Patriot women who admired young André for his bravery and good looks. They pleaded for his life in vain, nor were they able to upgrade him from the status of a common criminal in his execution.[61]

In August 1821 James Buchanan, the British consul in New York, risked life and limb by visiting Tarrytown, where André had been buried. He managed to disinter the corpse and examine it before a large gathering of townspeople. When they learned that Buchanan intended to return in order to retrieve the body for reburial in England, they objected vehemently: any honor bestowed on the spy would constitute a stain on the reputation of General Washington for having ordered him to be hanged and stripped of his officer's uniform prior to burial. Eventually, Buchanan did manage to take the remains to New York City and then to London, where a monument had already been erected to André's memory at Westminster Abbey. In 1833 Buchanan even published an account of the intensely politicized episode.[62]

What makes this saga especially noteworthy is that Hezekiah Niles, editor of *Niles Weekly Register*, promptly and correctly assumed that Buchanan's efforts had been inspired, or at least prompted, by the return of the remains of General Richard Montgomery from Canada and his reburial in New York in 1818, as well as William Cobbett's removal of Thomas Paine's bones in 1819. Buchanan reported that he had been "hourly annoyed by contrasts drawn from the conduct of the state of New York as to the remains of General Montgomery—while those of the British soldier, who was sacrificed in the service of his country, in the flower of his youth, (*by a doom, which, in the judgment of many, might have been commuted*), were abandoned and neglected." Exhuming Major André became a political quid pro quo.[63]

What transpired with the remains of Thomas Paine, the English émigré corset maker, the author of *Common Sense* in 1776, and one of the most influential (but also controversial) tract writers of all time, may well be the reductio ad absurdum among all these strange stories. Near the end of his life, Paine expressed the fear that his bones might eventually be dug up for malevolent reasons. When he died on June 8, 1809, in New York City, impoverished and by then rather obscure if not forgotten by the public, his corpse was arrayed in a shirt, a muslin gown tied at the neck and wrists with black ribbon, and stockings. A cap was placed beneath his head as a pillow because he never slept in a nightcap. He reposed in a mahogany coffin with his name and age engraved on a silver plate carefully attached and was buried in New Rochelle. His request for interment in a Quaker burying ground had been denied because he wrote the deistic *Age of Reason* (1794–96), so he was laid to rest in a corner section of his own farm. Because his friends surrounded the grave with a wall twelve feet square and planted four special trees, the site could be readily located. Ten years later William Cobbett, once Paine's bitter foe and an avidly pro-British journalist who wrote tracts under the pseudonym Peter Porcupine, went to New Rochelle, managed to dig up Paine's bones, and carried them off to England (fig. 9).[64]

After Cobbett died bankrupt in 1835, all of his property had to be submitted for public auction in order to satisfy his creditors. When the auctioneer refused to include Paine's bones in the proceedings, Cobbett's eldest son and executor petitioned the lord chancellor for relief, but the request was denied. What happened after that is anyone's guess. The son reputedly sold the bones to a neighboring Hampshire day laborer, but they more likely fell into the receivership of farmer George West along

Figure 9. "A Radical Reformer." Cartoon of William Cobbett carrying a sack of bones of Tom Paine from New Rochelle, New York, to England (1819). From Craig Nelson, *Thomas Paine* (New York: Viking, 1996).

with the remainder of Cobbett's unsold estate when the son himself was imprisoned for debt. Either the laborer or the farmer then sold Paine's remains to a London furniture salesman and onetime Cobbett secretary, who in turn seems to have sold at least part of the skeleton to an orthodox Anglican priest who insisted in 1854 that he owned the skull and the right hand but refused to let anyone see them. When a Paine disciple and researcher pursued this lead, he was told that the bones had been lost—which is the most familiar version of how the saga ended—but in fact those bones had apparently been taken by the priest's son to be examined by the Royal College of Surgeons, where an anatomist insisted that the putative skull was too small to have been a man's head.[65]

Meanwhile, the American press caught wind of what had happened following the failed auction and in 1837 expressed increasing outrage at the disgraceful treatment of a determined Revolutionary figure who had done so much to activate public sentiment in favor of independence early in 1776. The Philadelphia *Public Ledger* declared, "One of the grossest acts of indecency of which we ever heard, was the exhumation and transportation to England, of the remains of Paine. Nor can we regard with greater disgust, the still greater indecency of keeping them without internment [sic]." The *Ledger* demanded burial in either England or the United States "out of common Christian decency" and proclaimed the whole affair "disgraceful to both countries."[66]

Stories soon began to emerge that buttons had been carved from Paine's bones, and a rumor circulated for a while that his rib cage had surfaced in France, where Republicans felt indebted to his memory because of his antimonarchical tract *The Rights of Man* (1791–92). According to one other story, recorded in Cobbett's archives, some of Paine's hair and his blackened brain, taken from Cobbett's home in 1833, were later passed along to several other families and were eventually sold to Moncure D. Conway, Paine's American biographer (the biography was published in 1892), who gave them to a physician, who interred them in 1905 beneath an obelisk belonging to the Paine National Historical Association in New Rochelle. The dispersion and loss of Paine's remains is, indeed, one of the most bizarre and perplexing stories in the entire history of politically motivated exhumation.[67]

Adding more than a bit to the mystery, in July 1976 a seven-foot obelisk inscribed "in memory" of Thomas Paine was unearthed by a backhoe at Tivoli, New York, a town north of New Rochelle on the Hudson. It lay several feet beneath the roots of a hemlock tree and was uncovered only because a man had been asked to dig a ditch for a new septic field next to the home of a highway equipment operator. What has always been assumed to be Paine's true tombstone is much smaller and resides at the Thomas Paine Cottage and Museum in New Rochelle. Heightening the mystery, when the "new" obelisk was found, its top was broken and it also contained the name of John G. Lasher, a man descended from Palatine Germans who had first settled in the Tivoli area around 1710, and who died in 1877 at the age of eighty. Someone must have decided to "recycle" this imposing marker that had blank space to spare, just as Paine's remains got recycled in a different sense owing to their ongoing and seemingly perpetual mobility.[68]

It feels apt as well as ironic that while Paine was still very much alive and writing his impassioned installments of *The American Crisis* (December 1776–November 1778), he touched upon the topic of death and appropriate burials in a republican polity. In the fourth installment he addressed himself directly to General Sir William Howe, commander of British forces in North America: "The usual honours of the dead, to be sure, are not sufficiently sublime to escort a character like you to the republic of dust and ashes; for however men may differ in their ideas of grandeur or government here, the grave is nevertheless a perfect republic. Death is not the monarch of the dead, but of the dying. The moment he obtains a conquest he loses a subject, and, like the foolish King you serve, will, in the end, war himself out of all dominion."[69]

Paine had begun his life in that "foolish" monarchy and ended it in a republic, however imperfect. Yet in most surviving accounts his bones would haplessly disappear in the monarchy he had despised.[70]

✠

A sad story with an upbeat outcome will close this chapter devoted to the posthumous fate of famous figures from the Revolutionary era. Pierre L'Enfant, an artist, architect, and civil engineer, came to America in 1776 in order to serve in the Continental Army under George Washington's command. His cartographic skills made him invaluable, and he endeared himself to Washington. When New York City was selected in 1789 to serve as the new nation's temporary capital, Washington felt that L'Enfant was best qualified to redesign Federal Hall in lower Manhattan as a suitable site for the inaugural government. Because he accomplished that challenge quite successfully, Washington then invited L'Enfant to draw up a plan for the newly designated capital city on the Potomac, after Congress reached the compromise decision to have it located and built there between 1790 and 1800.[71]

The headstrong L'Enfant achieved a brilliant and enduring design in 1791–92 but was dismissed less than one year later by Secretary of State Thomas Jefferson because of disputes over the optimal schedule for publishing an engraved plan, which affected the value of house lots in the village and privately owned plots of land that would become the District of Columbia. In the years that followed, L'Enfant imprudently rejected the commission offered by Congress in payment for his services and demanded far more. Later, when he became willing to settle for a modest fee, an irritated Congress refused to pay him at all. He became the victim of his own arrogance, and the remainder of his life, like Paine's, devolved into a bitter struggle against poverty and obscurity.[72]

Benjamin Henry Latrobe, the gifted architect appointed by Jefferson to serve as the first surveyor of public buildings and to oversee "public construction" in the new capital, blamed L'Enfant for every setback and delay that occurred during the 1790s. He called his rival "this singular man, of whom it is not known whether he was ever educated to the profession, and who indubitably has neither good taste nor the slightest practical knowledge." Rather than returning to France, L'Enfant remained and continued to petition Congress for payment while living on sufferance at the estates of others. In 1824, when his final petition was nearing failure and he was forced to leave yet another temporary residence, a letter of salvation reached the old man from a nephew of Thomas Digges, inviting him to take up residence at Green Hill, a medium-sized plantation located along the "Eastern Branch" of the Potomac (the Anacostia River), just outside the Federal district that L'Enfant had so elegantly designed.[73]

The planner ended his days there as a "kind of eccentric elderly relative," spending much of his time tending flowers, studying the sky, intending to go into the city to pursue his claims but somehow never doing so. He died at Green Hill on June 15, 1825, just shy of his seventy-first birthday, and was buried at the base of a newly planted cedar sapling near the graves of servants and slaves to the Digges family. There was no public funeral, and only one obituary (little more than four hundred words) in the *National Intelligencer*, which lamented the absence of adequate materials for a biographical sketch. It acknowledged his plan for the capital but added that "he thought himself ill remunerated for this service, and, because full justice was not, as he thought, measured to him, he refused to receive what was tendered, and lived a life of sequestration from society, and austere privation, which attracted respect, whilst it excited compassion."[74]

Out of sight and very much out of mind for most of the nineteenth century, L'Enfant slowly began to regain public attention after 1881, when an anonymous article about him appeared in the *New-York Tribune*. Meanwhile, a retired Washington banker who now owned Green Hill decided to organize the architect's remaining effects, especially letters and documents of various sorts. In 1887 the Library of Congress published a facsimile edition of L'Enfant's plan for the District, and two years later Washington's newly organized Columbia Historical Society devoted its second volume of records to the origins of the city, including transcriptions of a selection of L'Enfant's memorials to Congress. By 1901–2 President Theodore Roosevelt had become quite friendly with Jules Jusserand, the French ambassador, who had strong interests in history and literature; they often played tennis together.[75]

Among Jusserand's goals while he enjoyed easy access to Roosevelt was calling greater attention to the role of French heroes during the Revolutionary era, ranging from Lafayette to L'Enfant. The crusade would prove effective: in May 1908 Congress allocated one thousand dollars "to remove and render accessible to the public the grave of Major Pierre Charles L'Enfant." Going even further, and quickly, in December of that year the secretary of war approved a prime grave site in Arlington National Cemetery. The process of giving L'Enfant his due, at least in terms of glory, was now under way. On April 22, 1909, the remains were exhumed—after a prudent pause until lightning and thunder abated. According to the *Washington Post*, witnesses found that a sadly decomposed coffin with "a layer of discolored mold three inches in thickness, two pieces of bone, and a tooth were all that remained of the great engineer."[76]

Those few surviving pieces were placed in a metal casket wrapped in an American flag and conveyed to Mount Olivet Cemetery along the Bladensburg Road, the route by which L'Enfant would have approached the village of Georgetown in March 1791 for a planning session with George Washington and others. On April 28, 1909, the casket arrived in Washington, escorted by an Army Corps of Engineers honor guard. It was brought into the Capitol rotunda and placed upon the very same catafalque that had supported the coffin of Abraham Lincoln (fig. 10). L'Enfant lay in state there, the very first foreign-born person and only the seventh individual to be given such a high honor. President William Howard Taft and his wife arrived at 10:30, surrounded by members of the Society of the Cincinnati and other dignitaries. Ambassador Jusserand praised his countryman for demonstrated skill and devotion. "For Major L'Enfant," he proclaimed, "the planning of the city of Washington was a work of love. . . . The streets were unexampled anywhere; gardens, parks, fountains, statues to famous men—all were devised in view of a great and powerful nation, the nation of today."[77]

Around noon, eight army engineers carried the casket out to the east front of the Capitol and placed it on an artillery caisson pulled by six bay mares. Cavalry from Fort Meyer across the Potomac led a cortège of five hundred persons and the Corps of Engineers band. The procession followed Pennsylvania Avenue to M Street in order to cross the Key Bridge in Georgetown, because the Memorial Bridge would not

Figure 10. Pierre L'Enfant's body lying in state in the Rotunda of the United States Capitol, April 28, 1909. Courtesy of the Washingtoniana Division, DC Public Library.

Figure 11. The dedication of Pierre L'Enfant's tomb and memorial at Arlington National Cemetery, April 29, 1909. Division of Prints and Photographs, Library of Congress.

be completed until 1929. Flags flew at half-mast along the way while children and teachers, given a holiday, lined the route to see the horse-drawn cart and its "solemn cargo." The new grave that awaited it had been situated on the highest promontory in Arlington Cemetery, beneath a huge oak standing less than twenty yards from the front steps of Arlington House, Robert E. Lee's former mansion. The view of the federal city from that spot is marvelous. In 1824 Lafayette had called it the greatest vista in the world (fig. 11).[78]

The grave into which the casket was lowered still lacked a permanent memorial cover; this had been authorized by Congress in 1908 but was still awaiting completion in Tennessee. Two years later it was ready, and in May 1911 several hundred distinguished visitors returned to gather on the porch of the Lee Mansion to witness L'Enfant's "second day of belated apotheosis." President Taft observed in his tribute, "There are not many who have to wait one hundred years to receive the reward to which they are entitled until the world shall make the progress which enables it to pay the just reward." Taft candidly alluded to L'Enfant's "highly artistic temperament" along with "the defects which not infrequently accompany that temperament."[79] The president made no bones about the handful of bones that had just been eulogized by the rector of St. Patrick's Church, where L'Enfant had once been a communicant.

The very large limestone cover for the grave had been carefully carved with an elaborate text, and at the top it displayed a part of the designer's own plan for the city that lay below, across the river. It is an exceedingly handsome tribute to this prickly genius who loved his adopted country despite rebuffs from his first patron, George Washington, rebukes from Secretary Jefferson, and repeated rejections by Congress. All of that now lay largely forgotten in the past, just as L'Enfant himself had been for almost a century.

✠

I find it remarkable that so many graves of Revolutionary heroes turned out to be sadly neglected yet were ultimately contested and then properly restored. Patriotic pride usually became the key determinant when people finally decided to do the right thing, including British patriots in the cases involving Major André and Thomas Paine. Although the Paine saga was sui generis as theater of the absurd, in general we can say that conflicts became intensified when partisans had divergent perceptions of what patriotic duty required.

The problematic search for reliably authentic first burial sites is another common denominator (see the Warren, Thomson, and Gwinnett scenarios), as is the competitive role of site-specific prestige in many instances. Finally, very substantial crowds turned out for many of the reburial events, most notably for the Wallabout martyrs, and for Montgomery, Greene, and even Button Gwinnett. These were highly public reburials, civic events that sparked sincere participation—perhaps more consistently so than many others that we will examine.

During the century between the partisan Republican notice taken of the prison ship victims (1808) and L'Enfant's federal restoration to a place of honor (1909), some of the reburials that took place owed their stimulus to sectional pride, though by the time of L'Enfant's memorialization, national reconciliation and a resurgent nationalism would prompt several of the most remarkable and notable of all American reinterments.

THREE

Honor, Dishonor, and Issues of Reputation

FROM SECTIONALISM TO NATIONALISM

"And this too shall pass away." How much it expresses! How chastening in the hour of pride! How consoling in the depths of affliction.

✝ Abraham Lincoln, address to Wisconsin State Agricultural Society, Milwaukee, September 30, 1859

*A*lthough issues of historical reputation and problems of group pride remained highly important with mid- and later nineteenth-century figures, narratives of neglected or forgotten burial sites became less common and less prominent, except of course for the many thousands of Yanks and Rebs who had the misfortune to die in the wrong region during the Civil War. Because the latter topic has been discussed recently and well by others, it will be dealt with mainly in passing here.[1] Pride of place and the growing significance of sectionalism and regionalism during much of the nineteenth century dominate the episodes that follow because survivors could not let the Civil War lapse from memory despite increasing calls toward the close of the century for sectional reconciliation. Reinterments often occurred because political and military leaders who died received burial far from home or else, once again, too far from the special site deemed most pertinent to their historical significance.

By the end of the nineteenth century and turn to the twentieth, however, sectionalism began giving way to nationalism as the main motive for several of the most notable exhumations and reburials in American history. Indeed, it is apropos to reference Theodore Roosevelt's New Nationalism here, because he will be a principal player and outspoken figure participating directly in our final two episodes.

Following the tragic conflict that took place from 1861 until 1865, it came to be accepted, at least among Northerners, that the federal government should bear responsibility for permanently honoring American military heroes. Hence the creation of Arlington National Cemetery, though not without considerable controversy and resentment from Southerners. But the kind of national pride that led to the reburial of adopted Virginian John Paul Jones in 1906 involved a whole different order of magnitude and symbolic meaning.

The achievement of belated recognition for sectional as well as national heroes provides us with a picture patterned with illumination as well as shadowy areas. The primary cause of such variations involves not only competing venues but also issues of overdue honor (or compensation for dishonor) among a galaxy of presidents and generals, admirals and justices. Gender also became an important factor, most notably in the South, where women aggressively insisted upon taking responsibility for ensuring proper burials in communities that had lost loved ones—loved ones who then became communities of the dead looked after by an array of proactive ladies' associations.

Resting in peace did not seem possible unless a personage reposed in just the right place. So the shared motif or common theme for American heroes, as the nation shifted back from sectionalism to nationalism, would be pride of place as compensation for death in the wrong locale. To some survivors the key issue remained, quite simply, "they shall not have died in vain." The Lost Cause lingered, to be sure, for more than a generation. But for others, mainly as the century reached its close, bestowing honor upon the deceased also meant achieving symbolic laurels for the United States as a whole. For persons imbued with that ideal, the motivation was not a lost cause so much as a *new* cause—the new nationalism that gave the twentieth century its jump-start.[2]

✠

James Monroe, a Virginian who became fifth president of the United States, married a New Yorker who predeceased him. Bereft and in ill-health by 1830, he decided to live with his daughter and moved to Manhattan, where he died on July 4, 1831, the same sacred day so rich in symbolism that had witnessed the demise of Adams and Jefferson in 1826. Officials in New York City asked Monroe's family for permission "to bury him, with appropriate honors, at the public cost." The funeral, held on July 7, became an elaborate affair. An honor guard escorted the body from the Gouverneur family residence of his children to a draped platform where the president of Columbia College delivered a moving eulogy. Following funeral services at St. Paul's, the procession moved up Broadway toward the Marble Cemetery at Second Street. Church bells tolled, guns sounded, and mourners in the cortège included members of the Society of the Cincinnati, national and local officials, foreign ministers and consuls. Although representatives from Virginia did not attend, a special church service was conducted in Richmond by the Episcopal bishop there.[3]

A quarter-century later, Virginians experienced a surge of new pride in their Revolutionary-era statesmen. But the initial idea to honor Monroe on the one-hundredth anniversary of his birth came from a transplanted Virginian living in New York who proposed that a monument be erected there to Monroe. While a Manhattan Council member agreed to seek municipal funding for it, Governor Henry A. Wise of Virginia was asked whether his state also had plans to honor the late president. Virginians apparently had not even considered the matter, but they mobilized swiftly. The General Assembly promptly passed a resolution appropriating two thousand dollars "for the removal of the remains of James Monroe . . . to the cemetery at the city of Richmond . . . for interment, provided that upon enquiry [the governor] may deem it proper, and such removal may meet with the approbation of the family." New York officials accepted the request graciously, and it pleased Monroe's children and grandchildren, who asked only for simplicity and privacy—neither of which would ultimately be provided.[4]

The Common Council of New York appointed a committee of arrangements that agreed the ceremonies should straddle July 4, which fell on a Sunday in 1858. They chose to exhume and ship Monroe's remains on July 3 for burial in Richmond on July 5; twenty-five hundred dollars was appropriated for the disinterment ceremonies, which included an offer by the Artillery Corps of Washington Grays to march in the funeral procession along with the New York Light Guard—a clear indication that sectional unity would be an ancillary goal (fig. 12). Once New York made it clear that pride of place would prompt the rituals there to be elaborate, Virginia clearly felt that it must follow suit, so the Monroe family had no choice but to allow public participation. When New York's socially elite Seventh Regiment announced that it would accompany the body to Richmond and stop in several cities on the way back, including Washington, where it would be reviewed by President Buchanan, the intensified current of regional tensions began to be felt. As one New York paper remarked of the regiment's journey to Richmond: "This handsome offer cannot but give the Southerners a higher opinion than they are accustomed to expect of the liberality and fraternal feeling of the people of the North. We trust in the future they will be disposed to accord to Northern chivalry a place in their vocabulary of compliment."[5]

Figure 12. Exhuming President James Monroe in New York, July 3, 1858. Wood engraving from *Harper's Weekly*, July 17, 1858. Division of Prints and Photographs, Library of Congress.

In Richmond, meanwhile, Governor Wise negotiated with Hollywood Cemetery, then still situated in a rustic area, to purchase not one but *three* prime lots on a hill in an ideal space reserved for very special dignitaries. The governor had an ambitious vision and scheme: to exhume what remained of Thomas Jefferson at Monticello and James Madison at Montpelier and rebury both founders along with Monroe as a kind of Old Dominion triumvirate. Descendants did not share this vision and declined, of course, just as George Washington's family had thirty-six years earlier.

On July 2 a delegation from Virginia joined with New York Virginians as well as Monroe's relatives and their guests for the opening of his tomb. The lead coffin was removed from its original casing and placed in a new, silver-handled mahogany casket. After the nameplate was transferred to the new container, it was surrounded by thirteen stars symbolic of the original states. The coffin, draped with a black pall, was then carried to a waiting hearse and taken to the Church of the Annunciation on West Fourteenth Street. At three in the afternoon, about ten thousand people who had gathered were admitted to view the coffin. A few hours later the coffin was replaced in a glass-covered hearse and became the focal point for an elaborate procession to City Hall, where it remained overnight with the Eighth New York Regiment as an honor guard.[6]

At eleven the next morning the mayor committed Monroe's remains to the Seventh New York Regiment, resplendent in dress uniform, along with the Virginia committee designated to accompany the body "home," even though home would not be his beloved Loudoun County. At Pier 13 the steamer *Jamestown*, newly painted and draped in mourning, awaited its 1:00 p.m. departure. Standing on the quarterdeck, Congressman John Cochrane delivered a farewell address on behalf of New York, to which the son of Virginia's governor responded with an apparent defense of his state's apparent delinquency in properly honoring Monroe: "James Monroe's head was bowed down to the grave, partly by a series of personal animosities and political acerbities, which chased him even to the tomb. Was it not, then, appropriate, exceedingly proper, that every memory of dissent, every voice of dissonance, and every discordant tone, should be allowed to die away, and be obliterated from the minds of men, before Virginia proceeded, in the fullness of time, to pay the merited honor to the remains of her illustrious dead?"[7] The firing of minute-guns from government forts continued until the *Jamestown* finally left the dock at 3:00 p.m.

The ship reached Norfolk late on Sunday afternoon, greeted by militia companies and large crowds. Following speeches, punch, and mint juleps, it proceeded up the James River to Richmond, where it was eagerly met on the morning of July 5. Flags hung at half-mast on buildings in town and ships in the harbor. Artillery salutes were fired from Capitol Square, and dockside ceremonies took place as the New York delegation was greeted by a host of Virginians. After an elaborate procession out to Hollywood Cemetery, Governor Wise delivered a eulogy that traced and celebrated Monroe's fifty-five-year career of distinguished public service. Welcoming the New Yorkers who had traveled that distance for the funeral of a hero they had gracefully surrendered, Wise once again alluded to the sectional differences so evident by 1858: "Who knows this day, this hour, here around this grave, that

New York is of the North and that Virginia is of the South? . . . They are one even as all the now proud and prominent thirty-two [states] are one" (fig. 13).[8]

Following the burial with prayers and powerful salvos, the Virginia militia accompanied the New York Regiment and many others to the huge Gallego flour mill, the only site in Richmond large enough to seat a vast throng for a celebratory banquet. A series of toasts saluted Independence Day first, then George Washington, then Monroe, and the fourth, given by a Richmond lawyer, mentioned Monroe's marriage to a New Yorker and finished with a tribute that captured the subtext of the entire event: "New York and Virginia, United in glory, united by interest and united by marriage, nothing but fanaticism can separate them."[9] As conflicting political positions soon gathered momentum, foretelling a brewing storm, that was not a sound prediction.

What remained to be done? The selection of a suitable monument. Governor Wise chose an elaborate gothic revival design by an Alsatian living in Richmond, a cast-iron structure that critics called the "bird

Figure 13. The ceremony at the grave of President James Monroe, Hollywood Cemetery, Richmond, Virginia, July 5, 1858. Wood engraving from *Harper's Weekly*, July 17, 1858. Division of Prints and Photographs, Library of Congress.

Figure 14. The tomb of President James Monroe, Hollywood Cemetery, Richmond, Virginia (1859; photo from 1908). Division of Prints and Photographs, Library of Congress.

cage," inspired by the delicate iron grills found around many statues located in or adjacent to European cathedrals (fig. 14). The twelve-foot-tall structure was placed above the new tomb late in 1859, almost the eve of the imminent and bitter Civil War that made such a mockery of all those vocal expressions of sectional harmony and cooperation.[10]

✦

On December 2, 1859, soon after his unsuccessful antislavery raid on Harper's Ferry, John Brown was executed by hanging in Charlestown, Virginia (soon to be West Virginia)—as ordered by the very same Governor Wise. The gallows had been set up in an open field outside of town. The doomed man rode there on a wagon, seated on his own coffin, accompanied by an armed escort. At the site, fifteen hundred cavalry and militia along with hundreds of spectators gathered to watch the grimly satisfying event. Observers on this occasion included one

John Wilkes Booth, standing in the ranks of the First Virginia Regiment and viewing the radical abolitionist with scorn: men like Brown were "the *only* traitors in the land." When authorities in charge removed Brown from the scaffold, they placed his body in a black walnut coffin, and most Southerners felt that justice had been done.[11]

One recalls a venerable, anonymous quotation that William Shakespeare incorporated into *Othello* as Iago's song: "It's pride that puts this country down; / Man, take thine old cloak about thee" (2.3.93).

While Southern sympathizers rejoiced, in the North many abolitionists bitterly lamented the death. At the widely publicized time of his execution, officials in Albany, New York, fired a one-hundred gun salute to honor Brown's martyrdom, and church bells tolled from New England to Kansas. In Lawrence, Kansas, antislavery settlers adopted eleven resolutions, three of which praised Brown's intentions at Harper's Ferry and asserted that "he had given his life for the liberty of man." At just the same time, Henry David Thoreau offered an address in Concord honoring the "crucified hero." Soon after, William Dean Howells, Edmund Clarence Stedman, Herman Melville, and Walt Whitman all wrote poems intended to immortalize Brown.[12]

When the train bearing Brown's body reached New York, a friend of the family decided that the martyr should not be buried in a *Southern* coffin and transferred the body to one made locally: a significantly symbolic "translation" even though not an ordinary exhumation. As the train headed to and through the Adirondacks, bells tolled with pride in every town and people gathered to observe the procession. When it reached Elizabethtown, New York, near North Elba, an honor guard stood watch until dawn, and then the coffin was placed in the main room of the Browns' farmhouse at North Elba so that neighbors could view their friend and hero for the last time. On December 8, 1859, final services were conducted at the home, and Wendell Phillips, an ardent abolitionist, gave the eulogy for that "marvellous old man" who "has loosened the roots of the slave system; it only breathes—it does not live—hereafter" (fig. 15).[13]

Historian Gary Laderman has observed that the meanings ascribed to John Brown's body "were related to the political strife, cultural dissension, and emotional turmoil erupting over the future of slavery in the years before the war—his corpse became a virtual arena where

Figure 15. John Brown's grave at North Elba, New York (c. 1897). Photograph by Seneca Ray Stoddard. Division of Prints and Photographs, Library of Congress.

larger social conflicts were represented for all sides in the debate."[14] In that sense and for those reasons, the politicization of his execution, funeral route home, and ultimate burial—in this instance there was no reburial, only the ideologically driven coffin change—foreshadowed the ideological politicization of reburials that took place in Europe following the fall of Communism in 1989.

✠

The grim narrative of Abraham Lincoln's assassination on Good Friday and subsequent death just before Easter Sunday, 1865, has been extensively related and analyzed.[15] Equally familiar is the mournful train trip home to Springfield, Illinois, with numerous stops in cities from Washington to New York and then west to Chicago so that a host of cities and citizens could express their grief. (The Lincolns' late son Willie, who had died at the age of eleven, was disinterred from Georgetown's Oak Hill Cemetery and sent along to be buried with his father.) The sixteenth president would be commemorated in death far more than he was ever celebrated in life. Less familiar to us today are the recorded sightings of country folk digging symbolic graves and burying the president "virtually" all along the funereal route.[16] Then there would be fierce conflicts over just where he should be buried and memorialized: in Chicago or at Springfield, as Mary Todd Lincoln defiantly demanded, and then in the heart of Springfield, as many residents preferred, or in the new Oak Ridge Cemetery situated on the outskirts, as Mary also insisted (figs. 16–17)?

Ultimately his remains would be moved numerous times, several of them for unexpected and bizarre reasons. The Lincoln Memorial Association swiftly emerged in Springfield to raise money for a suitably honorific tomb in Oak Ridge, with a hall inside the capacious structure that could serve as a museum and a caretaker to maintain decorum at the site and answer the questions of visitors, who eventually arrived in vast numbers. By the 1920s, so many people were making pilgrimages to visit the tomb that Chicago journalist Lloyd Lewis declared that more "pilgrims" came to pay their respects at this burial site than at any other in the world. More people may have visited Mount Vernon, but they did so primarily to see Washington's home, not his grave.[17]

On the night of November 7, 1876, a gang of four thugs working for a ring of big-time counterfeiters attempted to break into Lincoln's

Figure 16. Abraham Lincoln's magnificent hearse on the street at his funeral in Springfield, Illinois (May 4, 1865). The hearse was borrowed from the livery stable of a Mr. Arnot of St. Louis. Photograph by Samuel Montague Fassett. Division of Prints and Photographs, Library of Congress.

Figure 17. Abraham Lincoln's burial service at Oak Ridge Cemetery, May 4, 1865, Springfield, Illinois. Wood engraving after a sketch by W. Waud. *Harper's Weekly*, May 27, 1865. Division of Prints and Photographs, Library of Congress.

crypt to steal the body for a ransom of $200,000 in order to get the most skillful counterfeiter of them all out of jail. They intended to cart the remains all the way to the Indiana dunes and bury them there until the ransom was paid. Little did they know that one of their number, Lewis Swegles, was also an informer. The notified authorities waited in the ominously dark tomb until the grave robbers arrived, but then they bungled the capture: a police gun went off accidentally and gave the would-be robbers an opportunity to escape. They were soon apprehended in Chicago, however, through careful police work and imprudent behavior by the thieves—they had foolishly gathered at their favorite saloon.[18]

But what followed made the situation even stranger. The devoted caretaker, John Carroll Power, and a covert group of self-appointed guardians from Springfield became so nervous about the possibility of another attempt at theft that they removed Lincoln's coffin from its sarcophagus and reburied it, unmarked, at ground level where no one could conceivably find it. People living in Springfield could not keep a secret, however, and rumors circulated for years that the sarcophagus

Figure 18. The Lincoln tomb and monument as it appeared in 1883, when the president's body lay concealed in a shallow grave in the basement. Courtesy of the Abraham Lincoln Presidential Library and Museum, Springfield, Illinois.

on the main level was actually empty (fig. 18). So on April 14, 1887, the twenty-second anniversary of Lincoln's death, members of the Lincoln Monument Association opened the lead-sealed coffin to make sure the body was still inside (it was) and then rendered a proper reburial in its original sarcophagus.[19]

In order to minimize body snatching by medical students and doctors making anatomical studies, Illinois had passed a statute in 1845 making it a crime to disinter a body or remove a grave. The penalty was one year in prison. In 1879 the legislature augmented that law and changed the penalty to ten years for disturbing a grave or exhuming a body.[20]

Meanwhile, Robert Todd Lincoln, the president's only surviving son, escaped from his boredom as ambassador to England by taking on the presidency of George Pullman's Palace Car Company in Chicago. The despotic Pullman knew that he was hated by many people, and he feared that his remains might be dug up someday by those who had despised him in life, so he left explicit instructions to be buried in a steel-caged coffin beneath tons of cement. Robert Lincoln decided that that might be just the right solution for his father's apparently vulnerable remains. His advocacy led to the Springfield monument's redesign, and Lincoln and his wife were reunited in death, encased in lead, a cage of steel, and beneath tons of Portland cement (fig. 19).[21]

That reburial took place on September 26, 1901, but the saga doesn't end there. In 1930 it became apparent that the Lincolns' tomb needed significant repairs. As one writer has explained, "This time the coffins stayed put; but before the contractors went to work, everything else fragile or valuable was cleared out of the tomb." During the process the

Figure 19. The removal of Abraham Lincoln from his temporary tomb, April 30, 1901. A crowd gathered around the crate containing Lincoln's coffin. Division of Prints and Photographs, Library of Congress.

sarcophagus that had once held Lincoln's coffin was not locked away in a storage shed but left exposed out of doors. Alas, vandals once again entered the Oak Ridge Cemetery after dark, smashed the sarcophagus to bits, and carried off pieces, presumably as souvenirs. At least the Lincolns remained deeply secure.[22]

✛

Jefferson Davis served in the Black Hawk War (1832) but resigned his U.S. Army commission in 1835 to marry a daughter of General Zachary Taylor and became a planter in the Mississippi Delta. After leading the Mississippi Rifles in the Mexican War and participating in the Battle of Buena Vista, he entered the U.S. Senate and became chairman of the Committee on Military Affairs. In 1853 President Pierce made him secretary of war; but in 1857 he returned to the Senate, and eventually he became a reluctant secessionist. Soon after Mississippi left the Union, he accepted a major-generalship to prepare his state for defense, and in February 1861 he was unanimously chosen president of the Confederacy. Initially he tried to settle sectional differences peacefully around a conference table, but when Lincoln sent armed ships with reinforcements to Fort Sumter in Charleston harbor in April 1861, Davis tried unsuccessfully to enlist the support of Britain and France on behalf of his section's cause.

When the war ended in 1865, Davis and his cabinet fled southward from Richmond. He was captured by Federal forces in Georgia, imprisoned at Fort Monroe (named for the recently reburied fifth president) from 1865 until 1867, and indicted for treason but never actually brought to trial. His health shattered, he went to Canada and then Britain but was eventually allowed to return to the United States, where he settled on the Gulf Coast and completed his *Rise and Fall of the Confederate States* (1881).[23]

When Davis died late in 1889 after a lingering illness, people came to New Orleans from all over the South to pay their respects and participate in last rites for their historic leader. He was accompanied by the governors of nine states to what turned out to be a temporary tomb in Metairie Cemetery, as noted in this book's introduction. During the winter months of 1890, Southern legislatures all held solemn memorial sessions. More than three years following his death, in response to a request from citizens of Richmond, capital of the Confederacy, Davis's body was exhumed and taken to Hollywood Cemetery for burial on Memorial Day. Large crowds heard fond eulogies from men who had known him well, and in 1907 a statue honoring Davis (clothed as a cavalry commander) was erected at the west end of Monument Avenue, a kind of pendant to the great equestrian statue of Robert E. Lee already located at the east end.[24]

Albert Sidney Johnston, born in Kentucky, lived most of his life in Texas as a planter and soldier. Like Davis, he served under Zachary Taylor in the Mexican War. Although posted in California when the Civil War began, he swiftly returned eastward, and in May 1861 his friend Davis appointed him a general and commander of the Western Department. After several unsuccessful battles, he mounted a massive surprise attack on Ulysses S. Grant's forces at Shiloh in southwestern Tennessee and rallied his troops courageously, riding up and down the lines in a manner that made him legendary—especially after he was killed (most likely by friendly fire) on April 6, 1862. Davis considered him the finest Confederate general prior to the emergence of Robert E. Lee two months following the struggle at Shiloh. Johnston turned out to be the highest-ranking officer on either side killed during the Civil War.[25]

Following his death, Johnston's staff requested permission from General P. G. T. Beauregard to carry his body from the little church at Shiloh to New Orleans for burial. When Beauregard consented, a doctor injected whiskey into Johnston's blood vessels in order to preserve the body during the long journey south by wagon. A somber cavalcade accompanied the hearse to Corinth, Mississippi, where the remains were properly prepared for burial. At New Orleans the coffin was met by the mayor and the commander of Confederate troops defending the city. The body lay in state at City Hall for two days, after which Johnston's staff served as pallbearers and buried him in the St. Louis Cemetery.[26]

For nearly five years, Johnston's body remained there even though it was well known that he preferred burial in Texas. He had remarked to his brother-in-law, "When I die I want a handful of Texas earth on my breast." In the autumn of 1866, having secured the approval of Johnston's family, a joint resolution of the Texas legislature determined to bring Johnston to Austin for reinterment and appointed a committee of distinguished Texans to be the escorts for the body. On January 23, 1867, a religious service was held beside the tomb in New Orleans amidst a crowd of mourners and admirers. The pallbearers accompanying the body were all former Confederate generals.[27]

These were the early years of Reconstruction, however, and federal officials feared a demonstration of Confederate sympathy; consequently they had prohibited the funeral procession planned by Johnston's former comrades. This, however, served only to arouse Southern outrage. So thousands of people filed past the coffin once again as it lay on the wharf at Galveston, and the same response occurred when the body passed through Houston. When it reached Austin on February 1, Governor James W. Throckmorton welcomed it with an oration. While it lay in state at the capitol, vast numbers filed past the bier and covered the coffin with laurel and flowers. The next afternoon Johnston was laid to rest in a place of honor in the Texas State Cemetery. He had assisted in the founding of Austin, had lived there when it was the frontier capital of the independent Republic of Texas, and still later had liked living there with his family. In 1839 he had written to a friend: "Austin is in the . . . most beautiful & lovely country that the 'blazing eye' of the sun looks upon in his journey from the east to the west." Johnston had come home. In 1907 Elisabet Ney designed a graceful gothic monument, smaller but strikingly similar to James Monroe's "gilded cage," to be erected at his grave site.[28]

✛

The burials, reburials, and woefully neglected improper burials of the 620,000 combatants who died fighting in the Civil War constitute a very large and complex story that has been the subject of no fewer than five quite admirable recent books.[29] As early as 1862 Congress enacted legislation authorizing the president to purchase land "to be used as a national cemetery for the soldiers who shall die in the service of the country." That led to the requisition of Lee's Mansion and the eventual creation of Arlington National Cemetery. The following year General Lorenzo Thomas ordered the creation of a local cemetery for Federal troops who died in the prolonged battle of Chattanooga, and yet another for those killed at Stone's River, marking a transition from burial for convenient reasons of proximity to battle, and health considerations, to burial for purposes of commemoration as well.[30]

The narrative of Civil War reburials is also complex because the movement of bodies followed varied patterns in different phases as well as diverse locations, and persisted for more than a full generation following 1865. The Northern states whose men had fought at Gettysburg, for example, took the initiative in establishing the famous cemetery there; but the federal government assumed responsibility for its maintenance and gradually became the custodian of seventy-four national military cemeteries that served as the final resting places for well over 300,000 Union war dead (and eventually thousands of veterans of subsequent wars as well; fig. 20). Others who died in battle, usually coming from more affluent families that could pay searchers to locate bodies and bring them home, were taken back to their communities. Of the 5,100 Union soldiers killed or mortally wounded at Gettysburg, some 1,500 would be interred or reinterred in their hometown cemetery or family graveyard.[31]

Figure 20. Collecting the remains of Union soldiers for reinterment in national cemeteries. Wood engraving after Alexander Gardner, *Harper's Weekly*, November 24, 1866. Division of Prints and Photographs, Library of Congress.

The class and socioeconomic status of bereaved families made a considerable difference in the arrangements that might be worked out to respect the deceased and final wishes of their families. Late in 1864 General Larkin Dickason received seventy dollars and a request that a Union soldier who died in an Alexandria hospital be sent to his home: "Will you be kind enough to see that the body is properly exhumed and forwarded to my address. . . . The sum enclosed has been raised here by [the soldier's] friends out of respect for him and his relatives who are poor."[32]

In contrast, Stillman King Wightman of New York, who had connections with some important officials, resolved to find, collect, and ship home the remains of his son, who had died at Fort Fisher in North Carolina. After receiving a special pass from his old friend Secretary of the Navy Gideon Welles, Wightman made the long and difficult journey to the mouth of the Cape Fear River in North Carolina, found the marked grave of his son, Edward, and consulted with a surgeon, who explained that a lead coffin would be needed and might take months to procure. When Wightman refused to leave without the body, the surgeon conceded that it could be transported "in tolerable safety" if he used a regular coffin but filled all of the empty spaces with salt and rosin. Wightman attended to the exhumation and had the body wrapped in tent-cloth with pitch applied on the outside and then placed in a coffin that in turn was nailed shut inside a larger box. The body was then shipped to New York City at considerable expense and interred in the family burying ground next to the young soldier's sister.[33]

When the Gettysburg cemetery was created, it was assumed that only Union dead would repose there. A Gettysburg resident, F. W. Biesecker, won the contract to bury fallen soldiers at the rate of $1.59 per corpse; it stipulated that when ordered, "he shall open up graves and trenches for personal inspection of the remains, for the purpose of ascertaining whether they are bodies of Union soldiers, and close them over again when ordered to do so." Most of the soldiers who eventually received burial in the seventy-four national cemeteries had initially been placed in temporary graves, exhumed, and then reburied. Between 1865 and 1870 intensive efforts were made to reinter all Union dead in the newly created national cemeteries, which meant a great deal of checking based upon jackets (Federal blue), shoes (which differed by section), and even underwear (the quality of cotton varied North and South).[34]

Race mattered greatly, of course, though the practices varied inconsistently. For the most part, however, colored troops were buried with Union whites in national cemeteries, though often in separate sections. When Robert Gould Shaw, commander of the Negro Fifty-fourth Massachusetts Volunteers, was buried with his men in a mass grave at Fort Wagner, South Carolina, where they fell, many who knew of this were appalled, but the antislavery Shaw family in Boston totally approved and insisted that such an arrangement was exactly what he would have wanted. Shaw and his men were later exhumed and presumably buried as "unknowns" at Beaufort National Cemetery in South Carolina. Needless to say, integrated burial grounds were not acceptable in the South.[35]

What happened there, and to Southerners who died in the North, provoked the greatest amount of controversy, bitterness, and vexed reburials (fig. 21). At Antietam, for example, where the bloodiest single day of fighting occurred, a separate section was set aside for Confederates killed in Maryland (unlike the initial policy at Gettysburg). Rumors persisted in the North, however, that Southerners not only separated their own dead from Union losses but also severely abused

Figure 21. Graves of Confederate soldiers with board markers in Oakwood Cemetery, Richmond, Virginia, 1865. Division of Prints and Photographs, Library of Congress.

the bodies of fallen Federal troops. One Northern minister angrily insisted, "Not satisfied with the victory won, to add ignominy to defeat, the rebels buried our men with their faces downward, and took their bones for drumsticks and finger-rings, and their skulls for goblets and punchbowls."[36]

But bitterness over issues of reburial and memorialization lingered far longer in the South. In 1895, for example, Chicago's Ex-Confederate Association obtained permission from the secretary of war to erect a memorial within the soldiers' section of that city's Oak Woods Cemetery. During the war there had been a military prison in Chicago where at least forty-five hundred Confederates died from an outbreak of smallpox. After the war these Southerners were exhumed and reburied at Oak Woods, but largely in unmarked graves. The Ex-Confederate Association spent nearly twenty-five thousand dollars for a monument and appropriate dedication ceremonies. The monument displayed a soldier above a shaft of Georgia granite, rising from a broad plinth.[37]

From the close of the war onward, Southerners remained exceedingly vexed by what they considered the spiteful disrespect and indifference to Southerners who died in the North, especially in Pennsylvania and New York. (Southerners, of course, were deemed no more respectful of Yankees who died in the South.) Gettysburg became the greatest locus of anger, and provisional arrangements were made in 1869 for Confederates who had been buried in shallow mass graves there to be exhumed for reburial at Hollywood Cemetery. In 1872 the first group of 708 Confederate bodies reached Richmond. Five more shipments occurred during the next fourteen months, and eventually there would be 2,935 identified men and yet another 3,000 unknown dead.[38]

What remained the most distinctive feature of respect for deceased soldiers in the South was the very active role played by ladies' memorial associations, which insisted upon controlling everything to do with reburials and cemetery maintenance. The Hollywood Memorial Association in Richmond was one of the most active, of course, and largely managed the Gettysburg reinterment project. Long before the United Daughters of the Confederacy became politically active near the close of the century, these community-based associations of women operated independently, though they interacted for mutual support. They eventually relocated and reinterred the remains of 72,250 Confederates killed in the war, and they erected markers wherever possible, especially if the deceased could be identified.[39]

In 1900 and 1901 the United Daughters of the Confederacy, an organization then only six years old, bitterly contested the creation of a separate Confederate section at Arlington National Cemetery. Fearing that veterans belonging to the Grand Army of the Republic might still desecrate Confederate graves, they pleaded for the return of all Southern bones to their respective home states. For the most part they lost that struggle, mainly because programmatic sectional reconciliation was well under way by the start of the twentieth century.[40] In 1909 the widow of General George E. Pickett became the first woman and the second Confederate to deliver the annual Memorial Day address at Boston's Tremont Temple. In 1914 a Confederate memorial, built by the UDC, was erected at Arlington with Northern support and dedicated in a ceremony respectfully attended by federal authorities drawn from both camps, blue and gray.[41]

Variations on this theme and related ones persisted throughout the twentieth century and into the twenty-first. During the Civil War centennial, for example, the president of a historical society in Kansas City, Missouri, sent a proposal to President Lyndon B. Johnson aimed at marking Memorial Day in 1965 as the culmination of centennial observances. He felt that symbolic action was needed to minimize differences that still persisted between North and South. So he suggested the following: "Obtain permission from the families of the last survivor of the Union and Confederate Armies respectively, to have their bodies removed from their present resting places and placed side by side in a tomb to be erected in Arlington National Cemetery on the slope between the Lee Home and President Kennedy's tomb. . . . Not only would it be a reminder of, and a memorial to, the everlasting unity of the North and the South, but it would be a further tribute to the memory of our late President."[42] When the proposal was referred to Professor Bell Wiley at Emory University, a Civil War scholar and consultant to the commission, he responded with disdain: "I don't react positively to the idea of disinterring the remains of the last survivors and removing them to Arlington. Surely some more meaningful and appropriate ceremony can be arranged, and one that would not necessitate the transfer of bones and the erection of an expensive tomb." The proposal swiftly sank from view.[43]

In 1980 a more radical but also pragmatic proposal was implemented because the only national cemetery in West Virginia had been full for twenty years and veterans of World War II and Korea became concerned about whether they would be able to receive honored burial in a military cemetery. Many hundreds of Civil War soldiers, mostly unknown, were exhumed from the small national cemetery in Grafton, West Virginia, and all of their remains were reburied in one mass grave with a large and solemn memorial monument. The Veterans Administration speculated that if this project turned out to be successful, it might be expanded to include some 150,000 unknown Civil War soldiers across the United States. That does not seem to have happened, even though the concept did not cause a massive outcry.[44]

As recently as 2008, however, a thrust in the opposite direction — to *prevent* reburial — occurred. During the Civil War escaped slaves fled their plantations to join the Union Army and fight for freedom. More than three hundred who died during and after the war were buried in Talbird Cemetery on Hilton Head Island in South Carolina. By the twenty-first century the small plot of land where they lay had been overshadowed by multimillion-dollar condos and a private marina, signs of the transformation of a once predominantly black town into a cluster of gated communities for the very wealthy.

Yet for Howard Wright, the great-great-grandson of a former slave who fought in the war, Talbird was important to his family's heritage and, as he insisted, "an integral part of American history that should not be forgotten." Consequently he launched a campaign to get the Department of Veterans Affairs to provide proper headstones for the more than three thousand blacks in South Carolina who served in what was called the U.S. Colored Troops. Early in 2008 he received more than three hundred markers from the department, including one for his great-great grandfather, Caesar Kirk-Jones, who died in 1903 at the age of seventy-four.[45]

✛

More than any other writer from the Civil War era, Walt Whitman (who served as a hospital nurse for three years) is best remembered for his ruminations on what might help to redeem or countermand the catastrophe of mass death and the psychological consequences of terrible, lingering losses. Regarding the former, Whitman and others noted the positive effects of a "heroic-eminent death." With Abraham Lincoln very much in mind, he viewed a unifying and tragic loss, such as the president's, as "the cement of a death identified thoroughly with that people, at its head, and for its sake." Each ordinary soldier's death would also qualify as "heroic-eminent" if citizens could identify it with a just cause in defense of a people and on their behalf. Yet "strange, (is it not?)," he concluded, "that battles, martyrs, agonies, blood, even assassination, should so condense—perhaps only really, lastingly condense—a Nationality."[46]

When Ulysses S. Grant died of throat cancer in July 1885, his death qualified as "heroic-eminent" on several grounds. His reputation as the general who did the most to secure Union victory had grown steadily and eclipsed the corruption scandals and lapses of his presidency. His death also seemed heroic because he had bravely completed his memoirs while suffering from a most painful terminal illness. Because the memoirs became a best-seller, he achieved financial security for his family. In 1885 no one doubted that the burial place for such an American hero would have to be special and quite grand, but there would be rancorous disputes over the appropriate design for such a tomb, the campaign to raise a massive sum exceeding a million dollars, and above all, *location*. The Grant Monument Committee formed within a week of his death, mainly consisting of wealthy and prominent New Yorkers who seemed to assume that New York City must be the inevitable choice.[47]

In 1885 the body was placed in a temporary tomb in Manhattan, but as of early 1890, a suitable design had not yet been selected. Moreover, where to put him permanently remained equally vexing. He had died a resident of New York, but he had not lived there at all until returning from his much-touted tour around the world in 1879. In July 1885, not long before his death, Grant handed his son a slip of paper listing three possibilities: Illinois, his home state where he received his first general's commission; West Point—problematic because his wife could not be buried with him there; and New York, because, in Grant's words, "her people befriended me." Meanwhile, a U.S. senator from Kansas, a Civil War veteran himself, introduced a bill proposing the removal of Grant's remains to Washington for burial at Arlington National Cemetery. That suggestion met with strong approval on the grounds that many more people would visit the grave at the national cemetery with greatest prestige.[48]

During the course of 1890 the bill for reburial in Arlington was defeated, however, after intense bickering and high-pressure tactics exercised by a powerful coalition of New Yorkers. The latter, having raised the most money, felt determined to have their way, dodged the democratic logic of having an open design competition, and invited five prominent architects to submit plans. From that group it selected John H. Duncan, the designer of Brooklyn's Soldiers' and Sailors' Memorial Arch. Duncan's accepted plan took as its model the Roman mausoleum of Hadrian, a square Doric temple surmounted by a great granite dome. Five years earlier several journalists had suggested that a design from the middle period of Rome's imperial grandeur—a phase that fascinated Americans at the time—would be suitable, and now they saw their wish fulfilled.[49]

One more major decision remained: where in New York City should the memorial be placed? The committee took Grant's sons to three possible sites: on Central Park's Mall, on Watch Hill near Eighth Avenue and 110th Street, and in the new Riverside Park overlooking the Hudson. The Grant family chose the third, and when the tomb was dedicated in 1897, the crowds that gathered to mourn and celebrate General Grant would rank among the largest New York had ever seen. As historian Neil Harris has noted, Grant's Tomb "would become an important part of the city's public landscape, an anchor for great ceremonies." On April 27, 1897, nearly twelve years after his death, the Monument Association turned the tomb over to New York City (fig. 22). With sixty thousand marching troops, a parade of ships sailing up the Hudson River, choral societies, and bands, President McKinley and many other high-profile dignitaries reburied Grant. As one retired general wrote, "Since the transfer of Napoleon's remains from St. Helena to France, and their interment in the Hôtel des Invalides," no function had equaled "in solemnity and importance" the dedication of Grant's Tomb.[50] The sense of justice being done, along with commemorative euphoria, did much to overcome the disappointment felt by those who would have preferred Galena, Illinois, or Washington, or a structure that smacked less

Figure 22. Grant's Tomb, New York City (1901). Division of Prints and Photographs, Library of Congress.

of imperialism. The full realization of American empire lay two years in the future following the outcome of the Spanish-American War.

✛

Because of Southern disinterest in memorializing the victor of Appomattox, Grant's final entombment basically remained a sectional celebration, even though American nationalism had already begun a powerful and soon to be widespread revival. In President William McKinley's 1901 inaugural address he declared, "We are reunited. Sectionalism has disappeared." Although that insistence was not exactly true, it represented what a great many Americans wanted to believe at the dawn of the twentieth century.

In terms of reburials, three quite different episodes during the first decade of the new century epitomized the resurgence of interest in figures who had made special contributions. Each episode is indicative of diverse sentiments and motives, yet they reflect the rediscovery of pride in cultural institutions that served the nation (James Smithson), constitutional law (James Wilson), and above all, American maritime strength (John Paul Jones). Senator Charles Sumner of Massachusetts may have been just a generation premature when he pronounced the following in an 1867 address in New York City: "There is the national flag. He must be cold, indeed, who can look upon its folds rippling in the breeze without *pride of country*."[51]

Smithson, an illegitimate son of the widow of James Macie, was a direct descendant of King Henry VII, founder of the Tudor line in England. Educated at Oxford as an experimental chemist but barred from noble recognition at home because of his illegitimate birth, he spent most of his adult life in France and Italy. When Smithson died in Genoa in 1829, his will specified that his inherited fortune be left in trust to his bankers, with the income paid to his nephew. If the nephew died without heirs, the entire estate would go to the "United States of America, to found at Washington, under the name to [sic] the Smithsonian Institution, an establishment for the increase & diffusion of knowledge among men." The nephew built a handsome monument over Smithson's grave, but when he died childless in 1835, Smithson's bequest came to the United States in the form of a thousand gold sovereigns filling each of 105 bags, a fortune worth $508,418.46—a very considerable sum at the time.[52]

Early in the twentieth century the French consul at Genoa informed American officials of unsettling news. The city was building a huge jetty to protect its economically essential harbor, and stone for it was being quarried from the hill where the cemetery stood. Quite soon, the ground beneath Smithson's remains would disappear, and all of the bodies would be removed to unknown locations. When the Smithsonian regents learned of this, they responded with only mild interest—except for Gilbert Grosvenor, a son-in-law of Alexander Graham Bell and an energetic editor of what would shortly become the *National Geographic*. Grosvenor carried the case for reburying Smithson in the United States to the public by way of a carefully reasoned but impassioned letter to the New York *Herald*. The institution's regents then took the idea seriously and appointed Bell a committee of one to arrange for Smithson's bones to be brought to Washington "quietly" and "privately."[53]

Bell defied those low-key instructions and took the case to President

Figure 23. American Consul William Bishop holding the skull of James Smithson at the British Cemetery in Genoa (1904). Division of Prints and Photographs, Library of Congress.

Theodore Roosevelt, later noting in a letter, "I am proud of him [TR], for I am sure that the people of the United States recognize that it was the proper thing to do to accord a *national* reception, to the remains of the founder of the Smithsonian Institution." Bell and his wife arrived in Genoa late in December 1903, worked with the American consul there to cut through a tangled bureaucracy, and had Smithson's grave opened just as blasting and digging was beginning to erode the cemetery's hillside. After the last slab of stone covering the grave vault was removed, Smithson's skull stared up at the small group that had gathered to observe the proceedings (fig. 23). The coffin had crumbled to a reddish dust, but the bones remained dry and remarkably well preserved. They were carefully placed in a metal casket and stowed in a chapel for several days. The container was then wrapped in an American flag, nailed up in a heavy wooden box, and loaded aboard a German steamship bound for the United States. When it arrived off Sandy Hook, New Jersey, the USS *Dolphin* fired salutes and winched the casket aboard for the trip to Washington.[54]

On the morning of January 25, 1904, the Navy Department provided "as large a force of Marines as may be available" to escort the Marine Band as Smithson's casket, draped with American and British flags, was lifted from the *Dolphin*'s deck and carried slowly to the gate of the Navy Yard, where a troop of the Fifteenth Cavalry waited to escort carriages down Pennsylvania Avenue in a procession swelled with Smithsonian regents, the British ambassador, and a representative of President Roosevelt. Because Congress had not yet approved a final resting place for the remains, the casket was covered with a large American flag in a quiet upstairs room at the reddish sandstone Castle on the Mall. Soon after, the regents were authorized to place the casket in a handsome tomb situated at the main entryway to the Castle, surrounded by much of the original monument from Smithson's grave in Genoa (fig. 24).

Figure 24. James Smithson's crypt at the Castle of the Smithsonian Institution, Washington, DC. Courtesy of the Smithsonian Institution.

The regents, Congress, and the president had done their duty to what was rapidly becoming the nation's premier institution devoted to scientific research and museums of several kinds.[55]

✟

Less than two years later a very different story of exhumation and reinterment took place, one that helped restore the sullied reputation of an American nationalist who had been present to sign both the Declaration of Independence and the U.S. Constitution. James Wilson of Pennsylvania, associate justice of the first Supreme Court, died disgraced in 1798, fleeing from his creditors and on the verge of impeachment. Yet his significant role in drafting the Constitution had been second only to that of James Madison; a lawyer who attracted many clients, he was also regarded as a distinguished teacher of the law. The passion that proved to be his undoing was the accumulation of "private landed property," an ambition widely shared by prominent men of his generation—though few handled their financial affairs as badly as Wilson did. His downfall resulted from greed and imprudent investments in schemes to develop his land.[56]

In 1793, by then a widower in his early fifties, Wilson had married a nineteen-year-old woman. Three years later the general financial panic of 1796 caused his personal fortunes to collapse. When his work on the judicial circuit finished in 1797, Wilson and his young wife fled to Bethlehem, Pennsylvania, in order to escape angry creditors in Philadelphia. He promptly moved out of the state to New Jersey but was imprisoned briefly there because of the applications of a relentless creditor. Early in 1798 Wilson fled to Edenton, North Carolina, and sought refuge with his Supreme Court colleague Justice James Iredell, but he was still pursued by men to whom he owed substantial sums. His wife soon joined him, but malarial fever and high anxiety caused his death on August 21, 1798—a demise that saved him from certain removal from the Supreme Court by impeachment and conviction. Wilson was virtually destitute by then.[57]

Only a handful of mourners accompanied Wilson to his grave in the small rural cemetery close to Edenton, and Iredell, who returned home from Philadelphia (still the nation's capital in 1798) on the very day of Wilson's death, promptly informed the secretary of state of the vacancy on the Court and urged prompt appointment of a successor because so many cases were then pending. Newspapers made little mention of Wilson's death, and his colleagues on the bench did not even see fit to offer a eulogy. They seemed to be relieved that political embarrassment had been avoided. So Wilson remained largely forgotten—out of sight, out of mind, and disgraced—until late in the nineteenth century, when restoring his reputation was taken up as a cause by S. Weir Mitchell, a Philadelphia physician widely consulted for his rest-cure remedies for female neurasthenia but equally famous for his immensely popular historical novels about the Revolutionary era.[58]

Early in 1904 Mitchell approached the dean of the University of Pennsylvania Law School, urging him to mobilize his colleagues and Philadelphia lawyers more generally on behalf of a plan to bring Wilson's remains home for reburial in a "very great state affair" involving little public expense. The dean referred the matter to the chancellor of the Law Association, who lacked enthusiasm for the project because as a Democrat he feared the prospect of an elaborate state ceremony in which the Republican Theodore Roosevelt might participate or even preside. Given Wilson's best-known opinion for the Court (actually a form of dissent), *Chisholm v. Georgia* (1793), which Congress soon reversed with passage of the Eleventh Amendment, Wilson might be viewed as an apostle of the New Nationalism and an advocate of implied powers granted to the federal government under the Constitution.[59]

Weir Mitchell then acquired an energetic ally, however, in Burton Alva Konkle, an independent writer who decided to "give my life . . . to put Pennsylvania into national history as she ought to be." Disregarding the weak response to Mitchell's appeals, Konkle organized a James Wilson Memorial Committee, served as its secretary, and persuaded many prominent people to serve, including the chancellor of the Law Association. Konkle also recruited an equally energetic young member of the Philadelphia bar, Lucien H. Alexander, to act as his assistant. Alexander planned an entire agenda for the Wilson memorial proceedings: bringing Wilson's remains to Philadelphia on a warship provided by the secretary of the navy; carrying Wilson's coffin to Independence Hall, where it would lie in state; a solemn cortège of dignitaries who would accompany the remains to Christ Church; and the delivery of an address by a member of the Supreme Court, preferably the chief justice himself.[60]

Early in 1906 Alexander went to Hot Springs, Virginia, where Andrew Carnegie was vacationing, to appeal for his endorsement of the plan along with that of the St. Andrew's Society. Carnegie had come from the very same shire of Fife in Scotland that had been Wilson's birthplace. In June, Konkle and Alexander went to see Roosevelt in order to brief him on their plans and request that he attend the commemoration in Philadelphia. They also conferred with Chief Justice Fuller and the U.S. attorney general to secure their participation, and the secretary of the navy to gain his approbation. Only a short time before, in 1905, Roosevelt had played a prominent role in bringing the bones of John Paul Jones back to the United States from France, so 1906 marked a kind of apogee for such nationalistic reburials.[61]

When Roosevelt came to Harrisburg in October to dedicate the new state capitol building, he incorporated sentiments that had been handed to him by Konkle and Alexander: "I cannot do better than to base my theory of governmental action upon the words and deeds of one of Pennsylvania's greatest sons, Justice James Wilson." According to Roosevelt, Wilson had foreseen the need for a strong national government that had "full and complete power to work on behalf of the people."[62]

Early on November 18 the USS *Dubuque* steamed from Philadelphia to Norfolk with a Pennsylvania delegation on board, including Konkle, Alexander, a representative of the governor, and a special casket donated by the St. Andrew's Society. The delegation, swiftly expanded with other dignitaries, proceeded to Edenton with an honor guard from the Society of the Cincinnati and the Sons of the Revolution. North Carolina's lieutenant governor gave permission to exhume Wilson from his unmarked grave, a cordial luncheon took place at a nearby mansion, and the *Dubuque* steamed home with a grand salute from all the vessels in Norfolk's harbor, whose flags flew respectfully at half-mast. When the ship reached Philadelphia, the reception turned out to be even grander. A convoy of small craft moved out to meet the *Dubuque*, guns boomed in Wilson's honor, foreign vessels lowered their flags, and bells in the city began to toll.[63]

Sailors from the *Dubuque* carried the casket in a solemn procession to Independence Hall, where it was placed on a catafalque in the very room where Wilson and his fellow delegates had once gathered to discuss the Declaration and debate the Constitution. Previously this immense honor had only been bestowed upon the remains of John Quincy Adams, Henry Clay, and Abraham Lincoln. After citizens filed past for several hours, Wilson's coffin was escorted to a memorial service by three justices of the Supreme Court, led by the chief justice and Oliver Wendell Homes Jr. Christ Church was filled beyond capacity, and the justices sat in the pew that had belonged to George Washington during his two administrations. Speakers included Governor Samuel W. Pennypacker, Samuel Dickson as spokesman for the lawyers of Pennsylvania, the dean of the law faculty at Penn, where Wilson once taught, S.Weir Mitchell representing the realm of humane letters, Andrew Carnegie speaking for Scottish Americans, and Alton B. Parker, Roosevelt's Democratic opponent in 1904 and president of the American Bar Association, who tactfully praised Wilson's role in what had become "the greatest court in history."[64]

The U.S. attorney general, representing Roosevelt on this occasion, showed somewhat less finesse when he confessed, "It is one of the mysteries of history, which I have not been able to solve, why [Wilson's] fame has not kept pace with his service." The attorney general of Pennsylvania compensated with lavish praise for *Chisholm v. Georgia* as a masterpiece that "must be regarded as the climax of Federalism," even though it barely marked the beginning. A brief service followed in the venerable Christ Church graveyard at Fifth and Arch streets, the final resting place of such luminaries as Benjamin Franklin and Benjamin Rush. Wilson's remains were then lowered into the ground next to those of his first wife. By then Konkle and Alexander had become bitter enemies over who deserved the lion's share of credit for this triumphant outcome. Their mutual recriminations were noticed by the press, which ran such headlines as "Row Spoils Holy Rite."[65]

David W. Maxey, a Philadelphia attorney and historian by avocation who has pieced this story together, suggests in his conclusion that the entire episode "corresponds in strikingly similar ways, to the translation of the relics of saints in late antiquity and the medieval period. The modern mind may resist this comparison, but the continuities are there, including the discovery of the saint and the verification of sainthood, the ceremonies associated with the translation, the speeches given, the erection of a monument, and what an acute observer of this phenomenon has dubbed the 'impresarios' of the cult of saints."[66] Wilson's greed, financial collapse, and flight from his creditors were apparently forgiven if not fully forgotten. His reputation cleverly manipulated and miraculously restored, then raised from the dead like Lazarus, he rejoined the founding fathers as an American immortal.

There is an intriguing irony that must be added as a postscript to this strange story. In 1790 James Wilson delivered an important series, Lectures on Law, at the College of Philadelphia. Almost at the outset he declared that his new nation urgently needed a pantheon in Philadelphia so that her "patriots and her heroes" would be duly honored and remembered. Although no such hall of fame had been planned, he could envision it so clearly.

> The glorious dome already rises. Its architecture is of the neatest and chastest order: its dimensions are spacious: its proportions are elegant and correct. In its front a number of niches are formed. In some of them statues are placed. On the left of the portal, are the names and figures of Warren, Montgomery, Mercer [each one a patriot eventually exhumed and reinterred, as we have seen]. On the right hand, are the names and figures of Calvert [religious liberty], Penn, Franklin. In the middle is a niche of larger size, and decorated with peculiar ornaments. On the left side of it, are sculptured the trophies of war, on the right, the more precious emblems of peace. Above it, is represented the rising glory of the United States. It is without a statue and without a name. Beneath it, in letters very legible, are these words—"FOR THE MOST WORTHY." By the enraptured voice of grateful America—with the consenting plaudits of an admiring world, the designation is unanimously made. Late—very late—may the niche be filled.[67]

President George Washington sat in front when that lecture was delivered. He understood full well for whom the niche was envisioned. Perhaps James Wilson also imagined that one day, somewhere in his adopted city, there might also be a niche for himself.

✠

The story of John Paul Jones's exhumation in 1904 and trans-Atlantic reburial two years later is perhaps the most elaborate and grandly nationalistic in the entire American sequence of such episodes. Born in Scotland in 1747, Jones initially served on English ships engaged in the slave trade and then rose to command a merchant ship in the Caribbean. In 1773, however, he emigrated to Virginia, was commissioned by the Continental Congress two years later, and commanding the *Providence* he captured sixteen enemy ships. By 1777 he was carrying out crucial raids on British commercial shipping. In 1779, having remodeled an older French vessel that he renamed the *Bonhomme Richard*, Jones captured the *Serapis*, a more powerful British warship than his own, off the east coast of England and became the greatest American naval hero of the war.

Historically considered the first commodore (ultimately called vice-admiral) of the new American navy, he gave valiant and brilliant service during the War for Independence, often made possible by financing from King Louis XVI. In 1783 he went to Paris to arrange for settlement of prize monies for ships he had captured in European waters, but the complex legal procedures dragged on for several years. In 1787 Congress awarded him a gold medal. One year later he accepted a commission as rear admiral in the navy of Queen Catherine the Great of Russia, seeing action against the Turks; but when Jones's relationship with Catherine soured, he returned to Paris in 1790 and died there in 1792, amidst the political chaos that followed the first phase of the French Revolution.

According to some enthusiastic and intensely patriotic early twentieth-century accounts, both France and the United States claimed Jones as a national hero; French admirers are said to have proposed reburial in the Panthèon. In 1805 Napoleon lamented Jones's death, and a century afterward comparisons would be made between Jones's reinterment in the United States and the return of Napoleon's ashes from St. Helena to Paris in 1840. That brings to mind two sentences penned generations later by Charles de Gaulle: "Every man of action has a strong dose of egotism, pride, hardness, and cunning. But all those things will be forgiven him, indeed, they will be regarded as high qualities, if he can make of them the means to achieve great ends."[68]

The American minister to France in 1792, Gouverneur Morris, explaining rather lamely that it would be imprudent to spend the limited resources of the United States and Jones's heirs on a grand funeral, said, "I desired that he might be buried in a private and economical manner," which meant in the very modest Protestant cemetery in Paris. Even that involved considerable bureaucratic hassling in a Roman Catholic country, however, though a commissary for Louis XVI paid the 462 francs for public interment as fitting tribute to a man who felt grateful to the king and had earned royal respect by humiliating the archrival British navy. Jones's burial actually marked a new era of religious toleration within the highly unstable republican regime that was emerging in 1792, the very year Louis XVI was imprisoned. Despite objections that Jones was a Calvinist, he became the first Protestant to receive any sort of public interment in France.[69]

The ceremony turned out to be considerably more impressive than one might have expected under the circumstances—despite the fact that Morris felt his many social obligations (inconsequential, as it turned out) prevented him from attending. At eight o'clock in the evening on July 20, three primary groups appeared. First, a deputation from the French National Assembly was accompanied by a detachment of grenadiers, a bishop, and a vicar. A second group came from the consistory of Protestants in Paris, including a pastor chosen to make an address. And third, there were a number of friends and associates who had hovered over Jones during his final illness.[70]

With the passage of time, unfortunately, the small cemetery became densely crowded. Deceased persons were buried very close together, sometimes even two or three deep. Within a century the graveyard underwent so many changes and suffered from such neglect that it became nearly impossible to recognize who was buried where, and inaccurate reports eventually circulated that Jones may well have been relocated in either of two other graveyards, including Père Lachaise, famous for its flock of celebrities. In 1899 an American journalist, Julius Chambers, publicized the desirability of locating Jones's remains and taking them home. That led to a resolution's being introduced in Congress supporting such a plan, yet it died in committee. Undaunted, Chambers hired an agent at his own expense to seek out the exact location of the grave.[71]

During his term as ambassador to France, General Horace Porter followed Chambers's lead and made it his mission to locate Jones and take him back to the United States for proper burial. As he wrote when he launched the search, "Here was presented the spectacle of a hero whose fame once covered two continents, and whose name is still an inspiration to a world-famed navy, lying for more than a century in a forgotten grave, like an obscure outcast, relegated to oblivion in a squalid corner of a distant foreign city, buried in ground once consecrated, but since desecrated." The efforts that Porter went to in order to find Jones's remains in the abandoned and overbuilt St. Louis Cemetery were genuinely heroic, exceeding virtually any comparable quest on every measure: funds expended, supervision of the work, verification of the bones, arranging for the autopsy, "repackaging" Jones, and organizing an elaborate parade.[72]

Relying upon careful historical research and advance work done by Chambers's agent, associates recruited by Porter identified the correct cemetery. They knew from a letter written in 1792 that Jones had been buried in a "leaden coffin." Looking in what seemed to be the logical spot, they dug deep and found five leaden coffins, three of which bore the nameplates of other men. A fourth contained the skeleton of a person too tall to have been Jones, but the fifth held the remains of a man just the right size with a cap on which there appeared to be the initials *J* and *P*, the latter with an open loop when it was inverted. Anthropologists and pathologists then discovered kidney lesions, "which presented the appearance, very clearly, of chronic interstitial nephritis," the condition responsible for Jones's final illness and death. Twelve individuals, American and French, witnessed the site, the examination, and the identification (also relying upon samples of hair; fig. 25). They unanimously concurred that these were surely the remains of John Paul Jones.[73]

When news reached Washington in 1905, the government dispatched four war vessels, led by the USS *Brooklyn*, which remained in perfect column formation for the entire trans-Atlantic cruise and landed at Cherbourg in time for an elaborate French welcome and Fourth of July celebration. Two days later, the anniversary of Jones's birth, his remains were accompanied through Paris by five hundred American sailors and marines, a formal transfer of the body from French to American custody took place, and the decision was made to strike a note of victory rather than sounding a funereal tone. In remarks delivered as part of the service held at the American Church on July 6, special emissary Francis Loomis gave a speech celebrating Jones's achievements but acknowledging that "America unfortunately exemplified the adage that Republics are ungrateful, for in the stress and struggle of building a new country, she forgot for a time her departed hero."[74]

Figure 25. The place where the body of John Paul Jones was found in 1904. General Horace Porter seated at the left. A workman holds the point of his pick over the spot where he struck the lead coffin. From *John Paul Jones: Commemoration at Annapolis, April 24, 1906*, comp. Charles W. Stewart (Washington, DC: Government Printing Office, 1907).

That lament would echo Alexis de Tocqueville in his two-volume *Democracy in America* (1835–40), where several times he called attention to the memory lapses of a present-minded and future-oriented society. But at the farewell dinner arranged in Paris for General Porter, Colonel Henry Watterson proclaimed that Porter had "rescued John Paul Jones from fiction and restored him to history. He [Porter] ends his career in Paris by the rescue from a forgotten sepulcher of an immortal sea fighter."[75]

At five o'clock on July 6 a grand procession formed and proceeded along the Avenue de l'Alma to the Champs Elysées. The cortège bearing the coffin on a caisson included two regiments of French infantry with their orchestral bands, one regiment of cuirassiers, two batteries of artillery, two companies of American marines, and six companies of "blue jackets" from the four American warships. Enthusiastic and reverent spectators lined the route, which culminated at the Esplanade des Invalides, where the coffin was placed on a bier in a specially con-

Figure 26. The ceremonies in honor of John Paul Jones at the Naval Academy, July 24, 1905. From *John Paul Jones' Last Cruise and Final Resting Place. The United States Naval Academy* (Washington, DC: George E. Howard, 1906).

structed pavilion, under the flags of both countries and a profusion of flowers. Ambassadors and dignitaries from many nations surrounded the catafalque and listened respectfully to national anthems and a reading of the resolution by which Congress ordered a medal to be struck and presented to Jones in 1787, along with a letter written to the unfortunate Louis XVI informing him of that fact.[76]

A funeral train then carried the coffin and well-wishers from both countries to Cherbourg, where a French admiral gave a flowery address on July 8. The remains were then transferred to the *Brooklyn*, which steamed westward and was met by a naval escort of honor as it approached Hampton Roads, Virginia, at the mouth of the Chesapeake, where it docked on July 22. Two days later the coffin arrived at the Naval Academy in Annapolis, where it was placed in a temporary vault to the accompaniment of Chopin's funeral march (fig. 26). The final, triumphant commemorative ceremonies took place on April 24, 1906—the exact anniversary of Jones's glorious capture of the *Drake* off Carrickfergus in 1778—in the new Memorial Chapel whose cornerstone had been placed by Admiral Dewey, revered hero of the Spanish-American

War, on June 3, 1904, more than a year before the completed exhumation in Paris.[77]

The two-year time-lag between preparation of the new chapel and the final entombment was not at all unusual for Anglo-American state funerals, which required meticulous preparation of an elaborate burial site deemed to have sufficient national significance. I have already noted that to have been the case with Grant's Tomb during the 1890s. Also, a delay often occurred when mourners waited for a special anniversary occasion that seemed symbolically suitable or propitious. Well after the 1861 death of Queen Victoria's husband, Prince Albert, his coffin was brought from the royal vault beneath St. George's Chapel at Windsor and placed in a temporary sarcophagus in December 1862. It remained there until placed in an extraordinary gothic tomb in 1868.[78]

The planning and preparation for the final entombment of Jones could not have been more elaborate. The event coincided with the annual meeting of the Daughters of the American Revolution in Washington. On April 21 a French squadron of three armored cruisers arrived at Annapolis. Two days later the ranking officers of that squadron were welcomed at a White House reception, followed by two other receptions at the Navy Department and the War Department. In the evening many guests joined the French officers for dinner at the White House, followed by yet another reception. On April 24, the commemorative day, the presidential party and others were welcomed at a luncheon given by the superintendent of the Naval Academy. The next day, hardly an anticlimax, the secretary of the navy hosted a luncheon for the French officers, and that evening a gala dinner and reception took place at the French embassy. On April 26, French Ambassador Jules Jusserand (Roosevelt's favorite tennis partner) and Rear Admiral Paul Campion attended the laying of a cornerstone at Annapolis to honor French sailors and soldiers who had died in the American Revolution. The next day the French squadron departed from Annapolis toward home.[79]

The most important day during that weeklong celebration of Jones and the two nations was April 24, when President Roosevelt spoke for thirty minutes at Annapolis followed by Ambassador Jusserand, the indefatigable General Horace Porter, and Governor Edwin Warfield of Maryland, then a closing prayer by the chief naval chaplain. Roosevelt would use the occasion of James Wilson's reburial in Philadelphia to

praise the expansion of national power, and he voiced similar sentiments at the permanent entombment of Jones. The primary focus of
this recent winner of the Nobel Peace Prize for his mediation in the
Russo-Japanese War was military preparedness.

> We can afford as a people to differ on the ordinary party questions; but
> if we are both farsighted and patriotic we can not afford to differ on the
> all-important question of keeping the national defenses as they should
> be kept; of not alone keeping up, but of going on with building up of the
> United States navy, and of keeping our small army at least at its present
> size and making it the most efficient for its size that there is on the globe.
> Remember, you here who are listening to me, that to applaud patriotic
> sentiments and to turn out to do honor to the dead heroes who by land
> or by sea won honor for our flag is only worth while if we are prepared
> to show that our energies do not exhaust themselves in words.[80]

Within the imposing new chapel, the walls of the crypt surrounding Jones's sarcophagus displayed, in recessed cases, memorabilia from
his extraordinary career: his gold sword presented by Louis XVI, his
service sword, his captain's commission of October 10, 1776, signed by
John Hancock, and the two steel dies for his gold medal authorized by
Congress in 1787 (fig. 27). Close by stands one of the original plaster
busts of Jones executed during his life by Jean Antoine Houdon in Paris.
In addition to this handsome and moving memorial, in 1912 a bronze
statue of Jones was unveiled near the Tidal Basin in West Potomac Park.
The commission for that work went to the American sculptor Charles
Henry Niehaus, and the model for its handsome head would be the fine
bust by Houdon.[81] Following more than a century of distance and neglect, John Paul Jones had been doubly immortalized in the nation's
pantheon of larger-than-life heroes.

✚

Needless to say, nineteenth-century Americans were quite often inclined to be more than sentimental about death, despite its prevalence,
especially among the young. Some have even referred to a nineteenth-
century American "cult of death" that is readily seen in domestic iconography, especially "mourning pictures," and the writings of such
major figures as Bryant, Poe, and Whitman on Lincoln, Emily Dickin-

Figure 27. The sarcophagus and memorial to John Paul Jones in the chapel of the U.S. Naval Academy. Courtesy of the U.S. Naval Academy.

son, and others.[82] The artist William Sidney Mount (1807–68) received numerous commissions to paint the visages of recently deceased people, particularly women and children. One written request, for example, asked him to work from a "daguerreotype likeness, as I have one or two of my child that I lost about two months since [the child, not the likeness]. She was ten years old and the likenesses are very strong ones. I shall remove her from the vaulted grave in which she now rests to a family vault that we shall build as soon as the spring opens and will be ready about the first of May and then she can be seen if it will assist any in the painting of it as her coffin is so fixed that she can be looked at without exposing her to the air." Mount disliked these assignments but accepted this one and numerous others because they paid so well.[83]

Sentiments and episodes of that nature seem to have been common-place during the mid-nineteenth century.[84] By the close of the nine-teenth and start of the twentieth, however, as the vogue for spiritualism and necromancy waned, the impulse to immortalize by visual means gradually became less romantically ghoulish and gave way to memorial portraits as we now know them and the celebration of notable individuals in the interest of glorifying the nation and its institutions. Lurid voyeurism could take still other forms, though. The commercialization (even commodification) of dead celebrities and the idiosyncratic demands of survivors, most often family members, prompted still more instances of exhumation—the stimuli sometimes being just as much social or economic as political, and deeply personal as well.

— FOUR —

Problematic Graves, Tourism, and the Wishes of Survivors

We cannot know how much we learn
From those who never will return,
Until a flash of unforeseen
Remembrance falls on what has been.

✢ Edward Arlington Robinson, *Flammonde*

$\mathcal{B}$eyond the orbits of American statesmen and warriors, founders and fallen heroes, there are significant exhumation episodes involving an array of legendary figures, especially in literature and the arts—distinctive individuals like Edgar Allan Poe and Mark Rothko. What many of them shared in common beyond exhumation and reburial, or the restoration of a neglected gravesite, is that civic and personal survivors (most notably mothers and spouses) felt that the deceased had either not been interred properly or else, most important, not in the most appropriate location. Survivors (or members of the next generation) frequently insisted—sometimes despite evidence to the contrary—that the deceased had really wanted to be buried in a spot other than the one initially chosen, often for reasons of convenience at the time. Arguments over where the most appropriate site might be frequently persisted for decades, and in certain cases even longer.

With some significant exceptions, graves of the persons discussed here were not disinterred because a change had occurred in their reputations as historically significant individuals: few went from being utterly forgotten to being dramatically rediscovered. On the other hand, opening or moving graves, or else erecting new and more imposing monuments, did tend to enhance reputations and revitalize interest in the individuals' careers and contributions to American life and culture. In a few instances, most notably that of Daniel Boone, whose reburial would be among the most bitterly contested of all, interstate rivalry and pride figured prominently but also profits to be made from commercial tourism. Curiosity seekers, disciples, and pilgrims have played prominent parts in prompting reinterment. And they have often thrived in its aftermath. The outlaw Jesse James, the architect Frank Lloyd Wright, and the scout, explorer, and colonizer Boone provide prime examples, along with many others.

Boone was born in 1734 near Reading, Pennsylvania. As a young man he migrated south through the Appalachians to the frontier portion of North Carolina; in 1775 he led a group of settlers westward into what later became Kentucky and erected a fort at Boonesborough. As that region was still a very remote county of Virginia, Boone was elected to the Virginia state legislature in 1780 and became a sheriff and surveyor who speculated in land and often received payment for his services in land. Because he repeatedly failed to file and secure fair title to his real estate—Boone was as lackadaisical about matters of business as he was brilliant as a guide, woodsman, and, when necessary, Indian fighter— he lost control of all his holdings in Kentucky (by then a state) and moved to Missouri, where he lived on land given to him by Congress for his valiant services in defending against the British and their Indian allies during the War for Independence.[1]

When Boone died near St. Charles, Missouri, in 1820, he was buried near his beloved wife Rebecca in her Bryan family graveyard on Tuque Creek, a typical frontier burying ground at that time: "a small, unkempt, and unfrequented space into which the deceased members of the Boone settlement were crowded." Most of the graves, including Boone's, were initially unmarked—a predictable source of trouble and contestation.[2] Because Boonesborough had been the site of a wildly dramatic battle during the war, a commemorative celebration took place there in 1840. After the governor of Kentucky gave a rousing oration about Boone and his heroic legacy, some prominent Kentuckians proposed erecting a statue dedicated to Boone and the early settlers there. Meanwhile, St. Louis newspapers mentioned the possibility of placing a monument at the site of Boone's grave in what became Charette, Missouri, where the overgrown Bryan family farm was situated.[3]

In 1845, however, before the slow-moving Missourians had taken any action, Kentucky's legislature passed a resolution authorizing the reinterment of Boone's remains near the state capitol in Frankfort. The scheme actually originated with the proprietors of a new capital cemetery company, an entrepreneurial group improving a site perched high on a hill overlooking the city. While seeking the assistance of various prominent state figures, the proprietors appealed to Nathan Boone for permission to relocate his father's remains. Although Daniel Boone had left very clear instructions concerning his burial, which did *not* include Kentucky because he had refused to set foot in the state since 1799,[4] the state treasurer wrote to Nathan "that his remains were deposited in a remote village in Missouri. This should not be." A former governor declared that "Kentucky (and none other) is the place to contain the remains," adding that he felt certain that if Boone and his immediate relatives could speak "from the other world . . . they would prefer being buried in Kentucky to any part of the globe."[5]

In Missouri officials promptly appropriated five hundred dollars to erect a monument over Boone's grave and dispatched their own appeals to Boone's son to leave Daniel's body alone. At that point Boone's many grandchildren, his nephews, and others descended from his large family began to take sides, because some had remained in Kentucky while the larger group lived in Missouri. Harvey Griswold also became a crucial figure in the conflict, because he had purchased the Bryan farm on Tuque Creek. Griswold declared that he was "opposed to a removal of said remains from the place selected by the said Boone in his lifetime, and to any act which may deprive Missouri of the credit of doing appropriate honours." Nevertheless, a prominent Kentuckian, Senator John J. Crittenden, later the author of the 1861 Crittenden Resolves that sought to avert the Civil War, claimed in response that William Boone had produced "satisfactory evidence that the immediate relations to Col. Boone had been consulted and had given their written consent."[6]

The aggressively determined Kentucky organizers hired three local African Americans in Missouri to excavate the Boone family graves for them. At that point a series of bizarre developments began to unfold. Some years after Boone died, family members had placed markers where they *believed* the scout and his wife had been interred. More than thirty witnesses now gathered around those stones and watched the diggers turn up pieces of bone, shroud, and decayed coffins. Many of the bones disintegrated, but what could be salvaged was placed in pine boxes, while locals picked up and walked off with teeth and bits of bone scattered around the excavated site and kept them as relics. No one even bothered to backfill the graves, and such markers as there were fell over and cracked. A St. Louis paper then reported that assembled members of the Boone family had declared that the bones "were freely given up" with the expectation that Kentuckians would "faithfully carry out their object of doing suitable honors to the remains of their illustrious ancestor."[7]

Meanwhile, as historian John Mack Faragher has recounted, the Frankfort cemetery proprietors planned an elaborate reburial ceremony "under as imposing auspices as the occasion should demand."

On the evening prior to the celebratory day, prominent Kentuckians came to the capital to observe the transfer of the collected remains into appropriately new coffins. A youngster who had been present recalled much later that Boone's presumptive skull "was handled by the persons present and its peculiarities commented upon." As we have seen with Descartes, Swedenborg, and others, the skulls of famous men seem to exude a certain fascination—even prior to the Victorian generation's obsession with craniology.[8]

On Saturday, September 13, 1845, several thousand people gathered in the streets of Frankfort to watch marching bands, state officials, military companies, and fraternal organizations parading from the capitol building across the river and up the hill to the cemetery, preceded by four white horses drawing the hearse that bore the Boone coffins. At the grave site overlooking the Kentucky River valley, the authoritative Crittenden, so crucial to this disinterment of the great guide from Missouri, delivered an elaborate tribute to Daniel Boone.

Within a month, the Frankfort cemetery group announced the first public sale of lots and enjoyed quite a brisk business. The enterprising proprietors, however, failed to erect the pledged monument. A few years later when a group of proud Kentuckians tried to raise a private fund to underwrite such a monument, they met with indifference. Only in 1860, when the state legislature put up two thousand dollars for the purpose, did a monument to Boone finally materialize (fig. 28).[9] While the monument was being prepared, some workers uncovered the graves and opened the coffins, and an observer lamented that they shoveled up remains "as carelessly as if they had belonged to any ordinary mortal." One person, eager for a souvenir himself, fled with a fragment of what he believed to be one of Boone's vertebrae in his pocket.

During the half-century that followed, tourists chipped away at the monument until it was nearly ruined. In 1910, under pressure from the Rebecca Bryan Boone Chapter of the DAR, the Kentucky legislature appropriated funds to restore the monument, and cemetery officials surrounded it with a substantial fence to protect it from what Faragher has labeled "Boone's adoring public."[10]

Meanwhile, bitterness had been brewing in Missouri. According to the St. Louis *Globe Democrat* in 1888, Boone's original grave had been "desecrated to gratify a spasm of Kentucky pride." Soon, some Boone

Figure 28. Daniel Boone's grave and monument, first erected in 1860, Frankfort Cemetery, Frankfort, Kentucky. Following restoration in 1910, cemetery officials surrounded the monument with a substantial fence to protect it from souvenir hunters. Courtesy of the Kentucky Historical Society, Frankfort.

descendants began spreading rumors that the Kentuckians had actually failed to retrieve Boone. They insisted that when Boone was buried in 1820 another coffin already occupied the spot next to Rebecca's, so Daniel's coffin was placed at her feet. At the disinterment, therefore, angry descendants from Missouri had allowed the Kentuckians to uncover the wrong grave. According to this version, the family "considered it a smart deception and justifiable." Other members of Boone's extended family, however, dismissed this face-saving account. In October 1915, at the dedication ceremony for a DAR monument to Boone at the Tuque Creek graveyard before an assembled crowd of two thousand, a Boone descendant publicly repudiated the revisionist tale.[11]

Historians have observed that according to contemporary comments, the immediate family's consent was "freely given" and that despite disintegration, the coffins lying side by side in 1845 seem to have been identical. Yet one Missouri-based Bryan bitterly resented the imputation that family members might have been privy to a shameful deception, though the highly ambiguous assertion that he made seems more an act of faith than empirically grounded: "For shame!" he cried. "There was not a single body buried here that was not [connected to] some one living near to whom the memory was dear." So doubts lingered in Missouri, and they have endured. On several occasions Missouri officials have requested the return of Rebecca Boone's supposed remains from Kentucky so that she could be reinterred in her rightful place next to her husband, who they claim never left. In 1987 officials in Warren County, where the Bryan graveyard is located, asked the governor of Missouri to issue a proclamation declaring that Daniel Boone's bones had not departed from the state. He declined to do so.[12]

More than just pride of place was at stake in all this. Tourist dollars also mattered. To complicate matters and keep the controversy alive, in 1983 Kentucky's forensic anthropologist carefully examined the plaster cast of Boone's skull that had been made at the time of his death and announced that not only could it not have been Boone's but more likely "this really could be the skull of a Negro." He acknowledged that it was not a very good cast, but that did not prevent wire services from picking up the story and having it reprinted in newspapers all across the country. The record keeper at the cemetery in Frankfort insisted that "his remains are here"; but who knows?[13] No one does for certain, even if no devious trick was played on the Kentuckians in 1845, because both Boones were buried in a small and crowded space without reliable markers. Daniel Boone's mythic stature may be larger than life, but the tangible reality that remains is much less.

✦

Born in 1809 and orphaned at the age of three, as an adult Edgar Allan Poe led a peripatetic life as a writer of poetry and detective and horror stories, and as the literary editor for various journals. He called himself a "magazinist" and clearly had a precocious and wide-ranging intellect. In 1829 he moved to Baltimore, which became his home despite significant stints of work in New York and Philadelphia. In 1835 he married a cousin, Virginia Clemm, who was not quite fourteen at the time, and some later believed that her premature death upset his emotional balance. Accounts of his alcoholism and possible use of opium seem to have been exaggerated, though both may have contributed to his own early death in 1849.[14]

Although Poe's life story is starkly different from Boone's, some striking similarities are relevant because they call attention to certain patterns in nineteenth-century American culture, irrespective of differences between urban and frontier conditions. I have in mind, for example, the practice of unmarked graves for so many, though by no means all, and the persistence of poorly tended graves, even for individuals who had achieved a degree of fame or notoriety. The initial failure to erect monuments for such figures also recurs, as does the ongoing difficulty in raising public funds for memorials even when attention is called to this lamentable lapse. The desire to move the remains of people to a more prominent place of honor commonly arose within one generation after death; and because various permissions to move coffins or bodies are usually required, it was often difficult to achieve a consensus about *whether* to reinter, and if so where. Finally, and once again predictably, many more people are likely to be present for a ceremonial reburial than for the first funeral.

In 1844 Edgar Allan Poe published one of his less familiar stories in a little-known Philadelphia periodical called *Broadway Journal*. Titled "The Premature Burial," it begins with this sentence: "There are certain themes of which the interest is all-absorbing, but which are too entirely horrible for the purposes of legitimate fiction." It recounts a variety of episodes that had been reported in the press worldwide, sounding like bizarre items from *Ripley's Believe It or Not*, about people who were inadvertently buried alive and then tried to battle their way out of their grave, most often without success but in some cases causing a coffin to topple off its temporary supports. The sixth and seventh paragraphs in this piece concern the wife of a widely respected citizen, "a lawyer of eminence and a member of Congress."

> The lady was deposited in her family vault, which, for three subsequent years, was undisturbed. At the expiration of this term it was opened for the reception of a sarcophagus;—but, alas! How fearful a shock awaited the husband, who, personally, threw open the door. As its portals swung outwardly back, some white-appareled object fell rattling within his arms. It was the skeleton of his wife in her yet unmouldered shroud.

A careful investigation rendered it evident that she had revived within two days after her entombment—that her struggles within the coffin had caused it to fall from a ledge, or shelf, to the floor, where it was so broken as to permit her escape.[15]

The nature and preoccupations of this journalistic-seeming story, rather than its particular and horrific mix of narratives (some American and others European), provide an eerie but figurative anticipation of what happened some years after Poe himself died in Baltimore on October 7, 1849. He was buried the very next day in an unmarked grave at the Poe family plot behind the Westminster Presbyterian Church in Baltimore. The Reverend W. T. D. Clemm, a relative of Poe's wife and her mother, read the burial service, and George W. Spence officiated as sexton. Only eight or nine people attended the brief rites.

In 1873 Paul Hamilton Hayne, a southern poet of some renown, visited Poe's grave and felt so distressed by its unkempt condition that he wrote an article for newspaper publication in which he urged people to clear the grave of weeds and erect an appropriate monument. Hayne's article was widely reprinted and helped to revive lagging efforts to raise money for a suitable memorial. His hortatory essay was duly noticed not only throughout the United States but also in Europe, where Poe had achieved an admiring readership. A Baltimore teacher of elocution in the public schools led the two-year crusade for funds, using newspaper publicity along with Poe-related entertainments given by her students; but only when a Philadelphia philanthropist provided the final $650 was it possible to commission a suitable marker.[16]

The result was a large monument initially located in the back of the churchyard. The marker even bore a medallion with a portrait of Poe, based upon an image of him in the possession of a family member. The total cost of the monument and medallion exceeded $1,500. But in order to provide an adequate foundation for such a large monument, it became necessary to exhume Poe's remains and place them in the grave of his mother-in-law, Mrs. Clemm, who died in 1871 and had adored "Eddie." Late in October 1875 a reporter for the Baltimore *American* described the exhumation.

The laborers employed to perform the task, upon digging to a depth of about five feet, discovered the coffin in a good state of preservation, after having lain in its place nearly 26 years. The lid was removed, and the remains curiously examined by the few present. There before their gaze, was extended the skeleton, almost in perfect condition, and lying with the long bony hands reposing one upon the other, as they had been arranged in death. The skull bore marks of greater decay, the teeth from the upper jaw having become dislodged, but those in the lower were all in place, and some little hair was still clinging near the forehead. Beyond what has been described nothing was to be seen. The coffin was inclosed in another, and reinterred.[17]

Spence, the sexton who had officiated in 1849 supervised the exhumation as well. Three years later he told a visitor to the grave that when it was first opened in 1875 he lifted the head of Poe's skeleton and "his brain rattled around inside just like a lump of mud, sir." Meanwhile, the monument committee deferred to what it believed to be popular sentiment and agreed to relocate the burial site from the rear of the churchyard to the front, which meant a far more prominent spot at the corner of Fayette and Greene streets (note the honorific names of two Revolutionary War heroes). Descendants of the original owners of two large lots gave their permission, so Poe was exhumed once again and moved, along with Mrs. Clemm (fig. 29).[18]

Although the reinterment and transfer of the monument were achieved on November 6, 1875, the unveiling and formal dedication occurred eleven days later (fig. 30). In order to accommodate the large crowd and special guests, the dedication actually took place at the Western Female High School, where members of the Baltimore Philharmonic Society played and sang. The president of Baltimore City College made the principal address, and Sara Sigourney Rice, who had launched and led the fund-raising campaign, read aloud from laudatory letters written by such American and English literati as Henry Wadsworth Longfellow, Oliver Wendell Holmes, William Cullen Bryant, Algernon Swinburne, and Alfred Lord Tennyson.

The memorialists then moved to the actual grave site, where a carefully draped cloth was removed from the monument, revealing wreaths of ivy, lilies, and evergreens. A floral tribute in the shape of a raven, made from black immortelles, was placed upon the tomb by the acting company of Ford's Grand Opera House in Baltimore, as a way of honoring Poe's biological mother, who had been an actress in the Holliday

Figure 29. The grave of Edgar Allan Poe, Westminster Burial Ground, Baltimore, Maryland. Photograph courtesy of R. Owens, Westminster Preservation Trust, Inc.

Street Theatre. After the ceremonies ended, Walt Whitman approached the monument and, as a mark of respect for Poe, asked for and received a leaf of laurel and a half-opened bud. As one writer remarked, "The atmosphere of the occasion was rather that of a grand triumphal pageant than of a funeral service, [and] strictly religious exercises were conspicuous by their absence."[19]

In 1883 William F. Gill of Boston and New York, one of Poe's earliest biographers, visited the cemetery in Fordham, New York, where Virginia Clemm Poe had been buried in 1847, and he arrived just in the nick of time. Part of the cemetery was being razed, and, according to his report decades later in the Boston *Herald*, Gill encountered a sexton with Virginia's bones on a shovel, about to be thrown away because he knew of no one who wished to claim them. With the sexton's cooperation, Gill placed the bones in a small box, took them to his home in New York, corresponded with Poe family members in Baltimore, and eventually took the container there to be placed in a bronze casket and laid on Poe's left side. On January 19, 1885, the seventy-sixth anniversary of

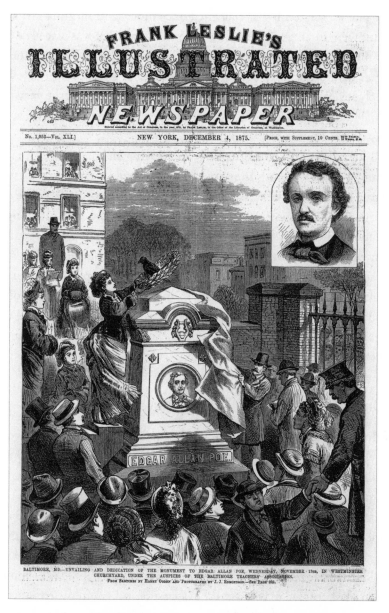

Figure 30. The unveiling of the Edgar Allan Poe Monument, November 15, 1875. Woodcut engraving from *Frank Leslie's Illustrated Newspaper*, December 4, 1875. The woman leaning against the monument, and placing a wreath with a raven on top, is Sara Sigourney Rice. In 1875 the monument stood on a grassy plot. The gate and a brick walkway were added in 1910. Image courtesy of Jess Savoye and the Edgar Allan Poe Society of Baltimore.

Poe's birth, the tomb was reopened once more, and Virginia Poe's remains were interred. It is unclear whether her casket was placed *next* to her husband's or, perhaps more likely, on top of his and her mother's. (That would not have been quite so quirky as it may sound. He had deeply loved them both.) The sexton who had officiated at the very first burial in 1849 and at the exhumation in 1875 was present yet again at the rites that reunited the trio in 1885.[20]

There is an intriguing epilogue. Starting in 1949, a mysterious stranger began placing the same birthday gift on Poe's grave every year: a half-full bottle of cognac and three red roses—the absence of a fourth rose signifying less than a full bottle of whiskey? According to the tour director for the Westminster Preservation Trust, an organization with oversight of the graveyard where Poe is buried, "It's a very personal tribute and we have never made any attempt to discover his identity." Every Halloween the Westminster Hall and Burying Ground Association provides a Poe impersonator who reads a work by the celebrated godfather of ghost stories.[21] Clearly, symbolic and sentimental tourism has become an increasingly significant part of the reburial phenomenon.

✦

If the adventures of Boone's and Poe's remains seem somewhat bizarre, an episode in 1889 provides a rather different example of attempts at bodily identification at a time when putting up memorial markers to historical personages was very much in vogue. During the summer of that year, *Mayflower* descendants in Massachusetts intended to dedicate a major monument to Miles (aka Myles) Standish, the Pilgrims' military adviser and defender immortalized by Longfellow in his romanticized narrative poem *The Courtship of Miles Standish* (1858). The monument was expected to be one of the largest of its kind in the country. As with many figures who died in the distant and storied past, the location where Standish had actually been laid to rest in 1656 remained utterly obscure several centuries later.

But in 1889 it came to light that a man who had died eighteen years earlier at the age of ninety-five had given testimony that Standish lay buried in a South Duxbury cemetery. How did he know? When he was a lad in Revolutionary times, his father had pointed out Standish's grave to him. Consequently, during the third week in April (when the Boston Marathon is now run to commemorate Paul Revere's heroic ride in 1775), the grave (*some* grave, at least) was dug up so that authorities could try to ascertain whether the skeleton found there might possibly be that of Miles Standish. Professor Albert Bushnell Hart of Harvard, an esteemed authority on early American history and especially New England's, joined various pathologists in this fruitless undertaking. The outcome was inconclusive, of course, but it received attention in the press because interest in Standish and the Pilgrim "fathers" was so intense at the time.[22]

Yet another episode from that period involves less romanticism and consequently may seem less intriguing, perhaps, than the never-ending Boone and Poe sagas. It is far more representative, however, because Americans were often exhumed either because an influential survivor preferred them to be permanently in a place most prominently associated with them historically or else because a such a person decided that they should be reunited in death with the spouse deemed to be the most appropriate—the "right" one or the "original" one.

Robert Dale Owen was born in Scotland in 1801, the son of a highly successful, wealthy, and reform-minded manufacturer. The family came to the United States in 1825, when the father, Robert Owen, bought and briefly took control of a thriving utopian community that had been created at New Harmony, Indiana, by German Rappites in 1805. The idealistic senior Owen was too busy with other concerns, political and entrepreneurial, to administer his colony effectively, despite help from a son strongly committed to his socialist views. After this second and less well managed phase of the utopian community failed, young Owen went back to Europe briefly, then moved to New York and wrote the first book published in the United States advocating birth control (by means of coitus interruptus), titled *Moral Physiology, or A Brief and Plain Treatise on the Population Question* (1830). Owen returned to Indiana in 1833 and served two terms in the State House of Representatives. In between he was elected to two terms in the U.S. Congress (1843–47) and drafted the bill providing for creation of the Smithsonian Institution.[23]

In 1853 President Franklin Pierce appointed Owen U.S. minister at Naples. After that he remained active in public life in various ways, mainly through his deep commitment to abolitionism and emancipation. In 1865 he submitted a radical early draft of the Fourteenth Amendment that, with modifications by others, became the basis for the final version. As a strong believer in spiritualism (despite being hoaxed at least once), he wrote two widely read works on the subject: *Footfalls on the Boundary of Another World* (1859) and *The Debatable Land between This World and the Next* (1872). After his wife died, his efforts to communicate with her failed, so very late in life he remarried.[24]

When Owen passed away in 1877 at his summer home on Lake George in the Adirondacks, he was buried in the quiet Caldwell community cemetery across the lake. Simple private services were conducted by the same Presbyterian minister who had performed the wedding ceremony a year before, "mute testimony that a once outstanding infidel had learned to live in peace with orthodoxy." On his gravestone, however, the titles of his two spiritualist works were carved. Owen remained in that serene lakeside spot for sixty years, until his aged daughter decided to disinter and move him back to New Harmony in 1937, on the banks of the Wabash, next to his first wife and deceased children.[25] Survivors have a way of prevailing in the long run.

✠

The death and ultimate resting place of the brilliant inventor John Ericsson warrants inclusion here because, in key respects, it harks back to the John Paul Jones saga, though in reverse—a trans-Atlantic passage from west to east. It sheds interesting light on ceremonial uses of the U.S. Navy in peacetime, when warships are readily available for ceremonial purposes.

Born in 1803, Ericsson was a Swedish mechanical engineer best known for devising the caloric (or hot air) engine during the later 1820s; his invention eventually made him a very wealthy man. He moved to New York in 1839 and between 1840 and 1842 oversaw the development of a new frigate class for the U.S. Navy. In 1843 the USS *Princeton* won a speed competition against the paddle steamer, regarded until then as the fastest ship afloat. In 1862 Ericsson designed the USS *Monitor* for the Union side, responding to Confederate development of the *Merrimack* and resulting in a memorable confrontation between the first two ironclad warships. The American Academy of Arts and Sciences promptly awarded Ericsson the Rumford Prize, a very considerable and well-deserved honor.

When Ericsson died of Bright's disease in New York City in March 1889, ripe with years and honors, some said that "he had so separated himself from his fellows, and so far outlived the era of his best known works, that few realized the historical significance of his death until they read the record of his achievements in the biographical notices filling the papers." On the day of his funeral, however, thirty-two pall-bearers, personal friends and representatives of various societies, especially Swedish American, gathered at his house and proceeded with little ceremony to Trinity Church on lower Broadway, where the burial service was read and the choir sang the familiar hymn "Lead, Kindly Light." His body was then carried to the Marble Cemetery, where James Monroe had been initially buried back in 1831. The procession was a simple one, and nothing in the nature of a civic funeral occurred. The coffin was placed in a receiving vault to await a decision about Ericsson's final resting place. A funeral hymn was sung by a Swedish glee club, and the Odd Fellows of Ericsson's lodge, the Amaranthus, performed their basic, rather secular rites.[26]

Various suggestions emerged for his final interment, including a proposition to place his remains in the Livingston Vault of Trinity churchyard right next to those of Robert Fulton, the "other" inventor of a steamboat. In May the New York state legislature passed an act authorizing the city to spend ten thousand dollars to erect a monument to Ericsson in one of the public parks. Congress passed two other bills totaling eighty thousand dollars for yet another monument. In April, however, Secretary of State James G. Blaine received a message from the American legation in Stockholm informing him that "Sweden would regard with extreme favor Ericsson's body sent home by man-of-war." Blaine passed this request on to the secretary of the navy, who dawdled but eventually responded in June 1890 that the USS *Essex*, an old and inferior vessel, was available to honor the request of the Swedish government. When public sentiment made it clear that this seemed inadequate recompense for the ingenious inventor of the *Monitor*, an impressive cruiser from the "new navy," the USS *Baltimore*, became available.[27]

On August 18 President Benjamin Harrison sent an order to the commandant of the Navy Yard in New York. It read in part:

> Upon the occasion of the embarkation of the remains of Captain Ericsson, it is the desire of the President to give solemn expression to the cordial and fraternal feeling that unites us with a kindred people, the parent source of a large body of our most valued citizens, of whom the late inventor, a Scandinavian by birth, and an American by adoption, was the most illustrious example. In recognition of this feeling and of the debt we owe to Sweden for the gift of Ericsson, whose genius rendered us the highest service in a moment of grave peril and anxiety, it is directed that at this other moment, when we give back his body to his native country, the flag of Sweden shall be saluted by the squadron.[28]

The Navy Department then followed with elaborate instructions for flags to be lowered to half-mast during the embarkation, minute guns to be fired from the monitor *Nantucket* as the body passed from the shore to the *Baltimore*, and then as that vessel passed through the squadron, Swedish ensigns to be displayed and a twenty-one-gun salute to be fired.

When Ericsson's remains were finally removed from the receiving vault at Marble Cemetery (also known as the Second Street cemetery), Swedish singing societies gathered and serenaded their dead countryman with Adolph Fredrik Lindblad's "Stridsbön," the battle prayer of Sweden. The captain of the *Baltimore* had received a message from one of the executors of Ericsson's estate that read in part:

> We send him back crowned with honor; proud of the life of fifty years he devoted to this nation, and with gratitude for the gifts he gave to us. Was he a dreamer? Yes. He dreamed of the practical application of screw propulsion, and the commerce of the world was revolutionized. He dreamed of making naval warfare more terrible, and the *Monitor* was built. . . . He dreamed of hot air, and behold ten thousand caloric engines. He dreamed of the sun's rays in sandy deserts, where water was hard to get, and the solar engine came.[29]

Following a voyage of nineteen days, the *Baltimore* reached Stockholm and transferred its charge to the Swedish government. Three officers of the Swedish navy and four of Ericsson's nephews had been

Figure 31. The White Squadron's farewell salute to the body of John Ericsson, New York Bay, August 23, 1890. 1900 engraving based upon the 1898 painting by Edward Moran, located at the U.S. Naval Academy. Division of Prints and Photographs, Library of Congress.

appointed a committee of reception. Sailors from the American man-of-war placed the coffin on a steam barge commanded by a captain of the Swedish navy, and it was followed ashore by a procession of boats with all flags flying at half-mast. At the landing, troops paraded as an escort while American sailors carried the coffin to a pavilion. After a simple service consisting of Swedish hymns and the recitation of a poem, a hearse followed by an escort including representatives of the royal family took the bier to a train waiting at the railway station, bound for Ericsson's final resting place in Filipstad.[30]

When it reached that town in Vermland, the body was borne by twelve miners into a church, where the Lutheran services for the dead were performed. On the morning of September 14, 1890, the coffin went to its ultimate site—a chapel especially prepared for its reception in an adjoining cemetery, said to be "the finest in Sweden." Like John Paul Jones, Ericsson received the ultimate distinction of burial in a brand-new chapel designed to honor him individually.

On November 7, 1884, Ericsson had written an illuminating letter that casts his fame and reputed fortune in an unexpected light. From my perspective, it supplies a most interesting kind of epitaph.

> They imagine in Sweden that I now possess a large fortune, not considering what it has cost me to be useful to my fellow-men, especially my native country, for which I have worked out a complete system of defence. They do not know that for nearly twenty years (during which time I have spent a million crowns), I have not worked for money. They know that during these years I have produced various machines that now pay well, but they do not know that I have resigned these inventions to certain mechanical manufacturers who most liberally consented to construct experimental machines for me at a time when I was not able to pay for the work.[31]

Part of his estate remained uncertain because he still had claims pending against the U.S. government for his investment in a ship called the Destroyer, not to mention partial recompense for his design of the *Princeton* back in 1841–42, which somehow still remained unsettled.

✛

From this story of a suitably honored hero we now shift to that of an infamous outlaw who eventually managed to become a legendary figure of folklore following an early death. Jesse James was born in 1847, the son of a commercial hemp farmer and sometime Baptist minister in Kearney, Missouri. (Hemp is the raw material used in making rope.) Missouri became a bitterly divided border state during the Civil War, and Kearney was situated in the section known as Little Dixie because of its pro-slavery Confederate partisanship. Jesse's older brother, Frank, and later Jesse himself joined a Southern guerrilla band eventually known as Quantrill's Raiders, active in harassing Federal troops in an arc extending from Missouri to Texas. In 1864 they came upon twenty-two unarmed Union soldiers and murdered them all in what came to be known as the Centralia Massacre. The band subsequently encountered another Union company and killed them as well. After the war, when the group was exiled from Missouri by U.S. military authorities, they became bushwhackers determined to attack those responsible for Radical Reconstruction.[32]

Without abandoning their impassioned political views, the alienated group soon turned to more lucrative outlaw activities, committing in 1866 the first armed bank robbery during peacetime in the United States. Others followed, and in 1869 Jesse began to achieve individual notoriety when he robbed a bank in Gallatin, Missouri, and killed a teller. The James gang teamed up with the Cole Younger band and began an astonishing string of armed robberies and murders across a long swath of territory that stretched from Iowa to Texas. In 1873 they turned to train robberies and achieved a kind of Robin Hood reputation because they bypassed individual passengers in favor of looting large commercial funds being transported in the baggage cars. Meanwhile, Jesse had married a woman named Zerelda, called Zee because her mother was also Zerelda.[33]

Tired of the James gang's ruthless depredations—nine consecutive years of successful train robberies—and eager to gain political capital from its demise, Missouri's Governor Thomas T. Crittenden offered a ten-thousand-dollar bounty for the capture of Jesse James. On the eve of a new robbery scheme aimed at Platte City, Missouri, in April 1882, one of the Ford brothers, new members of Jesse's outlaw gang, shot him in the back of the head while he stood on a chair in his St. Joseph house to dust a picture before departing for the impending hold-up. Crittenden denied that he had sanctioned the assassination, but he pardoned the Fords unconditionally following their convictions for murder. James's death and the subsequent trials sparked an immense wave of sensationalistic newspaper coverage that began in Kansas City and Kearney and spread swiftly across the country.[34]

James's body was placed in a casket and taken home to his mother by train in a baggage car carefully guarded by sheriffs. According to press accounts, the body "lay in state" in Kearney, observed by two thousand curiosity seekers along with supporters of the local bandit, who testified that the corpse "looked natural" with hands folded and a peaceful face. Funeral services were held on the afternoon of April 6 at the Kearney Baptist Church, where Jesse had been a boyhood member but later was "excluded" (fig. 32). The pallbearers were five local men and a mysterious stranger who seemed to be in charge. Some whispered that it was his older brother, Frank, who had been sequestered in hiding; but the stranger was stout, unlike the slender Frank, and an enigma remains. Two clergymen officiated, and one read a passage from the book of Job:

THE HOUSE IN WHICH
JESSE JAMES ➤ ➤ ➤
WAS KILLED.

THE HOME OF FRANK & JESSE JAMES

THE BAPTIST CHURCH
KEARNEY MO. IN WHICH THE
FUNERAL SERVICES WERE
HELD.

Figure 32. The home of Frank and Jesse James showing the Baptist Church in Kearney, Missouri, where the funeral of Jesse James took place. Division of Prints and Photographs, Library of Congress.

"Man that is born of woman is of few days and full of trouble." Jesse James was thirty-four years old.[35]

At the close of a standard funeral service in which James was alluded to only once, one of the pastors announced that James's mother had asked him to request that those present refrain from going to her farm, where interment would take place. Because her third husband, Reuben Samuel, was quite ill and the grave site situated close to the house, she feared that crowd noise might affect him adversely. "It is therefore requested that none but friends and relatives go to the grave." When members of the cortège reached the Samuel farmhouse, however, a considerable number of country folk had gathered anyway. They remained quiet and respectful as James was buried in a corner of the yard outside the house where he had been born, and "where his mother could look from her windows upon the mound at the foot of a big coffee-bean tree" (fig. 33).[36]

For the next twenty years Mrs. Samuel planted flowers on the grave and tended them with loving care. James had been buried seven feet deep rather than the usual five or six, to forestall any attempt to steal the body. Mrs. Samuel erected a tall white marble monument on which she had an inscription carved which read, in part: "In Loving Remembrance of My Beloved Son . . . Murdered by a Traitor and Coward Whose Name Is Not Worthy to Appear Here."[37] Eventually, desperate for money because she had always depended upon Jesse for financial support, she sold memorabilia from the house to souvenir hunters. Later, the house itself became a tourist attraction where customers could visit the grave and play golf for five dollars.

In 1898 the surviving Quantrill veterans began to hold reunions tinged with romantic nostalgia for the Lost Cause. Sentiment soon swelled to exhume Jesse from inconvenient access at the farmhouse and place his remains in Kearney's Mount Olivet Cemetery, where people like themselves would find it easier to pay their respects to the most famous rebel outlaw of his time—perhaps of the entire nineteenth century.

Figure 33. Jesse James's grave at the Samuel farm, Kearney, Missouri. From Frank Triplett, *The Life, Times, and Treacherous Death of Jesse James* (Chicago: Sage Books, Swallow Press, 1970).

The skeleton they disinterred on June 29, 1902, was indeed his—the evidence being Bob Ford's bullet hole in the head and numerous gold-filled teeth, visible to Jesse James the younger, who was familiar with his father's mouth.[38]

Several family members held the skull in their hands and scrutinized it. (It had rolled off the decayed and tipsy coffin-bottom twice and had to be retrieved each time by a gravedigger from the bottom of the deeply dug cavity.) James was reburied as a Confederate hero in a handsome new coffin. The Quantrill troopers then congregated for dinner in town and gathered afterward at the farmhouse to tell stories of their daring misdeeds during the war. His mother was present yet again for the 1902 reburial—a survivor who got her way more than once but not with finality. The younger Jesse James's reassurance about the authentic remains mattered because of several false, folkloric rumors that arose later.[39]

Jesse James's birthplace, boyhood home, and final resting place have since become celebrated, as he continues to be the most famous resident of Kearney and its environs and serves to boost tourism there. Each year during the third week of September a gala event is held at the Jesse James Festival Grounds. Visitors along with locals can experience a parade, carnival, rodeo, historical reenactments, a teen dance, and a barbecue cook-off—all in the name of community solidarity, hospitality, and much-needed commercial sustenance. A good time is had by all.

Yet tales continued to circulate that Jesse really did not die on April 3, 1882, but escaped to Texas, where he lived to be 103. Hence the need to exhume his bones one more time in 1995 for DNA testing and forensic study. This third exhumation required a request from the county coroner and prosecutor and then a court order. The remains found were indeed Jesse's. I'm not quite sure what has replaced the good old stories once told by the good old boys. But the answer would appear to be Hollywood films, the most recent one released in 2008.[40]

✛

There is an oddly parallel yet symptomatic ending to the reburial of a radically different figure than Jesse James: the English novelist, poet, and writer of short stories D. H. Lawrence. Recall the ultimate conflict between the wishes of James's mother and those of his Quantrill pals;

in Lawrence's case we encounter a conflict of wills between his widow and other strong-willed women who idolized him. There are no other parallels.

Born in 1885 to a puritanical schoolteacher and a drunken coal miner, Lawrence would develop an antipathy to industrialization and social convention, an attraction to primitive religions and a mystical philosophy of nature. In addition to his prolific literary output, he is remembered for his avant-garde theories of sex, morals, and society. He also possessed a restless soul that made extensive travel magnetic for his personal compass—one might almost say compulsive movement—perhaps in search of a congenial homeland and associates; and he shared that passion with his wife, Frieda von Richthofen, who was six years his senior. He met her in 1912, when she was married to Ernest Weekley, his former modern languages professor at the University of Nottingham. Following an intense affair, she divorced Weekley and eloped with Lawrence in 1914.[41]

Seven years later Lawrence received a letter from Mabel Dodge, an independently wealthy member of the modernist avant-garde who had been married twice and, between husbands, became the lover of radical writer John Reed before shifting her enthusiasm from running a salon for artists and intellectuals in Greenwich Village to roughing it in the more primitive environment of an artists' colony in Taos, near Santa Fe, New Mexico. There she shed her artist (second) husband in favor of Antonio Luhan, a statuesque and laconic Indian from the Taos Pueblo (who was eventually banned from the pueblo because of his liaison with Dodge). They married soon after he built a tipi for himself in the front yard of her rough-hewn but capacious lodging.

Because Luhan admired Lawrence's work, especially *Sea and Sardinia* (1921) at the time, she urged him to visit Taos and find inspiration in the mountainous desert area; she believed he would encounter like-minded souls as well as a natural setting that would suit him. He responded with strong interest but one concern: "Is there a colony of rather dreadful sub-arty people?" Then he promptly dismissed his own anxiety: "Even if there is, it couldn't be worse than Florence."[42]

Early in 1922 the strong-willed Frieda, who shared his curiosity about America in general and Taos in particular, wrote to Mabel Dodge, "We were coming *straight* to you at Taos but now we are not—L says he cant face America *yet*—He does'nt feel strong enough! So we are first going to the East to Ceylon—We have got friends there, two Americans, 'Mayflowerers,' and Buddhists. Strengthened with Buddha, noisy, rampageous America might be easier to tackle."[43] Eventually, of course, this famously peripatetic pair did reach Taos in September 1922, acquired property (later known as the Kiowa Ranch) in 1924 in exchange for the manuscript of *Sons and Lovers* (1913), and then made trips to Mexico, briefly back to England, then Taos once again. Because of poor health, they finally settled in a villa north of Florence in Italy.

Lawrence published *The Plumed Serpent* in 1926 and then *Lady Chatterley's Lover* in 1928, sparking a great scandal and protracted litigation because the latter was deemed obscene. He continued to write all manner of poetry, fiction, and reviews even as his tuberculosis worsened. Following a stint at a sanatorium, he went to Vence, situated in the hills above Nice, in France, and there endured his final illness in 1930, the year he published his last book, titled *The Virgin and the Gypsy*. After his burial in Vence, Frieda returned to Taos to commiserate with her friend and rival Mabel Dodge Luhan. Frieda was soon joined by her new lover, Angelo Ravagli, an Italian artist and artisan who later became her third husband. (He still had a wife in Italy.)[44]

In March 1935 a small group of admirers gathered at Lawrence's grave in Vence. One participant, a journalist for the London *Daily Express*, seems to have been deeply moved by the experience, and a headline in his paper soon announced that it was "The Last Wish of D. H. Lawrence" to be buried on Kiowa Ranch. The article declared, "An Italian friend was sent here by Mrs. Lawrence to exhume the body." The ashes would be placed "in a little temple which has been built by Mrs. Lawrence, Indians, and others who loved her husband," presumably a reference to Mabel.[45] There is no evidence that Lawrence had ever indicated where he wished his final resting place to be, but it seems clear that his most significant survivors, Frieda and Mabel, felt certain that spiritually he truly belonged somewhere near Taos, situated at seven thousand feet above sea level, a serene and mystical place that matched his temperament very well.

Ravagli had indeed built a small concrete chapel there, on a slope above the ranch, and had placed an agricultural wheel over the door to form a rustic kind of faux rose window. What the chapel lacked, of course, was Lawrence's body, so Frieda asked a friend, Earl Brewster, who was in France for other reasons, to help organize the translation. When Frieda learned the cost of transporting an intact body across the Atlantic, however, she decided that bringing his ashes would do just as well. Brewster agreed to supervise the exhumation and cremation, but when the requisite papers did not arrive in time, he informed Ravagli, who made periodic visits to Italy to see his wife, that *he* would have to go to Vence to deal with the difficult situation.[46]

The task became an unnerving challenge. Ravagli needed to deal with both French and American bureaucrats in order to procure the necessary documents, and his French was not much better than his English. Frieda, meanwhile, contracted double pneumonia and was convalescing with friends in Santa Fe when Ravagli and the ashes boarded the *Conte de Savoia* sailing from Marseilles. When he reached New York, U.S. customs officials were reluctant to admit a funerary urn containing human remains as part of the baggage of a tourist who was not an American citizen. So Alfred Stieglitz, the pioneering photographer, patron of modern art, and husband of Georgia O'Keeffe, who had already established her own presence near Santa Fe, interceded with the authorities. Ravagli and his precious cargo then boarded a series of trains and headed for the Southwest.[47]

When the last train on his segmented journey reached Lamy, New Mexico (still the nearest rail station to Santa Fe), Frieda and some friends were eagerly waiting to greet Ravagli after his six-month absence. Only when they had almost reached Santa Fe did they realize (according to legend, at least) that the precious urn had been left behind at the train station. So they returned to retrieve it. (In a different version of this episode, a friend accidentally overturned the urn and refilled it with ashes from a fireplace.) From Santa Fe the party headed for Taos, and once again, at least according to Ravagli, the ashes were left behind and needed to be fetched a few days later.[48]

A friend then warned Frieda that Mabel and Dorothy Brett, yet another woman devoted to Lawrence and his memory, were planning to steal the ashes and scatter them across the desert. Some such plot does seem to have existed. Brett always denied it, but Mabel never did. Brenda Maddox has summarized the situation well: "Mabel never denied her belief that Lawrence's ashes would have been more appropriately scattered to the desert winds than enshrined in a gimcrack chapel which she dubbed 'the Angelino temple.' The fear in the Taos colony was that Ravagli wanted to turn 'the shrine' into a tourist attraction and charge admission; alarm intensified when the local paper carried a public invitation from Frieda for everybody to come to the dedication ceremony at which a Mexican mariachi band would play."[49]

Mabel and Tony Luhan persuaded a local judge *not* to preside over the dedication ceremony. They asked the Indians not to attend as well, but a few showed up anyway and performed a ritual dance around a bonfire in front of the chapel at sunset. Frieda seemed pleased, and she had dealt (in her way) with the possibility of theft by Lawrence worshipers. While Ravagli mixed concrete for the slab that would become the altar of the chapel, she emptied the ashes into the concrete mix. She wrote to Una Jeffers (the wife of poet Robinson Jeffers) in Carmel: "When I remember how I had stood in front of Lawrence's narrow grave [in Vence] and thought Here lies the only thing that really ever was mine, he gave himself body & soul—And this 'my friends' wanted to steal from me. . . . Now I get over it. . . . I wish you had been at the ceremony, it was simple and beautiful."[50]

Would that the story ended there, but rumors and speculation persisted. Stieglitz wrote to Dorothy Brett that after he had helped Ravagli negotiate the hurdles at U.S. customs, he found the ashes in their urn standing outside the door of his American Place art gallery in Manhattan. "I left [sic] them go their natural way," he added enigmatically. "Someday I'll tell you the story. Nothing like it has ever happened. Angelo really has no idea of what did happen." And neither do we. In 1956, after Frieda's death and when Ravagli was about to return to Italy for good, he confessed that Lawrence's ashes had never left France. Fearing that heavy customs duties might be levied on the importation of human remains, he said, he had scattered the ashes in Vence, crossed the Atlantic with an empty urn, and then refilled it with ersatz ashes in New York. As Maddox observed, "If true, it would explain the irreverence with which Frieda and Ravagli kept giggling over, and losing, the sacred dust."[51]

In contrast, one thinks of Nicolas Poussin's beautiful early landscape painting *The Ashes of Phocion Collected by His Widow* (1648), located at the Walker Art Gallery in Liverpool. Phocion was a great Athenian general and statesman (fourth century BCE) who was accused of treason on false charges and forced to drink hemlock. Poussin purports to witness the genuinely grieving widow gathering his ashes in the foreground of the scene—a far cry from the apparent lightheartedness and exuberant behavior of Frieda Lawrence at Taos in 1935.

✦

After the American novelist F. Scott Fitzgerald died in Hollywood in 1940, his burial took place at the Union Cemetery in Rockville, Maryland, a municipal facility located about eight miles north of Washington, DC. (The Fitzgeralds originated as a Maryland family whose most famous member was Francis Scott Key.) The Catholic Church would not allow the lapsed Fitzgerald to be buried in ground under its jurisdiction because he had not attended a Catholic service for many years. When his wife Zelda was killed in a fire at the sanatorium in Asheville, North Carolina, where she had been institutionalized, her remains were then placed next to his despite his scandalous affair in Hollywood with gossip columnist Sheilah Graham. The Fitzgeralds' grave lay sadly neglected for many years, but in 1975 the Women's Club of Rockville decided to spruce it up as a bicentennial project. Members of the Rockville Civic Improvement Advisory Commission also urged that some appropriate action be taken.[52]

Not coincidentally, by 1975 the Fitzgeralds' daughter, Scottie Fitzgerald Smith, felt very strongly that her parents should be reburied in the family plot at the St. Mary's Roman Catholic Church cemetery, also in Rockville, which she regarded as "a quiet oasis in an otherwise turbulent world." Receiving permission from the church and from local government, the move occurred, and the little graveyard that accommodated the newcomers now overlooks one of the busiest intersections in densely populated Montgomery County.[53]

A Fitzgerald scholar, Russell E. Hamill Jr., helped Scottie obtain the necessary permission for disinterment and felt moved that "a daughter's love for her parents stayed the course, steady and true, throughout her life." Because he viewed Scottie Smith's mission as a family homecoming, he attended the reburial with his wife and children on the last Friday in October. The Prayers for Christian Burial recited at the small service came from the novelist's own missal, handed down from his mother and grandmother; it had been printed in 1806. A priest blessed the grave site as three generations of Fitzgeralds listened, and Hamill read a passage from *The Great Gatsby* (1925). Fitzgerald himself had in fact once written, "I wouldn't mind a bit if in a few years Zelda and I could snuggle up together under a stone in some old graveyard here. That is really a happy thought and not melancholy at all." He ultimately achieved that happy thought, albeit too late to enjoy it.[54]

✢

Gutzon Borglum is the American sculptor best remembered because he loved to work in granite on a gigantic scale. Born in Idaho in 1867, he worshiped Abraham Lincoln, as had his Danish immigrant father, and named his own son for the sixteenth president. His equestrian statue of General Philip Sheridan was so successful that castings were placed in Washington, DC, and then Chicago as well (1923). He moved on to a huge commission that would display heroes of the Confederacy on Stone Mountain, Georgia (nominally "finished" in 1923–25); but when his project did not please the United Daughters of the Confederacy, he left it and shifted to his most famous work, the four presidents on Mount Rushmore (1926–39).

When Borglum died suddenly in 1939 with his masterpiece not quite completed, the secretary to the Mount Rushmore Commission immediately asked Secretary of the Interior Harold Ickes whether he had any objection to the construction of a crypt "of a design approved by the Park Service and the Commission at an unobtrusive spot in the mountain." Although this would have been undertaken entirely with private funds and the park encompassed eighteen hundred acres with plenty of space to accommodate a crypt for the larger-than-life sculptor, Ickes and his staff strongly opposed the suggestion, explaining that burying a private citizen (even with legitimate professional and personal ties to the site) was contrary to established policy and would lead to countless requests for private burials in federal park areas.[55]

Despite National Park Service opposition, a congressman introduced a bill providing for Borglum's interment on the site of his best-known work. It passed, and President Roosevelt signed it. When private funds were not forthcoming, Congress passed a second bill in 1943; but no crypt was ever funded. Meanwhile, well before his death Borglum had extracted a promise from his son, Lincoln, that he would be buried amongst a plenitude of flowers in California. So he was eventually laid to rest in Forest Lawn Memorial Park Cemetery in Glendale, where a court of honor bears an inscription composed by his lifelong friend, Rupert Hughes. Borglum's son, the key survivor in this case, had honored his father's request, but apparently with reluctance. He, too, had wanted that honorific crypt beneath the presidents, facing the brilliant southern sun.[56]

✣

For an intriguing instance of total domination by the survivor who mattered most in terms of willpower, consider the fascinating case of Frank Lloyd Wright, born in April 1869 to a Welsh family in Richland Center, Wisconsin, not far from Madison. He became one of the most celebrated and distinctively American architects, having pioneered the low-lying Prairie Style and then proceeded to design many other types of structures, residential and public, always exploring the newest technologies to reconceive and reshape the built environment. He conceived the affordable Usonian house for ordinary Americans during the Depression, then the spectacular home he called "Fallingwater" near Pittsburgh for the Kaufmann family, later the extraordinary Johnson Wax administration building in Racine, Wisconsin, and finally the Solomon Guggenheim Museum in Manhattan. These all continue to be celebrated among his many masterpieces. Wright also created the Taliesin Fellowship as a community for his family, student-apprentices, and disciples, first in Wisconsin early in the 1930s and then Taliesin West near Scottsdale, Arizona, completed as a winter home seven years later.[57]

When Wright died in his ninetieth year in April 1959, a burial precedent was followed. Just as he had done almost half a century earlier after his mistress, Mamah Borthwick, was killed by a crazed servant, Wright's coffin was placed on a flower-strewn farm wagon drawn by a sturdy pair of horses (fig. 34). With forty-some family members and friends walking behind it, the wagon proceeded to the modest family burying ground at the foot of a hill a few hundred yards from Taliesin East. Under the supervision of his strong-willed third wife, Olgivanna, he was interred not far from the bodies of his mother and Mamah. For the next twenty-six years Olgivanna presided over the ongoing Taliesin Fellowship and studios, but primarily in Arizona, where she reigned like a queen bee.[58]

The writer Brendan Gill knew the Wrights and visited Taliesin West with some frequency. His account of the last Easter party that he

Figure 34. The cortége of Frank Lloyd Wright at Taliesin East, April 1959. From Brendan Gill, *Many Masks: A Life of Frank Lloyd Wright* (New York: G. P. Putnam's, 1987), 500. *Milwaukee Journal* photo from 1959.

attended, in 1984, provides a memorable vision of the elaborate festivities and high jinks that went on, but also a vivid portrait of the domineering woman who survived Wright and determined the fate of his earthly remains.

> Although Olgivanna was in her late eighties and almost totally deaf and blind, in her indomitable fashion she pretended to hear and see as well as ever. Under a hat broad-brimmed to ward off the sun and in a garb that may have owed something to Montenegro and certainly owed much to her imagination, she sat with me at lunch, smiling, dark-eyed, and handsome. As we chatted, I sensed her determination to preside with a show of undiminished strength and grace over a springtime ritual that now after almost half a century, was being gently wrested from her grasp. She had served as the priestess of a shrine whose god had steadily gained in puissance over the years; now she was failing, now against her will she was slipping away . . . but the god remained.[59]

She had kept Wright's spell and will alive by dominating the fellowship and the Frank Lloyd Wright Foundation, maintaining the two Taliesins more or less intact both physically and spiritually. Olgivanna had one last card to play, and she took the trick, thereby stunning a great many of her late husband's family, friends, and followers. When she died in Scottsdale on March 1, 1985, the only person with her was

Wright's former physician, who then called a meeting of the fellowship and informed them of her dying wish: that she, her late husband, and her daughter by her first marriage should all be cremated, with Wright himself removed to Taliesin West, where a special garden would be built, dedicated to all three, and their ashes mingled together. The wish did not appear in her will, and many felt that it had been a last-minute whim. But the remaining entourage at Taliesin, which had dwindled, lacked the will to defy Olgivanna's heart's desire—except for the inclusion of her own daughter. That demand was unequivocally set aside.[60]

Anticipating that there would be opposition to the exhumation, foundation officers moved secretly and quickly. They obtained the requisite approval from Iovanna Wright, the only child that Frank and Olgivanna had together, and from a coroner who also pledged his secrecy. Wright's body was exhumed in Wisconsin and cremated on March 25. When a local newspaper editor learned of it in Madison, too late, the hue and cry began. Iovanna remarked to one family member, "Daddy gets cold up there in Wisconsin." The relative added ruefully, "When Olgivanna told you to do something, you did it." Within a week Wright's ashes were taken to Scottsdale. It took several years to complete the memorial garden and surrounding wall overlooking Paradise Valley in which the ashes of FLW and Olgivanna would be "immured" together; but the story and attendant storm broke quickly in early April, on the twenty-sixth anniversary of Wright's death. It prompted an uproar among family members and some former students, associates, and architects around the country. Disbelief and anger were widespread.[61]

A former Wright apprentice who had researched Wright's wills for a book declared that he found no clear indication of where the architect wished to be buried. Yet he proclaimed his disappointment in no uncertain terms. "This is an example of their [the foundation's] insensitivity and of Mrs. Wright's arrogance because what they have done is overrule Mr. Wright's wishes. I feel that it was almost a sacrilegious act. It was an obscene thing to do to any person." Enraged family members agreed because they felt certain that *they* knew what Wright wanted. One of Wright's sons by his first wife, a retired antitrust lawyer in Washington, called the move "an act of vandalism." He insisted that his father *had* indicated that he wanted to be buried in the cemetery outside of Spring Green because that had been the family burying ground since 1886.[62]

A few family members acknowledged that they at least understood why Olgivanna, his soulmate for thirty-four years, had wanted their bodies to be mingled in death. The actress Anne Baxter, one of Wright's granddaughters, called the grave opening "painfully absurd" but added that "he may be laughing for all we know because his spirit is much bigger than his bones." A managing trustee of the Wright Foundation insisted that the request had not been a last-minute whim. "Mrs. Wright had been talking to many people about doing it for quite a few years," he contended. That is certainly possible, but precious few of those "many people" seem to have come forward in support of the statement.[63]

Karl E. Meyer, a historian of art and archaeology and author of *The Plundered Past* (1973), wrote an editorial for the *New York Times* noting that the remains had been "exhumed and stealthily transported to Arizona. To a Wisconsinite, that is equivalent to uprooting Jefferson from Monticello for reburial in Beverly Hills." Meyer acknowledged that while Wright lived his native state gave him no official commissions and that Madison voted down his project for a splendid civic center on Lake Monona (a decision it later reversed).[64] Nonetheless, he continued, "there is something sad and unfair about Wisconsin's losing yet more to the Sun Belt, where much of its industry has already fled. Frank Lloyd Wright belonged to the Middle West, and once wrote of its weather, 'The lightning in this region, always so crushing and severe, crashed and Taliesin smiled.' They will need a strong wall to contain that spirit amid the retirement condominiums in Paradise Valley."[65] Once again a willfully potent survivor had gotten her way, and in her case defied many others in order to do so.

✳

Less sensational (and somewhat less controversial) variations on that saga continue to occur right up to the present, of course. I shall close this chapter with two examples: one involving a noncelebrity family—ordinary folks, to whom these things also happen—and then a quite recent episode concerning a famous artist and his family.

The following was recounted in the *Washington Post* as a human interest story by a survivor with a very different situation and a less domineering temperament than Olgivanna Wright's. In 1989 an elderly woman in West Virginia called her granddaughter living in a New York

City suburb and said, "I want him to come home at last." She plaintively sought family permission to exhume her eldest son's remains from where he had died two decades earlier, of a brain aneurism that burst without warning when he was only thirty-four. The grandmother's voice was soft and trembling because she called from a nursing home where she was recovering from a stroke, and from the exhaustion of caring for her long-ailing husband, who lay in a bed next to her in a room that they shared. "We want to be ready," she said, and the grand-daughter had no need to ask, "Ready for what?" Ready for when they died and were laid to rest themselves. "I think for a while after we have hung up. I will do what she asks, but for my reasons. And I have only one. I do not remember the last time I said good night to my father." Having been only five when her father died, she wanted to put some difficult memories that she did not really trust behind her and thereby put the past to rest.[66]

Contacts with her father's parents had diminished over time. There may have been some acrimony between them and her mother—she couldn't quite be sure. "Such an unexpected death either yields close-ness or a desperate need to get as far away as possible from reminders of the pain." Her mother had remarried some time ago. Her older brother had recently become a doctor, and her younger brother was studying to be a lawyer. The grandparents had long been very remote, but her father seemed to belong more to them than to her, because her memories of him were so elusive. The ones that she did have she felt she had been told about, so that they were not even really her own memories. They were borrowed, or linked to some photographs that had been explained to her once upon a time, long ago.

So she began the complicated process of gathering and notarizing the necessary documentation to exhume her father's remains from the Cemetery of the Holy Rood in Westbury, New York. There were various forms and affidavits with numerous lines to be signed. Then there was the problematic stone monument atop the grave. It needed to be moved, and the cemetery didn't do that. What about the plot? Did the family want to sell it? The cemetery would pay only the price paid in 1968, even though that space now cost far more. She learned a great deal about disinterment. She was told that the exhumation could not be done in the summer months because of the heat. She discovered how expensive it is to move a body. And then there is the final paper to which every family member must give consent. The grandmother resisted repeatedly and perversely, despite her own initiative in the matter. "Why? Why? Why?" she asked. "It was hard enough to live through it the first time." Finally she relented. "I guess it's time to close that chapter for all of us," she quietly conceded, and signed.[67]

Visits to the nursing home in West Virginia followed, with stories told about her father as a boy, an adolescent, a student, a young man. She came to appreciate the father she never really knew. An unexpected closeness developed as the family history unfolded, sometimes with repetition, sometimes with variations on a theme. Meanwhile they all had to wait until the state regulatory agency "spits out its approval of our wishes. It will be around late fall by the time he's cremated and brought here, to be buried again with the first of his parents to die. That must be comforting to them, I think, that someone will be there when they leave the earth. And I feel more at peace too." The granddaughter still had one more "duty of my own," a visit to view the new cemetery. She did so, saw the lush landscape, the brilliant blue sky above the meadow and the mountain. She felt glad that she had come and had complied with her grandmother's request, despite all the complications. "Soon we will bring him here forever, home at last. I will say goodbye then, and remember it as long as I can."[68]

✠

Mark Rothko, the celebrated abstract expressionist painter, was born in Latvia in 1903 but came to New York at an early age. He endured years of penury but persisted stubbornly until he found his own distinctive style in the 1940s: large horizontal blocks of paint, one layer misting into another so that they must be viewed carefully and closely to appreciate the nuances of color—red melting into orange, for example, or overlapping green and blue tones that are related yet offsetting. By the time Rothko committed suicide in 1970, following years of depression, the value of his art had escalated, and it continues to do so today. A famous trial occurred, prolonged for more than a decade, after his children's guardians accused his three executors of selling works to the Marlborough Gallery in New York for less than market value while collecting exorbitant commissions and dividing the proceeds. In 1975 the executors were found guilty of negligence and conflict of interest, removed from their positions of trust, and fined, along with Marlborough, the sum of $9.2 million.[69]

When Rothko died he had been buried in a plot belonging to Theodore Stamos at East Marion, New York. Stamos was also an abstract expressionist, a close friend, and subsequently one of the three executors. East Marion is a small village nestled between Greenport and Orient Point on the North Fork of Long Island. In 2007 the artist's daughter and son petitioned the Supreme Court of the State of New York to make it possible to have their father's remains disinterred and reburied at a Jewish cemetery in Westchester County. The first request met with resistance from the owner of the initial burial plot, Stamos's sister. It was also upsetting to many of the residents of East Marion. As the secretary-treasurer of the East Marion Cemetery Association acknowledged, "He's our only notable person." She added, "There's quite an artistic community out here. And when this first started, people who knew who he was were quite alarmed that this was being contemplated."[70] Each side could have considered a line from Shakespeare's *Twelfth Night*: "Is there no respect of place, persons, nor time, in you?" (2.3.100).

Nonetheless, in March 2007 the cemetery association's board voted with one dissent to allow the exhumation. To protect itself against community wrath, however, board members decided to require Rothko's daughter to obtain a court order permitting removal of the remains. The two children (long since adults and both professional people) also sought to exhume their mother, estranged from the artist, who had died six months after their father and was buried at Knollwood Cemetery and Mausoleum in Cleveland. Their objective was to reinter her body with Rothko's in Kensico Cemetery in Valhalla, New York. The key document reads: "Petitioners have long wished to reunite their parents in a final resting place consistent with their parents' wishes and Mark Rothko's Jewish faith."[71]

On April 10, 2008, Justice Arthur G. Pitts of the State Supreme Court in Riverhead agreed to the Rothko family request. He noted that even before the petition was filed in 2007, the sister of Theodore Stamos (who died in Greece) had consented in writing to the proposed removal and reinterment. The fact that she wished to reconsider a year later was dismissed as irrelevant. "Although the Court has received numerous letters regarding the instant petition, no party has sought to intervene and the application must be deemed unopposed," the judge ruled. Nancy Poole, secretary-treasurer of the East Marion Cemetery Association, commented in response: "I think we really lost a piece of history here. A lot of people are going to be pretty miserable about it."[72] Those who maintain cemeteries cannot readily tolerate the premature departure of celebrities—even dead ones who never lived nearby.

Once more, the closest survivors eventually won out, even though in this instance, yet again, the wishes of each estranged parent remain unclear. In the absence of successful spiritualism or necromancy, instructions from beyond the grave are difficult to receive—or to decipher when one believes that they have actually been received.

✠

The deaths discussed in this chapter span the years from Boone's demise in 1820 until Rothko's in 1970, and their reburials from 1845 until 2008. Although the conflicts shifted from being highly public and political in Boone's case to far more personal in Rothko's, the pride-of-place issue persisted. The cemetery in East Marion, New York, did not want to give up its one illustrious figure any more than Missouri wanted to lose the luster associated with Boone's appealing legend. Much more than in the episodes in previous chapters, persuasive and immediate survivors of the famous figures here felt fiercely determined to control where the deceased would ultimately repose, fighting off the wishes of admirers in the case of D. H. Lawrence and disciples in that of Frank Lloyd Wright. Uncertainties about finding or possessing the "right" remains continued to be problematic. We have no more assurance that Boone's bones are really buried in Frankfort than we do that Lawrence's ashes actually made it to Taos.

By now the reader will surely have noticed the virtual absence of famous reburied women. For the most part, female reburials occurred when a dead spouse was relocated alongside her husband or else was reunited with a husband in cases where their original graves were sadly situated in different places, as with the wives of Rothko and Poe. There has been an exception, however, in the case of female missionaries, and we consider that situation next in the context of others involving religious figures.

— FIVE —

Disinterred by Devotion

RELIGION, RACE, AND SPIRITUAL REPOSE

I would rather sleep in the southern corner of a little country churchyard, than in the tomb of the Capulets. I should like, however, that my dust should mingle with kindred dust. The good old expression, "Family burying-ground," has something pleasing in it, at least to me.

✠ Edmund Burke to Michael Smith, c. 1750

*T*he American past provides numerous instances of reburial for which the word *enshrinement* is appropriate because they actually involved men of the cloth or laypersons deemed inspirational, in some cases missionaries who were not ordained but believed that they were doing the Lord's work. In certain situations the figures involved were entirely secular, yet their devoted followers felt that they deserved the kind of respect, even veneration, due the founder of a cause, or else the deceased was someone who had achieved an unusual "first" that had not been suitably recognized at the time of death, often owing to racial prejudice. Intense feelings about religion and race have sparked some of the most heated disputes about where people should be buried.

There is also the persistent issue of Native American burials as well as Indian remains belonging to museums and other public institutions. In those cases we encounter feelings similar to those aroused by heroes of the Revolutionary generation, but with a spiritual dimension added. Not only had many Indian chiefs not been interred in the most suitable places, but native religion *required* that they be moved to soil where their descendants could perform the requisite tribal rites. Just as we have seen with the founding Anglo-American generation from the later eighteenth century, sometimes two groups of Native Americans could not agree on which venue was the optimal or the most appropriate one. At times these conflicts even prompted attempts to steal the remains—the most famous figure in that regard being the great Sioux chief Sitting Bull.

✛

George Whitefield arrived in America from England in the later 1730s and became a pivotal figure in the Great Awakening, a broadly based religious revival that pulsed vibrantly in the North American colonies for a full generation. Whitefield emerged as the most widely known among all the notable itinerant preachers, and as a member of the Church of England who anticipated Methodism, he offered an ecumenical message that appealed to men and women of many denominations. Late in September 1770 his travels took him to Newburyport, Massachusetts, where ill-health and physical exhaustion caused his sudden death at age fifty-nine. As the news of his demise spread quickly, a spirited controversy arose over the question of where he should be buried. Because of his fame, it mattered very much, especially since he had no special relationship to Newburyport, where fate had left him almost at random. Eminent figures from Boston wanted him buried there because they perceived their city as the capital of American Calvinism. Portsmouth, New Hampshire, hoped that offering a fine new tomb "hew'd out of a rock" might bring him permanently there; even distant Georgia, where Whitefield had established an orphanage, sought his remains, and the colonial legislature appropriated money for that purpose.[1]

A friend of Whitefield for at least a decade, the Reverend Jonathan Parsons of Newburyport, along with his Presbyterian deacons and local residents, categorically refused to relinquish the body. Immediately following Whitefield's death they began to prepare the vault beneath the main level of their meetinghouse. When the offer arrived from Portsmouth, they responded that Whitefield's body was "not fit to be removed," which seemed to imply a rapid decomposition of the corpse, but that turns out not to have been the case at all. There is no indication that the dying man had expressed any desire to be buried at Newburyport, and one account suggests that he clearly did *not* wish to be. Various communities continued to vie with intensity for the honor of his entombment. He was, after all, the most famous evangelist in British North America.[2]

Whitefield's actual funeral, however, sparked much less controversy. The Reverend Parsons sent invitations to several external ministers requesting their participation. On October 2, 1770, six clergymen served as pallbearers for the procession, which stretched one full mile in length, with Parsons and his family walking immediately behind the coffin to make sure that nothing untoward happened. Mourners sang and wept during the hymns. Following the service they watched as the bier descended into the brick-lined vault. A brief prayer there concluded the service. Estimates vary, but as many as ten thousand worshipers attended the funeral in and around the meetinghouse. They came from near and far.[3]

The burial service itself had been similar to that for most clergymen; what made Whitefield's unusual was the amount of ongoing attention that people paid to the body and the tomb *afterward.* The immediate result was an outpouring of elegiac poems and hymns that highlighted themes of death, burial, but above all salvation, the distinctive aspect of such funeral rites at the time. Few of those tracts are at all memorable, but the most popular bore a hymn that Whitefield himself had composed to be sung over his own body. (He had not expected it would be put to use quite so soon.) Printers often decorated the black-bordered sheets on which these funereal poems and hymns were printed with a crude etching that depicted Whitefield lying on top of a coffin. No other preacher of that generation seems to have elicited the same degree of popular reverence, verging upon fetishism.[4]

Because Whitefield had been interred in a vault within the church rather than buried beneath the earth, people could view the body upon request. The first major viewing occurred in 1775, when the invasion force authorized by the Continental Congress to attack Montreal and Quebec headed north on its appointed mission. At the conclusion of a special service held at Newburyport on September 17, several officers, including Benedict Arnold and Daniel Morgan, approached the sexton with a request: they wanted to enter the burial vault and view the remains. When the sexton did not object, a small group descended below the Communion table, opened the door to the vault, and entered the chamber. The sexton pried open the lid of the coffin, and the group gazed at the fully clothed corpse. Bending over the body, officers cut away parts of the preacher's collar and his wristbands, which they snipped into smaller pieces to distribute among themselves as they departed for Canada—ecclesiastical relics for good fortune on the long journey ahead and in battle.[5]

That created a kind of precedent for subsequent and well-documented episodes when ministers and lay folk entered the vault to view the remains. In 1784 a Mr. Brown from England received permission to do so, having heard from friends that the body remained undecayed—a condition often regarded as an indication of sanctity. Brown wrote in the *Christian Magazine* in 1790 that the body was "perfect" aside from its discolored flesh, adding that "the skin immediately rose after I had touched it." If indeed Whitefield had remained in such a prime condition for two decades, it did not endure much longer. In 1796 a Newburyport resident and several companions opened the coffin to find the "flesh totally consumed."[6]

Lurid fascination with and reverence toward the tomb (along with pride of possession) persisted for generations. In 1829 the Reverend Dr. Proudfit received on behalf of the church the gift of a cenotaph from a prominent Newburyport merchant. The monument contained a description of Whitefield's ministry, which of course included information about how well prepared the tomb had been and an account of the rites performed in 1770 (fig. 35). In that same year, 1829, church fathers re-

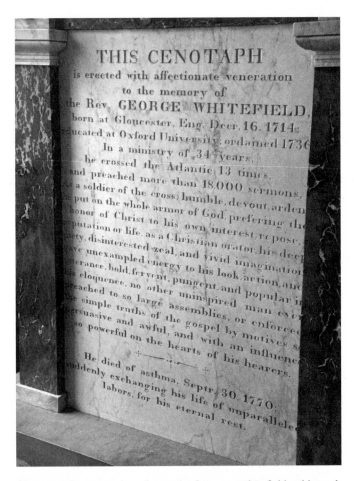

Figure 35. The cenotaph at the tomb of George Whitefield, Old South Presbyterian Church, Newburyport, Massachusetts. Photograph courtesy of Darryl Dash.

Figure 36. The open vault of George Whitefield's tomb, Old South Presbyterian Church, Newburyport, Massachusetts. Photograph courtesy of Robert E. Marshall.

moved the remains from their original coffin and placed them in a new mahogany version within a redone brick-lined vault—all part of a major renovation of the building. Proudfit actually conceived a grandiose plan to construct a "monumental temple" to honor Whitefield, but sufficient encouragement and adequate funds were not forthcoming—foreshadowing the fate of the temple envisioned for Jefferson Davis in New Orleans two generations later. By the close of the nineteenth century, however, visitors to the tomb could view Whitefield's remains in a coffin with a glass lid, as a gas-lit lamp illuminated the chamber. A cast of Whitefield's skull could also be seen in the interior of the vault (fig. 36).[7]

In 1835 a deputation of British Baptists arrived in Newburyport to see "our never to be forgotten evangelist." Once inside the vault, two ministers sat on top of adjacent coffins and peered into the open casket that was the object of their pilgrimage. As others had done and would continue to do, they took Whitefield's skull in their hands and contemplated it as they discussed his inspiring ministry. Another visiting clergyman from England who did exactly the same thing a year earlier had remarked that "more care should be taken to preserve these remains and less freedom used in exhibition of them."[8] As we have already seen, skulls retained their peculiar appeal as cynosures of greatness or notoriety—not to mention a sense of intimate connectedness between the quick and the dead.

Many of Whitefield's English admirers hoped that someday his bones would be brought home for burial in his native land. That would never be possible given the possessiveness and local pride of the church fondly known as Old South in Newburyport. But an English devotee, a Mr. Bolton, hoped for a small memento of the revered minister. In 1829 an unnamed friend of his made the pilgrimage to Massachusetts, gained access to the open casket, and stole Whitefield's right arm bone. According to one account, he had bribed the sexton's son, who permitted him to remove the bone unobserved, and he then shipped it in a tidy parcel to Great Britain. Needless to say, discovery of the missing member shocked the congregation and the town. It is said that Mr. Bolton was horrified when the bone reached his home, calling the robbery a "sacrilegious act." Nevertheless, he chose to keep the relic until 1849, when a new minister at the church received a package containing the missing piece along with a note attesting to the "genuineness of the restoration." The borrowed bone was replaced in the new coffin as part of a solemn ceremony "witnessed" at various removes by two thousand people. Not only did the bone get resituated in its original position, but the "little box" in which the relic had been shipped now adorned the coffin itself as an indication that integrity had triumphed.[9]

Because Methodism was a new denomination at the close of the eighteenth century, and because Whitefield was recognized as a close second to John Wesley, the English founder, Methodists also had special cause to come to Newburyport as pilgrims. Jason Lee, the first Methodist circuit rider in New England and later the founder of a Methodist mission to Oregon, was one of them. (His own reburial account lies just ahead.) After Francis Asbury, the tireless itinerant and founder of American Methodism, died in Spottsylvania, Virginia, in March 1816, his followers disinterred his body from a family cemetery six weeks later and transferred it to the Eutaw Street Church in Baltimore, where a huge public procession, much larger than Whitefield's in 1770, escorted the remains to a new vault beneath the pulpit. In 1854 Methodists removed Asbury yet again, along with two other early leaders, to Mount Olivet Cemetery, a burial ground "exclusively devoted to the Methodists."[10]

By the 1920s and '30s, visitation to Whitefield's tomb had declined; people continued to come, but they now paid a fee for admission to the vault. Commercial tourism and curiosity had caught up with religiosity. By the 1930s guidebooks to Massachusetts and New England barely mentioned the tomb, however, and in 1933 the church covered the coffin with slate tiles. The skeleton that had been so casually displayed for a century and a half was no longer visible. *Sic transit gloria mundi.*[11]

✠

American feelings about the nature and circumstances of physical remains would undergo notable changes during the course of the nineteenth century and into the twentieth. Essentially, the physical condition of a deceased person's body mattered more intensely to people during the first two-thirds of the nineteenth century than later, largely for inconsistently observed religious reasons rooted in traditional Protestantism—though not to the extent we might have expected. At a special moment in time, the second coming of Jesus Christ to earth, corpses (or what was left of them) were to be miraculously reconstituted and reunited with their previously disembodied souls. Gary Laderman explains this doctrine thus: "In spite of natural laws that had ordained bodily disintegration, God had the power to restore life to the dead and 'awaken' the body from its lifeless state."[12]

Nevertheless, the physical condition of a body at the time of burial was believed to matter very much indeed, and that provides one of the reasons that the deceased were normally viewed just prior to interment. Seeing the corpse meant more than extending a mournful farewell. Close inspection was coupled with due respect, and on more than one occasion respect suffered as a consequence of inspection carried to excess. L. M. Sargent, a Boston "sexton of the old school," remarked that the desire to scrutinize bodily decay—he called it a "morbid desire"—was especially prevalent among women; some even wanted to descend into tombs, lift the coffin lid, and "gaze upon the mouldering bones" of their parent or child. Sargent described the poignant intensity of a "female gaze," quite different from what we now mean by the male gaze. According to Laderman, however, this was by no means an exclusively female propensity. The need to contemplate (or even cut) locks of hair, and simply be with the deceased, "to sustain the last look, and to monitor early stages of decomposition—particularly of close relations—expressed a need for maintaining physical proximity and resisting the finality that comes with bodily disintegration."[13]

Gradually, over the course of time, sentiments concerning the *soul* of a loved one became considerably more important than concerns about bodily condition. When the latter came to be deemphasized during the later nineteenth century, decomposition caused less anxiety and watchfulness than before. What mattered most by the later Victorian period was the condition of the spirit at death, rather than the actual body. This shift involved more than changing theological emphases. A growing concern about infectious diseases, and especially about how readily cholera or smallpox might be spread, played a part. When exhumations occurred they prompted unease about the possibility of disease and contagion. For the same reason, burial directly beneath church sanctuaries began to meet with disapproval. Even burial out of doors in vaults became increasingly worrisome to many because of the odors that often emanated from such structures, making memorial visits to churchyards and cemeteries unpleasant. As a growing acceptance of the natural process of decay developed, arguments on behalf of prompt burials beneath the earth became more common. Bodies no longer lingered in open coffins for extended viewing in the parlors of people's homes.[14]

✛

In 1860 some local antiquarians in Providence, Rhode Island, decided that the time had come (actually, was long overdue) to remedy a lamentable oversight in that state's history: locating the burial site of Roger Williams, founder of the colony, precursor of the Baptist denomination in America, "the first theologian on this earth who ever theoretically advocated the separation of 'Church and State,' and the first statesman who practically established religious freedom as the constitutional basis of civil government." Members of the community intended to erect a monument above his "neglected ashes." When Williams died in 1683, however, he was buried on his own "plantation" (meaning home lot) without any marker ("not even a rough stone"), and hence "recourse must now [in 1860] be had to traditionary testimony which is fast disappearing."[15]

In 1771 a special committee had been appointed by the freemen of Providence to ascertain the burial spot and to draft an inscription for a monument that they intended to erect over the grave of the "Founder of this Town and Colony . . . but the troubles of the revolutionary war, which ensued, prevented any active exertions for ascertaining the exact spot, and for erecting thereon the proposed monument." The author of the 1860 narrative of a renewed search was born close to the spring where Williams lived and died. He undertook an extended inquiry into local traditions that might prove helpful. He had called upon Moses Brown prior to the latter's death in 1836 at the age of ninety-eight, and learned that a specific burial lot had always been considered the one used by the Williams family "but that his [actual] grave was unknown."[16]

Acknowledging that the pursuit of his quarry would hinge upon slender evidence, Zachariah Allen examined old newspaper accounts and interviewed various people who had known descendants of Roger Williams and could provide clues based upon family lore. Although acknowledging that Williams's grave had been "leveled many years with the surrounding graveyard," Allen learned from a letter that a woman who died at the age of eighty in 1855 had as a child "often visited the grave" of Roger Williams with her father, who in turn in early boyhood had been put into the grave next to it by his father. How and why? Some unspecified time earlier, in digging another grave for a new interment, "the spade man came upon the bones of Williams, being portions of his lower extremities. Many of the inhabitants gathered to see the bones of the Founder of Rhode Island, and her grandfather among them; who, actuated by a singular whim, lowered, his little son, her father, into the grave, probably thinking that the act would make an indelible impression of the discovery upon his son's memory." I should think that it very well might. Kids just love being lowered into graves![17]

Given such "helpful" clues about the proper site, on the first day of spring in 1860 Allen, with two gentlemen as witnesses and two "experienced superintendents of the public burial grounds," carefully directed excavation research. With no apparent doubt that they were working in just the right spot, they took "the utmost care . . . in scraping away the earth from the grave of Roger Williams. Not a vestige of any bone was discoverable, not even of the lime dust which usually remains after the gelatinous part of the bone is decomposed." Next to Williams's purported grave they found another that they assumed to be his wife's because they found one lock of braided hair, "being the sole remaining human relic."[18]

Then came the most remarkable revelation of all, the discovery of the root structure of an ancient apple tree that had the supernatural prescience to function like a divining rod.

> This tree had pushed downwards one of its main roots in a sloping direction and nearly straight course towards the precise spot that had been occupied by the skull of Roger Williams. There making a turn conforming with its circumference, the root followed the direction of the back bone to the hips, and thence divided into two branches, each one following a leg bone to the heel, where they both turned upwards to the extremities of the toes of the skeleton. One of the roots formed a slight crook at the part occupied by the knee joint, thus producing an increased resemblance to the outlines of the skeleton of Roger Williams, as if, indeed, moulded thereto by the powers of vegetable life.[19]

Mother Nature had provided nothing less than a precise outline of the very spot where Williams had slumbered for 177 years (fig. 37). Instead of lauding the apple tree as a sacred plant that had last touched the founder and guided their quest, however, Allen and his colleagues called it a "thief . . . for it had been caught in the act of robbing a grave and of appropriating its contents to its own use, re-incorporating them into its living trunk and branches." The tree had selfishly garnished Williams's remains for its own nourishment. Quite an unnatural act for a perfectly natural culprit.[20]

What purportedly remained of Williams and his wife was then moved to the tomb of a descendant in the North Burial Ground for interment. Finally, in 1936 those scant seventeenth-century fragments were put in a bronze container and placed beneath the base of a monument in Prospect Terrace Park in Providence. The infamous "Williams root" can now be seen in the collections of the Rhode Island Historical Society, where it is mounted on a panel in the basement of the John Brown House Museum. Family traditions are not always reliable, but sometimes they offer the only clues available. Some people prefer to have venerable memories as guidelines—even ones that defy credibility—than mere guesswork or nothing at all. A Roger Williams National Memorial was established in 1965 at a city park on the southern edge of Providence. His memory and significance live on in historical studies, of course, especially those devoted to works concerned with church-state

Figure 37. Roger Williams's Apple Tree Root. Providence, Rhode Island, March 22, 1860. Wood. Courtesy of the Rhode Island Historical Society (RHi X3 2943).

relations in America. One might even say that he enjoys a certain root-edness in the American canon.[21]

✛

Early Protestant missionaries to the Pacific Northwest have also figured prominently in narratives of exhumation and reburial, though in quite different ways from the Williams saga. Although Williams most certainly deserves to be considered a missionary himself, among his other leadership roles, the essence of his life involves a critical chapter in the history of civil religion. Those that follow are dramatic markers in American westward expansion and the belief in divine if not manifest destiny along with the persistent commitment to proselytize on behalf of Protestant Christianity.

Marcus Whitman (1802–47), trained in New York as a physician, applied to the American Board of Commissioners for Foreign Missions to go west in order to educate and Christianize Native Americans in an area still disputed between the United States and Great Britain. Because the board accepted only married couples, Whitman decided in 1835 to join the Ithaca-based missionary Samuel Parker, who raised the requisite funds among Presbyterians, and went to what became northwest Montana and Idaho in order to minister to bands of the Flathead and Nez Percé peoples. Upon his return the following year, Whitman heeded a renewed call from the ABCFM, which required wedded missionaries, and therefore married Narcissa Prentiss of western New York (almost sight unseen), a teacher of physics and chemistry who had been roused by the Second Great Awakening and also felt a call to undertake missionary work. In May 1836 the Whitmans joined a caravan of fur traders and headed west, led by a group of experienced mountain men. Narcissa Whitman and Eliza Spalding became the first European American women to cross the Rocky Mountains.[22]

The Whitmans established several new missions in the Walla Walla valley and settled at Waiilatpu, a word meaning "place of the rye grass" in the Cayuse language. There they farmed, he provided medical care, and she devoted herself to schooling for the native groups. In 1843 Marcus returned east and gathered and then led a large group of wagon trains westward from Fort Hall in eastern Idaho. Later coming to be known as the Great Emigration, this undertaking would establish the viability of the Oregon Trail for subsequent American homesteaders. But the large influx of newcomers brought unwelcome diseases to which the Indians were especially vulnerable, including a severe epidemic of measles in 1847. Indians customarily held medicine men responsible for medical crises. Consequently, on November 29, 1847, Cayuse tribal members murdered the Whitmans in their home along with twelve other whites. Most of the missionary buildings in what would soon become the Oregon Territory were destroyed as well.

By the 1860s, however, Walla Walla began to grow rapidly and money was raised to fulfill Marcus Whitman's dream of establishing a seminary in the vicinity of Waiilatpu. It began in 1866 as a private elementary school, added courses, and a few years later became Whitman Academy. By 1882 it had come under the sponsorship of the Congregational Education Society and was renamed Whitman College on what would have been Whitman's eightieth birthday. Although a modest monument had been put up following the Whitmans' burial early in 1848, a movement got under way late in the 1880s to erect a much grander one. Fundraising based in Portland did not go well at first, but the Whitman Monument Association, formed in March 1897, largely by residents of Walla Walla, fulfilled the dream as the fiftieth anniversary of the Whitmans' death approached.[23]

The Monument Association obtained title to eight acres of land that included the original mission cemetery with the large grave containing all of the massacre victims, as well as a hill more than one hundred feet high that rises adjacent to the cemetery. The total cost of the land and the elaborate memorial stones envisioned by the Association came to about twenty-five hundred dollars. Members erected a granite shaft on top of the hill, eighteen feet high and tapering at the top, square at the base and standing on a pedestal nine feet high with the name Whitman carved boldly on one side (fig. 38). There were also plans to set a memorial slab of Vermont marble over the large grave site. After the granite and marble stones arrived, the remains of all fourteen victims were placed in a large metal casket and reburied on January 29, 1898, basically at the same site where they had been placed by the Oregon militia volunteers half a century before. The names of all fourteen were inscribed on the huge marble slab, which is eleven feet long.[24]

When the remains were exhumed on October 22, 1897, only five skulls and some bones were found beneath the overturned wagon box that the volunteers had used as a temporary covering half a century before. Marcus Whitman's skull was readily identified by the gold filling in a posterior molar tooth. Because there was only one woman's skull among the five, it was presumed to be Narcissa's. To everyone's horror, however, it was discovered that both skulls had been sawed in half, most likely using Dr. Whitman's surgical saw, "the cut commencing at the nasal bones and extending back to the seat of the back wound. . . . The sawing was done unskillfully, probably when the body was lying on the ground face

Figure 38. The Whitman Monument (and "Great Grave") at Waiilaptu, Whitman Mission National Historic Site, Walla Walla, Washington. From Clifford M. Drury, *Marcus and Narcissa Whitman* (Glendale, Calif.: Arthur H. Clark, 1973). Courtesy of National Park Service– Whitman Mission National Historic Site.

upward." Various explanations were offered as to what had happened and why. The most plausible is that the deed was done by Joe Lewis, a man of mixed race who was known to have harbored deep grudges against both Whitmans and played a leading role in plotting their deaths.[25]

At the approach of the 1936 centennial of the arrival of the Whitman-Spalding mission in what became Oregon Territory (comprising both the subsequent states of Oregon and Washington), considerable interest was stimulated among church as well as secular groups. The Presbyterian Church U.S.A. became notably active in promoting centennial observances. The denomination's general assembly held a major commemorative service in Syracuse, New York, in May 1936. Communities like Lewiston, Idaho, and Walla Walla, Washington, put on elaborate celebrations lasting several days. The one in Walla Walla highlighted the Whitmans, and the hagiographic status they had already achieved was steadily enhanced during the decades that followed.[26]

The Whitmans were not the earliest missionaries to reach the Pacific Northwest, for there had been a competitive rivalry between ABCFM Presbyterians and Methodists to Christianize the Indians there. Jason Lee was born in 1803 in Stanstead, Quebec. A go-getter, he was self-supporting by the age of thirteen. After undergoing a conversion experience and education at the Wilbraham Academy, he served as a minister in the Stanstead area from 1830 to 1832. One year later he was chosen by the Methodist Episcopal Church to head a mission to the Flathead Indians. Traveling overland with his own party and then joined by another group, he reached Fort Vancouver on the Columbia River in 1834. When the first mission site proved unhealthy, Lee promptly led his people to the Willamette River, where they created a settlement ten miles northwest of the present site of Salem, Oregon. Following some hassles with the Hudson's Bay Company in 1835–36, he helped to draft a petition for the establishment of a territorial government, and in 1838 he made the arduous trip to Washington, DC, to present that petition to Congress, stopping first at the Whitman mission in Walla Walla to visit with Marcus and Narcissa Whitman.[27]

After returning to his own settlement, he continued to found missions and became vigorously active in the territorial organization of Oregon, cementing its ties with the United States even as the American dispute with Great Britain over this area became more heated. Between 1841 and 1843 he was instrumental in the formation of a provisional government for the territory. He also worked actively to promote educational development there and shaped the plan that led to the founding of the Oregon Institute, subsequently Willamette University. Some difficulties at the mission led him to return to New York in 1844. While visiting his sister in Stanstead during March of the following year, his health failed and he died at the age of forty-two. He was buried in the town of his birth.

In 1904 Mrs. Smith French of The Dalles, Oregon, wrote to a Colonel Butterfield of Derby Line, Vermont, suggesting the desirability of moving Lee's remains from Stanstead to the Lee Mission Cemetery in Salem. Butterfield agreed not only to superintend Lee's exhumation but to bear the entire cost of shipping the remains along with his tombstone to Portland and then on to Salem, provided that suitable arrangements could be made to receive and reinter them. When the Columbia River Annual Conference of the Methodist Episcopal Church met at The Dalles later that year, Mrs. French had a resolution ready to present, and the conference appointed a committee of arrangements to provide a program for the reburial. The remains were then expressed from Derby Line to Portland and deposited in the safety vault of the Title Guarantee and Trust Company in the Portland Chamber of Commerce Building. The date chosen for reinterment was June 15, 1906, in conjunction with the sixty-second annual commencement of Willamette University.[28]

An editorial that appeared in the Portland *Oregonian* echoed sentiments expressed in several of the eulogies offered on June 15:

> The return of the dust of Jason Lee to Oregon for final sepulture sixty-one years after his death, the final interment in the cemetery that bears his name, near the site of the old mission that he established away back in the years of a past century, was a grandly significant tribute to the memory of a man who was a moving force in the early settlement of Oregon. The sod in Lee Mission Cemetery has been broken many times since, according to the record, "it was broken to receive the body of Maria Pittman and her child, wife and son of Jason Lee"; but during all the intervening years no form has been more readily consigned to the bosom of our common mother [earth?] than Jason Lee's after all these years.[29]

The Honorable J. C. Moreland, who presided at the services of the Pioneer Association on June 15, recognized that the political importance of filling the newly opened territory with American citizens equaled if not surpassed the importance of Christianizing the Native Americans there. Moreland praised Lee because "he soon saw that when the final settlement of the ownership of this country between this nation and Great Britain then held under treaty of joint occupation should come, that ownership would largely be determined by the citizenship of its settlers." Lee's reburial set a significant precedent: in the years following, many other early missionaries were also exhumed and reburied at the Lee Mission Cemetery.[30]

✛

Father Junípero Serra, born in 1713, received an appointment in 1767 to be the Superior of a band of fifteen Franciscans responsible for the Indian missions of California. Ultimately, twenty-one missions were created by these intrepid proselytizers, and Serra had personal oversight over seven of them. (The chapel at Mission San Juan Capistrano, built in 1782, is believed to be the oldest building still standing in California. Known as Father Serra's Church, it has the distinction of being the only remaining church in which he is known to have officiated.) A man of remarkable energy and administrative ability, Serra died tragically of a snakebite in August 1784 and was initially buried at Mission San Carlos Borromeo de Carmelo (Mission Carmel).[31]

In 1870, when Father Antonio Casanova became the parish priest at Monterey, he made a careful inspection and found the floors of the old church at Mission Carmel buried beneath three feet of debris and covered by grass and weeds. He then determined to rescue the shrine from its ignominious condition. He uncovered four redwood coffins buried below the floor of the sanctuary and in the presence of four hundred faithful worshipers read the original entry in the burial register, including Serra's. Stone slabs were then replaced over the reinterred remains. In so doing, Casanova reawakened interest in the Roman Catholic mission movement and its history.[32] In 1937 the Church introduced the Cause for Serra's beatification, one step from canonization, and in 1988 he was finally beatified by Pope John Paul II, though over the strenuous objection of Native Americans who insisted that their ancestors had been mistreated by Serra.

✛

We even have an intriguing instance of a man who became notorious for his *anti*religious views yet was forgiven and reluctantly reburied thirty-three years following his death. Robert J. Ingersoll was born in 1833, the son of an abolitionist-leaning Presbyterian preacher in upstate New York. After serving in the Civil War, Ingersoll became prominent in the Republican Party and was elected attorney general of the State of Illinois, his home as an adult. Because he was a freethinker—the most notorious of the nineteenth century—he could rise no higher in political circles, but he made a successful career as an immensely popular orator. (His speeches were collected and published in twelve volumes.) Although he spoke on many topics, ranging from Shakespeare to Reconstruction, his best-known and most controversial speeches concerned agnosticism and the sanctity of the family. His radical views about slavery, racial prejudice, and woman suffrage also kept him controversial; but his audiences were never bored, even when he spoke for more than two hours or even three.[33]

After Ingersoll died in 1899, and following his funeral at Dobb's Ferry, New York, where there were readings from his own works and from the New York School of Ethical Culture, the body was taken to Fresh Pond, Long Island, where it was cremated. The noted sculptor George Gray Barnard (who created a controversial statue of young Abraham Lincoln in 1915) selected an urn that had been imported from France. It bore Ingersoll's name and the inscription "L'urne garde la poussière, le coeur, le souvenir" (this urn shelters the ashes, the heart, the memory). Until 1923, when his wife died, the agnostic's urn rested on the mantel of her bedroom. For the next nine years his urn and hers were placed on an altar at the home of their daughter.[34]

On May 4, 1932, both sets of ashes were reinterred at Arlington National Cemetery, on a green knoll across a small declivity from the resting place of the Unknown Soldier. Having been a colonel of the Eleventh Illinois Cavalry and compiled a record for gallantry during the Civil War, he was entitled to burial at Arlington, yet it had been denied at the time of his death because he had so brazenly poked fun at religious belief. He had become an object of pulpit venom all across the country. A few years before she died, however, his widow requested that he be reinterred at Arlington, and the request was honored, albeit reluctantly. Her ashes were placed with his in a grave covered with roses, lilies, and lilacs. Only a few family members and admirers were present for the brief military service.[35]

✛

Reburials involving race and racial issues run a striking gamut of conditions and circumstances, sometimes predictable but quite often not. In what may well be the most notable case, curious and unusual in several respects, there turned out to be a positive culmination in terms of national pride—in this instance Jamaican nationalism. Marcus Garvey, remembered as a journalist, publisher, Black Nationalist orator, and entrepreneur, was born in Jamaica in 1887. From 1912 to 1914 he lived in London, and in the latter year he founded the Universal Negro Improvement Association and African Communities League. During the decade that followed he advocated a pan-African philosophy that aimed to inspire a global mass movement focusing on Africa. Ultimately he created, at the peak of his success during the 1920s, the largest single movement among people of African descent in the black diaspora. His philosophy and charisma would become a source of inspiration for subsequent movements, ranging from the Nation of Islam to Rastafarianism.[36]

After corresponding with Booker T. Washington, Garvey came to the United States in 1916, built his movement from a base in Harlem, where he survived an assassination attempt in 1919, and addressed a throng of twenty-five thousand people at Madison Square Garden in 1925. He hoped to develop Liberia as a genuine and permanent homeland for black people. But he encountered opposition and hostile criticism from prominent figures like W. E. B. Du Bois, who regarded him as a megalomaniac with wildly unrealistic plans. After he worked out a strange entente with the Ku Klux Klan—arguing that its members were less hypocritical than most whites—he became an increasingly divisive figure. In 1935 he left Jamaica permanently for London; but two years later he collaborated with the archracist Senator Theodore Bilbo of Mississippi to promote a repatriation scheme in the U.S. Congress called the Greater Liberia Act.[37]

In 1940 Garvey died in London after suffering two strokes and reading a mistaken and negative obituary of himself in the *Chicago Defender*. Because of trans-Atlantic travel conditions during World War II, Garvey was interred at Kensal Green Cemetery in London. In 1956 what had been the Kingston Race Course in Jamaica, renamed the George VI Park, provided a dramatic scene when a bust of Garvey was unveiled. According to his second wife and widow, Amy Jacques Garvey,

> All classes of the island and foreign invitees were there to take part in the ceremony, which had its inception years before when Kenneth Hill, then mayor, proposed it, and the present mayor and councilors brought it to its climax. Sculptor Alvin Marriott, a Jamaican, had done, not only a good bust, but for years had pressed to have it bronzed and erected. The arrangements for the occasion were carefully and well planned by

the Corporation and representatives from government, military and social services—all willing to help, so that the ceremony would be truly representative of all Jamaica. Invitations had been sent out to persons representative of all walks of life. Thousands assembled.[38]

The entire scene seemed quite grand, and perhaps anticipatory. A military band paraded in the colorful zouave dress uniform of the Old West Indian Regiment. A police guard of honor appeared in formal attire, and there were Girl Guides, Boy Scout troops, and hundreds of children representing different schools. At 4:30 the governor arrived with his aide-de-camp (Jamaica was not yet independent), and there were speeches and eulogies, after which the bust was unveiled. Then came a laying-on of wreaths on behalf of the mayor and council and a eulogy by the president of the UNIA on behalf of the American organization. The bust was later placed on its pedestal near the east gate of the park, facing north, looking up to the hills.[39]

Garvey's last request in 1940 had been that his body be taken back to Jamaica and not left in a "land of Strangers." When Jamaica achieved its independence in 1962, Garvey was named one of the island's national heroes at the ceremonies marking autonomy. Two years later, in August 1964, his remains were disinterred from the catacombs of St. Mary's Catholic Church, to which they had been transferred, and taken to Kingston, where the government had erected a permanent shrine to house the bones of its "first national hero" in King George VI Memorial Park. A crowd of thirty thousand gathered at the rites to hear dignitaries of church and state proclaim their pride in this native son as he was reinterred in an emblematic star-shaped tomb of black marble. It seems fair to say that Garvey himself would have felt extremely gratified.[40]

✛

In 1909 Commander Robert E. Peary allegedly became the first American to reach the North Pole on foot and plant an American flag. But possibly not. A neglected American explorer named Frederick Cook may very well have achieved the same feat one year earlier, but that is a separate and complex story.[41] The highly competitive and self-promoting Peary has received most of the credit, and that is what matters here. He originally hired an African American named Matthew Alexander Henson to be his valet but later came to rely upon him as a navigator and hardy expert on cold-weather trekking. It is not clear which member of the Peary party was actually the very first to place his foot on the North Pole, but it may very well have been Henson who did so and promptly planted the stars and stripes in the ice.

When Peary died in 1920, by then an admiral and recognized worldwide as a great explorer, he was buried at Arlington National Cemetery beneath a globe-shaped monument on the crest of a hill (fig. 39). When Henson died in 1955 at the age of eighty-eight, he was buried in a simple grave at Woodlawn Cemetery in the Bronx, having spent most of his post-Arctic years in obscurity as a clerk in the Customs House of New York City. He was denied burial at Arlington, perhaps because of his race but also because he had never been a member of the U.S. military.[42]

On April 6, 1988, exactly seventy-nine years to the day after Henson and Peary had their historic moment, Henson received a hero's burial close to Peary at Arlington, and his wife, Lucy Ross Henson, was reinterred beside him. She had died in 1968 and had also been buried at Woodlawn. Relatives,

Figure 39. Mourners attending the memorial service for Admiral Richard Peary at Arlington National Cemetery (1920). Mourners include President-Elect and Mrs. Harding, Chief Justice and Mrs. Taft, and members of Peary's family. Division of Prints and Photographs, Library of Congress.

friends, and admirers, some of them Inuits from the Arctic, hailed the exhumation and reburial of Matthew Henson as an event that corrected a historic slight and signified a "new day" in race relations. The event also marked the culmination of a long campaign by Henson's family to rectify the "oversight," and he received military honors despite his lack of rank. The black granite marker above Henson's grave includes an inscribed likeness of him in cold-weather gear and several Arctic scenes. The printed inscription actually hails him as "Co-discoverer of the North Pole."[43]

Among those seated at graveside for the ceremony were four Inuits, direct descendants of a son that Henson fathered by a native woman in the Arctic. One of them, Qtdlag Henson, spoke for the Greenland branch of the family: "We are very proud," he said in his native language. "This is a very great day for us." The American branch was represented by a Henson niece, Olive Henson Fulton, who recalled that as a schoolgirl she had been punished by her teacher for insisting that a black man, her own relative, had helped to discover the North Pole. Peary himself had also fathered a son while in the Arctic, and a few years prior to Henson's reburial at Arlington, Kali Peary and Anaukaq Henson had come to the United States for a "North Pole Family Reunion" organized by the same Harvard professor of neurophysiology, S. Allen Counter, who helped lead the drive to recognize Henson's achievements. Dr. Counter, an African American himself, had managed to locate Henson's Inuit offspring.[44]

Speaking at the reinterment, Counter remarked that Henson had been denied his due recognition "because of the racial attitudes of his time." He declared, "We are assembled here today to right a tragic wrong. Welcome home, Matt Henson, to the company of your friend Robert Peary. Welcome home to a new day in America. Welcome home, brother." Along with Henson's relatives and admirers, Counter had to win an order from President Ronald Reagan to have Henson buried at Arlington because he had technically not been enlisted in the military. So recognition and justice were achieved, however belatedly.[45]

✠

An African burial ground (originally known as the Negros [sic] Burial Ground) was created at an unwanted field in lower Manhattan by 1712; it was used exclusively for African American burials until 1790, as blacks had been barred from interment in most New York City churchyards after the 1690s. Owing to rapid growth and new construction, by 1820 builders had deposited vast amounts of fill on top of this site, and it remained largely forgotten until 1991, when excavation for a huge new $276 million federal office building began to reveal unexpected remains. The General Services Administration (GSA) contracted with archaeologists to document and remove them, but when it became clear that significant burials had been unearthed, improper storage had damaged remains, and the archaeological project lacked a proper research design, concerned citizens, especially blacks, protested and pressured politicians to halt excavation. Congress then passed a law in 1992 that stopped excavation on the lot immediately adjacent to the new structure—the primary burial site—and allocated three million dollars for on-site reburial and a memorial.[46]

Ultimately, the remains of more than four hundred individuals were exhumed and examined. When it became apparent that even more might also be disinterred, religious institutions called a halt to the exhumations. The GSA then contracted with a new team of predominantly African American scholars to study the remains, which were transferred to Howard University in Washington, DC, for scientific studies that revealed the West African origins of many of the deceased, most notably from Ghana (based upon patterns of filed teeth, particular kinds of beads surrounding skeletons, etc.).[47]

Nonhuman physical remains from the site were largely kept in New York; these included coins, shells, glass, buttons, beads, clay pipes, coral, and other artifacts that had been found in what survived of wooden coffins. In 1993 the site received National Historic Landmark status, the GSA established an Office of Public Education and Interpretation for the African Burial Ground, and New York City's Landmark Preservation Commission created the African Burial Ground and Commons Historic District, a designation requiring review of any construction or excavation projects proposed for the area. All of the exhumed remains and their associated artifacts were eventually reinterred in 2003, following additional research about the site and the African American community in colonial New York.[48]

✠

The recorded history of Native American remains, burial grounds, and reburials dates back several centuries. During the early American Republic, when white settlers crossed the Appalachians and moved into the Old Northwest, they became fascinated by the great burial mounds made by Indians in long and elaborate configurations, sometimes serpentine in shape. The poet Philip Freneau, author of *The Rising Glory of America* (1771) and decades later the editor of an ardently Jeffersonian newspaper, reflected that interest in 1788 by celebrating Native American practices in a lengthy poem titled "The Indian Burying Ground." Here are just five stanzas.

> In spite of all the learned have said,
> I still my old opinion keep;
> The *posture*, that *we* give the dead,
> Points out the soul's eternal sleep.

> Not so the ancients of these lands—
> The Indian, when from life released,
> Again is seated with his friends,
> And shares again the joyous feast.

> His imaged birds, and painted bowl,
> And venison, for a journey dressed,
> Bespeak the nature of the soul
> ACTIVITY that knows no rest.

> His bow, for action ready bent,
> And arrows, with a head of stone,
> Can only mean that life is spent,
> And not the old ideas gone.

> Thou, stranger, that shalt come this way,
> No fraud upon the dead commit—
> Observe the swelling turf, and say
> They do not *lie*, but here they *sit*.[49]

So long as the romanticized ideal of the Noble Savage persisted, curiosity about the wondrous Indian mounds located in several states prompted positive speculation about their meaning. In 1821 William Cullen Bryant, soon to become the best-known poet in America, wrote "The Ages" (for delivery to the Phi Beta Kappa Society at Harvard), in which he referred wistfully to the "mound-builder" civilization. A decade later Thomas Cole, considered the founder of the Hudson River Valley school of painting, also speculated about their mystery.[50] The mounds subsequently became significant tourist attractions, especially after twentieth-century guidebooks offered explanations and pointed people to the sites.

Within more recent decades, however, the question of repatriation and reburial of Indian remains has become far more complex for a variety of reasons, ranging from the dislocation of burial grounds to make way for "progress" to a resurgence of Native American pride and religious sentiments. White regrets and guilt have also played a part. On Memorial Day in 1979, for example, the skeletal remains of Spokane and Colville Indians unearthed during construction of the Grand Coulee Dam in 1939–40, which had been given to the Eastern Washington State Historical Museum, were reburied "with dignity and respect" at the Colville Indian Reservation in Washington.[51]

The final years of the 1980s turned out to be a pivotal time for widespread changes in attitudes concerning the custody of Indian remains. In 1990 Congress passed legislation called the Native American Graves Protection and Repatriation Act (NAGPRA), which led, to take just one prominent example from April 2006, to the reburial of skeletal remains of 1,590 people within Mesa Verde National Park. The actual burial site was omitted from public announcements in order to deter curiosity seekers and looters. Representatives of the Hopi Nation along with people from the Zuni, Zia, and Acoma pueblos had worked out the details with federal officials.[52]

A major shift in curatorial sentiment had actually preceded the passage of NAGPRA, largely resulting from pressure brought by Native American groups.[53] Early in 1990 the Dickson Mounds Museum in Lewiston, Illinois, decided voluntarily to close an exhibit featuring the exposed graves of 234 prehistoric American Indians because of "heightened sensitivity to display of human remains." The museum director explained that there had not been protests or even complaints but that such a display was a "living-on-borrowed-time sort of thing."[54]

Later that year the remains of sixty-one Native Americans, mostly from a University of Minnesota archaeological collection excavated from mounds throughout the state between the 1930s and 1950s, were reburied in special ceremonies at Indian Mounds Park in St. Paul. That event was only the first in a series of Minnesota reburials planned for an estimated two thousand Indians. The bones buried at Mounds Park in sixty-one swaths of red cloth were estimated to range from three hundred to several thousand years old. According to Paul Little, a spiritual leader of the Devil's Lake Sioux Tribe in North Dakota, "They were kept in boxes and locked up so their spirit didn't go anywhere. When they're released today . . . they'll be free forever."[55]

Episodes involving Indian "celebrities" fit this book's focus more closely, so we turn to a famous failure of long standing and then to the uncertain fate of two great chiefs. When Pocahontas died of smallpox in England in 1617, she was buried at the aptly named Gravesend. The idea of bringing her remains "home" was bruited about from time to time but went nowhere. As the bicentennial of the American Revolution approached in 1975, for example, Representative G. William Whitehurst, Republican of Virginia and formerly a history professor at Norfolk's Old Dominion College for eighteen years, introduced a resolution in Congress to have the American and British governments coordinate arrangements for her return. "It would be a real fine gesture," Whitehurst declared, "if her bones could be returned to the banks of the James [River] where she roamed as a little Indian girl." The resolution died from nonsupport.[56]

In 1947 a state senator from Charleston, South Carolina, proposed moving the grave of Osceola, the famous Seminole chief who died in prison at Fort Moultrie on nearby Sullivan's Island in 1838. His carefully marked grave was situated at the fort, which had been abandoned by the army. Therefore, if the state acquired the military property as it proposed to do, Senator Wallace intended to introduce a bill in the General Assembly to return the body to custody of the Seminole Tribe in Florida. Wallace quite rightly observed that Osceola's capture, "which was under a flag of truce, and his death in prison was a disgrace to the United States, and I want to make amends as far as possible. His body should be somewhere in Florida, near where he lived and ruled over his tribe."[57]

That proposal did not gain any more supporters than Whitehurst's had; but in 1966 a Miami businessman, Otis W. Shriver, claimed that he had dug up Osceola and placed his bones in a bank vault in order to bury them at a tourist destination in Rainbow Springs. Shriver traveled around the state the following year drumming up support for his commercial project, but without success. Subsequently archaeologists proved that what Shriver had were merely animal bones and that what was left of Osceola remained in his coffin. In 1979 the Seminole Nation bought Osceola's bandolier and other items at auction from Sotheby's. But material objects served as inadequate substitutes for his remains, which would have been vastly more meaningful.[58]

The saga of Sitting Bull, the great Sioux chief (1834–90), is even more poignant and complex because he was reburied at least three times, most likely four. In 1889 he retired to the Standing Rock Reservation, which straddles the Dakotas. A revival of the Ghost Dance, in which he placed no faith, brought dancers close to his cabin on Grand River, and fearing that he might decide to lead an uprising, a group of Indian Agency policemen were sent to arrest him. Their charge was merely to "bring him in." When one of them was shot by a follower of Sitting Bull, however, the police returned fire and killed the venerable warrior.

At the post cemetery in Fort Yates, located in what is now North Dakota, three U.S. Army officers stood next to an open grave. In it a rough wooden box contained the canvas-wrapped body of Sitting Bull. As a "pagan" he did not qualify for burial in either the Catholic cemetery or the small frame church of the Congregational mission just south of the Indian Agency. In any case, agency police objected to any sort of service, so a detail of four soldiers, actually prisoners from the guard house, shoveled dirt into the hole and covered the coffin of one of the greatest Native American statesmen—a tragic and undeserved end in the reservation's equivalent of a pauper's grave.[59]

He had been buried less than two months when a North Dakota senator urged the Indian Office to move swiftly to acquire as many of the chief's personal effects as possible. What the state wanted most, and successfully got, was Sitting Bull's cabin to form part of the state's exhibition at the Chicago World's Fair of 1893. With approval from the Interior Department, state agents entered into negotiations with the chief's widow and by the end of 1891 had removed the cabin, log by log, for reconstruction in Chicago. How to present and interpret it became a matter of contention, but the general public simply viewed it as the home of the notorious warrior who had wiped out George Armstrong Custer and his troops at the Little Big Horn in 1876.[60]

Meanwhile, others sought ownership of many of Sitting Bull's personal effects, by hook or by crook, and rumors began to circulate in the press that the coffin placed in the pauper's grave really did not contain

Figure 40. Sitting Bull's grave, North Dakota (c. 1906). Photograph by Frank Bennett Fiske. Division of Prints and Photographs, Library of Congress.

Sitting Bull at all. Such gossip may have been prompted because in 1908 the military graves at Fort Yates were disinterred for reburial, most likely including Sitting Bull's; however, the federal government's Indian agent at the reservation had ordered that the Sioux's bones be returned (fig. 40).[61]

The rumors were refuted by the Fort Yates post surgeon and other military officers who had helped to dispose of the body. Yet Hunkpapa tribal leaders (one branch of the Lakota Sioux) who had greatly admired the chief agitated to have his body removed from the military cemetery to his boyhood home thirty miles south on Grand River, where it could be suitably memorialized. White Indian agents and some of their Native allies arduously resisted this request. Clarence Gray Eagle, a son of Sitting Bull's brother-in-law, kept the cause of reburial alive with much passion, but failed. Meanwhile, in 1932 Sitting Bull was reinterred at Fort Yates, once again for logistical reasons.[62]

Problems arose following World War II when construction of the Missouri River dams got under way. Initial plans called for the Fort Yates flatlands to be inundated, prompting Gray Eagle to resume his campaign to remove the chief to Grand River. He pointed out that the great chief's grave had been neglected for years, but state officials of North Dakota swiftly spruced up the grave as a tourist attraction because they did not want to lose their biggest celebrity. The state refused to grant a permit for exhumation. In April 1953 Gray Eagle led an expedition (with an undertaker and diggers) from Mobridge, South Dakota, located in the southeastern corner of the Standing Rock Reservation, that "swooped down on the gravesite in the dark of night and carried off the object of all the controversy." They reburied Sitting Bull on a scenic site overlooking the Missouri a short distance below where the mouth of the Grand River lay beneath a huge reservoir. Twenty tons of steel rails and concrete were placed on top to make sure that he could not be moved again, and a bust sculpted by Korczak Ziolkowski provided memorialization.[63]

But is Sitting Bull really there? Subsequent research by North Dakota historians established a reasonable doubt that Gray Eagle's grave robbers actually removed Sitting Bull or at least obtained *all* of his bones. Dike work in 1962 accidentally exposed other bones that purportedly matched descriptions of Sitting Bull's. The grave was excavated at that time, and a small box with bones was interred once again. In 1984 the curator of collections for the State Historical Society of North Dakota proclaimed that the robbers must have taken the wrong remains—by then a familiar refrain. The North Dakota site, which in the end was not flooded after all, now bears a marker that leaves the issue permanently ambiguous. It simply states that "he was buried here but his grave has been vandalized many times."[64]

Who could possibly have imagined in 1876, when Custer died, or in 1890, when Sitting Bull was killed, that less than a century later North and South Dakota would be battling for possession of these remains, the reasons being partially sentimental and tribal but also touristic and commercial?

✛

We cannot overlook the historical phenomenon of collections of Native American relics, and the current revival of reburial practices among North American Indians, owing partially to the remarkable number of human remains that have been repatriated by anthropological and archaeological museums and major institutions like the Smithsonian Institution in Washington and the American Museum of Natural History in New York. Although much has recently been written about these topics, ranging from Indian religious imperatives to legal issues, this narrative would be incomplete without briefly acknowledging at least two aspects of this complex phenomenon that date back historically further than some might assume. One is the fascination shared by many Americans, especially in the twentieth century, with Native American culture prior to the arrival of Europeans. The other is rather belated respect for the significance of suitable burial in Indian religious beliefs and practices.

Historically many white Americans were fascinated by arrowheads and other items that in the nineteenth century could still be readily spotted on the surface of the ground, especially by observant woodsmen or by people who watched carefully as they made their way by canoe along riverbanks. Henry David Thoreau and his brother John were among these collectors during their youth in the 1820s and '30s. Oddly enough, however, during the depths of the Great Depression in 1933–34, interest in what has been called the Indian curio market notably intensified, perhaps because those who dealt in relics needed pot hunters and grave robbers. Some unemployed people found that they could eke out a living by finding goods for which someone might pay them a pittance, and if they were really enterprising or lucky, more than that. "Pots, pipes, and points" became a kind of shorthand for what diggers hoped to unearth, piece together, and sell.

As the market developed, especially after World War II, but even in the 1930s, the most highly prized artifacts were those produced before the Indians had been relocated on reservations. That meant that excavating and exploring Indian mounds became especially tempting, and in some instances the mounds situated on privately owned land were the most vulnerable to archaeologists as well as unauthorized diggers and grave robbers. To take just one example, a very considerable cluster of Indian mounds existed in eastern Oklahoma just south of the Arkansas River, largely on private farmland. Early in the twentieth century these were simply called the Mound Builders Mounds. Later, as curiosity seekers took note of them, they became the Fort Coffee Mounds because of the proximity of an abandoned fort not far away. By the 1930s they were known as the Spiro Mounds, while several of the larger ones had their own particular names.[65]

A very large main mound came to be called the Craig Mound because the Craig family owned the farm on which it was located, though later—when its extraordinary contents became known—it would be renamed the Great Temple Mound. It stood 33 feet high and ran 180 feet in length and 120 feet wide. Once excavated, it turned out to cover a long-abandoned Indian town complete with all sorts of structures that seem to have been suddenly collapsed by some natural catastrophe, most likely an earthquake but possibly a tornado. Inside, an archaeologist found two sets of burials. The four people situated in one set appear to have died simultaneously, as if their house had been utterly flattened on them in the middle of the night. "Later, the ruins had been burned with the dead inside, and dirt had been piled over it until a small mound resulted. Thirty-two additional skeletons had been inserted into the mound sometime later. Along with the skeletons [Joseph B.] Thoburn found numerous artifacts, including T-shaped pipes, spear points, bowls, and even copper ax-heads."[66]

Relic hunters swiftly formed consortiums to which they gave spurious names, such as the Pocola Mining Company, and the craze to collect grave goods and bones grew in intensity. Not only were valuable grave goods found, but—germane to our focus—crematoriums and charnel houses were also discovered in the ruins. The charnel houses turned out to be especially interesting, as they revealed that distinctions had clearly been made in this prehistoric civilization between commoners and royal families. The bodies of commoners were simply piled into large mortuaries where they might remain for some time, their bones all jumbled together. After months or even years, once this space had been filled it would be cleaned out, and the bones or skeletons would be buried in cemeteries at the very edge of the mounds, or even at the fringe of town, mostly in mass graves. For the nobility, however, burial seems to have been much more elaborate and respectful. The bones of nobles were carefully arranged and eventually placed in a jar or box woven from river cane and then buried. Contemporary grave goods were interred with them.[67]

Although such mounds have surrendered their secrets slowly and much about these civilizations remains altogether mysterious, it is clear from the many levels and layers that have been excavated that burial and reburial practices changed over time.

✝

There is also a contemporary reburial movement among Native peoples in North America, particularly among those that are less fully engaged with the economic and technological complexities of modern life. One representative group whose practices have been carefully examined are called the Lakes' People living at Vallican in south-central British Columbia, between a pair of north-south running ranges, the Monashee Mountains and the Selkirk Mountains. For the Lakes' People, putting exhumed ancestors back into the earth reestablishes a reciprocal relationship between them and their Sinixt tribal members from earlier times, "to bring space and time together," as Paula Pryce has observed, to "reinforce the strength of ethnic longevity, and make the universe function properly once again." Returning bodies to their rightful places becomes a symbolic way of reordering a disruptive and confusing world, of "piecing together the crumbling shards of a precarious existence and making logic out of chaos."[68]

Put differently, reburial for the Sinixt is a "symbolic salve" for the distressing circumstances of contemporary life. By exhuming and reinterring, the Sinixt at Vallican enable their ancestors to fulfill their spiritual commitments of reciprocity by uniting them once again with their land and their descendants. And by placing ancestral remains back into the earth, members of this tribal group believe that they are infusing the land with their own presence, thereby committing themselves and future generations to that land. As Pryce has pointed out, such acts have *political* implications as well, because reburial "asserts their presence in this territory despite the dominant society's view that they do not belong there." So reburial memorializes the longevity of their cultural presence in that region.[69]

The anthropologist Marshall Sahlins has noted that such an ethos and behavior is more than an expression of ethnic identity. Rather, the act of exhumation and reburial reflects and incorporates "the people's attempt to control their relationships with the dominant society, including control of the technical and political means that up to now have been used to victimize them."[70] Considering the discontent and anger of Native Americans prior to 1990 about the "incarceration" of their ancestors in museums controlled by Euro-Americans, one is reminded of two lines from Robert Frost's early poem "The Death of the Hired Man": "And nothing to look backward to with pride / And nothing to look forward to with hope."[71] Happily, that unfortunately hopeless situation is changing.

In June 2008 nearly fifty Native Americans entered the American Museum of Natural History in Manhattan, ahead of the usual throng of visitors. Their cheeks were smeared with rust-colored dye, and red and white woven bands encircled their heads. As one report remarked, "They were at the end of a journey that had, in its way, taken years." Unlike the thousands of schoolchildren who normally fill the museum's halls on a Monday, the forty-six visitors had come to take their ancestors home. "Our people are humans; we aren't tokens," declared Chief Vern Jacks, who heads the Tseycum First Nation, a tiny tribe from northern Vancouver Island in British Columbia. With the museum's complete consent, the Tseycum tribe repatriated the remains of fifty-five of their ancestors.[72]

✢

If only in terms of symbolic gestures, actions, and statements, what has been occurring among North American tribal groups since the late 1980s is not so different from what happened in Eastern Europe, most notably in Hungary, Poland, and Romania following the fall of Communist control in 1989. Both situations had an ideological component, and both arose from feelings of deep resentment and a need to reject persistent domination by others.

A resurgence of religion, the revival of churches, and the resurrection and reburial of political martyrs all reflected an earnest desire to reestablish norms of social and ethical life that had been repressed for decades in Eastern Europe, and in some parts of the Soviet Bloc, for several generations. Therefore we need to conclude by going to such places and noting the disinterment practices that emerged swiftly once the dictators had been displaced and freedom of action and expression became possible.

— SIX —

*Repossessing the
Dead Elsewhere
in Our Time*

I will talk of things heavenly, or things earthly; things moral, or things evangelical; things sacred, or things profane; things past or things to come; things foreign, or things at home; things more essential, or things circumstantial.

✠ John Bunyan, *Pilgrim's Progress* (1678)

*S*un Yat-sen, leader of the remarkable Chinese Revolution in 1911 and the founder of modern China, died in 1925 in Beijing, where he was attempting to unify his politically unwieldy country. Despite visiting an area controlled by men unsympathetic to him, his body lay in state for two weeks, and massive throngs of supporters appeared with thousands of long funeral scrolls to adorn the route to his burial place at the Azure Cloud Temple. His dying wish, however, was to be buried at Nanjing in a tomb similar to that of Lenin, a man he greatly admired. So late in the spring of 1929 General Chiang Kai-shek orchestrated a spectacular ceremonial reburial in the new capital city as a way of mobilizing support for his Nationalist Party and consolidating its control over the country.[1]

An impressive funeral train reminiscent of Abraham Lincoln's in April 1865 carried the coffin in June to Nanjing, where it lay in state at the central headquarters of Chiang's party. The concept for Sun's enormous mausoleum, located near but even larger than that of the last Ming emperor, derived from the symbolic notions behind Lenin's glorification five years earlier. The architect who chose the design had actually been trained in the United States, and the influence of the Lincoln Memorial is clear, not so much as a stylistic copy as in the way the tomb is situated. Though hard to imagine, the Greek Temple on the Mall in Washington influenced the concept for Sun's final resting place: a temple resembling a bell to remind the masses that Sun had awakened China.[2] It is more than intriguing to consider that a combination of Lincoln and Lenin as heroic national leaders shaped the thinking of those who would memorialize Sun Yat-sen in 1929.

Other ironies abound. When Sun was inaugurated in 1912, the public outpouring of welcome and enthusiasm had been spontaneous, as was the genuine grief when he died in 1925. By contrast, the masses seem to have been rather disinterested in, almost apathetic about, the carefully staged, slow procession of ten thousand marchers (organized by political groups and the military supporting Chiang) that escorted Sun to his mausoleum on July 1, 1929. Those who did not fully support Chiang's party were not included. As Henrietta Harrison has explained very well, the event looked more like an imperial funeral than the burial of an anticolonial and revolutionary modernizer.[3] This very grand interment exercise was highly politicized—its symbolism maximized for the advantage of a new leader still striving to consolidate his power.

On September 30, 1989, an equally massive procession, intended to achieve a comparable outcome, accompanied the remains of Juan Manuel de Rosas (whose death had occurred more than a century before) along a fifty-five-block route to La Recoleta cemetery, the most elite and famous necropolis in Buenos Aires. A military carriage bearing the casket was escorted and accompanied by many dignitaries, including the president of Argentina, his cabinet and government officials, and descendants of the deceased but also of the powerful nineteenth-century generals who had bitterly opposed Rosas during his reign and beyond. Next came grenadiers, and then an escort of federal police arrayed in period uniforms from the middle third of the nineteenth century (actually, the very uniforms of the *mazorca*, Rosas's once widely feared henchmen). Five thousand gauchos from all across Argentina and Uruguay brought up the rear, along with members of the Pro-Repatriation Committee, who had waited nearly four decades for this moment.

Rosas is remembered as the most famous figure in nineteenth-century Argentine history—but also the most notorious. He had been the leader and governor of the Argentine Confederation from 1829 until 1852, when he was defeated in battle and sought exile in England, where he died in 1877 and received burial in a modest Catholic cemetery. Although he had served as a symbol of national unification and a passionate defender of Argentine sovereignty, he was also remembered as a ruthless dictator intolerant of any opposition. Consequently the nation's official historiography had long since developed a strong anti-Rosista tradition.[4]

When Juan Perón returned from *his* exile in 1973, he felt that the time had come for what was left of Rosas to be repatriated, and supporters of that notion even wanted him to be buried in the Cathedral of Buenos Aires, the resting place of José de San Martín, founder of the nation. Rosas remained too controversial to receive that ultimate honor; but after the fiercely anti-Communist rule of military leaders ended and democracy returned to Argentina in 1983, President Carlos

Saúl Menem eventually determined to bring Rosas's remains home as an act of reconciliation between conservatives and liberals. Rosas had wanted to be buried in his native land. The act of reinterment with so much official pomp and vast numbers watching meant different things to different people, yet it did serve Menem's purpose: a moving and highly visible moment of national unification if not instantaneous healing. Rosas found his rest not far from the burial site of Eva Perón, the people's darling. Although it was not the cathedral, he had achieved a place of honor.[5]

An even more sensational and widely noticed reburial involved the revolutionary Che Guevara. He was killed in 1967 by CIA-authorized Bolivian troops and buried with five others in a secret mass grave near an obscure mountain village. In 1995 the Bolivian government, responding to international pressure, reluctantly authorized a search that finally located the site, and the remains were eventually verified. Following agreements with Bolivia and Argentina, countries that had claims to Guevara (the second by birth), he was reburied as a heroic martyr on October 17, 1997, in a specially built mausoleum in the central Cuban city of Santa Clara, the site of his best-known military triumph. Fidel Castro presided over a pomp-filled state funeral with a ringing tribute.[6]

✟

The reasons for exhumations and reburials in modern times range from nationalism in the decade following World War I to the rehabilitation of political reputations as a symptom and symbol of anti-Communist fervor in Eastern Europe following 1989. A desire for national unification has been a prominent motive in recent events as well, not just in China and Argentina but also in Germany after the Berlin Wall came down, not to mention the Balkans following World War II. There are also causes that we have encountered earlier in this book, such as bringing legendary figures home as a gesture of repossession if not always respect.

Religion continues to matter in important ways because individuals seen as saintly often require a more appropriate interment than the one originally received. John Henry Cardinal Newman's burial site is a current case in point, still unresolved as of this writing and posing a dilemma for the Vatican as well as segments of British society. Then there are men like Friedrich Nietzsche, buried in obscure local cemeteries that are threatened either by "progress" (otherwise known as entrepreneurial urban and suburban development) or else by lapses of memory and the physical damage done by time and tourists at grave sites. In some instances, once again for political reasons, issues arise over whether and where to reinter someone whose reputation may have changed or been altered.

To cite a prime American example, when Major Marcus Reno died in disgrace in 1889, he was buried in an unmarked grave at Oak Hill Cemetery in Washington, DC, because he had received a dishonorable discharge from the U.S. Army on grounds of "cowardice" while mobilizing in support of General George A. Custer at the Battle of the Little Big Horn in 1876. Reno had been the highest-ranking officer serving under Custer. Later that year he was also accused of making advances toward the wife of another officer, and in 1880 he received a court-martial for drunkenness. The testimonial record regarding some of these charges is unclear and seems to have been altered by unknown hands; although his decimated company's location was such that he could not have known of Custer's desperate plight, the accusations related to alcohol abuse do seem to have been justified.[7]

In 1967 the Army Board of Corrections cleared Reno of all those unverified charges, and he was reburied in September at what then was still called the Custer Battlefield National Cemetery. (Custer's name has since been removed from the cemetery and national park, which is now simply called the Little Bighorn National Park.) As the mayor of Billings put it in September 1967, the reinterment would be "an occasion of prideful pomp and circumstance" for Reno. And it was.[8]

We might compare that reversal of reputation with an equally remarkable one in France, where late in 2007 the French government requested the return of the remains of its first president and last emperor, Louis Napoleon III. After a number of foreign adventures and misadventures during the 1860s, his forces were defeated in the Franco-Prussian War of 1870, prompting him to flee with his wife, Empress Eugenie, to Chislehurst, Kent, where he remained in exile until his death in 1873. Despite the ignominy of his last years in power, Napoleon III did play a major role in physically reconfiguring Paris into an elegant modern city, replacing those unhealthful medieval streets with wide boulevards. Under his regime major parks were built along with apartment blocks for the middle class and new sewage systems. Hence the request for his ashes (which had lain in a crypt at an English abbey for 120 years) to be repatriated to the French republic over which he presided before proclaiming himself emperor. He is once again home.[9]

It has not been unusual, in America and abroad, for national chauvinism to trump the last wishes of a deceased man who is widely esteemed. Alexandre Dumas *père* (1802–70), a mixed-race novelist best known for such swashbuckling romances as *The Three Musketeers* (1844) and *The Count of Monte Cristo* (also 1844), chose to be buried quite simply and with his parents in his native town of Villers-Cotterets; yet in 2002 his remains were exhumed and reburied with solemnity at the Panthèon in Paris. His central role in the popular national patrimony apparently meant more than respect for his personal preference.

Quite a different saga that also culminated at the Panthèon is intriguing for two reasons: first for what it reveals about French politics under Charles de Gaulle, and second because it has no real counterpart in American annals, unless we make a very approximate comparison with the way that many of those who had opposed Lincoln's presidency later joined in remembering him as a martyr in the cause of preserving the Union.[10] Jean Moulin (1899–1943), founder and leader of the French Resistance during World War II, was arrested in June 1943, was interrogated in Lyon by Klaus Barbie (head of the Gestapo there) but revealed nothing to him about the Resistance's organization, and died the next month on a Paris to Berlin train that was heading to a concentration camp. It is unclear whether he committed suicide or was beaten to death by Barbie.[11]

Following liberation in 1944, Moulin's remains were cremated and his ashes buried at Père Lachaise Cemetery. In 1963, however, the Union des Résistants, Déportés, Internés, et des Familles des Morts proposed that his ashes be exhumed and reinterred at the Panthèon. The leftist opposition took up their cause in Parliament. In 1964, the twentieth anniversary of liberation, as it happened, the French government chose to invent a new historical version of the German occupation so that French chauvinists could claim that France had *always* resisted invaders. Charles de Gaulle, the president, and André Malraux, his esteemed minister of culture, essentially appropriated the compelling idea of reburying Moulin as a way of glorifying de Gaulle, linking him more closely to the Resistance and equating him with the very soul of the French nation. Instead of gaining approval through a legislative vote, the government issued an executive order, thereby making the measure its own.[12]

Reburial of the ashes became an elaborately scripted two-day affair. On December 18 they were removed from Père Lachaise, and the urn was placed in a new container and then in a coffin with a simple inscription: only the hero's name. In the afternoon that casket was taken to the Ile de la Cité, where, to the accompaniment of a funeral march, it was temporarily placed with military honors in the crypt of the Monument to the Martyrs of the Deportation. Much elaborate protocol followed, with an honor guard consisting of 194 members of the Resistance along with leaders from all parties and movements. At ten o'clock that evening a cortège formed, led by the Garde Républicaine of Paris and followed by the flags of various Resistance groups.[13]

This procession carried the remains of Jean Moulin to the Panthèon, where the next day de Gaulle presided over a very formal state ceremony at which his deputy Malraux delivered the eulogy. The casket had been placed at the center of the Panthèon on a temporary altar beneath the cupola, and final interment occurred later in the Panthèon's northern crypt. In a very literal sense, the government in power had co-opted from the Left the ultimate symbol of French Resistance in the name of French political unity following a bitterly divisive war in Algeria. In effect, the glory of Moulin's courageous leadership had to be shared with President de Gaulle. This shabby attempt at political unification following a politically troublesome war was a curious harbinger of the Rosas episode in Argentina twenty-five years later.[14]

✛

Now we turn to a different sort of heroic story of reburial for national pride and honor. Manfred Baron von Richthofen was only twenty-two when World War I broke out in 1914.[15] As a skilled and courageous fighter pilot, he downed many Allied planes in single combat and became the most glamorous hero of the German war effort. Films and postcards were made of the Red Baron preparing for battle, and in 1917 he was awarded the nation's highest military honor. When he was killed in action pursuing an enemy plane over the Somme in April 1918, it seemed not only a national tragedy but a frightful omen for Germany. The British actually buried him with military honors in France, and subsequently the French exhumed and reburied him in a larger cemetery, though still in France. In 1925 the Richthofen family decided that the time had come to bring the body home, and the project swiftly became a momentous national event.[16]

The train from France bearing the Red Baron's remains crossed into Germany on November 17. As it moved through the country toward Berlin, many thousands of people turned out to watch it pass, just as somber Americans had turned out in vast numbers to see Lincoln's funeral train make its circuitous way to Springfield in April 1865. In Frankfurt veterans from the nationalist Stahlhelm, the republican Reichsbanner, and the Jewish Reichsbund Jüdischer Frontsoldaten created an honor guard to meet the train. When it reached Berlin on November 18, a huge crowd was waiting despite the dark and the cold. The following day a continuous stream of people walked past the coffin in the Gnadenkirche. At the funeral two days later, President Paul von Hindenberg led the official delegation. Soldiers beat muffled drums and led a riderless horse in a procession to the Invaliden Cemetery for interment. The grave quickly became a German shrine.[17]

Some years later Manfred's brother Bolko reflected on the symbolic meaning of this powerfully moving funeral: "Not all of the hundreds of thousands who gave their lives for Germany, and who were laid to rest in foreign soil, could be brought home. And so, the thousands of people who streamed to greet our Manfred saw him as the representative of the self-sacrificing German hero, and honored in him the sons and brothers who had given themselves for the fatherland." The event had much to do with a resurgence of German nationalism, of course. But as historian Robert Whalen has observed, "Mass mourning for the Red Baron, then, was more than a reaffirmation of the heroic. Mixed in the mourning was not a little nostalgia for the time when the heroic had meaning, and grief that the heroic was gone. The Red Baron was home, but the Red Baron was dead."[18]

Sixty-six years later Germans would find themselves intensely divided over the decision to disinter King Frederick the Great from what had been West Germany until 1990 and rebury him at Sans Souci, his palace at Potsdam, once the royal suburb of Berlin. The story of Frederick's migratory remains is an intriguing and intensely politicized one. Having somehow claimed the enlightened Prussian king as a forebear of the Nazi movement, Adolf Hitler had his corpse dug up from his original site at a Potsdam garrison church in 1944 and hidden away in a salt mine in order to protect it from seizure by the advancing Red Army. After the war, however, American occupying forces located the royal sarcophagus and gave it a new funeral, after which Frederick's Hohenzollern descendants retrieved the remains and reinterred them at the family castle. In 1991, ten months after the reunification of Germany, Chancellor Helmut Kohl and his conservative Christian Democratic Party decided to celebrate the nation's restored unity by exhuming Frederick yet again for reburial once more at Potsdam in the east on August 17, declaring that the former ruler "should be neither mythologized nor demonized." From Kohl's perspective, the reburial of "Old Fritz" would supply the ideal sign of Germany made whole again, the "crowning moment."[19]

Opposition politicians and historians weighed in critically against Kohl's decision to lend his prestige to the ceremony. Historian Golo Mann called Kohl's role "absolute tastelessness" and remarked that Kohl's blessing of this symbolic gesture "demonstrates the kind of mentality that prompts cheers among the stupid but causes awkward fears in European capitals." Meanwhile, and more important, the opposition party, Social Democrats, also attacked participation by Kohl and the army as a nationalistic display that sent exactly the wrong message about the new Germany. Hadn't Hitler made a dramatic pilgrimage to Frederick's tomb to usher in the Nazis' acquisition of power? Didn't Frederick preside over two of Europe's bloodiest wars: the Seven Years' War and the War of the Austrian Succession? As one Social Democratic party leader said to reporters, "Any historical to-do over Frederick's bones . . . could be understood wrongly."[20] So a gesture conceived as a symbol of reunification instead came to be emblematic of sharp divisiveness over German history and identity. But the enlightened Frederick was now at home once more in Potsdam, and all the intense passion faded away as political discourse moved on to more critical issues.

Much less contested but no less embarrassing in terms of national pride is the bizarre afterlife of Johann Friedrich von Schiller (1759–1805), the great German poet, dramatist, historian, and philosopher of the romantic era, best remembered in the English-speaking world for his play *Maria Stuart*, or *Mary Queen of Scots* (1800). When Schiller died, he was buried in the communal vault at Weimar, not far from Jena in eastern Germany, where he had served as professor of history at the university. According to legend, however, Schiller's skull was entrusted for some months to his close friend, the even more famous writer Johann Wolfgang von Goethe (1749–1832), whose family home (now a fine museum) is in Frankfurt but who, like Schiller, is also associated with the culturally rich and bucolic community of Weimar. A handsome monument to both men stands in front of the German National Theater there.

In the two decades following Schiller's death his reputation grew incrementally, and with it the sentiment that he should not lie in a common grave in Jacob's Cemetery, even though such burial had been standard practice through the eighteenth century, even for many celebrities. So in 1826 the mayor of Weimar entered the communal vault to seek Schiller's remains. He came back with no fewer than twenty-three skulls (and related bones), one of which was determined by two doctors and Schiller's son to belong to the writer, and then a more honorific reburial took place. A debate persisted for generations, however, over whether the designated remains truly belonged to Schiller. In 1911 a prominent anatomist descended into the vault once again and this time emerged with sixty-three additional skulls! He made a new selection with a seemingly matching skeleton, and they were placed in a special coffin in a side room of the ducal vault. Yet questions and doubts understandably persisted.[21]

While the country was politically divided after World War II, with Weimar located in East Germany, a team examined both sets of skeletons in 1959, but inconclusively. Little more than a decade later, in 1970, a group of scientists decided to exhume Goethe's remains in the middle of the night, photographing and treating the bones with chemicals to help preserve them. What remained of the two immortals was then deposited in a pair of matched oak coffins in a place of particular honor at Weimar. In 2007 yet another forensic inquiry was undertaken to determine which bones truly belonged to Schiller, this time using DNA from five members of the Schiller family at a cost of $170,000 to conduct chemical analysis and facial reconstruction—all of which was recorded by a German documentary film company. Ultimately it was decided that *neither* set of Schiller's putative remains was authentic, because the two skeletons included the bones of at least six different people.[22]

The net result of these macabre activities, in what has been aptly described as "a tale more Gothic than Classicist," is that Schiller's coffin is now empty. Hellmut Seemann, president of the Foundation of Weimar Classics, which is responsible for everything from museums and parks in Weimar to the famed Goethe-Schiller Archive, who had cooperated with the German public television station in making the film, declared that the search for Schiller was now finished. His goal would no longer be to find Schiller's true remains but only to settle questions about the ones they had in hand, so to speak. "It is like with a painting," he explained. "Is it by Rembrandt or only a workshop painting? You have also responsibility for the skulls you have." Local officials complained that adverse publicity about an empty Schiller coffin could be very bad for tourism in Weimar, but interviews made with local citizens and tourists at the bronze monument—thus far, at least—have not revealed any great disenchantment, only disappointment and more than a bit of bemusement.[23] As we have seen more than once, decisions made about reinterments in the United States have frequently hinged upon commercial concerns about tourism.

After almost half a century, Germany was still trying to redeem its reputation from the barbarisms committed before and during World War II—the repercussions of that catastrophe, of course continue to be felt to this day. Not long before the Allies liberated northern Holland in the spring of 1945, German military agents had murdered some 422 Dutch nationals and members of the Dutch resistance. Early in May 1945 the remains were found buried in the dunes at Kennemer. Eventually, forty-five separate sites were located, but the task of identifying bodies remained difficult. Most had been robbed of personal belongings and clothing, so that only dentures could reveal who was who. Dentists nationwide participated in the laborious project, and most of the victims were ultimately identified. An imprisoned undertaker had initially been instructed to take those bodies to the sand dunes and leave them "in a tidily orderly manner." His meticulously organized lists and notebooks were very helpful, and by now only two of the 422 people remain unknown.[24]

The first of many reburials at the dunes took place in a new Remembrance Cemetery on November 27, 1945, in the presence of the Dutch royal family. The final reinterment occurred ten years later. Eight large memorial stones serve as reminders of where the bodies were found, and on the stones is inscribed how many murdered members of the resistance are buried there. Victims from other sites have subsequently been added to the Remembrance Cemetery, which now has 373 graves. As with many who died during the American Civil War, some of the 422 victims have since been reburied in family graves, in hometown cemeteries, or even at the place of their execution. Every year on May 4 large numbers of people come from all over the Netherlands to stand in solemn, respectful vigil at this site. It is perhaps the most moving occasion of the Dutch calendar year.[25]

✛

A notable and germane yet little-known work of historical fiction by an Albanian writer provides an interesting parallel with the regional and sectional search for bodies to be brought "home" during and after the American Civil War. Ismail Kadare, born in 1936, was educated in history and philology at the University of Tirana (the capital of Albania). In 1990, immediately before the fall of Communism in Albania, he sought political asylum in France, and since then he has divided his time between Albania and France. In 2005 he won the Inaugural Booker International Prize.

In 1963 Kadare published *The General of the Dead Army*, which was translated into French in 1970 and English in 1991. A kind of summary parable appears as an interlude between chapters two-thirds of the way through the novel.

> Once upon a time a general and a priest [his chaplain] set off on an adventure together. They were going to collect together all the remains of their soldiers who had been killed in a big war. They walked and walked, they crossed lots of mountains and lots of plains, always hunting for those bones and collecting them up. The country was nasty and rough. But they didn't turn back, they kept on further and further. They collected as many bones as they could and then they came back to count them. But they realized that there were still a lot they hadn't found. So they pulled on their boots and their raincoats and they set

off on their search again. . . . They were quite exhausted; they felt they were being crushed into the ground by their task. Neither the wind nor the rain would tell them where to look for the soldiers they were seeking. But they collected as many as they could and came back once again to count them. Many of the ones they had been looking for still hadn't been found.[26]

The novel relates the complex story of an Italian general sent on a mission in 1963 by his government, at the behest of many Italian families, to recover the bodies of an army known as the Blue Battalion that was defeated by Albanian partisans and guerrillas in 1943. The families wanted their husbands and sons brought home for honorable burial. The thankless and exhausting task spans two years, and in the process the general discovers that a one-armed German general and his staff are in Albania for exactly the same reason. (The Germans placed an occupation force there after the Italians defected, but it was driven out by Communist partisans in 1944.) On occasion the Italian general and his chaplain are shocked to find graves that have been opened and the contents removed. At first they assume to their dismay that Albanians have desecrated these graves, but they eventually discover that the rival German team had reached each spot first.[27]

About halfway through the novel a passage printed in italics conveys the interior thoughts of the Italian general when excessive brandy causes him to second-guess his own mission.

> *I don't see why our comrades' remains should be restored to their families. I don't believe that was their last wish, as some people claim. To us, to all old soldiers, such displays of sentimentality seem very puerile. A soldier, living or dead, never feels at ease except among his comrades. So leave them together. Don't split them up. Let the serried graves keep the old warlike spirit of yesterday still alive in us. Don't listen to those chicken-hearted people always ready to yell at the sight of a drop of blood. Listen to us, we fought here and we know.*[28]

Kadare's message would seem to be that military men and civilians think differently about the importance of permanent reburial "at home" as a matter of personal and national honor. It becomes a thankless job to look for the remains of dead souls merely to bring them back for a decent burial. Is it really worth the effort? Does it not involve a misguided sense of national pride?

At the outset, the general had no doubts. "He would do everything in his power to acquit himself worthily of such a sacred task. Not one of his countrymen should be forgotten, not one should be left behind in this foreign land."[29] Two years of frustrating labor prompt a change of heart. It is twenty years too late, and two years of futility are too many. When the general learns that his subordinates have made grievous mistakes in the identification of remains, he is appalled. Attempts at rationalization would be humiliating. "I would be rather more inclined to say that they rebaptized the bones of unknown soldiers with the names of those men they had been particularly requested to look out for. In short, if the story is true, then we are dealing with a gross and appalling fraud. The remains have been sent to families to whom they did not rightfully belong." The disillusioned general concludes: "A nasty business altogether."[30] Sending unknown and unknowable dead men back across the Adriatic had clearly been a colossal blunder.

At the very end, the two generals meet at a hotel in Tirana, the Italian drinking brandy, the German drinking *raki*, the anise-flavored alcoholic beverage beloved in the Balkans, Turkey, and Greece. Because they each have lists of men with particular height specifications whose bodies they were supposed to send back, they cynically contemplate swapping German bodies for Italians so that each one can fulfill his specific mandate. Ultimately they do not, and the one-armed German general philosophizes: "The remains we dig up constitute war's very essence, you might say. What remains when it is all over; the precipitate after a chemical reaction." Mutual recognition of cynical beliefs and behavior thereby gives way to banal sophistries.[31]

A full generation later, however, we discover a distinctive sign of new and changing attitudes toward the ethical imperative of repatriating those who were lost in war. On May 27, 2008, the German press reported that Germany's War Graves Authority had signed an agreement for the remains of some four thousand German soldiers killed in the former Czechoslovakia during World War II to be buried at a special site in the western Czech town of Cheb. In a move hailed by both sides as an act of reconciliation, the Czechs decided to build a military cemetery for the German war dead next to the town graveyard. That felt like a triumph of good faith and reconciliation over cynical recriminations.[32]

✠

The body of Benito Mussolini underwent one of the most intensely politicized migrations of all, from an ad hoc gallows to a blessed sanctuary—all in all, a tortuous rite of passage for his bitterly divided country. After he was captured and killed by anti-Fascist partisans near Lake Como in April 1945, his corpse and those of his mistress and a few associates were taken to Milan, where they were hanged upside down from an elevated pole at a gasoline station, making possible the infamous photos that inspired the Left and enraged the Right for years thereafter. Following autopsies and indecision, in June Mussolini and Clara Petacci were secretly buried in unmarked graves at Musocco Cemetery in Milan. The authorities wanted to keep his resting place from becoming a symbolic marker for the significant number of Il Duce admirers who persisted. The latter had wanted him buried at the Altar of the Nation in Rome's Piazza Venezia, the site of his famous balcony speeches. Although they could not achieve that, on Easter 1946 they did successfully steal the body and took it to a fifteenth-century monastery outside Pavia, where Franciscan monks helped to conceal it. The purpose of this plot was to transform clandestine neo-Fascism into a legitimate political force.[33]

In the process of Mussolini's exhumation and transportation, several of his fingers fell off; they were subsequently fetishized as relics by the Right. Meanwhile the police swung into action and made numerous arrests among known neo-Fascists in the Milan area. Even more momentous, Italians voted in a referendum to abolish the monarchy and establish a republic. After one hundred days of aggressive police work with informers and arrested insiders, police discovered the body sealed in a trunk, wrapped in two rubberized sacks, and hidden in a closet in one of the monk's cells on the monastery's ground floor. Along with Il Duce's remains ("a skeleton falling to pieces") authorities also found a declaration by the Fascist Party that envisioned the day when his body would be buried on Rome's Capitoline Hill. Photos taken of the small trunk at police headquarters became almost as familiar as the grim images photographed at the Milan gas station.[34]

Thereafter Mussolini's remains would be secretly hidden for reasons of state until 1957. On orders from the prime minister and with the agreement of Cardinal Ildefonso Schuster, archbishop of Milan, the government kept Mussolini's remains concealed in the chapel of the convent of Cerro Maggiore, near Milan, thereby honoring a commitment that the police chief had made to a priest to give the dictator a Christian yet secret resting place. For the next eleven years, only a tiny group of politicians, clerics, and civil servants knew the exact location of the "tomb." Given all of that secrecy, of course, by 1950 a Buried in Italy Campaign had begun—rumors spread like wildfire that he was buried here, there, and everywhere. Schemes and searches abounded.[35]

The Italian government resisted requests that he be reinterred in the cemetery at Predappio in Emilia-Romagna, his birthplace, where his grave could easily turn into a pilgrimage site for neo-Fascists or a site of vandalism for his foes. During the summer of 1957, however, the Italian Social Movement newspaper engaged in a forceful campaign to have the remains restored to Predappio. Mussolini's widow, Rachele, negotiated details for the body's return with Prime Minister Adone Zoli, a conservative Christian Democrat. Decoy vehicles were used to deter journalists, and the remains, placed in a wooden box marked "church documents," were accompanied by police and monks from the Lombard convent to the Mussolini family crypt at the San Casciano cemetery on August 31. Neo-Fascist faithful were present for the entombment, and predictably, the site has remained a shrine for political pilgrims ever since.[36]

✝

Joseph Stalin's encounters with death and burial were numerous, fascinating, and virtually without any counterpart in American historical experience. Born in 1878, he married his first wife, called Kato, in 1906. Although he adored her, he also neglected her because of his intense political commitments and ceaseless travel to raise money for Lenin and revolution. On November 22, 1907, Kato died of typhus and dysentery. At her church funeral he declared, "This creature softened my heart of stone. She died and with her died my last warm feelings for humanity." At the burial his composure totally cracked, and he threw himself fully into her grave on top of the coffin. After being hauled out by friends, he spotted members of the czar's secret police entering the graveyard, raced to the back, vaulted the fence, and disappeared for two months.

Eventually he returned to his mother's home in Georgia to grieve. "My personal life is shattered," he sobbed. "Nothing attaches me to life except socialism. I'm going to dedicate my existence to that."[37]

When Stalin died of a cerebral hemorrhage on March 5, 1953, he was elaborately embalmed and placed under glass in the Lenin Mausoleum in Red Square (actually the third one constructed for Lenin). Three years later, however, Nikita Khrushchev addressed the Twentieth Party Congress in a secret session and denounced Stalin's "cult of personality" and his "violation of Leninist norms of legality." Because more than fourteen hundred delegates heard the speech, it did not remain secret for very long. Khrushchev subsequently arranged for his friend Nikolai Podgorny, a future head of state, to propose that the continued presence of Stalin's body next to Lenin's was "no longer appropriate" on account of his "abuse of power, mass repressions against honourable Soviet people, and other activities in the period of the personality cult." At the Twenty-second Party Congress in 1961, Podgorny made that proposal and it carried unanimously.[38]

On the night of October 31, 1961, Stalin's remains were secretly removed from the mausoleum, on which a notice then appeared that it was "closed for repairs." Stalin's name was also removed from the entrance, his body was cremated, and the ashes were buried below the Kremlin wall near those of four former comrades. His new "resting place" was marked by a black granite slab with the simple inscription "J. V. Stalin, 1879–1953." During the winter months of 1961–62, countless statues and portraits of the once-feared dictator were removed throughout the Soviet Union. Resistance was encountered only in Stalin's native Georgia, where a huge statue overlooked the venerable city of Tbilisi. Even that statue eventually disappeared, just before Khrushchev's visit to Georgia with Fidel Castro. In 1970, however, a small bust of Stalin was added to the ultra-brief inscription at his new grave site.[39]

✴

We must turn next to nearby Hungary, where multiple exhumations and reburials since 1988 have been politicized perhaps more intensively than anywhere else. Episodes there are remarkably symptomatic of ideological regime change and a desire to make amends for serious political "sins" of the recent past by honoring as national heroes the martyrs who epitomize integrity, courage, and creativity.[40] It is difficult to identify comparable phenomena in American political culture, because we have not experienced a 180-degree reversal and rebirth comparable to what happened in Hungary beginning in 1988.

The reputations of national heroes wax and wane everywhere. In the United States, for example, esteem for Woodrow Wilson's reputation has gradually declined, whereas Harry S. Truman's aura rose upon reconsideration and because of the political uses to which his persona could be put by subsequent presidents, such as Gerald Ford. But such shifts have depended upon the ebb and flow of historical revisionism and public opinion. In the United States we have not had the kind of overt *manipulation* (as opposed to resuscitation, perhaps) of reputations that has characterized Hungary during the last two decades, and the contrast can be instructive.[41]

As I noted briefly while discussing Rachmaninoff in chapter 1, the composer Bela Bartók died in New York in 1945, somewhat disillusioned with the United States, but having emigrated from Hungary at the beginning of World War II to protest the encroachment of Nazism in Hungarian politics and society. In the spring of 1988 his two sons, one living in the United States and the other in Budapest, decided that their father's remains really should be returned to his homeland. As it happens, the socialist government had been wanting just that for some while, but the timing could not have been more convenient, because nationalist sentiment was then reaching fever pitch.

During the fortnight between his exhumation and reburial, Hungarian newspapers and magazines became obsessed with Bartók. Instead of being flown directly from New York to Budapest, the coffin traveled by ocean liner to England and then by motorcade from France through Germany and Austria, with celebratory concerts held in Southampton, Cherbourg, Paris, Strasbourg, Munich, and Vienna. When the coffin crossed the border into Hungary, people lined the highway to watch the motorcade pass through their villages.[42]

As Susan Gal has observed, it is difficult to imagine a similar welcome, more than four decades following death, for a classical composer, especially an often difficult and musically dissonant one, in the United States or even in Western Europe. Gal believes that Bartók's funeral can best be understood "as a move by intellectuals closely associated with state socialism and the Communist Party to celebrate a national hero who would evoke the sympathy and confidence of a broad internal audience (including opposition intellectuals in both the populist and the urbanist camps) while appealing to an international one as well."[43]

Keep in mind, however, that in his youth Bartók had written a concerto dedicated to Lajos Kossuth, leader of the 1848 Revolution in Hungary, and that Bartók had been inspired by authentic Hungarian folk music. Moreover, he was not a genuine émigré, someone who simply abandoned his country, but had lived in self-imposed exile because he opposed both Fascism and Communism. He also became closely identified with populism when the return of his body was compared with the 1894 return of Kossuth's body and the 1906 return of the remains of Rákóczi, also a leader of Hungarian rebellion against Habsburg rule from Vienna.[44]

In identifying Bartók's reburial with the homecomings of Kossuth and Rákóczi, both of them exiled revolutionaries, the state implicitly offered critical and opposition intellectuals a body they had not even requested while remaining conspicuously silent about the body that the democratic, urbanist opposition had been seeking for years: that of Imre Nagy, leader of the 1956 anti-Soviet uprising who was brutally murdered and placed in an unmarked grave. Because Bartók had opposed Fascism so vehemently, his return meant that symbolically his spirit found Communist Hungary a politically and ethically acceptable place. By that logic, as Gal has remarked, "the return of Bartók's body justified, legitimated, and strengthened the Hungarian government's very weak moral claims on the population."[45]

The composer had actually requested in his will that no great ceremony accompany his funeral. Although it may have turned out to be grander than he envisioned or desired, it actually became a relatively modest skirmish in the discursive battle among Hungarian elites. With the demise of the Hungarian Communist Party the following year, a difficult tension between the desire for distinctive national identity on one hand and pan-European sentiments on the other persisted in the contest between new political parties formed in 1989 in the wake of earlier opposition groups. A certain synthesis of specifically Hungarian qualities along with the broader European culture had been ascribed to Bartók and pleased many Hungarians. It even impressed those who found the funeral rhetoric inappropriate because it stressed a fundamental cultural duality. The idea that Hungarian nationalism could be reconciled with Europeanness became attractive to Hungarians because it helped to resolve a long-standing intellectual and political tension in the Hungarian sense of self.[46]

Hungary may very well have the most notable history of exhuming and reburying political leaders who fell from grace because of revolutionary changes. Count Lajos Batthyány, chosen as prime minister of the 1848 Revolution, was executed on October 6, 1849, but eventually reburied in the renamed Kerepesi Common Cemetery in 1870. During the later nineteenth century this cemetery increasingly became the final resting place for rich or famous Hungarians. A special section was set aside for persons who had committed suicide or been executed and therefore could not receive an ecclesiastical burial. On March 15, 1860, students organized a celebration in front of the cemetery to commemorate the outbreak of the 1848 Revolution. When police shot into the crowd, killing a law student, his funeral turned into the largest anti-Habsburg demonstration the city had seen. The martyr, Géza Forinyák, was buried in the cemetery wall.[47]

The most notorious and carefully studied modern example of political rehabilitation and exhumation, however, involves Imre Nagy, prime minister of Soviet-controlled Hungary in the early 1950s who led the anti-Soviet revolt in 1956. Once that rebellion had been crushed, Nagy and four "coconspirators" were convicted in a closed trial, hanged in 1958, and secretly buried in the courtyard of their prison. Three years later, their pseudonymously identified bodies were moved to an unmarked mass grave in the largest cemetery in Budapest. Rumors emanated from drunken gravediggers that they had been placed in plot 301, situated in an obscure corner of the burial ground. During the early 1980s, on the anniversary of the execution, family members and surviving victims of the abortive revolution began placing flowers on the ground at the presumed resting place. Their guess must have been correct, because in 1982 the police started closing that part of the cemetery on October 23, the anniversary of the day when the 1956 Revolution began.[48]

In July 1988 the last secretary-general of the Hungarian Communist Party announced that the family of Imre Nagy would be allowed to rebury him in private. By then, however, he had already received a symbolic public burial—but elsewhere. On June 16, 1988, the thirtieth anniversary of his death, a commemorative monument to Nagy was erected at Père Lachaise Cemetery in Paris, courtesy of then mayor Jacques Chirac. The monument took the form of a shipwrecked boat—meant to be emblematic of the fate of utopian Communism—designed by László Rajk, son of the executed minister of foreign affairs, the most famous victim of the notorious Hungarian show trials at the end of the 1940s. When the symbolic burial of Nagy occurred in Paris, a demonstration took place in Budapest at the Eternal Sacred Flame honoring Batthyány, the executed and already reburied prime minister of 1848–49. Following the suggestion of one of the organizers of the demonstration, the Eternal Sacred Flame was renamed the Batthyány-Imre Nagy Flame.[49]

The ideological and political transformation of Hungary in 1989 occurred with such nonviolent smoothness that it barely qualified as a revolution. Changes occurred by means of radical reform. The most symbolic and memorable event took place on June 16, when Nagy was reburied on Heroes' Square in front of the Millenary Monument, which had been erected as part of observances of the thousand-year anniversary of the Hungarians' arrival in the Carpathian Basin. As the historian István Rév has written in his thorough account, "The monument links a Magyar past with the Hungarian Holy Crown that represents the country's Christian and European civilizing mission in the Carpathian Basin."[50]

Within a month of his widely noted ceremony, the political rehabilitation of Nagy was complete. This pattern of honorific exhumation, reburial, and restoration would continue for some years and would be replicated with various other heroic figures in Hungary. After János Kádár, the Communist leader for thirty-three years, died in 1989, the son of László Rajk, who had been betrayed by Kádár while he served as foreign minister, decided to remove his father from his ignominious grave so that he would not lie anywhere near his executioner. The son had him reinterred close to the exiled and reburied president Count Károlyi in a *depositio ad sanctos*, a practice carried over from antiquity when Christian noblemen buried their relatives in close proximity to martyrs of the church. (As Rév has noted of these ironic *danses maca-*

bres, Kádár died at *exactly* the hour when Nagy received legal rehabilitation from the Supreme Court of Hungary.)[51]

Admiral Miklós Horthy had served as Hungary's interwar regent and eventually guided Hungary into an alliance with Hitler in return for the redemption of pieces of Hungarian territory. Horthy died in 1944, unmourned after the war by Communists. When he was exhumed and reburied in 1993 at the request of Hungary's first prime minister following the revolution (a former history teacher, as it happens),[52] Horthy's new entombment was deemed the obliteration of Communism from national memory. But as Rév has written, "Those weeping over Horthy's new grave mourned the hundreds of thousands of soldiers who fell along the Don River in the Second World War against the Soviet Union just [even] as they mourned the man who sent them to their death, and they sought to camouflage their own recent past with the corpse of the regent. . . . Those who were present at the funeral hoped that their physical proximity to the regent's remains would prove that they had always been implacable anti-Communists, the secret opponents of his enemies."[53]

It's very curious the way complex memories and shadowy reputations change when the political context has been altered. We have already seen that to be true in the case of such Americans as James Wilson and Jefferson Davis—both men the victims and then the beneficiaries of shifting political climates.

✠

The outcome and the legacy of most of these European episodes has been more than national reconciliation and the notable rehabilitation of selected reputations for leadership and courage. Their heritage has also involved historical revisionism on a large scale—revisionism that has not only been accepted but embraced, partially for reasons of partisan satisfaction but mainly in the interest of truth—correcting the record. Here we must distinguish between two related yet rather different forms of "revisionism." I am profoundly struck by the contrast with the United States, where we have learned, especially in recent decades, that what most Americans understand by "revisionist history" is mistrusted. It is not readily acceptable to the lay public and has frequently been denounced on the floor of Congress by well-educated and well-meaning senators and representatives, ranging from liberals like Dianne Feinstein of California to conservatives like Alan Simpson of Wyoming, not to mention Lynne Cheney's notorious attack during the 1990s on the new History Standards for secondary schools in the United States.

The frequent refrain of resistance runs along these lines: "Why can't they just leave history alone—the way it really happened and got recorded?" There seems to be an American assumption that the first attempts at historical narration and understanding get it all quite right. Much of the public believes that the books we once read in school were authoritative. More often than not, new information and challenging interpretations seem to be suspect because troublesome: they require the reconsideration of cherished assumptions. "Historical revisionism" has not been well received in America, not ordinarily and certainly not in recent decades.[54]

Revisionism and its potential for conflict take unexpected forms in diverse venues, however, and the varied examples never cease to compel attention. Some are especially awkward in terms of challenges to institutional authority. Still others pose a problem for popular beliefs. Consider several from 2008. A Capuchin monk called Padre Pio died in 1968 at the age of eighty-one in his hometown of San Giovanni Rotondo, located not far from Puglia, on the heel of Italy's boot. In April 2008 his body was exhumed and put on display until the end of the year because he had become the most popular saint in Italy, having been canonized by Pope John Paul II (who canonized more saints than any other pope). Padre Pio's appeal and mystery arose from the fact that he claimed to have stigmata similar to the wounds of Christ, from which he bled and could feel actual pain. Pope John XXIII had considered him a fraud and a womanizer, accusing him of "immense deception."[55]

Nevertheless, he is beloved by the masses. There is no lack of testimony from witnesses. "He was suffering," explained a woman with a German friend who saw him in 1966. "He had blood coming out of his hands. If you saw it, you would believe it." More than 750,000 people made reservations to view the body during the seven-month span while it was displayed in 2008. Padre Pio seems to appeal to something mystically spiritual, which many feel the Vatican does not—at least not sufficiently. Moreover, the hospitality industry in southern Italy promoted the viewing opportunity with all its might because that area receives the least amount of tourism in Italy. The man in charge of tourism for the Puglia region put it quite frankly: "This is an opportunity we have to turn religious tourism into mass tourism." Replicas of Padre Pio's "famous" half-gloves could be purchased for the equivalent of eight dollars; a snow globe of Padre Pio went for for $4.75.[56]

Unfortunately, when Padre Pio's crypt had been opened a few months earlier, in bitter cold, his hands were reported to be in perfect condition with no signs of stigmata at all. The archbishop who presided at the exhumation, Domenico D'Ambrosio, would say only the following: "As soon as we got inside we could clearly make out the beard. The top part of the skull is partly skeletal, but the chin is perfect and the rest of the body is well preserved." According to medical experts who peered at the body, neither the feet nor the hands showed any signs of the wounds expected of someone who supposedly bled spontaneously, on and off, for more than fifty years. Whether Padre Pio was duplicitous remained to be determined during the months of visitation, but the Vatican placed strict limits on the number of people who could be present when the tomb was opened. What the millions would see, and their understanding of what they saw, well, . . . differences persisted, perhaps predictably. The outcome remains inconclusive.[57]

In the summer of 2008 the Vatican requested the exhumation of England's most renowned convert to Roman Catholicism as part of his elevation toward sainthood. When John Henry Cardinal Newman died in August 1890, he was buried in the rustic cemetery at Rednal Hill, Birmingham, at the country house of the Birmingham Oratory. He shares a grave and memorial stone there with his lifelong friend Ambrose St. John, who converted to Catholicism at the same time as Newman. The pall above Newman's coffin bears his motto, "Cor ad Cor Loquitur" (Heart speaks to heart). The Vatican wants Newman's remains to be moved to a marble sarcophagus in the Birmingham Oratory, where people can pay tribute to him more easily because of urban access. It is unclear whether the two beloved friends will now be separated in death if the cardinal achieves sainthood.[58]

✝

For quite a different scenario of potential revisionism, we turn to a contested case where exhumation and reburial elsewhere is demanded because an individual's celebrated reputation has gone from philanthropic benefactor to exploitative racist. Cecil John Rhodes (1853–1902) did much to develop Zimbabwe (formerly Southern Rhodesia) and South Africa by founding the De Beers Company and the Gold Fields of South Africa. When he died a very rich man, he was buried, as he requested, on the massive *dwala* that forms the center of a dramatic site that he named the "View of the World." Although he is best remembered in the Anglo-American sphere as the generous donor of Rhodes scholarships, he is increasingly recalled in Zimbabwe as a man who sequestered land and placed locals in a condition close to slavery as they worked in mines, on farms, and in the industrial and commercial sectors.[59]

A Harare-based pressure group, mainly consisting of highly vocal Shona-speaking activists, insists that the hill where Rhodes is buried is really sacred ground on which indigenous kings were laid to rest. They have campaigned since the 1990s for the removal of the grave and demand that Rhodes's remains be either repatriated to England or else thrown into the Zambezi River. Not everyone in Zimbabwe agrees, however, that "View of the World" truly was a sacred burial site—it is a matter of tradition unsupported by any historical evidence—and because the site is a designated national monument protected by the National Museums and Monuments of Zimbabwe (NMMZ), the site has considerable touristic value. Hence the domestic division over Rhodes's possible reinterment elsewhere.[60]

A compromise solution under consideration is to leave Rhodes where he is but redefine the concept of "national heritage" to include more native sites. Meanwhile, Cecil Rhodes remains in situ despite activists' threats to toss him into the Zambezi.[61] Rhodes's case is intriguing both because of the obvious postcolonial backlash, but also as an example of exhumation being demanded because of a dramatic *decline* in reputation locally, rather than a rediscovery and redemption in historical esteem.

✛

Turning to a totally different type of recent "revisionism," this one resulting from new radiocarbon dating techniques, the English site we know as Stonehenge, located on the Salisbury Plain, has been at least partially demystified—not how it was built but its genesis. Archaeologists based at the University of Sheffield have determined from human cremation burials among and around the massive stones that the site was first used as a cemetery, from about 3,000 BCE until *after* the megaliths were erected sometime around 2,500 BCE. What appeared to be the head of a stone mace, a symbol of authority, was found in one grave, suggesting that this must have been a grave site for the ruling dynasty responsible for erecting Stonehenge. In medieval literature there are stories speaking of Stonehenge as a memorial to the dead—anecdotal evidence, to be sure, but consistent with what the archaeologists are now indicating.[62]

They estimate that as many as 240 people were buried at Stonehenge, all of them as cremation deposits. Evidence from elsewhere in the British Isles indicates that skeletal burials were quite rare at that time and that cremation was the normative custom for the elite. Yet another member of the research team from Sheffield proposes the likelihood that the burials at Stonehenge actually represent generations of a single royal family. Why? The number of burials in the earliest phase (3000 BCE) was relatively small, with larger numbers of burials occurring in the later stages, thereby suggesting a multiplication of offspring. The Stonehenge Riverside Project has been excavating since 2003 with support from the National Geographic Society. Most of the cremated remains were actually uncovered decades ago, but only in recent years have improved methods of radiocarbon dating made it possible to analyze burned bones with reliable accuracy.[63]

✠

When we consider European reburials with an unusually high degree of symbolic content and public performance, such as Jean Moulin's in 1964, two for Imre Nagy in 1988–89 (first in Paris and then in Budapest), or Frederick the Great's political fracas in 1991, American situations come to mind that were similarly high in civic symbolism for contemporaries, albeit much less recent: James Monroe in 1831, Daniel Boone in 1845, Jefferson Davis in 1893, James Wilson and John Paul Jones in 1905–6. During the past century, however, Europe quite clearly exceeds the United States in emblematic exhumations as ideological referenda.

And that raises the question why. As a speculative answer, consider just six lines drawn from W. H. Auden's famous poem about the start of World War II, titled "September 1, 1939":

Exiled Thucydides knew
All that a speech can say
About Democracy,
And what dictators do,
The elderly rubbish they talk
To an apathetic grave.

Nation-states elsewhere have had a marked history of political leaders (and dictators) determined to use exhumation and reburial as a political tool or weapon, which eventually, more often than not, elicits a responsive determination to set the record straight. One thinks of Chiang Kai-shek's exploitation of Sun Yat-sen, Hitler's of Frederick the Great, Juan Perón and Carlos Menem's resuscitation of Juan Manuel de Rosas, and the anti-Communists' resurrection of Imre Nagy. Some Americans have considered Abraham Lincoln's wartime policies as dictatorial yet unavoidable, or similarly regard Franklin Roosevelt's quasi-constitutional measures to fight the Great Depression, but we really have no history of dictatorial leaders who have grievously manipulated death for partisan advantage. John Adams did not do so when Washington died in 1799. Nor was it done by Andrew Johnson in 1865, nor Theodore Roosevelt in 1901, and it was done only minimally by Lyndon B. Johnson after 1963.

Although as we have seen there are many parallels and similarities between celebrity reburials in the Old World and the New, I am ultimately more impressed by several fundamental contrasts. To mention a significant though hardly the most important one first, issues of religious conformity versus heterodoxy in Europe often posed problems largely unknown in the United States. The contested cases of Lajos Kossuth (a Lutheran), Adam Mickiewicz (a lapsed Catholic), William Butler Yeats (a nonobservant Catholic), Vladimir Jabotinsky (a radically revisionist Jew), all discussed in the first chapter, and Padre Pio (a self-dramatizing priest) come promptly to mind. Robert Ingersoll's atheism and F. Scott Fitzgerald's lapsed Catholicism provide rather unusual but minor blips on the American side.

The relationship and connections between exhumation/reburial and nationalism lead us to a much more meaningful basis for comparison.

Issues involving national unity or identity seem to have been more press-ing, persistent, impassioned, and politicized in Europe, as we have seen, for example, in the cases of Frederick the Great, Adam Mickiewicz, and Communist Hungary's symbolic need for Bela Bartók's body in 1988.

Amid the sectional tensions that troubled nineteenth-century Amer-ica, especially in the decades before and following the Civil War, New York nevertheless gave James Monroe back to Virginia very graciously in 1858, and Rhode Island quite reasonably acceded to Georgia's request to keep the remains of Nathanael Greene in 1902. The relocation of Confederate dead from Northern battlegrounds to Southern cemeter-ies, noted in chapter 3, might be cited, but those partisan and intensely felt issues were resolved fairly promptly because the North felt no great need or desire to keep the remains of vanquished rebels—quite the con-trary. And the Northern press covered the reburial of Jefferson Davis with considerable interest but little recrimination. The federal govern-ment never even brought Davis to trial for treason, though it very well could have.

✛

In June 2008 the former (and final) Soviet leader, Mikhail Gorbachev, urged that the embalmed body of Vladimir Lenin, leader of the Bolshe-vik Revolution in 1917, should be moved from its reverential mausoleum in Red Square, where it has rested since his death in 1924, and given a standard burial. Lenin's literal and symbolic presence in the heart of Moscow has provided an ongoing source of controversy since the collapse of the Soviet Union in 1991. Gorbachev explained that, in his view, "we should not be occupied right now with grave-digging. But we will necessarily come to a time when the mausoleum will have lost its meaning and we will bury [Lenin], give him up to the earth as his family had wanted. I think the time will come." Perhaps he is right, but the Communists still remain the second largest political party in Russia. Although the Orthodox Church has also called for Lenin's exhumation and reburial, echoing the suggestion made initially by Boris Yeltsin, the first post-Soviet leader, Communists insist that the founding father of the Soviet Union should stay put. Vladimir Putin acknowledged that the issue is an emotional one and has not committed himself to either side. So the outcome remains unclear. The great irony, of course, though scarcely remembered, is that Lenin and his wife, just like John Calvin and Baron Von Steuben, personally disapproved of visibly memorializing the dead![64]

What also remains unclear is our ability to generalize about the historical "democratization" (a term used advisedly) of burial and reinterment. Those who would prefer to have Lenin receive a much less honorific interment would seem to be tending in that direction—perhaps as an end to Soviet sanctification. As noted in chapter 3, democratization also appears to have been the rationale behind look-alike tombstones in national military cemeteries in the United States and later in Western Europe. Once upon a time, long, long ago, those with high political status received far more elaborate burial in preferred sites, as we know from ancient Egypt, Stonehenge, and the Spiro Mounds in eastern Oklahoma. Ordinary folks were either cremated or interred on the periphery of a special burial ground, often impermanently. Their bones were disposable. No democracy of the dead in those days.[65]

Next consider the transition from the eighteenth to the mid-nineteenth century in the United States. Civil society shifted from comparatively low-key burials with few or modest grave markers in the colonial period to an era when affluent people began to outdo themselves in erecting elaborate vaults and monuments in the "natural paradise" that Mount Auburn and its emulating suburban cemeteries aspired to be. The key distinction to keep in mind, of course, is that government-run cemeteries could be readily democratized after the Civil War, but for those people in the private sector where families owned their own plots, options remained at the discretion of affluent purchasers. In the twentieth century, however, a trend away from grandiosity gradually became apparent, even at private burial grounds. Conspicuous consumption in death diminished somewhat.

Ultimately, European conflicts involving reburial were more likely to become not only intensely politicized—note the fanatical democratization of death that accompanied the French Revolution, yet also the deconsecration of the Panthèon as a site for special reinterments—but often *internationalized*, as we have seen in the episodes concerning Adam Mickiewicz on the Continent, Baron von Richthofen in France and Germany, Lajos Kossuth, and Imre Nagy (keeping in mind the 1988 French embarrassment of Hungary by its honoring of Nagy at Père Lachaise Cemetery, a famous site that also figures in several other episodes that we have considered).[66] The reinterments of John Howard Payne ("Home Sweet Home") and John Paul Jones are rather unusual examples of Americans requiring international action. There is much to be learned from the diverse narratives of American burials, and much more illumination is to be had by observing the contrasts with disputatious stories of contestation that took place in foreign lands.

✝

A major stimulus for this project occurred when I encountered two excellent books dealing with Eastern Europe: anthropologist Katherine Verdery's *The Political Lives of Dead Bodies* (1999) and cultural historian István Rév's *Retroactive Justice* (2005). Although I was already familiar with numerous sagas of exhumation and reburial in the United States, duly noticed out of sheer curiosity and serendipity over a span of several decades, their political resonance and the persistent role of pride were not immediately apparent to me. The recorded narratives of figures like John Paul Jones and Daniel Boone initially seemed rather different from each other and from their European counterparts. In recent years, and with closer scrutiny of many more episodes, although significant contrasts remain, the differences cluster within discernible patterns. Certain similarities have seemed increasingly noteworthy, such as the rehabilitation of individual reputations, pride of possession, devoted adulation of celebrities, and especially the imperatives of commercial tourism. The last is definitely not a distinctively American thing.

Moreover, exhumation and reburial have more often been a tradition-oriented phenomenon with conservative or "preservationist" appeal rather than a cause customarily taken up by progressives, and that is true everywhere. Within the United States I think of the Masonic Dr. Joseph Warren, James Monroe, John Trumbull, and Jefferson Davis as prime examples of tradition-oriented causes. The fates of Robert Ingersoll and Matthew Henson, however, represent progressive outcomes in which invidious distinctions of disbelief and color were overcome. Elsewhere one thinks of Jean Moulin (1964), Juan Manuel de Rosas (1989), and Frederick the Great (1991) as exhumations that served the needs of conciliating nationalists and were stridently opposed by leftist liberals, at least initially.

In contrast, when Karl Marx, who had lived in most of the major European capitals, died in March 1883, he was buried in what is now the rather crowded and funky Highgate Cemetery in North London, joined there fifteen months later by his wife Jenny. No one has proposed relocating them. To the best of my knowledge, his birthplace in Trier (situated in Prussia) has never asked for him.

We must also consider that with each of the striking categories of comparison just mentioned, human agency has been crucial. It matters even more than contingency. Reburials rarely occur by accident or serendipity; they are very carefully planned material events. Recall these four lines penned by Richard Wilbur in 1956:

> What is our praise or pride
> But to imagine excellence, and try to make it.
> What does it say over the door of Heaven
> But *homo fecit*?[67]

The challenging contrast that remains, however, clearly lies in the realm of political sentiment and discourse. Here, perhaps, we find the most important contrasts between the United States and elsewhere. Although many American reburials were quite obviously motivated politically, they mostly seem to have lacked the ongoing ideological edge and intensity of those European reburials where feelings were fiercely fired by anti-Communism (see Nagy) or pro- and anti-Fascism (see Mussolini) or anti-clericalism (see Voltaire).

Revisiting Alexis de Tocqueville's *Democracy in America* brings to mind once again his emphasis upon the American republican consensus and its legacy. A brief passage from each volume of *Democracy* (1835 and 1840) highlights his theme of how very much Americans shared in common compared with Europeans.

> What is meant by a republic in the United States is the slow and quiet action of society upon itself. It is an orderly state founded in reality upon the enlightened will of the nation. It is a conciliatory government where resolutions ripen over time, are discussed slowly and executed only when fully matured. . . . Americans frequently change their laws but the basis of the constitution is respected.[68]

I have often noticed that theories which are by their nature revolutionary, in that they can be realized only by a complete and sometimes sudden upheaval in the rights of property or the status of persons, are infinitely less to people's liking in the United States than in the great monarchies of Europe.[69]

Because Americans had less interest in political theory and were less ideological, their society was more stable despite its penchant for perpetual change. Never having had an *ancien régime* or hence a reaction against it, the United States never developed a strong tradition of socialism, a point reiterated and embellished in the twentieth century by the German sociologist Werner Sombart and the American political scientist Louis Hartz. In 1955 Hartz devoted an influential book to a recondite elaboration of Tocqueville and of Lionel Trilling's observation in 1950 that "in the United states at this time liberalism is not only the dominant but even the sole intellectual tradition."[70]

As Tocqueville so astutely noticed, using his innovative approach to the study of politics and society, Americans could very clearly differ among themselves, but not (save for 1861–65) with the enduring and irreconcilable ferocity of monarchists versus republicans, socialists versus capitalists, or Communists versus liberal democrats in Europe. It is not that partisanship has been lacking in America. It began in earnest quite early in George Washington's first administration, when Hamiltonians and Jeffersonians differed on domestic as well as foreign policy. But partisanship here has not, for the most part, had quite the same unbridgeable ideological chasm that has been endemic in European history, and this has had important consequences in contrasting our episodes of exhumation.

Given that long historical context and comparative framework, I believe we are now better situated to comprehend many of the apparent differences between Old and New World experiences with the politics of reburial. While similarities are not unexpected, the differences appear more pronounced. The explanation lies in the contrasts between two kinds of political cultures—one more nearly univocal in terms of basic democratic values, the other with partisans speaking past one another.

NOTES

INTRODUCTION

1. Donald E. Collins, *The Death and Resurrection of Jefferson Davis* (Lanham, Md.: Rowman and Littlefield, 2005), 67–88, the quotation at 88.

2. Ibid., 90–94.

3. Ibid., 95–111, the quotation at 103. For an explanation of the etymology of *translation*, see Russell Shorto, *Descartes' Bones: A Skeletal History of the Conflict between Faith and Reason* (New York: Doubleday, 2008), 51–52.

4. Collins, *Death and Resurrection of Jefferson Davis*, 96.

5. Ibid., 110–21; the general is quoted on 154.

6. Ibid., 118, 122–25.

7. *Richmond Dispatch*, September 18, 1892.

8. Collins, *Death and Resurrection of Davis*, 137–47.

9. Ibid., 149–53.

10. Herodotus, *The Persian Wars*, trans. George Rawlinson (New York: Modern Library, 1942), 36–38, the quotation at 37.

11. Plutarch, *The Rise and Fall of Athens: Nine Greek Lives*, trans. Ian Scott-Kilvert (London: Penguin, 1960), 149–50. I am indebted to classicist Hunter R. Rawlings for these citations.

CHAPTER ONE

1. See George Mosse, *Fallen Soldiers: Reshaping the Memory of the World Wars* (New York: Oxford University Press, 1990), 39–40. William Wordsworth preferred the cypress. See John Morley, *Death, Heaven, and the Victorians* (Pittsburgh: University of Pittsburgh Press, 1971), 49.

2. Mosse, *Fallen Soldiers*, 40–41, 82–84; Jay Winter, *Sites of Memory, Sites of Mourning: The Great War in European Cultural History* (Cambridge: Cambridge University Press, 1995).

3. See Blanche M. G. Linden, *Silent City on a Hill: Picturesque Landscapes of Memory and Boston's Mount Auburn Cemetery*, 2nd ed. (Amherst: University of Massachusetts Press, 2007), 19–20, 24, 227.

4. See Allan I. Ludwig, *Graven Images: New England Stonecarving and Its Symbols, 1650–1815* (Middletown, Conn.: Wesleyan University Press, 1966); James A. Hijiya, "American Gravestones and Attitudes toward Death: A Brief History," *Proceedings of the American Philosophical Society*, 127, no. 5 (1983), 339–63.

5. Marilyn Yalom, *The American Resting Place: Four Hundred Years of History through Our Cemeteries and Burial Grounds* (Boston: Houghton Mifflin, 2008), 11–12.

6. Joseph B. Doyle, *Frederick William Von Steuben and the American Revolution* (Steubenville, Ohio: H. C. Cook, 1913), 351, 354.

7. Ibid., 376; *New York Times*, October 1, 1872, 1; John McCauley Palmer, *General Von Steuben* (New Haven, Conn.: Yale University Press, 1937), 403–4. In 1936 a replica of Von Steuben's log home was built in the park, based upon a sketch made in 1802 by a traveling clergyman.

8. Linden, *Silent City on a Hill*, 4, 23, 26–27, 86, 163.

9. Mark S. Schantz, *Awaiting the Heavenly Country: The Civil War and America's Culture of Death* (Ithaca, N.Y.: Cornell University Press, 2008), 38, 40, 47, 50. The last quotation (italics mine) is from Rufus W. Clark, *Heaven and Its Scrip-*

tural Emblems (Boston: John P. Jewell, 1853), 80.

10. Schantz, *Awaiting the Heavenly Country*, 53, 56.

11. Quoted in Debby Applegate, *The Most Famous Man in America: The Biography of Henry Ward Beecher* (New York: Doubleday, 2006), 36.

12. Linden, *Silent City on a Hill*, 24, 127–28, 137–38.

13. Schantz, *Awaiting the Heavenly Country*, 80–81. The "vile bodies" passage is from Philippians 3:20–21.

14. The "culture of melancholy" seems to be customarily ascribed to the second through the fourth decades of the nineteenth century, demarked especially by William Cullen Bryant's poem "Thanatopsis" (1817) and the "melancholy pleasure" of visiting rural cemeteries during the 1830s and into the 40s.

15. See Gary Laderman, *The Sacred Remains: American Attitudes toward Death, 1799–1883* (New Haven, Conn.: Yale University Press, 1996); James J. Farrell, *Inventing the American Way of Death* (Philadelphia: Temple University Press, 1980).

16. See David Charles Sloane, *The Last Great Necessity: Cemeteries in American History* (Baltimore: Johns Hopkins University Press, 1991), 1–6.

17. See Jessica Mitford, *The American Way of Death* (New York: Simon and Schuster, 1963); Drew Gilpin Faust, *The Republic of Suffering: Death and the American Civil War* (New York: Alfred A. Knopf, 2008).

18. Peter Metcalf and Richard Huntington, *Celebrations of Death: The Anthropology of Mortuary Ritual*, 2nd ed. (New York: Cambridge University Press, 1991); David Stannard, ed., *Death in America* (Philadelphia: University of Pennsylvania Press, 1975); Margaretta J. Darnall, "The American Cemetery as Picturesque Landscape: Bellefontaine Cemetery, St. Louis," *Winterthur Portfolio* 19 (Winter 1983), 249–69.

19. See Annette Becker, "War Memorials: A Legacy of Total War?" in *On the Road to Total War: The American Civil War and the German Wars of Unification, 1861–1871*, ed. Stig Förster and Jörg Nagler, (Washington, D.C.: German Historical Institute, 1997); Sanford Levinson, *Written in Stone: Public Monuments in Changing Societies* (Durham, N.C.: Duke University Press, 1998); Hijiya, "American Gravestones and Attitudes towards Death."

20. For an excellent example of Federalist versus Republican partisanship and conflict in 1813 involving three burials of the first American "martyr" in the War of 1812, see Robert E. Cray Jr., "The Death and Burials of Captain James Lawrence: Wartime Mourning in the Early Republic," *New York History* 83 (Spring 2002): 133–64.

21. See "Bodies of Civil War Dead Moved to Provide New Veteran Graves," *New York Times*, June 29, 1980, 30; Michael C. Kearl and Anoel Rinaldi, "The Political Uses of the Dead as Symbols in Contemporary Civil Religions," *Social Forces* 61 (March 1983): 701.

22. See Annette Gordon-Reed, *Thomas Jefferson and Sally Hemings: An American Controversy* (Charlottesville: University of Virginia Press, 1997); "DNA Tests Confirm the Deaths of the Last Missing Romanovs," *New York Times*, May 1, 2008, A12.

23. Robert Pogue Harrison, *The Dominion of the Dead* (Chicago: University of Chicago Press, 2003), xi.

24. See Cray, "Death and Burials of Captain James Lawrence," 133–64.

25. See http://www.congressionalcemetery.org. I am indebted to Mary Wright, stewardship program director at the Congressional Cemetery, for providing me with an abundant amount of printed information about the cemetery and its history.

26. Peter Andrews, *In Honored Glory: The Story of Arlington* (New York: G. P. Putnam's Sons, 1966), chap. 2.

27. Zora Neale Hurston to W. E. B. Du Bois, June 11, 1945, in *The Correspondence of W. E. B. Du Bois*, ed. Herbert Aptheker (Amherst: University of Massachusetts Press, 1978), 3:41–42. Du Bois replied on July 11, 1945, that the idea "has its attractions but I am afraid that the practical difficulties are too great" (ibid., 43).

28. In March 2008, President Vladimir Putin of Russia launched the creation of a Federal Military Memorial Cemetery, designed to be Russia's counterpart to Arlington National Cemetery, possibly to be located on a wasteland in northern Moscow. Putin hopes to be buried there himself, somewhere close to Stalin, his hero. It is due for completion in 2010.

29. Eric M. Meyers, *Jewish Ossuaries: Reburial and Rebirth, Secondary Burials in Their Near Eastern Setting* (Rome: Biblical Institute Press, 1971), 15–16, 31, 63, 72.

30. G. E. Mylonas, "Homeric and Mycenaean Burial Customs," *American Journal of Archaeology* 52 (January 1948): 56–81. In the Homeric epics the dead are cremated; but we know from archaeological evidence that in Mycenaean times the deceased were inhumed—an interesting discrepancy.

31. Christopher Columbus has two "official" tombs, one in Seville, where he was buried in the cathedral, and another in Santo Domingo.

32. Caroline Walker Bynum, *The Resurrection of the Body in Western Christianity, 200–1336* (New York: Columbia University Press, 1995), 201–3, 212. See also Katharine Park, "The Life of the Corpse: Division and Dissection in Late Medieval Europe," *Journal of the History of Medicine and Allied Sciences* 50 (1995): 111–32.

33. Johan Huizinga, *The Waning of the Middle Ages* (1924, reprint Garden City, N.Y.: Doubleday, 1956), 143–44; Jacob Burckhardt, *The Civilization of the Renaissance in Italy* (1876, reprint New York: Harper and Row, 1958), 2:466; Russell Shorto, *Descartes' Bones: A Skeletal History of the Conflict between Faith and Reason* (New York: Doubleday, 2008), 50–52.

34. See Philippe Ariès, *Images of Man and Death* (Cambridge, Mass.: Harvard University Press, 1985), 14, 19; Peter Brown, *The Cult of the Saints: Its Rise and Function in Late Christianity* (Chicago: University of Chicago Press, 1981).

35. I am indebted for the following to Shorto, *Descartes' Bones*.

36. Ibid., 42, 47–48.

37. Ibid., 69.

38. Ibid., 106, 109–10, 118, 126–29.

39. Ibid., 127, 139, 212, and passim.

40. In 2009 Descartes' skull was relocated to the school in La Fiche where he studied as a boy.

41. See Roger Pearson, *Voltaire Almighty: A Life in Pursuit of Freedom* (New York: Bloomsbury, 2005), 387–91; Haydn Mason, *Voltaire: A Biography* (Baltimore: Johns Hopkins University Press, 1981), 149–51; Craig Nelson, *Thomas Paine: Enlightenment, Revolution, and the Birth of Modern Nations* (New York: Viking, 2006), 329.

42. Gail S. Altman, *Fatal Links: The Curious Deaths of Beethoven and the Two Napoleons* (Tallahassee, Fla.: Anubian, 1999).

43. Michelle Vovelle, "Le Deuil Bourgeois: Du faire-part à la statuaire funéraire," *Le Débat*, no. 12 (May 1981): 60–82; Jean Seznec, "Michelet in Germany: A Journey in Self-Discovery," *History and Theory* 16, no. 1 (1977): 3. For an 1897 image of a man lifting his fiancée from her tomb, see Ariès, *Images of Man and Death*, plate 306. For a nineteenth-century view of Père Lachaise Cemetery, see Ariès, plate 342.

44. Peter Karsten, *Patriot-Heroes in England and America: Political Symbolism and Changing Values over Three Centuries* (Madison: University of Wisconsin Press, 1978), 114, 129, 161; Barbara

Graustark in "Newsmakers," *Newsweek*, March 20, 1978, 67.

45. Martha Lampland, "Death of a Hero: Hungarian National Identity and the Funeral of Lajos Kossuth," *Hungarian Studies* 8, no. 1 (1993): 29–35.

46. Patrice M. Dabrowski, "Eloquent Ashes: The Translation of Adam Mickiewicz's Remains," chapter 3 in *Commemorations and the Shaping of Modern Poland* (Bloomington: Indiana University Press, 2004). I am indebted to this fine book for all that follows.

47. Ibid., 84–86.

48. Ibid., 86–87.

49. Ibid., 88.

50. Ibid., 90.

51. Ibid., 96–99.

52. R. F. Foster, *W. B. Yeats: A Life*, vol. 2, *The Arch-Poet, 1915–1939* (Oxford: Oxford University Press, 2003), 653–55.

53. Ibid., 656–57.

54. Ibid., 657.

55. Alan Cowell, "Ancestors Are Revered and Living Well in Madagascar," *New York Times*, July 26, 1983, A2; the quotation from Katherine Verdery, *The Political Lives of Dead Bodies: Reburial and Postsocialist Change* (New York: Columbia University Press, 1999), 42.

56. Ralph Waldo Emerson, "Works and Days" (1857), in *The Complete Works* (Boston, 1904), 7:177. In the preceding paragraph he insisted that "the use of history is to give value to the present hour and its duty."

57. Wallace Evan Davies, *Patriotism on Parade: The Story of Veterans' and Hereditary Organizations in America, 1783–1900* (Cambridge, Mass.: Harvard University Press, 1955); D. O. S. Lowell, "The Quest of Ancestors," *Munsey's Magazine* 34 (February 1906): 543–48; Florida Pier, "The Power of Ancestors," *Century* 71 (January 1906): 445–47. For an early but significant example of this impulse, see François Weil, "John Farmer and the Making of American Genealogy," *New England Quarterly* 80 (September 2007): 408–34.

58. See Levinson, *Written in Stone*, 38–68.

59. See David Lowenthal, *The Past Is a Foreign Country* (Cambridge: Cambridge University Press, 1985), 321–24.

60. "Rossini's Remains Exhumed," *Washington Post*, May 3, 1887, 1; "Payne," in *Dictionary of American Biography*.

61. "Rachmaninoff, Buried in New York, May Return to Russia," *New York Times*, April 1, 1992, 31. To view Rachmaninoff's grave, go to the Kensico website, http://kensico.org/historic-scenic-tour .asp, and click on #27.

62. "Reburial of Herzl in Jerusalem Set," *Washington Post*, August 8, 1949, 3.

63. Myron J. Aronoff (Rutgers University), "The Origins of Israeli Political Culture," paper prepared for an international conference, Israeli Democracy under Stress: Cultural and Institutional Perspectives, held at the Hoover Institute, Stanford, June 27–July 1, 1990, 13.

64. Ibid.

65. Louise Hall Tharp, *Saint-Gaudens and the Gilded Era* (Boston: Little, Brown, 1969), 119. It is noteworthy that Polybius reported comparable practices when members of the Roman political and military elite died. See *Polybius on Roman Imperialism: The Histories of Polybius*, ed. Alvin H. Bernstein (South Bend, Ind.: Regnery, 1980), 215–16.

66. *Journals of Ralph Waldo Emerson, 1856–1863*, ed. E. W. Emerson and W. E. Forbes (Boston: Houghton Mifflin, 1913), 9:102–3. It is very odd that this rather curious act by Emerson is not mentioned in the standard biographies.

67. Kenneth A. Lockridge, *The Diary and Early Life of William Byrd II of Virginia, 1674–1744* (Chapel Hill: University of North Carolina Press, 1987), 43; Pierre Marambaud, *William Byrd of Westover, 1674–1744* (Charlottesville: University Press of Virginia, 1971).

68. Quoted in Laderman, *Sacred Remains*, 36.

CHAPTER TWO

1. See John J. Pullen, *Patriotism in America: A Study of Changing Devotions, 1770–1970* (New York: American Heritage, 1971); Cecilia O'Leary, *To Die For: The Paradox of American Patriotism* (Princeton, N.J.: Princeton University Press, 1999); Stuart McConnell, "Nationalism," in *Encyclopedia of the United States in the Twentieth Century*, ed. Stanley Kutler (New York: Charles Scribner's Sons, 1996), 1:251–71.

2. See Hans Kohn, *American Nationalism: An Interpretive Essay* (New York: Macmillan, 1957); John Breuilly, *Nationalism and the State* (Chicago: University of Chicago Press, 1984); Wilbur Zelinsky, *Nation into State: The Shifting Symbolic Foundations of American Nationalism* (Chapel Hill: University of North Carolina Press, 1988); John Pettegrew, " 'The Soldier's Faith': Turn-of-the-Century Memory of the Civil War and the Emergence of Modern American Nationalism," *Journal of Contemporary History* 31 (January 1996): 49–73; Ronald Beiner, ed., *Theorizing Nationalism* (Albany: SUNY Press, 1999); Anatol Lieven, *America Right or Wrong: An Anatomy of American Nationalism* (New York: Oxford University Press, 2004).

3. Robert Cray Jr., "Commemorating the Prison Ship Dead: Revolutionary Memory and the Politics of Sepulture in the Early Republic, 1776–1808," *William and Mary Quarterly*, 3rd ser., 56 (July 1999): 565–90.

4. Ibid., 573, 583–84, 587. See also Matthew Dennis, "Patriotic Remains: Bones of Contention in the Early Republic," in *Mortal Remains: Death in Early America*, ed. Nancy Isenberg and Andrew Burstein (Philadelphia: University of Pennsylvania Press, 2003), 144–47.

5. Walt Whitman, *The Complete Poetry and Prose*, ed. Malcolm Cowley (New York: Pellegrini and Cudahy, 1948), 434–35. Whitman's poem seems to date from 1888. The highly significant tomb of Alexander the Great became obscure and lost in antiquity, despite claims by several Egyptian Ptolemies to know its location and therefore to be Alexander's political heirs.

6. Cray, "Commemorating the Prison Ship Dead," 588–90.

7. John Cary, *Joseph Warren: Physician, Politician, Patriot* (Urbana: University of Illinois Press, 1961), 222–23; Blanche Linden-Ward, *Silent City on a Hill: Landscapes of Memory and Boston's Mount Auburn Cemetery* (Columbus: Ohio State University Press, 1989), 148.

8. A Bostonian, *Biographical Sketch of Gen. Joseph Warren . . . with the Celebrated Eulogy Pronounced by Perez Morton, M.M., on the Re-interment of the Remains by the Masonic Order, at King's Chapel in 1776* (Boston: Shepard, Clark, and Brown, 1857), 67, 73, 75–76, 78, 80–81. For the centrality of antebellum eschatology, see Mark Schantz, *Awaiting the Heavenly Country: The Civil War and America's Culture of Death* (Ithaca, N.Y.: Cornell University Press, 2008), chap. 2.

9. General Hugh Mercer, who may have persuaded George Washington to cross the Delaware River in December 1776, was killed in a skirmish with the British just prior to the Battle of Princeton and died a painful death on January 12, 1777. Originally interred at the Christ Church Burial Ground in Philadelphia, in 1840 he was exhumed and reinterred at Laurel Hill Cemetery. See his Wikipedia entry for excellent recent photographs of his burial site and monument at Laurel Hill. His original gravestone was brought from Christ Church and rests in front of the elaborate 1840s monument.

10. George Vaux, "Settlers in Merion—The Harrison Family and Harriton Plantation," *Pennsylvania Magazine of History and Biography* 13, no. 4 (1889): 453–54. This version of what occurred in 1838, and at whose initiative, has been

contested. Resolution awaits publication of an essay by historian Elliott Shore of Bryn Mawr College, who has been kind enough to share with me his work-in-progress "A Philadelphia Story."

11. Vaux, "Settlers in Merion," 455. Shore is skeptical of Vaux's version that it occurred in the "middle of the night." Nevertheless, he quotes ("A Philadelphia Story," 11) from a contemporary who owned the original burial site and lamented *"the clandestine manner* it was removed to a public cemetery for the purpose of giving éclat to a particular locality."

12. Vaux, "Settlers in Merion," 455–57. For a succinct variant of this scenario that closely follows the Vaux account, see Boyd Stanley Schlenther, *Charles Thomson: A Patriot's Pursuit* (Newark: University of Delaware Press, 1990), 222–23, which properly calls attention to the conflicting property interests among divided descendants of Charles and Hannah Thompson.

13. J. Edwin Hendricks, *Charles Thomson and the Making of a New Nation, 1729–1824* (Rutherford, N.J.: Fairleigh Dickinson University Press, 1979), 190–91, also calls attention to the possibility that the wrong bodies were unearthed because of inadequate markers.

14. Blanche M. G. Linden, *Silent City on a Hill: Picturesque Landscapes of Memory and Boston's Mount Auburn Cemetery*, 2nd ed. (Amherst: University of Massachusetts Press, 2007), 190–91, 195; Marilyn Yalom, *The American Resting Place: Four Hundred Years of History through Our Cemeteries and Burial Grounds* (Boston: Houghton Mifflin, 2008), 102–3.

15. The most complete account, on which I rely here, is by Michael P. Gabriel, *Major General Richard Montgomery: The Making of an American Hero* (Madison, N.J.: Fairleigh Dickinson University Press, 2002), 190–93.

16. Ibid., 193–94. According to one older but apparently reliable source, the efforts of John Pintard, founder of the New-York Historical Society, were instrumental in having Montgomery's remains buried at St. Paul's. See James Grant Wilson, *The Life and Letters of Fitz-Greene Halleck* (New York: D. Appleton, 1869), 512.

17. Gabriel, *Richard Montgomery*, 194–95.

18. Ibid., 196–97. Italics mine.

19. Ibid., 197–98.

20. Ibid., 199.

21. I have depended most heavily on Paul David Nelson, *Anthony Wayne: Soldier of the Early Republic* (Bloomington: Indiana University Press, 1985).

22. Ibid., 300–301.

23. Ibid., 302.

24. Ibid., 302–3.

25. Kirk Savage, "The Self-Made Monument: George Washington and the Fight to Erect a National Memorial," *Winterthur Portfolio* 22 (Winter 1987): 225–42, esp. 231. In 1930–31, when Washington's birthplace was being excavated and reconstructed in Wakefield, Virginia, remains of his ancestors were disinterred from the family burying ground and reburied in an impressive ceremony, and a new memorial was erected. See Seth C. Bruggeman, *Here George Washington Was Born: Memory, Material Culture, and the Public History of a National Monument* (Athens: University of Georgia Press, 2008), 195.

26. "Washington's Remains," *New York Times*, August 3, 1889, 4. Nevertheless, relics related to Washington were distributed among members of his circle. At the museum home of Elizabeth Powel in Philadelphia there is a kind of relic case containing a lock of Washington's hair and a fragment from his casket, given to Powel as mementoes of her departed friend. I am indebted to David W. Maxey for this information.

27. Theodore Sizer, ed., *The Autobiography of Colonel John Trumbull: Patriot-Artist,*

1756–1843 (New York: Da Capo, 1970), 378–80 (an appendix reprinted from the Walpole Society *Note Book*, 1948).

28. Ibid., 380–81.

29. Ibid., 381–82.

30. Ibid., 382.

31. See Gerald M. Carbone, *Nathanael Greene: A Biography of the American Revolution* (New York: Palgrave Macmillan, 2008).

32. Terry Golway, *Washington's General: Nathanael Greene and the Triumph of the American Revolution* (New York: Henry Holt, 2005), chaps. 11–12.

33. Russell F. Weigley, "Nathanael Greene," in *Encyclopedia of American Biography*, ed. John A. Garraty (New York: Harper & Row, 1974), 451–53; Carbone, *Nathanael Greene*, chap. 6.

34. *The Remains of Major General Nathanael Greene* (Providence, R.I.: E. L. Freeman and Sons, 1903), 95–96. This very rare book is much more revealing for our purposes than any biography of Greene.

35. Ibid., 105–11, 113, 229.

36. Ibid., 111, 118, 122.

37. Ibid., 135, 140.

38. Ibid., 123, 126–27.

39. Ibid., 128–30. Italics mine.

40. Ibid., 143–44.

41. Ibid., 113, 123, 130, 137. See David W. Blight, *Race and Reunion: The Civil War in American Memory* (Cambridge, Mass.: Harvard University Press, 2001), esp. chaps. 5–7; Paul H. Buck, *The Road to Reunion, 1865–1900* (Boston: Little, Brown, 1937), chaps. 11, 13.

42. Don Higginbotham, *Daniel Morgan: Revolutionary Rifleman* (Chapel Hill: University of North Carolina Press, 1961), 130–55.

43. Quoted in North Callahan, *Daniel Morgan: Ranger of the Revolution* (New York: Holt, Rinehart, and Winston, 1961), 297.

44. William L. Clark, in *Dedication of Mount Hebron Cemetery, in Winchester, Virginia, June 22, 1844* . . . (Winchester, Va.: Republican Office, 1845), 20. My italics.

45. Ibid., 13.

46. Ibid., 6.

47. Callahan, *Daniel Morgan*, 298; Higginbotham, *Daniel Morgan*, 214. For reasons unknown, a Daniel Morgan Monument Association was formed in 1911 in Portland, Maine; but it too did nothing for the new burial site.

48. "Court Gets Reburial Fight," *Washington Post*, August 13, 1951, B1; "Who Gets the General's Body?" *Life* 31 (September 3, 1951): 53–54.

49. Higginbotham, *Daniel Morgan*, 215; Callahan, *Daniel Morgan*, 298.

50. Roger M. Williams, "Who's Got Button's Bones?" *American Heritage* 17 (February 1966): 28–29.

51. Ibid., 30.

52. Ibid., 31.

53. Ibid.

54. Ibid., 31–32.

55. Ibid., 102.

56. Ibid; "Button Gwinnett Is Buried Again," *Washington Post*, October 3, 1964, C31.

57. "Lord Howe's Bones Found," *New York Times*, October 11, 1889, 1.

58. James Austin Holden, "New Historical Light on the Real Burial Place of George Augustus Lord Viscount Howe, 1758," in *Proceedings of the New York Historical Association* 10 (1911): 302. The 1910 meeting of NYSHA was actually held at Fort Ticonderoga, which made the contents of these proceedings especially lively.

59. Ibid., 304–5.

60. Ibid., 306–7.

61. Michael Meranze, "Major André's Exhumation," in *Mortal Remains: Death in Early America*, ed. Nancy Isenberg and Andrew Burstein (Philadelphia: University of Pennsylvania Press, 2003), 124–26, 128–29. Given the bitter feelings about Washington's unyielding treatment of André, it is fascinating that when James Lawrence, captain of the USS *Chesapeake*, was killed in a naval battle off the coast of Massachusetts in 1813, the British victors took his body to

Halifax, Nova Scotia, and buried him with full military honors. See Robert E. Cray Jr., "The Death and Burials of Captain James Lawrence: Wartime Mourning in the Early Republic," *New York History* 83 (Spring 2002): 145–46.

62. Meranze, "Major André's Exhumation," 126–29; James Buchanan, "Narrative of the Exhumation of the Remains of Major André," *United Service Journal and Naval and Military Magazine* (London), pt. 3 (1833), 307–8.

63. *Niles Weekly Register*, August 18, 1821, 386; Buchanan quoted in Meranze, "Major André's Exhumation," 130, italics in the original.

64. Leo A. Bressler, "Peter Porcupine and the Bones of Thomas Paine," *Pennsylvania Magazine of History and Biography* 82 (April 1958): 176–85; Moncure Daniel Conway, *The Life of Thomas Paine . . . To Which Is Added a Sketch of Paine by William Cobbett* (New York: G. P. Putnam's Sons, 1892), 2:451–55; David Hawke, *Paine* (New York: Harper and Row, 1974), 401; Craig Nelson, *Thomas Paine: Enlightenment, Revolution, and the Birth of Modern Nations* (New York: Viking, 2006), 323, 327.

65. Nelson, *Thomas Paine*, 327–28; J. Watson, *A Brief History of the Remains of the Late Thomas Paine from the Time of Their Disinterment in 1819 by the Late William Cobbett, M.P., Down to the Year 1846* (London: J. Watson, 1847).

66. Philadelphia *Public Ledger*, January 6, 1837, 4, and February 11, 1837, 2.

67. Nelson, *Thomas Paine*, 328–30; Conway, *Life of Thomas Paine*, esp. 2:429–59.

68. James Feron, "Paine Tombstone Uncovered Upstate," *New York Times*, July 19, 1976, 31.

69. Thomas Paine, *Collected Writings*, ed. Eric Foner (New York: Library of America, 1995), 152.

70. When Alexander the Great died of a fever in Babylon in 323 BCE, his body was preserved in golden honey, interred in a golden coffin mounted on a golden temple, and hauled westward by sixty-four mules, each one wearing a golden crown. Along the way the conveyance was intercepted by one of his most trusted generals, Ptolemy, who had just become the ruler of Egypt. Ptolemy stole the body and took it back to Egypt, where his descendants showed it to such luminaries as Julius Caesar. When the Ptolemies lost their throne in 30 BCE, the mummified Alexander was lost to history, though scholars have searched for centuries. Heather Pringle, *The Mummy Congress: Science, Obsession, and the Everlasting Dead* (New York: Hyperion, 2001), 134–35.

71. Fergus M. Bordewich, *Washington: The Making of the American Capital* (New York: Amistad, 2008), 12–14, 29–30.

72. Ibid., 73–75; 81–89; Scott W. Berg, *Grand Avenues: The Story of the French Visionary Who Designed Washington, D.C.* (New York: Pantheon, 2007); Saul K. Padover, ed., *Thomas Jefferson and the Nation's Capital . . . 1783–1818* (Washington, D.C.: Government Printing Office, 1946).

73. Berg, *Grand Avenues*, 232–33, 237.

74. Ibid., 233–34, 243–44.

75. Ibid., 272–74.

76. Quoted in ibid., 274.

77. Ibid., 274–75.

78. Ibid., 275–76.

79. Ibid., 276–77.

CHAPTER THREE

1. See William A. Blair, *Cities of the Dead: Contesting the Memory of the Civil War in the South, 1865–1914* (Chapel Hill: University of North Carolina Press, 2004); Caroline E. Janney, *Burying the Dead but Not the Past: Ladies' Memorial Associations and the Lost Cause* (Chapel Hill: University of North Carolina Press, 2008); John R. Neff, *Honoring the*

Civil War Dead: Commemoration and the Problem of Reconciliation (Lawrence: University Press of Kansas, 2005).

2. See Caroline E. Janney, " 'One of the Best Loved, North and South': The Appropriation of National Reconciliation by LaSalle Corbell Pickett," *Virginia Magazine of History and Biography* 116 (October 2008): 371–406.

3. Mary H. Mitchell, *Hollywood Cemetery: The History of a Southern Shrine* (Richmond: Virginia State Library, 1985), 35–36.

4. Ibid., 36–37.

5. Ibid., 38–39.

6. Ibid., 40.

7. Ibid.

8. Ibid., 41–42.

9. Ibid., 42–43.

10. Ibid., 44–45.

11. Stephen B. Oates, *To Purge This Land with Blood: A Biography of John Brown*, 2nd ed. (Amherst: University of Massachusetts Press, 1984), 351–53.

12. Ibid., 354–56.

13. Ibid., 357–58. Late in August 1899, on the exact anniversary of John Brown's raid at Ossawatomie, Kansas, in 1856, some of his comrades were reburied not far from his grave in North Elba, New York. *New York Times*, August 26, 1899, 6.

14. Gary Laderman, *The Sacred Remains: American Attitudes toward Death, 1799–1883* (New Haven, Conn.: Yale University Press, 1996), 90–91.

15. See Thomas J. Craughwell, *Stealing Lincoln's Body* (Cambridge, Mass.: Harvard University Press, 2007), 1–15; Neff, *Honoring the Civil War Dead*, chap. 2.

16. Lloyd Lewis, *Myths after Lincoln* (New York: Harcourt, Brace, 1929), viii, 260–61. See also Millard Lampell, "The Lonesome Train," a classic cantata about Lincoln's funeral train, first produced in 1944 on the prestigious Columbia Presents Norman Corwin radio series.

17. Lewis, *Myths after Lincoln*, 259.

18. Craughwell, *Stealing Lincoln's Body*, chaps. 2–5.

19. *New York Times*, April 14, 1887, 1; ibid., April 15, 1887, 1.

20. Craughwell, *Stealing Lincoln's Body*, 131, 208.

21. Ibid., 185–86, 193–95; Dorothy Meserve Kunhardt, "Strange History Brought to Light: Rare Photos of Lincoln Exhumation," *Life*, February 15, 1963, 86–88. The photograph on p. 86 shows the exposed coffin in 1901.

22. Craughwell, *Stealing Lincoln's Body*, 198.

23. See Hudson Strode, *Jefferson Davis* (New York: Harcourt, Brace, 1955–56), 3 vols.

24. Donald E. Collins, *The Death and Resurrection of Jefferson Davis* (Lanham, Md.: Rowman and Littlefield, 2005), chaps. 3–4; Robert Penn Warren, *Jefferson Davis Gets His Citizenship Back* (Lexington: University Press of Kentucky, 1980), 107.

25. When Stonewall Jackson was fatally wounded at Chancellorsville on May 3, 1863, his left arm was amputated and buried there with a marker. He died eight days later. In 1929 the arm was exhumed, placed in a steel box, and reburied on a plantation known as Ellwood in the Wilderness Battlefield. The only gravestone there belongs to Jackson's arm and can be visited with National Park Service permission. See http://www.roadsideamerica.com/set/arms.html.

26. Charles P. Roland, *Albert Sidney Johnston: Soldier of Three Republics* (Austin: University of Texas Press, 1964), 352–53.

27. Ibid., 353.

28. Ibid., 353–54; Thomas L. Connelly, *The Marble Man: Robert E. Lee and His Image in American Society* (New York: Alfred A. Knopf, 1977), 25.

29. Neff, *Honoring the Civil War Dead*; Blair, *Cities of the Dead*; Drew Gilpin Faust, *This Republic of Suffering: Death and the American Civil War* (New York: Alfred

A. Knopf, 2008); Janney, *Burying the Dead but Not the Past*; and Mark S. Schantz, *Awaiting the Heavenly Country: The Civil War and America's Culture of Death* (Ithaca, N.Y.: Cornell University Press, 2008).

30. Neff, *Honoring the Civil War Dead*, 108, 126.

31. James McPherson, "Dark Victories," *New York Review of Books*, April 17, 2008, 78–79.

32. Laderman, *Sacred Remains*, 110.

33. Ibid., 111–12.

34. Neff, *Honoring the Civil War Dead*, 111–15, 128.

35. Ibid., 63–64; Walter Muir Whitehill, *Boston and the Civil War* (Boston: Boston Athenaeum, 1963), 10–11.

36. Neff, *Honoring the Civil War Dead*, 56–57, 116–17.

37. Ibid., 3.

38. Janney, *Burying the Dead but Not the Past*, 46, 120–24. See also the insightful essay-review by Joan Marie Johnson, *Reviews in American History* 36 (December 2008): 529–36.

39. Janney, *Burying the Dead but Not the Past*, 9, 49, 119–32, 142–46. See also A. V. Huff Jr., "The Democratization of Art: Memorializing the Confederate Dead in South Carolina, 1866–1914," in *Art in the Lives of South Carolinians*, ed. David Moltke-Hansen (Charleston: Carolina Art Association, 1978), AH 1–8.

40. "Reburial of Confederates," *New York Times*, May 2, 1901, 5.

41. Janney, "One of the Best Loved North and South," 371. When La Salle Pickett died in 1931, Richmond's Hollywood Cemetery refused to bury her beside her husband. Instead her remains were placed in a mausoleum near Arlington National Cemetery. But in 1998 the Virginia Division of the UDC reinterred her remains next to her husband's at Hollywood (ibid., 391).

42. Conrad L. Eckert to Lyndon B. Johnson, April 1, 1964, Papers of the Civil War Centennial Commission, box 99, National Archives, Washington, D.C.

43. Bell Wiley to Edmund C. Gass, April 22, 1964, Papers of the Civil War Centennial Commission, box 99, National Archives, Washington, D.C.

44. "Bodies of Civil War Dead Moved to Provide New Veteran Graves," *New York Times*, June 29, 1980, A30. For the exhumation of the remains of sixty-seven Civil War soldiers, women, and children, mainly African American, from a national cemetery in south-central New Mexico, see "Soldiers' Remains Secretly Exhumed," *New York Times*, April 9, 2008, A19. Exhumation and reburial elsewhere occurred because widespread grave-looting was discovered.

45. "Man on a Mission to Get Recognition for Slaves Who Fought for the Union," MCT News Service, March 4, 2008, History Network News, Breaking News, March 5, 2008.

46. Quoted in Neff, *Honoring the Civil War Dead*, 10–11. See Daniel Aaron, *The Unwritten War: American Writers and the Civil War* (New York: Alfred A. Knopf, 1973), 62–72, in his chapter on Whitman.

47. Neil Harris, "The Battle for Grant's Tomb," *American Heritage* 36 (August 1985): 71–72, 74.

48. Ibid., 75–76.

49. Ibid., 77.

50. Ibid., 78–79.

51. Sumner, *Are We a Nation? Address of Hon. Charles Sumner . . . at the Cooper Institute, November 19, 1867* (New York: Young Men's Republican Union, 1867); my italics.

52. Melville Bell Grosvenor, "How James Smithson Came to Rest in the Institution He Never Knew," *Smithsonian Magazine* 6 (January 1976): 31–33.

53. Ibid., 34.

54. Ibid., 34–35; S. P. Langley, "The Removal of the Remains of James Smithson," *Smithsonian Miscellaneous Collections* 45 (October 1903): 243–51.

55. Grosvenor, "How James Smithson Came to Rest," 35–36. See also *Proceedings of the Board of Regents for the Year Ending June 30, 1904* (Washington, D.C., 1905), xvi–xxxiv, 7–10; ibid for 1905 (Washington, D.C., 1906), xi–xii, xv, xix, 3, 5–6.

56. See Page Smith, *James Wilson: Founding Father, 1742–1798* (Chapel Hill: University of North Carolina Press, 1956), chap. 25; Geoffrey Seed, *James Wilson* (Millwood, N.Y.: KTO Press, 1978).

57. David W. Maxey, "The Translation of James Wilson," in *Journal of Supreme Court History: 1990 Yearbook of the Supreme Court Historical Society* (Washington, D.C.: [Blackwell], 1991), 29–31.

58. Ibid., 32–33; Smith, *James Wilson*, 390.

59. Maxey, "Translation of James Wilson," 33–34. The majority opinion written by Chief Justice John Jay provided that federal judicial power should not extend to suits against one of the states initiated by citizens of another state or a foreign nation. Within less than a generation the nationalistic Marshall Court diminished the force of that amendment by means of several rulings.

60. Maxey, "Translation of James Wilson," 34.

61. Ibid., 35–36.

62. Ibid., 36.

63. Ibid., 37–38.

64. Ibid., 38–39.

65. Ibid., 40–41.

66. Ibid., 41.

67. James Wilson, "Lectures on Law," in *The Works of James Wilson*, ed. Robert Green McCloskey (Cambridge, Mass.: Harvard University Press, 1967), 1:70–71.

68. H. Marion, *John Paul Jones' Last Cruise and Final Resting Place, the United States Naval Academy* (Washington, D.C.: George E. Howard, 1906), 11–12. This valuable volume includes dozens of photographs, showing scenes ranging from workmen unearthing Jones's coffin through every stage of the many eulogies and ceremonies attendant upon his exhumation, public display in Paris, Franco-American celebrations, and the trip to Cherbourg. Very clearly, an official photographer had been assigned to make a complete visual record of the process. See Charles de Gaulle, *Le fil de l'épée* (Paris: Berger-Levrault, 1944).

69. Lincoln Lorenz, *John Paul Jones: Fighter for Freedom and Glory* (Annapolis, Md.: U.S. Naval Institute, 1943), 751–52.

70. Ibid., 753–54.

71. Ibid., 756.

72. Ibid., 755–56.

73. Ibid., 757–58.

74. Marion, *John Paul Jones' Last Cruise*, 33, 36.

75. Quoted in ibid., 21.

76. Ibid., 41, 45.

77. Ibid., 53, 56, 74.

78. John Morley, *Death, Heaven, and the Victorians* (Pittsburgh: University of Pittsburgh Press, 1971), 201.

79. Charles W. Stewart and others, *John Paul Jones: Commemoration at Annapolis, April 24, 1906* (Washington, D.C.: Government Printing Office, 1907), 12–13.

80. Ibid., 18–19.

81. Lorenz, *John Paul Jones*, 759, 765.

82. See Schantz, chap. 6, "The Court of Death," in *Awaiting the Heavenly Country*.

83. Alfred Frankenstein, *William Sidney Mount* (New York: Harry N. Abrams, 1975), 11, 260, 285, and the quotation at 248.

84. For a fascinating example of a lifelike painting of two dead children (1865), commissioned by an older sibling and based upon photographs, see Angela Miller, "Death and Resurrection in an Artist's Studio," *American Art* 20 (Spring 2006): 84–95, esp. 92–93. For a study of the residual fascination with images of the dead, especially dead children, during the late Victorian era, see Michael Lesy, *Wisconsin Death Trip* (New York: Pantheon, 1973).

CHAPTER FOUR

1. See John Mack Faragher, *Daniel Boone: The Life and Legend of an American Pioneer* (New York: Holt, 1992); Robert Morgan, *Boone: A Biography* (Chapel Hill, N.C.: Algonquin, 2007).

2. Following a visit by Mr. Peck in 1818, he reported that for "several years he [Boone] had kept his coffin constantly under the bunk in which he slept, and used to sit and regard it with a melancholy satisfaction. . . . And he felt already at rest, in knowing where his body was going to lie when it had finished its earthly service. That ridge overlooking the Missouri was never out of his mind." George Canning Hill, *Daniel Boone: The Pioneer of Kentucky* (New York: Worthington, 1890), 256.

3. Faragher, *Daniel Boone*, 354–55.

4. According to more than one early biographer, however, the men sent from Kentucky to dig up Boone's remains undertook a "holy mission of bearing him back to the land he had loved so well." W. H. Bogart, *Daniel Boone and the Hunters of Kentucky* (Auburn, N.Y.: Miller, Orton, and Mulligan, 1854), 384.

5. Faragher, *Daniel Boone*, 355–56.

6. Ibid., 356.

7. Ibid., 357–58.

8. Ibid., 358.

9. Ibid., 358–59.

10. Ibid., 359.

11. Ibid., 359–60. Two of the most widely read nineteenth-century biographies of Boone acknowledge that his original burial place in Missouri was "the grave he had chosen," yet neither book ever mentions Missouri's dismay and discontent with his removal to Frankfort. The 1890 volume assumes that Kentucky deserved the body even though Boone had made an explicit request on behalf of "the spot his own eyes had selected." See Bogart, *Daniel Boone and the Hunters*, 384–86; Hill, *Daniel Boone*, 259–61.

12. Faragher, *Daniel Boone*, 360–61.

13. Ibid., 361–62; "The Body in Daniel Boone's Grave May Not Be His," *New York Times*, July 21, 1983, C13.

14. See Kenneth Silverman, *Edgar Allan Poe: Mournful and Never Ending Remembrance* (New York: HarperCollins, 1991); Edward Wagenknecht, *Edgar Allan Poe: The Man behind the Legend* (New York: Oxford University Press, 1963).

15. Poe, "The Premature Burial," in *The Complete Works of Edgar Allan Poe*, ed. James A. Harrison (New York: AMS Press, 1965), vol. 5 overall, *Tales* 4:255, 257. For Poe's views concerning death and immortality, see Wagenknecht, *Edgar Allan Poe*, 210–15.

16. John C. Miller, "The Exhumation and Reburials of Edgar and Virginia Poe and Mrs. Clemm," *Poe Studies* 7 (December 1974): 46–47.

17. Ibid., 46.

18. Ibid., 47.

19. Ibid.

20. Ibid. In the late summer of 2008 Poe devotees who insist that he wrote his most important works in Philadelphia began seriously agitating to have his grave removed from Baltimore to Philadelphia. Ian Urbina, "Baltimore Has Poe; Philadelphia Wants Him," *New York Times*, September 6, 2008, A10.

21. Mary Jane Solomon, "Where the Somebodies Are Buried," *Washington Post*, October 25, 1991, 6.

22. "Grave of Miles Standish," *New York Times*, April 20, 1889, 5.

23. Richard W. Leopold, *Robert Dale Owen: A Biography* (Cambridge, Mass.: Harvard University Press, 1940).

24. Ibid.

25. Ibid., 414; Thomas C. Wheeler, ed., *A Vanishing America: The Life and Times of the Small Town* (New York: Holt, Rinehart, and Winston, 1964), 92.

26. William Conant Church, *The Life of John Ericsson* (New York: C. Scribner's Sons, 1907), 2:322–24.

27. Ibid., 325–26.

28. Quoted in ibid., 328.

29. Quoted in ibid., 329.

30. Ibid., 330–31.

31. Quoted in ibid., 332.

32. Ted P. Yeatman, *Frank and Jesse James: The Story behind the Legend* (Nashville: Cumberland House, 2000), 54–58.

33. Robertus Love, *The Rise and Fall of Jesse James* (New York: G. P. Putnam's Sons, 1926), esp. chaps. 6–7, 11–12, 14, 22, 25.

34. Ibid., ch. 26.

35. T .J. Stiles, *Jesse James: Last Rebel of the Civil War* (New York: Alfred A. Knopf, 2002), 377–78; Love, *Rise and Fall of Jesse James*, 366–70.

36. Love, *Rise and Fall*, 370–71.

37. Ibid., 371.

38. "Jesse James's Remains Disinterred and Removed," *New York Times*, June 30, 1902, 1.

39. Love, *Rise and Fall*, 377–81.

40. Yeatman, *Frank and Jesse James*, appendix H, 371–76.

41. Brenda Maddox, *D. H. Lawrence: The Story of a Marriage* (New York: Simon and Schuster, 1994).

42. Ibid., 286.

43. Ibid., 292.

44. Janet Byrne, *A Genius for Living: The Life of Frieda Lawrence* (New York: HarperCollins, 1995), 338–40, 350. Byrne refers to him as Angelino rather than Angelo.

45. Maddox, *D. H. Lawrence*, 499. For much of the saga that follows I am indebted to Brenda Maddox's careful but tongue-in-cheek account.

46. Ibid.

47. Ibid., 499–500. Byrne's narrative in *Genius for Living*, 363, 365–68, basically agrees with Maddox's version and adds some amusing anecdotes.

48. Maddox, *D. H. Lawrence*, 500.

49. Ibid.

50. Ibid., 501. A dancing party followed the dedication, at which a local Mexican orchestra hired by Frieda played and a bonfire was lit. "The guests—some were strangers who had arrived in response to an open notice placed by Frieda in a Santa Fe paper—feasted on hot dogs and red wine." Byrne, *Genius for Living*, 367–68.

51. Maddox, *D. H. Lawrence*, 500–501.

52. Cynthia Gorney, "Fitzgerald Reburied in Simple Ceremony," *Washington Post*, November 8, 1975, A15.

53. Solomon, "Where the Somebodies Are Buried," 7.

54. Ibid.; Gorney, "Fitzgerald Reburied," A15, A28.

55. Gilbert C. Fite, *Mount Rushmore* (Norman: University of Oklahoma Press, 1952), 220.

56. "Authorizing the Construction of a Crypt for the Remains of Gutzon Borglum," April 16, 1941, H.R. 3857, 77th Congress, First Session (Washington, D.C.: Government Printing Office, 1941), 1–12; Robert J. Casey and Mary Borglum, *Give the Man Room: The Story of Gutzon Borglum* (Indianapolis: Bobbs Merrill, 1952), 316–17.

57. Meryle Secrest, *Frank Lloyd Wright* (New York: Alfred A. Knopf, 1992).

58. Brendan Gill, *Many Masks: A Life of Frank Lloyd Wright* (New York: G. P. Putnam's Sons, 1987), 499.

59. Ibid., 514.

60. Secrest, *Frank Lloyd Wright*, 14–15.

61. Ibid., 16–18; Iver Peterson, "Reburial of Frank Lloyd Wright Touches Off Stormy Debate," *New York Times*, April 10, 1985, A14.

62. Peterson, "Reburial of Frank Lloyd Wright."

63. Ibid.

64. The Monona Terrace Convention Center finally got built in the later 1990s on Monona Bay.

65. Karl E. Meyer, "Frank Lloyd Wright Goes West," *New York Times*, April 19, 1985, A30.

66. Kara Swisher, "My Father's Homecoming," *Washington Post*, August 20, 1989, F1.

67. Ibid., F4.

68. Ibid. For a comparable yet different episode, see Amy Dickinson, "Father's Death Leaves Grieving Kin Split over His Final Resting Place," *Ithaca Journal*, March 26, 2008, 2C.

69. Lee Seldes, *The Legacy of Mark Rothko* (New York: Holt, Rinehart, and Winston, 1978).

70. Kathryn Shattuck, "Rothko Kin Sue to Transfer his Remains," *New York Times*, April 8, 2008, E1.

71. Ibid., E5. See Wilbur Zelinsky, "A Toponymic Approach to the Geography of American Cemeteries," *Names* 38 (September 1990): 209–29.

72. Kathryn Shattuck, "38 Years after Artist's Suicide, His Remains Are on the Move," *New York Times*, March 16, 2008, B5.

CHAPTER FIVE

1. Robert E. Cray Jr., "Memorialization and Enshrinement: George White-field and Popular Religious Culture, 1770–1850," *Journal of the Early Republic* 10 (Fall 1990): 343–44.

2. Ibid., 344–45. I am indebted to Cray's exhaustive monograph for most of what follows.

3. Ibid., 347.

4. Ibid., 348.

5. Ibid., 349; Alan Heimert, *Religion and the American Mind from the Great Awakening to the Revolution* (Cambridge, Mass.: Harvard University Press, 1966), 483.

6. Cray, "Memorialization and Enshrinement," 350–51.

7. Ibid., 351–52.

8. Ibid., 357.

9. Ibid., 357–58.

10. Herbert Asbury, *A Methodist Saint: The Life of Bishop Asbury* (New York: Alfred A. Knopf, 1927), 305; L. C. Rudolph, *Francis Asbury* (Nashville: Abingdon, 1966), 220.

11. Cray, "Memorialization and Enshrinement," 359–60.

12. Gary Laderman, *The Sacred Remains: American Attitudes toward Death, 1799–1883* (New Haven, Conn.: Yale University Press, 1996), 53–54.

13. Ibid., 76. The decomposition of Abraham Lincoln's corpse, especially his face, when displayed in New York City on April 24–25, 1865, became a major issue, though mainly for aesthetic reasons. See David Herbert Donald and Harold Holzer, eds., *Lincoln in the Times: The Life of Abraham Lincoln as Originally Reported in the New York Times* (New York: St. Martin's, 2005), 330–31.

14. Laderman, *Sacred Remains*, 51, 70–72, 169–70. For parallel sentiments arising slightly earlier in England, see John Morley, *Death, Heaven, and the Victorians* (Pittsburgh: University of Pittsburgh Press, 1971), 34–39.

15. Zachariah Allen, "Memorial of Roger Williams," paper read before the Rhode Island Historical Society, Providence, May 18, 1860, 1.

16. Ibid., 2

17. Ibid., 3–4.

18. Ibid., 6.

19. Ibid., 7.

20. Ibid., 8–9.

21. See Edmund S. Morgan, *Roger Williams: The Church and the State* (New York: Harcourt, Brace, and World, 1967); Edwin S. Gaustad, *Liberty of Conscience: Roger Williams in America* (Grand Rapids, Mich.: Eerdmans, 1991).

22. Julie Roy Jeffrey, *Converting the West: A Biography of Narcissa Whitman* (Norman: University of Oklahoma Press, 1991).

23. Clifford M. Drury, *Marcus and Narcissa Whitman and the Opening of Old Oregon* (Glendale, Calif.: Arthur H. Clark, 1973), 2:341–42.

24. Ibid., 342–43.

25. Ibid., 344.

26. Ibid., 344–45.

27. Robert J. Loewenberg, *Equality on the Oregon Frontier: Jason Lee and the Methodist Mission, 1834–1843* (Seattle: University of Washington Press, 1876).

28. Cornelius Brosnan, *Jason Lee: Prophet of the New Oregon* (New York: Macmillan, 1932), 323.

29. Ibid., appendix 8, "An Echo from the Past."

30. Moreland is quoted in "Memorial Services at Re-interment of Remains of Jason Lee. Salem, Oregon, June 15, 1906" (n.p., n.d.), 9; E. W. Potter, *Idaho: A Bicentennial History* (New York: W. W. Norton, 1977), 105.

31. Maynard J. Geiger, *The Life and Times of Fray Junípero Serra, O.F.M., or The Man Who Never Turned Back, 1713–1784*, 2 vols. (Washington, D.C.: Academy of American Franciscan History, 1959).

32. Kenneth M. King, *Mission to Paradise: The Story of Junípero Serra and the Missions of California* (Chicago: Franciscan Herald, 1975), 182–85.

33. Orvin Larson, *American Infidel: Robert J. Ingersoll* (New York: Citadel, 1962).

34. C. H. Cramer, *Royal Bob: The Life of Robert G. Ingersoll* (Indianapolis: Bobbs-Merrill, 1952), 257, 261–62, 264.

35. "Reburial for Ingersoll," *New York Times*, May 5, 1932, 22.

36. Edmund D. Cronon, *Black Moses: The Story of Marcus Garvey and the Universal Negro Improvement Association* (Madison: University of Wisconsin Press, 1955); Rupert Lewis and Maureen Warner-Lewis, *Garvey: Africa, Europe, the Americas* (Trenton, N.J.: Africa World Press, 1986, 1994).

37. Colin Grant, *Negro with a Hat: The Rise and Fall of Marcus Garvey and His Dream of Mother Africa* (New York: Oxford University Press, 2008).

38. Amy Jacques Garvey, *Garvey and Garveyism* (New York: Collier Macmillan, 1970), 289–90.

39. Ibid., 290–94.

40. John Henrik Clarke, *Marcus Garvey and the Vision of Africa* (New York: Random House, 1974), 344; "Garvey Reburial in Jamaica," *New York Times*, August 14, 1964, 6; Elton C. Fax, *Garvey: The Story of a Pioneer Black Nationalist* (New York: Dodd, Mead, 1972), 278–79.

41. See Bruce Henderson, *True North: Peary, Cook, and the Race to the Pole* (New York: W. W. Norton, 2005).

42. B. Drummond Ayres Jr., "Matt Henson, Aide at Pole, Rejoins Peary," *New York Times*, April 7, 1988, A16.

43. Ibid.

44. See http://www.matthewhenson.com/counter.htm and http://www.people.fas.harvard.edu/~counter/culture.html.

45. Ayres, "Matt Henson, Aide at Pole." For the significant case of Felix Longoria, a Mexican American soldier killed in the Philippines in 1945 who received honorific reburial at Arlington in 1949 through the efforts of Senator Lyndon Johnson, after being denied a place in a Texas cemetery, see http://www.tshaonline.org/handbook/online/articles/FF/vef1.html. I owe this reference to my colleague Maria Cristina Garcia.

46. Andrea E. Frohne, "The African Burial Ground in New York City: Manifesting and Representing Spirituality of Space" (PhD diss., SUNY Binghamton, 2002).

47. Anne-Marie E. Cantwell and Diana di Zerega Wall, *Unearthing Gotham: The Archaeology of New York City* (New Haven, Conn.: Yale University Press, 2001), chap. 16.

48. Cheryl LaRoche and Michael Blakey, "Seizing Intellectual Power: The Dialogue at the New York African Burial Ground," *Historical Archaeology* 31, no. 3 (1997): 84–106; Marilyn Yalom, *The American Resting Place: Four Hundred Years of History through Our Cemeteries and Burial Grounds* (Boston: Houghton Mifflin, 2008), 92.

49. Philip Freneau, *The Poems of Philip Freneau, Poet of the American Revolution*, ed. Fred Lewis Pattee (Princeton, N.J.: Princeton Historical Society, 1903), 2:369.

50. Thomas M. Allen, *A Republic in Time:*

Temporality and Social Imagination in Nineteenth-Century America (Chapel Hill: University of North Carolina Press, 2008), 50–52.

51. "Indian Remains from Dam Site to Be Reburied 'with Respect,'" *New York Times*, November 26, 1978, 71.

52. Douglas H. Ubelaker and Lauryn Guttenplan Grant, "Human Skeletal Remains: Preservation or Reburial?" *Yearbook of Physical Anthropology* 32 (1989): 249–87; "Repatriation: An Interdisciplinary Dialogue," special issue of *American Indian Quarterly* 20 (Spring 1996); "NAGPRA: Respectful Reburial Returns Remains to Proper Setting," *Cortez Journal*, April 25, 2006, http://www.cortezjournal.com/asp-bin/article.asp/article.

53. See Devon A. Mihesuah, ed., *Repatriation Reader: Who Owns American Indian Remains* (Lincoln: University of Nebraska Press, 2000), 123–68, 180–210; Robert Layton, ed., *Conflict in the Archaeology of Living Traditions* (London: Unwin Hyman, 1989), chaps. 11, 14, and 16; Jane Hubert, "A Proper Place for the Dead: A Critical Review of the 'Reburial Issue,'" *Journal of Indigenous Studies* 1, no. 1 (1989): 34–45.

54. "Illinois Museum to End Exhibit of Indian Remains," *New York Times*, January 5, 1990, A17; "Illinois to Shut an Exhibit of Indian Skeletons," *New York Times*, November 29, 1991, A30.

55. "Native American Reburials," *Christian Century* 107 (October 17, 1990): 928.

56. This information appeared in a brief list in the *New York Times*, November 5, 1975, 59.

57. "Osceola Reburial Urged," *New York Times*, September 1, 1947, 21. The post surgeon who attended Osceola's death cut off his head and kept it as a souvenir in his own home. He later sent it to another doctor in New York, who is believed to have lost it in a fire in 1866. See Alvin Josephy, *The Patriot Chiefs: A Chronicle of American Indian Leadership* (New York: Viking, 1961), 208; chapter 6 covers the circumstances of Osceola's death.

58. "Osceola," in *Wikipedia*, http://en.wikipedia.org/wiki/Osceola. For the nineteenth-century story of Chief Lone Wolf the Elder (?–1879) and his determination to find and rebury the remains of his son, Tau-ankia, see J. Lee Jones Jr., *Red Raiders Retaliate: The Story of Lone Wolf the Elder (Guipagho), Famous Kiowa Indian Chief* (n.p.: Pioneer Book, 1980).

59. Robert M. Utley, *The Lance and the Shield: The Life and Times of Sitting Bull* (New York: Holt, 1993), 306–7.

60. Ibid., 312.

61. Ibid. Apache Chief Geronimo died a prisoner of war at Fort Sill, Oklahoma, in 1909. It is believed that Prescott S. Bush and some Yale classmates broke into the grave during World War I and made off with the skull, and it has reposed ever since in a glass case at Skull and Bones, a Yale secret society whose house is called The Tomb. Geronimo's heirs have brought suit for the recovery and repatriation of his skull. James C. McKinley Jr., "Geronimo's Heirs Sue Secret Yale Society over His Skull," *New York Times*, February 20, 1909, A13.

62. "Historians Contend Raiders Didn't Get Sitting Bull Bones," *New York Times*, November 11, 1984, 71.

63. Utley, *Lance and the Shield*, 313; "Bones of Sitting Bull Go South from One Dakota to the Other," *New York Times*, April 9, 1953, 29.

64. "Historians Contend Raiders Didn't Get Sitting Bull's Bones," 71.

65. David La Vere, *Looting Spiro Mounds: An American King Tut's Tomb* (Norman: University of Oklahoma Press, 2007).

66. Ibid., 13–14.

67. Ibid., 119–25, esp. 123.

68. Paula Pryce, *"Keeping the Lakes' Way": Reburial and the Re-creation of a*

Moral World among an Invisible People (Toronto: University of Toronto Press, 1999), 139.

69. Ibid., 140.

70. Quoted in ibid.

71. From the collection *North of Boston* in *Complete Poems of Robert Frost, 1949* (New York: Henry Holt, 1949), 52.

72. Cara Buckley, "After 100 Years, Tribe's Ancestors Head Home," *New York Times*, June 10, 2008, http://www.nytimes.com/2008/06/10/nyregion/10remains.html.

CHAPTER SIX

1. Henrietta Harrison, *The Making of the Republican Citizen: Political Ceremonies and Symbols in China, 1911–1929* (Oxford: Oxford University Press, 2000), 133–44.

2. Ibid., 207–9.

3. Ibid., 226–30. See also Marie-Claire Bergère, *Sun Yat-sen* (Stanford, Calif.: Stanford University Press, 1998), chap. 11. The whole event was carefully recorded and photographed at the time, and accounts of it appear in numerous memoirs.

4. Jeffrey Shumway, "'Sometimes Knowing How to Forget Is Also Having a Memory': The Repatriation of Juan Manuel de Rosas and the Healing of Argentina," in *Body Politics: Death, Dismemberment, and Memory in Latin America*, ed. Lyman L. Johnson (Albuquerque: University of New Mexico Press, 2004), 105–40, esp. 105, 126–27.

5. Ibid., 119–30. See also Donna J. Guy, "Life and the Commodification of Death in Argentina: Juan and Eva Perón," in *Body Politics*, ed. Johnson, 245–72.

6. Jon Lee Anderson, *Che Guevara: A Revolutionary Life* (New York: Grove, 1997), xv; Richard L. Harris, *Death of a Revolutionary: Che Guevara's Last Mission* (New York: W. W. Norton, 2007), 272–77.

7. See John Upton Terrell and Colonel George Walton, *Faint the Trumpet Sounds: The Life and Trial of Major Reno* (New York: David McKay, 1966).

8. "Major Reno to Be Reburied," *New York Times*, September 6, 1967, 31; Ottie W. Reno, *Reno and Apsaalooka Survive Custer* (New York: Cornwall, 1997), chaps. 39–40, esp. 294–303.

9. London *Telegraph*, December 11, 2007; History Network News, Breaking News, December 11, 2007.

10. See Michael Kammen, "Mourning for a Lost Captain: New York City Comes to Terms with the National Tragedy," in *Lincoln and New York*, ed. Harold Holzer (New York: New-York Historical Society, 2009), 223–57.

11. Patrick Marnham, *Resistance and Betrayal: The Death and Life of the Greatest Hero of the French Resistance* (New York: Random House, 2002); Alan Clinton, *Jean Moulin, 1899–1943: The French Resistance and the Republic* (New York: Palgrave, 2002), 1–2, 196–99.

12. The entire story is told in fascinating detail by Henry Rousso in *The Vichy Syndrome: History and Memory in France since 1944* (Cambridge, Mass.: Harvard University Press, 1991), 81–84.

13. Ibid., 84–86.

14. Ibid., 87–89; Pierre Péan, *Vies et morts de Jean Moulin: Éléments d'une biographie* (Paris: Fayard, 1998), chaps. 33–34, for a detailed French perspective.

15. Von Richthofen was Frieda Lawrence's cousin.

16. Robert Weldon Whalen, *Bitter Wounds: German Victims of the Great War, 1914–1939* (Ithaca, N.Y.: Cornell University Press, 1984), 28–29, 33. For British survivors' pilgrimages to the Western Front during the 1920s to pay homage to their war dead, see Tom Lawson, "'The Free-Masonry of Sorrow'? English National Identities and the Memorialization of the Great War in Britain, 1919–1931," *History and Memory*

20 (Spring 2008): 89–120, esp. 100 and 113. See also Jay Winter, *Sites of Memory: The Great War in European Cultural History* (Cambridge: Cambridge University Press, 1995).

17. Whalen, *Bitter Wounds*, 34.

18. Both quoted in ibid., 34–35. For the many World War I memorials dedicated by Serbia's King Alexander I during the 1920s and the intensification of Serbian national sentiment, see Melissa Boko-voy, "Scattered Graves, Ordered Cemeteries: Commemorating Serbia's Wars of National Liberation, 1912–1918," in *Staging the Past: The Politics of Commemoration in Habsburg Central Europe, 1848 to the Present*, ed. Nancy Wingfield and Maria Bucur (West Lafayette, Ind.: Purdue University Press, 2001), 236–54. During the war the Serbs were allied with Britain and France against Germany, the Habsburgs, and the Ottoman Empire.

19. Marc Fisher, "Frederick: The Grave Germany Split over Prussian's Reburial," *Washington Post*, August 17, 1991, C1.

20. Ibid., C5.

21. Nicholas Kulish, "A Postscript for a Writer, 200 Years in the Works," *New York Times*, May 9, 2008, A8.

22. Ibid.; "Where's Schiller?" *New York Times*, May 5, 2008, E2.

23. Kulish, "Postscript for a Writer," A8; Nicholas Kulish, "2 More Skulls, but Still No Schiller," *International Herald Tribune*, May 9, 2008, 3.

24. Willemien Spook, "In These Kennemerdunes Sleep Our Dead," *Haarlems Dagblad*, May 4, 1993. Translated by Donata Trace de Reus of the University of Northumbria for the Dunes' website.

25. Ibid. I am grateful to Elisabeth Hopperus Buma for providing me with the journalistic account and information about the ongoing observance.

26. Ismail Kadare, *The General of the Dead Army* (New York: New Amsterdam Books, 1991), 181.

27. Ibid., 146.

28. Ibid., 130–31.

29. Ibid., 10.

30. Ibid., 228.

31. Ibid., 235, 249.

32. *Deutsche Welle*, May 27, 2008, posted on History Network News, Breaking News, May 29, 2008.

33. Sergio Luzzatto, *The Body of Il Duce: Mussolini's Corpse and the Fortunes of Italy* (New York: Metropolitan Books, 2005), 92–112.

34. Ibid., 105–12.

35. Ibid., 117–18.

36. Ibid., 207–11. On p. 210 there is a vivid photograph of the sarcophagus, a bust of Mussolini above it, fasces right and left of the portrait, and a guest book filled with signatures on a table in front of the railing. For the ongoing fetishization of Mussolini's grave by admirers, especially young ones, see Geert Mak, *In Europe: Travels through the Twentieth Century* (New York: Vintage, 2008), 297–98.

37. Simon Sebag Montefiore, *Young Stalin* (New York: Alfred A. Knopf, 2007), 191–94, the quotation at 193.

38. Georges Bortoli, *Death of Stalin* (New York: Praeger, 1975), 160–63; H. Montgomery Hyde, *Stalin: The History of a Dictator* (New York: Farrar, Straus, and Giroux, 1997), 605.

39. Hyde, *Stalin*, 605–6; Bortoli, *Death of Stalin*, 196.

40. For excellent context, see Alice Freifeld, "The Cult of March 15: Sustaining the Hungarian Myth of Revolution, 1849–1999," in *Staging the Past: The Politics of Commemoration in Habsburg Central Europe, 1848 to the Present*, ed. Nancy Wingfield and Maria Bucur (West Lafayette, Ind.: Purdue University Press, 2001), esp. 265–69 (for Kossuth), and 270–73, 276 (for Petőfi).

41. But see James W. Loewen, *Lies across America: What Our Historic Sites Get Wrong* (New York: New Press, 1999).

42. Susan Gal, "Bartók's Funeral: Rep-resentations of Europe in Hungarian Political Rhetoric," *American Ethnologist* 18 (August 1991): 449.

43. Ibid., 450.

44. Alex Ross, *The Rest Is Noise: Listening to the Twentieth Century* (New York: Far-rar, Straus, and Giroux, 2007), 88–90, 94–97, 121–22, 284, 327. For American perceptions, see Tibor Frank, "The Changing Image of Hungary in the United States," *Hungarian Quarterly* 38 (Winter 1997): 116–24.

45. Gal, "Bartók's Funeral," 451–52.

46. Ibid.

47. István Rév, *Retroactive Justice: Prehistory of Post-Communism* (Stanford, Calif.: Stanford University Press, 2005), 103.

48. Ibid., 24–25.

49. Ibid., 25–26.

50. Ibid., 19–21, 24–25.

51. Ibid., 28–29.

52. Freifeld notes that the Hungarian Revo-lution of 1989 was the most historically minded of all the revolutions that took place in 1989 ("Cult of March 15").

53. Rév, *Retroactive Justice*, 44–45.

54. See Frances FitzGerald, *America Re-vised: History Schoolbooks in the Twentieth Century* (Boston: Little, Brown, 1979); James W. Loewen, *Lies My Teacher Told Me: Everything Your American History Textbook Got Wrong* (New York: New Press, 1995); Gary B. Nash, Charlotte Crabtree, and Ross E. Dunn, *History on Trial: Culture Wars and the Teaching of the Past* (New York: Alfred A. Knopf, 1997). Even well-educated figures like John and Jacqueline Kennedy preferred to read history that was heroic and inspiring rather than disillusioning. See Sam Tanenhaus, "A Fumbled Handoff of the Torch," *New York Times*, January 25, 2009, Opinion sec., 2.

55. Ian Fisher, "Italian Saint Stirs Up a Mix of Faith and Commerce," *New York Times*, April 25, 2008, A9.

56. Ibid.

57. *The Independent* (UK), March 9, 2008, reported on the History News Network, Breaking News, March 9, 2008. For one of the many Web sites still devoted to his memory in 2009, see http://www.padrepio.com.

58. London *Telegraph*, July 15, 2008, reported in History News Network, Breaking News, July 16, 2008.

59. Svinurayi Joseph Muringaniza, "Heri-tage That Hurts: The Case of the Grave of Cecil John Rhodes in the Matopos National Park, Zimbabwe," in *The Dead and Their Possessions: Repatria-tion in Principle, Policy, and Practice*, ed. Cressida Fforde et al. (London: Rout-ledge, 2002), 317–25.

60. Ibid.

61. Ibid.

62. John Noble Wilford, "Stonehenge Began as Cemetery, Data Shows," *New York Times*, May 30, 2008, A11.

63. Ibid.; "For Centuries Stonehenge Was a Burial Site," Associated Press, May 29, 2008, posted on History News Network, Breaking News, May 29, 2008.

64. "Bury Lenin's Body, Says Gorbachev," *The Independent* (UK), June 5, 2008, reported on History News Network, Breaking News, June 6, 2008. See the prescient comment by Ernesto Laclau: "The cycle of events which opened with the Russian Revolution has definitely closed . . . as a force of irradiation in the collective memory of the interna-tional left. . . . The corpse of Leninism, stripped of all the trappings of power, now reveals its pathetic and deplor-able reality." Laclau, *New Reflections on the Revolution of Our Time* (London: Verso, 1990), ix. See Heather Pringle, *The Mummy Congress: Science, Obsession, and the Everlasting Dead* (New York: Hyperion, 2001), 278–82.

65. With the passage of time, mummi-fication in Egypt became partially "democratized." As the art of embalm-ing became perfected, people other than

kings and queens were increasingly mummified. See Pringle, *Mummy Congress*, 41–42.

66. In a notable coincidence, Père Lachaise was created in 1804 and the Congressional Cemetery in Washington in 1807—both designed to be the new type of garden-style cemetery within city limits, an improvement upon the spatially crowded urban graveyards of the past but not yet the suburban cemeteries portended by Mount Auburn, Massachusetts, in 1831.

67. Richard Wilbur, "For the New Railway Station in Rome," in *Things of This World* (1956), in Wilbur, *New and Collected Poems* (San Diego: Harcourt, Brace, Jovanovich, 1988), 277–78. The poem has eight stanzas. For reasons that remain unclear, the final two are set in quotation marks. This is one.

68. Alexis de Tocqueville, *Democracy in America*, ed. Isaac Kramnick (New York: Penguin, 2003), 464, 468.

69. Ibid., 742.

70. See Jean Heffer and Jeanine Rovet, eds., *Why Is There No Socialism in the United States?* (Paris: École des Hautes Études en Sciences Sociales, 1988), 37–85; Louis Hartz, *The Liberal Tradition in America* (New York: Harcourt, Brace, 1955); Lionel Trilling, *The Liberal Imagination: Essays on Literature and Society* (New York: Viking, 1950), vii.

INDEX

Page references in italics refer to illustrations.